TEN GREAT MYSTERIES

TEN GREAT MYSTERIES

Edited by HOWARD HAYCRAFT

and JOHN BEECROFT

Doubleday & Company, Inc.
GARDEN CITY, NEW YORK

Printed in the United States of America

Table of Contents

Introduction

AS EVERY READER KNOWS, there is virtually no limit to the number of ways a mystery anthology can be put together. Most readers today are familiar with the anthology constructed on historical principles, or nationalistic lines, or the scholarly collection of special types of stories. A lighter-hearted method is to bring together mystery stories having a similar setting or subject matter—such as travel, sports, food, love, or humor. All these patterns have produced excellent and often amusing books, and your present editors have no quarrel with any of them.

In assembling the present volume, however, we have elected to follow a simpler method. From the mass of detective and mystery fiction that has poured from the printing presses in the last three decades, we have chosen a balanced menu of ten stories—long, short, and medium—which have seemed to us really memorable in conception and execution. If the stories selected have a common denominator, we believe that it is quality—each in its own type and style.

Perhaps a few words about the individual selections will add to the reader's enjoyment.

Dashiell Hammett, whose spare, hard-hitting novel *The Maltese Falcon* we have chosen to open the volume, has been called the most influential detective story writer of this century. He is certainly the most imitated. If not the originator of the American hardboiled detective story, he is (to quote his disciple the late Raymond Chandler) its "ace performer," and more than externally. Acknowledged as a classic of its kind, *The Maltese Falcon* was also made into a notable moving picture. No one who saw the film is likely to forget the performances of Humphrey Bogart, Sydney Greenstreet, or Peter Lorre as Spade, Gutman, and Joel Cairo. Readers who know Hammett only as the creator of *The Thin Man* are due for a surprise in depth.

It would be difficult to think of an author farther removed from Hammett, on the surface, than the English writer Dorothy Sayers, the creator of Lord Peter Wimsey. Yet as long as detective stories are read, it is likely that her literate, almost scholarly novels such as *The Nine Tailors* and *Gaudy Night* will be relished and remembered. In the fact that the same reader can enjoy both Hammett and Sayers lies much of the strength of the modern detective story. *The Learned Adventure of the Dragon's Head,* the Lord Peter story chosen for inclusion here, reveals the author and her titled detective in one of their lighter moods and problems.

By common consent, Erle Stanley Gardner's Perry Mason novels are recognized as the best-selling detective stories of modern times, perhaps of all time. In recent years a successful television series has increased their already vast audience. In *The Case of the Crying Swallow* it is our pleasure to present one of the best but least known adventures of the famous California lawyer-sleuth.

Agatha Christie, the author of *The Murder of Roger Ackroyd* and more than fifty other volumes of crime fiction, needs no introduction to anyone who has ever read a mystery story. Late in her distinguished career she turned to playwriting, and in a single season had four plays running simultaneously in London and New York. Most highly praised of these was *The Witness for the Prosecution,* which subsequently became an outstanding motion picture. We offer here the unforgettable story of the same title on which both the stage and screen successes were based.

"Ellery Queen *is* the American detective story," in the words of mystery critic Anthony Boucher. Ellery Queen (the author) "is" also two cousins, Frederic Dannay and Manfred Lee, who have been writing novels and short stories about Ellery Queen (the detective) ever since 1929. In their spare time they edit *Ellery Queen's Mystery Magazine.* Ellery, too, has had his audience recently widened by television. *The Adventure of the President's Half Disme* finds him matching his famous wits against none other than the Father of His Country.

On any list of English authors and fictional detectives whose exploits are equally popular in America, the names of Margery Allingham and her quiet but effective Albert Campion stand high indeed. *The Case of the Late Pig* is one of Campion's most attractive and entertaining adventures, and one that has been too little known.

Although Daphne du Maurier has won principal renown in the realm of "straight" fiction, there are few who will deny that her *Rebecca* is one of the great mystery classics of all time. *No Motive,* the story selected for inclusion here, is not only one of her finest and most compassionate tales, but a detective story in the truest sense of the term.

It is doubtful if any pair of sleuths since the immortal Holmes and Watson have inspired a more personal or affectionate following than Rex Stout's elephantine Nero Wolfe and his irrepressible assistant Archie Goodwin. Latest intelligence as these words are written is that they too are to have a televised incarnation. Their bearded creator received a unique honor from his fellow craftsmen in 1959 when the Mystery Writers of America voted him the coveted title of "Grand Master" of his art. *Die Like a Dog* tells what happens when a handsome canine specimen decides to adopt Nero and Archie, with unfortunate results for a callous killer.

The one really significant structural development in mystery fiction, since the introduction of the hardboiled novel by Hammett and his colleagues, has been the growth of the so-called suspense story. In this field William Irish (who also writes as Cornell Woolrich) has few equals. *The Dancing Detective* is one of his most representative and powerful stories. Warning: fasten your seat-belts!

When, if ever, the ledgers are closed on the detective story at some future millennial date, the name of Josephine Tey seems as assured of pride of place as any writer of our time. All of the Tey novels are rewarding; some are merely better than others. Outstanding, perhaps, are two: *The Daughter of Time* and the present selection *The Franchise Affair*, a stunning modern-dress reconstruction of the historic real-life Elizabeth Canning case, which, moreover, has something to say about life and living in any age. But, like good wine, *The Franchise Affair* needs no bush. It speaks—most satisfyingly—for itself.

Certainly, of the thousands of stories available, another editor or pair of editors might have chosen quite differently—but these are our choices. We hope that you enjoy them as much as we have.

Howard Haycraft

men decided to adopt Nero and Archie with unlimited [illegible] for a [illegible] kill[illegible].

The one really significant structural development in mystery fiction since the introduction of the [illegible] novel, by Hammett and his colleagues, has been the growth of the [illegible] suspense story. In the field William Irish (in [illegible] Cornell Woolrich) has few equals. *The Phantom Lady* [illegible] some of his most [illegible] and powerful stories. [illegible] your seat belt!

[illegible] closed on the detective story at some future moment, the [illegible] Tey seems as [illegible] of pride of place as any writer of our time. All of [illegible] novels are [illegible], some are merely better than others. Connoisseurs [illegible] *The Daughter of Time* [illegible] the present selection *The Franchise Affair*, a stunning and [illegible] reconstruction of the [illegible] eighteenth century case which, moreover, has some time to say about life and human [illegible]. But, [illegible] *The Franchise Affair* needs no [illegible], it speaks—and [illegible] makes—for itself.

Certainly, of the thousands of stories available, another editor or pair of editors might have chosen quite differently—but these are our choices. We hope that you enjoy them as much as we have.

[illegible] Haycraft

The Maltese Falcon

BY DASHIELL HAMMETT

CHAPTER I

Spade & Archer

SAMUEL SPADE'S JAW was long and bony, his chin a jutting v under the more flexible v of his mouth. His nostrils curved back to make another, smaller, v. His yellow-grey eyes were horizontal. The v *motif* was picked up again by thickish brows rising outward from twin creases above a hooked nose, and his pale brown hair grew down—from high flat temples—in a point on his forehead. He looked rather pleasantly like a blond satan.

He said to Effie Perine: "Yes, sweetheart?"

She was a lanky sunburned girl whose tan dress of thin woolen stuff clung to her with an effect of dampness. Her eyes were brown and playful in a shiny boyish face. She finished shutting the door behind her, leaned against it, and said: "There's a girl wants to see you. Her name's Wonderly."

"A customer?"

"I guess so. You'll want to see her anyway: she's a knockout."

"Shoo her in, darling," said Spade. "Shoo her in."

Effie Perine opened the door again, following it back into the outer office, standing with a hand on the knob while saying: "Will you come in, Miss Wonderly?"

A voice said, "Thank you," so softly that only the purest articulation made the words intelligible, and a young woman came through the doorway. She advanced slowly, with tentative steps, looking at Spade with cobalt-blue eyes that were both shy and probing.

She was tall and pliantly slender, without angularity anywhere. Her body was erect and high-breasted, her legs long, her hands and feet narrow. She wore two shades of blue that had been selected because of her eyes. The hair curling from under her blue hat was darkly red, her full lips more brightly red. White teeth glistened in the crescent her timid smile made.

Spade rose bowing and indicating with a thick-fingered hand the oaken armchair beside his desk. He was quite six feet tall. The steep rounded slope of his shoulders made his body seem almost conical—no broader than it was thick—and kept his freshly pressed grey coat from fitting very well.

Miss Wonderly murmured, "Thank you," softly as before and sat down on the edge of the chair's wooden seat.

Spade sank into his swivel-chair, made a quarter-turn to face her, smiled politely. He smiled without separating his lips. All the v's in his face grew longer.

The tappity-tap-tap and the thin bell and muffled whir of Effie Perine's typewriting came through the closed door. Somewhere in a neighboring office a power-driven machine vibrated dully. On Spade's desk a limp cigarette smoldered in a brass tray filled with the remains of limp cigarettes. Ragged grey flakes of cigarette-ash dotted the yellow top of the desk and the green blotter and the papers that were there. A buff-curtained window, eight or ten inches open, let in from the court a current of air faintly scented with ammonia. The ashes on the desk twitched and crawled in the current.

Miss Wonderly watched the grey flakes twitch and crawl. Her eyes were uneasy. She sat on the very edge of the chair. Her feet were flat on the floor, as if she were about to rise. Her hands in dark gloves clasped a flat dark handbag in her lap.

Spade rocked back in his chair and asked: "Now what can I do for you, Miss Wonderly?"

She caught her breath and looked at him. She swallowed and said hurriedly: "Could you—? I thought—I—that is—" Then she tortured her lower lip with glistening teeth and said nothing. Only her dark eyes spoke now, pleading.

Spade smiled and nodded as if he understood her, but pleasantly, as if nothing serious were involved. He said: "Suppose you tell me about it, from the beginning, and then we'll know what needs doing. Better begin as far back as you can."

"That was in New York."

"Yes."

"I don't know where she met him. I mean I don't know where in New York. She's five years younger than I—only seventeen—and we didn't have the same friends. I don't suppose we've ever been as close as sisters should be. Mama and Papa are in Europe. It would kill them. I've got to get her back before they come home."

"Yes," he said.

"They're coming home the first of the month."

Spade's eyes brightened. "Then we've two weeks," he said.

"I didn't know what she had done until her letter came. I was frantic." Her lips trembled. Her hands mashed the dark handbag in her lap. "I was too afraid she had done something like this to go to the police, and the fear that something had happened to her kept urging me to go. There wasn't anyone I could go to for advice. I didn't know what to do. What could I do?"

"Nothing, of course," Spade said, "but then her letter came?"

"Yes, and I sent her a telegram asking her to come home. I sent it to General Delivery here. That was the only address she gave me. I waited a whole week, but no answer came, not another word from her. And Mama and Papa's return was drawing nearer and nearer. So I came to San Francisco to get her. I wrote her I was coming. I shouldn't have done that, should I?"

"Maybe not. It's not always easy to know what to do. You haven't found her?"

"No, I haven't. I wrote her that I would go to the St. Mark, and I begged her to come and let me talk to her even if she didn't intend to go home with me. But she didn't come. I waited three days, and she didn't come, didn't even send me a message of any sort."

Spade nodded his blond satan's head, frowned sympathetically, and tightened his lips together.

"It was horrible," Miss Wonderly said, trying to smile. "I couldn't sit there like that—waiting—not knowing what had happened to her, what might be happening to her." She stopped trying to smile. She shuddered. "The only address I had was General Delivery. I wrote her another letter, and yesterday afternoon I went to the Post Office. I stayed there until after dark, but I didn't see her. I went there again this morning, and still didn't see Corinne, but I saw Floyd Thursby."

Spade nodded again. His frown went away. In its place came a look of sharp attentiveness.

"He wouldn't tell me where Corinne was," she went on, hopelessly. "He wouldn't tell me anything, except that she was well and happy. But how can I believe that? That is what he would tell me anyhow, isn't it?"

"Sure," Spade agreed. "But it might be true."

"I hope it is. I do hope it is," she exclaimed. "But I can't go back home like this, without having seen her, without even having talked to her on the phone. He wouldn't take me to her. He said she didn't want to see me. I can't believe that. He promised to tell her he had seen me, and to bring her to see me—if she would come—this evening at the hotel. He said he knew she wouldn't. He promised to come himself if she wouldn't. He—"

She broke off with a startled hand to her mouth as the door opened.

The man who had opened the door came in a step, said, "Oh, excuse me!" hastily took his brown hat from his head, and backed out.

"It's all right, Miles," Spade told him. "Come in. Miss Wonderly, this is Mr. Archer, my partner."

Miles Archer came into the office again, shutting the door behind him, ducking his head and smiling at Miss Wonderly, making a vaguely polite gesture with the hat in his hand. He was of medium height, solidly built, wide in the shoulders, thick in the neck, with a jovial heavy-jawed red face and some grey in his close-trimmed hair. He was apparently as many years past forty as Spade was past thirty.

Spade said: "Miss Wonderly's sister ran away from New York with a fellow named Floyd Thursby. They're here. Miss Wonderly has seen Thursby and has a date with him tonight. Maybe he'll bring the sister with him. The chances are he won't. Miss Wonderly wants us to find the sister and get her away from him and back home." He looked at Miss Wonderly. "Right?"

"Yes," she said indistinctly. The embarrassment that had gradually been driven away by Spade's ingratiating smiles and nods and assurances was pinkening her face again. She looked at the bag in her lap and picked nervously at it with a gloved finger.

Spade winked at his partner.

Miles Archer came forward to stand at a corner of the desk. While the girl looked at her bag he looked at her. His little brown eyes ran their bold appraising gaze from her lowered face to her feet and up to her face again. Then he looked at Spade and made a silent whistling mouth of appreciation.

Spade lifted two fingers from the arm of his chair in a brief warning gesture and said:

"We shouldn't have any trouble with it. It's simply a matter of having a man at the hotel this evening to shadow him away when he leaves, and shadow him until he leads us to your sister. If she comes with him, and you persuade her to return with you, so much the better. Otherwise—if she doesn't want to leave him after we've found her—well, we'll find a way of managing that."

Archer said: "Yeh." His voice was heavy, coarse.

Miss Wonderly looked up at Spade, quickly, puckering her forehead between her eyebrows.

"Oh, but you must be careful!" Her voice shook a little, and her lips shaped the words with nervous jerkiness. "I'm deathly afraid of him, of what he might do. She's so young and his bringing her here from New York is such a serious— Mightn't he—mightn't he do—something to her?"

Spade smiled and patted the arms of his chair.

"Just leave that to us," he said. "We'll know how to handle him."

"But mightn't he?" she insisted.

"There's always a chance." Spade nodded judicially. "But you can trust us to take care of that."

"I do trust you," she said earnestly, "but I want you to know that he's a dangerous man. I honestly don't think he'd stop at anything. I don't believe he'd hesitate to—to kill Corinne if he thought it would save him. Mightn't he do that?"

"You didn't threaten him, did you?"

"I told him that all I wanted was to get her home before Mama and Papa came so they'd never know what she had done. I promised him

I'd never say a word to them about it if he helped me, but if he didn't Papa would certainly see that he was punished. I—I don't suppose he believed me, altogether."

"Can he cover up by marrying her?" Archer asked.

The girl blushed and replied in a confused voice: "He has a wife and three children in England. Corinne wrote me that, to explain why she had gone off with him."

"They usually do," Spade said, "though not always in England." He leaned forward to reach for pencil and pad of paper. "What does he look like?"

"Oh, he's thirty-five years old, perhaps, and as tall as you, and either naturally dark or quite sunburned. His hair is dark too, and he has thick eyebrows. He talks in a rather loud, blustery, way and has a nervous, irritable, manner. He gives the impression of being—of violence."

Spade, scribbling on the pad, asked without looking up: "What color eyes?"

"They're blue-grey and watery, though not in a weak way. And—oh, yes —he has a marked cleft in his chin."

"Thin, medium, or heavy build?"

"Quite athletic. He's broad-shouldered and carries himself erect, has what could be called a decidedly military carriage. He was wearing a light grey suit and a grey hat when I saw him this morning."

"What does he do for a living?" Spade asked as he laid down his pencil.

"I don't know," she said. "I haven't the slightest idea."

"What time is he coming to see you?"

"After eight o'clock."

"All right, Miss Wonderly, we'll have a man there. It'll help if—"

"Mr. Spade, could either you or Mr. Archer?" She made an appealing gesture with both hands. "Could either of you look after it personally? I don't mean that the man you'd send wouldn't be capable, but—oh!— I'm so afraid of what might happen to Corinne. I'm afraid of him. Could you? I'd be—I'd expect to be charged more, of course." She opened her handbag with nervous fingers and put two hundred-dollar bills on Spade's desk. "Would that be enough?"

"Yeh," Archer said, "and I'll look after it myself."

Miss Wonderly stood up, impulsively holding a hand out to him.

"Thank you! Thank you!" she exclaimed, and then gave Spade her hand, repeating: "Thank you!"

"Not at all," Spade said over it. "Glad to. It'll help some if you either meet Thursby downstairs or let yourself be seen in the lobby with him at some time."

"I will," she promised, and thanked the partners again.

"And don't look for me," Archer cautioned her. "I'll see you all right."

Spade went to the corridor-door with Miss Wonderly. When he returned to his desk Archer nodded at the hundred-dollar bills there, growled complacently, "They're right enough," picked one up, folded it, and tucked it into a vest-pocket. "And they had brothers in her bag."

Spade pocketed the other bill before he sat down. Then he said: "Well, don't dynamite her too much. What do you think of her?"

"Sweet! And you telling me not to dynamite her." Archer guffawed suddenly without merriment. "Maybe you saw her first, Sam, but I spoke first." He put his hands in his trousers-pockets and teetered on his heels.

"You'll play hell with her, you will." Spade grinned wolfishly, showing the edges of teeth far back in his jaw. "You've got brains, yes you have." He began to make a cigarette.

CHAPTER II

Death in the Fog

A TELEPHONE-BELL RANG in darkness. When it had rung three times bed-springs creaked, fingers fumbled on wood, something small and hard thudded on a carpeted floor, the springs creaked again, and a man's voice said:

"Hello. . . . Yes, speaking. . . . Dead? . . . Yes. . . . Fifteen minutes. Thanks."

A switch clicked and a white bowl hung on three gilded chains from the ceiling's center filled the room with light. Spade, barefooted in green and white checked pajamas, sat on the side of his bed. He scowled at the telephone on the table while his hands took from beside it a packet of brown papers and a sack of Bull Durham tobacco.

Cold steamy air blew in through two open windows, bringing with it half a dozen times a minute the Alcatraz foghorn's dull moaning. A tinny alarm-clock, insecurely mounted on a corner of Duke's *Celebrated Criminal Cases of America*—face down on the table—held its hands at five minutes past two.

Spade's thick fingers made a cigarette with deliberate care, sifting a measured quantity of tan flakes down into curved paper, spreading the flakes so that they lay equal at the ends with a slight depression in the middle, thumbs rolling the paper's inner edge down and up under the outer edge as forefingers pressed it over, thumbs and fingers sliding to the paper cylinder's ends to hold it even while tongue licked the flap, left forefinger and thumb pinching their end while right forefinger and thumb smoothed the damp seam, right forefinger and thumb twisting their end and lifting the other to Spade's mouth.

He picked up the pigskin and nickel lighter that had fallen to the floor, manipulated it, and with the cigarette burning in a corner of his mouth stood up. He took off his pajamas. The smooth thickness of his arms, legs, and body, the sag of his big rounded shoulders, made his body like a bear's. It was like a shaved bear's: his chest was hairless. His skin was childishly soft and pink.

He scratched the back of his neck and began to dress. He put on a thin white union-suit, grey socks, black garters, and dark brown shoes. When he had fastened his shoes he picked up the telephone, called Graystone 4500, and ordered a taxicab. He put on a green-striped white shirt, a soft white collar, a green necktie, the grey suit he had worn that day, a loose tweed overcoat, and a dark grey hat. The street-door-bell rang as he stuffed tobacco, keys, and money into his pockets.

Where Bush Street roofed Stockton before slipping downhill to Chinatown, Spade paid his fare and left the taxicab. San Francisco's night-fog, thin, clammy, and penetrant, blurred the street. A few yards from where Spade had dismissed the taxicab a small group of men stood looking up an alley. Two women stood with a man on the other side of Bush Street, looking at the alley. There were faces at windows.

Spade crossed the sidewalk between iron-railed hatchways that opened above bare ugly stairs, went to the parapet, and, resting his hands on the damp coping, looked down into Stockton Street.

An automobile popped out of the tunnel beneath him with a roaring swish, as if it had been blown out, and ran away. Not far from the tunnel's mouth a man was hunkered on his heels before a billboard that held advertisements of a moving picture and a gasoline across the front of a gap between two store-buildings. The hunkered man's head was bent almost to the sidewalk so he could look under the billboard. A hand flat on the paving, a hand clenched on the billboard's green frame, held him in this grotesque position. Two other men stood awkwardly together at one end of the billboard, peeping through the few inches of space between it and the building at that end. The building at the other end had a blank grey sidewall that looked down on the lot behind the billboard. Lights flickered on the sidewall, and the shadows of men moving among lights.

Spade turned from the parapet and walked up Bush Street to the alley where men were grouped. A uniformed policeman chewing gum under an enameled sign that said *Burritt St.* in white against dark blue put out an arm and asked:

"What do you want here?"

"I'm Sam Spade. Tom Polhaus phoned me."

"Sure you are." The policeman's arm went down. "I didn't know you at first. Well, they're back there." He jerked a thumb over his shoulder. "Bad business."

"Bad enough," Spade agreed, and went up the alley.

Half-way up it, not far from the entrance, a dark ambulance stood. Behind the ambulance, to the left, the alley was bounded by a waist-high fence, horizontal strips of rough boarding. From the fence dark ground fell away steeply to the billboard on Stockton Street below.

A ten-foot length of the fence's top rail had been torn from a post at one end and hung dangling from the other. Fifteen feet down the slope a flat boulder stuck out. In the notch between boulder and slope Miles Archer lay on his back. Two men stood over him. One of them held the beam of an electric torch on the dead man. Other men with lights moved up and down the slope.

One of them hailed Spade, "Hello, Sam," and clambered up to the alley, his shadow running up the slope before him. He was a barrel-bellied tall man with shrewd small eyes, a thick mouth, and carelessly shaven dark jowls. His shoes, knees, hands, and chin were daubed with brown loam.

"I figured you'd want to see it before we took him away," he said as he stepped over the broken fence.

"Thanks, Tom," Spade said. "What happened?" He put an elbow on a fence-post and looked down at the men below, nodding to those who nodded to him.

Tom Polhaus poked his own left breast with a dirty finger. "Got him right through the pump—with this." He took a fat revolver from his coat-pocket and held it out to Spade. Mud inlaid the depressions in the revolver's surface. "A Webley. English, ain't it?"

Spade took his elbow from the fence-post and leaned down to look at the weapon, but he did not touch it.

"Yes," he said, "Webley-Fosbery automatic revolver. That's it. Thirty-eight, eight shot. They don't make them any more. How many gone out of it?"

"One pill." Tom poked his breast again. "He must've been dead when he cracked the fence." He raised the muddy revolver. "Ever seen this before?"

Spade nodded. "I've seen Webley-Fosberys," he said without interest, and then spoke rapidly: "He was shot up here, huh? Standing where you are, with his back to the fence. The man that shot him stands here." He went around in front of Tom and raised a hand breast-high with leveled forefinger. "Lets him have it and Miles goes back, taking the top off the fence and going on through and down till the rock catches him. That it?"

"That's it," Tom replied slowly, working his brows together. "The blast burnt his coat."

"Who found him?"

"The man on the beat, Shilling. He was coming down Bush, and just as he got here a machine turning threw headlights up here, and he saw the top off the fence. So he came up to look at it, and found him."

"What about the machine that was turning around?"

"Not a damned thing about it, Sam. Shilling didn't pay any attention to it, not knowing anything was wrong then. He says nobody didn't come out of here while he was coming down from Powell or he'd've seen them. The only other way out would be under the billboard on Stockton. Nobody went that way. The fog's got the ground soggy, and the only marks are where Miles slid down and where this here gun rolled."

"Didn't anybody hear the shot?"

"For the love of God, Sam, we only just got here. Somebody must've heard it, when we find them." He turned and put a leg over the fence. "Coming down for a look at him before he's moved?"

Spade said: "No."

Tom halted astride the fence and looked back at Spade with surprised small eyes.

Spade said: "You've seen him. You'd see everything I could."

Tom, still looking at Spade, nodded doubtfully and withdrew his leg over the fence.

"His gun was tucked away on his hip," he said. "It hadn't been fired. His overcoat was buttoned. There's a hundred and sixty-some bucks in his clothes. Was he working, Sam?"

Spade, after a moment's hesitation, nodded.

Tom asked: "Well?"

"He was supposed to be tailing a fellow named Floyd Thursby," Spade said, and described Thursby as Miss Wonderly had described him.

"What for?"

Spade put his hands into his overcoat-pockets and blinked sleepy eyes at Tom.

Tom repeated impatiently: "What for?"

"He was an Englishman, maybe. I don't know what his game was, exactly. We were trying to find out where he lived." Spade grinned faintly and took a hand from his pocket to pat Tom's shoulder. "Don't crowd me." He put the hand in his pocket again. "I'm going out to break the news to Miles's wife." He turned away.

Tom, scowling, opened his mouth, closed it without having said anything, cleared his throat, put the scowl off his face, and spoke with a husky sort of gentleness:

"It's tough, him getting it like that. Miles had his faults same as the rest of us, but I guess he must've had some good points too."

"I guess so," Spade agreed in a tone that was utterly meaningless, and went out of the alley.

In an all-night drug-store on the corner of Bush and Taylor Streets, Spade used a telephone.

"Precious," he said into it a little while after he had given a number, "Miles has been shot. . . . Yes, he's dead. . . . Now don't get excited. . . . Yes. . . . You'll have to break it to Iva. . . . No, I'm damned if I will. You've got to do it. . . . That's a good girl. . . . And keep her away from the office. . . . Tell her I'll see her—uh—some time. . . . Yes, but don't tie me up to anything. . . . That's the stuff. You're an angel. 'Bye."

Spade's tinny alarm-clock said three-forty when he turned on the light in the suspended bowl again. He dropped his hat and overcoat on the bed and went into his kitchen, returning to the bedroom with a wine-glass and a tall bottle of Bacardi. He poured a drink and drank it standing. He put bottle and glass on the table, sat on the side of the bed facing them, and rolled a cigarette. He had drunk his third glass of Bacardi and was lighting his fifth cigarette when the street-door-bell rang. The hands of the alarm-clock registered four-thirty.

Spade sighed, rose from the bed, and went to the telephone-box beside his bathroom door. He pressed the button that released the street-door-lock. He muttered, "Damn her," and stood scowling at the black telephone-box, breathing irregularly while a dull flush grew in his cheeks.

The grating and rattling of the elevator-door opening and closing came from the corridor. Spade sighed again and moved towards the corridor-door. Soft heavy footsteps sounded on the carpeted floor outside, the footsteps of two men. Spade's face brightened. His eyes were no longer harassed. He opened the door quickly.

"Hello, Tom," he said to the barrel-bellied tall detective with whom he had talked in Burritt Street, and, "Hello, Lieutenant," to the man beside Tom. "Come in."

They nodded together, neither saying anything, and came in. Spade shut the door and ushered them into his bedroom. Tom sat on an end of the sofa by the windows. The Lieutenant sat on a chair beside the table.

The Lieutenant was a compactly built man with a round head under short-cut grizzled hair and a square face behind a short-cut grizzled mustache. A five-dollar-gold-piece was pinned to his necktie and there was a small elaborate diamond-set secret-society-emblem on his lapel.

Spade brought two wine-glasses in from the kitchen, filled them and his own with Bacardi, gave one to each of his visitors, and sat down with his on the side of the bed. His face was placid and uncurious. He raised his glass, and said, "Success to crime," and drank it down.

Tom emptied his glass, set it on the floor beside his feet, and wiped his mouth with a muddy forefinger. He stared at the foot of the bed as if trying to remember something of which it vaguely reminded him.

The Lieutenant looked at his glass for a dozen seconds, took a very small sip of its contents, and put the glass on the table at his elbow. He examined the room with hard deliberate eyes, and then looked at Tom.

Tom moved uncomfortably on the sofa and, not looking up, asked: "Did you break the news to Miles's wife, Sam?"

Spade said: "Uh-huh."

"How'd she take it?"

Spade shook his head. "I don't know anything about women."

Tom said softly: "The hell you don't."

The Lieutenant put his hands on his knees and leaned forward. His greenish eyes were fixed on Spade in a peculiarly rigid stare, as if their focus were a matter of mechanics, to be changed only by pulling a lever or pressing a button.

"What kind of gun do you carry?" he asked.

"None. I don't like them much. Of course there are some in the office."

"I'd like to see one of them," the Lieutenant said. "You don't happen to have one here?"

"No."

"You sure of that?"

"Look around." Spade smiled and waved his empty glass a little. "Turn the dump upside-down if you want. I won't squawk—if you've got a search-warrant."

Tom protested: "Oh, hell, Sam!"

Spade set his glass on the table and stood up facing the Lieutenant.

"What do you want, Dundy?" he asked in a voice hard and cold as his eyes.

Lieutenant Dundy's eyes had moved to maintain their focus on Spade's. Only his eyes had moved.

Tom shifted his weight on the sofa again, blew a deep breath out through his nose, and growled plaintively: "We're not wanting to make any trouble, Sam."

Spade, ignoring Tom, said to Dundy: "Well, what do you want? Talk turkey. Who in hell do you think you are, coming in here trying to rope me?"

"All right," Dundy said in his chest, "sit down and listen."

"I'll sit or stand as I damned please," said Spade, not moving.

"For Christ's sake be reasonable," Tom begged. "What's the use of us having a row? If you want to know why we didn't talk turkey it's because when I asked you who this Thursby was you as good as told me it was none of my business. You can't treat us that way, Sam. It ain't right and it won't get you anywheres. We got our work to do."

Lieutenant Dundy jumped up, stood close to Spade, and thrust his square face up at the taller man's.

"I've warned you your foot was going to slip one of these days," he said.

Spade made a depreciative mouth, raising his eyebrows. "Everybody's foot slips sometime," he replied with derisive mildness.

"And this is yours."

Spade smiled and shook his head. "No, I'll do nicely, thank you." He stopped smiling. His upper lip, on the left side, twitched over his eyetooth. His eyes became narrow and sultry. His voice came out deep as the Lieutenant's. "I don't like this. What are you sucking around for? Tell me, or get out and let me go to bed."

"Who's Thursby?" Dundy demanded.

"I told Tom what I knew about him."

"You told Tom damned little."

"I knew damned little."

"Why were you tailing him?"

"I wasn't. Miles was—for the swell reason that we had a client who was paying good United States money to have him tailed."

"Who's the client?"

Placidity came back to Spade's face and voice. He said reprovingly: "You know I can't tell you that until I've talked it over with the client."

"You'll tell it to me or you'll tell it in court," Dundy said hotly. "This is murder and don't you forget it."

"Maybe. And here's something for you to not forget, sweetheart. I'll tell it or not as I damned please. It's a long while since I burst out crying because policemen didn't like me."

Tom left the sofa and sat on the foot of the bed. His carelessly shaven mud-smeared face was tired and lined.

"Be reasonable, Sam," he pleaded. "Give us a chance. How can we turn up anything on Miles's killing if you won't give us what you've got?"

"You needn't get a headache over that," Spade told him. "I'll bury my dead."

Lieutenant Dundy sat down and put his hands on his knees again. His eyes were warm green discs.

"I thought you would," he said. He smiled with grim content. "That's just exactly why we came to see you. Isn't it, Tom?"

Tom groaned, but said nothing articulate.

Spade watched Dundy warily.

"That's just exactly what I said to Tom," the Lieutenant went on. "I said: 'Tom, I've got a hunch that Sam Spade's a man to keep the family-troubles in the family.' That's just what I said to him."

The wariness went out of Spade's eyes. He made his eyes dull with boredom. He turned his face around to Tom and asked with great carelessness: "What's itching your boy-friend now?"

Dundy jumped up and tapped Spade's chest with the ends of two bent fingers.

"Just this," he said, taking pains to make each word distinct, emphasizing them with his tapping finger-ends: "Thursby was shot down in front of his hotel just thirty-five minutes after you left Burritt Street."

Spade spoke, taking equal pains with his words: "Keep your God-damned paws off me."

Dundy withdrew the tapping fingers, but there was no change in his voice: "Tom says you were in too much of a hurry to even stop for a look at your partner."

Tom growled apologetically: "Well, damn it, Sam, you did run off like that."

"And you didn't go to Archer's house to tell his wife," the Lieutenant said. "We called up and that girl in your office was there, and she said you sent her."

Spade nodded. His face was stupid in its calmness.

Lieutenant Dundy raised his two bent fingers towards Spade's chest, quickly lowered them, and said: "I give you ten minutes to get to a phone and do your talking to the girl. I give you ten minutes to get to Thursby's joint—Geary near Leavenworth—you could do it easy in that time, or fifteen at the most. And that gives you ten or fifteen minutes of waiting before he showed up."

"I knew where he lived?" Spade asked. "And I knew he hadn't gone straight home from killing Miles?"

"You knew what you knew," Dundy replied stubbornly. "What time did you get home?"

"Twenty minutes to four. I walked around thinking things over."

The Lieutenant wagged his round head up and down. "We knew you weren't home at three-thirty. We tried to get you on the phone. Where'd you do your walking?"

"Out Bush Street a way and back."

"Did you see anybody that—?"

"No, no witnesses," Spade said and laughed pleasantly. "Sit down, Dundy. You haven't finished your drink. Get your glass, Tom."

Tom said: "No, thanks, Sam."

Dundy sat down, but paid no attention to his glass of rum.

Spade filled his own glass, drank, set the empty glass on the table, and returned to his bedside-seat.

"I know where I stand now," he said, looking with friendly eyes from one of the police-detectives to the other. "I'm sorry I got up on my hind legs, but you birds coming in and trying to put the work on me made me nervous. Having Miles knocked off bothered me, and then you birds cracking foxy. That's all right now, though, now that I know what you're up to."

Tom said: "Forget it."

The Lieutenant said nothing.

Spade asked: "Thursby die?"

While the Lieutenant hesitated Tom said: "Yes."

Then the Lieutenant said angrily: "And you might just as well know it—if you don't—that he died before he could tell anybody anything."

Spade was rolling a cigarette. He asked, not looking up: "What do you mean by that? You think I did know it?"

"I meant what I said," Dundy replied bluntly.

Spade looked up at him and smiled, holding the finished cigarette in one hand, his lighter in the other.

"You're not ready to pinch me yet, are you, Dundy?" he asked.

Dundy looked with hard green eyes at Spade and did not answer him.

"Then," said Spade, "there's no particular reason why I should give a damn what you think, is there, Dundy?"

Tom said: "Aw, be reasonable, Sam."

Spade put the cigarette in his mouth, set fire to it, and laughed smoke out.

"I'll be reasonable, Tom," he promised. "How did I kill this Thursby? I've forgotten."

Tom grunted disgust. Lieutenant Dundy said: "He was shot four times in the back, with a forty-four or forty-five, from across the street, when he started to go in the hotel. Nobody saw it, but that's the way it figures."

"And he was wearing a Luger in a shoulder-holster," Tom added. "It hadn't been fired."

"What do the hotel-people know about him?" Spade asked.

"Nothing except that he'd been there a week."

"Alone?"

"Alone."

"What did you find on him? or in his room?"

Dundy drew his lips in and asked: "What'd you think we'd find?"

Spade made a careless circle with his limp cigarette. "Something to tell you who he was, what his store was. Did you?"

"We thought you could tell us that."

Spade looked at the Lieutenant with yellow-grey eyes that held an almost exaggerated amount of candor. "I've never seen Thursby, dead or alive."

Lieutenant Dundy stood up looking dissatisfied. Tom rose yawning and stretching.

"We've asked what we came to ask," Dundy said, frowning over eyes hard as green pebbles. He held his mustached upper lip tight to his teeth, letting his lower lip push the words out. "We've told you more than you've told us. That's fair enough. You know me, Spade. If you did or you didn't you'll get a square deal out of me, and most of the breaks. I don't know that I'd blame you a hell of a lot—but that wouldn't keep me from nailing you."

"Fair enough," Spade replied evenly. "But I'd feel better about it if you'd drink your drink."

Lieutenant Dundy turned to the table, picked up his glass, and slowly emptied it. Then he said, "Good night," and held out his hand. They shook hands ceremoniously. Tom and Spade shook hands ceremoniously. Spade let them out. Then he undressed, turned off the lights, and went to bed.

CHAPTER III

Three Women

WHEN SPADE REACHED his office at ten o'clock the following morning Effie Perine was at her desk opening the morning's mail. Her boyish face was pale under its sunburn. She put down the handful of envelopes and the brass paper-knife she held and said: "She's in there." Her voice was low and warning.

"I asked you to keep her away," Spade complained. He too kept his voice low.

Effie Perine's brown eyes opened wide and her voice was irritable as his: "Yes, but you didn't tell me how." Her eyelids went together a little and her shoulders drooped. "Don't be cranky, Sam," she said wearily. "I had her all night."

Spade stood beside the girl, put a hand on her head, and smoothed her hair away from its parting. "Sorry, angel, I haven't—" He broke off as the inner door opened. "Hello, Iva," he said to the woman who had opened it.

"Oh, Sam!" she said.

She was a blonde woman of a few more years than thirty. Her facial prettiness was perhaps five years past its best moment. Her body for all its sturdiness was finely modeled and exquisite. She wore black clothes from hat to shoes. They had as mourning an impromptu air. Having spoken, she stepped back from the door and stood waiting for Spade.

He took his hand from Effie Perine's head and entered the inner office, shutting the door. Iva came quickly to him, raising her sad face for his kiss. Her arms were around him before his held her. When they had kissed he made a little movement as if to release her, but she pressed her face to his chest and began sobbing.

He stroked her round back, saying: "Poor darling." His voice was tender. His eyes, squinting at the desk that had been his partner's, across the room from his own, were angry. He drew his lips back over his teeth in an impatient grimace and turned his chin aside to avoid contact with the crown of her hat. "Did you send for Miles's brother?" he asked.

"Yes, he came over this morning." The words were blurred by her sobbing and his coat against her mouth.

He grimaced again and bent his head for a surreptitious look at the watch on his wrist. His left arm was around her, the hand on her left shoulder. His cuff was pulled back far enough to leave the watch uncovered. It showed ten-ten.

The woman stirred in his arms and raised her face again. Her blue eyes were wet, round, and white-ringed. Her mouth was moist.

"Oh, Sam," she moaned, "did you kill him?"

Spade stared at her with bulging eyes. His bony jaw fell down. He took his arms from her and stepped back out of her arms. He scowled at her and cleared his throat.

She held her arms up as he had left them. Anguish clouded her eyes, partly closed them under eyebrows pulled up at the inner ends. Her soft damp red lips trembled.

Spade laughed a harsh syllable, "Ha!" and went to the buff-curtained window. He stood there with his back to her looking through the curtain into the court until she started towards him. Then he turned quickly and went to his desk. He sat down, put his elbows on the desk, his chin between his fists, and looked at her. His yellowish eyes glittered between narrowed lids.

"Who," he asked coldly, "put that bright idea in your head?"

"I thought—" She lifted a hand to her mouth and fresh tears came to her eyes. She came to stand beside the desk, moving with easy sure-footed grace in black slippers whose smallness and heel-height were extreme. "Be kind to me, Sam," she said humbly.

He laughed at her, his eyes still glittering. "You killed my husband, Sam, be kind to me." He clapped his palms together and said: "Jesus Christ."

She began to cry audibly, holding a white handkerchief to her face.

He got up and stood close behind her. He put his arms around her. He kissed her neck between ear and coat-collar. He said: "Now, Iva, don't." His face was expressionless. When she had stopped crying he put his mouth to her ear and murmured: "You shouldn't have come here today, precious. It wasn't wise. You can't stay. You ought to be home."

She turned around in his arms to face him and asked: "You'll come tonight?"

He shook his head gently. "Not tonight."

"Soon?"

"Yes."

"How soon?"

"As soon as I can."

He kissed her mouth, led her to the door, opened it, said, "Good-bye, Iva," bowed her out, shut the door, and returned to his desk.

He took tobacco and cigarette-papers from his vest-pockets, but did not roll a cigarette. He sat holding the papers in one hand, the tobacco in the other, and looked with brooding eyes at his dead partner's desk.

Effie Perine opened the door and came in. Her brown eyes were uneasy. Her voice was careless. She asked: "Well?"

Spade said nothing. His brooding gaze did not move from his partner's desk.

The girl frowned and came around to his side. "Well," she asked in a louder voice, "how did you and the widow make out?"

"She thinks I shot Miles," he said. Only his lips moved.

"So you could marry her?"

Spade made no reply to that.

The girl took his hat from his head and put it on the desk. Then she leaned over and took the tobacco-sack and the papers from his inert fingers.

"The police think I shot Thursby," he said.

"Who is he?" she asked, separating a cigarette-paper from the packet, sifting tobacco into it.

"Who do you think I shot?" he asked.

When she ignored that question he said: "Thursby's the guy Miles was supposed to be tailing for the Wonderly girl."

Her thin fingers finished shaping the cigarette. She licked it, smoothed it, twisted its ends, and placed it between Spade's lips. He said, "Thanks, honey," put an arm around her slim waist, and rested his cheek wearily against her hip, shutting his eyes.

"Are you going to marry Iva?" she asked, looking down at his pale brown hair.

"Don't be silly," he muttered. The unlighted cigarette bobbed up and down with the movement of his lips.

"She doesn't think it's silly. Why should she—the way you've played around with her?"

He sighed and said: "I wish to Christ I'd never seen her."

"Maybe you do now." A trace of spitefulness came into the girl's voice. "But there was a time."

"I never know what to do or say to women except that way," he grumbled, "and then I didn't like Miles."

"That's a lie, Sam," the girl said. "You know I think she's a louse, but I'd be a louse too if it would give me a body like hers."

Spade rubbed his face impatiently against her hip, but said nothing.

Effie Perine bit her lip, wrinkled her forehead, and, bending over for a better view of his face, asked: "Do you suppose she could have killed him?"

Spade sat up straight and took his arm from her waist. He smiled at her. Her smile held nothing but amusement. He took out his lighter, snapped on the flame, and applied it to the end of his cigarette. "You're an angel," he said tenderly through smoke, "a nice rattle-brained angel."

She smiled a bit wryly. "Oh, am I? Suppose I told you that your Iva hadn't been home many minutes when I arrived to break the news at three o'clock this morning?"

"Are you telling me?" he asked. His eyes had become alert though his mouth continued to smile.

"She kept me waiting at the door while she undressed or finished undressing. I saw her clothes where she had dumped them on a chair. Her hat and coat were underneath. Her singlette, on top, was still warm. She said she had been asleep, but she hadn't. She had wrinkled up the bed, but the wrinkles weren't mashed down."

Spade took the girl's hand and patted it. "You're a detective, darling, but"—he shook his head—"she didn't kill him."

Effie Perine snatched her hand away. "That louse wants to marry you, Sam," she said bitterly.

He made an impatient gesture with his head and one hand.

She frowned at him and demanded: "Did you see her last night?"

"No."

"Honestly?"

"Honestly. Don't act like Dundy, sweetheart. It ill becomes you."

"Has Dundy been after you?"

"Uh-huh. He and Tom Polhaus dropped in for a drink at four o'clock."

"Do they really think you shot this what's-his-name?"

"Thursby." He dropped what was left of his cigarette into the brass tray and began to roll another.

"Do they?" she insisted.

"God knows." His eyes were on the cigarette he was making. "They did have some such notion. I don't know how far I talked them out of it."

"Look at me, Sam."

He looked at her and laughed so that for the moment merriment mingled with the anxiety in her face.

"You worry me," she said, seriousness returning to her face as she talked. "You always think you know what you're doing, but you're too slick for your own good, and some day you're going to find it out."

He sighed mockingly and rubbed his cheek against her arm. "That's what Dundy says, but you keep Iva away from me, sweet, and I'll manage to survive the rest of my troubles." He stood up and put on his hat. "Have the *Spade & Archer* taken off the door and *Samuel Spade* put on. I'll be back in an hour, or phone you."

Spade went through the St. Mark's long purplish lobby to the desk and asked a red-haired dandy whether Miss Wonderly was in. The red-haired dandy turned away, and then back shaking his head. "She checked out this morning, Mr. Spade."

"Thanks."

Spade walked past the desk to an alcove off the lobby where a plump young-middle-aged man in dark clothes sat at a flat-topped mahogany desk. On the edge of the desk facing the lobby was a triangular prism of mahogany and brass inscribed *Mr. Freed.*

The plump man got up and came around the desk holding out his hand.

"I was awfully sorry to hear about Archer, Spade," he said in the tone of one trained to sympathize readily without intrusiveness. "I've just seen it in the *Call*. He was in here last night, you know."

"Thanks, Freed. Were you talking to him?"

"No. He was sitting in the lobby when I came in early in the evening. I didn't stop. I thought he was probably working and I know you fellows like to be left alone when you're busy. Did that have anything to do with his—?"

"I don't think so, but we don't know yet. Anyway, we won't mix the house up in it if it can be helped."

"Thanks."

"That's all right. Can you give me some dope on an ex-guest, and then forget that I asked for it?"

"Surely."

"A Miss Wonderly checked out this morning. I'd like to know the details."

"Come along," Freed said, "and we'll see what we can learn."

Spade stood still, shaking his head. "I don't want to show in it."

Freed nodded and went out of the alcove. In the lobby he halted suddenly and came back to Spade.

"Harriman was the house-detective on duty last night," he said. "He's sure to have seen Archer. Shall I caution him not to mention it?"

Spade looked at Freed from the corners of his eyes. "Better not. That won't make any difference as long as there's no connection shown with this Wonderly. Harriman's all right, but he likes to talk, and I'd as lief not have him think there's anything to be kept quiet."

Freed nodded again and went away. Fifteen minutes later he returned.

"She arrived last Tuesday, registering from New York. She hadn't a trunk, only some bags. There were no phone-calls charged to her room, and she doesn't seem to have received much, if any, mail. The only one anybody remembers having seen her with was a tall dark man of thirty-six or so. She went out at half-past nine this morning, came back an hour later, paid her bill, and had her bags carried out to a car. The boy who carried them says it was a Nash touring car, probably a hired one. She left a forwarding address—the Ambassador, Los Angeles."

Spade said, "Thanks a lot, Freed," and left the St. Mark.

When Spade returned to his office Effie Perine stopped typing a letter to tell him: "Your friend Dundy was in. He wanted to look at your guns."

"And?"

"I told him to come back when you were here."

"Good girl. If he comes back again let him look at them."

"And Miss Wonderly called up."

"It's about time. What did she say?"

"She wants to see you." The girl picked up a slip of paper from her desk and read the memorandum penciled on it: "She's at the Coronet, on California Street, apartment one thousand and one. You're to ask for Miss Leblanc."

Spade said, "Give me," and held out his hand. When she had given him the memorandum he took out his lighter, snapped on the flame, set it to the slip of paper, held the paper until all but one corner was curling black ash, dropped it on the linoleum floor, and mashed it under his shoe-sole.

The girl watched him with disapproving eyes.

He grinned at her, said, "That's just the way it is, dear," and went out again.

CHAPTER IV

The Black Bird

MISS WONDERLY, in a belted green crêpe silk dress, opened the door of apartment 1001 at the Coronet. Her face was flushed. Her dark red hair, parted on the left side, swept back in loose waves over her right temple, was somewhat tousled.

Spade took off his hat and said: "Good morning."

His smile brought a fainter smile to her face. Her eyes, of blue that was almost violet, did not lose their troubled look. She lowered her head and said in a hushed, timid, voice: "Come in, Mr. Spade."

She led him past open kitchen-, bathroom-, and bedroom-doors into a cream and red living-room, apologizing for its confusion: "Everything is upside-down. I haven't even finished unpacking."

She laid his hat on a table and sat down on a walnut settee. He sat on a brocaded oval-backed chair facing her.

She looked at her fingers, working them together, and said: "Mr. Spade, I've a terrible, terrible confession to make."

Spade smiled a polite smile, which she did not lift her eyes to see, and said nothing.

"That—that story I told you yesterday was all—a story," she stammered, and looked up at him now with miserable frightened eyes.

"Oh, that," Spade said lightly. "We didn't exactly believe your story."

"Then—?" Perplexity was added to the misery and fright in her eyes.

"We believed your two hundred dollars."

"You mean—?" She seemed to not know what he meant.

"I mean that you paid us more than if you'd been telling the truth," he explained blandly, "and enough more to make it all right."

Her eyes suddenly lighted up. She lifted herself a few inches from the settee, settled down again, smoothed her skirt, leaned forward, and spoke eagerly: "And even now you'd be willing to—?"

Spade stopped her with a palm-up motion of one hand. The upper part of his face frowned. The lower part smiled. "That depends," he said. "The hell of it is, Miss—— Is your name Wonderly or Leblanc?"

She blushed and murmured: "It's really O'Shaughnessy—Brigid O'Shaughnessy."

"The hell of it is, Miss O'Shaughnessy, that a couple of murders"—she winced—"coming together like this get everybody stirred up, make the police think they can go the limit, make everybody hard to handle and expensive. It's not—"

He stopped talking because she had stopped listening and was waiting for him to finish.

"Mr. Spade, tell me the truth." Her voice quivered on the verge of hysteria. Her face had become haggard around desperate eyes. "Am I to blame for—for last night?"

Spade shook his head. "Not unless there are things I don't know about," he said. "You warned us that Thursby was dangerous. Of course you lied to us about your sister and all, but that doesn't count: we didn't believe you." He shrugged his sloping shoulders. "I wouldn't say it was your fault."

She said, "Thank you," very softly, and then moved her head from side to side. "But I'll always blame myself." She put a hand to her throat. "Mr. Archer was so—so alive yesterday afternoon, so solid and hearty and—"

"Stop it," Spade commanded. "He knew what he was doing. They're the chances we take."

"Was—was he married?"

"Yes, with ten thousand insurance, no children, and a wife who didn't like him."

"Oh, please don't!" she whispered.

Spade shrugged again. "That's the way it was." He glanced at his watch and moved from his chair to the settee beside her. "There's no time for worrying about that now." His voice was pleasant but firm. "Out there a flock of policemen and assistant district attorneys and reporters are running around with their noses to the ground. What do you want to do?"

"I want you to save me from—from it all," she replied in a thin tremulous voice. She put a timid hand on his sleeve. "Mr. Spade, do they know about me?"

"Not yet. I wanted to see you first."

"What—what would they think if they knew about the way I came to you—with those lies?"

"It would make them suspicious. That's why I've been stalling them till I could see you. I thought maybe we wouldn't have to let them know all of it. We ought to be able to fake a story that will rock them to sleep, if necessary."

"You don't think I had anything to do with the—the murders—do you?"

Spade grinned at her and said: "I forgot to ask you that. Did you?"

"No."

"That's good. Now what are we going to tell the police?"

She squirmed on her end of the settee and her eyes wavered between heavy lashes, as if trying and failing to free their gaze from his. She seemed smaller, and very young and oppressed.

"Must they know about me at all?" she asked. "I think I'd rather die than that, Mr. Spade. I can't explain now, but can't you somehow manage so that you can shield me from them, so I won't have to answer their questions? I don't think I could stand being questioned now. I think I would rather die. Can't you, Mr. Spade?"

"Maybe," he said, "but I'll have to know what it's all about."

She went down on her knees at his knees. She held her face up to him. Her face was wan, taut, and fearful over tight-clasped hands.

"I haven't lived a good life," she cried. "I've been bad—worse than you could know—but I'm not all bad. Look at me, Mr. Spade. You know I'm not all bad, don't you? You can see that, can't you? Then can't you trust me a little? Oh, I'm so alone and afraid, and I've got nobody to help me if you won't help me. I know I've no right to ask you to trust me if I won't trust you. I do trust you, but I can't tell you. I can't tell you now. Later I will, when I can. I'm afraid, Mr. Spade. I'm afraid of trusting you. I don't mean that. I do trust you, but—I trusted Floyd and—I've nobody else, nobody else, Mr. Spade. You can help me. You've said you can help me. If I hadn't believed you could save me I would have run away today instead of sending for you. If I thought anybody else could save me would I be down on my knees like this? I know this isn't fair of me. But be generous, Mr. Spade, don't ask me to be fair. You're strong, you're resourceful, you're brave. You can spare me some of that strength and resourcefulness and courage, surely. Help me, Mr. Spade. Help me because I need help so badly, and because if you don't where will I find anyone who can, no matter how willing? Help me. I've no right to ask you to help me blindly, but I do ask you. Be generous, Mr. Spade. You can help me. Help me."

Spade, who had held his breath through much of this speech, now emptied his lungs with a long sighing exhalation between pursed lips and said: "You won't need much of anybody's help. You're good. You're very good. It's chiefly your eyes, I think, and that throb you get into your voice when you say things like 'Be generous, Mr. Spade.'"

She jumped up on her feet. Her face crimsoned painfully, but she held her head erect and she looked Spade straight in the eyes.

"I deserve that," she said. "I deserve it, but—oh!—I did want your help so much. I do want it, and need it, so much. And the lie was in the way I said it, and not at all in what I said." She turned away, no longer holding herself erect. "It is my own fault that you can't believe me now."

Spade's face reddened and he looked down at the floor, muttering: "Now you are dangerous."

Brigid O'Shaughnessy went to the table and picked up his hat. She came back and stood in front of him holding the hat, not offering it to him, but holding it for him to take if he wished. Her face was white and thin.

Spade looked at his hat and asked: "What happened last night?"

"Floyd came to the hotel at nine o'clock, and we went out for a walk. I suggested that so Mr. Archer could see him. We stopped at a restaurant in Geary Street, I think it was, for supper and to dance, and came back to the hotel at about half-past twelve. Floyd left me at the door and I stood inside and watched Mr. Archer follow him down the street, on the other side."

"Down? You mean towards Market Street?"

"Yes."

"Do you know what they'd be doing in the neighborhood of Bush and Stockton, where Archer was shot?"

"Isn't that near where Floyd lived?"

"No. It would be nearly a dozen blocks out of his way if he was going from your hotel to his. Well, what did you do after they had gone?"

"I went to bed. And this morning when I went out for breakfast I saw the headlines in the papers and read about—you know. Then I went up to Union Square, where I had seen automobiles for hire, and got one and went to the hotel for my luggage. After I found my room had been searched yesterday I knew I would have to move, and I had found this place yesterday afternoon. So I came up here and then telephoned your office."

"Your room at the St. Mark was searched?" he asked.

"Yes, while I was at your office." She bit her lip. "I didn't mean to tell you that."

"That means I'm not supposed to question you about it?"

She nodded shyly.

He frowned.

She moved his hat a little in her hands.

He laughed impatiently and said: "Stop waving the hat in my face. Haven't I offered to do what I can?"

She smiled contritely, returned the hat to the table, and sat beside him on the settee again.

He said: "I've got nothing against trusting you blindly except that I won't be able to do you much good if I haven't some idea of what it's all about. For instance, I've got to have some sort of a line on your Floyd Thursby."

"I met him in the Orient." She spoke slowly, looking down at a pointed finger tracing eights on the settee between them. "We came here from Hongkong last week. He was—he had promised to help me. He took advantage of my helplessness and dependence on him to betray me."

"Betray you how?"

She shook her head and said nothing.

Spade, frowning with impatience, asked: "Why did you want him shadowed?"

"I wanted to learn how far he had gone. He wouldn't even let me know where he was staying. I wanted to find out what he was doing, whom he was meeting, things like that."

"Did he kill Archer?"

She looked up at him, surprised. "Yes, certainly," she said.

"He had a Luger in a shoulder-holster. Archer wasn't shot with a Luger."

"He had a revolver in his overcoat-pocket," she said.

"You saw it?"

"Oh, I've seen it often. I know he always carries one there. I didn't see it last night, but I know he never wears an overcoat without it."

"Why all the guns?"

"He lived by them. There was a story in Hongkong that he had come out there, to the Orient, as bodyguard to a gambler who had had to leave the States, and that the gambler had since disappeared. They said Floyd knew about his disappearing. I don't know. I do know that he always went heavily armed and that he never went to sleep without covering the floor around his bed with crumpled newspaper so nobody could come silently into his room."

"You picked a nice sort of playmate."

"Only that sort could have helped me," she said simply, "if he had been loyal."

"Yes, if." Spade pinched his lower lip between finger and thumb and looked gloomily at her. The vertical creases over his nose deepened, drawing his brows together. "How bad a hole are you actually in?"

"As bad," she said, "as could be."

"Physical danger?"

"I'm not heroic. I don't think there's anything worse than death."

"Then it's that?"

"It's that as surely as we're sitting here"—she shivered—"unless you help me."

He took his fingers away from his mouth and ran them through his hair. "I'm not Christ," he said irritably. "I can't work miracles out of thin air." He looked at his watch. "The day's going and you're giving me nothing to work with. Who killed Thursby?"

She put a crumpled handkerchief to her mouth and said, "I don't know," through it.

"Your enemies or his?"

"I don't know. His, I hope, but I'm afraid—I don't know."

"How was he supposed to be helping you? Why did you bring him here from Hongkong?"

She looked at him with frightened eyes and shook her head in silence. Her face was haggard and pitifully stubborn.

Spade stood up, thrust his hands into the pockets of his jacket, and scowled down at her. "This is hopeless," he said savagely. "I can't do anything for you. I don't know what you want done. I don't even know if you know what you want."

She hung her head and wept.

He made a growling animal noise in his throat and went to the table for his hat.

"You won't," she begged in a small choked voice, not looking up, "go to the police?"

"Go to them!" he exclaimed, his voice loud with rage. "They've been running me ragged since four o'clock this morning. I've made myself God knows how much trouble standing them off. For what? For some crazy notion that I could help you. I can't. I won't try." He put his hat on his head and pulled it down tight. "Go to them? All I've got to do is stand still and they'll be swarming all over me. Well, I'll tell them what I know and you'll have to take your chances."

She rose from the settee and held herself straight in front of him though her knees were trembling, and she held her white panic-stricken face up high though she couldn't hold the twitching muscles of mouth and chin still. She said: "You've been patient. You've tried to help me. It is hopeless, and useless, I suppose." She stretched out her right hand. "I thank you for what you have done. I—I'll have to take my chances."

Spade made the growling animal noise in his throat again and sat down on the settee. "How much money have you got?" he asked.

The question startled her. Then she pinched her lower lip between her teeth and answered reluctantly: "I've about five hundred dollars left."

"Give it to me."

She hesitated, looking timidly at him. He made angry gestures with mouth, eyebrows, hands, and shoulders. She went into her bedroom, returning almost immediately with a sheaf of paper money in one hand.

He took the money from her, counted it, and said: "There's only four hundred here."

"I had to keep some to live on," she explained meekly, putting a hand to her breast.

"Can't you get any more?"

"No."

"You must have something you can raise money on," he insisted.

"I've some rings, a little jewelry."

"You'll have to hock them," he said, and held out his hand. "The Remedial's the best place—Mission and Fifth."

She looked pleadingly at him. His yellow-grey eyes were hard and implacable. Slowly she put her hand inside the neck of her dress, brought out a slender roll of bills, and put them in his waiting hand.

He smoothed the bills out and counted them—four twenties, four tens, and a five. He returned two of the tens and the five to her. The others he put in his pocket. Then he stood up and said: "I'm going out and see what I can do for you. I'll be back as soon as I can with the best news I can manage. I'll ring four times—long, short, long, short—so you'll know it's me. You needn't go to the door with me. I can let myself out."

He left her standing in the center of the floor looking after him with dazed blue eyes.

Spade went into a reception-room whose door bore the legend *Wise, Merican & Wise*. The red-haired girl at the switchboard said: "Oh, hello, Mr. Spade."

"Hello, darling," he replied. "Is Sid in?"

He stood beside her with a hand on her plump shoulder while she manipulated a plug and spoke into the mouthpiece: "Mr. Spade to see you, Mr. Wise." She looked up at Spade. "Go right in."

He squeezed her shoulder by way of acknowledgment, crossed the reception-room to a dully lighted inner corridor, and passed down the corridor to a frosted glass door at its far end. He opened the frosted glass door and went into an office where a small olive-skinned man with a tired oval face under thin dark hair dotted with dandruff sat behind an immense desk on which bales of paper were heaped.

The small man flourished a cold cigar-stub at Spade and said: "Pull a chair around. So Miles got the big one last night?" Neither his tired face nor his rather shrill voice held any emotion.

"Uh-huh, that's what I came in about." Spade frowned and cleared his throat. "I think I'm going to have to tell a coroner to go to hell, Sid. Can I hide behind the sanctity of my clients' secrets and identities and what-not, all the same priest or lawyer?"

Sid Wise lifted his shoulders and lowered the ends of his mouth. "Why not? An inquest is not a court-trial. You can try, anyway. You've gotten away with more than that before this."

"I know, but Dundy's getting snotty, and maybe it is a little bit thick this time. Get your hat, Sid, and we'll go see the right people. I want to be safe."

Sid Wise looked at the papers massed on his desk and groaned, but he got up from his chair and went to the closet by the window. "You're a son of a gun, Sammy," he said as he took his hat from its hook.

Spade returned to his office at ten minutes past five that evening. Effie Perine was sitting at his desk reading *Time*. Spade sat on the desk and asked: "Anything stirring?"

"Not here. You look like you'd swallowed the canary."

He grinned contentedly. "I think we've got a future. I always had an idea that if Miles would go off and die somewhere we'd stand a better chance of thriving. Will you take care of sending flowers for me?"

"I did."

"You're an invaluable angel. How's your woman's intuition today?"

"Why?"

"What do you think of Wonderly?"

"I'm for her," the girl replied without hesitation.

"She's got too many names," Spade mused, "Wonderly, Leblanc, and she says the right one's O'Shaughnessy."

"I don't care if she's got all the names in the phone-book. That girl is all right, and you know it."

"I wonder." Spade blinked sleepily at Effie Perine. He chuckled. "Anyway she's given up seven hundred smacks in two days, and that's all right."

Effie Perine sat up straight and said: "Sam, if that girl's in trouble and you let her down, or take advantage of it to bleed her, I'll never forgive you, never have any respect for you, as long as I live."

Spade smiled unnaturally. Then he frowned. The frown was unnatural. He opened his mouth to speak, but the sound of someone's entrance through the corridor-door stopped him.

Effie Perine rose and went into the outer office. Spade took off his hat and sat in his chair. The girl returned with an engraved card—*Mr. Joel Cairo.*

"This guy is queer," she said.

"In with him, then, darling," said Spade.

Mr. Joel Cairo was a small-boned dark man of medium height. His hair was black and smooth and very glossy. His features were Levantine. A square-cut ruby, its sides paralleled by four baguette diamonds, gleamed against the deep green of his cravat. His black coat, cut tight to narrow shoulders, flared a little over slightly plump hips. His trousers fitted his round legs more snugly than was the current fashion. The uppers of his patent-leather shoes were hidden by fawn spats. He held a black derby hat in a chamois-gloved hand and came towards Spade with short, mincing, bobbing steps. The fragrance of *chypre* came with him.

Spade inclined his head at his visitor and then at a chair, saying: "Sit down, Mr. Cairo."

Cairo bowed elaborately over his hat, said, "I thank you," in a high-pitched thin voice and sat down. He sat down primly, crossing his ankles, placing his hat on his knees, and began to draw off his yellow gloves.

Spade rocked back in his chair and asked: "Now what can I do for you, Mr. Cairo?" The amiable negligence of his tone, his motion in the chair, were precisely as they had been when he had addressed the same question to Brigid O'Shaughnessy on the previous day.

Cairo turned his hat over, dropping his gloves into it, and placed it bottom-up on the corner of the desk nearest him. Diamonds twinkled on the second and fourth fingers of his left hand, a ruby that matched the one in his tie even to the surrounding diamonds on the third finger of his right hand. His hands were soft and well cared for. Though they were not large their flaccid bluntness made them seem clumsy. He rubbed his palms together and said over the whispering sound they made: "May a stranger offer condolences for your partner's unfortunate death?"

"Thanks."

"May I ask, Mr. Spade, if there was, as the newspapers inferred, a certain—ah—relationship between that unfortunate happening and the death a little later of the man Thursby?"

Spade said nothing in a blank-faced definite way.

Cairo rose and bowed. "I beg your pardon." He sat down and placed his hands side by side, palms down, on the corner of the desk. "More than idle curiosity made me ask that, Mr. Spade. I am trying to recover an—ah—ornament that has been—shall we say?—mislaid. I thought, and hoped, you could assist me."

Spade nodded with eyebrows lifted to indicate attentiveness.

"The ornament is a statuette," Cairo went on, selecting and mouthing his words carefully, "the black figure of a bird."

Spade nodded again, with courteous interest.

"I am prepared to pay, on behalf of the figure's rightful owner, the sum of five thousand dollars for its recovery." Cairo raised one hand from the desk-corner and touched a spot in the air with the broad-nailed tip of an ugly forefinger. "I am prepared to promise that—what is the phrase? —no questions will be asked." He put his hand on the desk again beside the other and smiled blandly over them at the private detective.

"Five thousand is a lot of money," Spade commented, looking thoughtfully at Cairo. "It—"

Fingers drummed lightly on the door.

When Spade had called, "Come in," the door opened far enough to admit Effie Perine's head and shoulders. She had put on a small dark felt hat and a dark coat with a grey fur collar.

"Is there anything else?" she asked.

"No. Good night. Lock the door when you go, will you?"

"Good night," she said and disappeared behind the closing door.

Spade turned in his chair to face Cairo again, saying: "It's an interesting figure."

The sound of the corridor-door's closing behind Effie Perine came to them.

Cairo smiled and took a short compact flat black pistol out of an inner pocket. "You will please," he said, "clasp your hands together at the back of your neck."

CHAPTER V

The Levantine

SPADE DID NOT LOOK at the pistol. He raised his arms and, leaning back in his chair, intertwined the fingers of his two hands behind his head. His eyes, holding no particular expression, remained focused on Cairo's dark face.

Cairo coughed a little apologetic cough and smiled nervously with lips that had lost some of their redness. His dark eyes were humid and bashful and very earnest. "I intend to search your offices, Mr. Spade. I warn you that if you attempt to prevent me I shall certainly shoot you."

"Go ahead." Spade's voice was as empty of expression as his face.

"You will please stand," the man with the pistol instructed him at whose thick chest the pistol was aimed. "I shall have to make sure that you are not armed."

Spade stood up pushing his chair back with his calves as he straightened his legs.

Cairo went around behind him. He transferred the pistol from his right hand to his left. He lifted Spade's coat-tail and looked under it. Holding the pistol close to Spade's back, he put his right hand around

Spade's side and patted his chest. The Levantine face was then no more than six inches below and behind Spade's right elbow.

Spade's elbow dropped as Spade spun to the right. Cairo's face jerked back not far enough: Spade's right heel on the patent-leathered toes anchored the smaller man in the elbow's path. The elbow struck him beneath the cheek-bone, staggering him so that he must have fallen had he not been held by Spade's foot on his foot. Spade's elbow went on past the astonished dark face and straightened when Spade's hand struck down at the pistol. Cairo let the pistol go the instant that Spade's fingers touched it. The pistol was small in Spade's hand.

Spade took his foot off Cairo's to complete his about-face. With his left hand Spade gathered together the smaller man's coat-lapels—the ruby-set green tie bunching out over his knuckles—while his right hand stowed the captured weapon away in a coat-pocket. Spade's yellow-grey eyes were somber. His face was wooden, with a trace of sullenness around the mouth.

Cairo's face was twisted by pain and chagrin. There were tears in his dark eyes. His skin was the complexion of polished lead except where the elbow had reddened his cheek.

Spade by means of his grip on the Levantine's lapels turned him slowly and pushed him back until he was standing close in front of the chair he had lately occupied. A puzzled look replaced the look of pain in the lead-colored face. Then Spade smiled. His smile was gentle, even dreamy. His right shoulder raised a few inches. His bent right arm was driven up by the shoulder's lift. Fist, wrist, forearm, crooked elbow, and upper arm seemed all one rigid piece, with only the limber shoulder giving them motion. The fist struck Cairo's face, covering for a moment one side of his chin, a corner of his mouth, and most of his cheek between cheek-bone and jaw-bone.

Cairo shut his eyes and was unconscious.

Spade lowered the limp body into the chair, where it lay with sprawled arms and legs, the head lolling back against the chair's back, the mouth open.

Spade emptied the unconscious man's pockets one by one, working methodically, moving the lax body when necessary, making a pile of the pockets' contents on the desk. When the last pocket had been turned out he returned to his own chair, rolled and lighted a cigarette, and began to examine his spoils. He examined them with grave unhurried thoroughness.

There was a large wallet of dark soft leather. The wallet contained three hundred and sixty-five dollars in United States bills of several sizes; three five-pound notes; a much-visaed Greek passport bearing Cairo's name and portrait; five folded sheets of pinkish onionskin paper covered with what seemed to be Arabic writing; a raggedly clipped newspaper-account of the finding of Archer's and Thursby's bodies; a post-card-photograph of a dusky woman with bold cruel eyes and a tender drooping mouth; a large silk handkerchief, yellow with age and somewhat cracked along its folds; a thin sheaf of Mr. Joel Cairo's engraved cards; and a ticket for an orchestra seat at the Geary Theatre that evening.

Besides the wallet and its contents there were three gaily colored silk handkerchiefs fragrant of *chypre*; a platinum Longines watch on a platinum and red gold chain, attached at the other end to a small pear-shaped pendant of some white metal; a handful of United States, British, French, and Chinese coins; a ring holding half a dozen keys; a silver and onyx fountain-pen; a metal comb in a leatherette case; a nail-file in a leatherette case; a small street-guide to San Francisco; a Southern Pacific baggage-check; a half-filled package of violet pastilles; a Shanghai insurance-broker's business-card; and four sheets of Hotel Belvedere writing paper, on one of which was written in small precise letters Samuel Spade's name and the addresses of his office and his apartment.

Having examined these articles carefully—he even opened the back of the watch-case to see that nothing was hidden inside—Spade leaned over and took the unconscious man's wrist between finger and thumb, feeling his pulse. Then he dropped the wrist, settled back in his chair, and rolled and lighted another cigarette. His face while he smoked was, except for occasional slight and aimless movements of his lower lip, so still and reflective that it seemed stupid; but when Cairo presently moaned and fluttered his eyelids Spade's face became bland, and he put the beginning of a friendly smile into his eyes and mouth.

Joel Cairo awakened slowly. His eyes opened first, but a full minute passed before they fixed their gaze on any definite part of the ceiling. Then he shut his mouth and swallowed, exhaling heavily through his nose afterward. He drew in one foot and turned a hand over on his thigh. Then he raised his head from the chair-back, looked around the office in confusion, saw Spade, and sat up. He opened his mouth to speak, started, clapped a hand to his face where Spade's fist had struck and where there was now a florid bruise.

Cairo said through his teeth, painfully: "I could have shot you, Mr. Spade."

"You could have tried," Spade conceded.

"I did not try."

"I know."

"Then why did you strike me after I was disarmed?"

"Sorry," Spade said, and grinned wolfishly, showing his jaw-teeth, "but imagine my embarrassment when I found that five-thousand-dollar offer was just hooey."

"You are mistaken, Mr. Spade. That was, and is, a genuine offer."

"What the hell?" Spade's surprise was genuine.

"I am prepared to pay five thousand dollars for the figure's return."

Cairo took his hand away from his bruised face and sat up prim and business-like again. "You have it?"

"No."

"If it is not here"—Cairo was very politely skeptical—"why should you have risked serious injury to prevent my searching for it?"

"I should sit around and let people come in and stick me up?" Spade flicked a finger at Cairo's possessions on the desk. "You've got my apartment-address. Been up there yet?"

"Yes, Mr. Spade. I am ready to pay five thousand dollars for the figure's return, but surely it is natural enough that I should try first to spare the owner that expense if possible."

"Who is he?"

Cairo shook his head and smiled. "You will have to forgive my not answering that question."

"Will I?" Spade leaned forward smiling with tight lips. "I've got you by the neck, Cairo. You've walked in and tied yourself up, plenty strong enough to suit the police, with last night's killings. Well, now you'll have to play with me or else."

Cairo's smile was demure and not in any way alarmed. "I made somewhat extensive inquiries about you before taking any action," he said, "and was assured that you were far too reasonable to allow other considerations to interfere with profitable business relations."

Spade shrugged. "Where are they?" he asked.

"I have offered you five thousand dollars for—"

Spade thumped Cairo's wallet with the backs of his fingers and said: "There's nothing like five thousand dollars here. You're betting your eyes. You could come in and say you'd pay me a million for a purple elephant, but what in hell would that mean?"

"I see, I see," Cairo said thoughtfully, screwing up his eyes. "You wish some assurance of my sincerity." He brushed his red lower lip with a fingertip. "A retainer, would that serve?"

"It might."

Cairo put his hand out towards his wallet, hesitated, withdrew the hand, and said: "You will take, say, a hundred dollars?"

Spade picked up the wallet and took out a hundred dollars. Then he frowned, said, "Better make it two hundred," and did.

Cairo said nothing.

"Your first guess was that I had the bird," Spade said in a crisp voice when he had put the two hundred dollars into his pocket and had dropped the wallet on the desk again. "There's nothing in that. What's your second?"

"That you know where it is, or, if not exactly that, that you know it is where you can get it."

Spade neither denied nor affirmed that: he seemed hardly to have heard it. He asked: "What sort of proof can you give me that your man is the owner?"

"Very little, unfortunately. There is this, though: nobody else can give you any authentic evidence of ownership at all. And if you know as much about the affair as I suppose—or I should not be here—you know that the means by which it was taken from him shows that his right to it was more valid than anyone else's—certainly more valid than Thursby's."

"What about his daughter?" Spade asked.

Excitement opened Cairo's eyes and mouth, turned his face red, made his voice shrill. "*He* is not the owner!"

Spade said, "Oh," mildly and ambiguously.

"Is he here, in San Francisco, now?" Cairo asked in a less shrill, but still excited, voice.

Spade blinked his eyes sleepily and suggested: "It might be better all around if we put our cards on the table."

Cairo recovered composure with a little jerk. "I do not think it would be better." His voice was suave now. "If you know more than I, I shall profit by your knowledge, and so will you to the extent of five thousand dollars. If you do not then I have made a mistake in coming to you, and to do as you suggest would be simply to make that mistake worse."

Spade nodded indifferently and waved his hand at the articles on the desk, saying: "There's your stuff"; and then, when Cairo was returning them to his pockets: "It's understood that you're to pay my expenses while I'm getting this black bird for you, and five thousand dollars when it's done?"

"Yes, Mr. Spade; that is, five thousand dollars less whatever moneys have been advanced to you—five thousand in all."

"Right. And it's a legitimate proposition." Spade's face was solemn except for wrinkles at the corners of his eyes. "You're not hiring me to do any murders or burglaries for you, but simply to get it back if possible in an honest and lawful way."

"If possible," Cairo agreed. His face also was solemn except for the eyes. "And in any event with discretion." He rose and picked up his hat. "I am at the Hotel Belvedere when you wish to communicate with me—room six-thirty-five. I confidently expect the greatest mutual benefit from our association, Mr. Spade." He hesitated. "May I have my pistol?"

"Sure. I'd forgotten it."

Spade took the pistol out of his coat-pocket and handed it to Cairo.

Cairo pointed the pistol at Spade's chest.

"You will please keep your hands on the top of the desk," Cairo said earnestly. "I intend to search your offices."

Spade said: "I'll be damned." Then he laughed in his throat and said: "All right. Go ahead. I won't stop you."

CHAPTER VI

The Undersized Shadow

FOR HALF AN HOUR after Joel Cairo had gone Spade sat alone, still and frowning, at his desk. Then he said aloud in the tone of one dismissing a problem, "Well, they're paying for it," and took a bottle of Manhattan cocktail and a paper drinking-cup from a desk-drawer. He filled the cup two-thirds full, drank, returned the bottle to the drawer, tossed the cup into the wastebasket, put on his hat and overcoat, turned off the lights, and went down to the night-lit street.

An undersized youth of twenty or twenty-one in neat grey cap and overcoat was standing idly on the corner below Spade's building.

Spade walked up Sutter Street to Kearny, where he entered a cigar-store to buy two sacks of Bull Durham. When he came out the youth was one of four people waiting for a street-car on the opposite corner.

Spade ate dinner at Herbert's Grill in Powell Street. When he left the Grill, at a quarter to eight, the youth was looking into a nearby haberdasher's window.

Spade went to the Hotel Belvedere, asking at the desk for Mr. Cairo. He was told that Cairo was not in. The youth sat in a chair in a far corner of the lobby.

Spade went to the Geary Theatre, failed to see Cairo in the lobby, and posted himself on the curb in front, facing the theatre. The youth loitered with other loiterers before Marquard's restaurant below.

At ten minutes past eight Joel Cairo appeared, walking up Geary Street with his little mincing bobbing steps. Apparently he did not see Spade until the private detective touched his shoulder. He seemed moderately surprised for a moment, and then said: "Oh, yes, of course you saw the ticket."

"Uh-huh. I've got something I want to show you." Spade drew Cairo back towards the curb a little away from the other waiting theatre-goers. "The kid in the cap down by Marquard's."

Cairo murmured, "I'll see," and looked at his watch. He looked up Geary Street. He looked at a theatre-sign in front of him on which George Arliss was shown costumed as Shylock, and then his dark eyes crawled sidewise in their sockets until they were looking at the kid in the cap, at his cool pale face with curling lashes hiding lowered eyes.

"Who is he?" Spade asked.

Cairo smiled up at Spade. "I do not know him."

"He's been tailing me around town."

Cairo wet his lower lip with his tongue and asked: "Do you think it was wise, then, to let him see us together?"

"How do I know?" Spade replied. "Anyway, it's done."

Cairo removed his hat and smoothed his hair with a gloved hand. He replaced his hat carefully on his head and said with every appearance of candor: "I give you my word I do not know him, Mr. Spade. I give you my word I have nothing to do with him. I have asked nobody's assistance except yours, on my word of honor."

"Then he's one of the others?"

"That may be."

"I just wanted to know, because if he gets to be a nuisance I may have to hurt him."

"Do as you think best. He is not a friend of mine."

"That's good. There goes the curtain. Good night," Spade said, and crossed the street to board a westbound street-car.

The youth in the cap boarded the same car.

Spade left the car at Hyde Street and went up to his apartment. His rooms were not greatly upset, but showed unmistakable signs of having been searched. When Spade had washed and had put on a fresh shirt and collar he went out again, walked up to Sutter Street, and boarded a westbound car. The youth boarded it also.

Within half a dozen blocks of the Coronet Spade left the car and went into the vestibule of a tall brown apartment-building. He pressed three bell-buttons together. The street-door-lock buzzed. He entered, passed the elevator and stairs, went down a long yellow-walled corridor to the rear of the building, found a back door fastened by a Yale lock, and let himself out into a narrow court. The court led to a dark back street, up which Spade walked for two blocks. Then he crossed over to California Street and went to the Coronet. It was not quite half-past nine o'clock.

The eagerness with which Brigid O'Shaughnessy welcomed Spade suggested that she had been not entirely certain of his coming. She had put on a satin gown of the blue shade called Artoise that season, with chalcedony shoulder-straps, and her stockings and slippers were Artoise. The red and cream sitting-room had been brought to order and livened with flowers in squat pottery vases of black and silver. Three small rough-barked logs burned in the fireplace. Spade watched them burn while she put away his hat and coat.

"Do you bring me good news?" she asked when she came into the room again. Anxiety looked through her smile, and she held her breath.

"We won't have to make anything public that hasn't already been made public."

"The police won't have to know about me?"

"No."

She sighed happily and sat on the walnut settee. Her face relaxed and her body relaxed. She smiled up at him with admiring eyes. "However did you manage it?" she asked more in wonder than in curiosity.

"Most things in San Francisco can be bought, or taken."

"And you won't get into trouble? Do sit down." She made room for him on the settee.

"I don't mind a reasonable amount of trouble," he said with not too much complacence.

He stood beside the fireplace and looked at her with eyes that studied, weighed, judged her without pretense that they were not studying, weighing, judging her. She flushed slightly under the frankness of his scrutiny, but she seemed more sure of herself than before, though a becoming shyness had not left her eyes. He stood there until it seemed plain that he meant to ignore her invitation to sit beside her, and then crossed to the settee.

"You aren't," he asked as he sat down, "exactly the sort of person you pretend to be, are you?"

"I'm not sure I know what you mean," she said in her hushed voice, looking at him with puzzled eyes.

"Schoolgirl manner," he explained, "stammering and blushing and all that."

She blushed and replied hurriedly, not looking at him: "I told you this afternoon that I've been bad—worse than you could know."

"That's what I mean," he said. "You told me that this afternoon in the same words, same tone. It's a speech you've practiced."

After a moment in which she seemed confused almost to the point of tears she laughed and said: "Very well, then, Mr. Spade, I'm not at all the sort of person I pretend to be. I'm eighty years old, incredibly wicked, and an iron-molder by trade. But if it's a pose it's one I've grown into, so you won't expect me to drop it entirely, will you?"

"Oh, it's all right," he assured her. "Only it wouldn't be all right if you were actually that innocent. We'd never get anywhere."

"I won't be innocent," she promised with a hand on her heart.

"I saw Joel Cairo tonight," he said in the manner of one making polite conversation.

Gaiety went out of her face. Her eyes, focused on his profile, became frightened, then cautious. He had stretched his legs out and was looking at his crossed feet. His face did not indicate that he was thinking about anything.

There was a long pause before she asked uneasily:

"You—you know him?"

"I saw him tonight." Spade did not look up and he maintained his light conversational tone. "He was going to see George Arliss."

"You mean you talked to him?"

"Only for a minute or two, till the curtain-bell rang."

She got up from the settee and went to the fireplace to poke the fire. She changed slightly the position of an ornament on the mantelpiece, crossed the room to get a box of cigarettes from a table in a corner, straightened a curtain, and returned to her seat. Her face now was smooth and unworried.

Spade grinned sidewise at her and said: "You're good. You're very good."

Her face did not change. She asked quietly: "What did he say?"

"About what?"

She hesitated. "About me."

"Nothing." Spade turned to hold his lighter under the end of her cigarette. His eyes were shiny in a wooden satan's face.

"Well, what did he say?" she asked with half-playful petulance.

"He offered me five thousand dollars for the black bird."

She started, her teeth tore the end of her cigarette, and her eyes, after a swift alarmed glance at Spade, turned away from him.

"You're not going to go around poking at the fire and straightening up the room again, are you?" he asked lazily.

She laughed a clear merry laugh, dropped the mangled cigarette into a tray, and looked at him with clear merry eyes. "I won't," she promised. "And what did you say?"

"Five thousand dollars is a lot of money."

She smiled, but when, instead of smiling, he looked gravely at her, her smile became faint, confused, and presently vanished. In its place came a hurt, bewildered look. "Surely you're not really considering it," she said.

"Why not? Five thousand dollars is a lot of money."

"But, Mr. Spade, you promised to help me." Her hands were on his arm. "I trusted you. You can't—" She broke off, took her hands from his sleeve and worked them together.

Spade smiled gently into her troubled eyes. "Don't let's try to figure out how much you've trusted me," he said. "I promised to help you—sure—but you didn't say anything about any black birds."

"But you must've known or—or you wouldn't have mentioned it to me. You do know now. You won't—you can't—treat me like that." Her eyes were cobalt-blue prayers.

"Five thousand dollars is," he said for the third time, "a lot of money."

She lifted her shoulders and hands and let them fall in a gesture that accepted defeat. "It is," she agreed in a small dull voice. "It is far more than I could ever offer you, if I must bid for your loyalty."

Spade laughed. His laughter was brief and somewhat bitter. "That is good," he said, "coming from you. What have you given me besides money? Have you given me any of your confidence? any of the truth? any help in helping you? Haven't you tried to buy my loyalty with money and nothing else? Well, if I'm peddling it, why shouldn't I let it go to the highest bidder?"

"I've given you all the money I have." Tears glistened in her white-ringed eyes. Her voice was hoarse, vibrant. "I've thrown myself on your mercy, told you that without your help I'm utterly lost. What else is there?" She suddenly moved close to him on the settee and cried angrily: "Can I buy you with my body?"

Their faces were few inches apart. Spade took her face between his hands and he kissed her mouth roughly and contemptuously. Then he sat back and said: "I'll think it over." His face was hard and furious.

She sat still holding her numb face where his hands had left it.

He stood up and said: "Christ! there's no sense to this." He took two steps towards the fireplace and stopped, glowering at the burning logs, grinding his teeth together.

She did not move.

He turned to face her. The two vertical lines above his nose were deep clefts between red wales. "I don't give a damn about your honesty," he told her, trying to make himself speak calmly. "I don't care what kind of tricks you're up to, what your secrets are, but I've got to have something to show that you know what you're doing."

"I do know. Please believe that I do, and that it's all for the best, and—"

"Show me," he ordered. "I'm willing to help you. I've done what I could so far. If necessary I'll go ahead blindfolded, but I can't do it without more confidence in you than I've got now. You've got to convince me that you know what it's all about, that you're not simply fiddling around by guess and by God, hoping it'll come out all right somehow in the end."

"Can't you trust me just a little longer?"

"How much is a little? And what are you waiting for?"

She bit her lip and looked down. "I must talk to Joel Cairo," she said almost inaudibly.

"You can see him tonight," Spade said, looking at his watch. "His show will be out soon. We can get him on the phone at his hotel."

She raised her eyes, alarmed. "But he can't come here. I can't let him know where I am. I'm afraid."

"My place," Spade suggested.

She hesitated, working her lips together, then asked: "Do you think he'd go there?"

Spade nodded.

"All right," she exclaimed, jumping up, her eyes large and bright. "Shall we go now?"

She went into the next room. Spade went to the table in the corner and silently pulled the drawer out. The drawer held two packs of playing-cards, a pad of score-cards for bridge, a brass screw, a piece of red string, and a gold pencil. He had shut the drawer and was lighting a cigarette when she returned wearing a small dark hat and a grey kidskin coat, carrying his hat and coat.

Their taxicab drew up behind a dark sedan that stood directly in front of Spade's street-door. Iva Archer was alone in the sedan, sitting at the wheel. Spade lifted his hat to her and went indoors with Brigid O'Shaughnessy. In the lobby he halted beside one of the benches and asked: "Do you mind waiting here a moment? I won't be long."

"That's perfectly all right," Brigid O'Shaughnessy said, sitting down. "You needn't hurry."

Spade went out to the sedan. When he had opened the sedan's door Iva spoke quickly: "I've got to talk to you, Sam. Can't I come in?" Her face was pale and nervous.

"Not now."

Iva clicked her teeth together and asked sharply: "Who is she?"

"I've only a minute, Iva," Spade said patiently. "What is it?"

"Who is she?" she repeated, nodding at the street-door.

He looked away from her, down the street. In front of a garage on the next corner an undersized youth of twenty or twenty-one in neat grey cap and overcoat loafed with his back against a wall. Spade frowned and returned his gaze to Iva's insistent face. "What is the matter?" he asked. "Has anything happened? You oughtn't to be here at this time of night."

"I'm beginning to believe that," she complained. "You told me I oughtn't to come to the office, and now I oughtn't to come here. Do you mean I oughtn't to chase after you? If that's what you mean why don't you say it right out?"

"Now, Iva, you've got no right to take that attitude."

"I know I haven't. I haven't any rights at all, it seems, where you're concerned. I thought I did. I thought your pretending to love me gave me—"

Spade said wearily: "This is no time to be arguing about that, precious. What was it you wanted to see me about?"

"I can't talk to you here, Sam. Can't I come in?"

"Not now."

"Why can't I?"

Spade said nothing.

She made a thin line of her mouth, squirmed around straight behind the wheel, and started the sedan's engine, staring angrily ahead.

When the sedan began to move Spade said, "Good night, Iva," shut the door, and stood at the curb with his hat in his hand until it had been driven away. Then he went indoors again.

Brigid O'Shaughnessy rose smiling cheerfully from the bench and they went up to his apartment.

CHAPTER VII

G in the Air

IN HIS BEDROOM that was a living-room now the wall-bed was up, Spade took Brigid O'Shaughnessy's hat and coat, made her comfortable in a padded rocking chair, and telephoned the Hotel Belvedere. Cairo had not returned from the theatre. Spade left his telephone-number with the request that Cairo call him as soon as he came in.

Spade sat down in the armchair beside the table and without any preliminary, without an introductory remark of any sort, began to tell the girl about a thing that had happened some years before in the Northwest. He talked in a steady matter-of-fact voice that was devoid of emphasis or pauses, though now and then he repeated a sentence slightly rearranged, as if it were important that each detail be related exactly as it had happened.

At the beginning Brigid O'Shaughnessy listened with only partial attentiveness, obviously more surprised by his telling the story than interested in it, her curiosity more engaged with his purpose in telling the story than with the story he told; but presently, as the story went on, it caught her more and more fully and she became still and receptive.

A man named Flitcraft had left his real-estate-office, in Tacoma, to go to luncheon one day and had never returned. He did not keep an engagement to play golf after four that afternoon, though he had taken the initiative in making the engagement less than half an hour before he went out to luncheon. His wife and children never saw him again. His wife and he were supposed to be on the best of terms. He had two children, boys, one five and the other three. He owned his house in a Tacoma suburb, a new Packard, and the rest of the appurtenances of successful American living.

Flitcraft had inherited seventy thousand dollars from his father, and, with his success in real estate, was worth something in the neighborhood of two hundred thousand dollars at the time he vanished. His affairs were in order, though there were enough loose ends to indicate that he had not been setting them in order preparatory to vanishing. A deal that would have brought him an attractive profit, for instance, was to have been concluded the day after the one on which he disappeared. There was nothing to suggest that he had more than fifty or sixty dollars in his immediate possession at the time of his going. His habits for months past could be accounted for too thoroughly to justify any suspicion of secret vices, or even of another woman in his life, though either was barely possible.

"He went like that," Spade said, "like a fist when you open your hand."

When he had reached this point in his story the telephone-bell rang.

"Hello," Spade said into the instrument. "Mr. Cairo? . . . This is Spade. Can you come up to my place—Post Street—now? . . . Yes, I think it is." He looked at the girl, pursed his lips, and then said rapidly: "Miss O'Shaughnessy is here and wants to see you."

Brigid O'Shaughnessy frowned and stirred in her chair, but did not say anything.

Spade put the telephone down and told her: "He'll be up in a few minutes. Well, that was in 1922. In 1927 I was with one of the big detective agencies in Seattle. Mrs. Flitcraft came in and told us somebody had seen a man in Spokane who looked a lot like her husband. I went over there. It was Flitcraft, all right. He had been living in Spokane for a couple of years as Charles—that was his first name—Pierce. He had an automobile-business that was netting him twenty or twenty-five thousand a year, a wife, a baby son, owned his home in a Spokane suburb, and usually got away to play golf after four in the afternoon during the season."

Spade had not been told very definitely what to do when he found Flitcraft. They talked in Spade's room at the Davenport. Flitcraft had no feeling of guilt. He had left his first family well provided for, and what he had done seemed to him perfectly reasonable. The only thing that bothered him was a doubt that he could make that reasonableness clear to Spade. He had never told anybody his story before, and thus had not had to attempt to make its reasonableness explicit. He tried now.

"I got it all right," Spade told Brigid O'Shaughnessy, "but Mrs. Flitcraft never did. She thought it was silly. Maybe it was. Anyway, it came out all right. She didn't want any scandal, and, after the trick he had played on her—the way she looked at it—she didn't want him. So they were divorced on the quiet and everything was swell all around.

"Here's what had happened to him. Going to lunch he passed an office-building that was being put up—just the skeleton. A beam or something fell eight or ten stories down and smacked the sidewalk alongside him. It brushed pretty close to him, but didn't touch him, though a piece of the sidewalk was chipped off and flew up and hit his cheek. It only took a piece of skin off, but he still had the scar when I saw him. He rubbed it with his finger—well, affectionately—when he told me about it. He was scared stiff of course, he said, but he was more shocked than really frightened. He felt like somebody had taken the lid off life and let him look at the works."

Flitcraft had been a good citizen and a good husband and father, not by any outer compulsion, but simply because he was a man who was most comfortable in step with his surroundings. He had been raised that way. The people he knew were like that. The life he knew was a clean orderly sane responsible affair. Now a falling beam had shown him that life was fundamentally none of these things. He, the good citizen-husband-father, could be wiped out between office and restaurant by the accident of a falling beam. He knew then that men died at haphazard like that, and lived only while blind chance spared them.

It was not, primarily, the injustice of it that disturbed him: he accepted that after the first shock. What disturbed him was the discovery that in sensibly ordering his affairs he had got out of step, and not into step, with life. He said he knew before he had gone twenty feet from the fallen beam that he would never know peace again until he had adjusted himself to this new glimpse of life. By the time he had eaten his luncheon he had found his means of adjustment. Life could be ended for him at random by a falling beam: he would change his life at random by simply going away. He loved his family, he said, as much as he supposed was usual, but he knew he was leaving them adequately provided for, and his love for them was not of the sort that would make absence painful.

"He went to Seattle that afternoon," Spade said, "and from there by boat to San Francisco. For a couple of years he wandered around and then drifted back to the Northwest, and settled in Spokane and got married. His second wife didn't look like the first, but they were more alike than they were different. You know, the kind of women that play fair games of golf and bridge and like new salad-recipes. He wasn't sorry for what he had done. It seemed reasonable enough to him. I don't think he even knew he had settled back naturally into the same groove he had jumped out of in Tacoma. But that's the part of it I always liked. He adjusted himself to beams falling, and then no more of them fell, and he adjusted himself to them not falling."

"How perfectly fascinating," Brigid O'Shaughnessy said. She left her chair and stood in front of him, close. Her eyes were wide and deep. "I don't have to tell you how utterly at a disadvantage you'll have me, with him here, if you choose."

Spade smiled slightly without separating his lips. "No, you don't have to tell me," he agreed.

"And you know I'd never have placed myself in this position if I hadn't trusted you completely." Her thumb and forefinger twisted a black button on his blue coat.

Spade said, "That again!" with mock resignation.

"But you know it's so," she insisted.

"No, I don't know it." He patted the hand that was twisting the button. "My asking for reasons why I should trust you brought us here. Don't let's confuse things. You don't have to trust me, anyhow, as long as you can persuade me to trust you."

She studied his face. Her nostrils quivered.

Spade laughed. He patted her hand again and said: "Don't worry about that now. He'll be here in a moment. Get your business with him over, and then we'll see how we'll stand."

"And you'll let me go about it—with him—in my own way?"

"Sure."

She turned her hand under his so that her fingers pressed his. She said softly: "You're a God-send."

Spade said: "Don't overdo it."

She looked reproachfully at him, though smiling, and returned to the padded rocker.

Joel Cairo was excited. His dark eyes seemed all irises and his high-pitched thin-voiced words were tumbling out before Spade had the door half-open.

"That boy is out there watching the house, Mr. Spade, that boy you showed me, or to whom you showed me, in front of the theatre. What am I to understand from that, Mr. Spade? I came here in good faith, with no thought of tricks or traps."

"You were asked in good faith." Spade frowned thoughtfully. "But I ought to've guessed he might show up. He saw you come in?"

"Naturally. I could have gone on, but that seemed useless, since you had already let him see us together."

Brigid O'Shaughnessy came into the passageway behind Spade and asked anxiously: "What boy? What is it?"

Cairo removed his black hat from his head, bowed stiffly, and said in a prim voice: "If you do not know, ask Mr. Spade. I know nothing about it except through him."

"A kid who's been trying to tail me around town all evening," Spade said carelessly over his shoulder, not turning to face the girl. "Come on in, Cairo. There's no use standing here talking for all the neighbors."

Brigid O'Shaughnessy grasped Spade's arm above the elbow and demanded: "Did he follow you to my apartment?"

"No. I shook him before that. Then I suppose he came back here to try to pick me up again."

Cairo, holding his black hat to his belly with both hands, had come into the passageway. Spade shut the corridor-door behind him and they went into the living-room. There Cairo bowed stiffly over his hat once more and said: "I am delighted to see you again, Miss O'Shaughnessy."

"I was sure you would be, Joe," she replied, giving him her hand.

He made a formal bow over her hand and released it quickly.

She sat in the padded rocker she had occupied before. Cairo sat in the armchair by the table. Spade, when he had hung Cairo's hat and coat in the closet, sat on an end of the sofa in front of the windows and began to roll a cigarette.

Brigid O'Shaughnessy said to Cairo: "Sam told me about your offer for the falcon. How soon can you have the money ready?"

Cairo's eyebrows twitched. He smiled. "It is ready." He continued to smile at the girl for a little while after he had spoken, and then looked at Spade.

Spade was lighting his cigarette. His face was tranquil.

"In cash?" the girl asked.

"Oh, yes," Cairo replied.

She frowned, put her tongue between her lips, withdrew it, and asked: "You are ready to give us five thousand dollars, now, if we give you the falcon?"

Cairo held up a wriggling hand. "Excuse me," he said. "I expressed myself badly. I did not mean to say that I have the money in my pockets, but that I am prepared to get it on a very few minutes' notice at any time during banking hours."

"Oh!" She looked at Spade.

Spade blew cigarette-smoke down the front of his vest and said: "That's probably right. He had only a few hundred in his pockets when I frisked him this afternoon."

When her eyes opened round and wide he grinned.

The Levantine bent forward in his chair. He failed to keep eagerness from showing in his eyes and voice. "I can be quite prepared to give you the money at, say, half-past ten in the morning. Eh?"

Brigid O'Shaughnessy smiled at him and said: "But I haven't got the falcon."

Cairo's face was darkened by a flush of annoyance. He put an ugly hand on either arm of his chair, holding his small-boned body erect and stiff between them. His dark eyes were angry. He did not say anything.

The girl made a mock-placatory face at him. "I'll have it in a week at the most, though," she said.

"Where is it?" Cairo used politeness of mien to express skepticism.

"Where Floyd hid it."

"Floyd? Thursby?"

She nodded.

"And you know where that is?" he asked.

"I think I do."

"Then why must we wait a week?"

"Perhaps not a whole week. Whom are you buying it for, Joe?"

Cairo raised his eyebrows. "I told Mr. Spade. For its owner."

Surprise illuminated the girl's face. "So you went back to him?"

"Naturally I did."

She laughed softly in her throat and said: "I should have liked to have seen that."

Cairo shrugged. "That was the logical development." He rubbed the back of one hand with the palm of the other. His upper lids came down to shade his eyes. "Why, if I in turn may ask a question, are you willing to sell to me?"

"I'm afraid," she said simply, "after what happened to Floyd. That's why I haven't it now. I'm afraid to touch it except to turn it over to somebody else right away."

Spade, propped on an elbow on the sofa, looked at and listened to them impartially. In the comfortable slackness of his body, in the easy stillness of his features, there was no indication of either curiosity or impatience.

"Exactly what," Cairo asked in a low voice, "happened to Floyd?"

The tip of Brigid O'Shaughnessy's right forefinger traced a swift G in the air.

Cairo said, "I see," but there was something doubting in his smile. "Is he here?"

"I don't know." She spoke impatiently. "What difference does it make?"

The doubt in Cairo's smile deepened. "It might make a world of difference," he said, and rearranged his hands in his lap so that, intentionally or not, a blunt forefinger pointed at Spade.

The girl glanced at the pointing finger and made an impatient motion with her head. "Or me," she said, "or you."

"Exactly, and shall we add more certainly the boy outside?"

"Yes," she agreed and laughed. "Yes, unless he's the one you had in Constantinople."

Sudden blood mottled Cairo's face. In a shrill enraged voice he cried: "The one you couldn't make?"

Brigid O'Shaughnessy jumped up from her chair. Her lower lip was between her teeth. Her eyes were dark and wide in a tense white face. She took two quick steps towards Cairo. He started to rise. Her right hand went out and cracked sharply against his cheek, leaving the imprint of fingers there.

Cairo grunted and slapped her cheek, staggering her sidewise, bringing from her mouth a brief muffled scream.

Spade, wooden of face, was up from the sofa and close to them by then. He caught Cairo by the throat and shook him. Cairo gurgled and put a hand inside his coat. Spade grasped the Levantine's wrist, wrenched it away from the coat, forced it straight out to the side, and twisted it until the clumsy flaccid fingers opened to let the black pistol fall down on the rug.

Brigid O'Shaughnessy quickly picked up the pistol.

Cairo, speaking with difficulty because of the fingers on his throat, said: "This is the second time you've put your hands on me." His eyes, though the throttling pressure on his throat made them bulge, were cold and menacing.

"Yes," Spade growled. "And when you're slapped you'll take it and like it." He released Cairo's wrist and with a thick open hand struck the side of his face three times, savagely.

Cairo tried to spit in Spade's face, but the dryness of the Levantine's mouth made it only an angry gesture. Spade slapped the mouth, cutting the lower lip.

The door-bell rang.

Cairo's eyes jerked into focus on the passageway that led to the corridor-door. His eyes had become unangry and wary. The girl had gasped and turned to face the passageway. Her face was frightened. Spade stared gloomily for a moment at the blood trickling from Cairo's lip, and then stepped back, taking his hand from the Levantine's throat.

"Who is it?" the girl whispered, coming close to Spade; and Cairo's eyes jerked back to ask the same question.

Spade gave his answer irritably: "I don't know."

The bell rang again, more insistently.

"Well, keep quiet," Spade said, and went out of the room, shutting the door behind him.

Spade turned on the light in the passageway and opened the door to the corridor. Lieutenant Dundy and Tom Polhaus were there.

"Hello, Sam," Tom said. "We thought maybe you wouldn't've gone to bed yet."

Dundy nodded, but said nothing.

Spade said good-naturedly: "Hello. You guys pick swell hours to do your visiting in. What is it this time?"

Dundy spoke then, quietly: "We want to talk to you, Spade."

"Well?" Spade stood in the doorway, blocking it. "Go ahead and talk."

Tom Polhaus advanced saying: "We don't have to do it standing here, do we?"

Spade stood in the doorway and said: "You can't come in." His tone was very slightly apologetic.

Tom's thick-featured face, even in height with Spade's, took on an expression of friendly scorn, though there was a bright gleam in his small shrewd eyes. "What the hell, Sam?" he protested and put a big hand playfully on Spade's chest.

Spade leaned against the pushing hand, grinned wolfishly, and asked: "Going to strong-arm me, Tom?"

Tom grumbled, "Aw, for God's sake," and took his hand away.

Dundy clicked his teeth together and said through them: "Let us in."

Spade's lip twitched over his eyetooth. He said: "You're not coming in. What do you want to do about it? Try to get in? Or do your talking here? Or go to hell?"

Tom groaned.

Dundy, still speaking through his teeth, said: "It'd pay you to play along with us a little, Spade. You've got away with this and you've got away with that, but you can't keep it up forever."

"Stop me when you can," Spade replied arrogantly.

"That's what I'll do." Dundy put his hands behind him and thrust his hard face up towards the private detective's. "There's talk going around that you and Archer's wife were cheating on him."

Spade laughed. "That sounds like something you thought up yourself."

"Then there's not anything to it?"

"Not anything."

"The talk is," Dundy said, "that she tried to get a divorce out of him so's she could put in with you, but he wouldn't give it to her. Anything to that?"

"No."

"There's even talk," Dundy went on stolidly, "that that's why he was put on the spot."

Spade seemed mildly amused. "Don't be a hog," he said. "You oughtn't try to pin more than one murder at a time on me. Your first idea that I knocked Thursby off because he'd killed Miles falls apart if you blame me for killing Miles too."

"You haven't heard me say you killed anybody," Dundy replied. "You're the one that keeps bringing that up. But suppose I did. You could have blipped them both. There's a way of figuring it."

"Uh-huh. I could've butchered Miles to get his wife, and then Thursby so I could hang Miles's killing on him. That's a hell of a swell system, or will be when I can give somebody else the bump and hang Thursby's on them. How long am I supposed to keep that up? Are you going to put your hand on my shoulder for all the killings in San Francisco from now on?"

Tom said: "Aw, cut the comedy, Sam. You know damned well we don't like this any more than you do, but we got our work to do."

"I hope you've got something to do besides pop in here early every morning with a lot of damned fool questions."

"And get damned lying answers," Dundy added deliberately.

"Take it easy," Spade cautioned him.

Dundy looked him up and down and then looked him straight in the eyes. "If you say there was nothing between you and Archer's wife," he said, "you're a liar, and I'm telling you so."

A startled look came into Tom's small eyes.

Spade moistened his lips with the tip of his tongue and asked: "Is that the hot tip that brought you here at this ungodly time of night?"

"That's one of them."

"And the others?"

Dundy pulled down the corners of his mouth. "Let us in." He nodded significantly at the doorway in which Spade stood.

Spade frowned and shook his head.

Dundy's mouth-corners lifted in a smile of grim satisfaction. "There must've been something to it," he told Tom.

Tom shifted his feet and, not looking at either man, mumbled: "God knows."

"What's this?" Spade asked. "Charades?"

"All right, Spade, we're going." Dundy buttoned his overcoat. "We'll be in to see you now and then. Maybe you're right in bucking us. Think it over."

"Uh-huh," Spade said, grinning. "Glad to see you any time, Lieutenant, and whenever I'm not busy I'll let you in."

A voice in Spade's living-room screamed: "Help! Help! Police! Help!" The voice, high and thin and shrill, was Joel Cairo's.

Lieutenant Dundy stopped turning away from the door, confronted Spade again, and said decisively: "I guess we're going in."

The sounds of a brief struggle, of a blow, of a subdued cry, came to them.

Spade's face twisted into a smile that held little joy. He said, "I guess you are," and stood out of the way.

When the police-detectives had entered he shut the corridor-door and followed them back to the living-room.

CHAPTER VIII

Horse Feathers

BRIGID O'SHAUGHNESSY WAS HUDDLED in the armchair by the table. Her forearms were up over her cheeks, her knees drawn up until they hid the lower part of her face. Her eyes were white-circled and terrified.

Joel Cairo stood in front of her, bending over her, holding in one hand the pistol Spade had twisted out of his hand. His other hand was clapped to his forehead. Blood ran through the fingers of that hand and down under them to his eyes. A smaller trickle from his cut lip made three wavy lines across his chin.

Cairo did not heed the detectives. He was glaring at the girl huddled in front of him. His lips were working spasmodically, but no coherent sound came from between them.

Dundy, the first of the three into the living-room, moved swiftly to Cairo's side, put a hand on his own hip under his overcoat, a hand on the Levantine's wrist, and growled: "What are you up to here?"

Cairo took the red-smeared hand from his head and flourished it close to the Lieutenant's face. Uncovered by the hand, his forehead showed a three-inch ragged tear. "This is what she has done," he cried. "Look at it."

The girl put her feet down on the floor and looked warily from Dundy, holding Cairo's wrist, to Tom Polhaus, standing a little behind them, to Spade, leaning against the door-frame. Spade's face was placid. When his gaze met hers his yellow-grey eyes glinted for an instant with malicious humor and then became expressionless again.

"Did you do that?" Dundy asked the girl, nodding at Cairo's cut head.

She looked at Spade again. He did not in any way respond to the appeal in her eyes. He leaned against the door-frame and observed the occupants of the room with the polite detached air of a disinterested spectator.

The girl turned her eyes up to Dundy's. Her eyes were wide and dark and earnest. "I had to," she said in a low throbbing voice. "I was all alone in here with him when he attacked me. I couldn't—I tried to keep him off. I—I couldn't make myself shoot him."

"Oh, you liar!" Cairo cried, trying unsuccessfully to pull the arm that held his pistol out of Dundy's grip. "Oh, you dirty filthy liar!" He twisted himself around to face Dundy. "She's lying awfully. I came here in good faith and was attacked by both of them, and when you came he went out to talk to you, leaving her here with this pistol, and then she said they were going to kill me after you left, and I called for help, so you wouldn't leave me here to be murdered, and then she struck me with the pistol."

"Here, give me this thing," Dundy said, and took the pistol from Cairo's hand. "Now let's get this straight. What'd you come here for?"

"He sent for me." Cairo twisted his head around to stare defiantly at Spade. "He called me up on the phone and asked me to come here."

Spade blinked sleepily at the Levantine and said nothing.

Dundy asked: "What'd he want you for?"

Cairo withheld his reply until he had mopped his bloody forehead and chin with a lavender-barred silk handkerchief. By then some of the indignation in his manner had been replaced by caution. "He said he wanted—they wanted—to see me. I didn't know what about."

Tom Polhaus lowered his head, sniffed the odor of *chypre* that the mopping handkerchief had released in the air, and turned his head to scowl interrogatively at Spade. Spade winked at him and went on rolling a cigarette.

Dundy asked: "Well, what happened then?"

"Then they attacked me. She struck me first, and then he choked me and took the pistol out of my pocket. I don't know what they would have done next if you hadn't arrived at that moment. I dare say they would have murdered me then and there. When he went out to answer the bell he left her here with the pistol to watch over me."

Brigid O'Shaughnessy jumped out of the armchair crying, "Why don't you make him tell the truth?" and slapped Cairo on the cheek.

Cairo yelled inarticulately.

Dundy pushed the girl back into the chair with the hand that was not holding the Levantine's arm and growled: "None of that now."

Spade, lighting his cigarette, grinned softly through smoke and told Tom: "She's impulsive."

"Yeah," Tom agreed.

Dundy scowled down at the girl and asked: "What do you want us to think the truth is?"

"Not what he said," she replied. "Not anything he said." She turned to Spade. "Is it?"

"How do I know?" Spade responded. "I was out in the kitchen mixing an omelette when it all happened, wasn't I?"

She wrinkled her forehead, studying him with eyes that perplexity clouded.

Tom grunted in disgust.

Dundy, still scowling at the girl, ignored Spade's speech and asked her: "If he's not telling the truth, how come he did the squawking for help, and not you?"

"Oh, he was frightened to death when I struck him," she replied, looking contemptuously at the Levantine.

Cairo's face flushed where it was not blood-smeared. He exclaimed: "Pfoo! Another lie!"

She kicked his leg, the high heel of her blue slipper striking him just below the knee. Dundy pulled him away from her while big Tom came to stand close to her, rumbling: "Behave, sister. That's no way to act."

"Then make him tell the truth," she said defiantly.

"We'll do that all right," he promised. "Just don't get rough."

Dundy, looking at Spade with green eyes hard and bright and satisfied, addressed his subordinate: "Well, Tom, I don't guess we'll go wrong pulling the lot of them in."

Tom nodded gloomily.

Spade left the door and advanced to the center of the room, dropping his cigarette into a tray on the table as he passed it. His smile and manner were amiably composed. "Don't be in a hurry," he said. "Everything can be explained."

"I bet you," Dundy agreed, sneering.

Spade bowed to the girl. "Miss O'Shaughnessy," he said, "may I present Lieutenant Dundy and Detective-sergeant Polhaus." He bowed to Dundy. "Miss O'Shaughnessy is an operative in my employ."

Joel Cairo said indignantly: "That isn't so. She—"

Spade interrupted him in a quite loud, but still genial, voice: "I hired her just recently, yesterday. This is Mr. Joel Cairo, a friend—an acquaintance, at any rate—of Thursby's. He came to me this afternoon and tried to hire me to find something Thursby was supposed to have on him when he was bumped off. It looked funny, the way he put it to me, so I wouldn't touch it. Then he pulled a gun—well, never mind that unless it comes to a point of laying charges against each other. Anyway, after talking it over with Miss O'Shaughnessy, I thought maybe I could get something out of him about Miles's and Thursby's killings, so I asked him to come up here. Maybe we put the questions to him a little rough, but he wasn't hurt any, not enough to have to cry for help. I'd already had to take his gun away from him again."

As Spade talked anxiety came into Cairo's reddened face. His eyes moved jerkily up and down, shifting their focus uneasily between the floor and Spade's bland face.

Dundy confronted Cairo and bruskly demanded: "Well, what've you got to say to that?"

Cairo had nothing to say for nearly a minute while he stared at the Lieutenant's chest. When he lifted his eyes they were shy and wary. "I don't know what I should say," he murmured. His embarrassment seemed genuine.

"Try telling the facts," Dundy suggested.

"The facts?" Cairo's eyes fidgeted, though their gaze did not actually leave the Lieutenant's. "What assurance have I that the facts will be believed?"

"Quit stalling. All you've got to do is swear to a complaint that they took a poke at you and the warrant-clerk will believe you enough to issue a warrant that'll let us throw them in the can."

Spade spoke in an amused tone: "Go ahead, Cairo. Make him happy. Tell him you'll do it, and then we'll swear to one against you, and he'll have the lot of us."

Cairo cleared his throat and looked nervously around the room, not into the eyes of anyone there.

Dundy blew breath through his nose in a puff that was not quite a snort and said: "Get your hats."

Cairo's eyes, holding worry and a question, met Spade's mocking gaze. Spade winked at him and sat on the arm of the padded rocker. "Well, boys and girls," he said, grinning at the Levantine and at the girl with nothing but delight in his voice and grin, "we put it over nicely."

Dundy's hard square face darkened the least of shades. He repeated peremptorily: "Get your hats."

Spade turned his grin on the Lieutenant, squirmed into a more comfortable position on the chair-arm, and asked lazily: "Don't you know when you're being kidded?"

Tom Polhaus's face became red and shiny.

Dundy's face, still darkening, was immobile except for lips moving stiffly to say: "No, but we'll let that wait till we get down to the Hall."

Spade rose and put his hands in his trousers-pockets. He stood erect so he might look that much farther down at the Lieutenant. His grin was a taunt and self-certainty spoke in every line of his posture.

"I dare you to take us in, Dundy," he said. "We'll laugh at you in every newspaper in San Francisco. You don't think any of us is going to swear to any complaints against the others, do you? Wake up. You've been kidded. When the bell rang I said to Miss O'Shaughnessy and Cairo: 'It's those damned bulls again. They're getting to be nuisances. Let's play a joke on them. When you hear them going one of you scream, and then we'll see how far we can string them along before they tumble.' And—"

Brigid O'Shaughnessy bent forward in her chair and began to laugh hysterically.

Cairo started and smiled. There was no vitality in his smile, but he held it fixed on his face.

Tom, glowering, grumbled: "Cut it out, Sam."

Spade chuckled and said: "But that's the way it was. We—"

"And the cut on his head and mouth?" Dundy asked scornfully. "Where'd they come from?"

"Ask him," Spade suggested. "Maybe he cut himself shaving."

Cairo spoke quickly, before he could be questioned, and the muscles of his face quivered under the strain of holding his smile in place while he spoke. "I fell. We intended to be struggling for the pistol when you came in, but I fell. I tripped on the end of the rug and fell while we were pretending to struggle."

Dundy said: "Horse feathers."

Spade said: "That's all right, Dundy, believe it or not. The point is that that's our story and we'll stick to it. The newspapers will print it whether they believe it or not, and it'll be just as funny one way as the other, or more so. What are you going to do about it? It's no crime to kid a copper, is it? You haven't got anything on anybody here. Everything we told you was part of the joke. What are you going to do about it?"

Dundy put his back to Spade and gripped Cairo by the shoulders. "You can't get away with that," he snarled, shaking the Levantine. "You belched for help and you've got to take it."

"No, sir," Cairo sputtered. "It was a joke. He said you were friends of his and would understand."

Spade laughed.

Dundy pulled Cairo roughly around, holding him now by one wrist and the nape of his neck. "I'll take you along for packing the gun, anyway," he said. "And I'll take the rest of you along to see who laughs at the joke."

Cairo's alarmed eyes jerked sidewise to focus on Spade's face.

Spade said: "Don't be a sap, Dundy. The gun was part of the plant.

It's one of mine." He laughed. "Too bad it's only a thirty-two, or maybe you could find it was the one Thursby and Miles were shot with."

Dundy released Cairo, spun on his heel, and his right fist clicked on Spade's chin.

Brigid O'Shaughnessy uttered a short cry.

Spade's smile flickered out at the instant of the impact, but returned immediately with a dreamy quality added. He steadied himself with a short backward step and his thick sloping shoulders writhed under his coat. Before his fist could come up Tom Polhaus had pushed himself between the two men, facing Spade, encumbering Spade's arms with the closeness of his barrel-like belly and his own arms.

"No, no, for Christ's sake!" Tom begged.

After a long moment of motionlessness Spade's muscles relaxed. "Then get him out of here quick," he said. His smile had gone away again, leaving his face sullen and somewhat pale.

Tom, staying close to Spade, keeping his arms on Spade's arms, turned his head to look over his shoulder at Lieutenant Dundy. Tom's small eyes were reproachful.

Dundy's fists were clenched in front of his body and his feet were planted firm and a little apart on the floor, but the truculence in his face was modified by thin rims of white showing between green irises and upper eyelids.

"Get their names and addresses," he ordered.

Tom looked at Cairo, who said quickly: "Joel Cairo, Hotel Belvedere."

Spade spoke before Tom could question the girl. "You can always get in touch with Miss O'Shaughnessy through me."

Tom looked at Dundy. Dundy growled: "Get her address."

Spade said: "Her address is in care of my office."

Dundy took a step forward, halting in front of the girl. "Where do you live?" he asked.

Spade addressed Tom: "Get him out of here. I've had enough of this."

Tom looked at Spade's eyes—hard and glittering—and mumbled: "Take it easy, Sam." He buttoned his coat and turned to Dundy, asking, in a voice that aped casualness, "Well, is that all?" and taking a step towards the door.

Dundy's scowl failed to conceal indecision.

Cairo moved suddenly towards the door, saying: "I'm going too, if Mr. Spade will be kind enough to give me my hat and coat."

Spade asked: "What's the hurry?"

Dundy said angrily: "It was all in fun, but just the same you're afraid to be left here with them."

"Not at all," the Levantine replied, fidgeting, looking at neither of them, "but it's quite late and—and I'm going. I'll go out with you if you don't mind."

Dundy put his lips together firmly and said nothing. A light was glinting in his green eyes.

Spade went to the closet in the passageway and fetched Cairo's hat and coat. Spade's face was blank. His voice held the same blankness when he stepped back from helping the Levantine into his coat and said to Tom: "Tell him to leave the gun."

Dundy took Cairo's pistol from his overcoat-pocket and put it on the table. He went out first, with Cairo at his heels. Tom halted in front of Spade, muttering, "I hope to God you know what you're doing," got no response, sighed, and followed the others out. Spade went after them as far as the bend in the passageway, where he stood until Tom had closed the corridor-door.

CHAPTER IX

Brigid

SPADE RETURNED to the living-room and sat on an end of the sofa, elbows on knees, cheeks in hands, looking at the floor and not at Brigid O'Shaughnessy smiling weakly at him from the armchair. His eyes were sultry. The creases between brows over his nose were deep. His nostrils moved in and out with his breathing.

Brigid O'Shaughnessy, when it became apparent that he was not going to look up at her, stopped smiling and regarded him with growing uneasiness.

Red rage came suddenly into his face and he began to talk in a harsh guttural voice. Holding his maddened face in his hands, glaring at the floor, he cursed Dundy for five minutes without break, cursed him obscenely, blasphemously, repetitiously, in a harsh guttural voice.

Then he took his face out of his hands, looked at the girl, grinned sheepishly, and said: "Childish, huh? I know, but, by God, I do hate being hit without hitting back." He touched his chin with careful fingers. "Not that it was so much of a sock at that." He laughed and lounged back on the sofa, crossing his legs. "A cheap enough price to pay for winning." His brows came together in a fleeting scowl. "Though I'll remember it."

The girl, smiling again, left her chair and sat on the sofa beside him. "You're absolutely the wildest person I've ever known," she said. "Do you always carry on so high-handed?"

"I let him hit me, didn't I?"

"Oh, yes, but a police official."

"It wasn't that," Spade explained. "It was that in losing his head and slugging me he overplayed his hand. If I'd mixed it with him then he couldn't've backed down. He'd've had to go through with it, and we'd've had to tell that goofy story at headquarters." He stared thoughtfully at the girl, and asked: "What did you do to Cairo?"

"Nothing." Her face became flushed. "I tried to frighten him into keeping still until they had gone and he either got too frightened or stubborn and yelled."

"And then you smacked him with the gun?"

"I had to. He attacked me."

"You don't know what you're doing." Spade's smile did not hide his annoyance. "It's just what I told you: you're fumbling along by guess and by God."

"I'm sorry," she said, face and voice soft with contrition, "Sam."

"Sure you are." He took tobacco and papers from his pockets and began to make a cigarette. "Now you've had your talk with Cairo. Now you can talk to me."

She put a fingertip to her mouth, staring across the room at nothing with widened eyes, and then, with narrower eyes, glanced quickly at Spade. He was engrossed in the making of his cigarette. "Oh, yes," she began, "of course—" She tock the finger away from her mouth and smoothed her blue dress over her knees She frowned at her knees.

Spade licked his cigarette, sealed it, and asked, "Well?" while he felt for his lighter.

"But I didn't," she said, pausing between words as if she were selecting them with great care, "have time to finish talking to him." She stopped frowning at her knees and looked at Spade with clear candid eyes. "We were interrupted almost before we had begun."

Spade lighted his cigarette and laughed his mouth empty of smoke. "Want me to phone him and ask him to come back?"

She shook her head, not smiling. Her eyes moved back and forth between her lids as she shook her head, maintaining their focus on Spade's eyes. Her eyes were inquisitive.

Spade put an arm across her back, cupping his hand over the smooth bare white shoulder farthest from him. She leaned back into the bend of his arm. He said: "Well, I'm listening."

She twisted her head around to smile up at him with playful insolence, asking: "Do you need your arm there for that?"

"No." He removed his hand from her shoulder and let his arm drop down behind her.

"You're altogether unpredictable," she murmured.

He nodded and said amiably: "I'm still listening."

"Look at the time!" she exclaimed, wriggling a finger at the alarm-clock perched atop the book saying two-fifty with its clumsily shaped hands.

"Uh-huh, it's been a busy evening."

"I must go." She rose from the sofa. "This is terrible."

Spade did not rise. He shook his head and said: "Not until you've told me about it."

"But look at the time," she protested, "and it would take hours to tell you."

"It'll have to take them then."

"Am I a prisoner?" she asked gaily.

"Besides, there's the kid outside. Maybe he hasn't gone home to sleep yet."

Her gaiety vanished. "Do you think he's still there?"

"It's likely."

She shivered. "Could you find out?"

"I could go down and see."

"Oh, that's—will you?"

Spade studied her anxious face for a moment and then got up from the sofa saying: "Sure." He got a hat and overcoat from the closet. "I'll be gone about ten minutes."

"Do be careful," she begged as she followed him to the corridor-door.

He said, "I will," and went out.

Post Street was empty when Spade issued into it. He walked east a block, crossed the street, walked west two blocks on the other side, recrossed it, and returned to his building without having seen anyone except two mechanics working on a car in a garage.

When he opened his apartment-door Brigid O'Shaughnessy was standing at the bend in the passageway, holding Cairo's pistol straight down at her side.

"He's still there," Spade said.

She bit the inside of her lip and turned slowly, going back into the living-room. Spade followed her in, put his hat and overcoat on a chair, said, "So we'll have time to talk," and went into the kitchen.

He had put the coffee-pot on the stove when she came to the door, and was slicing a slender loaf of French bread. She stood in the doorway and watched him with preoccupied eyes. The fingers of her left hand idly caressed the body and barrel of the pistol her right hand still held.

"The table-cloth's in there," he said, pointing the bread-knife at a cupboard that was one breakfast-nook partition.

She set the table while he spread liverwurst on, or put cold corned beef between, the small ovals of bread he had sliced. Then he poured the coffee, added brandy to it from a squat bottle, and they sat at the table. They sat side by side on one of the benches. She put the pistol down on the end of the bench nearer her.

"You can start now, between bites," he said.

She made a face at him, complained, "You're the most insistent person," and bit a sandwich.

"Yes, and wild and unpredictable. What's this bird, this falcon, that everybody's all steamed up about?"

She chewed the beef and bread in her mouth, swallowed it, looked attentively at the small crescent its removal had made in the sandwich's rim, and asked: "Suppose I wouldn't tell you? Suppose I wouldn't tell you anything at all about it? What would you do?"

"You mean about the bird?"

"I mean about the whole thing."

"I wouldn't be too surprised," he told her, grinning so that the edges of his jaw-teeth were visible, "to know what to do next."

"And that would be?" She transferred her attention from the sandwich to his face. "That's what I wanted to know: what would you do next?"

He shook his head.

Mockery rippled in a smile on her face. "Something wild and unpredictable?"

"Maybe. But I don't see what you've got to gain by covering up now. It's coming out bit by bit anyhow. There's a lot of it I don't know, but there's some of it I do, and some more that I can guess at, and, give me another day like this, I'll soon be knowing things about it that you don't know."

"I suppose you do now," she said, looking at her sandwich again, her face serious. "But—oh!—I'm so tired of it, and I do so hate having to talk about it. Wouldn't it—wouldn't it be just as well to wait and let you learn about it as you say you will?"

Spade laughed. "I don't know. You'll have to figure that out for yourself. My way of learning is to heave a wild and unpredictable monkey-wrench into the machinery. It's all right with me, if you're sure none of the flying pieces will hurt you."

She moved her bare shoulders uneasily, but said nothing. For several minutes they ate in silence, he phlegmatically, she thoughtfully. Then she said in a hushed voice: "I'm afraid of you, and that's the truth."

He said: "That's not the truth."

"It is," she insisted in the same low voice. "I know two men I'm afraid of and I've seen both of them tonight."

"I can understand your being afraid of Cairo," Spade said. "He's out of your reach."

"And you aren't?"

"Not that way," he said and grinned.

She blushed. She picked up a slice of bread encrusted with grey liverwurst. She put it down on her plate. She wrinkled her white forehead and she said: "It's a black figure, as you know, smooth and shiny, of a bird, a hawk or falcon, about that high." She held her hands a foot apart.

"What makes it important?"

She sipped coffee and brandy before she shook her head. "I don't know," she said. "They'd never tell me. They promised me five hundred pounds if I helped them get it. Then Floyd said afterward, after we'd left Joe, that he'd give me seven hundred and fifty."

"So it must be worth more than seventy-five hundred dollars?"

"Oh, much more than that," she said. "They didn't pretend that they were sharing equally with me. They were simply hiring me to help them."

"To help them how?"

She lifted her cup to her lips again. Spade, not moving the domineering stare of his yellow-grey eyes from her face, began to make a cigarette. Behind them the percolator bubbled on the stove.

"To help them get it from the man who had it," she said slowly when she had lowered her cup, "a Russian named Kemidov."

"How?"

"Oh, but that's not important," she objected, "and wouldn't help you" —she smiled impudently—"and is certainly none of your business."

"This was in Constantinople?"

She hesitated, nodded, and said: "Marmora."

He waved his cigarette at her, saying: "Go ahead, what happened then?"

"But that's all. I've told you. They promised me five hundred pounds to help them and I did and then we found that Joe Cairo meant to desert us, taking the falcon with him and leaving us nothing. So we did exactly that to him, first. But then I wasn't any better off than I had been before, because Floyd hadn't any intention at all of paying me the seven hundred and fifty pounds he had promised me. I had learned that by the time we got here. He said we would go to New York, where he would sell it and give me my share, but I could see he wasn't telling me the truth." Indignation had darkened her eyes to violet. "And that's why I came to you to get you to help me learn where the falcon was."

"And suppose you'd got it? What then?"

"Then I'd have been in a position to talk terms with Mr. Floyd Thursby."

Spade squinted at her and suggested: "But you wouldn't have known where to take it to get more money than he'd give you, the larger sum that you knew he expected to sell it for?"

"I did not know," she said.

Spade scowled at the ashes he had dumped on his plate. "What makes it worth all that money?" he demanded. "You must have some idea, at least be able to guess."

"I haven't the slightest idea."

He directed the scowl at her. "What's it made of?"

"Porcelain or black stone. I don't know. I've never touched it. I've only seen it once, for a few minutes. Floyd showed it to me when we'd first got hold of it."

Spade mashed the end of his cigarette in his plate and made one draught of the coffee and brandy in his cup. His scowl had gone away. He wiped his lips with his napkin, dropped it crumpled on the table, and spoke casually: "You *are* a liar."

She got up and stood at the end of the table, looking down at him with dark abashed eyes in a pinkening face. "I am a liar," she said. "I have always been a liar."

"Don't brag about it. It's childish." His voice was good-humored. He came out from between table and bench. "Was there any truth at all in that yarn?"

She hung her head. Dampness glistened on her dark lashes. "Some," she whispered.

"How much?"

"Not—not very much."

Spade put a hand under her chin and lifted her head. He laughed into her wet eyes and said: "We've got all night before us. I'll put some more brandy in some more coffee and we'll try again."

Her eyelids drooped. "Oh, I'm so tired," she said tremulously, "so tired of it all, of myself, of lying and thinking up lies, and of not knowing what is a lie and what is the truth. I wish I—"

She put her hands up to Spade's cheeks, put her open mouth hard against his mouth, her body flat against his body.

Spade's arms went around her, holding her to him, muscles bulging his blue sleeves, a hand cradling her head, its fingers half lost among red hair, a hand moving groping fingers over her slim back. His eyes burned yellowly.

CHAPTER X

The Belvedere Divan

BEGINNING DAY had reduced night to a thin smokiness when Spade sat up. At his side Brigid O'Shaughnessy's soft breathing had the regularity of utter sleep. Spade was quiet leaving bed and bedroom and shutting the bedroom-door. He dressed in the bathroom. Then he examined the sleeping girl's clothes, took a flat brass key from the pocket of her coat, and went out.

He went to the Coronet, letting himself into the building and into her apartment with the key. To the eye there was nothing furtive about his going in: he entered boldly and directly. To the ear his going in was almost unnoticeable: he made as little sound as might be.

In the girl's apartment he switched on all the lights. He searched the place from wall to wall. His eyes and thick fingers moved without apparent haste, and without ever lingering or fumbling or going back, from one inch of their fields to the next, probing, scrutinizing, testing with expert certainty. Every drawer, cupboard, cubbyhole, box, bag, trunk—locked or unlocked—was opened and its contents subjected to examination by eyes and fingers. Every piece of clothing was tested by hands that felt for telltale bulges and ears that listened for the crinkle of paper between pressing fingers. He stripped the bed of bedclothes. He looked under rugs and at the under side of each piece of furniture. He pulled down blinds to see that nothing had been rolled up in them for concealment. He leaned through windows to see that nothing hung below them on the outside. He poked with a fork into powder and cream-jars on the dressing-table. He held atomizers and bottles up against the light. He examined dishes and pans and food and food-containers. He emptied the garbage-can on spread sheets of newspaper. He opened the top of the flush-box in the bathroom, drained the box, and peered down into it. He examined and tested the metal screens over the drains of bathtub, washbowl, sink, and laundry-tub.

He did not find the black bird. He found nothing that seemed to have any connection with a black bird. The only piece of writing he found was a week-old receipt for the month's apartment-rent Brigid O'Shaughnessy had paid. The only thing he found that interested him enough to delay his search while he looked at it was a double-handful of rather fine jewelry in a polychrome box in a locked dressing-table-drawer.

When he had finished he made and drank a cup of coffee. Then he unlocked the kitchen-window, scarred the edge of its lock a little with his pocket-knife, opened the window—over a fire-escape—got his hat and overcoat from the settee in the living-room, and left the apartment as he had come.

On his way home he stopped at a store that was being opened by a puffy-eyed shivering plump grocer and bought oranges, eggs, rolls, butter, and cream.

Spade went quietly into his apartment, but before he had shut the corridor-door behind him Brigid O'Shaughnessy cried: "Who is that?"

"Young Spade bearing breakfast."

"Oh, you frightened me!"

The bedroom-door he had shut was open. The girl sat on the side of the bed, trembling, with her right hand out of sight under a pillow.

Spade put his packages on the kitchen-table and went into the bedroom. He sat on the bed beside the girl, kissed her smooth shoulder, and said: "I wanted to see if that kid was still on the job, and to get stuff for breakfast."

"Is he?"

"No."

She sighed and leaned against him. "I awakened and you weren't here and then I heard someone coming in. I was terrified."

Spade combed her red hair back from her face with his fingers and said: "I'm sorry, angel. I thought you'd sleep through it. Did you have that gun under your pillow all night?"

"No. You know I didn't. I jumped up and got it when I was frightened."

He cooked breakfast—and slipped the flat brass key into her coat-pocket again—while she bathed and dressed.

She came out of the bathroom whistling *En Cuba*. "Shall I make the bed?" she asked.

"That'd be swell. The eggs need a couple of minutes more."

Their breakfast was on the table when she returned to the kitchen. They sat where they had sat the night before and ate heartily.

"Now about the bird?" Spade suggested presently as they ate.

She put her fork down and looked at him. She drew her eyebrows together and made her mouth small and tight. "You can't ask me to talk about that this morning of all mornings," she protested. "I don't want to and I won't."

"It's a stubborn damned hussy," he said sadly and put a piece of roll into his mouth.

The youth who had shadowed Spade was not in sight when Spade and Brigid O'Shaughnessy crossed the sidewalk to the waiting taxicab. The taxicab was not followed. Neither the youth nor another loiterer was visible in the vicinity of the Coronet when the taxicab arrived there.

Brigid O'Shaughnessy would not let Spade go in with her. "It's bad enough to be coming home in evening dress at this hour without bringing company. I hope I don't meet anybody."

"Dinner tonight?"

"Yes."

They kissed. She went into the Coronet. He told the chauffeur: "Hotel Belvedere."

When he reached the Belvedere he saw the youth who had shadowed him sitting in the lobby on a divan from which the elevators could be seen. Apparently the youth was reading a newspaper.

At the desk Spade learned that Cairo was not in. He frowned and pinched his lower lip. Points of yellow light began to dance in his eyes. "Thanks," he said softly to the clerk and turned away.

Sauntering, he crossed the lobby to the divan from which the elevators could be seen and sat down beside—not more than a foot from—the young man who was apparently reading a newspaper.

The young man did not look up from his newspaper. Seen at this scant distance, he seemed certainly less than twenty years old. His features were small, in keeping with his stature, and regular. His skin was very fair. The whiteness of his cheeks was as little blurred by any considerable growth of beard as by the glow of blood. His clothing was neither new nor of more than ordinary quality, but it, and his manner of wearing it, was marked by a hard masculine neatness.

Spade asked casually, "Where is he?" while shaking tobacco down into a brown paper curved to catch it.

The boy lowered his paper and looked around, moving with a purposeful sort of slowness, as of a more natural swiftness restrained. He looked with small hazel eyes under somewhat long curling lashes at Spade's chest. He said, in a voice as colorless and composed and cold as his young face: "What?"

"Where is he?" Spade was busy with his cigarette.

"Who?"

"The fairy."

The hazel eyes' gaze went up Spade's chest to the knot of his maroon tie and rested there. "What do you think you're doing, Jack?" the boy demanded. "Kidding me?"

"I'll tell you when I am." Spade licked his cigarette and smiled amiably at the boy. "New York, aren't you?"

The boy stared at Spade's tie and did not speak. Spade nodded as if the boy had said yes and asked: "Baumes rush?"

The boy stared at Spade's tie for a moment longer, then raised his newspaper and returned his attention to it. "Shove off," he said from the side of his mouth.

Spade lighted his cigarette, leaned back comfortably on the divan, and spoke with good-natured carelessness: "You'll have to talk to me before you're through, sonny—some of you will—and you can tell G. I said so."

The boy put his paper down quickly and faced Spade, staring at his necktie with bleak hazel eyes. The boy's small hands were spread flat over his belly. "Keep asking for it and you're going to get it," he said, "plenty." His voice was low and flat and menacing. "I told you to shove off. Shove off."

Spade waited until a bespectacled pudgy man and a thin-legged blonde girl had passed out of hearing. Then he chuckled and said: "That would go over big back on Seventh Avenue. But you're not in Romeville now. You're in my burg." He inhaled cigarette-smoke and blew it out in a long pale cloud. "Well, where is he?"

The boy spoke two words, the first a short guttural verb, the second "you."

"People lose teeth talking like that." Spade's voice was still amiable though his face had become wooden. "If you want to hang around you'll be polite."

The boy repeated his two words.

Spade dropped his cigarette into a tall stone jar beside the divan and with a lifted hand caught the attention of a man who had been standing at an end of the cigar-stand for several minutes. The man nodded and came towards them. He was a middle-aged man of medium height, round and sallow of face, compactly built, tidily dressed in dark clothes.

"Hello, Sam," he said as he came up.

"Hello, Luke."

They shook hands and Luke said: "Say, that's too bad about Miles."

"Uh-huh, a bad break." Spade jerked his head to indicate the boy on the divan beside him. "What do you let these cheap gunmen hang out in your lobby for, with their tools bulging their clothes?"

"Yes?" Luke examined the boy with crafty brown eyes set in a suddenly hard face. "What do you want here?" he asked.

The boy stood up. Spade stood up. The boy looked at the two men, at their neckties, from one to the other. Luke's necktie was black. The boy looked like a schoolboy standing in front of them.

Luke said: "Well, if you don't want anything, beat it, and don't come back."

The boy said, "I won't forget you guys," and went out.

They watched him go out. Spade took off his hat and wiped his damp forehead with a handkerchief.

The hotel-detective asked: "What is it?"

"Damned if I know," Spade replied. "I just happened to spot him. Know anything about Joel Cairo—six-thirty-five?"

"Oh, that one!" The hotel detective leered.

"How long's he been here?"

"Four days. This is the fifth."

"What about him?"

"Search me, Sam. I got nothing against him but his looks."

"Find out if he came in last night?"

"Try to," the hotel-detective promised and went away. Spade sat on the divan until he returned. "No," Luke reported, "he didn't sleep in his room. What is it?"

"Nothing."

"Come clean. You know I'll keep my clam shut, but if there's anything wrong we ought to know about it so's we can collect our bill."

"Nothing like that," Spade assured him. "As a matter of fact, I'm doing a little work for him. I'd tell you if he was wrong."

"You'd better. Want me to kind of keep an eye on him?"

"Thanks, Luke. It wouldn't hurt. You can't know too much about the men you're working for these days."

It was twenty-one minutes past eleven by the clock over the elevator-doors when Joel Cairo came in from the street. His forehead was bandaged. His clothes had the limp unfreshness of too many hours' consecutive wear. His face was pasty, with sagging mouth and eyelids.

Spade met him in front of the desk. "Good morning," Spade said easily.

Cairo drew his tired body up straight and the drooping lines of his face tightened. "Good morning," he responded without enthusiasm.

There was a pause.

Spade said: "Let's go some place where we can talk."

Cairo raised his chin. "Please excuse me," he said. "Our conversations in private have not been such that I am anxious to continue them. Pardon my speaking bluntly, but it is the truth."

"You mean last night?" Spade made an impatient gesture with head and hands. "What in hell else could I do? I thought you'd see that. If you pick a fight with her, or let her pick one with you, I've got to throw in with her. I don't know where that damned bird is. You don't. She does. How in hell are we going to get it if I don't play along with her?"

Cairo hesitated, said dubiously: "You have always, I must say, a smooth explanation ready."

Spade scowled. "What do you want me to do? Learn to stutter? Well, we can talk over here." He led the way to the divan. When they were seated he asked: "Dundy take you down to the Hall?"

"Yes."

"How long did they work on you?"

"Until a very little while ago, and very much against my will." Pain and indignation were mixed in Cairo's face and voice. "I shall certainly take the matter up with the Consulate General of Greece and with an attorney."

"Go ahead, and see what it gets you. What did you let the police shake out of you?"

There was prim satisfaction in Cairo's smile. "Not a single thing. I adhered to the course you indicated earlier in your rooms." His smile went away. "Though I certainly wished you had devised a more reasonable story. I felt decidedly ridiculous repeating it."

Spade grinned mockingly. "Sure," he said, "but its goofiness is what makes it good. You sure you didn't give them anything?"

"You may rely upon it, Mr. Spade, I did not."

Spade drummed with his fingers on the leather seat between them. "You'll be hearing from Dundy again. Stay dummied-up on him and you'll be all right. Don't worry about the story's goofiness. A sensible one would've had us all in the cooler." He rose to his feet. "You'll want sleep if you've been standing up under a police-storm all night. See you later."

Effie Perine was saying, "No, not yet," into the telephone when Spade entered his outer office. She looked around at him and her lips shaped a silent word: "Iva." He shook his head. "Yes, I'll have him call you as soon as he comes in," she said aloud and replaced the receiver on its prong. "That's the third time she's called up this morning," she told Spade.

He made an impatient growling noise.

The girl moved her brown eyes to indicate the inner office. "Your Miss O'Shaughnessy's in there. She's been waiting since a few minutes after nine."

Spade nodded as if he had expected that and asked: "What else?"

"Sergeant Polhaus called up. He didn't leave any message."

"Get him for me."

"And G. called up."

Spade's eyes brightened. He asked: "Who?"

"G. That's what he said." Her air of personal indifference to the subject was flawless. "When I told him you weren't in he said: 'When he comes in, will you please tell him that G., who got his message, phoned and will phone again?' "

Spade worked his lips together as if tasting something he liked. "Thanks, darling," he said. "See if you can get Tom Polhaus." He opened the inner door and went into his private office, pulling the door to behind him.

Brigid O'Shaughnessy, dressed as on her first visit to the office, rose from a chair beside his desk and came quickly towards him. "Somebody has been in my apartment," she exclaimed. "It is all upside-down, every which way."

He seemed moderately surprised. "Anything taken?"

"I don't think so. I don't know. I was afraid to stay. I changed as fast as I could and came down here. Oh, you must've let that boy follow you there!"

Spade shook his head. "No, angel." He took an early copy of an afternoon paper from his pocket, opened it, and showed her a quarter-column headed SCREAM ROUTS BURGLAR.

A young woman named Carolin Beale, who lived alone in a Sutter Street apartment, had been awakened at four that morning by the sound of somebody moving in her bedroom. She had screamed. The mover had run away. Two other women who lived alone in the same building had discovered, later in the morning, signs of the burglar's having visited their apartments. Nothing had been taken from any of the three.

"That's where I shook him," Spade explained. "I went into that building and ducked out the back door. That's why all three were women who lived alone. He tried the apartments that had women's names in the vestibule-register, hunting for you under an alias."

"But he was watching your place when we were there," she objected.

Spade shrugged. "There's no reason to think he's working alone. Or maybe he went to Sutter Street after he had begun to think you were going to stay all night in my place. There are a lot of maybes, but I didn't lead him to the Coronet."

She was not satisfied. "But he found it, or somebody did."

"Sure." He frowned at her feet. "I wonder if it could have been Cairo. He wasn't at his hotel all night, didn't get in till a few minutes ago. He told me he had been standing up under a police-grilling all night. I wonder." He turned, opened the door, and asked Effie Perine: "Got Tom yet?"

"He's not in. I'll try again in a few minutes."

"Thanks." Spade shut the door and faced Brigid O'Shaughnessy.

She looked at him with cloudy eyes. "You went to see Joe this morning?" she asked.

"Yes."

She hesitated. "Why?"

"Why?" He smiled down at her. "Because, my own true love, I've got to keep in some sort of touch with all the loose ends of this dizzy affair if I'm ever going to make heads or tails of it." He put an arm around her shoulders and led her over to his swivel-chair. He kissed the tip of her nose lightly and set her down in the chair. He sat on the desk in front of her. He said: "Now we've got to find a new home for you, haven't we?"

She nodded with emphasis. "I won't go back there."

He patted the desk beside his thighs and made a thoughtful face. "I think I've got it," he said presently. "Wait a minute." He went into the outer office, shutting the door.

Effie Perine reached for the telephone, saying: "I'll try again."

"Afterwards. Does your woman's intuition still tell you that she's a madonna or something?"

She looked sharply up at him. "I still believe that no matter what kind of trouble she's gotten into she's all right, if that's what you mean."

"That's what I mean," he said. "Are you strong enough for her to give her a lift?"

"How?"

"Could you put her up for a few days?"

"You mean at home?"

"Yes. Her joint's been broken into. That's the second burglary she's had this week. It'd be better for her if she wasn't alone. It would help a lot if you could take her in."

Effie Perine leaned forward, asking earnestly: "Is she really in danger, Sam?"

"I think she is."

She scratched her lip with a fingernail. "That would scare Ma into a green hemorrhage. I'll have to tell her she's a surprise-witness or something that you're keeping under cover till the last minute."

"You're a darling," Spade said. "Better take her out there now. I'll get her key from her and bring whatever she needs over from her apartment.

Let's see. You oughtn't to be seen leaving here together. You go home now. Take a taxi, but make sure you aren't followed. You probably won't be, but make sure. I'll send her out in another in a little while, making sure she isn't followed."

CHAPTER XI

The Fat Man

THE TELEPHONE-BELL was ringing when Spade returned to his office after sending Brigid O'Shaughnessy off to Effie Perine's house. He went to the telephone.

"Hello. . . . Yes, this is Spade. . . . Yes, I got it. I've been waiting to hear from you. . . . Who? . . . Mr. Gutman? Oh, yes, sure! . . . Now —the sooner the better. . . . Twelve C. . . . Right. Say fifteen minutes. . . . Right."

Spade sat on the corner of his desk beside the telephone and rolled a cigarette. His mouth was a hard complacent v. His eyes, watching his fingers make the cigarette, smoldered over lower lids drawn up straight.

The door opened and Iva Archer came in.

Spade said, "Hello, honey," in a voice as lightly amiable as his face had suddenly become.

"Oh, Sam, forgive me! forgive me!" she cried in a choked voice. She stood just inside the door, wadding a black-bordered handkerchief in her small gloved hands, peering into his face with frightened red and swollen eyes.

He did not get up from his seat on the desk-corner. He said: "Sure. That's all right. Forget it."

"But, Sam," she wailed, "I sent those policemen there. I was mad, crazy with jealousy, and I phoned them that if they'd go there they'd learn something about Miles's murder."

"What made you think that?"

"Oh, I didn't! But I was mad, Sam, and I wanted to hurt you."

"It made things damned awkward." He put his arm around her and drew her nearer. "But it's all right now, only don't get any more crazy notions like that."

"I won't," she promised, "ever. But you weren't nice to me last night. You were cold and distant and wanted to get rid of me, when I had come down there and waited so long to warn you, and you—"

"Warn me about what?"

"About Phil. He's found out about—about you being in love with me, and Miles had told him about my wanting a divorce, though of course *he* never knew what for, and now Phil thinks we—you killed his brother because he wouldn't give me the divorce so we could get married. He told me he believed that, and yesterday he went and told the police."

"That's nice," Spade said softly. "And you came to warn me, and because I was busy you got up on your ear and helped this damned Phil Archer stir things up."

"I'm sorry," she whimpered, "I know you won't forgive me. I—I'm sorry, sorry, sorry."

"You ought to be," he agreed, "on your own account as well as mine. Has Dundy been to see you since Phil did his talking? Or anybody from the bureau?"

"No." Alarm opened her eyes and mouth.

"They will," he said, "and it'd be just as well to not let them find you here. Did you tell them who you were when you phoned?"

"Oh, no! I simply told them that if they'd go to your apartment right away they'd learn something about the murder and hung up."

"Where'd you phone from?"

"The drug-store up above your place. Oh, Sam, dearest, I—"

He patted her shoulder and said pleasantly: "It was a dumb trick, all right, but it's done now. You'd better run along home and think up things to tell the police. You'll be hearing from them. Maybe it'd be best to say 'no' right across the board." He frowned at something distant. "Or maybe you'd better see Sid Wise first." He removed his arm from around her, took a card out of his pocket, scribbled three lines on its back, and gave it to her. "You can tell Sid everything." He frowned. "Or almost everything. Where were you the night Miles was shot?"

"Home," she replied without hesitating.

He shook his head, grinning at her.

"I was," she insisted.

"No," he said, "but if that's your story it's all right with me. Go see Sid. It's up on the next corner, the pinkish building, room eight-twenty-seven."

Her blue eyes tried to probe his yellow-grey ones. "What makes you think I wasn't home?" she asked slowly.

"Nothing except that I know you weren't."

"But I was, I was." Her lips twisted and anger darkened her eyes. "Effie Perine told you that," she said indignantly. "I saw her looking at my clothes and snooping around. You know she doesn't like me, Sam. Why do you believe things she tells you when you know she'd do anything to make trouble for me?"

"Jesus, you women," Spade said mildly. He looked at the watch on his wrist. "You'll have to trot along, precious. I'm late for an appointment now. You do what you want, but if I were you I'd tell Sid the truth or nothing. I mean leave out the parts you don't want to tell him, but don't make up anything to take its place."

"I'm not lying to you, Sam," she protested.

"Like hell you're not," he said and stood up.

She strained on tiptoe to hold her face nearer his. "You don't believe me?" she whispered.

"I don't believe you."

"And you won't forgive me for—for what I did?"

"Sure I do." He bent his head and kissed her mouth. "That's all right. Now run along."

She put her arms around him. "Won't you go with me to see Mr. Wise?"

"I can't, and I'd only be in the way." He patted her arms, took them from around his body, and kissed her left wrist between glove and sleeve. He put his hands on her shoulders, turned her to face the door, and released her with a little push. "Beat it," he ordered.

The mahogany door of suite 12-C at the Alexandria Hotel was opened by the boy Spade had talked to in the Belvedere lobby. Spade said, "Hello," good-naturedly. The boy did not say anything. He stood aside holding the door open.

Spade went in. A fat man came to meet him.

The fat man was flabbily fat with bulbous pink cheeks and lips and chins and neck, with a great soft egg of a belly that was all his torso, and pendant cones for arms and legs. As he advanced to meet Spade all his bulbs rose and shook and fell separately with each step, in the manner of clustered soap-bubbles not yet released from the pipe through which they had been blown. His eyes, made small by fat puffs around them, were dark and sleek. Dark ringlets thinly covered his broad scalp. He wore a black cutaway coat, black vest, black satin Ascot tie holding a pinkish pearl, striped grey worsted trousers, and patent-leather shoes.

His voice was a throaty purr. "Ah, Mr. Spade," he said with enthusiasm and held out a hand like a fat pink star.

Spade took the hand and smiled and said: "How do you do, Mr. Gutman?"

Holding Spade's hand, the fat man turned beside him, put his other hand to Spade's elbow, and guided him across a green rug to a green plush chair beside a table that held a siphon, some glasses, and a bottle of Johnnie Walker whiskey on a tray, a box of cigars—Coronas del Ritz—two newspapers, and a small and plain yellow soapstone box.

Spade sat in the green chair. The fat man began to fill two glasses from bottle and siphon. The boy had disappeared. Doors set in three of the room's walls were shut. The fourth wall, behind Spade, was pierced by two windows looking out over Geary Street.

"We begin well, sir," the fat man purred, turning with a proffered glass in his hand. "I distrust a man that says when. If he's got to be careful not to drink too much it's because he's not to be trusted when he does."

Spade took the glass and, smiling, made the beginning of a bow over it.

The fat man raised his glass and held it against a window's light. He nodded approvingly at the bubbles running up in it. He said: "Well, sir, here's to plain speaking and clear understanding."

They drank and lowered their glasses.

The fat man looked shrewdly at Spade and asked: "You're a close-mouthed man?"

Spade shook his head. "I like to talk."

"Better and better!" the fat man exclaimed. "I distrust a close-mouthed man. He generally picks the wrong time to talk and says the wrong things. Talking's something you can't do judiciously unless you keep in practice." He beamed over his glass. "We'll get along, sir, that we will." He set his glass on the table and held the box of Coronas del Ritz out to Spade. "A cigar, sir."

Spade took a cigar, trimmed the end of it, and lighted it. Meanwhile the fat man pulled another green plush chair around to face Spade's within convenient distance and placed a smoking-stand within reach of both chairs. Then he took his glass from the table, took a cigar from the box, and lowered himself into his chair. His bulbs stopped jouncing and settled into flabby rest. He sighed comfortably and said: "Now, sir, we'll talk if you like. And I'll tell you right out that I'm a man who likes talking to a man that likes to talk."

"Swell. Will we talk about the black bird?"

The fat man laughed and his bulbs rode up and down on his laughter. "Will we?" he asked and, "We will," he replied. His pink face was shiny with delight. "You're the man for me, sir, a man cut along my own lines. No beating about the bush, but right to the point. 'Will we talk about the black bird?' We will. I like that, sir. I like that way of doing business. Let us talk about the black bird by all means, but first, sir, answer me a question, please, though maybe it's an unnecessary one, so we'll understand each other from the beginning. You're here as Miss O'Shaughnessy's representative?"

Spade blew smoke above the fat man's head in a long slanting plume. He frowned thoughtfully at the ash-tipped end of his cigar. He replied deliberately: "I can't say yes or no. There's nothing certain about it either way, yet." He looked up at the fat man and stopped frowning. "It depends."

"It depends on—?"

Spade shook his head. "If I knew what it depends on I could say yes or no."

The fat man took a mouthful from his glass, swallowed it, and suggested: "Maybe it depends on Joel Cairo?"

Spade's prompt "Maybe" was noncommittal. He drank.

The fat man leaned forward until his belly stopped him. His smile was ingratiating and so was his purring voice. "You could say, then, that the question is which one of them you'll represent?"

"You could put it that way."

"It will be one or the other?"

"I didn't say that."

The fat man's eyes glistened. His voice sank to a throaty whisper asking: "Who else is there?"

Spade pointed his cigar at his own chest. "There's me," he said.

The fat man sank back in his chair and let his body go flaccid. He blew his breath out in a long contented gust. "That's wonderful, sir," he purred. "That's wonderful. I do like a man that tells you right out he's looking out for himself. Don't we all? I don't trust a man that says he's not. And the man that's telling the truth when he says he's not I distrust most of all, because he's an ass and an ass that's going contrary to the laws of nature."

Spade exhaled smoke. His face was politely attentive. He said: "Uh-huh. Now let's talk about the black bird."

The fat man smiled benevolently. "Let's," he said. He squinted so that fat puffs crowding together left nothing of his eyes but a dark gleam visible. "Mr. Spade, have you any conception of how much money can be made out of that black bird?"

"No."

The fat man leaned forward again and put a bloated pink hand on the arm of Spade's chair. "Well, sir, if I told you—by Gad, if I told you half!—you'd call me a liar."

Spade smiled. "No," he said, "not even if I thought it. But if you won't take the risk just tell me what it is and I'll figure out the profits."

The fat man laughed. "You couldn't do it, sir. Nobody could do it that hadn't had a world of experience with things of that sort, and"—he paused impressively—"there aren't any other things of that sort." His bulbs jostled one another as he laughed again. He stopped laughing, abruptly. His fleshy lips hung open as laughter had left them. He stared at Spade with an intentness that suggested myopia. He asked: "You mean you don't know what it is?" Amazement took the throatiness out of his voice.

Spade made a careless gesture with his cigar. "Oh, hell," he said lightly, "I know what it's supposed to look like. I know the value in life you people put on it. I don't know what it is."

"She didn't tell you?"

"Miss O'Shaughnessy?"

"Yes. A lovely girl, sir."

"Uh-huh. No."

The fat man's eyes were dark gleams in ambush behind pink puffs of flesh. He said indistinctly, "She must know," and then, "And Cairo didn't either?"

"Cairo is cagey. He's willing to buy it, but he won't risk telling me anything I don't know already."

The fat man moistened his lips with his tongue. "How much is he willing to buy it for?" he asked.

"Ten thousand dollars."

The fat man laughed scornfully. "Ten thousand, and dollars, mind you, not even pounds. That's the Greek for you. Humph! And what did you say to that?"

"I said if I turned it over to him I'd expect the ten thousand."

"Ah, yes, *if!* Nicely put, sir." The fat man's forehead squirmed in a flesh-blurred frown. "They must know," he said only partly aloud, then: "Do they? Do they know what the bird is, sir? What was your impression?"

"I can't help you there," Spade confessed. "There's not much to go by. Cairo didn't say he did and he didn't say he didn't. She said she didn't, but I took it for granted that she was lying."

"That was not an injudicious thing to do," the fat man said, but his mind was obviously not on his words. He scratched his head. He frowned until his forehead was marked by raw red creases. He fidgeted in his chair as much as his size and the size of the chair permitted fidgeting. He shut his eyes, opened them suddenly—wide—and said to Spade: "Maybe they don't." His bulbous pink face slowly lost its worried frown and then, more quickly, took on an expression of ineffable happiness. "If they don't," he cried, and again: "If they don't I'm the only one in the whole wide sweet world who does!"

Spade drew his lips back in a tight smile. "I'm glad I came to the right place," he said.

The fat man smiled too, but somewhat vaguely. Happiness had gone out of his face, though he continued to smile, and caution had come into his eyes. His face was a watchful-eyed smiling mask held up between his thoughts and Spade. His eyes, avoiding Spade's, shifted to the glass at Spade's elbow. His face brightened. "By Gad, sir," he said, "your glass is empty." He got up and went to the table and clattered glasses and siphon and bottle mixing two drinks.

Spade was immobile in his chair until the fat man, with a flourish and a bow and a jocular "Ah, sir, this kind of medicine will never hurt you!" had handed him his refilled glass. Then Spade rose and stood close to the fat man, looking down at him, and Spade's eyes were hard and bright. He raised his glass. His voice was deliberate, challenging: "Here's to plain speaking and clear understanding."

The fat man chuckled and they drank. The fat man sat down. He held his glass against his belly with both hands and smiled up at Spade. He said: "Well, sir, it's surprising, but it well may be a fact that neither of them does know exactly what that bird is, and that nobody in all this whole wide sweet world knows what it is, saving and excepting only your humble servant, Casper Gutman, Esquire."

"Swell." Spade stood with legs apart, one hand in his trousers-pocket, the other holding his glass. "When you've told me there'll only be two of us who know."

"Mathematically correct, sir"—the fat man's eyes twinkled—"but"—his smile spread—"I don't know for certain that I'm going to tell you."

"Don't be a damned fool," Spade said patiently. "You know what it is. I know where it is. That's why we're here."

"Well, sir, where is it?"

Spade ignored the question.

The fat man bunched his lips, raised his eyebrows, and cocked his head a little to the left. "You see," he said blandly, "I must tell you what I know, but you will not tell me what you know. That is hardly equitable, sir. No, no, I do not think we can do business along those lines."

Spade's face became pale and hard. He spoke rapidly in a low furious voice: "Think again and think fast. I told that punk of yours that you'd have to talk to me before you got through. I'll tell you now that you'll do your talking today or you are through. What are you wasting my time for? You and your lousy secret! Christ! I know exactly what that stuff is that they keep in the subtreasury vaults, but what good does that do me? I can get along without you. God damn you! Maybe you could have got along without me if you'd kept clear of me. You can't now. Not in San Francisco. You'll come in or you'll get out—and you'll do it today."

He turned and with angry heedlessness tossed his glass at the table. The glass struck the wood, burst apart, and splashed its contents and glittering fragments over table and floor. Spade, deaf and blind to the crash, wheeled to confront the fat man again.

The fat man paid no more attention to the glass's fate than Spade did: lips pursed, eyebrows raised, head cocked a little to the left, he had maintained his pink-faced blandness throughout Spade's angry speech, and he maintained it now.

Spade, still furious, said: "And another thing, I don't want—"

The door to Spade's left opened. The boy who had admitted Spade came in. He shut the door, stood in front of it with his hands flat against his flanks, and looked at Spade. The boy's eyes were wide open and dark with wide pupils. Their gaze ran over Spade's body from shoulders to knees, and up again to settle on the handkerchief whose maroon border peeped from the breast-pocket of Spade's brown coat.

"Another thing," Spade repeated, glaring at the boy: "Keep that gunsel away from me while you're making up your mind. I'll kill him. I don't like him. He makes me nervous. I'll kill him the first time he gets in my way. I won't give him an even break. I won't give him a chance. I'll kill him."

The boy's lips twitched in a shadowy smile. He neither raised his eyes nor spoke.

The fat man said tolerantly: "Well, sir, I must say you have a most violent temper."

"Temper?" Spade laughed crazily. He crossed to the chair on which he had dropped his hat, picked up the hat, and set it on his head. He held out a long arm that ended in a thick forefinger pointing at the fat man's belly. His angry voice filled the room. "Think it over and think like hell. You've got till five-thirty to do it in. Then you're either in or out, for keeps." He let his arm drop, scowled at the bland fat man for a moment, scowled at the boy, and went to the door through which he had entered. When he opened the door he turned and said harshly: "Five-thirty—then the curtain."

The boy, staring at Spade's chest, repeated the two words he had twice spoken in the Belvedere lobby. His voice was not loud. It was bitter.

Spade went out and slammed the door.

CHAPTER XII

Merry-Go-Round

SPADE RODE DOWN from Gutman's floor in an elevator. His lips were dry and rough in a face otherwise pale and damp. When he took out his handkerchief to wipe his face he saw his hand trembling. He grinned at it and said, "Whew!" so loudly that the elevator-operator turned his head over his shoulder and asked: "Sir?"

Spade walked down Geary Street to the Palace Hotel, where he ate luncheon. His face had lost its pallor, his lips their dryness, and his hand its trembling by the time he had sat down. He ate hungrily without haste, and then went to Sid Wise's office.

When Spade entered, Wise was biting a fingernail and staring at the window. He took his hand from his mouth, screwed his chair around to face Spade, and said: " 'Lo. Push a chair up."

Spade moved a chair to the side of the big paper-laden desk and sat down. "Mrs. Archer come in?" he asked.

"Yes." The faintest of lights flickered in Wise's eyes. "Going to marry the lady, Sammy?"

Spade sighed irritably through his nose. "Christ, now you start that!" he grumbled.

A brief tired smile lifted the corners of the lawyer's mouth. "If you don't," he said, "you're going to have a job on your hands."

Spade looked up from the cigarette he was making and spoke sourly: "You mean you are? Well, that's what you're for. What did she tell you?"

"About you?"

"About anything I ought to know."

Wise ran fingers through his hair, sprinkling dandruff down on his shoulders. "She told me she had tried to get a divorce from Miles so she could—"

"I know all that," Spade interrupted him. "You can skip it. Get to the part I don't know."

"How do I know how much she—?"

"Quit stalling, Sid." Spade held the flame of his lighter to the end of his cigarette. "What did she tell you that she wanted kept from me?"

Wise looked reprovingly at Spade. "Now, Sammy," he began, "that's not—"

Spade looked heavenward at the ceiling and groaned: "Dear God, he's my own lawyer that's got rich off me and I have to get down on my knees and beg him to tell me things!" He lowered at Wise. "What in hell do you think I sent her to you for?"

Wise made a weary grimace. "Just one more client like you," he complained, "and I'd be in a sanatarium—or San Quentin."

"You'd be with most of your clients. Did she tell you where she was the night he was killed?"

"Yes."

"Where?"

"Following him."

Spade sat up straight and blinked. He exclaimed incredulously: "Jesus, these women!" Then he laughed, relaxed, and asked: "Well, what did she see?"

Wise shook his head. "Nothing much. When he came home for dinner that evening he told her he had a date with a girl at the St. Mark, ragging her, telling her that was her chance to get the divorce she wanted. She thought at first he was just trying to get under her skin. He knew—"

"I know the family history," Spade said. "Skip it. Tell me what she did."

"I will if you'll give me a chance. After he had gone out she began to think that maybe he might have had that date. You know Miles. It would have been like him to—"

"You can skip Miles's character too."

"I oughtn't to tell you a damned thing," the lawyer said. "So she got their car from the garage and drove down to the St. Mark, sitting in the car across the street. She saw him come out of the hotel and she saw that he was shadowing a man and a girl—she says she saw the same girl with you last night—who had come out just ahead of him. She knew then that he was working, had been kidding her. I suppose she was disappointed, and mad—she sounded that way when she told me about it. She followed Miles long enough to make sure he was shadowing the pair, and then she went up to your apartment. You weren't home."

"What time was that?" Spade asked.

"When she got to your place? Between half-past nine and ten the first time."

"The first time?"

"Yes. She drove around for half an hour or so and then tried again. That would make it, say, ten-thirty. You were still out, so she drove back downtown and went to a movie to kill time until after midnight, when she thought she'd be more likely to find you in."

Spade frowned. "She went to a movie at ten-thirty?"

"So she says—the one on Powell Street that stays open till one in the morning. She didn't want to go home, she said, because she didn't want to be there when Miles came. That always made him mad, it seems, especially if it was around midnight. She stayed in the movie till it closed." Wise's words came out slower now and there was a sardonic glint in his eye. "She says she had decided by then not to go back to your place again. She says she didn't know whether you'd like having her drop in that late. So she went to Tait's—the one on Ellis Street—had something to eat and then went home—alone." Wise rocked back in his chair and waited for Spade to speak.

Spade's face was expressionless. He asked: "You believe her?"

"Don't you?" Wise replied.

"How do I know? How do I know it isn't something you fixed up between you to tell me?"

Wise smiled. "You don't cash many checks for strangers, do you, Sammy?"

"Not basketfuls. Well, what then? Miles wasn't home. It was at least two o'clock by then—must've been—and he was dead."

"Miles wasn't home," Wise said. "That seems to have made her mad again—his not being home first to be made mad by her not being home. So she took the car out of the garage again and went back to your place."

"And I wasn't home. I was down looking at Miles's corpse. Jesus, what a swell lot of merry-go-round riding. Then what?"

"She went home, and her husband still wasn't there, and while she was undressing your messenger came with the news of his death."

Spade didn't speak until he had with great care rolled and lighted another cigarette. Then he said: "I think that's an all right spread. It seems to click with most of the known facts. It ought to hold."

Wise's fingers, running through his hair again, combed more dandruff down on his shoulders. He studied Spade's face with curious eyes and asked: "But you don't believe it?"

Spade plucked his cigarette from between his lips. "I don't believe it or disbelieve it, Sid. I don't know a damned thing about it."

A wry smile twisted the lawyer's mouth. He moved his shoulders wearily and said: "That's right—I'm selling you out. Why don't you get an honest lawyer—one you can trust?"

"That fellow's dead." Spade stood up. He sneered at Wise. "Getting touchy, huh? I haven't got enough to think about: now I've got to remember to be polite to you. What did I do? Forget to genuflect when I came in?"

Sid Wise smiled sheepishly. "You're a son of a gun, Sammy," he said.

Effie Perine was standing in the center of Spade's outer office when he entered. She looked at him with worried brown eyes and asked: "What happened?"

Spade's face grew stiff. "What happened where?" he demanded.

"Why didn't she come?"

Spade took two long steps and caught Effie Perine by the shoulders. "She didn't get there?" he bawled into her frightened face.

She shook her head violently from side to side. "I waited and waited and she didn't come, and I couldn't get you on the phone, so I came down."

Spade jerked his hands away from her shoulders, thrust them far down in his trousers-pockets, said, "Another merry-go-round," in a loud enraged voice, and strode into his private office. He came out again. "Phone your mother," he commanded. "See if she's come yet."

He walked up and down the office while the girl used the telephone. "No," she said when she had finished. "Did—did you send her out in a taxi?"

His grunt probably meant yes.

"Are you sure she— Somebody must have followed her!"

Spade stopped pacing the floor. He put his hands on his hips and glared at the girl. He addressed her in a loud savage voice: "Nobody followed her. Do you think I'm a God-damned schoolboy? I made sure of it before I put her in the cab, I rode a dozen blocks with her to be more sure, and I checked her another half-dozen blocks after I got out."

"Well, but—"

"But she didn't get there. You've told me that. I believe it. Do you think I think she did get there?"

Effie Perine sniffed. "You certainly act like a God-damned schoolboy," she said.

Spade made a harsh noise in his throat and went to the corridor-door. "I'm going out and find her if I have to dig up sewers," he said. "Stay here till I'm back or you hear from me. For Christ's sake let's do something right."

He went out, walked half the distance to the elevators, and retraced his steps. Effie Perine was sitting at her desk when he opened the door. He said: "You ought to know better than to pay any attention to me when I talk like that."

"If you think I pay any attention to you you're crazy," she replied, "only"—she crossed her arms and felt her shoulders, and her mouth twitched uncertainly—"I won't be able to wear an evening gown for two weeks, you big brute."

He grinned humbly, said, "I'm no damned good, darling," made an exaggerated bow, and went out again.

Two yellow taxicabs were at the corner-stand to which Spade went. Their chauffeurs were standing together talking. Spade asked: "Where's the red-faced blond driver that was here at noon?"

"Got a load," one of the chauffeurs said.

"Will he be back here?"

"I guess so."

The other chauffeur ducked his head to the east. "Here he comes now."

Spade walked down to the corner and stood by the curb until the red-faced blond chauffeur had parked his cab and got out. Then Spade went up to him and said: "I got into your cab with a lady at noontime. We went out Stockton Street and up Sacramento to Jones, where I got out."

"Sure," the red-faced man said, "I remember that."

"I told you to take her to a Ninth Avenue number. You didn't take her there. Where did you take her?"

The chauffeur rubbed his cheek with a grimy hand and looked doubtfully at Spade. "I don't know about this."

"It's all right," Spade assured him, giving him one of his cards. "If you want to play safe, though, we can ride up to your office and get your superintendent's OK."

"I guess it's all right. I took her to the Ferry Building."

"By herself?"

"Yeah. Sure."

"Didn't take her anywhere else first?"

"No. It was like this: after we dropped you I went on out Sacramento, and when we got to Polk she rapped on the glass and said she wanted to get a newspaper, so I stopped at the corner and whistled for a kid, and she got her paper."

"Which paper?"

"The *Call*. Then I went on out Sacramento some more, and just after we'd crossed Van Ness she knocked on the glass again and said take her to the Ferry Building."

"Was she excited or anything?"

"Not so's I noticed."

"And when you got to the Ferry Building?"

"She paid me off, and that was all."

"Anybody waiting for her there?"

"I didn't see them if they was."

"Which way did she go?"

"At the Ferry? I don't know. Maybe upstairs, or towards the stairs."

"Take the newspaper with her?"

"Yeah, she had it tucked under her arm when she paid me."

"With the pink sheet outside, or one of the white?"

"Hell, Cap, I don't remember that."

Spade thanked the chauffeur, said, "Get yourself a smoke," and gave him a silver dollar.

Spade bought a copy of the *Call* and carried it into an office-building-vestibule to examine it out of the wind.

His eyes ran swiftly over the front-page-headlines and over those on the second and third pages. They paused for a moment under SUSPECT ARRESTED AS COUNTERFEITER on the fourth page, and again on page five under BAY YOUTH SEEKS DEATH WITH BULLET. Pages six and seven held nothing to interest him. On eight 3 BOYS ARRESTED AS S. F. BURGLARS AFTER SHOOTING held his attention for a moment, and after that nothing until he reached the thirty-fifth page, which held news of the weather, shipping, produce, finance, divorce, births, marriages, and deaths. He read the list of dead, passed over pages thirty-six and thirty-seven—financial news—found nothing to stop his eyes on the thirty-eighth and last page, sighed, folded the newspaper, put it in his coat-pocket, and rolled a cigarette.

For five minutes he stood there in the office-building-vestibule smoking and staring sulkily at nothing. Then he walked up to Stockton Street, hailed a taxicab, and had himself driven to the Coronet.

He let himself into the building and into Brigid O'Shaughnessy's apartment with the key she had given him. The blue gown she had worn the previous night was hanging across the foot of her bed. Her blue stockings and slippers were on the bedroom floor. The polychrome box that had held jewelry in her dressing-table-drawer now stood empty on the dressing-table-top. Spade frowned at it, ran his tongue across his lips, strolled through the rooms, looking around but not touching anything, then left the Coronet and went downtown again.

In the doorway of Spade's office-building he came face to face with the boy he had left at Gutman's. The boy put himself in Spade's path, blocking the entrance, and said: "Come on. He wants to see you."

The boy's hands were in his overcoat-pockets. His pockets bulged more than his hands need have made them bulge.

Spade grinned and said mockingly: "I didn't expect you till five-twenty-five. I hope I haven't kept you waiting."

The boy raised his eyes to Spade's mouth and spoke in the strained voice of one in physical pain: "Keep on riding me and you're going to be picking iron out of your navel."

Spade chuckled. "The cheaper the crook, the gaudier the patter," he said cheerfully. "Well, let's go."

They walked up Sutter Street side by side. The boy kept his hands in his overcoat-pockets. They walked a little more than a block in silence. Then Spade asked pleasantly: "How long have you been off the gooseberry lay, son?"

The boy did not show that he had heard the question.

"Did you ever—?" Spade began, and stopped. A soft light began to glow in his yellowish eyes. He did not address the boy again.

They went into the Alexandria, rode up to the twelfth floor, and walked down the corridor towards Gutman's suite. Nobody else was in the corridor.

Spade lagged a little, so that, when they were within fifteen feet of Gutman's door, he was perhaps a foot and a half behind the boy. He leaned sidewise suddenly and grasped the boy from behind by both arms, just beneath the boy's elbows. He forced the boy's arms forward so that the boy's hands, in his overcoat-pockets, lifted the overcoat up before him. The boy struggled and squirmed, but he was impotent in the big man's grip. The boy kicked back, but his feet went between Spade's spread legs.

Spade lifted the boy straight up from the floor and brought him down hard on his feet again. The impact made little noise on the thick carpet. At the moment of impact Spade's hands slid down and got a fresh grip on the boy's wrists. The boy, teeth set hard together, did not stop straining against the man's big hands, but he could not tear himself loose, could not keep the man's hands from crawling down over his own hands. The boy's teeth ground together audibly, making a noise that mingled with the noise of Spade's breathing as Spade crushed the boy's hands.

They were tense and motionless for a long moment. Then the boy's arms became limp. Spade released the boy and stepped back. In each of Spade's hands, when they came out of the boy's overcoat-pockets, there was a heavy automatic pistol.

The boy turned and faced Spade. The boy's face was a ghastly white blank. He kept his hands in his overcoat-pockets. He looked at Spade's chest and did not say anything.

Spade put the pistols in his own pockets and grinned derisively. "Come on," he said. "This will put you in solid with your boss."

They went to Gutman's door and Spade knocked.

CHAPTER XIII

The Emperor's Gift

GUTMAN OPENED the door. A glad smile lighted his fat face. He held out a hand and said: "Ah, come in, sir! Thank you for coming. Come in."

Spade shook the hand and entered. The boy went in behind him. The fat man shut the door. Spade took the boy's pistols from his pockets and held them out to Gutman. "Here. You shouldn't let him run around with these. He'll get himself hurt."

The fat man laughed merrily and took the pistols. "Well, well," he said, "what's this?" He looked from Spade to the boy.

Spade said: "A crippled newsie took them away from him, but I made him give them back."

The white-faced boy took the pistols out of Gutman's hands and pocketed them. The boy did not speak.

Gutman laughed again. "By Gad, sir," he told Spade, "you're a chap worth knowing, an amazing character. Come in. Sit down. Give me your hat."

The boy left the room by the door to the right of the entrance.

The fat man installed Spade in a green plush chair by the table, pressed a cigar upon him, held a light to it, mixed whiskey and carbonated water, put one glass in Spade's hand, and, holding the other, sat down facing Spade.

"Now, sir," he said, "I hope you'll let me apologize for—"

"Never mind that," Spade said. "Let's talk about the black bird."

The fat man cocked his head to the left and regarded Spade with fond eyes. "All right, sir," he agreed. "Let's." He took a sip from the glass in his hand. "This is going to be the most astounding thing you've ever heard of, sir, and I say that knowing that a man of your caliber in your profession must have known some astounding things in his time."

Spade nodded politely.

The fat man screwed up his eyes and asked: "What do you know, sir, about the Order of the Hospital of St. John of Jerusalem, later called the Knights of Rhodes and other things?"

Spade waved his cigar. "Not much—only what I remember from history in school—Crusaders or something."

"Very good. Now you don't remember that Suleiman the Magnificent chased them out of Rhodes in 1523?"

"No."

"Well, sir, he did, and they settled in Crete. And they stayed there for seven years, until 1530 when they persuaded the Emperor Charles V to give them"—Gutman held up three puffy fingers and counted them—"Malta, Gozo, and Tripoli."

"Yes?"

"Yes, sir, but with these conditions: they were to pay the Emperor each year the tribute of one"—he held up a finger—"falcon in acknowledgment that Malta was still under Spain, and if they ever left the island it was to revert to Spain. Understand? He was giving it to them, but not unless they used it, and they couldn't give or sell it to anybody else."

"Yes."

The fat man looked over his shoulders at the three closed doors, hunched his chair a few inches nearer Spade's, and reduced his voice to a husky whisper: "Have you any conception of the extreme, the immeasurable, wealth of the Order at that time?"

"If I remember," Spade said, "they were pretty well fixed."

Gutman smiled indulgently. "Pretty well, sir, is putting it mildly." His whisper became lower and more purring. "They were rolling in wealth, sir. You've no idea. None of us has any idea. For years they had preyed on the Saracens, had taken nobody knows what spoils of gems, precious metals, silks, ivories—the cream of the cream of the East. That is history, sir. We all know that the Holy Wars to them, as to the Templars, were largely a matter of loot.

"Well, now, the Emperor Charles has given them Malta, and all the rent he asks is one insignificant bird per annum, just as a matter of form. What could be more natural than for these immeasurably wealthy Knights to look around for some way of expressing their gratitude? Well, sir, that's exactly what they did, and they hit on the happy thought of sending Charles for the first year's tribute, not an insignificant live bird, but a glorious golden falcon encrusted from head to foot with the finest jewels in their coffers. And—remember, sir—they had fine ones, the finest out of Asia." Gutman stopped whispering. His sleek dark eyes examined Spade's face, which was placid. The fat man asked: "Well, sir, what do you think of that?"

"I don't know."

The fat man smiled complacently. "These are facts, historical facts, not schoolbook history, not Mr. Wells's history, but history nevertheless." He leaned forward. "The archives of the Order from the twelfth century on are still at Malta. They are not intact, but what is there holds no less than three"—he held up three fingers—"references that can't be to anything else but this jeweled falcon. In J. Delaville Le Roulx's *Les Archives de l'Ordre de Saint-Jean* there is a reference to it—oblique to be sure, but a reference still. And the unpublished—because unfinished at the time of his death—supplement to Paoli's *Dell' origine ed instituto del sacro militar ordine* has a clear and unmistakable statement of the facts I am telling you."

"All right," Spade said.

"All right, sir. Grand Master Villiers de l'Isle d'Adam had this foot-high jeweled bird made by Turkish slaves in the castle of St. Angelo and sent it to Charles, who was in Spain. He sent it in a galley commanded by a French knight named Cormier or Corvere, a member of the Order." His voice dropped to a whisper again. "It never reached Spain." He smiled with compressed lips and asked: "You know of Barbarossa, Redbeard, Khair-ed-Din? No? A famous admiral of buccaneers sailing out of Algiers then. Well, sir, he took the Knights' galley and he took the bird. The bird went to Algiers. That's a fact. That's a fact that the French historian Pierre Dan put in one of his letters from Algiers. He wrote that the bird had been there for more than a hundred years, until it was carried away by Sir Francis Verney, the English adventurer who was with the Algerian buccaneers for a while. Maybe it wasn't, but Pierre Dan believed it was, and that's good enough for me.

"There's nothing said about the bird in Lady Frances Verney's *Memoirs of the Verney Family during the Seventeenth Century*, to be sure. I looked. And it's pretty certain that Sir Francis didn't have the bird when he died in a Messina hospital in 1615. He was stony broke. But, sir, there's no denying that the bird *did* go to Sicily. It was there and it came into the possession there of Victor Amadeus II some time after he became king in 1713, and it was one of his gifts to his wife when he married in Chambéry after abdicating. That is a fact, sir. Carutti, the author of *Storia del Regno di Vittorio Amadeo II*, himself vouched for it.

"Maybe they—Amadeo and his wife—took it along with them to Turin when he tried to revoke his abdication. Be that as it may, it turned up next in the possession of a Spaniard who had been with the army that took Naples in 1734—the father of Don José Monino y Redondo, Count of Floridablanca, who was Charles III's chief minister. There's nothing to show that it didn't stay in that family until at least the end of the Carlist War in '40. Then it appeared in Paris at just about the time that Paris was full of Carlists who had had to get out of Spain. One of them must have brought it with him, but, whoever he was, it's likely he knew nothing about its real value. It had been—no doubt as a precaution during the Carlist trouble in Spain—painted or enameled over to look like nothing more than a fairly interesting black statuette. And in that disguise, sir, it was, you might say, kicked around Paris for seventy years by private owners and dealers too stupid to see what it was under the skin."

The fat man paused to smile and shake his head regretfully. Then he went on: "For seventy years, sir, this marvelous item was, as you might say, a football in the gutters of Paris—until 1911 when a Greek dealer named Charilaos Konstantinides found it in an obscure shop. It didn't take Charilaos long to learn what it was and to acquire it. No thickness of enamel could conceal value from his eyes and nose. Well, sir, Charilaos was the man who traced most of its history and who identified it as what it actually was. I got wind of it and finally forced most of the history out of him, though I've been able to add a few details since.

"Charilaos was in no hurry to convert his find into money at once. He knew that—enormous as its intrinsic value was—a far higher, a terrific, price could be obtained for it once its authenticity was established beyond doubt. Possibly he planned to do business with one of the modern descendents of the old Order—the English Order of St. John of Jerusalem, the Prussian Johanniterorden, or the Italian or German *langues* of the Sovereign Order of Malta—all wealthy orders."

The fat man raised his glass, smiled at its emptiness, and rose to fill it and Spade's. "You begin to believe me a little?" he asked as he worked the siphon.

"I haven't said I didn't."

"No," Gutman chuckled. "But how you looked." He sat down, drank generously, and patted his mouth with a white handkerchief. "Well, sir, to hold it safe while pursuing his researches into its history, Charilaos had re-enameled the bird, apparently just as it is now. One year to the very day after he had acquired it—that was possibly three months after I'd made him confess to me—I picked up the *Times* in London and read that his establishment had been burglarized and him murdered. I was in Paris the next day." He shook his head sadly. "The bird was gone. By Gad, sir, I was wild. I didn't believe anybody else knew what it was. I didn't believe he had told anybody but me. A great quantity of stuff had been stolen. That made me think that the thief had simply taken the bird along with the rest of his plunder, not knowing what it was. Because I assure you that a thief who knew its value would not burden himself with anything else—no, sir—at least not anything less than crown jewels."

He shut his eyes and smiled complacently at an inner thought. He opened his eyes and said: "That was seventeen years ago. Well, sir, it took me seventeen years to locate that bird, but I did it. I wanted it, and I'm not a man that's easily discouraged when he wants something." His smile grew broad. "I wanted it and I found it. I want it and I'm going to have it." He drained his glass, dried his lips again, and returned his handkerchief to his pocket. "I traced it to the home of a Russian general —one Kemidov—in a Constantinople suburb. He didn't know a thing about it. It was nothing but a black enameled figure to him, but his natural contrariness—the natural contrariness of a Russian general—kept him from selling it to me when I made him an offer. Perhaps in my eagerness I was a little unskillful, though not very. I don't know about that. But I did know I wanted it and I was afraid this stupid soldier might begin to investigate his property, might chip off some of the enamel. So I sent some—ah—agents to get it. Well, sir, they got it and I haven't got it." He stood up and carried his empty glass to the table. "But I'm going to get it. Your glass, sir."

"Then the bird doesn't belong to any of you," Spade asked, "but to a General Kemidov?"

"Belong?" the fat man said jovially. "Well, sir, you might say it belonged to the King of Spain, but I don't see how you can honestly grant anybody else clear title to it—except by right of possession." He clucked. "An article of that value that has passed from hand to hand by such means is clearly the property of whoever can get hold of it."

"Then it's Miss O'Shaughnessy's now?"

"No, sir, except as my agent."

Spade said, "Oh," ironically.

Gutman, looking thoughtfully at the stopper of the whiskey-bottle in his hand, asked: "There's no doubt that she's got it now?"

"Not much."

"Where?"

"I don't know exactly."

The fat man set the bottle on the table with a bang. "But you said you did," he protested.

Spade made a careless gesture with one hand. "I meant to say I know where to get it when the time comes."

The pink bulbs of Gutman's face arranged themselves more happily. "And you do?" he asked.

"Yes."

"Where?"

Spade grinned and said: "Leave that to me. That's my end."

"When?"

"When I'm ready."

The fat man pursed his lips and, smiling with only slight uneasiness, asked: "Mr. Spade, where is Miss O'Shaughnessy now?"

"In my hands, safely tucked away."

Gutman smiled with approval. "Trust you for that, sir," he said. "Well now, sir, before we sit down to talk prices, answer me this: how soon can you—or how soon are you willing to—produce the falcon?"

"A couple of days."

The fat man nodded. "That is satisfactory. We— But I forget our nourishment." He turned to the table, poured whiskey, squirted charged water into it, set a glass at Spade's elbow and held his own aloft. "Well, sir, here's to a fair bargain and profits large enough for both of us."

They drank. The fat man sat down. Spade asked: "What's your idea of a fair bargain?"

Gutman held his glass up to the light, looked affectionately at it, took another long drink, and said: "I have two proposals to make, sir, and either is fair. Take your choice. I will give you twenty-five thousand dollars when you deliver the falcon to me, and another twenty-five thousand as soon as I get to New York; or I will give you one quarter—twenty-five per cent—of what I realize on the falcon. There you are, sir: an almost immediate fifty thousand dollars or a vastly greater sum within, say, a couple of months."

Spade drank and asked: "How much greater?"

"Vastly," the fat man repeated. "Who knows how much greater? Shall I say a hundred thousand, or a quarter of a million? Will you believe me if I name the sum that seems the probable minimum?"

"Why not?"

The fat man smacked his lips and lowered his voice to a purring murmur. "What would you say, sir, to half a million?"

Spade narrowed his eyes. "Then you think the dingus is worth two million?"

Gutman smiled serenely. "In your own words, why not?" he asked.

Spade emptied his glass and set it on the table. He put his cigar in his mouth, took it out, looked at it, and put it back in. His yellow-grey eyes were faintly muddy. He said: "That's a hell of a lot of dough."

The fat man agreed: "That's a hell of a lot of dough." He leaned forward and patted Spade's knee. "That is the absolute rock-bottom minimum—or Charilaos Konstantinides was a blithering idiot—and he wasn't."

Spade removed the cigar from his mouth again, frowned at it with distaste, and put it on the smoking-stand. He shut his eyes hard, opened them again. Their muddiness had thickened. He said: "The—the minimum, huh? And the maximum?" An unmistakable *sh* followed the x in maximum as he said it.

"The maximum?" Gutman held his empty hand out, palm up. "I refuse to guess. You'd think me crazy. I don't know. There's no telling how high it could go, sir, and that's the one and only truth about it."

Spade pulled his sagging lower lip tight against the upper. He shook his head impatiently. A sharp frightened gleam awoke in his eyes—and was smothered by the deepening muddiness. He stood up, helping himself up with his hands on the arms of his chair. He shook his head again and took an uncertain step forward. He laughed thickly and muttered: "God damn you."

Gutman jumped up and pushed his chair back. His fat globes jiggled. His eyes were dark holes in an oily pink face.

Spade swung his head from side to side until his dull eyes were pointed at—if not focused on—the door. He took another uncertain step.

The fat man called sharply: "Wilmer!"

A door opened and the boy came in.

Spade took a third step. His face was grey now, with jaw-muscles standing out like tumors under his ears. His legs did not straighten again after his fourth step and his muddy eyes were almost covered by their lids. He took his fifth step.

The boy walked over and stood close to Spade, a little in front of him, but not directly between Spade and the door. The boy's right hand was inside his coat over his heart. The corners of his mouth twitched.

Spade essayed his sixth step.

The boy's leg darted out across Spade's leg, in front. Spade tripped over the interfering leg and crashed face-down on the floor. The boy, keeping his right hand under his coat, looked down at Spade. Spade tried to get up. The boy drew his right foot far back and kicked Spade's temple. The kick rolled Spade over on his side. Once more he tried to get up, could not, and went to sleep.

CHAPTER XIV

La Paloma

SPADE, COMING AROUND the corner from the elevator at a few minutes past six in the morning, saw yellow light glowing through the frosted glass of his office-door. He halted abruptly, set his lips together, looked up and down the corridor, and advanced to the door with swift quiet strides.

He put his hand on the knob and turned it with care that permitted neither rattle nor click. He turned the knob until it would turn no farther: the door was locked. Holding the knob still, he changed hands, taking it now in his left hand. With his right hand he brought his keys out of his pocket, carefully, so they could not jingle against one another. He separated the office-key from the others and, smothering the others together in his palm, inserted the office-key in the lock. The insertion was soundless. He balanced himself on the balls of his feet, filled his lungs, clicked the door open, and went in.

Effie Perine sat sleeping with her head on her forearms, her forearms on her desk. She wore her coat and had one of Spade's overcoats wrapped cape-fashion around her.

Spade blew his breath out in a muffled laugh, shut the door behind him, and crossed to the inner door. The inner office was empty. He went over to the girl and put a hand on her shoulder.

She stirred, raised her head drowsily, and her eyelids fluttered. Suddenly she sat up straight, opening her eyes wide. She saw Spade, smiled, leaned back in her chair, and rubbed her eyes with her fingers. "So you finally got back?" she said. "What time is it?"

"Six o'clock. What are you doing here?"

She shivered, drew Spade's overcoat closer around her, and yawned. "You told me to stay till you got back or phoned."

"Oh, you're the sister of the boy who stood on the burning deck?"

"I wasn't going to—" She broke off and stood up, letting his coat slide down on the chair behind her. She looked with dark excited eyes at his temple under the brim of his hat and exclaimed; "Oh, your head! What happened?"

His right temple was dark and swollen.

"I don't know whether I fell or was slugged. I don't think it amounts to much, but it hurts like hell." He barely touched it with his fingers, flinched, turned his grimace into a grim smile, and explained: "I went visiting, was fed knockout-drops, and came to twelve hours later all spread out on a man's floor."

She reached up and removed his hat from his head. "It's terrible," she said. "You'll have to get a doctor. You can't walk around with a head like that."

"It's not as bad as it looks, except for the headache, and that might be mostly from the drops." He went to the cabinet in the corner of the office and ran cold water on a handkerchief. "Anything turn up after I left?"

"Did you find Miss O'Shaughnessy, Sam?"

"Not yet. Anything turn up after I left?"

"The District Attorney's office phoned. He wants to see you."

"Himself?"

"Yes, that's the way I understood it. And a boy came in with a message —that Mr. Gutman would be delighted to talk to you before five-thirty."

Spade turned off the water, squeezed the handkerchief, and came away from the cabinet holding the handkerchief to his temple. "I got that," he said. "I met the boy downstairs, and talking to Mr. Gutman got me this."

"Is that the G. who phoned, Sam?"

"Yes."

"And what—?"

Spade stared through the girl and spoke as if using speech to arrange his thoughts: "He wants something he thinks I can get. I persuaded him I could keep him from getting it if he didn't make the deal with me before five-thirty. Then—uh-huh—sure—it was after I'd told him he'd have to wait a couple of days that he fed me the junk. It's not likely he thought I'd die. He'd know I'd be up and around in ten or twelve hours. So maybe the answer's that he figured he could get it without my help in that time if I was fixed so I couldn't butt in." He scowled. "I hope to Christ he was wrong." His stare became less distant. "You didn't get any word from the O'Shaughnessy?"

The girl shook her head no and asked: "Has this got anything to do with her?"

"Something."

"This thing he wants belongs to her?"

"Or to the King of Spain. Sweetheart, you've got an uncle who teaches history or something over at the University?"

"A cousin. Why?"

"If we brightened his life with an alleged historical secret four centuries old could we trust him to keep it dark awhile?"

"Oh, yes, he's good people."

"Fine. Get your pencil and book."

She got them and sat in her chair. Spade ran more cold water on his handkerchief and, holding it to his temple, stood in front of her and dictated the story of the falcon as he had heard it from Gutman, from Charles V's grant to the Hospitallers up to—but no further than—the enameled bird's arrival in Paris at the time of the Carlist influx. He stumbled over the names of authors and their works that Gutman had mentioned, but managed to achieve some sort of phonetic likeness. The rest of the history he repeated with the accuracy of a trained interviewer.

When he had finished the girl shut her notebook and raised a flushed smiling face to him. "Oh, isn't this thrilling?" she said. "It's—"

"Yes, or ridiculous. Now will you take it over and read it to your cousin and ask him what he thinks of it? Has he ever run across anything that might have some connection with it? Is it probable? Is it possible—even barely possible? Or is it the bunk? If he wants more time to look it up, OK, but get some sort of opinion out of him now. And for God's sake make him keep it under his hat."

"I'll go right now," she said, "and you go see a doctor about that head."

"We'll have breakfast first."

"No, I'll eat over in Berkeley. I can't wait to hear what Ted thinks of this."

"Well," Spade said, "don't start boo-hooing if he laughs at you."

After a leisurely breakfast at the Palace, during which he read both morning papers, Spade went home, shaved, bathed, rubbed ice on his bruised temple, and put on fresh clothes.

He went to Brigid O'Shaughnessy's apartment at the Coronet. Nobody was in the apartment. Nothing had been changed in it since his last visit.

He went to the Alexandria Hotel. Gutman was not in. None of the other occupants of Gutman's suite was in. Spade learned that these other occupants were the fat man's secretary, Wilmer Cook, and his daughter Rhea, a brown-eyed fair-haired smallish girl of seventeen whom the hotel-staff said was beautiful. Spade was told that the Gutman party had arrived at the hotel, from New York, ten days before, and had not checked out.

Spade went to the Belvedere and found the hotel-detective eating in the hotel-café.

"Morning, Sam. Set down and bite an egg." The hotel-detective stared at Spade's temple. "By God, somebody maced you plenty!"

"Thanks, I've had mine," Spade said as he sat down, and then, referring to his temple: "It looks worse than it is. How's my Cairo's conduct?"

"He went out not more than half an hour behind you yesterday and I ain't seen him since. He didn't sleep here again last night."

"He's getting bad habits."

"Well, a fellow like that alone in a big city. Who put the slug to you, Sam?"

"It wasn't Cairo." Spade looked attentively at the small silver dome covering Luke's toast. "How's chances of giving his room a casing while he's out?"

"Can do. You know I'm willing to go all the way with you all the time." Luke pushed his coffee back, put his elbows on the table, and screwed up his eyes at Spade. "But I got a hunch you ain't going all the way with me. What's the honest-to-God on this guy, Sam? You don't have to kick back on me. You know I'm regular."

Spade lifted his eyes from the silver dome. They were clear and candid. "Sure, you are," he said. "I'm not holding out. I gave you it straight. I'm doing a job for him, but he's got some friends that look wrong to me and I'm a little leery of him."

"The kid we chased out yesterday was one of his friends."

"Yes, Luke, he was."

"And it was one of them that shoved Miles across."

Spade shook his head. "Thursby killed Miles."

"And who killed him?"

Spade smiled. "That's supposed to be a secret, but, confidentially, I did," he said, "according to the police."

Luke grunted and stood up saying: "You're a tough one to figure out, Sam. Come on, we'll have that look-see."

They stopped at the desk long enough for Luke to "fix it so we'll get a ring if he comes in," and went up to Cairo's room. Cairo's bed was smooth and trim, but paper in wastebasket, unevenly drawn blinds, and a couple of rumpled towels in the bathroom showed that the chambermaid had not yet been in that morning.

Cairo's luggage consisted of a square trunk, a valise, and a Gladstone bag. His bathroom-cabinet was stocked with cosmetics—boxes, cans, jars, and bottles of powders, creams, unguents, perfumes, lotions, and tonics. Two suits and an overcoat hung in the closet over three pairs of carefully treed shoes.

The valise and smaller bag were unlocked. Luke had the trunk unlocked by the time Spade had finished searching elsewhere.

"Blank so far," Spade said as they dug down into the trunk.

They found nothing there to interest them.

"Any particular thing we're supposed to be looking for?" Luke asked as he locked the trunk again.

"No. He's supposed to have come here from Constantinople. I'd like to know if he did. I haven't seen anything that says he didn't."

"What's his racket?"

Spade shook his head. "That's something else I'd like to know." He crossed the room and bent down over the wastebasket. "Well, this is our last shot."

He took a newspaper from the basket. His eyes brightened when he saw it was the previous day's *Call*. It was folded with the classified-advertising-page outside. He opened it, examined that page, and nothing there stopped his eyes.

He turned the paper over and looked at the page that had been folded inside, the page that held financial and shipping news, the weather, births, marriages, divorces, and deaths. From the lower left-hand corner, a little more than two inches of the bottom of the second column had been torn out.

Immediately above the tear was a small caption *Arrived Today* followed by:

12:20 A. M.—Capac from Astoria.
5:05 A. M.—Helen P. Drew from Greenwood.
5:06 A. M.—Albarado from Bandon.

The tear passed through the next line, leaving only enough of its letters to make *from Sydney* inferable.

Spade put the *Call* down on the desk and looked into the wastebasket again. He found a small piece of wrapping-paper, a piece of string, two hosiery tags, a haberdasher's sale-ticket for half a dozen pairs of socks, and, in the bottom of the basket, a piece of newspaper rolled into a tiny ball.

He opened the ball carefully, smoothed it out on the desk, and fitted it into the torn part of the *Call*. The fit at the sides was exact, but between the top of the crumpled fragment and the inferable *from Sydney* half an inch was missing, sufficient space to have held announcement of six or seven boats' arrival. He turned the sheet over and saw that the other side of the missing portion could have held only a meaningless corner of a stockbroker's advertisement.

Luke, leaning over his shoulder, asked: "What's this all about?"

"Looks like the gent's interested in a boat."

"Well, there's no law against that, or is there?" Luke said while Spade was folding the torn page and the crumpled fragment together and putting them into his coat-pocket. "You all through here now?"

"Yes. Thanks a lot, Luke. Will you give me a ring as soon as he comes in?"

"Sure."

Spade went to the Business Office of the *Call*, bought a copy of the previous day's issue, opened it to the shipping-news-page, and compared it with the page taken from Cairo's wastebasket. The missing portion had read:

5:17 A. M.–Tahiti from Sydney and Papeete.
6:05 A. M.–Admiral Peoples from Astoria.
8:07 A. M.–Caddopeak from San Pedro.
8:17 A. M.–Silverado from San Pedro.
8:05 A. M.–La Paloma from Hongkong.
9:03 A. M.–Daisy Gray from Seattle.

He read the list slowly and when he had finished he underscored *Hongkong* with a fingernail, cut the list of arrivals from the paper with his pocket-knife, put the rest of the paper and Cairo's sheet into the wastebasket, and returned to his office.

He sat down at his desk, looked up a number in the telephone-book, and used the telephone.

"Kearny one four o one, please. . . . Where is the *Paloma*, in from Hongkong yesterday morning, docked?" He repeated the question. "Thanks."

He held the receiver-hook down with his thumb for a moment, released it, and said: "Davenport two o two o, please. . . . Detective bureau, please. . . . Is Sergeant Polhaus there? . . . Thanks. . . . Hello, Tom, this is Sam Spade. . . . Yes, I tried to get you yesterday afternoon. . . . Sure, suppose you go to lunch with me. . . . Right."

He kept the receiver to his ear while his thumb worked the hook again. "Davenport o one seven o, please. . . . Hello, this is Samuel Spade. My secretary got a phone-message yesterday that Mr. Bryan wanted to see me. Will you ask him what time's the most convenient for him? . . . Yes, Spade, S-p-a-d-e." A long pause. "Yes. . . . Two-thirty? All right. Thanks."

He called a fifth number and said: "Hello, darling, let me talk to Sid? . . . Hello, Sid—Sam. I've got a date with the District Attorney at half-past two this afternoon. Will you give me a ring—here or there—around four, just to see that I'm not in trouble? . . . Hell with your Saturday afternoon golf: your job's to keep me out of jail. . . . Right, Sid. 'Bye."

He pushed the telephone away, yawned, stretched, felt his bruised temple, looked at his watch, and rolled and lighted a cigarette. He smoked sleepily until Effie Perine came in.

Effie Perine came in smiling, bright-eyed and rosy-faced. "Ted says it could be," she reported, "and he hopes it is. He says he's not a specialist in that field, but the names and dates are all right, and at least none of your authorities or their works are out-and-out fakes. He's all excited over it."

"That's swell, as long as he doesn't get too enthusiastic to see through it if it's phoney."

"Oh, he wouldn't—not Ted! He's too good at his stuff for that."

"Uh-huh, the whole damned Perine family's wonderful," Spade said, "including you and the smudge of soot on your nose."

"He's not a Perine, he's a Christy." She bent her head to look at her nose in her vanity-case-mirror. "I must've got that from the fire." She scrubbed the smudge with the corner of a handkerchief.

"The Perine-Christy enthusiasm ignite Berkeley?" he asked.

She made a face at him while patting her nose with a powdered pink disc. "There was a boat on fire when I came back. They were towing it out from the pier and the smoke blew all over our ferry-boat."

Spade put his hands on the arms of his chair. "Were you near enough to see the name of the boat?" he asked.

"Yes. *La Paloma*. Why?"

Spade smiled ruefully. "I'm damned if I know why, sister," he said.

CHAPTER XV

Every Crackpot

SPADE AND Detective-sergeant Polhaus ate pickled pigs' feet at one of Big John's tables at the States Hof Brau.

Polhaus, balancing pale bright jelly on a fork halfway between plate and mouth, said: "Hey, listen, Sam! Forget about the other night. He was dead wrong, but you know anybody's liable to lose their head if you ride them thataway."

Spade looked thoughtfully at the police-detective. "Was that what you wanted to see me about?" he asked.

Polhaus nodded, put the forkful of jelly into his mouth, swallowed it, and qualified his nod: "Mostly."

"Dundy send you?"

Polhaus made a disgusted mouth. "You know he didn't. He's as bull-headed as you are."

Spade smiled and shook his head. "No, he's not, Tom," he said. "He just thinks he is."

Tom scowled and chopped at his pig's foot with a knife. "Ain't you ever going to grow up?" he grumbled. "What've you got to beef about? He didn't hurt you. You came out on top. What's the sense of making a grudge of it? You're just making a lot of grief for yourself."

Spade placed his knife and fork carefully together on his plate, and put his hands on the table beside his plate. His smile was faint and devoid of warmth. "With every bull in town working overtime trying to pile up grief for me a little more won't hurt. I won't even know it's there."

Polhaus's ruddiness deepened. He said: "That's a swell thing to say to me."

Spade picked up his knife and fork and began to eat. Polhaus ate.

Presently Spade asked: "See the boat on fire in the bay?"

"I saw the smoke. Be reasonable, Sam. Dundy was wrong and he knows it. Why don't you let it go at that?"

"Think I ought to go around and tell him I hope my chin didn't hurt his fist?"

Polhaus cut savagely into his pig's foot.

Spade said: "Phil Archer been in with any more hot tips?"

"Aw, hell! Dundy didn't think you shot Miles, but what else could he do except run the lead down? You'd've done the same thing in his place, and you know it."

"Yes?" Malice glittered in Spade's eyes. "What made him think I didn't do it? What makes you think I didn't? Or don't you?"

Polhaus's ruddy face flushed again. He said: "Thursby shot Miles."

"You think he did?"

"He did. That Webley was his, and the slug in Miles came out of it."

"Sure?" Spade demanded.

"Dead sure," the police-detective replied. "We got hold of a kid—a bellhop at Thursby's hotel—that had seen it in his room just that morning. He noticed it particular because he'd never saw one just like it before. I never saw one. You say they don't make them any more. It ain't likely there'd be another around and—anyway—if that wasn't Thursby's what happened to his? And that's the gun the slug in Miles come out of." He started to put a piece of bread into his mouth, withdrew it, and asked: "You say you've seen them before: where was that at?" He put the bread into his mouth.

"In England before the war."

"Sure, there you are."

Spade nodded and said: "Then that leaves Thursby the only one I killed."

Polhaus squirmed in his chair and his face was red and shiny. "Christ's sake, ain't you never going to forget that?" he complained earnestly.

"That's out. You know it as well as I do. You'd think you wasn't a dick yourself the way you bellyache over things. I suppose you don't never pull the same stuff on anybody that we pulled on you?"

"You mean that you tried to pull on me, Tom—just tried."

Polhaus swore under his breath and attacked the remainder of his pig's foot.

Spade said: "All right. You know it's out and I know it's out. What does Dundy know?"

"He knows it's out."

"What woke him up?"

"Aw, Sam, he never really thought you'd—" Spade's smile checked Polhaus. He left the sentence incomplete and said: "We dug up a record on Thursby."

"Yes? Who was he?"

Polhaus's shrewd small brown eyes studied Spade's face. Spade exclaimed irritably: "I wish to God I knew half as much about this business as you smart guys think I do!"

"I wish we all did," Polhaus grumbled. "Well, he was a St. Louis gunman the first we hear of him. He was picked up a lot of times back there for this and that, but he belonged to the Egan mob, so nothing much was ever done about any of it. I don't know howcome he left that shelter, but they got him once in New York for knocking over a row of stuss-games—his twist turned him up—and he was in a year before Fallon got him sprung. A couple of years later he did a short hitch in Joliet for pistol-whipping another twist that had given him the needle, but after that he took up with Dixie Monahan and didn't have any trouble getting out whenever he happened to get in. That was when Dixie was almost as big a shot as Nick the Greek in Chicago gambling. This Thursby was Dixie's bodyguard and he took the run-out with him when Dixie got in wrong with the rest of the boys over some debts he couldn't or wouldn't pay off. That was a couple of years back—about the time the Newport Beach Boating Club was shut up. I don't know if Dixie had any part in that. Anyways, this is the first time him or Thursby's been seen since."

"Dixie's been seen?" Spade asked.

Polhaus shook his head. "No." His small eyes became sharp, prying. "Not unless you've seen him or know somebody's seen him."

Spade lounged back in his chair and began to make a cigarette. "I haven't," he said mildly. "This is all new stuff to me."

"I guess it is," Poulhaus snorted.

Spade grinned at him and asked: "Where'd you pick up all this news about Thursby?"

"Some of it's on the records. The rest—well—we got it here and there."

"From Cairo, for instance?" Now Spade's eyes held the prying gleam.

Polhaus put down his coffee-cup and shook his head. "Not a word of it. You poisoned that guy for us."

Spade laughed. "You mean a couple of high-class sleuths like you and Dundy worked on that lily-of-the-valley all night and couldn't crack him?"

"What do you mean—all night?" Polhaus protested. "We worked on him for less than a couple of hours. We saw we wasn't getting nowhere, and let him go."

Spade laughed again and looked at his watch. He caught John's eye and asked for the check. "I've got a date with the D. A. this afternoon," he told Polhaus while they waited for his change.

"He send for you?"

"Yes."

Polhaus pushed his chair back and stood up, a barrel-bellied tall man, solid and phlegmatic. "You won't be doing me any favor," he said, "by telling him I've talked to you like this."

A lathy youth with salient ears ushered Spade into the District Attorney's office. Spade went in smiling easily, saying easily: "Hello, Bryan!"

District Attorney Bryan stood up and held his hand out across his desk. He was a blond man of medium stature, perhaps forty-five years old, with aggressive blue eyes behind black-ribboned nose-glasses, the over-large mouth of an orator, and a wide dimpled chin. When he said, "How do you do, Spade?" his voice was resonant with latent power.

They shook hands and sat down.

The District Attorney put his finger on one of the pearl buttons in a battery of four on his desk, said to the lathy youth who opened the door again, "Ask Mr. Thomas and Healy to come in," and then, rocking back in his chair, addressed Spade pleasantly: "You and the police haven't been hitting it off so well, have you?"

Spade made a negligent gesture with the fingers of his right hand. "Nothing serious," he said lightly. "Dundy gets too enthusiastic."

The door opened to admit two men. The one to whom Spade said, "Hello, Thomas!" was a sunburned stocky man of thirty in clothing and hair of a kindred unruliness. He clapped Spade on the shoulder with a freckled hand, asked, "How's tricks?" and sat down beside him. The second man was younger and colorless. He took a seat a little apart from the others and balanced a stenographer's notebook on his knee, holding a green pencil over it.

Spade glanced his way, chuckled, and asked Bryan: "Anything I say will be used against me?"

The District Attorney smiled. "That always holds good." He took his glasses off, looked at them, and set them on his nose again. He looked through them at Spade and asked: "Who killed Thursby?"

Spade said: "I don't know."

Bryan rubbed his black eyeglass-ribbon between thumb and fingers and said knowingly: "Perhaps you don't, but you certainly could make an excellent guess."

"Maybe, but I wouldn't."

The District Attorney raised his eyebrows.

"I wouldn't," Spade repeated. He was serene. "My guess might be excellent, or it might be crummy, but Mrs. Spade didn't raise any children dippy enough to make guesses in front of a district attorney, an assistant district attorney, and a stenographer."

"Why shouldn't you, if you've nothing to conceal?"

"Everybody," Spade responded mildly, "has something to conceal."

"And you have—?"

"My guesses, for one thing."

The District Attorney looked down at his desk and then up at Spade. He settled his glasses more firmly on his nose. He said: "If you'd prefer not having the stenographer here we can dismiss him. It was simply as a matter of convenience that I brought him in."

"I don't mind him a damned bit," Spade replied. "I'm willing to have anything I say put down and I'm willing to sign it."

"We don't intend asking you to sign anything," Bryan assured him. "I wish you wouldn't regard this as a formal inquiry at all. And please don't think I've any belief—much less confidence—in those theories the police seem to have formed."

"No?"

"Not a particle."

Spade sighed and crossed his legs. "I'm glad of that." He felt in his pockets for tobacco and papers. "What's your theory?"

Bryan leaned forward in his chair and his eyes were hard and shiny as the lenses over them. "Tell me who Archer was shadowing Thursby for and I'll tell you who killed Thursby."

Spade's laugh was brief and scornful. "You're as wrong as Dundy," he said.

"Don't misunderstand me, Spade," Bryan said, knocking on the desk with his knuckles. "I don't say your client killed Thursby or had him killed, but I do say that, knowing who your client is, or was, I'll mighty soon know who killed Thursby."

Spade lighted his cigarette, removed it from his lips, emptied his lungs of smoke, and spoke as if puzzled: "I don't exactly get that."

"You don't? Then suppose I put it this way: where is Dixie Monahan?"

Spade's face retained its puzzled look. "Putting it that way doesn't help much," he said. "I still don't get it."

The District Attorney took his glasses off and shook them for emphasis. He said: "We know Thursby was Monahan's bodyguard and went with him when Monahan found it wise to vanish from Chicago. We know Monahan welshed on something like two-hundred-thousand-dollars' worth of bets when he vanished. We don't know—not yet—who his creditors were." He put the glasses on again and smiled grimly. "But we all know what's likely to happen to a gambler who welshes, and to his bodyguard, when his creditors find him. It's happened before."

Spade ran his tongue over his lips and pulled his lips back over his teeth in an ugly grin. His eyes glittered under pulled-down brows. His reddening neck bulged over the rim of his collar. His voice was low and hoarse and passionate. "Well, what do you think? Did I kill him for his creditors? Or just find him and let them do their own killing?"

"No, no!" the District Attorney protested. "You misunderstand me."

"I hope to Christ I do," Spade said.

"He didn't mean that," Thomas said.

"Then what did he mean?"

Bryan waved a hand. "I only mean that you might have been involved in it without knowing what it was. That could—"

"I see," Spade sneered. "You don't think I'm naughty. You just think I'm dumb."

"Nonsense." Bryan insisted: "Suppose someone came to you and engaged you to find Monahan, telling you they had reasons for thinking he was in the city. The someone might give you a completely false story—any one of a dozen or more would do—or might say he was a debtor who had run away, without giving you any of the details. How could you tell what was behind it? How would you know it wasn't an ordinary piece of detective work? And under those circumstances you certainly couldn't be held responsible for your part in it unless"—his voice sank to a more impressive key and his words came out spaced and distinct—"you made yourself an accomplice by concealing your knowledge of the murderer's identity or information that would lead to his apprehension."

Anger was leaving Spade's face. No anger remained in his voice when he asked: "That's what you meant?"

"Precisely."

"All right. Then there's no hard feelings. But you're wrong."

"Prove it."

Spade shook his head. "I can't prove it to you now. I can tell you."

"Then tell me."

"Nobody ever hired me to do anything about Dixie Monahan."

Bryan and Thomas exchanged glances. Bryan's eyes came back to Spade and he said: "But, by your own admission, somebody did hire you to do something about his bodyguard Thursby."

"Yes, about his ex-bodyguard Thursby."

"Ex?"

"Yes, ex."

"You know that Thursby was no longer associated with Monahan? You know that positively?"

Spade stretched out his hand and dropped the stub of his cigarette into an ashtray on the desk. He spoke carelessly: "I don't know anything positively except that my client wasn't interested in Monahan, had never been interested in Monahan. I heard that Thursby took Monahan out to the Orient and lost him."

Again the District Attorney and his assistant exchanged glances.

Thomas, in a tone whose matter-of-factness did not quite hide excitement, said: "That opens another angle. Monahan's friends could have knocked Thursby off for ditching Monahan."

"Dead gamblers don't have any friends," Spade said.

"It opens up two new lines," Bryan said. He leaned back and stared at the ceiling for several seconds, then sat upright quickly. His orator's face was alight. "It narrows down to three things. Number one: Thursby was killed by the gamblers Monahan had welshed on in Chicago. Not knowing Thursby had sloughed Monahan—or not believing it—they killed him because he had been Monahan's associate, or to get him out of the way so they could get to Monahan, or because he had refused to lead them to Monahan. Number two: he was killed by friends of Monahan. Or number three: he sold Monahan out to his enemies and then fell out with them and they killed him."

"Or number four," Spade suggested with a cheerful smile: "he died of old age. You folks aren't serious, are you?"

The two men stared at Spade, but neither of them spoke. Spade turned his smile from one to the other of them and shook his head in mock pity. "You've got Arnold Rothstein on the brain," he said.

Bryan smacked the back of his left hand down into the palm of his right. "In one of those three categories lies the solution." The power in his voice was no longer latent. His right hand, a fist except for protruding forefinger, went up and then down to stop with a jerk when the finger was leveled at Spade's chest. "And you can give us the information that will enable us to determine the category."

Spade said, "Yes?" very lazily. His face was somber. He touched his lower lip with a finger, looked at the finger, and then scratched the back of his neck with it. Little irritable lines had appeared in his forehead. He blew his breath out heavily through his nose and his voice was an ill-humored growl. "You wouldn't want the kind of information I could give you, Bryan. You couldn't use it. It'd poop this gambler's-revenge-scenario for you."

Bryan sat up straight and squared his shoulders. His voice was stern without blustering. "You are not the judge of that. Right or wrong, I am nonetheless the District Attorney."

Spade's lifted lip showed his eyetooth. "I thought this was an informal talk."

"I am a sworn officer of the law twenty-four hours a day," Bryan said, "and neither formality nor informality justifies your withholding from me evidence of crime, except of course"—he nodded meaningly—"on certain constitutional grounds."

"You mean if it might incriminate me?" Spade asked. His voice was placid, almost amused, but his face was not. "Well, I've got better grounds than that, or grounds that suit me better. My clients are entitled to a decent amount of secrecy. Maybe I can be made to talk to a Grand Jury or even a Coroner's Jury, but I haven't been called before either yet, and it's a cinch I'm not going to advertise my clients' business until I have to. Then again, you and the police have both accused me of being mixed up in the other night's murders. I've had trouble with both of you before. As far as I can see, my best chance of clearing myself of the trouble you're trying to make for me is by bringing in the murderers—all tied up. And my only chance of ever catching them and tying them up and bringing them in is by keeping away from you and the police, because neither of you show any signs of knowing what in hell it's all about." He rose and turned his head over his shoulder to address the stenographer: "Getting this all right, son? Or am I going too fast for you?"

The stenographer looked at him with startled eyes and replied: "No, sir, I'm getting it all right."

"Good work," Spade said and turned to Bryan again. "Now if you want to go to the Board and tell them I'm obstructing justice and ask them to revoke my license, hop to it. You've tried it before and it didn't get you anything but a good laugh all around." He picked up his hat.

Bryan began: "But look here—"

Spade said: "And I don't want any more of these informal talks. I've got nothing to tell you or the police and I'm God-damned tired of being called things by every crackpot on the city payroll. If you want to see me pinch me or subpœna me or something and I'll come down with my lawyer." He put his hat on his head, said, "See you at the inquest, maybe," and stalked out.

CHAPTER XVI

The Third Murder

SPADE WENT into the Hotel Sutter and telephoned the Alexandria. Gutman was not in. No member of Gutman's party was in. Spade telephoned the Belvedere. Cairo was not in, had not been in that day.

Spade went to his office.

A swart greasy man in notable clothes was waiting in the outer room.

Effie Perine, indicating the swart man, said: "This gentleman wishes to see you, Mr. Spade."

Spade smiled and bowed and opened the inner door. "Come in." Before following the man in Spade asked Effie Perine: "Any news on that other matter?"

"No, sir."

The swart man was the proprietor of a moving-picture-theatre in Market Street. He suspected one of his cashiers and a doorman of colluding to defraud him. Spade hurried him through the story, promised to "take care of it," asked for and received fifty dollars, and got rid of him in less than half an hour.

When the corridor-door had closed behind the showman Effie Perine came into the inner office. Her sunburned face was worried and questioning. "You haven't found her yet?" she asked.

He shook his head and went on stroking his bruised temple lightly in circles with his fingertips.

"How is it?" she asked.

"All right, but I've got plenty of headache."

She went around behind him, put his hand down, and stroked his temple with her slender fingers. He leaned back until the back of his head over the chair-top rested against her breast. He said: "You're an angel."

She bent her head forward over his and looked down into his face. "You've got to find her, Sam. It's more than a day and she—"

He stirred and impatiently interrupted her: "I haven't got to do anything, but if you'll let me rest this damned head a minute or two I'll go out and find her."

She murmured, "Poor head," and stroked it in silence awhile. Then she asked: "You know where she is? Have you any idea?"

The telephone-bell rang. Spade picked up the telephone and said: "Hello. . . . Yes, Sid, it came out all right, thanks. . . . No. . . . Sure. He got snotty, but so did I. . . . He's nursing a gambler's-war pipe-dream. . . . Well, we didn't kiss when we parted. I declared my weight and walked out on him. . . . That's something for you to worry about. . . . Right. 'Bye." He put the telephone down and leaned back in his chair again.

Effie Perine came from behind him and stood at his side. She demanded: "Do you think you know where she is, Sam?"

"I know where she went," he replied in a grudging tone.

"Where?" She was excited.

"Down to the boat you saw burning."

Her eyes opened until their brown was surrounded by white. "You went down there." It was not a question.

"I did not," Spade said.

"Sam," she cried angrily, "she may be—"

"She went down there," he said in a surly voice. "She wasn't taken. She went down there instead of to your house when she learned the boat was in. Well, what the hell? Am I supposed to run around after my clients begging them to let me help them?"

"But, Sam, when I told you the boat was on fire!"

"That was at noon and I had a date with Polhaus and another with Bryan."

She glared at him between tightened lids. "Sam Spade," she said, "you're the most contemptible man God ever made when you want to be. Because she did something without confiding in you you'd sit here and do nothing when you know she's in danger, when you know she might be—"

Spade's face flushed. He said stubbornly: "She's pretty capable of taking care of herself and she knows where to come for help when she thinks she needs it, and when it suits her."

"That's spite," the girl cried, "and that's all it is! You're sore because she did something on her own hook, without telling you. Why shouldn't she? You're not so damned honest, and you haven't been so much on the level with her, that she should trust you completely."

Spade said: "That's enough of that."

His tone brought a brief uneasy glint into her hot eyes, but she tossed her head and the glint vanished. Her mouth was drawn taut and small. She said: "If you don't go down there this very minute, Sam, I will and I'll take the police down there." Her voice trembled, broke, and was thin and wailing. "Oh, Sam, go!"

He stood up cursing her. Then he said: "Christ! It'll be easier on my head than sitting here listening to you squawk." He looked at his watch. "You might as well lock up and go home."

She said: "I won't. I'm going to wait right here till you come back."

He said, "Do as you damned please," put his hat on, flinched, took it off, and went out carrying it in his hand.

An hour and a half later, at twenty minutes past five, Spade returned. He was cheerful. He came in asking: "What makes you so hard to get along with, sweetheart?"

"Me?"

"Yes, you." He put a finger on the tip of Effie Perine's nose and flattened it. He put his hands under her elbows, lifted her straight up, and kissed her chin. He set her down on the floor again and asked: "Anything doing while I was gone?"

"Luke—what's his name?—at the Belvedere called up to tell you Cairo has returned. That was about half an hour ago."

Spade snapped his mouth shut, turned with a long step, and started for the door.

"Did you find her?" the girl called.

"Tell you about it when I'm back," he replied without pausing and hurried out.

A taxicab brought Spade to the Belvedere within ten minutes of his departure from his office. He found Luke in the lobby. The hotel-detective came grinning and shaking his head to meet Spade. "Fifteen minutes late," he said. "Your bird has fluttered."

Spade cursed his luck.

"Checked out—gone bag and baggage," Luke said. He took a battered memorandum-book from a vest-pocket, licked his thumb, thumbed pages, and held the book out open to Spade. "There's the number of the taxi that hauled him. I got that much for you."

"Thanks." Spade copied the number on the back of an envelope. "Any forwarding address?"

"No. He just come in carrying a big suitcase and went upstairs and packed and come down with his stuff and paid his bill and got a taxi and went without anybody being able to hear what he told the driver."

"How about his trunk?"

Luke's lower lip sagged. "By God," he said, "I forgot that! Come on."

They went up to Cairo's room. The trunk was there. It was closed, but not locked. They raised the lid. The trunk was empty.

Luke said: "What do you know about that!"

Spade did not say anything.

Spade went back to his office. Effie Perine looked up at him, inquisitively.

"Missed him," Spade grumbled and passed into his private room.

She followed him in. He sat in his chair and began to roll a cigarette. She sat on the desk in front of him and put her toes on a corner of his chair-seat.

"What about Miss O'Shaughnessy?" she demanded.

"I missed her too," he replied, "but she had been there."

"On the *La Paloma*?"

"The *La* is a lousy combination," he said.

"Stop it. Be nice, Sam. Tell me."

He set fire to his cigarette, pocketed his lighter, patted her shins, and said: "Yes, *La Paloma*. She got down there at a little after noon yesterday." He pulled his brows down. "That means she went straight there after leaving the cab at the Ferry Building. It's only a few piers away. The Captain wasn't aboard. His name's Jacobi and she asked for him by name. He was uptown on business. That would mean he didn't expect her, or not at that time anyway. She waited there till he came back at four o'clock. They spent the time from then till meal-time in his cabin and she ate with him."

He inhaled and exhaled smoke, turned his head aside to spit a yellow tobacco-flake off his lip, and went on: "After the meal Captain Jacobi had three more visitors. One of them was Gutman and one was Cairo and one was the kid who delivered Gutman's message to you yesterday. Those three came together while Brigid was there and the five of them did a lot of talking in the Captain's cabin. It's hard to get anything out of the crew, but they had a row and somewhere around eleven o'clock that night a gun went off there, in the Captain's cabin. The watchman beat it down there, but the Captain met him outside and told him everything was all right. There's a fresh bullet-hole in one corner of the cabin, up high enough to make it likely that the bullet didn't go through anybody to get there. As far as I could learn there was only the one shot. But as far as I could learn wasn't very far."

He scowled and inhaled smoke again. "Well, they left around midnight—the Captain and his four visitors all together—and all of them seem to have been walking all right. I got that from the watchman. I haven't been able to get hold of the Custom-House-men who were on duty there then. That's all of it. The Captain hasn't been back since. He didn't keep a date he had this noon with some shipping-agents, and they haven't found him to tell him about the fire."

"And the fire?" she asked.

Spade shrugged. "I don't know. It was discovered in the hold, aft—in the rear basement—late this morning. The chances are it got started some time yesterday. They got it out all right, though it did damage enough. Nobody liked to talk about it much while the Captain's away. It's the—"

The corridor-door opened. Spade shut his mouth. Effie Perine jumped down from the desk, but a man opened the connecting door before she could reach it.

"Where's Spade?" the man asked.

His voice brought Spade up erect and alert in his chair. It was a voice harsh and rasping with agony and with the strain of keeping two words from being smothered by the liquid bubbling that ran under and behind them.

Effie Perine, frightened, stepped out of the man's way.

He stood in the doorway with his soft hat crushed between his head and the top of the door-frame: he was nearly seven feet tall. A black overcoat cut long and straight and like a sheath, buttoned from throat to knees, exaggerated his leanness. His shoulders stuck out, high, thin, angular. His bony face—weather-coarsened, age-lined—was the color of wet sand and was wet with sweat on cheeks and chin. His eyes were dark and bloodshot and mad above lower lids that hung down to show pink inner membrane. Held tight against the left side of his chest by a black-sleeved arm that ended in a yellowish claw was a brown-paper-wrapped parcel bound with thin rope—an ellipsoid somewhat larger than an American football.

The tall man stood in the doorway and there was nothing to show that he saw Spade. He said, "You know—" and then the liquid bubbling came up in his throat and submerged whatever else he said. He put his other hand over the hand that held the ellipsoid. Holding himself stiffly straight, not putting his hands out to break his fall, he fell forward as a tree falls.

Spade, wooden-faced and nimble, sprang from his chair and caught the falling man. When Spade caught him the man's mouth opened and a little blood spurted out, and the brown-wrapped parcel dropped from the man's hands and rolled across the floor until a foot of the desk stopped it. Then the man's knees bent and he bent at the waist and his thin body became limber inside the sheathlike overcoat, sagging in Spade's arms so that Spade could not hold it up from the floor.

Spade lowered the man carefully until he lay on the floor on his left side. The man's eyes—dark and bloodshot, but not now mad—were wide open and still. His mouth was open as when blood had spurted from it, but no more blood came from it, and all his long body was as still as the floor it lay on.

Spade said: "Lock the door."

While Effie Perine, her teeth chattering, fumbled with the corridor-door's lock Spade knelt beside the thin man, turned him over on his back, and ran a hand down inside his overcoat. When he withdrew the hand presently it came out smeared with blood. The sight of his bloody hand brought not the least nor briefest of changes to Spade's face. Holding that hand up where it would touch nothing, he took his lighter out of his pocket with his other hand. He snapped on the flame and held the flame close to first one and then the other of the thin man's eyes. The eyes—lids, balls, irises, and pupils—remained frozen, immobile.

Spade extinguished the flame and returned the lighter to his pocket. He moved on his knees around to the dead man's side and, using his one clean hand, unbuttoned and opened the tubular overcoat. The inside of the overcoat was wet with blood and the double-breasted blue jacket beneath it was sodden. The jacket's lapels, where they crossed over the man's chest, and both sides of his coat immediately below that point, were pierced by soggy ragged holes.

Spade rose and went to the washbowl in the outer office.

Effie Perine, wan and trembling and holding herself upright by means of a hand on the corridor-door's knob and her back against its glass, whispered: "Is—is he—?"

"Yes. Shot through the chest, maybe half a dozen times." Spade began to wash his hands.

"Oughtn't we—?" she began, but he cut her short: "It's too late for a doctor now and I've got to think before we do anything." He finished washing his hands and began to rinse the bowl. "He couldn't have come far with those in him. If he— Why in hell couldn't he have stood up long enough to say something?" He frowned at the girl, rinsed his hands again, and picked up a towel. "Pull yourself together. For Christ's sake don't get sick on me now!" He threw the towel down and ran fingers through his hair. "We'll have a look at that bundle."

He went into the inner office again, stepped over the dead man's legs, and picked up the brown-paper-wrapped parcel. When he felt its weight his eyes glowed. He put it on his desk, turning it over so that the knotted part of the rope was uppermost. The knot was hard and tight. He took out his pocket-knife and cut the rope.

The girl had left the door and, edging around the dead man with her face turned away, had come to Spade's side. As she stood there—hands on a corner of the desk—watching him pull the rope loose and push aside brown paper, excitement began to supplant nausea in her face. "Do you think it is?" she whispered.

"We'll soon know," Spade said, his big fingers busy with the inner husk of coarse grey paper, three sheets thick, that the brown paper's removal had revealed. His face was hard and dull. His eyes were shining. When he had put the grey paper out of the way he had an egg-shaped mass of pale excelsior, wadded tight. His fingers tore the wad apart and then he had the foot-high figure of a bird, black as coal and shiny where its polish was not dulled by wood-dust and fragments of excelsior.

Spade laughed. He put a hand down on the bird. His wide-spread fingers had ownership in their curving. He put his other arm around Effie Perine and crushed her body against his. "We've got the damned thing, angel," he said.

"Ouch!" she said, "you're hurting me."

He took his arm away from her, picked the black bird up in both hands, and shook it to dislodge clinging excelsior. Then he stepped back holding it up in front of him and blew dust off it, regarding it triumphantly.

Effie Perine made a horrified face and screamed, pointing at his feet.

He looked down at his feet. His last backward step had brought his left heel into contact with the dead man's hand, pinching a quarter-inch of flesh at a side of the palm between heel and floor. Spade jerked his foot away from the hand.

The telephone-bell rang.

He nodded at the girl. She turned to the desk and put the receiver to her ear. She said: "Hello. . . . Yes. . . . Who? . . . Oh, yes!" Her eyes became large. "Yes. . . . Yes. . . . Hold the line. . . ." Her mouth suddenly stretched wide and fearful. She cried: "Hello! Hello! Hello!" She rattled the prong up and down and cried, "Hello!" twice. Then she sobbed and spun around to face Spade, who was close beside her by now. "It was Miss O'Shaughnessy," she said wildly. "She wants you. She's at the Alexandria—in danger. Her voice was—oh, it was awful, Sam!—

and something happened to her before she could finish. Go help her, Sam!"

Spade put the falcon down on the desk and scowled gloomily. "I've got to take care of this fellow first," he said, pointing his thumb at the thin corpse on the floor.

She beat his chest with her fists, crying: "No, no—you've got to go to her. Don't you see, Sam? He had the thing that was hers and he came to you with it. Don't you see? He was helping her and they killed him and now she's— Oh, you've got to go!"

"All right." Spade pushed her away and bent over his desk, putting the black bird back into its nest of excelsior, bending the paper around it, working rapidly, making a larger and clumsy package. "As soon as I've gone phone the police. Tell them how it happened, but don't drag any names in. You don't know. I got the phone-call and I told you I had to go out, but I didn't say where." He cursed the rope for being tangled, yanked it into straightness, and began to bind the package. "Forget this thing. Tell it as it happened, but forget he had a bundle." He chewed his lower lip. "Unless they pin you down. If they seem to know about it you'll have to admit it. But that's not likely. If they do then I took the bundle away with me, unopened." He finished tying the knot and straightened up with the parcel under his left arm. "Get it straight, now. Everything happened the way it did happen, but without this dingus unless they already know about it. Don't deny it—just don't mention it. And I got the phone-call—not you. And you don't know anything about anybody else having any connection with this fellow. You don't know anything about him and you can't talk about my business until you see me. Got it?"

"Yes, Sam. Who—do you know who he is?"

He grinned wolfishly. "Uh-uh," he said, "but I'd guess he was Captain Jacobi, master of *La Paloma*." He picked up his hat and put it on. He looked thoughtfully at the dead man and then around the room.

"Hurry, Sam," the girl begged.

"Sure," he said absent-mindedly, "I'll hurry. Might not hurt to get those few scraps of excelsior off the floor before the police come. And maybe you ought to try to get hold of Sid. No." He rubbed his chin. "We'll leave him out of it awhile. It'll look better. I'd keep the door locked till they come." He took his hand from his chin and rubbed her cheek. "You're a damned good man, sister," he said and went out.

CHAPTER XVII

Saturday Night

CARRYING THE PARCEL lightly under his arm, walking briskly, with only the ceaseless shifting of his eyes to denote wariness, Spade went, partly by way of an alley and a narrow court, from his office-building to Kearny and Post Streets, where he hailed a passing taxicab.

The taxicab carried him to the Pickwick Stage terminal in Fifth Street. He checked the bird at the Parcel Room there, put the check into a stamped envelope, wrote *M. F. Holland* and a San Francisco Post Office box-number on the envelope, sealed it, and dropped it into a mail-box. From the stage-terminal another taxicab carried him to the Alexandria Hotel.

Spade went up to suite 12-C and knocked on the door. The door was opened, when he had knocked a second time, by a small fair-haired girl in a shimmering yellow dressing-gown—a small girl whose face was white and dim and who clung desperately to the inner doorknob with both hands and gasped: "Mr. Spade?"

Spade said, "Yes," and caught her as she swayed.

Her body arched back over his arm and her head dropped straight back so that her short fair hair hung down her scalp and her slender throat was a firm curve from chin to chest.

Spade slid his supporting arm higher up her back and bent to get his other arm under her knees, but she stirred then, resisting, and between parted lips that barely moved blurred words came: "No! Ma' me wa'!"

Spade made her walk. He kicked the door shut and he walked her up and down the green-carpeted room from wall to wall. One of his arms around her small body, that hand under her armpit, his other hand gripping her other arm, held her erect when she stumbled, checked her swaying, kept urging her forward, but made her tottering legs bear all her weight they could bear. They walked across and across the floor, the girl falteringly, with incoördinate steps, Spade surely on the balls of his feet with balance unaffected by her staggering. Her face was chalk-white and eyeless, his sullen, with eyes hardened to watch everywhere at once.

He talked to her monotonously: "That's the stuff. Left, right, left, right. That's the stuff. One, two, three, four, one, two, three, now we turn." He shook her as they turned from the wall. "Now back again. One, two, three, four. Hold your head up. That's the stuff. Good girl. Left, right, left, right. Now we turn again." He shook her again. "That's the girl. Walk, walk, walk, walk. One, two, three, four. Now we go around." He shook her, more roughly, and increased their pace. "That's the trick. Left, right, left, right. We're in a hurry. One, two, three. . . ."

She shuddered and swallowed audibly. Spade began to chafe her arm and side and he put his mouth nearer her ear. "That's fine. You're doing fine. One, two, three, four. Faster, faster, faster, faster. That's it. Step, step, step, step. Pick them up and lay them down. That's the stuff. Now we turn. Left, right, left, right. What'd they do—dope you? The same stuff they gave me?"

Her eyelids twitched up then for an instant over dulled golden-brown eyes and she managed to say all of "Yes" except the final consonant.

They walked the floor, the girl almost trotting now to keep up with Spade, Spade slapping and kneading her flesh through yellow silk with both hands, talking and talking while his eyes remained hard and aloof and watchful. "Left, right, left, right, left, right, turn. That's the girl. One, two, three, four, one, two, three, four. Keep the chin up. That's the stuff. One, two . . ."

Her lids lifted again a bare fraction of an inch and under them her eyes moved weakly from side to side.

"That's fine," he said in a crisp voice, dropping his monotone. "Keep them open. Open them wide—wide!" He shook her.

She moaned in protest, but her lids went farther up, though her eyes were without inner light. He raised his hand and slapped her cheek half a dozen times in quick succession. She moaned again and tried to break away from him. His arm held her and swept her along beside him from wall to wall.

"Keep walking," he ordered in a harsh voice, and then: "Who are you?"

Her "Rhea Gutman" was thick but intelligible.

"The daughter?"

"Yes." Now she was no farther from the final consonant than *sh*.

"Where's Brigid?"

She twisted convulsively around in his arms and caught at one of his hands with both of hers. He pulled his hand away quickly and looked at it. Across its back was a thin red scratch an inch and a half or more in length.

"What the hell?" he growled and examined her hands. Her left hand was empty. In her right hand, when he forced it open, lay a three-inch jade-headed steel bouquet-pin. "What the hell?" he growled again and held the pin up in front of her eyes.

When she saw the pin she whimpered and opened her dressing-gown. She pushed aside the cream-colored pajama-coat under it and showed him her body below her left breast—white flesh crisscrossed with thin red lines, dotted with tiny red dots, where the pin had scratched and punctured it. "To stay awake . . . walk . . . till you came. . . . She said you'd come . . . were so long." She swayed.

Spade tightened his arm around her and said: "Walk."

She fought against his arm, squirming around to face him again. "No . . . tell you . . . sleep . . . save her . . ."

"Brigid?" he demanded.

"Yes . . . took her . . . Bur-Burlingame . . . twenty-six Ancho . . . hurry . . . too late . . ." Her head fell over on her shoulder.

Spade pushed her head up roughly. "Who took her there? Your father?"

"Yes . . . Wilmer . . . Cairo." She writhed and her eyelids twitched but did not open. ". . . kill her." Her head fell over again and again he pushed it up.

"Who shot Jacobi?"

She did not seem to hear the question. She tried pitifully to hold her head up, to open her eyes. She mumbled: "Go . . . she . . ."

He shook her brutally. "Stay awake till the doctor comes."

Fear opened her eyes and pushed for a moment the cloudiness from her face. "No, no," she cried thickly, "father . . . kill me . . . swear you won't . . . he'd know . . . I did . . . for her . . . promise . . . won't . . . sleep . . . all right . . . morning . . ."

He shook her again. "You're sure you can sleep the stuff off all right?"

"Ye'." Her head fell down again.

"Where's your bed?"

She tried to raise a hand, but the effort had become too much for her before the hand pointed at anything except the carpet. With the sigh of a tired child she let her whole body relax and crumple.

Spade caught her up in his arms—scooped her up as she sank—and, holding her easily against his chest, went to the nearest of the three doors. He turned the knob far enough to release the catch, pushed the door open with his foot, and went into a passageway that ran past an open bathroom-door to a bedroom. He looked into the bathroom, saw it was empty, and carried the girl into the bedroom. Nobody was there. The clothing that was in sight and things on the chiffonier said it was a man's room.

Spade carried the girl back to the green-carpeted room and tried the opposite door. Through it he passed into another passageway, past another empty bathroom, and into a bedroom that was feminine in its accessories. He turned back the bedclothes and laid the girl on the bed, removed her slippers, raised her a little to slide the yellow dressing-gown off, fixed a pillow under her head, and put the covers up over her.

Then he opened the room's two windows and stood with his back to them staring at the sleeping girl. Her breathing was heavy but not troubled. He frowned and looked around, working his lips together. Twilight was dimming the room. He stood there in the weakening light for perhaps five minutes. Finally he shook his thick sloping shoulders impatiently and went out, leaving the suite's outer door unlocked.

Spade went to the Pacific Telephone and Telegraph Company's station in Powell Street and called Davenport 2020. "Emergency Hospital, please. . . . Hello, there's a girl in suite twelve C at the Alexandria Hotel who has been drugged. . . . Yes, you'd better send somebody to take a look at her. . . . This is Mr. Hooper of the Alexandria."

He put the receiver on its prong and laughed. He called another number and said: "Hello, Frank. This is Sam Spade. . . . Can you let me have a car with a driver who'll keep his mouth shut? . . . To go down the peninsula right away. . . . Just a couple of hours. . . . Right. Have him pick me up at John's, Ellis Street, as soon as he can make it."

He called another number—his office's—held the receiver to his ear for a little while without saying anything, and replaced it on its hook.

He went to John's Grill, asked the waiter to hurry his order of chops, baked potato, and sliced tomatoes, ate hurriedly, and was smoking a cigarette with his coffee when a thick-set youngish man with a plaid cap set askew above pale eyes and a tough cheery face came into the Grill and to his table.

"All set, Mr. Spade. She's full of gas and rearing to go."

"Swell." Spade emptied his cup and went out with the thick-set man. "Know where Ancho Avenue, or Road, or Boulevard, is in Burlingame?"

"Nope, but if she's there we can find her."

"Let's do that," Spade said as he sat beside the chauffeur in the dark Cadillac sedan. "Twenty-six is the number we want, and the sooner the better, but we don't want to pull up at the front door."

"Correct."

They rode half a dozen blocks in silence. The chauffeur said: "Your partner got knocked off, didn't he, Mr. Spade?"

"Uh-huh."

The chauffeur clucked. "She's a tough racket. You can have it for mine."

"Well, hack-drivers don't live forever."

"Maybe that's right," the thick-set man conceded, "but, just the same, it'll always be a surprise to me if I don't."

Spade stared ahead at nothing and thereafter, until the chauffeur tired of making conversation, replied with uninterested yeses and noes.

At a drug-store in Burlingame the chauffeur learned how to reach Ancho Avenue. Ten minutes later he stopped the sedan near a dark corner, turned off the lights, and waved his hand at the block ahead. "There she is," he said. "She ought to be on the other side, maybe the third or fourth house."

Spade said, "Right," and got out of the car. "Keep the engine going. We may have to leave in a hurry."

He crossed the street and went up the other side. Far ahead a lone street-light burned. Warmer lights dotted the night on either side where houses were spaced half a dozen to a block. A high thin moon was cold and feeble as the distant street-light. A radio droned through the open windows of a house on the other side of the street.

In front of the second house from the corner Spade halted. On one of the gateposts that were massive out of all proportion to the fence flanking them a 2 and a 6 of pale metal caught what light there was. A square white card was nailed over them. Putting his face close to the card, Spade could see that it was a *For Sale or Rent* sign. There was no gate between the posts. Spade went up the cement walk to the house. He stood still on the walk at the foot of the porch-steps for a long moment. No sound came from the house. The house was dark except for another pale square card nailed on its door.

Spade went up to the door and listened. He could hear nothing. He tried to look through the glass of the door. There was no curtain to keep his gaze out, but inner darkness. He tiptoed to a window and then to another. They, like the door, were uncurtained except by inner darkness. He tried both windows. They were locked. He tried the door. It was locked.

He left the porch and, stepping carefully over dark unfamiliar ground, walked through weeds around the house. The side-windows were too high to be reached from the ground. The back door and the one back window he could reach were locked.

Spade went back to the gatepost and, cupping the flame between his hands, held his lighter up to the *For Sale or Rent* sign. It bore the printed name and address of a San Mateo real-estate-dealer and a line penciled in blue: *Key at 31.*

Spade returned to the sedan and asked the chauffeur: "Got a flash-light?"

"Sure." He gave it to Spade. "Can I give you a hand at anything?"

"Maybe." Spade got into the sedan. "We'll ride up to number thirty-one. You can use your lights."

Number 31 was a square grey house across the street from, but a little farther up than, 26. Lights glowed in its downstairs-windows. Spade went up on the porch and rang the bell. A dark-haired girl of fourteen or fifteen opened the door. Spade, bowing and smiling, said: "I'd like to get the key to number twenty-six."

"I'll call Papa," she said and went back into the house calling: "Papa!"

A plump red-faced man, bald-headed and heavily mustached, appeared, carrying a newspaper.

Spade said: "I'd like to get the key to twenty-six."

The plump man looked doubtful. He said: "The juice is not on. You couldn't see anything."

Spade patted his pocket. "I've a flashlight."

The plump man looked more doubtful. He cleared his throat uneasily and crumpled the newspaper in his hand.

Spade showed him one of his business-cards, put it back in his pocket, and said in a low voice: "We got a tip that there might be something hidden there."

The plump man's face and voice were eager. "Wait a minute," he said. "I'll go over with you."

A moment later he came back carrying a brass key attached to a black and red tag. Spade beckoned to the chauffeur as they passed the car and the chauffeur joined them.

"Anybody been looking at the house lately?" Spade asked.

"Not that I know of," the plump man replied. "Nobody's been to me for the key in a couple of months."

The plump man marched ahead with the key until they had gone up on the porch. Then he thrust the key into Spade's hand, mumbled, "Here you are," and stepped aside.

Spade unlocked the door and pushed it open. There was silence and darkness. Holding the flashlight—dark—in his left hand, Spade entered. The chauffeur came close behind him and then, at a little distance, the plump man followed them. They searched the house from bottom to top, cautiously at first, then, finding nothing, boldly. The house was empty—unmistakably—and there was nothing to indicate that it had been visited in weeks.

Saying, "Thanks, that's all," Spade left the sedan in front of the Alexandria. He went into the hotel, to the desk, where a tall young man with a dark grave face said: "Good evening, Mr. Spade."

"Good evening." Spade drew the young man to one end of the desk. "These Gutmans—up in twelve C—are they in?"

The young man replied, "No," darting a quick glance at Spade. Then he looked away, hesitated, looked at Spade again, and murmured: "A funny thing happened in connection with them this evening, Mr. Spade. Somebody called the Emergency Hospital and told them there was a sick girl up there."

"And there wasn't?"

"Oh, no, there was nobody up there. They went out earlier in the evening."

Spade said: "Well, these practical-jokers have to have their fun. Thanks."

He went to a telephone-booth, called a number, and said: "Hello. . . . Mrs. Perine? . . . Is Effie there? . . . Yes, please. . . . Thanks.

Hello, angel! What's the good word? . . . Fine, fine! Hold it. I'll be out in twenty minutes. . . . Right."

Half an hour later Spade rang the doorbell of a two-story brick building in Ninth Avenue. Effie Perine opened the door. Her boyish face was tired and smiling. "Hello, boss," she said. "Enter." She said in a low voice: "If Ma says anything to you, Sam, be nice to her. She's all up in the air."

Spade grinned reassuringly and patted her shoulder.

She put her hands on his arm. "Miss O'Shaughnessy?"

"No," he growled. "I ran into a plant. Are you sure it was her voice?"

"Yes."

He made an unpleasant face. "Well, it was hooey."

She took him into a bright living-room, sighed, and slumped down on one end of a Chesterfield, smiling cheerfully up at him through her weariness.

He sat beside her and asked: "Everything went OK? Nothing said about the bundle?"

"Nothing. I told them what you told me to tell them, and they seemed to take it for granted that the phone-call had something to do with it, and that you were out running it down."

"Dundy there?"

"No. Hoff and O'Gar and some others I didn't know. I talked to the Captain too."

"They took you down to the Hall?"

"Oh, yes, and they asked me loads of questions, but it was all—you know—routine."

Spade rubbed his palms together. "Swell," he said and then frowned, "though I guess they'll think up plenty to put to me when we meet. That damned Dundy will, anyway, and Bryan." He moved his shoulders. "Anybody you know, outside of the police, come around?"

"Yes." She sat up straight. "That boy—the one who brought the message from Gutman—was there. He didn't come in, but the police left the corridor-door open while they were there and I saw him standing there."

"You didn't say anything?"

"Oh, no. You had said not to. So I didn't pay any attention to him and the next time I looked he was gone."

Spade grinned at her. "Damned lucky for you, sister, that the coppers got there first."

"Why?"

"He's a bad egg, that lad—poison. Was the dead man Jacobi?"

"Yes."

He pressed her hands and stood up. "I'm going to run along. You'd better hit the hay. You're all in."

She rose. "Sam, what is—?"

He stopped her words with his hand on her mouth. "Save it till Monday," he said. "I want to sneak out before your mother catches me and gives me hell for dragging her lamb through gutters."

Midnight was a few minutes away when Spade reached his home. He put his key into the street-door's lock. Heels clicked rapidly on the sidewalk behind him. He let go the key and wheeled. Brigid O'Shaughnessy ran up the steps to him. She put her arms around him and hung on him, panting: "Oh, I thought you'd never come!" Her face was haggard, distraught, shaken by the tremors that shook her from head to foot.

With the hand not supporting her he felt for the key again, opened the door, and half lifted her inside. "You've been waiting?" he asked.

"Yes." Panting spaced her words. "In a—doorway—up the—street."

"Can you make it all right?" he asked. "Or shall I carry you?"

She shook her head against his shoulder. "I'll be—all right—when I —get where—I can—sit down."

They rode up to Spade's floor in the elevator and went around to his apartment. She left his arm and stood beside him—panting, both hands to her breast—while he unlocked his door. He switched on the passageway light. They went in. He shut the door and, with his arm around her again, took her back towards the living-room. When they were within a step of the living-room-door the light in the living-room went on.

The girl cried out and clung to Spade.

Just inside the living-room-door fat Gutman stood smiling benevolently at them. The boy Wilmer came out of the kitchen behind them. Black pistols were gigantic in his small hands. Cairo came from the bathroom. He too had a pistol.

Gutman said: "Well, sir, we're all here, as you can see for yourself. Now let's come in and sit down and be comfortable and talk."

CHAPTER XVIII

The Fall-Guy

SPADE, WITH HIS ARMS around Brigid O'Shaughnessy, smiled meagerly over her head and said: "Sure, we'll talk."

Gutman's bulbs jounced as he took three waddling backward steps away from the door.

Spade and the girl went in together. The boy and Cairo followed them in. Cairo stopped in the doorway. The boy put away one of his pistols and came up close behind Spade.

Spade turned his head far around to look down over his shoulder at the boy and said: "Get away. You're not going to frisk me."

The boy said: "Stand still. Shut up."

Spade's nostrils went in and out with his breathing. His voice was level. "Get away. Put your paw on me and I'm going to make you use the gun. Ask your boss if he wants me shot up before we talk."

"Never mind, Wilmer," the fat man said. He frowned indulgently at Spade. "You are certainly a most headstrong individual. Well, let's be seated."

Spade said, "I told you I didn't like that punk," and took Brigid O'Shaughnessy to the sofa by the windows. They sat close together, her head against his left shoulder, his left arm around her shoulders. She had stopped trembling, had stopped panting. The appearance of Gutman and his companions seemed to have robbed her of that freedom of personal movement and emotion that is animal, leaving her alive, conscious, but quiescent as a plant.

Gutman lowered himself into the padded rocking chair. Cairo chose the armchair by the table. The boy Wilmer did not sit down. He stood in the doorway where Cairo had stood, letting his one visible pistol hang down at his side, looking under curling lashes at Spade's body. Cairo put his pistol on the table beside him.

Spade took off his hat and tossed it to the other end of the sofa. He grinned at Gutman. The looseness of his lower lip and the droop of his upper eyelids combined with the v's in his face to make his grin lewd as a satyr's. "That daughter of yours has a nice belly," he said, "too nice to be scratched up with pins."

Gutman's smile was affable if a bit oily.

The boy in the doorway took a short step forward, raising his pistol as far as his hip. Everybody in the room looked at him. In the dissimilar eyes with which Brigid O'Shaughnessy and Joel Cairo looked at him there was, oddly, something identically reproving. The boy blushed, drew back his advanced foot, straightened his legs, lowered the pistol and stood as he had stood before, looking under lashes that hid his eyes at Spade's chest. The blush was pale enough and lasted for only an instant, but it was startling on his face that habitually was so cold and composed.

Gutman turned his sleek-eyed fat smile on Spade again. His voice was a suave purring. "Yes, sir, that was a shame, but you must admit that it served its purpose."

Spade's brows twitched together. "Anything would've," he said. "Naturally I wanted to see you as soon as I had the falcon. Cash customers—why not? I went to Burlingame expecting to run into this sort of a meeting. I didn't know you were blundering around, half an hour late, trying to get me out of the way so you could find Jacobi again before he found me."

Gutman chuckled. His chuckle seemed to hold nothing but satisfaction. "Well, sir," he said, "in any case, here we are having our little meeting, if that's what you wanted."

"That's what I wanted. How soon are you ready to make the first payment and take the falcon off my hands?"

Brigid O'Shaughnessy sat up straight and looked at Spade with surprised blue eyes. He patted her shoulder inattentively. His eyes were steady on Gutman's. Gutman's twinkled merrily between sheltering fat-puffs. He said: "Well, sir, as to that," and put a hand inside the breast of his coat.

Cairo, hands on thighs, leaned forward in his chair, breathing between parted soft lips. His dark eyes had the surface-shine of lacquer. They shifted their focus warily from Spade's face to Gutman's, from Gutman's to Spade's.

Gutman repeated, "Well, sir, as to that," and took a white envelope from his pocket. Ten eyes—the boy's now only half obscured by his lashes—looked at the envelope. Turning the envelope over in his swollen hands, Gutman studied for a moment its blank white front and then it's back, unsealed, with the flap tucked in. He raised his head, smiled amiably, and scaled the envelope at Spade's lap.

The envelope, though not bulky, was heavy enough to fly true. It struck the lower part of Spade's chest and dropped down on his thighs. He picked it up deliberately and opened it deliberately, using both hands, having taken his left arm from around the girl. The contents of the envelope were thousand-dollar bills, smooth and stiff and new. Spade took them out and counted them. There were ten of them. Spade looked up smiling. He said mildly: "We were talking about more money than this."

"Yes, sir, we were," Gutman agreed, "but we were talking then. This is actual money, genuine coin of the realm, sir. With a dollar of this you can buy more than with ten dollars of talk." Silent laughter shook his bulbs. When their commotion stopped he said more seriously, yet not altogether seriously: "There are more of us to be taken care of now." He moved his twinkling eyes and his fat head to indicate Cairo. "And—well, sir, in short—the situation has changed."

While Gutman talked Spade had tapped the edges of the ten bills into alignment and had returned them to their envelope, tucking the flap in over them. Now, with forearms on knees, he sat hunched forward, dangling the envelope from a corner held lightly by finger and thumb down between his legs. His reply to the fat man was careless: "Sure. You're together now, but I've got the falcon."

Joel Cairo spoke. Ugly hands grasping the arms of his chair, he leaned forward and said primly in his high-pitched thin voice: "I shouldn't think it would be necessary to remind you, Mr. Spade, that though you may have the falcon yet we certainly have you."

Spade grinned. "I'm trying to not let that worry me," he said. He sat up straight, put the envelope aside—on the sofa—and addressed Gutman: "We'll come back to the money later. There's another thing that's got to be taken care of first. We've got to have a fall-guy."

The fat man frowned without comprehension, but before he could speak Spade was explaining: "The police have got to have a victim—somebody they can stick for those three murders. We—"

Cairo, speaking in a brittle excited voice, interrupted Spade. "Two—only two—murders, Mr. Spade. Thursby undoubtedly killed your partner."

"All right, two," Spade growled. "What difference does that make? The point is we've got to feed the police some—"

Now Gutman broke in, smiling confidently, talking with good-natured assurance: "Well, sir, from what we've seen and heard of you I don't think we'll have to bother ourselves about that. We can leave the handling of the police to you, all right. You won't need any of our inexpert help."

"If that's what you think," Spade said, "you haven't seen or heard enough."

"Now come, Mr. Spade. You can't expect us to believe at this late date that you are the least bit afraid of the police, or that you are not quite able to handle—"

Spade snorted with throat and nose. He bent forward, resting forearms on knees again, and interrupted Gutman irritably: "I'm not a damned bit afraid of them and I know how to handle them. That's what I'm trying to tell you. The way to handle them is to toss them a victim, somebody they can hang the works on."

"Well, sir, I grant you that's one way of doing it, but—"

"'But' hell!" Spade said. "It's the only way." His eyes were hot and earnest under a reddening forehead. The bruise on his temple was liver-colored. "I know what I'm talking about. I've been through it all before and expect to go through it again. At one time or another I've had to tell everybody from the Supreme Court down to go to hell, and I've got away with it. I got away with it because I never let myself forget that a day of reckoning was coming. I never forget that when the day of reckoning comes I want to be all set to march into headquarters pushing a victim in front of me, saying: 'Here, you chumps, is your criminal.' As long as I can do that I can put my thumb to my nose and wriggle my fingers at all the laws in the book. The first time I can't do it my name's Mud. There hasn't been a first time yet. This isn't going to be it. That's flat."

Gutman's eyes flickered and their sleekness became dubious, but he held his other features in their bulbous pink smiling complacent cast and there was nothing of uneasiness in his voice. He said: "That's a system that's got a lot to recommend it, sir—by Gad, it has! And if it was anyway practical this time I'd be the first to say: 'Stick to it by all means, sir.' But this just happens to be a case where it's not possible. That's the way it is with the best of systems. There comes a time when you've got to make exceptions, and a wise man just goes ahead and makes them. Well, sir, that's just the way it is in this case and I don't mind telling you that I think you're being very well paid for making an exception. Now maybe it will be a little more trouble to you than if you had your victim to hand over to the police, but"—he laughed and spread his hands—"you're not a man that's afraid of a little bit of trouble. You know how to do things and you know you'll land on your feet in the end, no matter what happens." He pursed his lips and partly closed one eye. "You'll manage that, sir."

Spade's eyes had lost their warmth. His face was dull and lumpy. "I know what I'm talking about," he said in a low, consciously patient, tone. "This is my city and my game. I could manage to land on my feet—sure—this time, but the next time I tried to put over a fast one they'd stop me so fast I'd swallow my teeth. Hell with that. You birds'll be in New York or Constantinople or some place else. I'm in business here."

"But surely," Gutman began, "you can—"

"I can't," Spade said earnestly. "I won't. I mean it." He sat up straight. A pleasant smile illuminated his face, erasing its dull lumpishness. He spoke rapidly in an agreeable, persuasive, tone: "Listen to me, Gutman. I'm telling you what's best for all of us. If we don't give the police a fall-guy it's ten to one they'll sooner or later stumble on information about the falcon. Then you'll have to duck for cover with it—no matter where you are—and that's not going to help you make a fortune off it. Give them a fall-guy and they'll stop right there."

"Well, sir, that's just the point," Gutman replied, and still only in his eyes was uneasiness faintly apparent. "Will they stop right there? Or won't the fall-guy be a fresh clew that as likely as not will lead them to information about the falcon? And, on the other hand, wouldn't you say they were stopped right now, and that the best thing for us to do is leave well enough alone?"

A forked vein began to swell in Spade's forehead. "Jesus! you don't know what it's all about either," he said in a restrained tone. "They're not asleep, Gutman. They're lying low, waiting. Try to get that. I'm in it up to my neck and they know it. That's all right as long as I do something when the time comes. But it won't be all right if I don't." His voice became persuasive again. "Listen, Gutman, we've absolutely got to give them a victim. There's no way out of it. Let's give them the punk." He nodded pleasantly at the boy in the doorway. "He actually did shoot both of them—Thursby and Jacobi—didn't he? Anyway, he's made to order for the part. Let's pin the necessary evidence on him and turn him over to them."

The boy in the doorway tightened the corners of his mouth in what may have been a minute smile. Spade's proposal seemed to have no other effect on him. Joel Cairo's dark face was open-mouthed, open-eyed, yellowish, and amazed. He breathed through his mouth, his round effeminate chest rising and falling, while he gaped at Spade. Brigid O'Shaughnessy had moved away from Spade and had twisted herself around on the sofa to stare at him. There was a suggestion of hysterical laughter behind the startled confusion in her face.

Gutman remained still and expressionless for a long moment. Then he decided to laugh. He laughed heartily and lengthily, not stopping until his sleek eyes had borrowed merriment from his laughter. When he stopped laughing he said: "By Gad, sir, you're a character, that you are!" He took a white handkerchief from his pocket and wiped his eyes. "Yes, sir, there's never any telling what you'll do or say next, except that it's bound to be something astonishing."

"There's nothing funny about it." Spade did not seem offended by the fat man's laughter, nor in any way impressed. He spoke in the manner of one reasoning with a recalcitrant, but not altogether unreasonable, friend. "It's our best bet. With him in their hands, the police will—"

"But, my dear man," Gutman objected, "can't you see? If I even for a moment thought of doing it— But that's ridiculous too. I feel towards Wilmer just exactly as if he were my own son. I really do. But if I even for a moment thought of doing what you propose, what in the world do you think would keep Wilmer from telling the police every last detail about the falcon and all of us?"

Spade grinned with stiff lips. "If we had to," he said softly, "we could have him killed resisting arrest. But we won't have to go that far. Let him talk his head off. I promise you nobody'll do anything about it. That's easy enough to fix."

The pink flesh on Gutman's forehead crawled in a frown. He lowered his head, mashing his chins together over his collar, and asked: "How?" Then, with an abruptness that set all his fat bulbs to quivering and tumbling against one another, he raised his head, squirmed around to look at the boy, and laughed uproariously. "What do you think of this, Wilmer? It's funny, eh?"

The boy's eyes were cold hazel gleams under his lashes. He said in a low distinct voice: "Yes, it's funny—the son of a bitch."

Spade was talking to Brigid O'Shaughnessy: "How do you feel now, angel? Any better?"

"Yes, much better, only"—she reduced her voice until the last words would have been unintelligible two feet away—"I'm frightened."

"Don't be," he said carelessly and put a hand on her grey-stockinged knee. "Nothing very bad's going to happen. Want a drink?"

"Not now, thanks." Her voice sank again. "Be careful, Sam."

Spade grinned and looked at Gutman, who was looking at him. The fat man smiled genially, saying nothing for a moment, and then asked: "How?"

Spade was stupid. "How what?"

The fat man considered more laughter necessary then, and an explanation: "Well, sir, if you're really serious about this—this suggestion of yours, the least we can do in common politeness is to hear you out. Now how are you going about fixing it so that Wilmer"—he paused here to laugh again—"won't be able to do us any harm?"

Spade shook his head. "No," he said, "I wouldn't want to take advantage of anybody's politeness, no matter how common, like that. Forget it."

The fat man puckered up his facial bulbs. "Now come, come," he protested, "you make me decidedly uncomfortable. I shouldn't have laughed, and I apologize most humbly and sincerely. I wouldn't want to seem to ridicule anything you'd suggest, Mr. Spade, regardless of how much I disagreed with you, for you must know that I have the greatest respect and admiration for your astuteness. Now mind you, I don't see how this suggestion of yours can be in any way practical—even leaving out the fact that I couldn't feel any different towards Wilmer if he was my own flesh and blood—but I'll consider it a personal favor as well as a sign that you've accepted my apologies, sir, if you'll go ahead and outline the rest of it."

"Fair enough," Spade said. "Bryan is like most district attorneys. He's more interested in how his record will look on paper than in anything else. He'd rather drop a doubtful case than try it and have it go against him. I don't know that he ever deliberately framed anybody he believed innocent, but I can't imagine him letting himself believe them innocent if he could scrape up, or twist into shape, proof of their guilt. To be sure of convicting one man he'll let half a dozen equally guilty accomplices go free—if trying to convict them all might confuse his case.

"That's the choice we'll give him and he'll gobble it up. He wouldn't want to know about the falcon. He'll be tickled pink to persuade himself that anything the punk tells him about it is a lot of chewing-gum, an attempt to muddle things up. Leave that end to me. I can show him that if he starts fooling around trying to gather up everybody he's going to have a tangled case that no jury will be able to make heads or tails of, while if he sticks to the punk he can get a conviction standing on his head."

Gutman wagged his head sidewise in a slow smiling gesture of benign disapproval. "No, sir," he said, "I'm afraid that won't do, won't do at all. I don't see how even this District Attorney of yours can link Thursby and Jacobi and Wilmer together without having to—"

"You don't know district attorneys," Spade told him. "The Thursby angle is easy. He was a gunman and so's your punk. Bryan's already got a theory about that. There'll be no catch there. Well, Christ! they can only hang the punk once. Why try him for Jacobi's murder after he's been convicted of Thursby's? They simply close the record by writing it up against him and let it go at that. If, as is likely enough, he used the same gun on both, the bullets will match up. Everybody will be satisfied."

"Yes, but—" Gutman began, and stopped to look at the boy.

The boy advanced from the doorway, walking stiff-legged, with his legs apart, until he was between Gutman and Cairo, almost in the center of the floor. He halted there, leaning forward slightly from the waist, his shoulders raised towards the front. The pistol in his hand still hung at his side, but his knuckles were white over its grip. His other hand was a small hard fist down at his other side. The indelible youngness of his face gave an indescribably vicious—and inhuman—turn to the white-hot hatred and the cold white malevolence in his face. He said to Spade in a voice cramped by passion: "You bastard, get up on your feet and go for your heater!"

Spade smiled at the boy. His smile was not broad, but the amusement in it seemed genuine and unalloyed.

The boy said: "You bastard, get up and shoot it out if you've got the guts. I've taken all the riding from you I'm going to take."

The amusement in Spade's smile deepened. He looked at Gutman and said: "Young Wild West." His voice matched his smile. "Maybe you ought to tell him that shooting me before you get your hands on the falcon would be bad for business."

Gutman's attempt at a smile was not successful, but he kept the resultant grimace on his mottled face. He licked dry lips with a dry tongue. His voice was too hoarse and gritty for the paternally admonishing tone it tried to achieve. "Now, now, Wilmer," he said, "we can't have any of that. You shouldn't let yourself attach so much importance to these things. You—"

The boy, not taking his eyes from Spade, spoke in a choked voice out the side of his mouth: "Make him lay off me then. I'm going to fog him if he keeps it up and there won't be anything that'll stop me from doing it."

"Now, Wilmer," Gutman said and turned to Spade. His face and voice were under control now. "Your plan is, sir, as I said in the first place, not at all practical. Let's not say anything more about it."

Spade looked from one of them to the other. He had stopped smiling. His face held no expression at all. "I say what I please," he told them.

"You certainly do," Gutman said quickly, "and that's one of the things I've always admired in you. But this matter is, as I say, not at all practical, so there's not the least bit of use of discussing it any further, as you can see for yourself."

"I can't see it for myself," Spade said, "and you haven't made me see it, and I don't think you can." He frowned at Gutman. "Let's get this straight. Am I wasting time talking to you? I thought this was your show. Should I do my talking to the punk? I know how to do that."

"No, sir," Gutman replied, "you're quite right in dealing with me."

Spade said: "All right. Now I've got another suggestion. It's not as good as the first, but it's better than nothing. Want to hear it?"

"Most assuredly."

"Give them Cairo."

Cairo hastily picked up his pistol from the table beside him. He held it tight in his lap with both hands. Its muzzle pointed at the floor a little to one side of the sofa. His face had become yellowish again. His black eyes darted their gaze from face to face. The opaqueness of his eyes made them seem flat, two-dimensional.

Gutman, looking as if he could not believe he had heard what he had heard, asked: "Do what?"

"Give the police Cairo."

Gutman seemed about to laugh, but he did not laugh. Finally he exclaimed: "Well, by Gad, sir!" in an uncertain tone.

"It's not as good as giving them the punk," Spade said. "Cairo's not a gunman and he carries a smaller gun than Thursby and Jacobi were shot with. We'll have to go to more trouble framing him, but that's better than not giving the police anybody."

Cairo cried in a voice shrill with indignation: "Suppose we give them you, Mr. Spade, or Miss O'Shaughnessy? How about that if you're so set on giving them somebody?"

Spade smiled at the Levantine and answered him evenly: "You people want the falcon. I've got it. A fall-guy is part of the price I'm asking. As for Miss O'Shaughnessy"—his dispassionate glance moved to her white perplexed face and then back to Cairo and his shoulders rose and fell a fraction of an inch—"if you think she can be rigged for the part I'm perfectly willing to discuss it with you."

The girl put her hands to her throat, uttered a short strangled cry, and moved farther away from him.

Cairo, his face and body twitching with excitement, exclaimed: "You seem to forget that you are not in a position to insist on anything."

Spade laughed, a harsh derisive snort.

Gutman said, in a voice that tried to make firmness ingratiating: "Come now, gentlemen, let's keep our discussion on a friendly basis; but there certainly is"—he was addressing Spade—"something in what Mr. Cairo says. You must take into consideration the—"

"Like hell I must." Spade flung his words out with a brutal sort of carelessness that gave them more weight than they could have got from dramatic emphasis or from loudness. "If you kill me, how are you going to get the bird? If I know you can't afford to kill me till you have it, how are you going to scare me into giving it to you?"

Gutman cocked his head to the left and considered these questions. His eyes twinkled between puckered lids. Presently he gave his genial answer: "Well, sir, there are other means of persuasion besides killing and threatening to kill."

"Sure," Spade agreed, "but they're not much good unless the threat of death is behind them to hold the victim down. See what I mean? If you try anything I don't like I won't stand for it. I'll make it a matter of your having to call it off or kill me, knowing you can't afford to kill me."

"I see what you mean." Gutman chuckled. "That is an attitude, sir, that calls for the most delicate judgment on both sides, because, as you know, sir, men are likely to forget in the heat of action where their best interest lies and let their emotions carry them away."

Spade too was all smiling blandness. "That's the trick, from my side," he said, "to make my play strong enough that it ties you up, but yet not make you mad enough to bump me off against your better judgment."

Gutman said fondly: "By Gad, sir, you are a character!"

Joel Cairo jumped up from his chair and went around behind the boy and behind Gutman's chair. He bent over the back of Gutman's chair and, screening his mouth and the fat man's ear with his empty hand, whispered. Gutman listened attentively, shutting his eyes.

Spade grinned at Brigid O'Shaughnessy. Her lips smiled feebly in response, but there was no change in her eyes; they did not lose their numb stare. Spade turned to the boy: "Two to one they're selling you out, son."

The boy did not say anything. A trembling in his knees began to shake the knees of his trousers.

Spade addressed Gutman: "I hope you're not letting yourself be influenced by the guns these pocket-edition desperadoes are waving."

Gutman opened his eyes. Cairo stopped whispering and stood erect behind the fat man's chair.

Spade said: "I've practiced taking them away from both of them, so there'll be no trouble there. The punk is—"

In a voice choked horribly by emotion the boy cried, "All right!" and jerked his pistol up in front of his chest.

Gutman flung a fat hand out at the boy's wrist, caught the wrist, and bore it and the gun down while Gutman's fat body was rising in haste from the rocking chair. Joel Cairo scurried around to the boy's other side and grasped his other arm. They wrestled with the boy, forcing his arms down, holding them down, while he struggled futilely against them. Words came out of the struggling group: fragments of the boy's incoherent speech—"right . . . go . . . bastard . . . smoke"—Gutman's "Now, now, Wilmer!" repeated many times; Cairo's "No, please, don't" and "Don't do that, Wilmer."

Wooden-faced, dreamy-eyed, Spade got up from the sofa and went over to the group. The boy, unable to cope with the weight against him, had stopped struggling. Cairo, still holding the boy's arm, stood partly in front of him, talking to him soothingly. Spade pushed Cairo aside gently and drove his left fist against the boy's chin. The boy's head snapped back as far as it could while his arms were held, and then came forward. Gutman began a desperate "Here, what—?" Spade drove his right fist against the boy's chin.

Cairo dropped the boy's arm, letting him collapse against Gutman's great round belly. Cairo sprang at Spade, clawing at his face with the curved stiff fingers of both hands. Spade blew his breath out and pushed the Levantine away. Cairo sprang at him again. Tears were in Cairo's eyes and his red lips worked angrily, forming words, but no sound came from between them.

Spade laughed, grunted, "Jesus, you're a pip!" and cuffed the side of Cairo's face with an open hand, knocking him over against the table. Cairo regained his balance and sprang at Spade the third time. Spade stopped him with both palms held out on long rigid arms against his face. Cairo, failing to reach Spade's face with his shorter arms, thumped Spade's arms.

"Stop it," Spade growled. "I'll hurt you."

Cairo cried, "Oh, you big coward!" and backed away from him.

Spade stooped to pick up Cairo's pistol from the floor, and then the boy's. He straightened up holding them in his left hand, dangling them upside-down by their trigger-guards from his forefinger.

Gutman had put the boy in the rocking chair and stood looking at him with troubled eyes in an uncertainly puckered face. Cairo went down on his knees beside the chair and began to chafe one of the boy's limp hands.

Spade felt the boy's chin with his fingers. "Nothing cracked," he said. "We'll spread him on the sofa." He put his right arm under the boy's arm and around his back, put his left forearm under the boy's knees, lifted him without apparent effort, and carried him to the sofa.

Brigid O'Shaughnessy got up quickly and Spade laid the boy there. With his right hand Spade patted the boy's clothes, found his second pistol, added it to the others in his left hand, and turned his back on the sofa. Cairo was already sitting beside the boy's head.

Spade clinked the pistols together in his hand and smiled cheerfully at Gutman. "Well," he said, "there's our fall-guy."

Gutman's face was grey and his eyes were clouded. He did not look at Spade. He looked at the floor and did not say anything.

Spade said: "Don't be a dammed fool again. You let Cairo whisper to you and you held the kid while I pasted him. You can't laugh that off and you're likely to get yourself shot trying to."

Gutman moved his feet on the rug and said nothing.

Spade said: "And the other side of it is that you'll either say yes right now or I'll turn the falcon and the whole God-damned lot of you in."

Gutman raised his head and muttered through his teeth: "I don't like that, sir."

"You won't like it," Spade said. "Well?"

The fat man sighed and made a wry face and replied sadly: "You can have him."

Spade said: "That's swell."

CHAPTER XIX

The Russian's Hand

THE BOY LAY on his back on the sofa, a small figure that was—except for its breathing—altogether corpselike to the eye. Joel Cairo sat beside the boy, bending over him, rubbing his cheeks and wrists, smoothing his hair back from his forehead, whispering to him, and peering anxiously down at his white still face.

Brigid O'Shaughnessy stood in an angle made by table and wall. One of her hands was flat on the table, the other to her breast. She pinched her lower lip between her teeth and glanced furtively at Spade whenever he was not looking at her. When he looked at her she looked at Cairo and the boy.

Gutman's face had lost its troubled cast and was becoming rosy again. He had put his hands in his trousers-pockets. He stood facing Spade, watching him without curiosity.

Spade, idly jingling his handful of pistols, nodded at Cairo's rounded back and asked Gutman: "It'll be all right with him?"

"I don't know," the fat man replied placidly. "That part will have to be strictly up to you, sir."

Spade's smile made his v-shaped chin more salient. He said: "Cairo."

The Levantine screwed his dark anxious face around over his shoulder.

Spade said: "Let him rest awhile. We're going to give him to the police. We ought to get the details fixed before he comes to."

Cairo asked bitterly: "Don't you think you've done enough to him without that?"

Spade said: "No."

Cairo left the sofa and went close to the fat man. "Please don't do this thing, Mr. Gutman," he begged. "You must realize that—"

Spade interrupted him: "That's settled. The question is, what are you going to do about it? Coming in? Or getting out?"

Though Gutman's smile was a bit sad, even wistful in its way, he nodded his head. "I don't like it either," he told the Levantine, "but we can't help ourselves now. We really can't."

Spade asked: "What are you doing, Cairo? In or out?"

Cairo wet his lips and turned slowly to face Spade. "Suppose," he said, and swallowed. "Have I—? Can I choose?"

"You can," Spade assured him seriously, "but you ought to know that if the answer is *out* we'll give you to the police with your boy-friend."

"Oh, come, Mr. Spade," Gutman protested, "that is not—"

"Like hell we'll let him walk out on us," Spade said. "He'll either come in or he'll go in. We can't have a lot of loose ends hanging around." He scowled at Gutman and burst out irritably: "Jesus God! is this the first thing you guys ever stole? You're a fine lot of lollipops! What are you going to do next—get down and pray?" He directed his scowl at Cairo. "Well? Which?"

"You give me no choice." Cairo's narrow shoulders moved in a hopeless shrug. "I come in."

"Good," Spade said and looked at Gutman and at Brigid O'Shaughnessy. "Sit down."

The girl sat down gingerly on the end of the sofa by the unconscious boy's feet. Gutman returned to the padded rocking chair, and Cairo to the armchair. Spade put his handful of pistols on the table and sat on the table-corner beside them. He looked at the watch on his wrist and said: "Two o'clock. I can't get the falcon till daylight, or maybe eight o'clock. We've got plenty of time to arrange everything."

Gutman cleared his throat. "Where is it?" he asked and then added in haste: "I don't really care, sir. What I had in mind was that it would be best for all concerned if we did not get out of each other's sight until our business has been transacted." He looked at the sofa and at Spade again, sharply. "You have the envelope?"

Spade shook his head, looking at the sofa and then at the girl. He smiled with his eyes and said: "Miss O'Shaughnessy has it."

"Yes, I have it," she murmured, putting a hand inside her coat. "I picked it up. . . ."

"That's all right," Spade told her. "Hang on to it." He addressed Gutman: "We won't have to lose sight of each other. I can have the falcon brought here."

"That will be excellent," Gutman purred. "Then, sir, in exchange for the ten thousand dollars and Wilmer you will give us the falcon and an hour or two of grace—so we won't be in the city when you surrender him to the authorities."

"You don't have to duck," Spade said. "It'll be airtight."

"That may be, sir, but nevertheless we'll feel safer well out of the city when Wilmer is being questioned by your District Attorney."

"Suit yourself," Spade replied. "I can hold him here all day if you want." He began to roll a cigarette. "Let's get the details fixed. Why did he shoot Thursby? And why and where and how did he shoot Jacobi?"

Gutman smiled indulgently, shaking his head and purring: "Now come, sir, you can't expect that. We've given you the money and Wilmer. That is our part of the agreement."

"I do expect it," Spade said. He held his lighter to his cigarette. "A fall-guy is what I asked for, and he's not a fall-guy unless he's a cinch to take the fall. Well, to cinch that I've got to know what's what." He pulled his brows together. "What are you bellyaching about? You're not going to be sitting so damned pretty if you leave him with an out."

Gutman leaned forward and wagged a fat finger at the pistols on the table beside Spade's legs. "There's ample evidence of his guilt, sir. Both men were shot with those weapons. It's a very simple matter for the police-department-experts to determine that the bullets that killed the men were fired from those weapons. You know that; you've mentioned it yourself. And that, it seems to me, is ample proof of his guilt."

"Maybe," Spade agreed, "but the thing's more complicated than that and I've got to know what happened so I can be sure the parts that won't fit in are covered up."

Cairo's eyes were round and hot. "Apparently you've forgotten that you assured us it would be a very simple affair," Cairo said. He turned his excited dark face to Gutman. "You see! I advised you not to do this. I don't think—"

"It doesn't make a damned bit of difference what either of you think," Spade said bluntly. "It's too late for that now and you're in too deep. Why did he kill Thursby?"

Gutman interlaced his fingers over his belly and rocked his chair. His voice, like his smile, was frankly rueful. "You are an uncommonly difficult person to get the best of," he said. "I begin to think that we made a mistake in not letting you alone from the very first. By Gad, I do, sir!"

Spade moved his hand carelessly. "You haven't done so bad. You're staying out of jail and you're getting the falcon. What do you want?" He put his cigarette in a corner of his mouth and said around it: "Anyhow you know where you stand now. Why did he kill Thursby?"

Gutman stopped rocking. "Thursby was a notorious killer and Miss O'Shaughnessy's ally. We knew that removing him in just that manner would make her stop and think that perhaps it would be best to patch up her differences with us after all, besides leaving her without so violent a protector. You see, sir, I am being candid with you?"

"Yes. Keep it up. You didn't think he might have the falcon?"

Gutman shook his head so that his round cheeks wobbled. "We didn't think that for a minute," he replied. He smiled benevolently. "We had the advantage of knowing Miss O'Shaughnessy far too well for that and, while we didn't know then that she had given the falcon to Captain Jacobi in Hongkong to be brought over on the *Paloma* while they took a faster boat, still we didn't for a minute think that, if only one of them knew where it was, Thursby was the one."

Spade nodded thoughtfully and asked: "You didn't try to make a deal with him before you gave him the works?"

"Yes, sir, we certainly did. I talked to him myself that night. Wilmer had located him two days before and had been trying to follow him to wherever he was meeting Miss O'Shaughnessy, but Thursby was too crafty for that even if he didn't know he was being watched. So that night Wilmer went to his hotel, learned he wasn't in, and waited outside for him. I suppose Thursby returned immediately after killing your partner. Be that as it may, Wilmer brought him to see me. We could do nothing with him. He was quite determinedly loyal to Miss O'Shaughnessy. Well, sir, Wilmer followed him back to his hotel and did what he did."

Spade thought for a moment. "That sounds all right. Now Jacobi."

Gutman looked at Spade with grave eyes and said: "Captain Jacobi's death was entirely Miss O'Shaughnessy's fault."

The girl gasped, "Oh!" and put a hand to her mouth.

Spade's voice was heavy and even. "Never mind that now. Tell me what happened."

After a shrewd look at Spade, Gutman smiled. "Just as you say, sir," he said. "Well, Cairo, as you know, got in touch with me—I sent for him—after he left police headquarters the night—or morning—he was up here. We recognized the mutual advantage of pooling forces." He directed his smile at the Levantine. "Mr. Cairo is a man of nice judgment. The *Paloma* was his thought. He saw the notice of its arrival in the papers that morning and remembered that he had heard in Hongkong that Jacobi and Miss O'Shaughnessy had been seen together. That was when he had been trying to find her there, and he thought at first that she had left on the *Paloma,* though later he learned that she hadn't. Well, sir, when he saw the notice of arrival in the paper he guessed just what had happened: she had given the bird to Jacobi to bring here for her. Jacobi did not know what it was, of course. Miss O'Shaughnessy is too discreet for that."

He beamed at the girl, rocked his chair twice, and went on: "Mr. Cairo and Wilmer and I went to call on Captain Jacobi and were fortunate enough to arrive while Miss O'Shaughnessy was there. In many ways it was a difficult conference, but finally, by midnight we had persuaded Miss O'Shaughnessy to come to terms, or so we thought. We then left the boat and set out for my hotel, where I was to pay Miss O'Shaughnessy and receive the bird. Well, sir, we mere men should have known better than to suppose ourselves capable of coping with her. *En route,* she and Captain Jacobi and the falcon slipped completely through our fingers." He laughed merrily. "By Gad, sir, it was neatly done."

Spade looked at the girl. Her eyes, large and dark with pleading, met his. He asked Gutman: "You touched off the boat before you left?"

"Not intentionally, no, sir," the fat man replied, "though I dare say we—or Wilmer at least—were responsible for the fire. He had been out trying to find the falcon while the rest of us were talking in the cabin and no doubt was careless with matches."

"That's fine," Spade said. "If any slip-up makes it necessary for us to try him for Jacobi's murder we can also hang an arson-rap on him. All right. Now about the shooting."

"Well, sir, we dashed around town all day trying to find them and we found them late this afternoon. We weren't sure at first that we'd found them. All we were sure of was that we'd found Miss O'Shaughnessy's apartment. But when we listened at the door we heard them moving around inside, so we were pretty confident we had them and rang the bell. When she asked us who we were and we told her—through the door—we heard a window going up.

"We knew what that meant, of course; so Wilmer hurried downstairs as fast as he could and around to the rear of the building to cover the fire-escape. And when he turned into the alley he ran right plumb smack into Captain Jacobi running away with the falcon under his arm. That was a difficult situation to handle, but Wilmer did every bit as well as he could. He shot Jacobi—more than once—but Jacobi was too tough to either fall or drop the falcon, and he was too close for Wilmer to keep out of his way. He knocked Wilmer down and ran on. And this was in broad daylight, you understand, in the afternoon. When Wilmer got up he could see a policeman coming up from the block below. So he had to give it up. He dodged into the open back door of the building next to the Coronet, through into the street, and then up to join us—and very fortunate he was, sir, to make it without being seen.

"Well, sir, there we were—stumped again. Miss O'Shaughnessy had opened the door for Mr. Cairo and me after she had shut the window behind Jacobi, and she—" He broke off to smile at a memory. "We persuaded—that is the word, sir—her to tell us that she had told Jacobi to take the falcon to you. It seemed very unlikely that he'd live to go that far, even if the police didn't pick him up, but that was the only chance we had, sir. And so, once more, we persuaded Miss O'Shaughnessy to give us a little assistance. We—well—persuaded her to phone your office in an attempt to draw you away before Jacobi got there, and we sent Wilmer after him. Unfortunately it had taken us too long to decide and to persuade Miss O'Shaughnessy to—"

The boy on the sofa groaned and rolled over on his side. His eyes opened and closed several times. The girl stood up and moved into the angle of table and wall again.

"—coöperate with us," Gutman concluded hurriedly, "and so you had the falcon before we could reach you."

The boy put one foot on the floor, raised himself on an elbow, opened his eyes wide, put the other foot down, sat up, and looked around. When his eyes focused on Spade bewilderment went out of them.

Cairo left his armchair and went over to the boy. He put his arm on the boy's shoulders and started to say something. The boy rose quickly to his feet, shaking Cairo's arm off. He glanced around the room once and then fixed his eyes on Spade again. His face was set hard and he held his body so tense that it seemed drawn in and shrunken.

Spade, sitting on the corner of the table, swinging his legs carelessly, said: "Now listen, kid. If you come over here and start cutting up I'm going to kick you in the face. Sit down and shut up and behave and you'll last longer."

The boy looked at Gutman.

Gutman smiled benignly at him and said: "Well, Wilmer, I'm sorry indeed to lose you, and I want you to know that I couldn't be any fonder of you if you were my own son; but—well, by Gad!—if you lose a son it's possible to get another—and there's only one Maltese falcon."

Spade laughed.

Cairo moved over and whispered in the boy's ear. The boy, keeping his cold hazel eyes on Gutman's face, sat down on the sofa again. The Levantine sat beside him.

Gutman's sigh did not affect the benignity of his smile. He said to Spade: "When you're young you simply don't understand things."

Cairo had an arm around the boy's shoulders again and was whispering to him. Spade grinned at Gutman and addressed Brigid O'Shaughnessy: "I think it'd be swell if you'd see what you can find us to eat in the kitchen, with plenty of coffee. Will you? I don't like to leave my guests."

"Surely," she said and started towards the door.

Gutman stopped rocking. "Just a moment, my dear." He held up a thick hand. "Hadn't you better leave the envelope in here? You don't want to get grease-spots on it."

The girl's eyes questioned Spade. He said in an indifferent tone: "It's still his."

She put her hand inside her coat, took out the envelope, and gave it to Spade. Spade tossed it into Gutman's lap, saying: "Sit on it if you're afraid of losing it."

"You misunderstand me," Gutman replied suavely. "It's not that at all, but business should be transacted in a business-like manner." He opened the flap of the envelope, took out the thousand-dollar bills, counted them, and chuckled so that his belly bounced. "For instance there are only nine bills here now." He spread them out on his fat knees and thighs. "There were ten when I handed it to you, as you very well know." His smile was broad and jovial and triumphant.

Spade looked at Brigid O'Shaughnessy and asked: "Well?"

She shook her head sidewise with emphasis. She did not say anything, though her lips moved slightly, as if she had tried to. Her face was frightened.

Spade held his hand out to Gutman and the fat man put the money into it. Spade counted the money—nine thousand-dollar bills—and returned it to Gutman. Then Spade stood up and his face was dull and placid. He picked up the three pistols on the table. He spoke in a matter-of-fact voice. "I want to know about this. We"—he nodded at the girl, but without looking at her—"are going in the bathroom. The door will be open and I'll be facing it. Unless you want a three-story drop there's no way out of here except past the bathroom door. Don't try to make it."

"Really, sir," Gutman protested, "it's not necessary, and certainly not very courteous of you, to threaten us in this manner. You must know that we've not the least desire to leave."

"I'll know a lot when I'm through." Spade was patient but resolute. "This trick upsets things. I've got to find the answer. It won't take long." He touched the girl's elbow. "Come on."

In the bathroom Brigid O'Shaughnessy found words. She put her hands up flat on Spade's chest and her face up close to his and whispered: "I did not take that bill, Sam."

"I don't think you did," he said, "but I've got to know. Take your clothes off."

"You won't take my word for it?"

"No. Take your clothes off."

"I won't."

"All right. We'll go back to the other room and I'll have them taken off."

She stepped back with a hand to her mouth. Her eyes were round and horrified. "You would?" she asked through her fingers.

"I will," he said. "I've got to know what happened to that bill and I'm not going to be held up by anybody's maidenly modesty."

"Oh, it isn't that." She came close to him and put her hands on his chest again. "I'm not ashamed to be naked before you, but—can't you see?—not like this. Can't you see that if you make me you'll—you'll be killing something?"

He did not raise his voice. "I don't know anything about that. I've got to know what happened to the bill. Take them off."

She looked at his unblinking yellow-grey eyes and her face became pink and then white again. She drew herself up tall and began to undress. He sat on the side of the bathtub watching her and the open door. No sound came from the living-room. She removed her clothes swiftly, without fumbling, letting them fall down on the floor around her feet. When she was naked she stepped back from her clothing and stood looking at him. In her mien was pride without defiance or embarrassment.

He put his pistols on the toilet-seat and, facing the door, went down on one knee in front of her garments. He picked up each piece and examined it with fingers as well as eyes. He did not find the thousand-dollar bill. When he had finished he stood up holding her clothes out in his hands to her. "Thanks," he said. "Now I know."

She took the clothing from him. She did not say anything. He picked up his pistols. He shut the bathroom door behind him and went into the living-room.

Gutman smiled amiably at him from the rocking chair. "Find it?" he asked.

Cairo, sitting beside the boy on the sofa, looked at Spade with questioning opaque eyes. The boy did not look up. He was leaning forward, head between hands, elbows on knees, staring at the floor between his feet.

Spade told Gutman: "No, I didn't find it. You palmed it."

The fat man chuckled. "I palmed it?"

"Yes," Spade said, jingling the pistols in his hand. "Do you want to say so or do you want to stand for a frisk?"

"Stand for—?"

"You're going to admit it," Spade said, "or I'm going to search you. There's no third way."

Gutman looked up at Spade's hard face and laughed outright. "By Gad, sir, I believe you would. I really do. You're a character, sir, if you don't mind my saying so."

"You palmed it," Spade said.

"Yes, sir, that I did." The fat man took a crumpled bill from his vest-pocket, smoothed it on a wide thigh, took the envelope holding the nine bills from his coat-pocket, and put the smoothed bill in with the others. "I must have my little joke every now and then and I was curious to know what you'd do in a situation of that sort. I must say that you passed the test with flying colors, sir. It never occurred to me that you'd hit on such a simple and direct way of getting at the truth."

Spade sneered at him without bitterness. "That's the kind of thing I'd expect from somebody the punk's age."

Gutman chuckled.

Brigid O'Shaughnessy, dressed again except for coat and hat, came out of the bathroom, took a step towards the living-room, turned around, went to the kitchen, and turned on the light.

Cairo edged closer to the boy on the sofa and began whispering in his ear again. The boy shrugged irritably.

Spade, looking at the pistols in his hand and then at Gutman, went out into the passageway, to the closet there. He opened the door, put the pistols inside on the top of a trunk, shut the door, locked it, put the key in his trousers-pocket, and went to the kitchen door.

Brigid O'Shaughnessy was filling an aluminum percolator.

"Find everything?" Spade asked.

"Yes," she replied in a cool voice, not raising her head. Then she set the percolator aside and came to the door. She blushed and her eyes were large and moist and chiding. "You shouldn't have done that to me, Sam," she said softly.

"I had to find out, angel." He bent down, kissed her mouth lightly, and returned to the living-room.

Gutman smiled at Spade and offered him the white envelope, saying: "This will soon be yours; you might as well take it now."

Spade did not take it. He sat in the armchair and said: "There's plenty of time for that. We haven't done enough talking about the money-end. I ought to have more than ten thousand."

Gutman said: "Ten thousand dollars is a lot of money."

Spade said: "You're quoting me, but it's not all the money in the world."

"No, sir, it's not. I grant you that. But it's a lot of money to be picked up in as few days and as easily as you're getting it."

"You think it's been so damned easy?" Spade asked, and shrugged. "Well, maybe, but that's my business."

"It certainly is," the fat man agreed. He screwed up his eyes, moved his head to indicate the kitchen, and lowered his voice. "Are you sharing with her?"

Spade said: "That's my business too."

"It certainly is," the fat man agreed once more, "but"—he hesitated—"I'd like to give you a word of advice."

"Go ahead."

"If you don't—I dare say you'll give her some money in any event, but—if you don't give her as much as she thinks she ought to have, my word of advice is—be careful."

Spade's eyes held a mocking light. He asked: "Bad?"

"Bad," the fat man replied.

Spade grinned and began to roll a cigarette.

Cairo, still muttering in the boy's ear, had put his arm around the boy's shoulders again. Suddenly the boy pushed his arm away and turned on the sofa to face the Levantine. The boy's face held disgust and anger. He made a fist of one small hand and struck Cairo's mouth with it. Cairo cried out as a woman might have cried and drew back to the very end of the sofa. He took a silk handkerchief from his pocket and put it to his mouth. It came away daubed with blood. He put it to his mouth once more and looked reproachfully at the boy. The boy snarled, "Keep away from me," and put his face between his hands again. Cairo's handkerchief released the fragrance of *chypre* in the room.

Cairo's cry had brought Brigid O'Shaughnessy to the door. Spade, grinning, jerked a thumb at the sofa and told her: "The course of true love. How's the food coming along?"

"It's coming," she said and went back to the kitchen.

Spade lighted his cigarette and addressed Gutman: "Let's talk about money."

"Willingly, sir, with all my heart," the fat man replied, "but I might as well tell you frankly right now that ten thousand is every cent I can raise."

Spade exhaled smoke. "I ought to have twenty."

"I wish you could. I'd give it to you gladly if I had it, but ten thousand dollars is every cent I can manage, on my word of honor. Of course, sir, you understand that is simply the first payment. Later—"

Spade laughed. "I know you'll give me millions later," he said, "but let's stick to this first payment now. Fifteen thousand?"

Gutman smiled and frowned and shook his head. "Mr. Spade, I've told you frankly and candidly and on my word of honor as a gentleman that ten thousand dollars is all the money I've got—every penny—and all I can raise."

"But you didn't say positively."

Gutman laughed and said: "Positively."

Spade said gloomily: "That's not any too good, but if it's the best you can do—give it to me."

Gutman handed him the envelope. Spade counted the bills and was putting them in his pocket when Brigid O'Shaughnessy came in carrying a tray.

The boy would not eat. Cairo took a cup of coffee. The girl, Gutman, and Spade ate the scrambled eggs, bacon, toast, and marmalade she had prepared, and drank two cups of coffee apiece. Then they settled down to wait the rest of the night through.

Gutman smoked a cigar and read *Celebrated Criminal Cases of America,* now and then chuckling over or commenting on the parts of its contents that amused him. Cairo nursed his mouth and sulked on his end of the sofa. The boy sat with his head in his hands until a little after four o'clock. Then he lay down with his feet towards Cairo, turned his face to the window, and went to sleep. Brigid O'Shaughnessy, in the armchair, dozed, listened to the fat man's comments, and carried on wide-spaced desultory conversations with Spade.

Spade rolled and smoked cigarettes and moved, without fidgeting or nervousness, around the room. He sat sometimes on an arm of the girl's chair, on the table-corner, on the floor at her feet, on a straight-backed chair. He was wide-awake, cheerful, and full of vigor.

At half-past five he went into the kitchen and made more coffee. Half an hour later the boy stirred, awakened, and sat up yawning. Gutman looked at his watch and questioned Spade: "Can you get it now?"

"Give me another hour."

Gutman nodded and went back to his book.

At seven o'clock Spade went to the telephone and called Effie Perine's number. "Hello, Mrs. Perine? . . . This is Mr. Spade. Will you let me talk to Effie, please? . . . Yes, it is. . . . Thanks." He whistled two lines of *En Cuba,* softly. "Hello, angel. Sorry to get you up. . . . Yes, very. Here's the plot: in our Holland box at the Post Office you'll find an envelope addressed in my scribble. There's a Pickwick Stage parcel-room-check in it—for the bundle we got yesterday. Will you get the bundle and bring it to me—p. d. q.? . . . Yes, I'm home. . . . That's the girl—hustle. . . . 'Bye."

The street-door-bell rang at ten minutes of eight. Spade went to the telephone-box and pressed the button that released the lock. Gutman put down his book and rose smiling. "You don't mind if I go to the door with you?" he asked.

"OK," Spade told him.

Gutman followed him to the corridor-door. Spade opened it. Presently Effie Perine, carrying the brown-wrapped parcel, came from the elevator. Her boyish face was gay and bright and she came forward quickly, almost trotting. After one glance she did not look at Gutman. She smiled at Spade and gave him the parcel.

He took it saying: "Thanks a lot, lady. I'm sorry to spoil your day of rest, but this—"

"It's not the first one you've spoiled," she replied, laughing, and then, when it was apparent that he was not going to invite her in, asked: "Anything else?"

He shook his head. "No, thanks."

She said, "Bye-bye," and went back to the elevator.

Spade shut the door and carried the parcel into the living-room. Gutman's face was red and his cheeks quivered. Cairo and Brigid O'Shaughnessy came to the table as Spade put the parcel there. They were excited. The boy rose, pale and tense, but he remained by the sofa, staring under curling lashes at the others.

Spade stepped back from the table saying: "There you are."

Gutman's fat fingers made short work of cord and paper and excelsior, and he had the black bird in his hands. "Ah," he said huskily, "now, after seventeen years!" His eyes were moist.

Cairo licked his red lips and worked his hands together. The girl's lower lip was between her teeth. She and Cairo, like Gutman, and like Spade and the boy, were breathing heavily. The air in the room was chilly and stale, and thick with tobacco smoke.

Gutman set the bird down on the table again and fumbled at a pocket. "It's it," he said, "but we'll make sure." Sweat glistened on his round cheeks. His fingers twitched as he took out a gold pocket-knife and opened it.

Cairo and the girl stood close to him, one on either side. Spade stood back a little where he could watch the boy as well as the group at the table.

Gutman turned the bird upside-down and scraped an edge of its base with his knife. Black enamel came off in tiny curls, exposing blackened metal beneath. Gutman's knife-blade bit into the metal, turning back a thin curved shaving. The inside of the shaving, and the narrow plane its removal had left, had the soft grey sheen of lead.

Gutman's breath hissed between his teeth. His face became turgid with hot blood. He twisted the bird around and hacked at its head. There too the edge of his knife bared lead. He let knife and bird bang down on the table while he wheeled to confront Spade. "It's a fake," he said hoarsely.

Spade's face had become somber. His nod was slow, but there was no slowness in his hand's going out to catch Brigid O'Shaughnessy's wrist. He pulled her to him and grasped her chin with his other hand, raising her face roughly. "All right," he growled into her face. "You've had *your* little joke. Now tell us about it."

She cried: "No, Sam, no! That is the one I got from Kemidov. I swear—"

Joel Cairo thrust himself between Spade and Gutman and began to emit words in a shrill spluttering stream: "That's it! That's it! It was the Russian! I should have known! What a fool we thought him, and what fools he made of us!" Tears ran down the Levantine's cheeks and he danced up and down. "You bungled it!" he screamed at Gutman. "You and your stupid attempt to buy it from him! You fat fool! You let him know it was valuable and he found out how valuable and made a duplicate for us! No wonder we had so little trouble stealing it! No wonder he was so willing to send me off around the world looking for it! You imbecile! You bloated idiot!" He put his hands to his face and blubbered.

Gutman's jaw sagged. He blinked vacant eyes. Then he shook himself and was—by the time his bulbs had stopped jouncing—again a jovial fat man. "Come, sir," he said good-naturedly, "there's no need of going on like that. Everybody errs at times and you may be sure this is every bit as severe a blow to me as to anyone else. Yes, that is the Russian's hand, there's no doubt of it. Well, sir, what do you suggest? Shall we stand here and shed tears and call each other names? Or shall we"—he paused and his smile was a cherub's—"go to Constantinople?"

Cairo took his hands from his face and his eyes bulged. He stammered: "You are—?" Amazement coming with full comprehension made him speechless.

Gutman patted his fat hands together. His eyes twinkled. His voice was a complacent throaty purring: "For seventeen years I have wanted that little item and have been trying to get it. If I must spend another year on the quest—well, sir—that will be an additional expenditure in time of only"—his lips moved silently as he calculated—"five and fifteen-seventeenths per cent."

The Levantine giggled and cried: "I go with you!"

Spade suddenly released the girl's wrist and looked around the room. The boy was not there. Spade went into the passageway. The corridor-door stood open. Spade made a dissatisfied mouth, shut the door, and returned to the living-room. He leaned against the door-frame and looked at Gutman and Cairo. He looked at Gutman for a long time, sourly. Then he spoke, mimicking the fat man's throaty purr: "Well, sir, I must say you're a swell lot of thieves!"

Gutman chuckled. "We've little enough to boast about, and that's a fact, sir," he said. "But, well, we're none of us dead yet and there's not a bit of use thinking the world's come to an end just because we've run into a little setback." He brought his left hand from behind him and held it out towards Spade, pink smooth hilly palm up. "I'll have to ask you for that envelope, sir."

Spade did not move. His face was wooden. He said: "I held up my end. You got your dingus. It's your hard luck, not mine, that it wasn't what you wanted."

"Now come, sir," Gutman said persuasively, "we've all failed and there's no reason for expecting any one of us to bear the brunt of it, and—" He brought his right hand from behind him. In the hand was a small pistol, an ornately engraved and inlaid affair of silver and gold and mother-of-pearl. "In short, sir, I must ask you to return my ten thousand dollars."

Spade's face did not change. He shrugged and took the envelope from his pocket. He started to hold it out to Gutman, hesitated, opened the envelope, and took out one thousand-dollar bill. He put that bill into his trousers-pocket. He tucked the envelope's flap in over the other bills and held them out to Gutman. "That'll take care of my time and expenses," he said.

Gutman, after a little pause, imitated Spade's shrug and accepted the envelope. He said: "Now, sir, we will say good-bye to you, unless"—the fat puffs around his eyes crinkled—"you care to undertake the Constantinople expedition with us. You don't? Well, sir, frankly I'd like to have you along. You're a man to my liking, a man of many resources and nice judgment. Because we know you're a man of nice judgment we know we can say good-bye with every assurance that you'll hold the details of our little enterprise in confidence. We know we can count on you to appreciate the fact that, as the situation now stands, any legal difficulties that come to us in connection with these last few days would likewise and equally come to you and the charming Miss O'Shaughnessy. You're too shrewd not to recognize that, sir, I'm sure."

"I understand that," Spade replied.

"I was sure you would. I'm also sure that, now there's no alternative, you'll somehow manage the police without a fall-guy."

"I'll make out all right," Spade replied.

"I was sure you would. Well, sir, the shortest farewells are the best. Adieu." He made a portly bow. "And to you, Miss O'Shaughnessy, adieu. I leave you the *rara avis* on the table as a little memento."

CHAPTER XX

If They Hang You

FOR ALL OF FIVE MINUTES after the outer door had closed behind Casper Gutman and Joel Cairo, Spade, motionless, stood staring at the knob of the open living-room-door. His eyes were gloomy under a forehead drawn down. The clefts at the root of his nose were deep and red. His lips protruded loosely, pouting. He drew them in to make a hard v and went to the telephone. He had not looked at Brigid O'Shaughnessy, who stood by the table looking with uneasy eyes at him.

He picked up the telephone, set it on its shelf again, and bent to look into the telephone-directory hanging from a corner of the shelf. He turned the pages rapidly until he found the one he wanted, ran his finger down a column, straightened up, and lifted the telephone from the shelf again. He called a number and said:

"Hello, is Sergeant Polhaus there? . . . Will you call him, please? This is Samuel Spade. . . ." He stared into space, waiting. "Hello, Tom, I've got something for you. . . . Yes, plenty. Here it is: Thursby and Jacobi were shot by a kid named Wilmer Cook." He described the boy minutely. "He's working for a man named Casper Gutman." He described Gutman. "That fellow Cairo you met here is in with them too. . . . Yes, that's it. . . . Gutman's staying at the Alexandria, suite twelve C, or was. They've just left here and they're blowing town, so you'll have to move fast, but I don't think they're expecting a pinch. . . . There's a girl in it too—Gutman's daughter." He described Rhea Gutman. "Watch yourself when you go up against the kid. He's supposed to be pretty good with the gun. . . . That's right, Tom, and I've got some stuff here for you. I think I've got the guns he used. . . . That's right. Step on it—and luck to you!"

Spade slowly replaced receiver on prong, telephone on shelf. He wet his lips and looked down at his hands. Their palms were wet. He filled his deep chest with air. His eyes were glittering between straightened lids. He turned and took three long swift steps into the living-room.

Brigid O'Shaughnessy, startled by the suddenness of his approach, let her breath out in a little laughing gasp.

Spade, face to face with her, very close to her, tall, big-boned and thick-muscled, coldly smiling, hard of jaw and eye, said: "They'll talk when they're nailed—about us. We're sitting on dynamite, and we've only got minutes to get set for the police. Give me all of it—fast. Gutman sent you and Cairo to Constantinople?"

She started to speak, hesitated, and bit her lip.

He put a hand on her shoulder. "God damn you, talk!" he said. "I'm in this with you and you're not going to gum it. Talk. He sent you to Constantinople?"

"Y-yes, he sent me. I met Joe there and—and asked him to help me. Then we—"

"Wait. You asked Cairo to help you get it from Kemidov?"

"Yes."

"For Gutman?"

She hesitated again, squirmed under the hard angry glare of his eyes, swallowed, and said: "No, not then. We thought we would get it for ourselves."

"All right. Then?"

"Oh, then I began to be afraid that Joe wouldn't play fair with me, so—so I asked Floyd Thursby to help me."

"And he did. Well?"

"Well, we got it and went to Hongkong."

"With Cairo? Or had you ditched him before that?"

"Yes. We left him in Constantinople, in jail—something about a check."

"Something you fixed up to hold him there?"

She looked shamefacedly at Spade and whispered: "Yes."

"Right. Now you and Thursby are in Hongkong with the bird."

"Yes, and then—I didn't know him very well—I didn't know whether I could trust him. I thought it would be safer—anyway, I met Captain Jacobi and I knew his boat was coming here, so I asked him to bring a package for me—and that was the bird. I wasn't sure I could trust Thursby, or that Joe or—or somebody working for Gutman might not be on the boat we came on—and that seemed the safest plan."

"All right. Then you and Thursby caught one of the fast boats over. Then what?"

"Then—then I was afraid of Gutman. I knew he had people—connections—everywhere, and he'd soon know what we had done. And I was afraid he'd have learned that we had left Hongkong for San Francisco. He was in New York and I knew if he heard that by cable he would have plenty of time to get here by the time we did, or before.

He did. I didn't know that then, but I was afraid of it, and I had to wait here until Captain Jacobi's boat arrived. And I was afraid Gutman would find me—or find Floyd and buy him over. That's why I came to you and asked you to watch him for—"

"That's a lie," Spade said. "You had Thursby hooked and you knew it. He was a sucker for women. His record shows that—the only falls he took were over women. And once a chump, always a chump. Maybe you didn't know his record, but you'd know you had him safe."

She blushed and looked timidly at him.

He said: "You wanted to get him out of the way before Jacobi came with the loot. What was your scheme?"

"I—I knew he'd left the States with a gambler after some trouble. I didn't know what it was, but I thought that if it was anything serious and he saw a detective watching him he'd think it was on account of the old trouble, and would be frightened into going away. I didn't think—"

"You told him he was being shadowed," Spade said confidently. "Miles hadn't many brains, but he wasn't clumsy enough to be spotted the first night."

"I told him, yes. When we went out for a walk that night I pretended to discover Mr. Archer following us and pointed him out to Floyd." She sobbed. "But please believe, Sam, that I wouldn't have done it if I had thought Floyd would kill him. I thought he'd be frightened into leaving the city. I didn't for a minute think he'd shoot him like that."

Spade smiled wolfishly with his lips, but not at all with his eyes. He said: "If you thought he wouldn't you were right, angel."

The girl's upraised face held utter astonishment.

Spade said: "Thursby didn't shoot him."

Incredulity joined astonishment in the girl's face.

Spade said: "Miles hadn't many brains, but, Christ! he had too many years' experience as a detective to be caught like that by the man he was shadowing. Up a blind alley with his gun tucked away on his hip and his overcoat buttoned? Not a chance. He was as dumb as any man ought to be, but he wasn't quite that dumb. The only two ways out of the alley could be watched from the edge of Bush Street over the tunnel. You'd told us Thursby was a bad actor. He couldn't have tricked Miles into the alley like that, and he couldn't have driven him in. He was dumb, but not dumb enough for that."

He ran his tongue over the inside of his lips and smiled affectionately at the girl. He said: "But he'd've gone up there with you, angel, if he was sure nobody else was up there. You were his client, so he would have had no reason for not dropping the shadow on your say-so, and if you caught up with him and asked him to go up there he'd've gone. He was just dumb enough for that. He'd've looked you up and down and licked his lips and gone grinning from ear to ear—and then you could've stood as close to him as you liked in the dark and put a hole through him with the gun you had got from Thursby that evening."

Brigid O'Shaughnessy shrank back from him until the edge of the table stopped her. She looked at him with terrified eyes and cried: "Don't—don't talk to me like that, Sam! You know I didn't! You know—"

"Stop it." He looked at the watch on his wrist. "The police will be blowing in any minute now and we're sitting on dynamite. Talk!"

She put the back of a hand on her forehead. "Oh, why do you accuse me of such a terrible—?"

"Will you stop it?" he demanded in a low impatient voice. "This isn't the spot for the schoolgirl-act. Listen to me. The pair of us are sitting under the gallows." He took hold of her wrists and made her stand up straight in front of him. "Talk!"

"I—I— How did you know he—he licked his lips and looked—?"

Spade laughed harshly. "I knew Miles. But never mind that. Why did you shoot him?"

She twisted her wrists out of Spade's fingers and put her hands up around the back of his neck, pulling his head down until his mouth all but touched hers. Her body was flat against his from knees to chest. He put his arms around her, holding her tight to him. Her dark-lashed lids were half down over velvet eyes. Her voice was hushed, throbbing: "I didn't mean to, at first. I didn't, really. I meant what I told you, but when I saw Floyd couldn't be frightened I—"

Spade slapped her shoulder. He said: "That's a lie. You asked Miles and me to handle it ourselves. You wanted to be sure the shadower was somebody you knew and who knew you, so they'd go with you. You got the gun from Thursby that day—that night. You had already rented the apartment at the Coronet. You had trunks there and none at the hotel and when I looked the apartment over I found a rent-receipt dated five or six days before the time you told me you rented it."

She swallowed with difficulty and her voice was humble. "Yes, that's a lie, Sam. I did intend to if Floyd—I—I can't look at you and tell you this, Sam." She pulled his head farther down until her cheek was against his cheek, her mouth by his ear, and whispered: "I knew Floyd wouldn't be easily frightened, but I thought that if he knew somebody was shadowing him either he'd— Oh, I can't say it, Sam!" She clung to him, sobbing.

Spade said: "You thought Floyd would tackle him and one or the other of them would go down. If Thursby was the one then you were rid of him. If Miles was, then you could see that Floyd was caught and you'd be rid of him. That it?"

"S-something like that."

"And when you found that Thursby didn't mean to tackle him you borrowed the gun and did it yourself. Right?"

"Yes—though not exactly."

"But exact enough. And you had that plan up your sleeve from the first. You thought Floyd would be nailed for the killing."

"I—I thought they'd hold him at least until after Captain Jacobi had arrived with the falcon and—"

"And you didn't know then that Gutman was here hunting for you. You didn't suspect that or you wouldn't have shaken your gunman. You knew Gutman was here as soon as you heard Thursby had been shot. Then you knew you needed another protector, so you came back to me. Right?"

"Yes, but—oh, sweetheart!—it wasn't only that. I would have come back to you sooner or later. From the first instant I saw you I knew—"

Spade said tenderly: "You angel! Well, if you get a good break you'll be out of San Quentin in twenty years and you can come back to me then."

She took her cheek away from his, drawing her head far back to stare up without comprehension at him.

He was pale. He said tenderly: "I hope to Christ they don't hang you, precious, by that sweet neck." He slid his hands up to caress her throat.

In an instant she was out of his arms, back against the table, crouching, both hands spread over her throat. Her face was wild-eyed, haggard. Her dry mouth opened and closed. She said in a small parched voice: "You're not—" She could get no other words out.

Spade's face was yellow-white now. His mouth smiled and there were smile-wrinkles around his glittering eyes. His voice was soft, gentle. He said: "I'm going to send you over. The chances are you'll get off with life. That means you'll be out again in twenty years. You're an angel. I'll wait for you." He cleared his throat. "If they hang you I'll always remember you."

She dropped her hands and stood erect. Her face became smooth and untroubled except for the faintest of dubious glints in her eyes. She smiled back at him, gently. "Don't, Sam, don't say that even in fun. Oh, you frightened me for a moment! I really thought you— You know you do such wild and unpredictable things that—" She broke off. She thrust her face forward and stared deep into his eyes. Her cheeks and the flesh around her mouth shivered and fear came back into her eyes. "What—? Sam!" She put her hands to her throat again and lost her erectness.

Spade laughed. His yellow-white face was damp with sweat and though he held his smile he could not hold softness in his voice. He croaked: "Don't be silly. You're taking the fall. One of us has got to take it, after the talking those birds will do. They'd hang me sure. You're likely to get a better break. Well?"

"But—but, Sam, you can't! Not after what we've been to each other. You can't—"

"Like hell I can't."

She took a long trembling breath. "You've been playing with me? Only pretending you cared—to trap me like this? You didn't—care at all? You didn't—don't—l-love me?"

"I think I do," Spade said. "What of it?" The muscles holding his smile in place stood out like wales. "I'm not Thursby. I'm not Jacobi. I won't play the sap for you."

"That is not just," she cried. Tears came to her eyes. "It's unfair. It's contemptible of you. You know it was not that. You can't say that."

"Like hell I can't," Spade said. "You came into my bed to stop me asking questions. You led me out yesterday for Gutman with that phoney call for help. Last night you came here with them and waited outside for me and came in with me. You were in my arms when the trap was sprung—I couldn't have gone for a gun if I'd had one on me and couldn't have made a fight of it if I had wanted to. And if they didn't take you away with them it was only because Gutman's got too much sense to trust you except for short stretches when he has to and because he thought I'd play the sap for you and—not wanting to hurt you—wouldn't be able to hurt him."

Brigid O'Shaughnessy blinked her tears away. She took a step towards him and stood looking him in the eyes, straight and proud. "You called me a liar," she said. "Now you are lying. You're lying if you say you don't know down in your heart that, in spite of anything I've done, I love you."

Spade made a short abrupt bow. His eyes were becoming bloodshot, but there was no other change in his damp and yellowish fixedly smiling face. "Maybe I do," he said. "What of it? I should trust you? You who arranged that nice little trick for—for my predecessor, Thursby? You who knocked off Miles, a man you had nothing against, in cold blood, just like swatting a fly, for the sake of double-crossing Thursby? You who double-crossed Gutman, Cairo, Thursby—one, two, three? You who've never played square with me for half an hour at a stretch since I've known you? I should trust you? No, no, darling. I wouldn't do it even if I could. Why should I?"

Her eyes were steady under his and her hushed voice was steady when she replied: "Why should you? If you've been playing with me, if you do not love me, there is no answer to that. If you did, no answer would be needed."

Blood streaked Spade's eyeballs now and his long-held smile had become a frightful grimace. He cleared his throat huskily and said: "Making speeches is no damned good now." He put a hand on her shoulder. The hand shook and jerked. "I don't care who loves who, I'm not going to play the sap for you. I won't walk in Thursby's and Christ knows who else's footsteps. You killed Miles and you're going over for it. I could have helped you by letting the others go and standing off the police the best way I could. It's too late for that now. I can't help you now. And I wouldn't if I could."

She put a hand on his hand on her shoulder. "Don't help me then," she whispered, "but don't hurt me. Let me go away now."

"No," he said. "I'm sunk if I haven't got you to hand over to the police when they come. That's the only thing that can keep me from going down with the others."

"You won't do that for me?"

"I won't play the sap for you."

"Don't say that, please." She took his hand from her shoulder and held it to her face. "Why must you do this to me, Sam? Surely Mr. Archer wasn't as much to you as—"

"Miles," Spade said hoarsely, "was a son of a bitch. I found that out the first week we were in business together and I meant to kick him out as soon as the year was up. You didn't do me a damned bit of harm by killing him."

"Then what?"

Spade pulled his hand out of hers. He no longer either smiled or grimaced. His wet yellow face was set hard and deeply lined. His eyes burned madly. He said: "Listen. This isn't a damned bit of good. You'll never understand me, but I'll try once more and then we'll give it up. Listen. When a man's partner is killed he's supposed to do something about it. It doesn't make any difference what you thought of him. He was your partner and you're supposed to do something about it. Then it happens we were in the detective business. Well, when one of your organization gets killed it's bad business to let the killer get away with it. It's bad all around—bad for that one organization, bad for every detective everywhere. Third, I'm a detective and expecting me to run criminals down and then let them go free is like asking a dog to catch a rabbit and let it go. It can be done, all right, and sometimes it is done, but it's not the natural thing. The only way I could have let you go was by letting Gutman and Cairo and the kid go. That's—"

"You're not serious," she said. "You don't expect me to think that these things you're saying are sufficient reason for sending me to the—"

"Wait till I'm through and then you can talk. Fourth, no matter what I wanted to do now it would be absolutely impossible for me to let you go without having myself dragged to the gallows with the others. Next, I've no reason in God's world to think I can trust you and if I did this and got away with it you'd have something on me that you could use whenever you happened to want to. That's five of them. The sixth would be that, since I've also got something on you, I couldn't be sure you wouldn't decide to shoot a hole in *me* some day. Seventh, I don't even like the idea of thinking that there might be one chance in a hundred that you'd played me for a sucker. And eighth—but that's enough. All those on one side. Maybe some of them are unimportant. I won't argue about that. But look at the number of them. Now on the other side we've got what? All we've got is the fact that maybe you love me and maybe I love you."

"You know," she whispered, "whether you do or not."

"I don't. It's easy enough to be nuts about you." He looked hungrily from her hair to her feet and up to her eyes again. "But I don't know what that amounts to. Does anybody ever? But suppose I do? What of it? Maybe next month I won't. I've been through it before—when it lasted that long. Then what? Then I'll think I played the sap. And if I did it and got sent over then I'd be sure I was the sap. Well, if I send you over I'll be sorry as hell—I'll have some rotten nights—but that'll pass. Listen." He took her by the shoulders and bent her back, leaning over her. "If that doesn't mean anything to you forget it and we'll make it this: I won't because all of me wants to—wants to say to hell with the consequences and do it—and because—God damn you—you've counted on that with me the same as you counted on that with the others." He took his hands from her shoulders and let them fall to his sides.

She put her hands up to his cheeks and drew his face down again. "Look at me," she said, "and tell me the truth. Would you have done this to me if the falcon had been real and you had been paid your money?"

"What difference does that make now? Don't be too sure I'm as crooked as I'm supposed to be. That kind of reputation might be good business—bringing in high-priced jobs and making it easier to deal with the enemy."

She looked at him, saying nothing.

He moved his shoulders a little and said: "Well, a lot of money would have been at least one more item on the other side of the scales."

She put her face up to his face. Her mouth was slightly open with lips a little thrust out. She whispered: "If you loved me you'd need nothing more on that side."

Spade set the edges of his teeth together and said through them: "I won't play the sap for you."

She put her mouth to his, slowly, her arms around him, and came into his arms. She was in his arms when the door-bell rang.

Spade, left arm around Brigid O'Shaughnessy, opened the corridor-door. Lieutenant Dundy, Detective-sergeant Tom Polhaus, and two other detectives were there.

Spade said: "Hello, Tom. Get them?"

Polhaus said: "Got them."

"Swell. Come in. Here's another one for you." Spade pressed the girl forward. "She killed Miles. And I've got some exhibits—the boy's guns, one of Cairo's, a black statuette that all the hell was about, and a thousand-dollar bill that I was supposed to be bribed with." He looked at Dundy, drew his brows together, leaned forward to peer into the

Lieutenant's face, and burst out laughing. "What in hell's the matter with your little playmate, Tom? He looks heartbroken." He laughed again. "I bet, by God! when he heard Gutman's story he thought he had me at last."

"Cut it out, Sam," Tom grumbled. "We didn't think—"

"Like hell he didn't," Spade said merrily. "He came up here with his mouth watering, though you'd have sense enough to know I'd been stringing Gutman."

"Cut it out," Tom grumbled again, looking uneasily sidewise at his superior. "Anyways we got it from Cairo. Gutman's dead. The kid had just finished shooting him up when we got there."

Spade nodded. "He ought to have expected that," he said.

Effie Perine put down her newspaper and jumped out of Spade's chair when he came into the office at a little after nine o'clock Monday morning.

He said: "Morning, angel."

"Is that—what the papers have—right?" she asked.

"Yes, ma'am." He dropped his hat on the desk and sat down. His face was pasty in color, but its lines were strong and cheerful and his eyes, though still somewhat red-veined, were clear.

The girl's brown eyes were peculiarly enlarged and there was a queer twist to her mouth. She stood beside him, staring down at him.

He raised his head, grinned, and said mockingly: "So much for your woman's intuition."

Her voice was queer as the expression on her face. "You did that, Sam, to her?"

He nodded. "Your Sam's a detective." He looked sharply at her. He put his arm around her waist, his hand on her hip. "She did kill Miles, angel," he said gently, "offhand, like that." He snapped the fingers of his other hand.

She escaped from his arm as if it had hurt her. "Don't, please, don't touch me," she said brokenly. "I know—I know you're right. You're right. But don't touch me now—not now."

Spade's face became pale as his collar.

The corridor-door's knob rattled. Effie Perine turned quickly and went into the outer office, shutting the door behind her. When she came in again she shut it behind her.

She said in a small flat voice: "Iva is here."

Spade, looking down at his desk, nodded almost imperceptibly. "Yes," he said, and shivered. "Well, send her in."

The Learned Adventure of the Dragon's Head

BY DOROTHY L. SAYERS

"UNCLE PETER!"

"Half a jiff, Gherkins. No, I don't think I'll take the Catullus, Mr. Ffolliott. After all, thirteen guineas is a bit steep without either the title or the last folio, what? But you might send me round the Vitruvius and the Satyricon when they come in; I'd like to have a look at them, anyhow. Well, old man, what is it?"

"Do come and look at these pictures, Uncle Peter. I'm sure it's an awfully old book."

Lord Peter Wimsey sighed as he picked his way out of Mr. Ffolliott's dark back shop, strewn with the flotsam and jetsam of many libraries. An unexpected outbreak of measles at Mr. Bultridge's excellent preparatory school, coinciding with the absence of the Duke and Duchess of Denver on the Continent, had saddled his lordship with his ten-year-old nephew, Viscount St. George, more commonly known as Young Jerry, Jerrykins, or Pickled Gherkins. Lord Peter was not one of those born uncles who delight old nurses by their fascinating "way with" children. He succeeded, however, in earning tolerance on honourable terms by treating the young with the same scrupulous politeness which he extended to their elders. He therefore prepared to receive Gherkins's discovery with respect, though a child's taste was not to be trusted, and the book might quite well be some horror of woolly mezzotints or an inferior modern reprint adorned with leprous electros. Nothing much better was really to be expected from the "cheap shelf" exposed to the dust of the street.

"Uncle! there's such a funny man here, with a great long nose and ears and a tail and dogs' heads all over his body. *Monstrum hoc Cracoviæ*—that's a monster, isn't it? I should jolly well think it was. What's *Cracoviæ*, Uncle Peter?"

"Oh," said Lord Peter, greatly relieved, "the Cracow monster?" A portrait of that distressing infant certainly argued a respectable antiquity. "Let's have a look. Quite right, it's a very old book—Munster's *Cosmographia Universalis.* I'm glad you know good stuff when you see it, Gherkins. What's the *Cosmographia* doing out here, Mr. Ffolliott, at five bob?"

"Well, my lord," said the bookseller, who had followed his customers to the door, "it's in a very bad state, you see; covers loose and nearly all the double-page maps missing. It came in a few weeks ago—dumped in with a collection we bought from a gentleman in Norfolk—you'll find his name in it—Dr. Conyers of Yelsall Manor. Of course, we might keep it and try to make up a complete copy when we get another example. But it's rather out of our line, as you know, classical authors being our specialty. So we just put it out to go for what it would fetch in the *status quo,* as you might say."

"Oh, look!" broke in Gherkins. "Here's a picture of a man being chopped up in little bits. What does it say about it?"

"I thought you could read Latin."

"Well, but it's all full of sort of pothooks. What do they mean?"

"They're just contractions," said Lord Peter patiently. " '*Solent quoque hujus insulæ cultores'*— It is the custom of the dwellers in this island, when they see their parents stricken in years and of no further use, to take them down into the market-place and sell them to the cannibals, who kill them and eat them for food. This they do also with younger persons when they fall into any desperate sickness."

"Ha, ha!" said Mr. Ffolliott. "Rather sharp practice on the poor cannibals. They never got anything but tough old joints or diseased meat, eh?"

"The inhabitants seem to have had thoroughly advanced notions of business," agreed his lordship.

The viscount was enthralled.

"I *do* like this book," he said; "could I buy it out of my pocket-money, please?"

"Another problem for uncles," thought Lord Peter, rapidly ransacking his recollections of the *Cosmographia* to determine whether any of its illustrations were indelicate; for he knew the duchess to be strait-laced. On consideration, he could only remember one that was dubious, and there was a sporting chance that the duchess might fail to light upon it.

"Well," he said judicially, "in your place, Gherkins, I should be inclined to buy it. It's in a bad state, as Mr. Ffolliott has honourably told you—otherwise, of course, it would be exceedingly valuable; but, apart from the lost pages, it's a very nice clean copy, and certainly worth five shillings to you, if you think of starting a collection."

Till that moment, the viscount had obviously been more impressed by the cannibals than by the state of the margins, but the idea of figuring next term at Mr. Bultridge's as a collector of rare editions had undeniable charm.

"None of the other fellows collect books," he said; "they collect stamps, mostly. I think stamps are rather ordinary, don't you, Uncle Peter? I was rather thinking of giving up stamps. Mr. Porter, who takes us for history, has got a lot of books like yours, and he is a splendid man at footer."

Rightly interpreting this reference to Mr. Porter, Lord Peter gave it as his opinion that book-collecting could be a perfectly manly pursuit. Girls, he said, practically never took it up, because it meant so much learning about dates and type-faces and other technicalities which called for a masculine brain.

"Besides," he added, "it's a very interesting book in itself, you know. Well worth dipping into."

"I'll take it, please," said the viscount, blushing a little at transacting so important and expensive a piece of business; for the duchess did not encourage lavish spending by little boys, and was strict in the matter of allowances.

Mr. Ffolliott bowed, and took the *Cosmographia* away to wrap it up.

"Are you all right for cash?" enquired Lord Peter discreetly. "Or can I be of temporary assistance?"

"No, thank you, uncle; I've got Aunt Mary's half-crown and four shillings of my pocket-money, because, you see, with the measles happening, we didn't have our dormitory spread, and I was saving up for that."

The business being settled in this gentlemanly manner, and the budding bibliophile taking personal and immediate charge of the stout, square volume, a taxi was chartered which, in due course of traffic delays, brought the *Cosmographia* to 110A Piccadilly.

"And who, Bunter, is Mr. Wilberforce Pope?"

"I do not think we know the gentleman, my lord. He is asking to see your lordship for a few minutes on business."

"He probably wants me to find a lost dog for his maiden aunt. What it is to have acquired a reputation as a sleuth! Show him in. Gherkins, if this good gentleman's business turns out to be private, you'd better retire into the dining-room."

"Yes, Uncle Peter," said the viscount dutifully. He was extended on his stomach on the library hearthrug, laboriously picking his way through the more exciting-looking bits of the *Cosmographia*, with the aid of Messrs. Lewis & Short, whose monumental compilation he had hitherto looked upon as a barbarous invention for the annoyance of upper forms.

Mr. Wilberforce Pope turned out to be a rather plump, fair gentleman in the late thirties, with a prematurely bald forehead, horn-rimmed spectacles, and an engaging manner.

"You will excuse my intrusion, won't you?" he began. "I'm sure you must think me a terrible nuisance. But I wormed your name and address out of Mr. Ffolliott. Not his fault, really. You won't blame him, will you? I positively badgered the poor man. Sat down on his doorstep and refused to go, though the boy was putting up the shutters. I'm afraid you will think me very silly when you know what it's all about. But you really mustn't hold poor Mr. Ffolliott responsible, now, will you?"

"Not at all," said his lordship. "I mean, I'm charmed and all that sort of thing. Something I can do for you about books? You're a collector, perhaps? Will you have a drink or anything?"

"Well, no," said Mr. Pope, with a faint giggle. "No, not exactly a collector. Thank you very much, just a spot—no, no, literally a spot. Thank you; no"—he glanced round the bookshelves, with their rows of rich old leather bindings—"certainly not a collector. But I happen to be —er, interested—sentimentally interested—in a purchase you made yesterday. Really, such a very small matter. You will think it foolish. But I am told you are the present owner of a copy of Munster's *Cosmographia,* which used to belong to my uncle, Dr. Conyers."

Gherkins looked up suddenly, seeing that the conversation had a personal interest for him.

"Well, that's not quite correct," said Wimsey. "I was there at the time, but the actual purchaser is my nephew. Gerald, Mr. Pope is interested in your *Cosmographia.* My nephew, Lord St. George."

"How do you do, young man," said Mr. Pope affably. "I see that the collecting spirit runs in the family. A great Latin scholar, too, I expect, eh? Ready to decline *jusjurandum* with the best of us? Ha, ha! And what are you going to do when you grow up? Be Lord Chancellor, eh? Now, I bet you think you'd rather be an engine-driver, what, what?"

"No, thank you," said the viscount, with aloofness.

"What, not an engine-driver? Well, now, I want you to be a real business man this time. Put through a book deal, you know. Your uncle will see I offer you a fair price, what? Ha, ha! Now, you see, that picture-book of yours has a great value for me that it wouldn't have for anybody else. When *I* was a little boy of your age it was one of my very greatest joys. I used to have it to look at on Sundays. Ah, dear! the happy hours I used to spend with those quaint old engravings, and the funny old maps with the ships and salamanders and '*Hic dracones*'—you know what *that* means, I dare say. What does it mean?"

"Here are dragons," said the viscount, unwittingly but still politely.

"Quite right. I *knew* you were a scholar."

"It's a very attractive book," said Lord Peter. "My nephew was quite entranced by the famous Cracow monster."

"Ah yes—a glorious monster, isn't it?" agreed Mr. Pope, with enthusiasm. "Many's the time I've fancied myself as Sir Lancelot or somebody on a white war horse, charging that monster, lance in rest, with the captive princess cheering me on. Ah! childhood! You're living the happiest days of your life, young man. You won't believe me, but you are."

"Now what is it exactly you want my nephew to do?" enquired Lord Peter a little sharply.

"Quite right, quite right. Well now, you know, my uncle, Dr. Conyers, sold his library a few months ago. I was abroad at the time, and it was only yesterday, when I went down to Yelsall on a visit, that I learnt the dear old book had gone with the rest. I can't tell you how distressed I was. I know it's not valuable—a great many pages missing and all that—but I can't bear to think of its being gone. So, purely from sentimental reasons, as I said, I hurried off to Ffolliott's to see if I could get it back. I was quite upset to find I was too late, and gave poor Mr. Ffolliott no peace till he told me the name of the purchaser. Now, you see, Lord St. George, I'm here to make you an offer for the book. Come, now, double what you gave for it. That's a good offer, isn't it, Lord Peter? Ha, ha! And you will be doing me a very great kindness as well."

Viscount St. George looked rather distressed, and turned appealingly to his uncle.

"Well, Gerald," said Lord Peter, "it's your affair, you know. What do you say?"

The viscount stood first on one leg and then on the other. The career of a book collector evidently had its problems, like other careers.

"If you please, Uncle Peter," he said with embarrassment, "may I whisper?"

"It's not usually considered the thing to whisper, Gherkins, but you could ask Mr. Pope for time to consider his offer. Or you could say you would prefer to consult me first. That would be quite in order."

"Then, if you don't mind, Mr. Pope, I should like to consult my uncle first."

"Certainly, certainly; ha, ha!" said Mr. Pope. "Very prudent to consult a collector of greater experience, what? Ah! the younger generation, eh, Lord Peter? Regular little business men already."

"Excuse us, then, for one moment," said Lord Peter, and drew his nephew into the dining-room.

"I say, Uncle Peter," said the collector breathlessly, when the door was shut, "*need* I give him my book? I don't think he's a very nice man. I *hate* people who ask you to decline nouns for them."

"Certainly you needn't, Gherkins, if you don't want to. The book is yours, and you've a right to it."

"What would *you* do, uncle?"

Before replying, Lord Peter, in the most surprising manner, tiptoed gently to the door which communicated with the library and flung it suddenly open, in time to catch Mr. Pope kneeling on the hearthrug intently turning over the pages of the coveted volume, which lay as the owner had left it. He started to his feet in a flurried manner as the door opened.

"Do help yourself, Mr. Pope, won't you?" cried Lord Peter hospitably, and closed the door again.

"What is it, Uncle Peter?"

"If you want my advice, Gherkins, I should be rather careful how you had any dealings with Mr. Pope. I don't think he's telling the truth. He called those wood-cuts engravings—though, of course, that may be just his ignorance. But I can't believe that he spent all his childhood's Sunday afternoons studying those maps and picking out the dragons in them, because, as you may have noticed for yourself, old Munster put very few dragons into his maps. They're mostly just plain maps—a bit queer to our ideas of geography, but perfectly straightforward. That was why I brought in the Cracow monster, and, you see, he thought it was some sort of dragon."

"Oh, I say, uncle! So you said that on purpose!"

"If Mr. Pope wants the *Cosmographia,* it's for some reason he doesn't want to tell us about. And, that being so, I wouldn't be in too big a hurry to sell, if the book were mine. See?"

"Do you mean there's something frightfully valuable about the book, which we don't know?"

"Possibly."

"How exciting! It's just like a story in the *Boys' Friend Library.* What am I to say to him, uncle?"

"Well, in your place I wouldn't be dramatic or anything. I'd just say you've considered the matter, and you've taken a fancy to the book and have decided not to sell. You thank him for his offer, of course."

"Yes—er, won't you say it for me, uncle?"

"I think it would look better if you did it yourself."

"Yes, perhaps it would. Will he be very cross?"

"Possibly," said Lord Peter, "but, if he is, he won't let on. Ready?"

The consulting committee accordingly returned to the library. Mr. Pope had prudently retired from the hearthrug and was examining a distant bookcase.

"Thank you very much for your offer, Mr. Pope," said the viscount, striding stoutly up to him, "but I have considered it, and I have taken a—a—a fancy for the book and decided not to sell."

"Sorry and all that," put in Lord Peter, "but my nephew's adamant about it. No, it isn't the price; he wants the book. Wish I could oblige you, but it isn't in my hands. Won't you take something else before you go? Really? Ring the bell, Gherkins. My man will see you to the lift. *Good* evening."

When the visitor had gone, Lord Peter returned and thoughtfully picked up the book.

"We were awful idiots to leave him with it, Gherkins, even for a moment. Luckily, there's no harm done."

"You don't think he found out anything while we were away, do you, uncle?" gasped Gherkins, open-eyed.

"I'm sure he didn't."

"Why?"

"He offered me fifty pounds for it on the way to the door. Gave the game away. H'm! Bunter."

"My lord?"

"Put this book in the safe and bring me back the keys. And you'd better set all the burglar alarms when you lock up."

"Oo—er!" said Viscount St. George.

On the third morning after the visit of Mr. Wilberforce Pope, the viscount was seated at a very late breakfast in his uncle's flat, after the most glorious and soul-satisfying night that ever boy experienced. He was almost too excited to eat the kidneys and bacon placed before him by Bunter, whose usual impeccable manner was not in the least impaired by a rapidly swelling and blackening eye.

It was about two in the morning that Gherkins—who had not slept very well, owing to too lavish and grown-up a dinner and theatre the evening before—became aware of a stealthy sound somewhere in the direction of the fire-escape. He had got out of bed and crept very softly into Lord Peter's room and woken him up. He had said: "Uncle Peter, I'm sure there's burglars on the fire-escape." And Uncle Peter, instead of saying, "Nonsense, Gherkins, hurry up and get back to bed," had sat up and listened and said: "By Jove, Gherkins, I believe you're right." And had sent Gherkins to call Bunter. And on his return, Gherkins, who had always regarded his uncle as a very top-hatted sort of person, actually saw him take from his handkerchief-drawer an undeniable automatic pistol.

It was at this point that Lord Peter was apotheosed from the state of Quite Decent Uncle to that of Glorified Uncle. He said:

"Look here, Gherkins, we don't know how many of these blighters there'll be, so you must be jolly smart and do anything I say sharp, on the word of command—even if I have to say 'Scoot.' Promise?"

Gherkins promised, with his heart thumping, and they sat waiting in the dark, till suddenly a little electric bell rang sharply just over the head of Lord Peter's bed and a green light shone out.

"The library window," said his lordship, promptly silencing the bell by turning a switch. "If they heard, they may think better of it. We'll give them a few minutes."

They gave them five minutes, and then crept very quietly down the passage.

"Go round by the dining-room, Bunter," said his lordship; "they may bolt that way."

With infinite precaution, he unlocked and opened the library door, and Gherkins noticed how silently the locks moved.

A circle of light from an electric torch was moving slowly along the bookshelves. The burglars had obviously heard nothing of the counter-attack. Indeed, they seemed to have troubles enough of their own to keep their attention occupied. As his eyes grew accustomed to the dim light, Gherkins made out that one man was standing holding the torch, while the other took down and examined the books. It was fascinating to watch his apparently disembodied hands move along the shelves in the torch-light.

The men muttered discontentedly. Obviously the job was proving a harder one than they had bargained for. The habit of ancient authors of abbreviating the titles on the backs of their volumes, or leaving them completely untitled, made things extremely awkward. From time to time the man with the torch extended his hand into the light. It held a piece of paper, which they anxiously compared with the title-page of a book. Then the volume was replaced and the tedious search went on.

Suddenly some slight noise—Gherkins was sure *he* did not make it; it may have been Bunter in the dining-room—seemed to catch the ear of the kneeling man.

"Wot's that?" he gasped, and his startled face swung round into view.

"Hands up!" said Lord Peter, and switched the light on.

The second man made one leap for the dining-room door, where a smash and an oath proclaimed that he had encountered Bunter. The kneeling man shot his hands up like a marionette.

"Gherkins," said Lord Peter, "do you think you can go across to that gentleman by the bookcase and relieve him of the article which is so inelegantly distending the right-hand pocket of his coat? Wait a minute. Don't on any account get between him and my pistol, and mind you take the thing out *very* carefully. There's no hurry. That's splendid. Just point it at the floor while you bring it across, would you? Thanks. Bunter has managed for himself, I see. Now run into my bedroom, and in the bottom of my wardrobe you will find a bundle of stout cord. Oh! I beg your pardon; yes, put your hands down by all means. It must be very tiring exercise."

The arms of the intruders being secured behind their backs with a neatness which Gherkins felt to be worthy of the best traditions of Sexton Blake, Lord Peter motioned his captives to sit down and despatched Bunter for whisky-and-soda.

"Before we send for the police," said Lord Peter, "you would do me a great personal favour by telling me what you were looking for, and who sent you. Ah! thanks, Bunter. As our guests are not at liberty to use their hands, perhaps you would be kind enough to assist them to a drink. Now then, say when."

"Well, you're a gentleman, guv'nor," said the First Burglar, wiping his mouth politely on his shoulder, the back of his hand not being available. "If we'd a known wot a job this wos goin' ter be, blow me if we'd a touched it. The bloke said, ses 'e, 'It's takin' candy from a baby,' 'e ses. 'The gentleman's a reg'lar softie,' 'e ses, 'one o' these 'ere sersiety toffs wiv a maggot fer old books,' that's wot 'e ses, 'an' ef yer can find this 'ere old book fer me,' 'e ses, 'there's a pony fer yer.' Well! Sech a job! 'E didn't mention as 'ow there'd be five 'undred fousand bleedin' ole books all as alike as a regiment o' bleedin' dragoons. Nor as 'ow yer kept a nice little machine-gun like that 'andy by the bedside, *nor* yet as 'ow yer was so bleedin' good at tyin' knots in a bit o' string. No—'e didn't think ter mention them things."

"Deuced unsporting of him," said his lordship. "Do you happen to know the gentleman's name?"

"No—that was another o' them things wot 'e didn't mention. 'E's a stout, fair party, wiv 'orn rims to 'is goggles and a bald 'ead. One o' these 'ere philanthropists, I reckon. A friend o' mine, wot got inter trouble onct, got work froo 'im, and the gentleman comes round and ses to 'im, 'e ses, 'Could yer find me a couple o' lads ter do a little job?' 'e ses, an' my friend, finkin' no 'arm, you see, guv'nor, but wot it might be a bit of a joke like, 'e gets 'old of my pal an' me, an' we meets the gentleman in a pub dahn Whitechapel way. W'ich we was ter meet 'im there again Friday night, us 'avin' allowed that time fer ter git 'old of the book."

"The book being, if I may hazard a guess, the *Cosmographia Universalis?*"

"Sumfink like that, guv'nor. I got its jaw-breakin' name wrote down on a bit o' paper, wot my pal 'ad in 'is 'and. Wot did yer do wiv that 'ere bit o' paper, Bill?"

"Well, look here," said Lord Peter, "I'm afraid I must send for the police, but I think it likely, if you give us your assistance to get hold of your gentleman, whose name I strongly suspect to be Wilberforce Pope, that you will get off pretty easily. Telephone the police, Bunter, and then go and put something on that eye of yours. Gherkins, we'll give these gentlemen another drink, and then I think perhaps you'd better hop back to bed; the fun's over. No? Well, put a good thick coat on, there's a good fellow, because what your mother will say to me if you catch a cold I don't like to think."

So the police had come and taken the burglars away, and now Detective-Inspector Parker, of Scotland Yard, a great personal friend of Lord Peter's, sat toying with a cup of coffee and listening to the story.

"But what's the matter with the jolly old book, anyhow, to make it so popular?" he demanded.

"I don't know," replied Wimsey, "but after Mr. Pope's little visit the other day I got kind of intrigued about it and had a look through it. I've got a hunch it may turn out rather valuable, after all. Unsuspected beauties and all that sort of thing. If only Mr. Pope had been a trifle more accurate in his facts, he might have got away with something to which I feel pretty sure he isn't entitled. Anyway, when I'd seen—what I saw, I wrote off to Dr. Conyers of Yelsall Manor, the late owner——"

"Conyers, the cancer man?"

"Yes. He's done some pretty important research in his time, I fancy.

Getting on now, though; about seventy-eight, I fancy. I hope he's more honest than his nephew, with one foot in the grave like that. Anyway, I wrote (with Gherkins's permission, naturally) to say we had the book and had been specially interested by something we found there, and would he be so obliging as to tell us something of its history. I also——"

"But what did you find in it?"

"I don't think we'll tell him yet, Gherkins, shall we? I like to keep policemen guessing. As I was saying, when you so rudely interrupted me, I also asked him whether he knew anything about his good nephew's offer to buy it back. His answer has just arrived. He says he knows of nothing specially interesting about the book. It has been in the library untold years, and the tearing out of the maps must have been done a long time ago by some family vandal. He can't think why his nephew should be so keen on it, as he certainly never pored over it as a boy. In fact, the old man declares the engaging Wilberforce has never even set foot in Yelsall Manor to his knowledge. So much for the fire-breathing monsters and the pleasant Sunday afternoons."

"Naughty Wilberforce!"

"M'm. Yes. So, after last night's little dust-up, I wired the old boy we were tooling down to Yelsall to have a heart-to-heart talk with him about his picture-book and his nephew."

"Are you taking the book down with you?" asked Parker. "I can give you a police escort for it if you like."

"That's not a bad idea," said Wimsey. "We don't know where the insinuating Mr. Pope may be hanging out, and I wouldn't put it past him to make another attempt."

"Better be on the safe side," said Parker. "I can't come myself, but I'll send down a couple of men with you."

"Good egg," said Lord Peter. "Call up your myrmidons. We'll get a car round at once. You're coming, Gherkins, I suppose? God knows what your mother would say. Don't ever be an uncle, Charles; it's frightfully difficult to be fair to all parties."

Yelsall Manor was one of those large, decaying country mansions which speak eloquently of times more spacious than our own. The original late Tudor construction had been masked by the addition of a wide frontage in the Italian manner, with a kind of classical portico surmounted by a pediment and approached by a semi-circular flight of steps. The grounds had originally been laid out in that formal manner in which grove nods to grove and each half duly reflects the other. A late owner, however, had burst out into the more eccentric sort of landscape gardening which is associated with the name of Capability Brown. A Chinese pagoda, somewhat resembling Sir William Chambers's erection in Kew Gardens, but smaller, rose out of a grove of laurustinus towards the eastern extremity of the house, while at the rear appeared a large artificial lake, dotted with numerous islands, on which odd little temples, grottos, tea-houses, and bridges peeped out from among clumps of shrubs, once ornamental, but now sadly overgrown. A boat-house, with wide eaves like the designs on a willow-pattern plate, stood at one corner, its landing-stage fallen into decay and wreathed with melancholy weeds.

"My disreputable old ancestor, Cuthbert Conyers, settled down here when he retired from the sea in 1732," said Dr. Conyers, smiling faintly. "His elder brother died childless, so the black sheep returned to the fold with the determination to become respectable and found a family. I fear he did not succeed altogether. There were very queer tales as to where his money came from. He is said to have been a pirate, and to have sailed with the notorious Captain Blackbeard. In the village, to this day, he is remembered and spoken of as Cut-throat Conyers. It used to make the old man very angry, and there is an unpleasant story of his slicing the ears off a groom who had been heard to call him 'Old Cut-throat.' He was not an uncultivated person, though. It was he who did the landscape-gardening round at the back, and he built the pagoda for his telescope. He was reputed to study the Black Art, and there were certainly a number of astrological works in the library with his name on the fly-leaf, but probably the telescope was only a remembrance of his seafaring days.

"Anyhow, towards the end of his life he became more and more odd and morose. He quarrelled with his family, and turned his younger son out of doors with his wife and children. An unpleasant old fellow.

"On his deathbed he was attended by the parson—a good, earnest, God-fearing sort of man, who must have put up with a deal of insult in carrying out what he firmly believed to be the sacred duty of reconciling the old man to this shamefully treated son. Eventually, 'Old Cut-throat' relented so far as to make a will, leaving to the younger son 'My treasure which I have buried in Munster.' The parson represented to him that it was useless to bequeath a treasure unless he also bequeathed the information where to find it, but the horrid old pirate only chuckled spitefully, and said that, as he had been at the pains to collect the treasure, his son might well be at the pains of looking for it. Further than that he would not go, and so he died, and I dare say went to a very bad place.

"Since then the family has died out, and I am the sole representative of the Conyers, and heir to the treasure, whatever and wherever it is, for it was never discovered. I do not suppose it was very honestly come by, but, since it would be useless now to try and find the original owners, I imagine I have a better right to it than anybody living.

"You may think it very unseemly, Lord Peter, that an old, lonely man like myself should be greedy for a hoard of pirate's gold. But my whole life has been devoted to studying the disease of cancer, and I believe myself to be very close to a solution of one part at least of the terrible problem. Research costs money, and my limited means are very nearly exhausted. The property is mortgaged up to the hilt, and I do most urgently desire to complete my experiments before I die, and to leave a sufficient sum to found a clinic where the work can be carried on.

"During the last year I have made very great efforts to solve the mystery of 'Old Cut-throat's' treasure. I have been able to leave much of my experimental work in the most capable hands of my assistant, Dr. Forbes, while I pursued my researches with the very slender clue I had to go upon. It was the more expensive and difficult that Cuthbert had left no indication in his will whether Münster in Germany or Munster in Ireland was the hiding-place of the treasure. My journeys and my search in both places cost money and brought me no further on my quest. I returned, disheartened, in August, and found myself obliged to sell my library, in order to defray my expenses and obtain a little money with which to struggle on with my sadly delayed experiments."

"Ah!" said Lord Peter. "I begin to see light."

The old physician looked at him enquiringly. They had finished tea, and were seated around the great fireplace in the study. Lord Peter's interested questions about the beautiful, dilapidated old house and estate had led the conversation naturally to Dr. Conyers's family, shelving for the time the problem of the *Cosmographia*, which lay on a table beside them.

"Everything you say fits into the puzzle," went on Wimsey, "and I think there's not the smallest doubt what Mr. Wilberforce Pope was after, though how he knew that you had the *Cosmographia* here I couldn't say."

"When I disposed of the library, I sent him a catalogue," said Dr. Conyers. "As a relative, I thought he ought to have the right to buy anything he fancied. I can't think why he didn't secure the book then, instead of behaving in this most shocking fashion."

Lord Peter hooted with laughter.

"Why, because he never tumbled to it till afterwards," he said. "And oh, dear, how wild he must have been! I forgive him everything. Although," he added, "I don't want to raise your hopes too high, sir, for, even when we've solved old Cuthbert's riddle, I don't know that we're very much nearer to the treasure."

"To the *treasure?*"

"Well, now, sir. I want you first to look at this page, where there's a name scrawled in the margin. Our ancestors had an untidy way of signing their possessions higgledy-piggledy in margins instead of in a decent, Christian way in the fly-leaf. This is a handwriting of somewhere about Charles I's reign: 'Jac: Coniers.' I take it that goes to prove that the book was in the possession of your family at any rate as early as the first half of the seventeenth century, and has remained there ever since. Right. Now we turn to page 1099, where we find a description of the discoveries of Christopher Columbus. It's headed, you see, by a kind of map, with some of Mr. Pope's monsters swimming about in it, and apparently representing the Canaries, or, as they used to be called, the Fortunate Isles. It doesn't look much more accurate than old maps usually are, but I take

Liber V. 1099

DE NOVIS INSVLIS, quomodo, quando, & per quem illæ inuentæ sint.

CHristophorus Columbus natione Genuensis, cùm diu in aula regis Hispan' rum deuersatus fuisset, animum induxit, ut hactenus inaccessas orbis partes p aorares Petut praeterea à rege ut uoto suo non deesset, futurũ sibi & toti Hisp

it the big island on the right is meant for Lanzarote, and the two nearest to it may be Teneriffe and Gran Canaria."

"But what's that writing in the middle?"

"That's just the point. The writing is later than 'Jac: Coniers's' signature; I should put it about 1700—but, of course, it may have been written a good deal later still. I mean, a man who was elderly in 1730 would still use the style of writing he adopted as a young man, especially if, like your ancestor the pirate, he had spent the early part of his life in outdoor pursuits and hadn't done much writing."

"Do you mean to say, Uncle Peter," broke in the viscount excitedly, "that that's 'Old Cut-throat's' writing?"

"I'd be ready to lay a sporting bet it is. Look here, sir, you've been scouring round Münster in Germany and Munster in Ireland—but how about good old Sebastian Munster here in the library at home?"

"God bless my soul! Is it possible?"

"It's pretty nearly certain, sir. Here's what he says, written, you see, round the head of that sort of sea-dragon:

Hic in capite draconis ardet perpetuo Sol.
Here the sun shines perpetually upon the Dragon's Head.

Rather doggy Latin—sea-dog Latin, you might say, in fact."

"I'm afraid," said Dr. Conyers, "I must be very stupid, but I can't see where that leads us."

"No; 'Old Cut-throat' was rather clever. No doubt he thought that, if anybody read it, they'd think it was just an allusion to where it says, further down, that 'the islands were called *Fortunatæ* because of the wonderful temperature of the air and the clemency of the skies.' But the cunning old astrologer up in his pagoda had a meaning of his own. Here's a little book published in 1678—Middleton's *Practical Astrology*—just the sort of popular handbook an amateur like 'Old Cut-throat' would use. Here you are: 'If in your figure you find Jupiter or Venus or *Dragon's head*, you may be confident there is Treasure in the place supposed. . . . If you find *Sol* to be the Significator of the hidden Treasure, you may conclude there is Gold, or some jewels.' You know, sir, I think we may conclude it."

"Dear me!" said Dr. Conyers. "I believe, indeed, you must be right. And I am ashamed to think that if anybody had suggested to me that it could ever be profitable to me to learn the terms of astrology, I should have replied in my vanity that my time was too valuable to waste on such foolishness. I am deeply indebted to you."

"Yes," said Gherkins, "but where *is* the treasure, uncle?"

"That's just it," said Lord Peter. "The map is very vague; there is no latitude or longitude given; and the directions, such as they are, seem not even to refer to any spot on the islands, but to some place in the middle of the sea. Besides, it is nearly two hundred years since the treasure was hidden, and it may already have been found by somebody or other."

Dr. Conyers stood up.

"I am an old man," he said, "but I still have some strength. If I can by any means get together the money for an expedition, I will not rest till I have made every possible effort to find the treasure and to endow my clinic."

"Then, sir, I hope you'll let me give a hand to the good work," said Lord Peter.

Dr. Conyers had invited his guests to stay the night, and, after the excited viscount had been packed off to bed, Wimsey and the old man sat late, consulting maps and diligently reading Munster's chapter *"De*

Novis Insulis," in the hope of discovering some further clue. At length, however, they separated, and Lord Peter went upstairs, the book under his arm. He was restless, however, and, instead of going to bed, sat for a long time at his window, which looked out upon the lake. The moon, a few days past the full, was riding high among small, windy clouds, and picked out the sharp eaves of the Chinese tea-houses and the straggling tops of the unpruned shrubs. 'Old Cut-throat' and his landscape-gardening! Wimsey could have fancied that the old pirate was sitting now beside his telescope in the preposterous pagoda, chuckling over his riddling testament and counting the craters of the moon. "If *Luna*, there is silver." The water of the lake was silver enough; there was a great smooth path across it, broken by the sinister wedge of the boat-house, the black shadows of the islands, and, almost in the middle of the lake, a decayed fountain, a writhing Celestial dragon-shape, spiny-backed and ridiculous.

Wimsey rubbed his eyes. There was something strangely familiar about the lake; from moment to moment it assumed the queer unreality of a place which one recognises without having ever known it. It was like one's first sight of the Leaning Tower of Pisa—too like its picture to be quite believable. Surely, thought Wimsey, he knew that elongated island on the right, shaped rather like a winged monster, with its two little clumps of buildings. And the island to the left of it, like the British Isles, but warped out of shape. And the third island, between the others, and nearer. The three formed a triangle, with the Chinese fountain in the centre, the moon shining steadily upon its dragon head. *"Hic in capite draconis ardet perpetuo——"*

Lord Peter sprang up with a loud exclamation, and flung open the door into the dressing-room. A small figure wrapped in an eiderdown hurriedly uncoiled itself from the window-seat.

"I'm sorry, Uncle Peter," said Gherkins. "I was so *dreadfully* wide awake, it wasn't any good staying in bed."

"Come here," said Lord Peter, "and tell me if I'm mad or dreaming. Look out of the window and compare it with the map—Old Cut-throat's 'New Islands.' He made 'em, Gherkins; he put 'em here. Aren't they laid out just like the Canaries? Those three islands in a triangle, and the fourth down here in the corner? And the boat-house where the big ship is in the picture? And the dragon fountain where the dragon's head is? Well, my son, that's where your hidden treasure's gone to. Get your things on, Gherkins, and damn the time when all good little boys should be in bed! We're going for a row on the lake, if there's a tub in that boat-house that'll float."

"Oh, Uncle Peter! This is a *real* adventure!"

"All right," said Wimsey. "Fifteen men on the dead man's chest, and all that! Yo-ho-ho, and a bottle of Johnny Walker! Pirate expedition fitted out in dead of night to seek hidden treasure and explore the Fortunate Isles! Come on, crew!"

Lord Peter hitched the leaky dinghy to the dragon's knobbly tail and climbed out carefully, for the base of the fountain was green and weedy.

"I'm afraid it's your job to sit there and bail, Gherkins," he said. "All the best captains bag the really interesting jobs for themselves. We'd better start with the head. If the old blighter said head, he probably meant it." He passed an arm affectionately round the creature's neck for support, while he methodically pressed and pulled the various knobs and bumps of its anatomy. "It seems beastly solid, but I'm sure there's a spring somewhere. You won't forget to bail, will you? I'd simply hate to turn round and find the boat gone. Pirate chief marooned on island and all that. Well, it isn't its back hair, anyhow. We'll try its eyes. I say, Gherkins, I'm sure I felt something move, only it's frightfully stiff. We might have thought to bring some oil. Never mind; it's dogged as does it. It's coming. It's coming. Booh! Pah!"

A fierce effort thrust the rusted knob inwards, releasing a huge spout of water into his face from the dragon's gaping throat. The fountain, dry for many years, soared rejoicingly heavenwards, drenching the treasure-hunters, and making rainbows in the moonlight.

"I suppose this is 'Old Cut-throat's' idea of humour," grumbled Wimsey, retreating cautiously round the dragon's neck. "And now I can't turn it off again. Well, dash it all, let's try the other eye."

He pressed for a few moments in vain. Then, with a grinding clang, the bronze wings of the monster clapped down to its sides, revealing a deep square hole, and the fountain ceased to play.

"Gherkins!" said Lord Peter, "we've done it. (But don't neglect bailing on that account!) There's a box here. And it's beastly heavy. No; all right, I can manage. Gimme the boat-hook. Now I do hope the old sinner really did have a treasure. What a bore if it's only one of his little jokes. Never mind—hold the boat steady. There. Always remember, Gherkins, that you can make quite an effective crane with a boat-hook and a stout pair of braces. Got it? That's right. Now for home and beauty. . . . Hullo! what's all that?"

As he paddled the boat round, it was evident that something was happening down by the boat-house. Lights were moving about, and a sound of voices came across the lake.

"They think we're burglars, Gherkins. Always misunderstood. Give way, my hearties—

> *"A-roving, a-roving, since roving's been my ru-i-in,*
> *I'll go no more a-roving with you, fair maid."*

"Is that you, my lord?" said a man's voice as they drew in to the boat-house.

"Why, it's our faithful sleuths!" cried his lordship. "What's the excitement?"

"We found this fellow sneaking round the boat-house," said the man from Scotland Yard. "He says he's the old gentleman's nephew. Do you know him, my lord?"

"I rather fancy I do," said Wimsey. "Mr. Pope, I think. Good evening. Were you looking for anything? Not a treasure, by any chance? Because we've just found one. Oh! don't say that. *Maxima reverentia*, you know. Lord St. George is of tender years. And, by the way, thank you so much for sending your delightful friends to call on me last night. Oh, yes, Thompson, I'll charge him all right. You there, doctor? Splendid. Now, if anybody's got a spanner or anything handy, we'll have a look at Great-grandpapa Cuthbert. And if he turns out to be old iron, Mr. Pope, you'll have had an uncommonly good joke for your money."

An iron bar was produced from the boat-house and thrust under the hasp of the chest. It creaked and burst. Dr. Conyers knelt down tremulously and threw open the lid.

There was a little pause.

"The drinks are on you, Mr. Pope," said Lord Peter. "I think, doctor, it ought to be a jolly good hospital when it's finished."

"Why," [illegible] "should I be told [illegible]? What [illegible] this [illegible]?"

"We found this fellow prowling round the boathouse," said the man from Scotland Yard. "He says he's the old gentleman's nephew. Do you know him, my lord?"

"I rather fancy I do," said Wimsey. "Mr. Pope, I think. Good evening. Were you looking for anything? Not a treasure, by any chance? Because we've just found one. Oh! don't say that. Maximus [illegible] you know. Uncle George's [illegible] of tender years, and by the way, thank you so much for sending your delightful friends to call on me last night. Oh, yes, Thompson, I'll charge him all right. You there, doctor? [illegible] Now, if anybody's got a [illegible] or anything handy, we'll have a look at Great-grandpapa Cuthbert. And if it turns out to be old iron, Mr. Pope, you'll have had an uncommonly good joke for your pains."

An iron bar was produced from the boathouse and thrust under the hasp of the chest. It creaked and burst. The doctor knelt down eagerly and threw open the lid.

There was a little pause.

"The drinks are on you, Mr. Pope," said Lord Peter. "I think [illegible] going to be [illegible] good reading when it's finished!"

The Case of the Crying Swallow

BY ERLE STANLEY GARDNER

CHAPTER I

PERRY MASON, tilted back in his walnut desk chair, was studying a recent decision of the state supreme court when Della Street, his secretary, opened the door from the outer office, advanced to the desk and quietly laid ten crisp one-hundred-dollar bills on the blotter.

Mason, too engrossed to notice what she was doing, continued his reading.

Della Street said, "A client sends his card."

Mason straightened in the swivel chair and for the first time caught sight of the money which Della Street had so neatly spread out.

"He said his name was Mr. Cash," Della Street explained. "Then he handed me ten one-hundred-dollar bills and said these were his cards."

Mason grinned. "So the black market begins to turn yellow. What does Mr. Cash look like?"

"He's a floor walker."

Mason raised his eyebrows, glanced at the cash. "A *floorwalker?*"

"No, no, not a department store floorwalker! I mean that he's a floor *walker*, the same as you are. He paces the floor when he's worried. He's doing a carpet marathon out there right now."

Mason said, "I don't know whether civilization is breaking down the character of our criminals or whether the black market operators haven't been in business long enough to develop intestinal stamina. The bootleggers were a tougher breed. My own opinion is that these black market operators simply haven't had time to become accustomed to the fact that they're on the other side of society's legal fence. Give them another eighteen months and they'll be as tough as the old gangsters."

"He definitely *isn't* a black market operator," Della Street said positively. "He's distinguished-looking, has a slight limp, is deeply tanned, and . . . and I've seen him somewhere before. Oh, now I have it. I've seen his picture!"

"Give."

"Major Claude L. Winnett, polo player, yachtsman, millionaire playboy. When the war came, he quit being a playboy and became an aviator, bagged a whole flock of German planes and then was captured, liberated last fall, discharged because of his wound, returned to his doting mother and . . ."

Mason nodded. "I remember reading about the chap. He got a citation or something. Didn't he get married?"

"About four or five weeks ago," Della Street said. "That was where I first saw his picture—in the paper. Then again last week a reporter for the society supplement paid a visit to the Winnett home—one of the old-time country estates with stables of polo ponies, riding trails, hedges, private golf courses . . ."

"Show him in," Mason said. "But let him know first that you've placed him. It may save time."

Major Winnett, lean, fit, bronzed, and nervous, followed Della Street into the office. The excitement and anxiety of his manner were more noticeable than his slight limp. A well-modulated voice and patrician bearing made his surrender to emotion all the more impressive.

"Mr. Mason," he said as soon as he was in the room, "I had intended to keep my identity a secret and ask you to represent another person. Now that your secretary has recognized me, I'll put my cards on the table. My wife has disappeared. She needs your help. She's in trouble of some sort."

"Tell me about it," Mason said.

Major Winnett reached into his inside pocket, took out a folded piece of letter paper, and handed it to Mason.

The lawyer opened the letter, read:

"Claude, my darling, there are some things that I can't drag *you* into. I thought I had a way out, but I guess I didn't. Our happiness was such a beautiful thing. But beautiful things are always fragile. Don't worry about anything. I am responsible, and I am not going to let you suffer because of what you have done for me. Good-by, my darling.—MARCIA"

"What does she mean by saying she's responsible and not letting you suffer because of what you have done for her?" Mason asked.

Major Winnett's manner was uneasy. "My marriage was not exactly in accordance with the wishes of my mother. I went ahead with it despite her objections."

"Spoken objections?"

"Certainly not."

"Yet your wife knew of them?"

"Women feel many things without the necessity of words, Mr. Mason. I want you to find her and straighten things out for her."

"And then report to you?"

"Certainly."

Mason shook his head.

For a moment there was silence, broken only by the faint rumble of traffic and the breathing of Mason's client. Then Major Winnett said, "Very well. Do it your way."

"When did your wife leave?"

"Last night. I found this note on the dresser about midnight. I thought she had previously retired."

"Is there any reason why your wife would have been vulnerable to what we might call an outside influence?"

"Absolutely not—if you mean blackmail."

"Then tell me why your wife wasn't free to come to you with her troubles."

"I don't know, unless it's on account of my mother."

"What about her?"

"My mother is a very unusual person. When my father died, a dozen years ago, mother stepped in and took charge. She is living in a bygone era. She has old-fashioned ideas."

"The proprieties?" Mason asked.

"Not so much the proprieties as . . . well, class distinctions, the aristocracy of wealth and that sort of thing. I think she would have been more happy if I had married someone more in our own set."

"Who, for instance?"

"Oh, I didn't say any particular person," Major Winnett said hastily.

"I know you didn't. That's why I'm asking you."

"Well, perhaps Daphne Rexford."

"You think this caused your wife to leave?"

"No, no. Not directly. My mother has accepted Marcia into the family. Whatever may have been Mother's ideas about the marriage, Marcia is now one of us—a Winnett."

"Then suppose you tell me what you mean when you say 'not directly.'"

"Marcia would have done anything rather than subject me to any notoriety because she knew how my mother felt about that. You see, Mr. Mason, we live in a large, rather old-fashioned estate surrounded by hedges, with our private bridle paths, high wire fences, locked gates, no trespassing signs, and all the rest. The more the world moves in a way that meets with the disapproval of my mother, the more she tries to shut that part of the world out from her life."

"Anything unusual happen within the last few days?" the lawyer asked, probing his client's mind.

"A burglar entered our house Tuesday night."

"Take anything?" Mason asked.

"My wife's jewelry, valued at perhaps twenty-five or thirty thousand dollars, although I don't suppose a person could get that for it. It had been insured at fifteen thousand dollars."

"Had been?" Mason asked.

"Yes, my wife canceled the insurance. As it happened, only the day before the burglary."

Major Winnett glanced almost appealingly at the lawyer.

"Canceled her insurance," Mason said, "and then twenty-four hours later the burglary took place?"

"Yes."

"And you fail to see any connection between those two facts?"

"I am certain there is none," Major Winnett said hastily. "My wife's reasoning was absolutely sound. She had carried this insurance policy and paid high premiums on it while she was living in apartments and hotels because she wanted to keep her jewelry with her and wanted to wear it. But when she married me and came to live in Vista del Mar, it seemed hardly necessary to continue paying high premiums."

"Tell me more about that burglary and why you didn't report it to the police."

"How did you know we didn't report it to the police?"

"Your facial expression," Mason said dryly.

"That was purely on account of the fact that my mother . . . well, you know, the newspaper notoriety and . . ."

"Tell me about the burglary," Mason said.

Major Winnett spoke with the rhythm of a man who is carefully choosing his words. "I am a sound sleeper, Mr. Mason. My wife is not. On Tuesday night I was awakened by the sound of my wife's scream."

"What time?"

"I didn't look at my watch at the time but I did look at it a few minutes later and as nearly as I can place the time, it was around quarter to one."

"How long had you been in bed?"

"We retired about eleven."

"And you slept until your wife screamed?"

"Well, I have, in the back of my consciousness, a vague recollection of a swallow crying."

Mason raised his eyebrows.

"You are, of course, familiar," Major Winnett went on hastily, "with the famed swallows of the Mission of San Juan Capistrano?"

Mason nodded.

"The nesting place of those swallows is not confined to the Mission. They get more publicity at the Mission because they leave on a certain day and return on a certain day. I believe that the time of their return can be predicted almost to the hour. A very unusual sense of keeping a calendar. How they are able to return year after year . . ."

"And you have some of those swallows at your house?" Mason interrupted.

"Yes. They are a nuisance. Their nests are built out of mud, and are fastened to the eaves. Our gardener knocks them down as soon as he detects the birds building, but in case one of them eludes his vigilance and the nest is built, then we don't disturb it, because the birds lay eggs very soon after the nests are built."

"Go on," Mason said.

"Well, this particular swallow's nest was located in a very unfortunate place. The main residence at Vista del Mar is a large Spanish-type house with the tile roofs and a white exterior. My bedroom is on the second floor with a projecting balcony. The tile projects out over that balcony and the birds had made their nest in such a place that if a man climbed over the balcony rail, he'd be within a few feet of the nest."

"And a man did climb over that rail?"

"Evidently that is what happened. We found a ladder that had been placed against the side of the house. The intruder had climbed up the ladder. In doing so, he disturbed the swallows. When they're disturbed, they have a peculiar throaty chirp."

"And you heard that?"

"I either heard it or dreamed that I did. My wife doesn't remember it, and she is a much lighter sleeper than I am, but I don't think I was mistaken."

"Then you went back to sleep?"

"Apparently I did. I remember hearing the protestations of the swallows and, while I was aroused from a sound slumber, I didn't thoroughly waken. I dozed off again and was soon in a deep sleep from which I was awakened by my wife's scream."

"She saw the burglar?"

"She was aroused by some noise in the room. She saw this man standing at her dresser. At first she thought I had gone to the dresser for some purpose and she started to speak to me. Then she looked over and saw that I was in my bed . . ."

"There was enough light for that?"

"Yes. A late moon was giving some light."

"What happened?"

"The man heard the motion—some sound of the bed springs, I guess. He darted out to the balcony. My wife screamed and that awakened me, but it took me a few seconds to get oriented, to realize where I was and what was happening. By that time the man had made his escape."

"And you think the swallows were crying because the man disturbed them?"

"That's right. When he entered the building, he must have climbed over the balcony rail and touched the nest."

"When did your wife cancel the insurance?"

"Monday afternoon."

Mason toyed with his lead pencil, asked abruptly, "What happened Monday morning?"

"We all four breakfasted together."

"Who's the fourth?"

"Helen Custer, my mother's nurse."

"Your mother isn't well?"

"She has a bad heart. Her physician feels it's advisable to have a nurse in the house."

"She's been with you long?"

"For three years. We consider her very much one of the family."

"You breakfasted and then what?"

"I wrote letters. My mother . . . I don't know exactly where she *did* go. Marcia went riding."

"Where?"

"Heavens, I don't know. One of our bridle paths."

Mason said, "I believe it rained Sunday night, didn't it?"

Major Winnett looked at him curiously. "What," he asked, "does that have to do with it? . . . I mean what is the significance?"

"Skip it," Mason interrupted. "What happened next?"

"Nothing. My wife returned about eleven."

"When did she tell you she was going to cancel the insurance?"

"That was just before lunch. She telephoned to the insurance company; and then she wrote them a letter confirming her action."

"Did you notice anything unusual in your wife's manner?"

"Nothing," Major Winnett said so swiftly that it seemed the answer had been poised on his tongue, waiting merely for Mason's question.

Mason said, "Well, it's ten-thirty. I want to get Paul Drake of the Drake Detective Agency. We'll make a start out at your place and go on from there. I'll leave here about eleven. Does your mother know your wife has left?"

Major Winnett cleared his throat. "I told her my wife was visiting friends."

"How will you account for us?" Mason asked.

"How many will there be?"

"My secretary Miss Street, Paul Drake the detective, myself, and perhaps one of Mr. Drake's assistants."

Major Winnett said, "I'm working on a mining deal. I can explain to my mother that you're giving me some advice in connection with that. Your detective wouldn't mind posing as a mining expert?"

"Not at all."

"You'll come to the house and . . . will you want to stay there?"

Mason nodded. "I think we'd better. And I'll want photographs and a description of your wife."

Major Winnett took an envelope from his inside pocket, extracted nearly a dozen photographs. "I brought these along. They're snapshots. She's twenty-five, redheaded, bluish gray eyes, five feet two, a hundred and fifteen, and as nearly as I can tell from checking the clothes that are left in the closet, she's wearing a checkered suit, sort of a gray plaid. It's the one that she's wearing in this picture."

Mason studied the photographs, then reached for the envelope. "All right," he said, "we'll be out. You can go on ahead and see that all necessary arrangements are made."

CHAPTER II

THE CITY of Silver Strand Beach lay in a sheltered cove on the lee-side of a peninsula. The Winnett estate dominated this peninsula, its wire fences with forbidding "no trespassing" signs stretching for some two and a half miles. The Spanish-type house, perched on the summit some five hundred feet above the ocean, commanded a view in all directions.

Mason's car swept around the last curve in the graveled driveway, came to a stop in front of the imposing house as he said to Paul Drake, "I think the cancellation of that insurance policy is, perhaps, the first indication of what she had in mind, Paul. And I think that may have some connection with the horseback ride she took Monday morning."

Paul Drake's professionally lugubrious face didn't change expression in the least. "Anything to go on, Perry?"

"It rained Sunday night," Mason said. "It hasn't rained since. If you could find the path she took, it's quite possible you might be able to track her horse."

"For the love of Pete, do I have to ride a horse?"

"Sure. Tell the groom you'd like to ride. Ask him about some of the bridle paths."

"I can't see anything from a horse," Drake complained. "When a horse trots, I bounce. When I bounce, I see double."

"After you get out of sight of the house, you can lead the horse," Mason suggested.

"How about me?" Della Street asked.

"Try and get acquainted with the nurse," Mason suggested, "and take a look around."

Major Winnett himself answered Mason's ring; and the swift efficiency with which he installed them in rooms, introduced them to his mother, and Helen Custer, the nurse, showed that he had already made his preliminary explanations.

While Drake departed for the stables, after having expressed his spurious enthusiasm for horseflesh, Major Winnett took Mason on a tour of inspection.

Once they were alone in the upper corridors, Major Winnett asked quickly and in a low voice, "Is there anything in particular you want to see?"

"I'd like to get familiar with the entire house," Mason said guardedly. "But you might begin by showing me *your* room."

Major Winnett's room was on the south side. Glass doors opened on the balcony, from which the ocean could be seen shimmering in the sunlight.

"That's the swallow's nest?" Mason asked, indicating a gourd-like projection of mud which extended from the tiles just above the balcony.

"That's the swallow's nest. You can see that a person climbing a ladder . . ."

"Was the ladder already there?" Mason asked.

"Yes. The handy man had been doing some work on a pane of glass on the side of the bedroom. He had left the ladder in position that night, because he intended to finish it the next morning. Damn careless of him."

"In that case," Mason said, "your thief was an opportunist, since he didn't bring his own ladder."

"Yes, I suppose so."

"One who was, moreover, apparently familiar with the house. How about your servants?"

"You can't ever tell," Major Winnett said. "Particularly these days. But I *think* they're all right. Mother pays good wages and most of the help have been with her for some time. However, she *is* rather strict at times and there is a certain turnover."

"You own virtually all of the land on this peninsula?"

"Quite a bit of it, but not all of it. In a moment we'll go up to the observation tower and I can show you around from there. Generally, we take in about three-fourths of the peninsula. There is a strip out on the end where the county maintains a public camp ground."

"The public can reach that camp without crossing your estate?"

"Yes. Our line runs along by the grove of trees—beautiful oaks that offer a place for picnics. Picnickers are always scattering papers and plates around. We try to persuade them to go on down to the public camp grounds on the end of the peninsula."

"So anyone who came out here at night would have been definitely a trespasser?"

"Quite definitely."

"And having taken that risk, must have had some specific objective in mind, and would, therefore, if he were at all prudent, have arranged some manner of reaching his objective?"

"Yes, I suppose so."

"Therefore," Mason went on, "your burglar must either have been someone who knew that the ladder was here, or else it was an inside job."

"But how could anyone have known the ladder was here?"

Mason said, "If you can see the camp and the picnic grounds from here, it is quite possible that someone in the camp or picnic grounds could see the house."

"Yes, the house is quite a landmark. You can see it for miles."

"And perhaps a man, looking up here about dusk and noticing that a ladder had been left in place, would have decided it might be worthwhile to climb that ladder."

"Yes, I suppose so. However, Mr. Mason, I can't see that there is the slightest connection between the theft of my wife's jewelry and her disappearance."

"Probably not," Mason said.

They finished their tour with a trip up a flight of stairs to the place which Major Winnett described as "the tower."

Here was a belfry-like room, fifteen feet square, with plate glass windows on all sides. In the center, a pair of eighteen power binoculars attached to a swivel on a tripod could be turned and locked in any position.

"In times past," Major Winnett explained, "when there was more merchant shipping up and down the coast, we used to enjoy looking the boats over. You see, these binoculars can be swung in any direction. Now I'll point them toward town and . . ."

"Just a minute," Mason warned sharply, as Major Winnett reached for the binoculars. "They seem to be pointed toward that grove of trees. If you don't mind, I'd like to look through them."

"Why certainly. Help yourself."

Mason looked through the powerful prismatic binoculars. The right eye showed only a blur, but the left showed a shaded spot under the clump of big live oaks where the road crossed a mesa before dipping down through a little canyon to again come into view as it swung out toward the picnic and camping grounds on the extreme tip of the promontory.

"There's no central focusing screw," Major Winnett explained. "You have to adjust each eyepiece individually. Perhaps . . ."

"Yes, so I see," Mason said, removing his eyes from the binoculars.

"Here is what I mean," Major Winnett went on. "You simply screw this eyepiece . . ."

Mason courteously but firmly arrested the Major's hand. "Just a moment, Major," he said. "I want to look at that right eyepiece."

"Someone must have been tampering with it. It's way out of proper adjustment," the Major said.

"The left eyepiece is at zero adjustment. I take it that means a perfectly normal eye," Mason said, "whereas, on this right eyepiece, there is an adjustment of negative five. I take it those graduations are made so that a person can remember his own individual adjustment for infinity and adjust the binoculars readily."

"I suppose so. The figures represent diopters."

"And an adjustment of negative five certainly blurs the entire . . ."

"That can't be an adjustment," the Major interposed. "Someone has idly turned that eyepiece."

"I see your point," Mason said and promptly turned the eyepiece back to zero. "There," he announced, "that's better."

It was now possible to make out details in what had before been merely a patch of shadow.

Mason swung the binoculars to the picnic ground, and could see quite plainly the masonry barbecue pits, the tables and chairs. Beyond them, through the trees he caught a glimpse of the ocean.

"A beach down there?" he asked.

"Not a beach, but a very fine place for surf fishing."

Mason swung the binoculars once more toward the clump of trees and the wide place in the road. "And you say people picnic there?"

"Occasionally, yes."

"From that point," Mason said, "one could see the house quite plainly with binoculars."

"But the binoculars are up here."

"Not the only pair in the world surely."

The Major frowned. Mason turned the glasses on a moving object, saw a magnified image of Paul Drake walking slowly along a bridle path. The short, somewhat cramped steps indicated that his brief experience in the English riding saddle had been more than ample. The detective was leading the horse, his head bowed as he plodded along the bridle path.

CHAPTER III

MASON WAITED until he saw Major Winnett leave the house, walking toward the stables. Then the lawyer quietly opened the door of his room, walked down the corridor to Winnett's bedroom, crossed the balcony and climbed to the rail.

The entrance of the swallow's nest was too small to accommodate the lawyer's hand but he enlarged the entrance by chipping away bits of the dried mud with his thumb and forefinger.

From the inside of the nest came faint rustlings of motion. An immature beak pushed against Mason's finger.

The parent swallows cried protests as they swooped in swift, stabbing circles around the lawyer's head, but Mason, working rapidly, enlarged the opening so that he could insert his hand into the nest. He felt soft down-covered bodies. Down below them, his groping fingers encountered only the concave surface of the nest.

A frown of annoyance crossed the lawyer's face. He continued groping, however, gently moving the young birds to one side. Then the frown faded as the tips of his fingers struck a hard metallic object.

As the lawyer managed to remove this object, sunlight scintillated an emerald and diamond brooch into brilliance.

Mason swiftly pocketed the bit of jewelry, drew back from the fierce rushes of the swallows. He dropped to the floor of the balcony and returned to the bedroom.

Back in the bedroom he made a swift, thorough search of the various places where small objects might be concealed. A sole leather gun case in the back of a closet contained an expensive shotgun. Mason looked through the barrels. Both were plugged with oiled rags at breach and muzzle.

Mason's knife extracted one of the rags. He tilted up the barrels, and jewelry cascaded out into his palm, rings, earrings, brooches, a diamond and emerald necklace.

Mason replaced the jewelry, inserted the rag once more and put the barrels back in the leather case, returned the case to the closet.

Preparing to leave the room, he listened for a few moments at the bedroom door, then boldly opened it and stepped out, retracing his steps toward his own room.

He was halfway down the corridor when Mrs. Victoria Winnett appeared at an intersecting corridor and moved toward Mason with stately dignity and a calm purpose.

"Were you looking for something, Mr. Mason?" she asked.

The lawyer's smile was disarming. "Just getting acquainted with the house."

Victoria Winnett was the conventional composite of a bygone era. There were pouches beneath her eyes, sagging lines to her face, but the painstakingly careful manner in which every strand of hair had been carefully coiffed, her face massaged, powdered, and rouged, indicated the emphasis she placed on appearance, and there was a stately dignity about her manner which, as Della Street subsequently remarked, reminded one of an ocean liner moving sedately up to its pier.

Had she carefully rehearsed her entrance and been grooming herself for hours to convey just the right impression of dignified rebuke, Mrs. Victoria Winnett would not have needed to change so much as a line of her appearance. "I think my *son* wanted to show you around," she said as she fell into step at Mason's side.

"Oh, he's done that already," Mason said with breezy informality. "I was just looking the place over."

"You're Mr. *Perry* Mason, the lawyer, aren't you?"

"That's right."

"I had gathered from what I read about your cases that you specialize mostly in trial work."

"I do."

"*Murder* trials, do you not?"

"Oh, I handle lots of other cases. The murder cases get the most publicity."

"I see," she said in the tone of one who doesn't see at all.

"Nice place you have here," the lawyer went on. "I am very much interested in that observation cubicle on top of the house."

"It was my husband's idea. He liked to sit up there. Didn't I hear the swallows crying out there?"

"I thought *I* heard them too," Mason said.

She looked at him sharply. "We try to keep them from nesting here but occasionally the gardener fails to see a nest until it is completed; then we don't disturb the nest until after the young birds have hatched. They're noisy and talkative. You can hear them quite early in the mornings. I trust they won't disturb you. Are you a sound sleeper, Mr. Mason?"

They had paused at the head of the stairs. Mrs. Winnett apparently did not intend to go down, so Mason, standing poised on the upper stair tread, used strategy to terminate the interview.

"My friend, Drake, is looking over the horses, and if you'll pardon me I'll run down and join him."

He flashed her a smile and ran swiftly down the stairs, leaving her standing there, for the moment nonplussed at the manner in which the lawyer had so abruptly forestalled further questions.

CHAPTER IV

IN THE PATIO, Della Street caught Perry Mason's eye, gave him a significant signal and moved casually over to the driveway where she climbed into the car and sat down.

Mason walked over. "I think Paul Drake has something," he said. "I'm going down and look him up. He's just coming in on the bridle path. What have you got?"

"I can tell you something about the nurse, chief."

"What?"

"In the first place, if a woman's intuition counts for anything, she's in love with the Major—one of those hopeless affairs where she worships him from a distance. In the second place, I think she has a gambling habit of some sort."

"Races?"

"I don't know. I was up in the cupola just after you were. There was a pad of paper in the drawer of the little table up there. At first it looked completely blank. Then I tilted it so the light struck it at an angle and could see that someone had written on the top sheet with a fairly hard pencil so it had made an imprint on the bottom sheet. Then the top sheet had been torn off."

"Good girl! What was on the sheet of paper? I take it something significant."

"Evidently some gambling figures. I won't bother to show you the original at this time but here's a copy that I worked out. It reads like this: *These numbers* on the first line, then down below that, *led*; then down below that a space and 5″5936; down below that 6″8102; down below that 7″9835; down below that 8″5280; down below that 9″2640; down below that 10″1320."

"Anything else?" Mason asked.

"Then a line and below the line, the figure 49″37817. That looks like some sort of a lottery to me. I learned Mrs. Winnett has been up in the cupola lately and since *she'd* hardly be a gambler, I assume the nurse must have written down the figures."

Mason said thoughtfully, "Notice the last three numbers, Della, 5280, 2640, 1320. Does that sequence mean something to you?"

"No, why?"

Mason said, "5280 feet in a mile."

"Oh, yes, I get that."

"The next number, 2640 feet, is a half mile, and the last number, 1320 feet, is a quarter mile."

"Oh, yes, I see now. Then that double mark means inches, doesn't it?"

"It's an abbreviation of inches, yes. What does this nurse seem like, Della? Remember I only barely met her."

"Despite her muddy complexion, straight hair, and glasses, her eyes are really beautiful. You should see them light up when the Major's name comes up. My own opinion is this nurse could be good-looking. Then Mrs. Winnett would fire her. So she keeps herself looking plain and unattractive so she can be near the Major, whom she loves with a hopeless, helpless, unrequited passion."

"Look here," Mason said, "if you've noticed that within an hour and a half, how about Mrs. Victoria Winnett? Doesn't she know?"

"I think she does."

"And hasn't fired the nurse?"

"No. I think she doesn't mind if the nurse worships the ground the Major walks on but doesn't presume to raise her eyes to look at him, if you get what I mean."

"I get it," Mason said thoughtfully, "and I don't like it. Wait, here comes Paul now."

Drake, walking stiffly, joined them.

"Find anything, Paul?" Mason asked.

"I found something," Drake conceded, "and I don't know what it is."

"What does it look like, Paul?"

"In the first place," Drake said, "you can easily follow her tracks. She took the lower bridle path. After the first quarter mile, there's only one set of tracks going and coming. They were made when the ground was soft and they go down to a road and a gate that's locked. I didn't have a key but I could see where the horse tracks went through the gate and down onto the road, so I tied up my horse and managed to squeeze through the fence."

"Any tracks around those trees, Paul?"

"An automobile had been parked there," Drake said. "There must have been two automobiles. That's the only way I can figure it out but I still can't figure the tracks right."

"How come?"

Drake took a small thin book from his pocket. "This is a little pocket book which gives the tread designs of all makes of tires. Now an automobile was in there that had some fairly new tires. One of the wheels was worn too much to identify but I identified the track of a right front wheel. Then the track of the other front wheel and the other hind wheel and . . . well, there I bogged down, Perry."

"What do you mean?"

"Of course, you have to understand it's a little difficult trying to get those tracks all fitted into the proper sequence. They . . ."

"What are you getting at?" Mason said.

"Hang it, Perry, I got *three* wheels."

"And the fourth was worn smooth?"

"Not that—what I mean is, Perry, that I got three wheels *on a single side.*"

Mason frowned at the detective. "*Three* wheels on a side?"

"Three wheels on a side," Paul Drake insisted doggedly.

Mason said rather excitedly, "Paul, did you notice a circular spot in the ground, perhaps eight or ten inches in diameter?"

"How the deuce did you know that spot was there?" Drake demanded, his face showing bewilderment.

Mason said, "It was made by the bottom part of a bucket, Paul. And the three tracks on each side were all right. That's the way it should be."

"I don't get it."

"A house trailer," Mason explained. "An automobile and a house trailer were parked under the trees. The waste water from a trailer sink is carried out through a drain to the outside. A bucket is placed there to catch the water as it runs off."

"That's it, all right," Drake admitted, then added morosely, "I'm kicking myself for not thinking of it myself, Perry."

Mason said, "It now begins to look as though Marcia Winnett had kept an appointment on Monday with someone in a house trailer. And that seems to have been very much a turning point in her life."

Drake nodded. "On Monday—that's a cold trail, Perry."

"It's the only one we have," Mason pointed out.

CHAPTER V

MASON, STUDYING the tire tracks, said, "It was an automobile and a house trailer, Paul. The round place which marks the location of the spout bucket can be taken as being approximately in the middle of the trailer. You can see over here the mark of an auxiliary wheel attached to the front of the trailer to carry part of the weight while the trailer was parked. That enables us to estimate the length of the trailer."

Drake said, "The trailer must have been backed in between these trees, Perry."

Mason started prowling along the edge of the fence. "Took some clever handling to get it in there. Let's look around for garbage. If the trailer remained here overnight, there are probably some tin cans . . . potato peelings, stuff of that sort."

Mason, Della Street, and Drake separated, covering the ground carefully.

Abruptly Della said, "Chief, don't look too suddenly, but casually take a look up there at the big house on the hill. I think I saw someone moving in the glassed-in observation tower."

"I rather expected as much," Mason said, without even looking up. "However, it's something we can't help."

Drake exclaimed, "Here it is, Perry, a collection of tin cans and garbage."

Mason moved over to where Drake was standing. Here the water from the winter rains, rushing down the ditch at the side of the road, had eddied around one of the roots of the big live oak and formed a cave which extended some three feet back under the roots of the tree.

Mason, squatting on his heels, used two dry sticks to rake out the articles.

There were three cans which had been flattened under pressure, some peelings from onions and potatoes, waxed paper which had been wrapped around a loaf of bread, an empty glass container bearing a syrup label, and a crumpled paper bag.

Mason carefully segregated the items with his sticks. As he did so he kept up a running fire of conversation.

"That flattening of the cans is the trick of an old outdoor man," he said.

"Why flatten them?" Della inquired.

"Animals get their heads stuck in cans sometimes," Mason said. "Moreover, cans take up less room when they're flattened and require a smaller hole when they're buried. This little garbage pit tells quite a story. The occupant of the trailer must have been a man. Notice the canned beans, a can of chili con carne, potatoes, bread, onions—no tomato peelings, no lettuce leaves, no carrots, in fact, no fresh vegetables at all. A woman would have had a more balanced diet. These are the smallest cans obtainable and . . . hello, what's this?"

Mason had pulled apart the paper bag as he talked. Now he brought out a small oblong slip of paper on which figures had been stamped in purple ink.

Della Street said, "That's a cash register receipt from one of the cash and carry grocery stores."

Mason picked up the receipt. "And a very interesting one," he said. "The man bought fifteen dollars and ninety-four cents' worth of merchandise. There's a date on the back of the slip and this other figure refers to the time. The groceries were bought at five minutes past eight on Saturday morning. It begins to look, Paul, as though this is where you take over."

"What do you want me to do?" Drake asked.

Mason said, "Get a room in the hotel at Silver Strand Beach. Open up something of an office there. Get men on the job. Get lots of men. Have your men buy groceries. See if the printing on the slip from any cash register matches this. If it does, try and find out something about the single, sun-bronzed man who purchased fifteen dollars and ninety-four cents' worth of groceries at five minutes past eight on Saturday morning. A sale of that size to a man just a few minutes after the store opened might possibly have attracted attention."

"Okay," Drake said. "Anything else?"

"Lots else," Mason said. "Della, where's that slip of paper, the copy you made of what you found in the observation tower?"

Della ran to the glove compartment, brought back the square of paper on which she'd made the copy.

Drake looked at it, said, "What is it, Perry?"

"Stuff Della found in the observation tower. What do you make of it?"

"Some sort of dimensions," Drake said. "Here's this number 8 inches and 5280 feet, 9 inches and half a mile, 10 inches and quarter of a mile. What's the idea, Perry, why should the inches run 5, 6, 7, 8, 9, 10, and . . . ?"

"Suppose they aren't inches?" Mason said. "Suppose they're ditto marks."

"Well, it could be."

"Then what?" Mason asked.

Drake said, "Then the numbers could have something to do with a lottery of some sort."

"Add them up," Mason said dryly.

"The total is already here," Drake said, "49"37817."

Mason handed him a pencil.

Della Street, leaning over Drake's shoulder, was the first to get it. "Chief," she exclaimed, "the total isn't correct."

"I knew it wasn't," Mason said. "I didn't know just how much it was off, however. Let's find out."

Della Street said, "The total is . . . Wait a minute, Paul, I'll get it . . . 45″33113, but the total that's *marked* there is 49″37817."

"Subtract them," Mason said. "What do you get?"

Della Street's skillful fingers guided the pencil as she hastily wrote down numbers, performed the subtraction. "4″4704," she said.

Mason nodded. "I think," he said, "when we get this case solved, we'll find the important figure is the one that *isn't* there. Bear that figure in mind, Paul. It may turn up later."

CHAPTER VI

PERRY MASON TOOK the steep stairs to the observation tower two at a time.

There was no one in the cupola. The binoculars, however, had once more been swung so that they were pointing to the grove of trees where the trailer had been parked. Mason placed his eyes to the binoculars. The left eye showed a clear vision, the right was blurred.

Mason bent over to study the adjustment on the right lens, saw it was set once more at negative five, then he changed the focus on the binoculars.

As he did so, he heard motion behind him and straightened abruptly.

Mrs. Victoria Winnett was standing in the doorway. At her side was a slender brunette in riding clothes whose face showed startled surprise. Mrs. Winnett's face showed no expression whatever.

"I hardly expected to find *you* here," Mrs. Winnett said to Mason and then turning to the young woman at her side said, "Miss Rexford, permit me to present Mr. Perry Mason, the lawyer."

Daphne Rexford favored Mason with a smile which went only as far as her lips. Her eyes showed an emotion which might have been merely nervousness, might have been panic.

Mason acknowledged the introduction, then said, "I'm fascinated with the view you get from here, Mrs. Winnett."

"My late husband spent much of his time here. The place does hold something of a fascination. Daphne loves it."

"You're here frequently?" Mason asked Daphne Rexford.

"Yes, I study birds."

"I see."

"But," she went on hastily, "since you're here I'll postpone my bird study until some other time."

"On the contrary," Mason said, "I was just leaving. I wanted to get the lay of the land."

"He's working with Claude on a mining deal," Mrs. Winnett hastened to explain to Daphne Rexford. "There's a mining engineer with him. And Mr. Mason has his secretary. You'll meet them if you're over for dinner tonight."

"Oh, thank you, but I . . . I don't think I can make it for dinner tonight. If Claude's going to be busy . . . Where's Marcia?"

"Visiting friends," Mrs. Winnett said dryly. "*Please* come."

"Well, I . . . I should . . ."

Mason said as she hesitated, "Well, I must get down and hunt up my client. After all, I must earn my fee, you know."

"I feel quite sure you will," Mrs. Winnett said with a certain subtle significance. "Come, Daphne, dear. Draw up a chair. What was it you were saying about swallows?"

Daphne said hurriedly, "Oh, there's a meadow lark! I think there must be a nest down by that bush. I've seen that same lark so many times in that exact position . . ."

Mason quietly closed the door, walked down the stairs.

Major Winnett was in the drawing room. He looked up as Mason crossed toward the patio. "What luck?" he asked.

"Progress," Mason said.

Major Winnett's lips tightened. "Can't you do better than that? Can't you give me something definite? Or are you just running around in circles?"

"A good hound always runs around in circles to pick up a scent."

"Then you haven't anything definite yet?"

"I didn't say that."

"You intimated it."

Mason slid his right hand down into his trousers pocket, abruptly withdrew the diamond and emerald brooch he had taken from the swallow's nest.

"Seen this before?" he asked, extending his hand.

Major Winnett stiffened for a moment to rigid immobility. "It looks . . . Mr. Mason, that certainly is similar to a brooch my wife had."

"One that was stolen?"

"I believe so, yes."

"Thank you," Mason said and slipped the brooch back into his pocket.

"May I ask where you got that?" Claude Winnett asked excitedly.

"Not yet," Mason told him.

The telephone rang sharply. Major Winnett moved over to the library extension, picked up the receiver, said, "Hello," then turned to Mason. "It's for you."

Mason took the telephone. Drake's voice said, "We've got something, Perry."

"What?"

"That oblong slip of paper from the cash register. We've located the store. The girl that was on duty remembers our party. We've got a good description now. With that to go on, we had no trouble picking up his trail in a trailer camp. He registered under the name of Harry Drummond."

"There now?" Mason asked.

"Not now. He pulled out early yesterday morning. I've got men covering every trailer camp anywhere near here. We should pick him up soon. We have the license number and everything. And here's a funny one, Perry. There's a jane looking for him."

"You mean . . . ?"

"No, not the one we're interested in, another one. She's brunette, snaky, young and tall and she was asking the cashier about him earlier in the day. Had a good description. Wanted to know if such a man had been in."

"Are you located there in the hotel?"

"Yes. I've fixed up an office here and have half a dozen men out on the job, with more coming in all the time."

Mason said, "I'll be right up."

"Okay, be looking for you. Good-by."

Mason heard the click at the other end of the line but did not immediately hang up. He stood holding the receiver, frowning at the carpet.

Abruptly he heard another sharp click and the telephone bell in the library extension gave a little tinkle.

Mason dropped the receiver into place, turned to Major Winnett. "I take it," he said, "you have several extensions on the phone?"

"Four," Major Winnett said. "No, there's five. There's one up in the observation tower. I almost forgot about that."

"Thank you," Mason said, and then added after a moment, "so did I."

CHAPTER VII

PAUL DRAKE WAS TALKING on the phone as Mason entered the suite of rooms Drake was using for headquarters. In an adjoining room Della Street, a list of numbers at her elbow, was putting through a steady succession of calls.

"Come in, Perry," Drake said, hanging up the receiver. "I was trying to get you. We're getting results fast."

"Shoot."

"Our party is a man thirty-eight years old, bronzed, wears cowboy boots, a five-gallon hat, leather jacket, Pendleton trousers, rather chunky and has a wide, firm mouth. The license number of his automobile is 4E4705. He's driving a Buick automobile and has quite an elaborate house trailer painted green on the outside with aluminum paint on the roof. Up until Saturday morning he was in the Strand Trailer Camp. He left Saturday, showed up again late Monday night, pulled out again Wednesday morning and hasn't been seen since."

"How did you get it?" Mason asked.

"Just a lot of leg work."

"Give me the highlights."

"We located the store that has that cash register—the only one in town. Cash register gives the time and date of sale, the amount of the items and the total. This sale was made shortly after the store opened Saturday morning and the cashier remembers the man's general appearance. She particularly remembered the cowboy boots. We started covering trailer camps and almost immediately picked up our trail."

"What are you doing now?"

"I've got operatives scattered around with automobiles covering every trailer camp, every possible parking place for a house trailer anywhere in this part of the country. We're working in a constantly widening circle and should turn up something soon."

Mason took out his notebook. "The number is 4E4705?"

"That's right."

"Then our mysterious observer in the observation tower made a mistake in addition. Remember, we were looking for a number 4"4704. The first number must have been 4E4705 and ditto marks were beneath the E. The real total then should have been . . ."

He was interrupted by a knock on the door, a quick staccato knock which somehow contained a hint of hysteria.

Mason exchanged glances with Drake. The detective left the desk, crossed over, and opened the door.

The woman who stood on the threshold was twenty-seven or twenty-eight, a tall brunette with flashing black eyes, high cheekbones and an active, slender figure. A red brimless hat perched well back on her head emphasized the glossy darkness of her hair and harmonized with the red of her carefully made-up lips.

She smiled at Paul Drake, a stage smile which showed even, white teeth. "Are *you* Mr. Drake?" she asked, glancing from him to Mason.

Drake nodded.

"May I come in?"

Drake wordlessly stood to one side.

His visitor entered the room, nodded to Perry Mason, and said, "I'm *Mrs.* Drummond."

Drake started to glance at Mason, then caught himself in time, and managed to put only casual interest in his voice. "I'm Mr. Drake," he said, "and this is Mr. Mason. Is there something in particular, Mrs. Drummond?"

She said, "You're looking for my husband."

Drake merely raised his eyebrows.

"At the Strand Trailer Camp," she went on nervously. "And *I'm* looking for him *too*. I wonder if we can't sort of pool information?"

Mason interposed suavely. "*Your* husband, and you're looking for him, Mrs. Drummond?"

"Yes," she said, her large dark eyes appraising the lawyer.

"How long since you've seen him?" Mason asked.

"Two months."

"Perhaps if you want us to *pool* information, you'd better tell us a little more about the circumstances and how you happened to know we were looking for him."

She said, "I'd been at the Silver Strand Trailer Camp earlier in the day. The man promised me that he'd let me know if my husband returned. When your detectives appeared and started asking questions, he took the license number of their car, found out it belonged to the Drake Detective Agency, and . . ." She laughed nervously and said, "And that is where I started to do a little detective work on my own. Are you looking for him for the same reason I am?"

Mason smiled gravely. "That brings up the question of why you're looking for him."

She gave an indignant toss of her head. "After all, I have nothing to conceal. We were married a little over a year ago. It didn't click. Harry is an outdoor man. He's always chasing around on the trail of some mining deal or some cattle ranch. I don't like that sort of life and . . . well, about two months ago we separated. I sued for divorce."

"Have you got it yet?"

"Not yet. We had an understanding about a property settlement. When my lawyer sent my husband the papers, he sent them back with an insulting note and said he wouldn't pay me a red cent and that if I tried to get tough about it, he'd show that I didn't have any rights whatever."

"Why?"

"I don't know."

"And you want to find out just what he means by that?" Mason asked.

"That's right. And now suppose you tell me what *you* want him for. Has he done something?"

"Is he the type that would?" Mason asked.

"He's been in trouble before."

"What sort of trouble?"

"A mining swindle."

Drake glanced inquiringly at Mason.

"Where are you located?" Mason asked Mrs. Drummond.

"I'm right here at the hotel. And don't think they're the ones who told me about Mr. Drake's being here," she added hastily. "I found that out by . . . in another way."

"You spoke of *pooling* information," Mason said suggestively.

She laughed and said, "Well, what I meant was if you find him, will you let me know? And if I find him, I could let you know. After all, he shouldn't be difficult to locate with that trailer, but I want to catch him before he can get out of the state. If I can find out where he is, I have—some papers to serve."

"You have a car?" Mason asked.

She nodded, then added by way of explanation, "That is one thing I salvaged out of our marriage. I made him buy me a car, and that's one of the reasons I want to see him. The car's still in his name. He agreed to let me have it as part of the property settlement, but in his letter to my lawyer he said he could even take the car away from me if I tried to make trouble. Does either of you gentlemen have any idea what he meant by that?"

Mason shook his head and Drake joined in the gesture of negation.

"Perhaps," Mason suggested, "we might work out something. You see, even if your assumption is correct that we are looking for your husband, we would be representing some client in the matter and would naturally have to discuss things with that client."

"Is it because of something he's done?" she asked apprehensively. "Is he in more trouble? Will it mean all his money will go for lawyers again, just like it did before?"

"I'm sure I couldn't tell you," Mason said.

"That means you won't. Look, I'm in Room 613. Why don't you ask your *client* to come and see me?"

"Will you be there all during the evening?" Drake asked.

"Well . . ." She hesitated. "I'll be in and out. I'll . . . I'll tell you what I'll do. I'll keep in touch with the hotel and if there are any messages, I'll be where I can come and get them."

She flashed them a smile, moved toward the door with quick lithe grace, then almost as an afterthought, turned and gave them her hand, glancing curiously through the open door of the adjoining room to where Della Street was seated at the telephone. Then she gave Mason another smile as the lawyer held the door open for her, and left the room, walking with quick nervous steps.

Mason closed the door, cocked a quizzical eyebrow at Paul Drake.

"The guy's wise," Drake said. "That means we haven't much time, Perry."

"You think he was watching his back trail?"

Drake nodded. "She's an alert little moll who knows her way around.

This man Drummond has done something that he's trying to cover up. He left her to watch his back trail. She hypnotized the man who runs the trailer camp and then when my man showed up in an agency car . . ."

"But how about her asking questions at the cash-and-carry, Paul?"

Drake snapped his fingers. "Shucks, there's nothing to *that*. That's the way she builds up a background for herself. After all, she . . ."

The telephone interrupted. Drake picked up the receiver, said, "Drake talking . . . Okay, let's have it . . . When? . . . Where? . . . Okay, stay on the job . . . We'll be right down."

Drake hung up the receiver, said, "Well, that's it. We've got him located."

"Where?"

"Little down-at-the-heel trailer camp in a eucalyptus grove about three miles from here. Not much of a place, auto court cabins in front and, as an afterthought because there was lots of room, the owner strung up some wires and advertised trailer space in the rear. The conveniences aren't too good and it's patronized mostly by people who want to save two bits a day on the regular parking rate. The chief advantage is lots of elbow room. The grove consists of several acres and if a man wants to walk far enough to the bath and shower, he can pick his own parking place for the trailer."

"Any details?" Mason asked.

"One of my men just located it. The trailer came in yesterday night. The man who runs the place was busy selling gasoline at the time, and the driver of the car called out that he'd come back and register later. He tossed the man a silver dollar and the man told him to park any place he wanted to where he could find a plug for his electric connection."

Mason said, "Let's go. Della, you stay here and run the place. We'll telephone you in half an hour or so."

They drove down to the trailer camp in Mason's car. Drake's operative, lounging casually in the door of one of the auto cabins, gave the detective a surreptitious signal, and pointed toward the adjoining cabin.

Registering simply as "P. Drake," the detective rented the vacant cabin, then settled down with Perry Mason. A few moments later, Drake's operative came across to join them.

"Ever met Pete Brady?" Drake asked Mason.

Mason shook hands, said, "I've seen him once or twice before around your office."

"Glad to know you," Brady said to Mason, and then to Drake, "I'm not certain but what the guy who runs the place is getting a little suspicious. I asked too many questions."

"What's the dope?"

"The trailer's out there attached to the car. So far, I haven't had a glimpse of the man who is in it, but it's the license number of the car we want okay—4E4705."

"Let's take a look around," Mason said.

"You'll have to take it easy," Brady warned. "Just sort of saunter around."

"How about the gag of buying a trailer," Drake asked. "Have you used that?"

Brady shook his head.

"We'll try that," Drake said. "You can wait here for a while. What's the guy's name who runs the place?"

"Elmo, Sidney Elmo."

"Did he see you come over here?"

"No. I waited until he was selling gas."

"Okay. Stick around. I'll go tell the bird that we heard one of the trailers here was for sale. He won't know anything about it. That gives us an opportunity to go sauntering around looking them over."

Five minutes later when Drake returned, Mason joined him and they walked slowly out past the line of somewhat dilapidated cabins into the eucalyptus grove. Late afternoon shadows made the place seem cold and gloomy. The ground was still moist from the rain and the drippings of the trees when ocean fog enveloped that portion of the country.

"There's the outfit," Drake said. "What do we do? Go right up and knock and ask him if it's for sale?"

Mason said, "Let's try one of the other trailers first. We can talk loud enough so our voices will carry over here."

"Good idea," Drake said.

"Take this one," Mason suggested.

The two walked over to the small homemade trailer Mason had indicated. It was parked about a hundred feet from the green trailer. Electric lights showed a well-fleshed woman in her late forties cooking over the stove. On the outside, a man was taking advantage of the failing light to tinker with the bumper on the trailer. There was an Oklahoma license plate on the car.

"This the outfit that's for sale?" Mason asked.

The man looked up, a long thin mouth twisted into a smile. He said with a drawl, "I ain't saying yes, and I ain't saying no. You want to buy?"

"We're looking for a trailer that we heard was for sale here."

"What sort of a trailer?"

"We just heard it was a good one."

"That's the description of this job all right."

Drake interposed, "You're not the man who spoke to the manager of the Strand Trailer Park and said he wanted to sell, are you?"

"Nope. Fact is, I'm not particularly anxious to sell. But if you wanted to buy it, I'd be willing to listen."

"We're looking for a particular trailer that's for sale," Mason explained. "How about that green one over there? Know anything about it?"

"No. It just came in last night."

"Don't suppose you've talked with the people who own it?"

"I ain't seen 'em. They haven't been around all day."

Mason said, "That looks like it. Let's go over there, Paul."

"Take it easy," Mason said as they approached. "Ever use a house trailer, Paul?"

"No. Why?"

"The steady weight of the trailer has a tendency to wear out springs. So most trailers are equipped with an auxiliary wheel which can be screwed into position when the trailer is parked."

"There isn't any here," Drake said.

"That's just the point. Furthermore, no spout bucket has been put out under the spout. And to cap the climax, the cord hasn't been connected with the electric outlet."

"What are you getting at, Perry?"

By way of reply, Mason knocked loudly on the trailer door. When there was no response, the lawyer tentatively tried the knob.

The door swung open.

There was still enough afternoon light to show the sprawled figure lying in stark silence on the floor. The dark pool eddying out from under the body showed little jagged streaks of irregularity, but its ominous significance could not be misjudged.

"Oh-oh!" Drake exclaimed.

Mason stepped up and entered the trailer. Carefully avoiding the red pool, he looked down at the body. Then he bent over, touched the high heeled cowboy boot, moved it gently back and forth.

"Been dead for some time, Paul. Rigor mortis has set in."

"Come on out," Drake begged. "Let's play this one on the up-and-up and notify the police."

"Just a minute," Mason said. "I . . ." He bent over, and as he did so a shaft of light struck his face.

"What's that?" Drake asked.

Mason moved slightly so that the beam of light struck his eye.

"That," he announced, "is a hole in this trailer, directly in line with the window of that Oklahoma trailer. Light from the window over there where the woman is cooking comes through the hole in this trailer. The hole could have been made by a bullet."

"Okay, Perry. Let's notify the police."

Mason said, "First I want to find out a little more about that Oklahoma trailer."

"For the luvva Mike, Perry, have a heart! You're in the clear on this one—so far."

Mason, moving cautiously, left the trailer. He hesitated a moment when he stepped to the ground. Then he carefully polished the doorknob with his handkerchief.

"That's removing evidence," Drake said. "There are other prints there besides yours."

"How do you know?"

"It stands to reason."

"You can't prove it," Mason said. "The murderer probably wiped his fingerprints off the door just as I did."

Mason walked back to the trailer with the Oklahoma license. The man, still bent over the bumper at the rear of the trailer, seemed to be working aimlessly, stalling for time. The position of his head indicated an interest in what had been going on over at the other trailer.

"That the one?" he asked as Mason approached.

"I don't know. No one seems to be home."

"I ain't seen 'em leave. They couldn't go very far without their car."

"Seen any visitors over there?" Mason asked casually.

"Not today. There was a young woman called last night."

"What time?"

"I don't know. We'd gone to bed. Her headlights shone in the window and woke me up when she came. I sat up in bed and looked out the window."

"See her plain?"

"Yeah—a redhead. Checkered suit—trim looking package."

"She go in?"

"I guess so. She switched off her lights and I went back to sleep. Woke me up again when she left. Her car backfired a couple a times."

Mason glanced at Drake. "I'd like to find these people."

"I think there's only one—a man. He drove in last night and had quite a bit of trouble backing the trailer around. You take one of these big trailers and it's quite a job to park it. You try to back up and everything's just reversed from what it is when you're backing just a car. We went to bed pretty early and sometime after I'd got to sleep this other car came up. What really woke me up was headlights shining in my window. I looked out and seen this woman."

"Remember what sort of car she was driving?"

"It was a rented car."

"How do you know?"

"From the gasoline rationing stamp on the windshield."

"Your wife didn't wake up?"

"No."

"How long have *you* been here?" Mason asked.

"What's it to you?"

"Nothing."

"I thought not," the man said, suddenly suspicious, and then after a moment added, "You're asking a lot of questions."

"Sorry," Mason said.

The man hesitated a moment then, by way of dismissal, turned back to the bumper.

Mason glanced significantly at Paul Drake. Silently the two walked away.

"Okay, Paul," Mason said in a low voice. "Get Della on the phone. Tell her to put operatives on every drive-yourself car agency within a radius of fifty miles and see if we can find where the woman rented the car. When we spot the place, I'll handle the rest of it."

"I don't like it," Drake said.

"I don't like it myself," Mason told him. "But the young woman who called there last night was Marcia Winnett."

"And her car backfired," Drake said dryly.

Mason met his eyes. "Her car backfired, Paul. And in case it ever becomes necessary, remember that the only person who heard it said it was a backfire."

Drake nodded gloomily. "Not that *that* will do any good, Perry."

"It keeps us in the clear, Paul. You don't rush to the police to report that someone's car backfired."

"When you've discovered a body, you do."

"Who knows we've discovered any body?"

"I do."

Mason laughed. "Back to the hotel, Paul. We'll try and trace that car. And just to be on the safe side, we'll see where Mrs. Drummond was last night."

CHAPTER VIII

THE LAST TASK Mason had given Paul Drake turned out to be simple. Mrs. Drummond had been trying to locate her husband in the near-by trailer camps all the evening before, and she had arranged with a police officer who was off duty to accompany her.

Locating the rented car in which the girl in the checkered suit went to the trailer camp was another matter.

Despite all of Drake's efficiency, it was nearing eight o'clock when his detectives uncovered the lead Mason wanted. A man who operated a car rental agency in one of the coast cities, some twenty-five miles from Silver Strand Beach, had rented a car to a young woman who wore a checkered suit and who answered the description of Marcia Winnett.

Drake looked up from the telephone. "Want my man to try and pick up the trail from there or do you want to do it, Perry?"

Mason said, "I'll do it, Paul. And just to be on the safe side, let your man think that that isn't the trail we want."

"Okay," Drake said, and then into the telephone, "Describe her, Sam. Uh huh . . . uh huh, well, that's not the one. Keep working. Cover those other agencies and then report."

Drake hung up the phone. "Want me to come along, Perry?"

"Della and I'll handle it," Mason said. "Start calling your men in. Let them feel it turned out to be a false lead. And you'd better start checking on Mrs. Drummond, Paul. I wouldn't like to have her show up right now."

Drake nodded, said solicitously, "Watch your step, Perry."

"I'm watching it. Come on, Della."

The man who operated the car rental agency which had furnished a car to Marcia Winnett was not particularly communicative. It took diplomacy to get him in the mood to talk. Even then he confined his information to bare essentials.

He had never seen his customer before. She gave her name as Edith Bascom. She said her mother had died and it was necessary for her to use a car in connection with handling the estate. She was registered at the local hotel.

"Do you check on these stories?" Mason asked. "Or do you just rent cars?"

"Sometimes we just rent cars. Sometimes we check."

"What did you do in this case?"

"Cars are scarce now," the man said. "We checked."

"How?"

The man picked up a daily paper dated the day before and indicated the obituary column. Mason followed the man's finger to the stereotyped announcement of the death of Mrs. Shirley Bascom and the statement that funeral arrangements would be private.

Mason said, "I guess that covers it all right."

"What's your interest in it?"

"I'm a lawyer."

"I see. Well, she's okay. Rather upset on account of her mother's death, but a nice girl. You'll find her in the Palace Hotel, two blocks down the street."

"You checked on that?"

"I told you cars are scarce," the man said. "I checked on it."

It was but a matter of routine for Mason and his secretary to get the number of the room which had been assigned to Edith Bascom. Two minutes later Mason was knocking on the door.

There was no answer. Mason tried the knob. The door was locked.

Mason made a swift survey of the hall, stooped and held out his hands. "Step on my hands, Della. Take a quick look through the transom."

She braced herself with a hand on his shoulder, caught the lower ledge of the transom and peered through.

Mason, with his right hand on her hip, steadying her, felt her body stiffen. Then she was scrambling to get down.

"Chief," she said in an ominous whisper, "she's stretched out on the bed. She's . . . terribly still."

"Lights on?"

"No, but the shade is up and there's enough light coming in from the electric sign in front to make out the form on the bed."

Mason said, "There's a spring lock on the door . . . Better take another look, Della. See if she's breathing and . . . hold it. Here comes a chamber maid."

The chamber maid who wearily approached was aroused only momentarily from the lethargy of overwork by the bill Mason pushed into her palm.

"My wife and I seem to have left our key downstairs. If you could let us in, it would save us a trip down . . ."

"It's against the rules," she said, then added tonelessly, "but I guess it's okay," produced her passkey, and clicked back the latch on the door.

Mason boldly pushed open the door, stood aside for Della to enter, then followed her into the dimly lighted room, and closed the door behind him.

Della Street crossed over to the woman lying on the bed, as Mason groped for her pulse.

"She's alive!" Della Street said.

"The lights," Mason said crisply. "Pull the curtains first."

Della Street jerked down the shades, ran over and switched on the light.

Mason glanced at the bottle of sleeping tablets by the side of the bed, picked up the newspaper on the floor, glanced at it.

"She must have taken them yesterday," Della said. "We'll need a doctor and . . ."

"This afternoon," Mason interrupted curtly. "This is a late edition of the afternoon paper."

He dropped the paper, shook the sleeper, said, "Towels, Della. Cold water."

Della Street grabbed towels, turned on the cold water in the bathroom. Mason slapped Marcia Winnett with cold towels until the eyelids flickered open.

"What is it?" she asked thickly.

Mason said to Della Street, "Run down to the drugstore, Della. Get an emetic. Have room service send up some black coffee."

"How about a doctor?"

"Not if we can avoid it. Let's hope she hasn't had the tablets down long enough to get the full effects. Get an emetic."

Marcia Winnett tried to say something but the words were unintelligible. She dropped back against Mason's shoulder.

Mason calmly started removing her blouse. Della Street dashed from the room, headed for the drugstore.

Thirty minutes later Mason and Della Street assisted Marcia Winnett from the bathroom. There was a dead, lacklustre look about her eyes but she could talk now, and the coffee was beginning to take effect.

Mason said, "Concentrate on what I'm telling you. I'm a lawyer. I'm retained to represent you."

"By whom?"

"Your husband."

"No, no, he mustn't . . . he can't . . ."

Mason said, "I'm *your* lawyer. Your husband retained me to help you. I don't have to tell him anything."

She sighed wearily, said, "Let me go. It's better this way."

Mason shook her once more into wakefulness. "You went riding Monday morning. You talked with a man in a trailer. He made demands on you. You had to have money and have it at once. You didn't dare to ask your husband for it."

Mason waited for an answer. She made none. Her eyelids drooped and raised as if by a conscious effort.

Mason said, "You went back to the house. You canceled the insurance on your jewelry because you were too conscientious to stick the insurance company. You arranged to have some repairs made to a window on the side of your bedroom so a ladder would be handy. You got up in the night, went out to the balcony, and dumped your jewelry into the swallow's nest. Then you started screaming."

Her face might have been a wooden mask.

Mason went on, "You had waited until Tuesday to stage the burglary. You knew that it would be too obvious if it happened Monday night, the day you had canceled the insurance. Wednesday morning you found an opportunity to get most of the jewelry out of the swallow's nest. There was one piece you overlooked. Now then, suppose you tell me what happened after that."

She said, with the drowsy calm of one who discusses a distant event which can have no personal bearing, "I wanted to kill him. I can't remember whether I did or not."

"Did you shoot him?"

"I can't remember a thing that happened after . . . after I left the house."

Mason glanced at Della Street, said, "If I'm going to help you, I have to know what hold that man had on you."

"His name is Harry Drummond. He was my first husband."

"You were divorced?"

"I *thought* I was divorced. There were reasons why I couldn't go to Nevada. I gave him the money. He went to live in Nevada.

"From time to time he sent me reports of how things were coming.

Twice he asked for more money. Then he wrote me the divorce had been granted. He was lying. He'd gambled the money away. There never had been a divorce."

"When did you find this out?" Mason asked.

"Monday morning," she said. "He was clever. He'd kept in touch with me. He knew I rode down along that bridle path. He parked his trailer there. Mrs. Victoria Winnett doesn't like to have people camp there, so I rode down to ask whoever was in the trailer to please move on down to the public camp grounds."

"You had no idea who was in the trailer?"

"Not until Harry opened the door and said, 'Hello, Marcia. I thought it was about time you were showing up.' "

"What did he want?"

"Money."

"And he threatened you with—what?"

"The one weapon Claude couldn't stand, notoriety."

"So you promised to get him money?"

"I promised to get him my jewelry. He had to have money at once. He said someone was putting screws on him for cash."

"You were to meet him there when?"

"Wednesday morning."

"So you manipulated this fake burglary on Tuesday night after canceling your insurance on Monday. Then you took him the jewelry. Did he ask you how you had managed to secure the jewelry?"

"Yes. I told him the whole story. I told him it was all right to pawn it because the Winnetts wouldn't report the burglary to the police."

"And then what happened?"

"I can't remember."

"What can't you remember?"

"I can't remember a thing from the time . . : from the time Harry took the jewelry. He made some sneering remark, and I remember becoming very angry and then . . . then my mind went entirely blank."

"Did you have a revolver with you when you went down to the trailer Wednesday morning?" Mason asked.

"Yes."

"Where did you get it?"

"From a bureau drawer."

"Whose gun was it?"

"I don't know. I think it was . . . Mrs. Winnett's gun—pearl handled. I thought I might need some protection. It was a crazy idea. I took it along."

"Where is that gun now?"

"I don't know. I tell you I can't remember a thing that happened after I gave him the jewelry and he made that sneering remark."

"Did he make some further demands on you? Did he tell you you had to meet him at an isolated trailer park last night?"

"I don't know. I can't remember."

"*Did* you meet him there?"

"I can't remember."

"Did you," Mason asked, "rent an automobile from a drive-yourself agency about two blocks down the street?"

Her forehead puckered into a frown. "I seem to have some faint recollection of doing something like that, but I . . ." She shook her head. "No, it eludes me. I can't remember."

Mason said impatiently, "Why don't you come clean? You were clever enough to read the obituary notices and pretend to be the daughter of a woman who had just died. I'm trying to help you. At least tell me what I'm up against."

"I don't know. I can't remember."

Mason motioned toward the bottle of sleeping tablets. "And you thought you could take this way out and it would help?"

"I don't know. I guess I must have been . . . perhaps I was nervous. Perhaps I hadn't been sleeping at all and I just took too large a dose. I can't remember."

Mason turned to Della Street. "Willing to take a chance, Della?"

She nodded. "Anything you say, chief."

Mason said, "Put her in a car. Take her into Los Angeles. See that there's plenty of money in her purse. Take her to a *private* hospital. Under no circumstances give *your* name or address. Put on the rush act. Tell the first nurse you meet that this woman accosted you on the street and asked you to help her find out who she was. That you think it's a racket of some sort; but that she seems to have money and if she needs any assistance, the hospital is the place where she should be able to get it. Then turn and get out of the door fast."

Della nodded.

Mason turned to Marcia Winnett. "You heard what I said?"

"Yes . . . I . . . you mustn't take chances for me. I know that I must have killed him. I can't remember the details, Mr. Mason, but I killed him. I *think* it was in self-defense. I can't remember."

"I know," Mason said gently. "Don't worry about it. Remember you're a widow now. Don't get your memory back, and the next time you see me remember I'm a stranger. I'm going to try to help you. Get started, Della. Drive with the window open. Let her get lots of cold air. Get her to a hospital."

"How'll *you* get back?" Della asked.

"I'll have one of Drake's men pick me up."

Della looked at Marcia with cold contempt. "If you ask me," she blurted indignantly, "this act of hers . . ."

Mason gently closed one eye in an owlish wink. "Take her to the hospital, Della . . . and be sure you get out from under."

CHAPTER IX

THE GRAVEL on the driveway caused the wheels to slide as Mason slammed on the brakes. The car skidded at a sharp angle and Mason didn't even bother to straighten it out. He snapped off the lights and the ignition, leapt out and headed up the steps of the Winnett mansion, pushed open the door, and strode into the drawing room unannounced.

Mrs. Victoria Winnett and Daphne Rexford were lingering over liqueurs, talking in low voices.

Mrs. Winnett's smile was distantly friendly. "*Really*, Mr. Mason," she said, "you're rather late—for dinner."

The lawyer merely nodded, glanced at Daphne Rexford.

Mrs. Winnett reached for the bell. "I presume I can get you something," she said. "But after this, if you don't mind . . ."

"Let the food go," Mason said. "I want to talk with you."

The finger which had been touching the bell remained motionless. She said, "*Really*, Mr. Mason," in a voice that indicated a polite rebuke.

Daphne Rexford hurriedly arose. "If you'll excuse me, I have a telephone call I want to make . . ."

"Sit down, my dear. After all, I can't permit this human tornado to come bursting in on our tête-à-tête with . . ."

Mason caught Daphne Rexford's eye, jerked his head.

She made a feeble attempt at a smile and left the room.

"Really, Mr. Mason," Mrs. Winnett said, her voice now quite cold. "My attachment to my son is such that I am willing to make all allowances for his friends. Even so . . ."

She let her unfinished sentence carry its own meaning.

Mason drew up a chair and sat down. "Where's the Major?"

"He was called out about twenty minutes ago."

"You're fond of Daphne Rexford, aren't you?"

"Of course."

"Was she in the observation tower Monday?"

"Really, Mr. Mason. I'm not on the witness stand."

"You're going to be," Mason said.

"I'm afraid you've been drinking."

"If you think this is a joke," Mason said, "just keep on stalling. Time is precious. The officers may be out here any minute."

"Officers?"

"Officers. Cops. Bulls. Detectives. Plain-clothes men. Newspaper photographers. Walking around here with their hats on, throwing cigarettes on the rugs, taking flashlight pictures with captions— 'Society Leader Insists on Innocence.' "

That last did it. Mason saw her wince.

"You're a good poker player, but you can't bluff now. This is a showdown, Mrs. Winnett."

"Just what do you want?"

"To know all that you know."

She took a quick breath. "I know some trouble has developed between Marcia and Claude. I think that Marcia has left him. I hope she has."

"Why?"

"Because I don't feel that they are destined to be happy together . . ."

"No, I mean why has she left him?"

"I don't know."

"Make a guess."

"I can't."

"You know something about what happened on Monday?"

"On *Monday?* No."

"Was Daphne in the cupola on Monday?"

"I think she was."

"Did she come to you and tell you anything about what she saw either Monday or Wednesday?"

"Mr. Mason, you're being impertinent!"

Mason said, "You've found out something about Marcia. You thought she had involved the family good name, and took it on yourself to try and avoid notoriety. Your attempt backfired. I'm trying to find out just how badly it backfired."

"You can't prove any of these things you're saying, Mr. Mason."

"That," Mason said, "is only because I haven't the facilities at my command that the police have. The police may prove it."

"They won't," she said coldly. "I have told you absolutely everything I know."

Mason pushed back his chair, started for the door which led to the patio, then abruptly whirled, tiptoed swiftly back to the drawing room door, and jerked it open.

Daphne Rexford, plainly embarrassed, tried to pretend she had just been approaching the door. "Heavens," she said laughing, "I thought we were going to have a collision, Mr. Mason. You seem in a hurry." She tried to push easily on past him.

Mason barred her way. "You were listening."

"Mr. Mason, how *dare* you say anything like that?"

"Come in," Mason said. "Let's have it out. Let's . . . no, on second thought, I think I'll talk with you alone. Come on."

Mason took her arm. She drew back.

Mrs. Winnett said, "Mr. Mason is completely overstepping the prerogatives of a guest. I dislike to ask him to leave in my son's absence, but . . ."

Mason said to Daphne Rexford, "Police are going to be swarming over the place before midnight. Do you want to talk to me or do you want to talk to them?"

Daphne Rexford said over her shoulder to Mrs. Winnett, "Good heavens, Victoria, let's humor the man! I'll be back within a few minutes."

Without waiting for an answer from Victoria Winnett, she smiled disarmingly at Mason and moved away from the drawing room. "Come on, where do you want to talk?"

"Over here's good enough," Mason said, stopping in a corner of the library.

Daphne Rexford stood facing him. "What," she asked in a low voice, "are the police going to be investigating?"

Mason met her eyes. "Murder."

"Who . . . who was killed?"

"Let's talk first about what *you* know," Mason said. "You're the one who has the trick right eye. Mrs. Winnett has been covering up for you."

"I'm afraid I don't know what you mean."

"Whenever you look through the binoculars," Mason explained, "you have to move the right eyepiece quite a distance in order to see clearly, don't you?"

"What if I do?"

Mason said, "*You* were the one who was watching Marcia on Monday. What did you see?"

"Nothing. I . . ."

"Were you here Monday? Were you in the observation cupola?"

"I believe I was."

"You're over here quite a bit?"

"Yes. Victoria and I are great friends. She's an older woman, of course, but I like her. I like what she stands for and . . ."

"And like to be near Major Winnett and see as much of him as you can?"

"Certainly not," she said indignantly.

"We'll let it go at that for the time being," Mason said. "Now, about Monday, what did you see?"

"Nothing. I . . ."

"You were up in the tower?"

"Yes. I go there quite frequently. I study birds, and I write poetry. I can get inspiration up there, and . . ."

"And keep an eye on Major Winnett's wife when she's around the grounds, I suppose?"

"Mr. Mason, that's unfair and untrue."

"All right. You saw her Monday. What did you see?"

"I . . . nothing."

Mason said, "You saw her go into that orange trailer that was parked down in the trees. You watched her . . ."

"It wasn't orange. It was green."

Mason grinned at her.

"All right," she said. "Don't think you're trapping me. I just happened to notice Marcia riding, and then I saw a house trailer parked in the trees."

"Did you see her go in?"

"I saw her tie up her horse and walk over toward the trailer. I wasn't interested. I returned to the poetry I was writing."

"How long was she in there?"

"I don't know."

"Why did you watch her?"

"I didn't watch her. I was looking at birds."

"You had a pencil and a pad of paper up there with you?"

"Yes, of course. I told you I write poetry. One doesn't write on the walls, Mr. Mason. I keep pencil and paper in the drawer of the table up there."

"You used the binoculars to get the license number of the automobile. You marked it down, didn't you?"

"No."

"When were you up there last writing poetry?"

"Why . . . why, today."

"Do you go up there every day?"

"Not every day, but quite frequently."

"Have you been up every day this week?"

"I . . . I guess I have. Yes."

The telephone rang a sharp, strident, shrill summons.

Mason waited, listening, heard the butler answer it. Then the butler walked with unhurried dignity across the library to the drawing room, said something to Mrs. Winnett. She arose and went to the telephone. Mason heard her say, "Hello, Claude darling . . . Yes, dear . . . he's here . . . I'm afraid, Claude, that there has been some misunderstanding. Mr. Mason's activities are hardly such as one would connect with a mining matter. He has shown quite an interest in what Marcia . . ."

Mason walked over, gently pushed her aside, took the receiver from her hand, and said into the telephone, "Okay, Major, I've got it now. Get out here at once."

Major Winnett's voice was harsh with anger. "Just what do you mean, Mr. Mason? I'm afraid that you and I . . ."

Mason interrupted. "Your mother is trying to protect somebody. Daphne Rexford is trying to protect somebody. There's only one person I can think of whom they'd both go to such lengths to protect. That's you. If you get out here fast, we *may* be able to beat the police to it."

"What do you mean?"

"You know damn well what I mean," Mason said and hung up.

CHAPTER X

MAJOR WINNETT'S LIMP was more noticeable as he moved across the drawing room to confront Perry Mason. "I don't know exactly what's been going on here," he said angrily. "I don't know what prerogatives you have assumed, Mr. Mason. But as far as I'm concerned, our relationship is ended."

Mason said, "Sit down."

"I'm waiting to drive you to town, Mason, in case you don't have a car. If you do, I'll go with you to your room and you can pack up."

Mason said, "As nearly as I can put things together, you had previously discovered the trailer parked down in the trees. You were suspicious. You went up to the observation tower and saw Marcia go to the trailer and then later on saw the car and trailer go away. You took down the license number of the car. You looked up the man who owned that car. After that you kept a pretty close watch on what was going on.

"You didn't say anything when Marcia canceled the insurance on her jewelry and then had such an opportune burglary. You were very careful not to call the police because you knew the police would tab it as an inside job. You let your wife think it was because your mother didn't want any notoriety but you got the jewelry and hid it in that twelve-gauge shotgun. After that you kept a pretty good watch on your wife. Where did you get the jewelry?"

"Mason," Winnett said coldly. "In case you don't leave this house at once, I'm going to call the servants and have you put out."

Mason brushed aside Major Winnett's angry statement with a gesture. "You'll have to hire more servants, then," he said, and then went on. "When the trailer came back on Wednesday and Marcia went down there the second time, you decided to investigate. When you got down there, you found you had a fight on your hands. You killed Harry Drummond. Then you locked up the trailer, came back to the house, and waited until dark. Then you took the trailer with its gruesome evidence of murder, drove to a trailer camp . . ."

"Mason, watch what you're saying. By heaven, I'll throw you out myself!"

"Parked the trailer," Mason went on, as smoothly as though Major Winnett had said nothing, "but only after some difficulty; then got out and went home. Then you felt it would add an artistic touch to have two shots fired so the *time* of the killing could be definitely fixed. So you went back, sneaked in to the trailer park, stood in the dark *outside* the trailer and fired two shots in the air.

"You didn't realize that Marcia had been following you, and when she heard those shots she naturally thought you had killed Drummond out of jealousy, decided that she loved you too much to let you take the rap, and so skipped out. That's the reason you didn't go to a detective agency to get someone to try to find your wife. You wanted a lawyer who specialized in murder cases, *because you knew there was going to be a murder case.*"

Major Winnett snapped his fingers. "A lot of half-baked theories!"

"You see," Mason went on, "you made a couple of fatal mistakes. One of them was that the first shot you fired missed Drummond and went clean through the trailer leaving a hole in the double walls that clearly shows the direction taken by the bullet. When you parked that trailer in the automobile camp under the eucalyptus trees, it was dark and you didn't take the precaution of noticing where a bullet fired under such circumstances would have hit. That was a mistake, Major. As it happened, the hole in the trailer was lined up absolutely with the window of an adjoining trailer.

"At first the police will think the shot *might* have been fired from the other trailer. Then they'll make a more careful investigation and find that the direction of the bullet was the other way. Then they'll *know* that the murder wasn't committed there at the trailer park. There's another little thing you hadn't thought of. At the time you moved the trailer, the body had been dead for some time but the pool of blood hadn't entirely coagulated. Near the center of the pool there was blood that was still liquid. It spread around when the trailer swayed from side to side in going over irregularities in the road. That is what gives the pool of clotted blood the peculiar appearance of having little jagged streamers flowing from it."

Major Winnett was silent and motionless. His eyes were fixed on Mason with cold concentration. The anger had left his face, and it was quite plain the man's mind was desperately turning over Mason's words.

"So," Mason went on, "you knew that when the police started to investigate, they would find the dead man had been Marcia's first husband. You knew they would then start looking for her. When they found that she had skipped out, you knew what would happen. And so, you came to me."

Major Winnett cleared his throat. "You made a statement that Marcia had followed me. Do you have any evidence to back that up?"

Mason said, "It's a logical deduction from . . ."

"That's where you're wrong. Come to my room, I want to talk with you."

Mason said, "You haven't much time. The police have found the body.

They're going to be out here looking for Marcia as soon as they have completed an identification and checked up on the man's history."

"All right," Winnett said, "come with me. Mother, you and Daphne pretend you haven't heard any of this. I'll talk with you later."

Major Winnett led the way to his room, opened a portable bar, took out a bottle of Scotch.

Mason refused with a gesture, then when Winnett had poured out a drink, the lawyer reached over and poured half of that drink back into the bottle. "Just enough to give yourself a bracer," he warned, "not enough to give you a letdown afterwards. You're going to be talking with the police pretty soon. Start talking with me now."

Winnett said, "I didn't know Marcia went to visit the man in the trailer on Monday. I did know that Marcia went to the trailer on Wednesday."

"*How* did you know?"

"I was watching her."

"Why were you watching her?"

"Someone told me she had been to the trailer on Monday."

"Who?"

"My mother."

"What did you do?"

"After she left the trailer on Wednesday, I went down there to see who was in the trailer and see why my wife was having a rendezvous."

"What did you find?"

"I found the man dead. I found Marcia's jewelry spread out on a table in front of him. I realized what must have happened. I saw that one shot had gone into the man's heart. One had apparently gone past his head and into the wall of the trailer."

"All right," Mason said sarcastically, "it's your story. Go ahead with it. What did you do then?"

"I took Marcia's jewelry, I locked up the trailer. I came home. I waited until after dark, then I moved the trailer to a trailer camp I knew of, where I parked it. I got out and left the trailer and walked to where I had parked my own car earlier in the day. I had driven home before I realized that I could completely throw the police off the scent by letting it appear the murder had been committed late that night in the trailer camp. So, I returned, stood near the trailer, fired two shots into the air, then ran to my car and came back home. I thought Marcia was in bed. But when, after a couple of hours, I went up, I found she wasn't there, that she had left that note. That's why I came to you. I wanted your help. That's the truth, so help me."

Mason said, "You wrote down the license number of that automobile. Later on you tried to cover it up by adding some words and some figures. Then you added the total . . ."

"Mr. Mason, I swear I did not."

"Who did then?"

"I don't know."

"Someone wrote down the license number of the car," Mason said, "4E4705, then tried to camouflage it by working in a number of other figures and writing at the top *These numbers called*—but a mistake was made in the addition. I . . . wait a minute . . ."

Mason stood motionless, his eyes level-lidded with concentration.

"Perhaps," Major Winnett suggested, "it was . . ."

Mason motioned him to silence, then, after a moment, picked up the telephone, dialed the hotel where Drake had established an office, and when he had Drake on the line, said, "Hello, Paul, Perry talking. I think I've got it. There wasn't any mistake in the addition."

"I don't get it," Drake said, "the total should be 49″37818. Actually it's 49″37817."

"And that figure is right," Mason said. "The number we want is 4E4704."

"But the license number was 4E4705."

Mason said, "What happens when you have two cars? You are given license numbers in chronological order. Look up license number 4E4704. You can start your search in room 613 there at the hotel. Make it snappy."

Mason slammed up the telephone receiver and nodded to Major Winnett. "We've got one more chance. It's slim. The next time you go to a lawyer, don't be so damn smart. Tell him the truth. Where's your mother's room?"

"In the other wing at the far end of the corridor."

"And the nurse's room?" Mason asked. "That must be a communicating room?"

"It is."

Mason said, "Let's go."

Helen Custer, answering their knock, seemed somewhat flustered. "Why, good evening, I, ah . . . is there something . . ."

Mason pushed his way into the room. Major Winnett hesitated a moment, then followed. Mason kicked the door shut.

"Police are on their way out here," Mason said to the nurse.

"The police? What for?"

"To arrest you."

"For what?"

Mason said, "That's up to you."

"What do you mean?"

Mason said, "Playing it one way, it's blackmail. Playing it the other way, it's being an accessory after the fact on a murder charge. You'd better take the rap for blackmail."

"I . . . I . . . why, *what* are you talking about?"

Mason said, "I've practiced law long enough to know that a man should never torture clues to make them point in the direction he thinks they should go. When that column of figures added up to 49E37817 and I thought it should have been 49E37818, I assumed a mistake had been made in the addition. It wasn't a mistake. You marked down the number *Cal* 4E4704. You wanted to preserve that number but you didn't want anyone to think that it had any significance so you added the words at the top. *These numbers* and then inserted *led* after the *Cal,* so that made it read, These numbers called. Then you added other numbers after that number and then totaled the sum. Now then, you probably have less than five minutes to tell us why you wrote down 4E4704."

She glanced from Mason to Major Winnett. There was dismay in her eyes. "What makes you think I . . ."

Mason took out his watch, said, "If the police get here first you'll be an accessory after the fact. If you use your head, you *may* be able to get by with a rap for attempted blackmail."

"I . . . I . . . oh, Mr. Mason. I can't . . ."

Mason watched the hand ticking off the seconds.

"All right," she blurted. "It was yesterday morning. I was looking for Mrs. Victoria Winnett. I thought she was up in the observation tower. I went up there. She wasn't there. The binoculars were adjusted so they pointed down to that grove of trees. I just happened to look through them and saw the trailer. A light coupé was parked beside the big Buick that was attached to the trailer. A man and a woman were having a struggle of some sort. The man tried to strike her and the woman reached into her blouse. I saw the flash of a gun, then another flash. The man staggered back and the woman calmly closed the door of the trailer, got in her car and drove away.

"Through the binoculars I got a look at the number of her automobile. It was Cal 4E4704. I wrote it down on a piece of paper, intending to tell the police. Then . . . well, then I . . . thought . . . I . . ."

"What did you do with the piece of paper?" Mason asked.

"After a moment I realized that perhaps I could . . . well, you know. So I changed the focus on the binoculars back to . . ."

"So what did you do?" Mason asked.

"I didn't want that number to seem too conspicuous. I had written Cal 4E4704, so I wrote down other things, just as you said."

"The first number you wrote on a single sheet of paper that was on the table and not on the pad. When you wrote the rest of it, you had placed the paper on the pad."

"I . . . I guess I did."

Mason pointed to the telephone. "Ring up police headquarters," he said, "tell them what you saw. Tell them that it's been bothering you; that you thought you should have reported it to the police but that Mrs. Winnett is so opposed to any form of publicity that you didn't know just what to do; that tonight you asked Mrs. Winnett about it and she told you to telephone the police at once; that the reason you didn't do so before, was because the trailer was gone when you looked again and you supposed that the man hadn't been hurt and had driven the trailer away."

"If I do that," she said, "then I . . ."

"Then you stand about one chance in ten of beating the rap all around," Mason said grimly. "Don't do it, and you're stuck. What did you do—actually, I mean?"

"I looked up the license number. I found that the car was registered in the name of a Mrs. Harry Drummond. I located her and while I wasn't crude or anything . . . I wanted to open up a beauty shop and . . . well, she agreed to finance me."

Once more Mason pointed to the telephone. "Get police headquarters. Come on, Major. Let's go."

Out in the corridor Major Winnett said, "But how about my wife, Mason? How about my wife? That's the thing that bothers me. That . . ."

"And it damned well should bother you," Mason said. "She must have seen you driving the trailer Wednesday night and followed you to the place where you parked it. She went in, found Drummond dead and thought you had been trying to avenge the family's good name. You can see now what happened. She gave Drummond money to get a divorce. He told her he'd secured one. She married again. Drummond made the mistake of also marrying again. When the blow-off came, his second wife threatened to prosecute him for bigamy unless he gave her money. The only way he had to get money was to put the heat on Marcia. She was too conscientious to ask you for money or to try and stick the insurance company for money, so she staged a fake burglary, cached her jewelry in the swallow's nest, then turned over the jewelry to him. When the second Mrs. Drummond came for her money, all her husband had to offer her was jewelry. She thought it was hot. That started a fight and she shot him. And probably shot him in self-defense at that."

"But how am I going to explain—about moving the body?" Major Winnett asked.

Mason looked at him pityingly. "You're not going to explain one damn thing," he said. "What do you think you have a lawyer for? Get in my car. Leave the nurse to put the police on a hot trail."

CHAPTER XI

IT WAS NEARING MIDNIGHT when Perry Mason and Paul Drake walked into metropolitan police headquarters with a description of Marcia Winnett and a series of photographs.

"Of course," Mason explained to Sergeant Dorset, "the Major doesn't want any publicity. She had a spell of amnesia several years ago. He's afraid it *may* have returned."

Sergeant Dorset frowned down at a memo on his desk. "We've picked up a woman who answers that description—amnesia—a hospital telephoned in the report. How does it happen *you're* mixed in the case, Mason?"

"I handle the Winnetts' business."

"The deuce you do!"

"That's right."

Dorset regarded the memo on his desk. "The county teletype says a man named Drummond was murdered. Mrs. Winnett's nurse saw it all, phoned in a report. She had the license number of the murder car, Drummond's wife's."

"Indeed," Mason said, his voice showing courteous interest, but nothing else. "May we take a look at this amnesia case now? The Major is very anxious."

"And," Dorset went on, "when the county officers picked up Drummond's wife, she swore that not only was the killing in self-defense, but that the nurse had been blackmailing her. The nurse called her a liar. Mrs. Drummond's confession puts her in a poor position to claim blackmail. I understand the county is so pleased with having cracked the murder case they're washing their hands of all the rest of it."

Mason glared at Sergeant Dorset. "Will you kindly tell me what all this has to do with Major Winnett's wife?"

Dorset sighed. "I wish to hell I knew," he said, and then added significantly, "but I'll bet a hundred to one we never find out now."

Mason said, "Come down to earth. That murder case is county. The sheriff's office wouldn't like a city dick sticking his nose in."

Dorset nodded. "And by the same sign the way you've arranged it, the amnesia case is city and the county men won't mess around with *that*."

He regarded the lawyer with a certain scowling respect.

Mason said very positively, "I don't see what the murder has to do with all this if the sheriff's office has a solution and a confession, but one thing I do know is that if you have Major Winnett's wife here she's suffering from a nervous ailment and if you make it worse with a lot of fool notions, you'll wish you hadn't. Do I get her now, or do I get a *habeas corpus?*"

"Hell, you get her now," Dorset said disgustedly. "I can't help feeling that if I knew everything you'd been doing in the last twelve hours I'd get a promotion; and if I try to find out, I'll be back pounding pavements. Damn it!"

He picked up the telephone, said into the transmitter, "Send that amnesia case number eighty-four on the night bulletin up to my office."

The Witness for the Prosecution

BY AGATHA CHRISTIE

FROM "THE WITNESS FOR THE PROSECUTION AND OTHER STORIES" BY AGATHA CHRISTIE.

MR. MAYHERNE ADJUSTED his pince-nez and cleared his throat with a little dry-as-dust cough that was wholly typical of him. Then he looked again at the man opposite him, the man charged with willful murder.

Mr. Mayherne was a small man, precise in manner, neatly, not to say foppishly dressed, with a pair of very shrewd and piercing gray eyes. By no means a fool. Indeed, as a solicitor, Mr. Mayherne's reputation stood very high. His voice, when he spoke to his client, was dry but not unsympathetic.

"I must impress upon you again that you are in very grave danger, and that the utmost frankness is necessary."

Leonard Vole, who had been staring in a dazed fashion at the blank wall in front of him, transferred his glance to the solicitor.

"I know," he said hopelessly. "You keep telling me so. But I can't seem to realize yet that I'm charged with murder—*murder*. And such a dastardly crime too."

Mr. Mayherne was practical, not emotional. He coughed again, took off his pince-nez, polished them carefully, and replaced them on his nose. Then he said:

"Yes, yes, yes. Now, my dear Mr. Vole, we're going to make a determined effort to get you off—and we shall succeed—we shall succeed. But I must have all the facts. I must know just how damaging the case against you is likely to be. Then we can fix upon the best line of defense."

Still the young man looked at him in the same dazed, hopeless fashion. To Mr. Mayherne the case had seemed black enough, and the guilt of the prisoner assured. Now, for the first time, he felt a doubt.

"You think I'm guilty," said Leonard Vole, in a low voice. "But, by God, I swear I'm not! It looks pretty black against me, I know that. I'm like a man caught in a net—the meshes of it all round me, entangling me whichever way I turn. But I didn't do it, Mr. Mayherne, I didn't do it!"

In such a position a man was bound to protest his innocence. Mr. Mayherne knew that. Yet, in spite of himself, he was impressed. It might be, after all, that Leonard Vole was innocent.

"You are right, Mr. Vole," he said gravely. "The case does look very black against you. Nevertheless, I accept your assurance. Now, let us get to facts. I want you to tell me in your own words exactly how you came to make the acquaintance of Miss Emily French."

"It was one day in Oxford Street. I saw an elderly lady crossing the road. She was carrying a lot of parcels. In the middle of the street she dropped them, tried to recover them, found a bus was almost on top of her and just managed to reach the curb safely, dazed and bewildered by people having shouted at her. I recovered her parcels, wiped the mud off them as best I could, retied the string of one, and returned them to her."

"There was no question of your having saved her life?"

"Oh, dear me, no! All I did was to perform a common act of courtesy. She was extremely grateful, thanked me warmly, and said something about my manners not being those of most of the younger generation—I can't remember the exact words. Then I lifted my hat and went on. I never expected to see her again. But life is full of coincidences. That very evening I came across her at a party at a friend's house. She recognized me at once and asked that I should be introduced to her. I then found out that she was a Miss Emily French and that she lived at Cricklewood. I talked to her for some time. She was, I imagine, an old lady who took sudden and violent fancies to people. She took one to me on the strength of a perfectly simple action which anyone might have performed. On leaving, she shook me warmly by the hand, and asked me to come and see her. I replied, of course, that I should be very pleased to do so, and she then urged me to name a day. I did not want particularly to go, but it would have seemed churlish to refuse, so I fixed on the following Saturday. After she had gone, I learned something about her from my friends. That she was rich, eccentric, lived alone with one maid and owned no less than eight cats."

"I see," said Mr. Mayherne. "The question of her being well off came up as early as that?"

"If you mean that I inquired——" began Leonard Vole hotly, but Mr. Mayherne stilled him with a gesture.

"I have to look at the case as it will be presented by the other side. An ordinary observer would not have supposed Miss French to be a lady of means. She lived poorly, almost humbly. Unless you had been told the contrary, you would in all probability have considered her to be in poor circumstances—at any rate to begin with. Who was it exactly who told you that she was well off?"

"My friend, George Harvey, at whose house the party took place."

"Is he likely to remember having done so?"

"I really don't know. Of course it is some time ago now."

"Quite so, Mr. Vole. You see, the first aim of the prosecution will be to establish that you were in low water financially—that is true, is it not?"

Leonard Vole flushed.

"Yes," he said, in a low voice. "I'd been having a run of infernal bad luck just then."

"Quite so," said Mr. Mayherne again. "That being, as I say, in low water financially, you met this rich old lady and cultivated her acquaintance assiduously. Now if we are in a position to say that you had no idea she was well off, and that you visited her out of pure kindness of heart——"

"Which is the case."

"I dare say. I am not disputing the point. I am looking at it from the outside point of view. A great deal depends on the memory of Mr. Harvey. Is he likely to remember that conversation or is he not? Could he be confused by counsel into believing that it took place later?"

Leonard Vole reflected for some minutes. Then he said steadily enough, but with a rather paler face:

"I do not think that that line would be successful, Mr. Mayherne. Several of those present heard his remark, and one or two of them chaffed me about my conquest of a rich old lady."

The solicitor endeavored to hide his disappointment with a wave of the hand.

"Unfortunate," he said. "But I congratulate you upon your plain speaking, Mr. Vole. It is to you I look to guide me. Your judgment is quite right. To persist in the line I spoke of would have been disastrous. We must leave that point. You made the acquaintance of Miss French, you called upon her, the acquaintanceship progressed. We want a clear reason for all this. Why did you, a young man of thirty-three, good-looking, fond of sport, popular with your friends, devote so much of your time to an elderly woman with whom you could hardly have anything in common?"

Leonard Vole flung out his hands in a nervous gesture.

"I can't tell you—I really can't tell you. After the first visit, she pressed me to come again, spoke of being lonely and unhappy. She made it difficult for me to refuse. She showed so plainly her fondness and affection for me that I was placed in an awkward position. You see, Mr. Mayherne, I've got a weak nature—I drift—I'm one of those people who can't say 'No.' And believe me or not, as you like, after the third or fourth visit I paid her I found myself getting genuinely fond of the old thing. My mother died when I was young, an aunt brought me up, and she too died before I was fifteen. If I told you that I genuinely enjoyed being mothered and pampered, I dare say you'd only laugh."

Mr. Mayherne did not laugh. Instead he took off his pince-nez again and polished them, a sign with him that he was thinking deeply.

"I accept your explanation, Mr. Vole," he said at last. "I believe it to be psychologically probable. Whether a jury would take that view of it is another matter. Please continue your narrative. When was it that Miss French first asked you to look into her business affairs?"

"After my third or fourth visit to her. She understood very little of money matters, and was worried about some investments."

Mr. Mayherne looked up sharply.

"Be careful, Mr. Vole. The maid, Janet Mackenzie, declares that her mistress was a good woman of business and transacted all her own affairs, and this is borne out by the testimony of her bankers."

"I can't help that," said Vole earnestly. "That's what she said to me."

Mr. Mayherne looked at him for a moment or two in silence. Though he had no intention of saying so, his belief in Leonard Vole's innocence was at that moment strengthened. He knew something of the mentality of elderly ladies. He saw Miss French, infatuated with the good-looking young man, hunting about for pretexts that would bring him to the house. What more likely than that she should plead ignorance of business, and beg him to help her with her money affairs? She was enough of a woman of the world to realize that any man is slightly flattered by such an admission of his superiority. Leonard Vole had been flattered. Perhaps, too, she had not been averse to letting this young man know that she was wealthy. Emily French had been a strong-willed old woman, willing to pay her price for what she wanted. All this passed rapidly through Mr. Mayherne's mind, but he gave no indication of it, and asked instead a further question.

"And you did handle her affairs for her at her request?"

"I did."

"Mr. Vole," said the solicitor, "I am going to ask you a very serious question, and one to which it is vital I should have a truthful answer. You were in low water financially. You had the handling of an old lady's affairs—an old lady who, according to her own statement, knew little or nothing of business. Did you at any time, or in any manner, convert to your own use the securities which you handled? Did you engage in any transaction for your own pecuniary advantage which will not bear light of day?" He quelled the other's response. "Wait a minute before you answer. There are two courses open to us. Either we can make a feature of your probity and honesty in conducting her affairs whilst pointing out how unlikely it is that you would commit murder to obtain money which you might have obtained by such infinitely easier means. If, on the other hand, there is anything in your dealings which the prosecution will get hold of—if, to put it baldly, it can be proved that you swindled the old lady in any way, we must take the line that you had no motive for the murder, since she was already a profitable source of income to you. You perceive the distinction. Now, I beg of you, take your time before you reply."

But Leonard Vole took no time at all.

"My dealings with Miss French's affairs were all perfectly fair and above board. I acted for her interests to the very best of my ability, as any one will find who looks into the matter."

"Thank you," said Mr. Mayherne. "You relieve my mind very much. I pay you the compliment of believing that you are far too clever to lie to me over such an important matter."

"Surely," said Vole eagerly, "the strongest point in my favor is the lack of motive. Granted that I cultivated the acquaintanceship of a rich old lady in the hopes of getting money out of her—that, I gather, is the substance of what you have been saying—surely her death frustrates all my hopes?"

The solicitor looked at him steadily. Then, very deliberately, he repeated his unconscious trick with his pince-nez. It was not until they were firmly replaced on his nose that he spoke.

"Are you not aware, Mr. Vole, that Miss French left a will under which you are the principal beneficiary?"

"What?" The prisoner sprang to his feet. His dismay was obvious and unforced. "My God! What are you saying? She left her money to me?"

Mr. Mayherne nodded slowly. Vole sank down again, his head in his hands.

"You pretend you know nothing of this will?"

"Pretend? There's no pretense about it. I knew nothing about it."

"What would you say if I told you that the maid, Janet Mackenzie, swears that you *did* know? That her mistress told her distinctly that she had consulted you in the matter, and told you of her intentions?"

"Say? That she's lying! No, I go too fast. Janet is an elderly woman. She was a faithful watchdog to her mistress, and she didn't like me. She was jealous and suspicious. I should say that Miss French confided her intentions to Janet, and that Janet either mistook something she said, or else was convinced in her own mind that I had persuaded the old lady into doing it. I dare say that she herself believes now that Miss French actually told her so."

"You don't think she dislikes you enough to lie deliberately about the matter?"

Leonard Vole looked shocked and startled.

"No, indeed! Why should she?"

"I don't know," said Mr. Mayherne thoughtfully. "But she's very bitter against you."

The wretched young man groaned again.

"I'm beginning to see," he muttered. "It's frightful. I made up to her, that's what they'll say, I got her to make a will leaving her money to me, and then I go there that night, and there's nobody in the house—they find her the next day—oh! my God, it's awful!"

"You are wrong about there being nobody in the house," said Mr. Mayherne. "Janet, as you remember, was to go out for the evening. She went, but about half-past nine she returned to fetch the pattern of a blouse sleeve which she had promised to a friend. She let herself in by the back door, went upstairs and fetched it, and went out again. She heard voices in the sitting-room, though she could not distinguish what they said, but she will swear that one of them was Miss French's and one was a man's."

"At half-past nine," said Leonard Vole. "At half-past nine. . . ." He sprang to his feet. "But then I'm saved—saved——"

"What do you mean, saved?" cried Mr. Mayherne, astonished.

"By half-past nine I was at home again! My wife can prove that. I left Miss French about five minutes to nine. I arrived home about twenty past nine. My wife was there waiting for me. Oh, thank God—thank God! And bless Janet Mackenzie's sleeve pattern."

In his exuberance, he hardly noticed that the grave expression on the solicitor's face had not altered. But the latter's words brought him down to earth with a bump.

"Who, then, in your opinion, murdered Miss French?"

"Why, a burglar, of course, as was thought at first. The window was forced, you remember. She was killed with a heavy blow from a crowbar, and the crowbar was found lying on the floor beside the body. And several articles were missing. But for Janet's absurd suspicions and dislike of me, the police would never have swerved from the right track."

"That will hardly do, Mr. Vole," said the solicitor. "The things that were missing were mere trifles of no value, taken as a blind. And the marks on the window were not at all conclusive. Besides, think for yourself. You say you were no longer in the house by half-past nine. Who, then, was the man Janet heard talking to Miss French in the sitting-room? She would hardly be having an amicable conversation with a burglar?"

"No," said Vole. "No——" He looked puzzled and discouraged. "But, anyway," he added with reviving spirit, "it lets me out. I've got an alibi. You must see Romaine—my wife—at once."

"Certainly," acquiesced the lawyer. "I should already have seen Mrs. Vole but for her being absent when you were arrested. I wired to Scotland at once, and I understand that she arrives back tonight. I am going to call upon her immediately I leave here."

Vole nodded, a great expression of satisfaction settling down over his face.

"Yes, Romaine will tell you. My God! it's a lucky chance that."

"Excuse me, Mr. Vole, but you are very fond of your wife?"

"Of course."

"And she of you?"

"Romaine is devoted to me. She'd do anything in the world for me."

He spoke enthusiastically, but the solicitor's heart sank a little lower. The testimony of a devoted wife—would it gain credence?

"Was there anyone else who saw you return at nine-twenty. A maid, for instance?"

"We have no maid."

"Did you meet anyone in the street on the way back?"

"Nobody I knew. I rode part of the way in a bus. The conductor might remember."

Mr. Mayherne shook his head doubtfully.

"There is no one, then, who can confirm your wife's testimony?"

"No. But it isn't necessary, surely?"

"I dare say not. I dare say not," said Mr. Mayherne hastily. "Now there's just one thing more. Did Miss French know that you were a married man?"

"Oh, yes."

"Yet you never took your wife to see her. Why was that?"

For the first time, Leonard Vole's answer came halting and uncertain.

"Well—I don't know."

"Are you aware that Janet Mackenzie says her mistress believed you to be single, and contemplated marrying you in the future?"

Vole laughed.

"Absurd! There was forty years' difference in age between us."

"It has been done," said the solicitor drily. "The fact remains. Your wife never met Miss French?"

"No——" Again the constraint.

"You will permit me to say," said the lawyer, "that I hardly understand your attitude in the matter."

Vole flushed, hesitated, and then spoke.

"I'll make a clean breast of it. I was hard up, as you know. I hoped that Miss French might lend me some money. She was fond of me, but she wasn't at all interested in the struggles of a young couple. Early on, I found that she had taken it for granted that my wife and I didn't get on—were living apart. Mr. Mayherne—I wanted the money—for Romaine's sake. I said nothing, and allowed the old lady to think what she chose. She spoke of my being an adopted son to her. There was never any question of marriage—that must be just Janet's imagination."

"And that is all?"

"Yes—that is all."

Was there just a shade of hesitation in the words? The lawyer fancied so. He rose and held out his hand.

"Good-bye, Mr. Vole." He looked into the haggard young face and spoke with an unusual impulse. "I believe in your innocence in spite of the multitude of facts arrayed against you. I hope to prove it and vindicate you completely."

Vole smiled back at him.

"You'll find the alibi is all right," he said cheerfully.

Again he hardly noticed that the other did not respond.

"The whole thing hinges a good deal on the testimony of Janet Mackenzie," said Mr. Mayherne. "She hates you. That much is clear."

"She can hardly hate me," protested the young man.

The solicitor shook his head as he went out.

"Now for Mrs. Vole," he said to himself.

He was seriously disturbed by the way the thing was shaping.

The Voles lived in a small shabby house near Paddington Green. It was to this house that Mr. Mayherne went.

In answer to his ring, a big slatternly woman, obviously a charwoman, answered the door.

"Mrs. Vole? Has she returned yet?"

"Got back an hour ago. But I dunno if you can see her."

"If you will take my card to her," said Mr. Mayherne quietly, "I am quite sure that she will do so."

The woman looked at him doubtfully, wiped her hand on her apron and took the card. Then she closed the door in his face and left him on the step outside.

In a few minutes, however, she returned with a slightly altered manner.

"Come inside, please."

She ushered him into a tiny drawing-room. Mr. Mayherne, examining a drawing on the wall, started up suddenly to face a tall, pale woman who had entered so quietly that he had not heard her.

"Mr. Mayherne? You are my husband's solicitor, are you not? You have come from him? Will you please sit down?"

Until she spoke he had not realized that she was not English. Now, observing her more closely, he noticed the high cheekbones, the dense blue-black of the hair, and an occasional very slight movement of the hands that was distinctly foreign. A strange woman, very quiet. So quiet as to make one uneasy. From the very first Mr. Mayherne was conscious that he was up against something that he did not understand.

"Now, my dear Mrs. Vole," he began, "you must not give way——"

He stopped. It was so very obvious that Romaine Vole had not the slightest intention of giving way. She was perfectly calm and composed.

"Will you please tell me about it?" she said. "I must know everything. Do not think to spare me. I want to know the worst." She hesitated, then repeated in a lower tone, with a curious emphasis which the lawyer did not understand: "I want to know the worst."

Mr. Mayherne went over his interview with Leonard Vole. She listened attentively, nodding her head now and then.

"I see," she said, when he had finished. "He wants me to say that he came in at twenty minutes past nine that night?"

"He did come in at that time?" said Mr. Mayherne sharply.

"That is not the point," she said coldly. "Will my saying so acquit him? Will they believe me?"

Mr. Mayherne was taken aback. She had gone so quickly to the core of the matter.

"That is what I want to know," she said. "Will it be enough? Is there anyone else who can support my evidence?"

There was a suppressed eagerness in her manner that made him vaguely uneasy.

"So far there is no one else," he said reluctantly.

"I see," said Romaine Vole.

She sat for a minute or two perfectly still. A little smile played over her lips.

The lawyer's feeling of alarm grew stronger and stronger.

"Mrs. Vole——" he began. "I know what you must feel——"

"Do you?" she asked. "I wonder."

"In the circumstances——"

"In the circumstances—I intend to play a lone hand."

He looked at her in dismay.

"But, my dear Mrs. Vole—you are overwrought. Being so devoted to your husband——"

"I beg your pardon?"

The sharpness of her voice made him start. He repeated in a hesitating manner:

"Being so devoted to your husband——"

Romaine Vole nodded slowly, the same strange smile on her lips.

"Did he tell you that I was devoted to him?" she asked softly. "Ah! yes, I can see he did. How stupid men are! Stupid—stupid—stupid——"

She rose suddenly to her feet. All the intense emotion that the lawyer had been conscious of in the atmosphere was now concentrated in her tone.

"I hate him, I tell you! I hate him. I hate him. I hate him! I would like to see him hanged by the neck till he is dead."

The lawyer recoiled before her and the smoldering passion in her eyes.

She advanced a step nearer, and continued vehemently:

"Perhaps I shall see it. Supposing I tell you that he did not come in that night at twenty past nine, but at twenty past ten? You say that he tells you he knew nothing about the money coming to him. Supposing I tell you he knew all about it, and counted on it, and committed murder to get it? Supposing I tell you that he admitted to me that night when he came in what he had done? That there was blood on his coat? What then? Supposing that I stand up in court and say all these things?"

Her eyes seemed to challenge him. With an effort, he concealed his growing dismay, and endeavored to speak in a rational tone.

"You cannot be asked to give evidence against your husband——"

"He is not my husband!"

The words came out so quickly that he fancied he had misunderstood her.

"I beg your pardon? I——"

"He is not my husband."

The silence was so intense that you could have heard a pin drop.

"I was an actress in Vienna. My husband is alive but in a madhouse. So we could not marry. I am glad now."

She nodded defiantly.

"I should like you to tell me one thing," said Mr. Mayherne. He contrived to appear as cool and unemotional as ever. "Why are you so bitter against Leonard Vole?"

She shook her head, smiling a little.

"Yes, you would like to know. But I shall not tell you. I will keep my secret. . . ."

Mr. Mayherne gave his dry little cough and rose.

"There seems no point in prolonging this interview," he remarked. "You will hear from me again after I have communicated with my client."

She came closer to him, looking into his eyes with her own wonderful dark ones.

"Tell me," she said, "did you believe—honestly—that he was innocent when you came here today?"

"I did," said Mr. Mayherne.

"You poor little man," she laughed.

"And I believe so still," finished the lawyer. "Good evening, madam."

He went out of the room, taking with him the memory of her startled face.

"This is going to be the devil of a business," said Mr. Mayherne to himself as he strode along the street.

Extraordinary, the whole thing. An extraordinary woman. A very dangerous woman. Women were the devil when they got their knife into you.

What was to be done? That wretched young man hadn't a leg to stand upon. Of course, possibly he did commit the crime. . . .

"No," said Mr. Mayherne to himself. "No—there's almost too much evidence against him. I don't believe this woman. She was trumping up the whole story. But she'll never bring it into court."

He wished he felt more conviction on the point.

The police court proceedings were brief and dramatic. The principal witnesses for the prosecution were Janet Mackenzie, maid to the dead woman, and Romaine Heilger, Austrian subject, the mistress of the prisoner.

Mr. Mayherne sat in court and listened to the damning story that the latter told. It was on the lines she had indicated to him in their interview.

The prisoner reserved his defense and was committed for trial.

Mr. Mayherne was at his wits' end. The case against Leonard Vole was black beyond words. Even the famous K.C. who was engaged for the defense held out little hope.

"If we can shake that Austrian woman's testimony, we might do something," he said dubiously. "But it's a bad business."

Mr. Mayherne had concentrated his energies on one single point. Assuming Leonard Vole to be speaking the truth, and to have left the murdered woman's house at nine o'clock, who was the man Janet heard talking to Miss French at half-past nine?

The only ray of light was in the shape of a scapegrace nephew who had in bygone days cajoled and threatened his aunt out of various sums of money. Janet Mackenzie, the solicitor learned, had always been attached to this young man, and had never ceased urging his claims upon her mistress. It certainly seemed possible that it was this nephew who had been with Miss French after Leonard Vole left, especially as he was not to be found in any of his old haunts.

In all other directions, the lawyer's researches had been negative in their result. No one had seen Leonard Vole entering his own house, or leaving that of Miss French. No one had seen any other man enter or leave the house in Cricklewood. All inquiries drew blanks.

It was the eve of the trial when Mr. Mayherne received the letter which was to lead his thoughts in an entirely new direction.

It came by the six o'clock post. An illiterate scrawl, written on common paper and enclosed in a dirty envelope with the stamp stuck on crooked.

Mr. Mayherne read it through once or twice before he grasped its meaning.

"Dear Mister:

"Youre the lawyer chap wot acts for the young feller. If you want that painted foreign hussy showd up for wot she is an her pack of lies you come to 16 Shaw's Rents Stepney to-night It ull cawst you 2 hundred quid Arsk for Missis Mogson."

The solicitor read and reread this strange epistle. It might, of course, be a hoax, but when he thought it over, he became increasingly convinced that it was genuine, and also convinced that it was the one hope for the prisoner. The evidence of Romaine Heilger damned him completely, and the line the defense meant to pursue, the line that the evidence of a woman who had admittedly lived an immoral life was not to be trusted, was at best a weak one.

Mr. Mayherne's mind was made up. It was his duty to save his client at all costs. He must go to Shaw's Rents.

He had some difficulty in finding the place, a ramshackle building in an evil-smelling slum, but at last he did so, and on inquiry for Mrs. Mogson was sent up to a room on the third floor. On this door he knocked, and getting no answer, knocked again.

At this second knock, he heard a shuffling sound inside, and presently the door was opened cautiously half an inch and a bent figure peered out.

Suddenly the woman, for it was a woman, gave a chuckle and opened the door wider.

"So it's you, dearie," she said, in a wheezy voice. "Nobody with you, is there? No playing tricks? That's right. You can come in—you can come in."

With some reluctance the lawyer stepped across the threshold into the small dirty room, with its flickering gas jet. There was an untidy unmade bed in a corner, a plain deal table and two rickety chairs. For the first time Mr. Mayherne had a full view of the tenant of this unsavory apartment. She was a woman of middle age, bent in figure, with a mass of untidy gray hair and a scarf wound tightly round her face. She saw him looking at this and laughed again, the same curious, toneless chuckle.

"Wondering why I hide my beauty, dear? He, he, he. Afraid it may tempt you, eh? But you shall see—you shall see."

She drew aside the scarf and the lawyer recoiled involuntarily before the almost formless blur of scarlet. She replaced the scarf again.

"So you're not wanting to kiss me, dearie? He, he, I don't wonder. And yet I was a pretty girl once—not so long ago as you'd think, either. Vitriol, dearie, vitriol—that's what did that. Ah! but I'll be even with 'em——"

She burst into a hideous torrent of profanity which Mr. Mayherne tried vainly to quell. She fell silent at last, her hands clenching and unclenching themselves nervously.

"Enough of that," said the lawyer sternly. "I've come here because I have reason to believe you can give me information which will clear my client, Leonard Vole. Is that the case?"

Her eyes leered at him cunningly.

"What about the money, dearie?" she wheezed. "Two hundred quid, you remember."

"It is your duty to give evidence, and you can be called upon to do so."

"That won't do, dearie. I'm an old woman, and I know nothing. But you give me two hundred quid, and perhaps I can give you a hint or two. See?"

"What kind of hint?"

"What should you say to a letter? A letter from *her*. Never mind how I got hold of it. That's my business. It'll do the trick. But I want my two hundred quid."

Mr. Mayherne looked at her coldly, and made up his mind.

"I'll give you ten pounds, nothing more. And only that if this letter is what you say it is."

"Ten pounds?" She screamed and raved at him.

"Twenty," said Mr. Mayherne, "and that's my last word."

He rose as if to go. Then, watching her closely, he drew out a pocketbook, and counted out twenty one-pound notes.

"You see," he said. "That is all I have with me. You can take it or leave it."

But already he knew that the sight of the money was too much for her. She cursed and raved impotently, but at last she gave in. Going over to the bed, she drew something out from beneath the tattered mattress.

"Here you are, damn you!" she snarled. "It's the top one you want."

It was a bundle of letters that she threw to him, and Mr. Mayherne untied them and scanned them in his usual cool, methodical manner.

The woman, watching him eagerly, could gain no clue from his impassive face.

He read each letter through, then returned again to the top one and read it a second time. Then he tied the whole bundle up again carefully.

They were love letters, written by Romaine Heilger, and the man they were written to was not Leonard Vole. The top letter was dated the day of the latter's arrest.

"I spoke true, dearie, didn't I?" whined the woman. "It'll do for her, that letter?"

Mr. Mayherne put the letters in his pocket, then he asked a question.

"How did you get hold of this correspondence?"

"That's telling," she said with a leer. "But I know something more. I heard in court what that hussy said. Find out where she was at twenty past ten, the time she says she was at home. Ask at the Lion Road Cinema. They'll remember—a fine upstanding girl like that—curse her!"

"Who is the man?" asked Mr. Mayherne. "There's only a Christian name here."

The other's voice grew thick and hoarse, her hands clenched and unclenched. Finally she lifted one to her face.

"He's the man that did this to me. Many years ago now. She took him away from me—a chit of a girl she was then. And when I went after him—and went for him too—he threw the cursed stuff at me! And she laughed—damn her! I've had it in for her for years. Followed her, I have, spied upon her. And now I've got her! She'll suffer for this, won't she, Mr. Lawyer? She'll suffer?"

"She will probably be sentenced to a term of imprisonment for perjury," said Mr. Mayherne quietly.

"Shut away—that's what I want. You're going, are you? Where's my money? Where's that good money?"

Without a word, Mr. Mayherne put down the notes on the table. Then, drawing a deep breath, he turned and left the squalid room. Looking back, he saw the old woman crooning over the money.

He wasted no time. He found the cinema in Lion Road easily enough, and, shown a photograph of Romaine Heilger, the commissionaire recognized her at once. She had arrived at the cinema with a man some time after ten o'clock on the evening in question. He had not noticed her escort particularly, but he remembered the lady who had spoken to him about the picture that was showing. They stayed until the end, about an hour later.

Mr. Mayherne was satisfied. Romaine Heilger's evidence was a tissue of lies from beginning to end. She had evolved it out of her passionate hatred. The lawyer wondered whether he would ever know what lay behind that hatred. What had Leonard Vole done to her? He had seemed dumbfounded when the solicitor had reported her attitude to him. He had declared earnestly that such a thing was incredible—yet it had seemed to Mr. Mayherne that after the first astonishment his protests had lacked sincerity.

He did know. Mr. Mayherne was convinced of it. He knew, but he had no intention of revealing the fact. The secret between those two remained a secret. Mr. Mayherne wondered if some day he should come to learn what it was.

The solicitor glanced at his watch. It was late, but time was everything. He hailed a taxi and gave an address.

"Sir Charles must know of this at once," he murmured to himself as he got in.

The trial of Leonard Vole for the murder of Emily French aroused widespread interest. In the first place the prisoner was young and good-looking, then he was accused of a particularly dastardly crime, and there was the further interest of Romaine Heilger, the principal witness for the prosecution. There had been pictures of her in many papers, and several fictitious stories as to her origin and history.

The proceedings opened quietly enough. Various technical evidence came first. Then Janet Mackenzie was called. She told substantially the same story as before. In cross-examination counsel for the defense succeeded in getting her to contradict herself once or twice over her account of Vole's association with Miss French; he emphasized the fact that though she had heard a man's voice in the sitting-room that night, there was nothing to show that it was Vole who was there, and he managed to drive home a feeling that jealousy and dislike of the prisoner were at the bottom of a good deal of her evidence.

Then the next witness was called.

"Your name is Romaine Heilger?"

"Yes."

"You are an Austrian subject?"

"Yes."

"For the last three years you have lived with the prisoner and passed yourself off as his wife?"

Just for a moment Romaine Heilger's eyes met those of the man in the dock. Her expression held something curious and unfathomable.

"Yes."

The questions went on. Word by word the damning facts came out. On the night in question the prisoner had taken out a crowbar with him. He had returned at twenty minutes past ten, and had confessed to having killed the old lady. His cuffs had been stained with blood, and he had burned them in the kitchen stove. He had terrorized her into silence by means of threats.

As the story proceeded, the feeling of the court which had, to begin with, been slightly favorable to the prisoner, now set dead against him.

He himself sat with downcast head and moody air, as though he knew he were doomed.

Yet it might have been noted that her own counsel sought to restrain Romaine's animosity. He would have preferred her to be more unbiased.

Formidable and ponderous, counsel for the defense arose.

He put it to her that her story was a malicious fabrication from start to finish, that she had not even been in her own house at the time in question, that she was in love with another man and was deliberately seeking to send Vole to his death for a crime he did not commit.

Romaine denied these allegations with superb insolence.

Then came the surprising denouement, the production of the letter. It was read aloud in court in the midst of a breathless stillness.

"Max, beloved, the Fates have delivered him into our hands! He has been arrested for murder—but, yes, the murder of an old lady! Leonard, who would not hurt a fly! At last I shall have my revenge. The poor chicken! I shall say that he came in that night with blood upon him—that he confessed to me. I shall hang him, Max—and when he hangs he will know and realize that it was Romaine who sent him to his death. And then—happiness, Beloved! Happiness at last!"

There were experts present ready to swear that the handwriting was that of Romaine Heilger, but they were not needed. Confronted with the letter, Romaine broke down utterly and confessed everything. Leonard Vole had returned to the house at the time he said, twenty past nine. She had invented the whole story to ruin him.

With the collapse of Romaine Heilger, the case for the Crown collapsed also. Sir Charles called his few witnesses, the prisoner himself went into the box and told his story in a manly straightforward manner, unshaken by cross-examination.

The prosecution endeavored to rally, but without great success. The judge's summing up was not wholly favorable to the prisoner, but a reaction had set in and the jury needed little time to consider their verdict.

"We find the prisoner not guilty."

Leonard Vole was free!

Little Mr. Mayherne hurried from his seat. He must congratulate his client.

He found himself polishing his pince-nez vigorously, and checked himself. His wife had told him only the night before that he was getting a habit of it. Curious things, habits. People themselves never knew they had them.

An interesting case—a very interesting case. That woman, now, Romaine Heilger.

The case was dominated for him still by the exotic figure of Romaine Heilger. She had seemed a pale, quiet woman in the house at Paddington, but in court she had flamed out against the sober background, flaunting herself like a tropical flower.

If he closed his eyes he could see her now, tall and vehement, her exquisite body bent forward a little, her right hand clenching and unclenching itself unconsciously all the time.

Curious things, habits. That gesture of hers with the hand was her habit, he supposed. Yet he had seen someone else do it quite lately. Who was it now? Quite lately——

He drew in his breath with a gasp as it came back to him. The woman in Shaw's Rents. . . .

He stood still, his head whirling. It was impossible—impossible—— Yet, Romaine Heilger was an actress.

The K.C. came up behind him and clapped him on the shoulder.

"Congratulated our man yet? He's had a narrow shave, you know. Come along and see him."

But the little lawyer shook off the other's hand.

He wanted one thing only—to see Romaine Heilger face to face.

He did not see her until some time later, and the place of their meeting is not relevant.

"So you guessed," she said, when he had told her all that was in his mind. "The face? Oh! that was easy enough, and the light of that gas jet was too bad for you to see the make-up."

"But why—why——"

"Why did I play a lone hand?" She smiled a little, remembering the last time she had used the words.

"Such an elaborate comedy!"

"My friend—I had to save him. The evidence of a woman devoted to him would not have been enough—you hinted as much yourself. But I know something of the psychology of crowds. Let my evidence be wrung from me, as an admission, damning me in the eyes of the law, and a reaction in favor of the prisoner would immediately set in."

"And the bundle of letters?"

"One alone, the vital one, might have seemed like a—what do you call it?—put-up job."

"Then the man called Max?"

"Never existed, my friend."

"I still think," said little Mr. Mayherne, in an aggrieved manner, "that we could have got him off by the—er—normal procedure."

"I dared not risk it. You see you thought he was innocent——"

"And you knew it? I see," said little Mr. Mayherne.

"My dear Mr. Mayherne," said Romaine, "you do not see at all. I knew—he was guilty!"

The Adventure of The President's Half Disme

BY ELLERY QUEEN

THOSE FEW CURIOUS MEN who have chosen to turn off the humdrum highway to hunt for their pleasure along the back trails expect—indeed, they look confidently forward to—many strange encounters; and it is the dull stalk which does not turn up at least a hippogriff. But it remained for Ellery Queen to experience the ultimate excitement. On one of his prowls he collided with a President of the United States.

This would have been joy enough if it had occurred as you might imagine: by chance, on a dark night, in some back street of Washington, D.C., with Secret Service men closing in on the delighted Mr. Queen to question his motives by way of his pockets while a large black bullet-proof limousine rushed up to spirit the President away. But mere imagination fails in this instance. What is required is the power of fancy, for the truth is fantastic. Ellery's encounter with the President of the United States took place, not on a dark night, but in the unromantic light of several days (although the night played its role, too). Nor was it by chance: the meeting was arranged by a farmer's daughter. And it was not in Washington, D.C., for this President presided over the affairs of the nation from a different city altogether. Not that the meeting took place in that city, either; it did not take place in a city at all, but on a farm some miles south of Philadelphia. Oddest of all, there was no limousine to spirit the Chief Executive away, for while the President was a man of great wealth, he was still too poor to possess an automobile and, what is more, not all the resources of his Government—indeed, not all the riches of the world—could have provided one for him.

There are even more curious facets to this jewel of paradox. This was an encounter in the purest sense, and yet, physically, it did not occur at all. The President in question was dead. And while there are those who would not blink at a rubbing of shoulders or a clasping of hands even though one of the parties was in his grave, and to such persons the thought might occur that the meeting took place on a psychic plane—alas, Ellery Queen is not of their company. He does not believe in ghosts, consequently he never encounters them. So he did not collide with the President's shade, either.

And yet their meeting was as palpable as, say, the meeting between two chess masters, one in London and the other in New York, who never leave their respective armchairs and still play a game to a decision. It is even more wonderful than that, for while the chess players merely annihilate space, Ellery and the father of his country annihilated time—a century and a half of it.

In fine, this is the story of how Ellery Queen matched wits with George Washington.

Those who are finicky about their fashions complain that the arms of coincidence are too long; but in this case the Designer might say that He cut to measure. Or, to put it another way, an event often brews its own mood. Whatever the cause, the fact is The Adventure of the President's Half Disme, which was to concern itself with the events surrounding President Washington's fifty-ninth birthday, actually first engrossed Ellery on February the nineteenth and culminated three days later.

Ellery was in his study that morning of the nineteenth of February, wrestling with several reluctant victims of violence, none of them quite flesh and blood, since his novel was still in the planning stage. So he was annoyed when Nikki came in with a card.

"James Ezekiel Patch," growled the great man; he was never in his best humor during the planning stage. "I don't know any James Ezekiel Patch, Nikki. Toss the fellow out and get back to transcribing those notes on Possible Motives—"

"Why, Ellery," said Nikki. "This isn't like you at all."

"What isn't like me?"

"To renege on an appointment."

"Appointment? Does this Patch character claim—?"

"He doesn't merely claim it. He proves it."

"Someone's balmy," snarled Mr. Queen; and he strode into the living room to contend with James Ezekiel Patch. This, he perceived as soon as James Ezekiel Patch rose from the Queen fireside chair, was likely to be a heroic project. Mr. Patch, notwithstanding his mild, even studious, eyes, seemed to rise indefinitely; he was a large, a very large, man.

"Now what's all this, what's all this?" demanded Ellery fiercely; for after all Nikki was there.

"That's what I'd like to know," said the large man amiably. "What did you want with me, Mr. Queen?"

"What did I want with you! What did you want with me?"

"I find this very strange, Mr. Queen."

"Now see here, Mr. Patch, I happen to be extremely busy this morning—"

"So am I." Mr. Patch's large thick neck was reddening and his tone was no longer amiable. Ellery took a cautious step backward as his visitor lumbered forward to thrust a slip of yellow paper under his nose. "Did you send me this wire, or didn't you?"

Ellery considered it tactically expedient to take the telegram, although for strategic reasons he did so with a bellicose scowl.

IMPERATIVE YOU CALL AT MY HOME TOMORROW FEBRUARY NINETEEN PROMPTLY TEN A.M. SIGNED ELLERY QUEEN

"Well, sir?" thundered Mr. Patch. "Do you have something on Washington for me, or don't you?"

"Washington?" said Ellery absently, studying the telegram.

"*George* Washington, Mr. Queen! I'm Patch the antiquarian. I *collect* Washington. I'm an *authority* on Washington. I have a large fortune and I spend it all on Washington! I'd never have wasted my time this morning if your name hadn't been signed to this wire! This is my busiest week of the year. I have engagements to speak on Washington—"

"Desist, Mr. Patch," said Ellery. "This is either a practical joke, or—"

"The Baroness Tchek," announced Nikki clearly. "With another telegram." And then she added: "And Professor John Cecil Shaw, ditto."

The three telegrams were identical.

"Of course I didn't send them," said Ellery thoughtfully, regarding his three visitors. Baroness Tchek was a short powerful woman, resembling a dumpling with gray hair; an angry dumpling. Professor Shaw was lank and long-jawed, wearing a sack suit which hung in some places and failed in its purpose by inches at the extremities. Along with Mr. Patch, they constituted as deliciously queer a trio as had ever congregated in the Queen apartment. Their host suddenly determined not to let go of them. "On the other hand, someone obviously did, using my name . . ."

"Then there's nothing more to be said," snapped the Baroness, snapping her bag for emphasis.

"I should think there's a great deal more to be said," began Professor Shaw in a troubled way. "Wasting people's time this way—"

"It's not going to waste any more of *my* time," growled the large Mr. Patch. "Washington's Birthday only three days off—!"

"Exactly," smiled Ellery. "Won't you sit down? There's more in this than meets the eye . . . Baroness Tchek, if I'm not mistaken, you're the one who brought that fabulous collection of rare coins into the United States just before Hitler invaded Czechoslovakia? You're in the rare-coin business in New York now?"

"Unfortunately," said the Baroness coldly, "one must eat."

"And you, sir? I seem to know you."

"Rare books," said the Professor in the same troubled way.

"Of course. John Cecil Shaw, the rare-book collector. We've met at Mim's and other places. I abandon my first theory. There's a pattern here, distinctly unhumorous. An antiquarian, a coin dealer, and a collector of rare books—Nikki? Whom have you out there this time?"

"If this one collects anything," muttered Nikki into her employer's ear, "I'll bet it has two legs and hair on its chest. A darned pretty girl—"

"Named Martha Clarke," said a cool voice; and Ellery turned to find himself regarding one of the most satisfying sights in the world.

"Ah. I take it, Miss Clarke, you also received one of these wires signed with my name?"

"Oh, no," said the pretty girl. "I'm the one who sent them."

There was something about the comely Miss Clarke which inspired, if not confidence, at least an openness of mind. Perhaps it was the self-possessed manner in which she sat all of them, including Ellery, down in Ellery's living room while she waited on the hearth-rug, like a conductor on the podium, for them to settle in their chairs. And it was the measure of Miss Clarke's assurance that none of them was indignant, only curious.

"I'll make it snappy," said Martha Clarke briskly. "I did what I did the way I did it because, first, I had to make sure I could see Mr. Patch, Baroness Tchek, and Professor Shaw today. Second, because I may need a detective before I'm through . . . Third," she added, almost absently, "because I'm pretty desperate.

"My name is Martha Clarke. My father Tobias is a farmer. Our farm lies just south of Philadelphia, it was built by a Clarke in 1761, and it's been in our family ever since. I won't go gooey on you. We're broke and there's a mortgage. Unless Papa and I can raise six thousand dollars in the next couple of weeks we lose the old homestead."

Professor Shaw looked vague. But the Baroness said: "Deplorable, Miss Clarke. Now if I'm to run my auction this afternoon—"

And James Ezekiel Patch grumbled: "If it's money you want, young woman—"

"Certainly it's money I want. But I have something to sell."

"Ah!" said the Baroness.

"Oh?" said the Professor.

"Hm," said the antiquarian.

Mr. Queen said nothing, and Miss Porter jealously chewed the end of her pencil.

"The other day while I was cleaning out the attic, I found an old book."

"Well, now," said Professor Shaw indulgently. "An old book, eh?"

"It's called *The Diary of Simeon Clarke*. Simeon Clarke was Papa's great-great-great-something or other. His *Diary* was privately printed in 1792 in Philadelphia, Professor, by a second cousin of his, Jonathan, who was in the printing business there."

"Jonathan Clarke. *The Diary of Simeon Clarke*," mumbled the cadaverous book collector. "I don't believe I know either, Miss Clarke. Have you . . . ?"

Martha Clarke carefully unclasped a large Manila envelope and drew forth a single yellowed sheet of badly printed paper. "The title page was loose, so I brought it along."

Professor Shaw silently examined Miss Clarke's exhibit, and Ellery got up to squint at it. "Of course," said the Professor after a long scrutiny, in which he held the sheet up to the light, peered apparently at individual characters, and performed other mysterious rites, "mere age doesn't connote rarity, nor does rarity of itself constitute value. And while this page looks genuine for the purported period and is rare enough to be unknown to me, still . . ."

"Suppose I told you," said Miss Martha Clarke, "that the chief purpose of the *Diary*—which I have at home—is to tell the story of how George Washington visited Simeon Clarke's farm in the winter of 1791—"

"Clarke's farm? 1791?" exclaimed James Ezekiel Patch. "Preposterous. There's no record of—"

"And of what George Washington buried there," the farmer's daughter concluded.

By executive order, the Queen telephone was taken off its hook, the door was bolted, the shades were drawn, and the long interrogation began. By the middle of the afternoon, the unknown chapter in the life of the Father of His Country was fairly sketched.

Early on an icy gray February morning in 1791, Farmer Clarke had looked up from the fence he was mending to observe a splendid cortège galloping down on him from the direction of the City of Philadelphia. Outriders thundered in the van, followed by a considerable company of gentlemen on horseback and several great coaches-and-six driven by liveried Negroes. To Simeon Clarke's astonishment, the entire equipage stopped before his farmhouse. He began to run. He could hear the creak of springs and the snorting of sleek and sweating horses. Gentlemen and lackeys were leaping to the frozen ground and, by the time Simeon had reached the farmhouse, all were elbowing about the first coach, a magnificent affair bearing a coat of arms. Craning, the farmer saw within the coach a very large, great-nosed gentleman clad in a black velvet suit and a black cloak faced with gold; there was a cocked hat on his wigged head and a great sword in a white leather scabbard at his side. This personage was on one knee, leaning with an expression of considerable anxiety over a chubby lady of middle age, swathed in furs, who was half-sitting, half-lying on the upholstered seat, her eyes closed and her cheeks waxen under the rouge. Another gentleman, soberly attired, was stooping over the lady, his fingers on one pale wrist.

"I fear," he was saying with great gravity to the kneeling man, "that it would be imprudent to proceed another yard in this weather, Your Excellency. Lady Washington requires physicking and a warm bed immediately."

Lady Washington! Then the large, richly dressed gentleman was the President! Simeon Clarke pushed excitedly through the throng.

"Your Mightiness! Sir!" he cried. "I am Simeon Clarke. This is my farm. We have warm beds, Sarah and I!"

The President considered Simeon briefly. "I thank you, Farmer Clarke. No, no, Dr. Craik. I shall assist Lady Washington myself."

And George Washington carried Martha Washington into the little Pennsylvania farmhouse of Simeon and Sarah Clarke. An aide informed the Clarkes that President Washington had been on his way to Virginia to celebrate his fifty-ninth birthday in the privacy of Mount Vernon.

Instead, he passed his birthday on the Clarke farm, for the physician insisted that the President's lady could not be moved, even back to the nearby Capital, without risking complications. On His Excellency's order, the entire incident was kept secret. "It would give needless alarm to the people," he said. But he did not leave Martha's bedside for three days and three nights.

Presumably during those seventy-two hours, while his lady recovered from her indisposition, the President devoted some thought to his hosts, for on the fourth morning he sent black Christopher, his body servant, to summon the Clarkes. They found George Washington by the kitchen fire, shaven and powdered and in immaculate dress, his stern features composed.

"I am told, Farmer Clarke, that you and your good wife refuse reimbursement for the livestock you have slaughtered in the accommodation of our large company."

"You're my President, Sir," said Simeon. "I wouldn't take money."

"We—we wouldn't take money, Your Worship," stammered Sarah.

"Nevertheless, Lady Washington and I would acknowledge your hospitality in some kind. If you give me leave, I shall plant with my own hands a grove of oak saplings behind your house. And beneath one of the saplings I propose to bury two of my personal possessions." Washington's eyes twinkled ever so slightly. "It is my birthday—I feel a venturesome spirit. Come, Farmer Clarke and Mistress Clarke, would you like that?"

"What—what were they?" choked James Ezekiel Patch, the Washington collector. He was pale.

Martha Clarke replied: "The sword at Washington's side, in its white leather scabbard, and a silver coin the President carried in a secret pocket."

"Silver *coin?*" breathed Baroness Tchek, the rare-coin dealer. "What kind of coin, Miss Clarke?"

"The *Diary* calls it 'a half disme,' with an *s*," replied Martha Clarke, frowning. "I guess that's the way they spelled dime in those days. The book's full of queer spellings."

"A United States of America half disme?" asked the Baroness in a very odd way.

"That's what it says, Baroness."

"And this was in 1791?"

"Yes."

The Baroness snorted, beginning to rise. "I thought your story was too impossibly romantic, young woman. The United States Mint didn't begin to strike off half dismes until 1792!"

"Half dismes or any other U. S. coinage, I believe," said Ellery. "How come, Miss Clarke?"

"It was an experimental coin," said Miss Clarke coolly. "The *Diary* isn't clear as to whether it was the Mint which struck it off, or some private agency—maybe Washington himself didn't tell Simeon—but the President did say to Simeon that the half disme in his pocket had been coined from silver he himself had furnished and had been presented to him as a keepsake."

"There's a half disme with a story like that behind it in the possession of The American Numismatic Society," muttered the Baroness, "but it's definitely called one of the earliest coins struck off by the Mint. It's possible, I suppose, that in 1791, the preceding year, some specimen coins may have been struck off—"

"Possible my foot," said Miss Clarke. "It's so. The *Diary* says so. I imagine President Washington was pretty interested in the coins to be issued by the new country he was head of."

"Miss Clarke, I—I want that half disme. I mean—I'd like to buy it from you," said the Baroness.

"And I," said Mr. Patch carefully, "would like to ah . . . purchase Washington's sword."

"The *Diary*," moaned Professor Shaw. "I'll buy *The Diary of Simeon Clarke* from you, Miss Clarke!"

"I'll be happy to sell it to you, Professor Shaw—as I said, I found it in the attic and I have it locked up in a highboy in the parlor at home. But as for the other two things . . ." Martha Clarke paused, and Ellery looked delighted. He thought he knew what was coming. "I'll sell you the sword, Mr. Patch, and you the half disme, Baroness Tchek, provided—" and now Miss Clarke turned her clear eyes on Ellery "—provided you, Mr. Queen, will be kind enough to find them."

And there was the farmhouse in the frosty Pennsylvania morning, set in the barren winter acres, and looking as bleak as only a little Revolutionary house with a mortgage on its head can look in the month of February.

"There's an apple orchard over there," said Nikki as they got out of Ellery's car. "But where's the grove of oaks? I don't see any!" And then she added, sweetly: "Do you, Ellery?"

Ellery's lips tightened. They tightened further when his solo on the front-door knocker brought no response.

"Let's go around," he said briefly; and Nikki preceded him with cheerful step.

Behind the house there was a barn; and beyond the barn there was comfort, at least for Ellery. For beyond the barn there were twelve ugly holes in the earth, and beside each hole lay either a freshly felled oak tree and its stump, or an ancient stump by itself, freshly uprooted. On one of the stumps sat an old man in earth-stained blue jeans, smoking a corncob pugnaciously.

"Tobias Clarke?" asked Ellery.

"Yump."

"I'm Ellery Queen. This is Miss Porter. Your daughter visited me in New York yesterday—"

"Know all about it."

"May I ask where Martha is?"

"Station. Meetin' them there other folks." Tobias Clarke spat and looked away—at the holes. "Don't know what ye're all comin' down here for. Wasn't nothin' under them oaks. Dug 'em all up t'other day. Trees that were standin' and the stumps of the ones that'd fallen years back. Look at them holes. Hired hand and me dug down most to China. Washin'ton's Grove, always been called. Now look at it. Firewood—for someone else, I guess." There was iron bitterness in his tone. "We're losin' this farm, Mister, unless . . ." And Tobias Clarke stopped. "Well, maybe we won't," he said. "There's always that there book Martha found."

"Professor Shaw, the rare-book collector, offered your daughter two thousand dollars for it if he's satisfied with it, Mr. Clarke," said Nikki.

"So she told me last night when she got back from New York," said Tobias Clarke. "Two thousand—and we need six." He grinned, and he spat again.

"Well," said Nikki sadly to Ellery, "that's that." She hoped Ellery would immediately get into the car and drive back to New York—immediately.

But Ellery showed no disposition to be sensible. "Perhaps, Mr. Clarke, some trees died in the course of time and just disappeared, stumps, roots, and all. Martha"—Martha!—"said the *Diary* doesn't mention the exact number Washington planted here."

"Look at them holes. Twelve of 'em, ain't there? In a triangle. Man plants trees in a triangle, he plants trees in a triangle. Ye don't see no place between holes big enough for another tree, do ye? Anyways, there was the same distance between all the trees. No, sir, Mister, twelve was all there was ever; and I looked under all twelve."

"What's the extra tree doing in the center of the triangle? You haven't uprooted that one, Mr. Clarke."

Tobias Clarke spat once more. "Don't know much about trees, do ye? That's a cherry saplin' I set in myself six years ago. Ain't got nothin' to do with George Washington."

Nikki tittered.

"If you'd sift the earth in those holes—"

"I sifted it. Look, Mister, either somebody dug that stuff up a hundred years ago or the whole yarn's a Saturday night whopper. Which it most likely is. There's Martha now with them other folks." And Tobias Clarke added, spitting for the fourth time: "Don't let me be keepin' ye."

"It reveals Washington rather er . . . out of character," said James Ezekiel Patch that evening. They were sitting about the fire in the parlor, as heavy with gloom as with Miss Clarke's dinner; and that, at least in Miss Porter's view, was heavy indeed. Baroness Tchek wore the expression of one who is trapped in a cave; there was no further train until morning, and she had not yet resigned herself to a night in a farmhouse bed. The better part of the day had been spent poring over *The Diary of Simeon Clarke,* searching for a clue to the buried Washingtonia. But there was no clue; the pertinent passage referred merely to "a Triangle of Oake Trees behinde the red Barn, which His Excellency the President did plant with his own Hands, as he had promis'd me, and then did burie his Sworde and the Half Disme for his Pleasure in a Case of copper beneathe one of the Oakes, the which, he said (the Case), had been fashion'd by Mr. Revere of Boston who is experimenting with this Mettle in his Furnasses."

"How out of character, Mr. Patch?" asked Ellery. He had been staring into the fire for a long time, scarcely listening.

"Washington wasn't given to romanticism," said the large man dryly. "No folderol about him. I don't know of anything in his life which prepares us for such a yarn as this. I'm beginning to think—"

"But Professor Shaw himself says the *Diary* is no forgery!" cried Martha Clarke.

"Oh, the book's authentic enough." Professor Shaw seemed unhappy. "But it may simply be a literary hoax, Miss Clarke. The woods are full of them. I'm afraid that unless the story is confirmed by the discovery of that copper case with its contents . . ."

"Oh, dear," said Nikki impulsively; and for a moment she was sorry for Martha Clarke, she really was.

But Ellery said: "I believe it. Pennsylvania farmers in 1791 weren't given to literary hoaxes, Professor Shaw. As for Washington, Mr. Patch —no man can be so rigidly consistent. And with his wife just recovering from an illness—on his own birthday . . ." And Ellery fell silent again.

Almost immediately he leaped from his chair. "Mr. Clarke!"

Tobias stirred from his dark corner. "What?"

"Did you ever hear your father, or grandfather—anyone in your family—talk of *another barn behind the house?*"

Martha stared at him. Then she cried: "Papa, that's it! It was a different barn, in a different place, and the original Washington's Grove was cut down, or died—"

"Nope," said Tobias Clarke. "Never was but this one barn. Still got some of its original timbers. Ye can see the date burned into the crosstree—1761."

Nikki was up early. A steady *hack-hack-hack* borne on the frosty air woke her. She peered out of her back window, the coverlet up to her nose, to see Mr. Ellery Queen against the dawn, like a pioneer, wielding an ax powerfully.

Nikki dressed quickly, shivering, flung her mink-dyed muskrat over her shoulders, and ran downstairs, out of the house, and around it past the barn.

"Ellery! What do you think you're doing? It's practically the middle of the night!"

"Chopping," said Ellery, chopping.

"There's *mountains* of firewood stacked against the barn," said Nikki. "Really, Ellery, I think this is carrying a flirtation too far." Ellery did not reply. "And anyway, there's something—something gruesome and indecent about chopping up trees George Washington planted. It's vandalism."

"Just a thought," panted Ellery, pausing for a moment. "A hundred and fifty-odd years is a long time, Nikki. Lots of queer things could happen, even to a tree, in that time. For instance—"

"The copper case," breathed Nikki, visibly. "The roots grew *around* it. It's *in* one of these stumps!"

"Now you're functioning," said Ellery, and he raised the ax again.

He was still at it two hours later, when Martha Clarke announced breakfast.

At 11:30 A.M. Nikki returned from driving the Professor, the Baroness, and James Ezekiel Patch to the railroad station. She found Mr. Queen seated before the fire in the kitchen in his undershirt, while Martha Clarke caressed his naked right arm.

"Oh!" said Nikki faintly. "I *beg* your pardon."

"Where you going, Nikki?" said Ellery irritably. "Come in. Martha's rubbing liniment into my biceps."

"He's not very accustomed to chopping wood, is he?" asked Martha Clarke in a cheerful voice.

"Reduced those foul 'oakes' to splinters," groaned Ellery. "Martha, ouch!"

"I should think you'd be satisfied *now*," said Nikki coldly. "I suggest we imitate Patch, Shaw, and the Baroness, Ellery—there's a 3:05. We can't impose on Miss Clarke's hospitality forever."

To Nikki's horror, Martha Clarke chose this moment to burst into tears.

"Martha!"

Nikki felt like leaping upon her and shaking the cool look back into her perfidious eyes.

"Here—here, now, Martha." That's right, thought Nikki contemptuously. Embrace her in front of me! "It's those three rats. Running out that way! Don't worry—I'll find that sword and half disme for you yet."

"You'll never find them," sobbed Martha, wetting Ellery's undershirt. "Because they're not here. They *never* were here. When you s-stop to think of it . . . *burying* that coin, his sword . . . if the story were true, he'd have given them to Simeon and Sarah . . ."

"Not necessarily, not necessarily," said Ellery with a hateful haste. "The old boy had a sense of history, Martha. They all did in those days. They knew they were men of destiny and that the eyes of posterity were upon them. Burying 'em is *just* what Washington would have done!"

"Do you really th-think so?"

Oh . . . *pfui.*

"But even if he did bury them," Martha sniffled, "it doesn't stand to reason Simeon and Sarah would have let them *stay* buried. They'd have dug that copper box up like rabbits the minute G-George turned his back."

"Two simple countryfolk?" cried Ellery. "Salt of the earth? The new American earth? Disregard the wishes of His Mightiness, George Washington, First President of the United States? Are you out of your mind? And anyway, what would Simeon do with a dress-sword?"

Beat it into a plowshare, thought Nikki spitefully—*that's* what he'd do.

"And that half disme. How much could it have been worth in 1791? Martha, they're here under your farm somewhere. You wait and see—"

"I wish I could b-believe it . . . Ellery."

"Shucks, child. Now stop crying—"

From the door Miss Porter said stiffly: "You might put your shirt back on, Superman, before you catch pneumonia."

Mr. Queen prowled about the Clarke acres for the remainder of that day, his nose at a low altitude. He spent some time in the barn. He devoted at least twenty minutes to each of the twelve holes in the earth. He reinspected the oaken wreckage of his axwork, like a paleontologist examining an ancient petrifaction for the impression of a dinosaur foot. He measured off the distance between the holes; and, for a moment, a faint tremor of emotion shook him. George Washington had been a surveyor in his youth; here was evidence that his passion for exactitude had not wearied with the years. As far as Ellery could make out, the twelve oaks had been set into the earth at exactly equal distances, in an equilateral triangle.

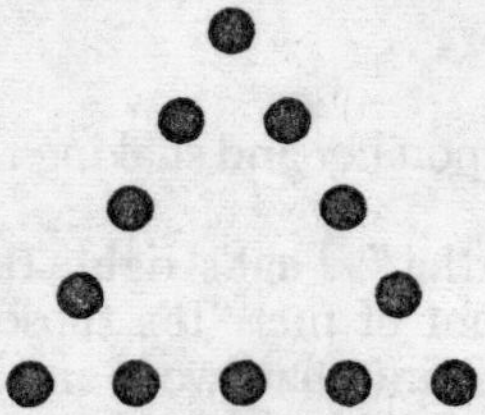

It was at this point that Ellery had seated himself upon the seat of a cultivator behind the barn, wondering at his suddenly accelerated circulation. Little memories were knocking at the door. And as he opened to admit them, it was as if he were admitting a personality. It was, of course, at this time that the sense of personal conflict first obtruded. He had merely to shut his eyes in order to materialize a tall, large-featured man carefully pacing off the distances between twelve points—pacing them off in a sort of objective challenge to the unborn future. George Washington . . .

The man Washington had from the beginning possessed an affinity for numbers. It had remained with him all his life. To count things, not so much for the sake of the things, perhaps, as for the counting, had been of the utmost importance to him. As a boy in Mr. Williams's school in Westmoreland, he excelled in arithmetic. Long division, subtraction, weights and measures—to calculate cords of wood and pecks of peas, pints and gallons and avoirdupois—young George delighted in these as other boys delighted in horseplay. As a man, he merely directed his passion into the channel of his possessions. Through his possessions he apparently satisfied his curious need for enumeration. He was not content simply to keep accounts of the acreage he owned, its yield, his slaves, his pounds and pence. Ellery recalled the extraordinary case of Washington and the seed. He once calculated the number of seeds in a pound troy weight of red clover. Not appeased by the statistics on red clover, Washington then went to work on a pound of timothy seed. His conclusions were: 71,000 and 298,000. His appetite unsatisfied, he thereupon fell upon the problem of New River grass. Here he tackled a calculation worthy of his prowess: his mathematical labors produced the great, pacifying figure of 844,800.

This man was so obsessed with numbers, Ellery thought, staring at the ruins of Washington's Grove, that he counted the windows in each house of his Mount Vernon estate and the number of "Paynes" in each window of each house, and then triumphantly recorded the exact number of each in his own handwriting.

It was like a hunger, requiring periodic appeasement. In 1747, as a boy of fifteen, George Washington drew "A Plan of Major Law: Washingtons Turnip Field as Survey'd by me." In 1786, at the age of fifty-four, General Washington, the most famous man in the world, occupied himself with determining the exact elevation of his piazza above the Potomac's high-water mark. No doubt he experienced a warmer satisfaction thereafter for knowing that when he sat upon his piazza looking down upon the river he was sitting exactly 124 feet 10½ inches above it.

And in 1791, as President of the United States, Ellery mused, he was striding about right here, setting saplings into the ground, twelve of them in an equilateral triangle, and beneath one of them he buried a copper case containing his sword and the half disme coined from his own silver. Beneath one of them . . . But it was not beneath one of them. Or had it been? And had long ago been dug up by a Clarke? But the story had apparently died with Simeon and Sarah. On the other hand . . .

Ellery found himself irrationally reluctant to conclude the obvious. George Washington's lifelong absorption with figures kept intruding. Twelve trees, equidistant, in an equilateral triangle.

"What is it?" he kept asking himself, almost angrily. "Why isn't it satisfying me?"

And then, in the gathering dusk, a very odd explanation insinuated itself. *Because it wouldn't have satisfied him!*

That's silly, Ellery said to himself abruptly. It has all the earmarks of a satisfying experience. There is no more satisfying figure in all geometry than an equilateral triangle. It is closed, symmetrical, definite, a whole and balanced and finished thing.

But it wouldn't have satisfied George Washington . . . for all its symmetry and perfection.

Then perhaps there is a symmetry and perfection beyond the cold beauty of figures?

At this point, Ellery began to question his own postulates . . . lost in the dark and to his time . . .

They found him at ten-thirty, crouched on the cultivator seat, numb and staring.

He permitted himself to be led into the house, he suffered Nikki to subject him to the indignity of having his shoes and socks stripped off and his frozen feet rubbed to life, he ate Martha Clarke's dinner—all with a detachment and indifference which alarmed the girls and even made old Tobias look uneasy.

"If it's going to have this effect on him," began Martha, and then she said: "Ellery, give it up. Forget it." But she had to shake him before he heard her.

He shook his head. "They're there."

"*Where?*" cried the girls simultaneously.

"In Washington's Grove."

"Ye found 'em?" croaked Tobias Clarke, half-rising.

"No."

The Clarkes and Nikki exchanged glances.

"Then how can you be so certain they're buried there, Ellery?" asked Nikki gently.

Ellery looked bewildered. "Darned if I know *how* I know," he said, and he even laughed a little. "Maybe George Washington told me." Then he stopped laughing and went into the firelit parlor and—pointedly—slid the doors shut.

At ten minutes past midnight Martha Clarke gave up the contest.

"Isn't he *ever* going to come out of there?" she said, yawning.

"You never can tell what Ellery will do," replied Nikki.

"Well, I can't keep my eyes open another minute."

"Funny," said Nikki. "I'm not the least bit sleepy."

"You city girls."

"You country girls."

They laughed. Then they stopped laughing, and for a moment there was no sound in the kitchen but the patient sentry-walk of the grandfather clock and the snores of Tobias assaulting the ceiling from above.

"Well," said Martha. Then she said: "I just *can't*. Are you staying up, Nikki?"

"For a little while. You go to bed, Martha."

"Yes. Well. Good night."

"Good night, Martha."

At the door Martha turned suddenly: "Did he say *George Washington told him?*"

"Yes."

Martha went rather quickly up the stairs.

Nikki waited fifteen minutes. Then she tiptoed to the foot of the stairs and listened. She heard Tobias snuffling and snorting as he turned over in his bed, and an uneasy moan from the direction of Martha's bedroom, as if she were dreaming an unwholesome dream. Nikki set her jaw grimly and went to the parlor doors and slid them open.

Ellery was on his knees before the fire. His elbows were resting on the floor. His face was propped in his hands. In this attitude his posterior was considerably higher than his head.

"Ellery!"

"Huh?"

"Ellery, what on earth—?"

"Nikki. I thought you'd gone to bed long ago." In the firelight his face was haggard.

"But what have you been *doing*? You look exhausted!"

"I am. I've been wrestling with a man who could bend a horseshoe with his naked hands. A very strong man. In more ways than one."

"What are you talking about? Who?"

"George Washington. Go to bed, Nikki."

"George . . . Washington?"

"Go to bed."

". . . *Wrestling* with him?"

"Trying to break through his defenses. Get into his mind. It's not an easy mind to get into. He's been dead such a long time—that makes the difference. The dead are stubborn, Nikki. Aren't you going to bed?"

Nikki backed out shivering.

The house *was* icy.

* * *

It was even icier when an inhuman bellow accompanied by a thunder that shook the Revolutionary walls of her bedroom brought Nikki out of bed with a yelping leap.

But it was only Ellery.

He was somewhere up the hall, in the first glacial light of dawn, hammering on Martha Clarke's door.

"Martha. *Martha!* Wake up, damn you, and tell me where I can find a book in this damned house! A biography of Washington—a history of the United States—an almanac . . . *anything!*"

The parlor fire had long since given up the ghost. Nikki and Martha in wrappers, and Tobias Clarke in an ancient bathrobe over his marbled long underwear, stood around shivering and bewildered as a disheveled, daemonic Ellery leafed eagerly through a 1921 edition of *The Farmer's Fact Book and Complete Compendium.*

"Here it is!" The words shot out of his mouth like bullets, leaving puffs of smoke.

"What is it, Ellery?"

"What on earth are you looking for?"

"He's loony, I tell ye!"

Ellery turned with a look of ineffable peace, closing the book.

"That's it," he said. "That's it."

"What's it?"

"Vermont. The State of Vermont."

"Vermont . . . ?"

"Ver*mont?*"

"Vermont. What in the crawlin' creepers's Vermont got to do with—?"

"Vermont," said Ellery with a tired smile, "did not enter the Union until March fourth, 1791. So that proves it, don't you see?"

"Proves *what?*" shrieked Nikki.

"Where George Washington buried his sword and half disme."

"Because," said Ellery in the rapidly lightening dawn behind the barn,

"Vermont was the fourteenth State to do so. The *fourteenth*. Tobias, would you get me an ax, please?"

"An ax," mumbled Tobias. He shuffled away, shaking his head.

"Come on, Ellery, I'm d-dying of c-cold!" chattered Nikki, dancing up and down before the cultivator.

"Ellery," said Martha Clarke piteously, "I don't understand *any* of this."

"It's very simple, Martha—oh, thank you, Tobias—as simple," said Ellery, "as simple arithmetic. Numbers, my dears—numbers tell this remarkable story. Numbers and their influence on our first President who was, above all things, a number-man. That was my key. I merely had to discover the lock to fit it into. Vermont was the lock. And the door's open."

Nikki seated herself on the cultivator. You had to give Ellery his head in a situation like this; you couldn't drive him for beans. Well, she thought grudgingly, seeing how pale and how tired-looking he was after a night's wrestling with George Washington, he's earned it.

"The number was wrong," said Ellery solemnly, leaning on Tobias's ax. "Twelve trees. Washington apparently planted twelve trees—Simeon Clarke's *Diary* never did mention the number twelve, but the evidence seemed unquestionable—there were twelve oaks in an equilateral triangle, each one an equal distance from its neighbor.

"And yet . . . I felt that *twelve* oaks couldn't be, perfect as the triangle was. Not if they were planted by George Washington. Not on February the twenty-second, New Style, in the year of our Lord 1791.

"Because on February the twenty-second, 1791—in fact, until March the fourth, when Vermont entered the Union to swell its original number by one—there was *another* number in the United States so important, so revered, so much a part of the common speech and the common living—and dying—that it was more than a number; it was a solemn and sacred thing; almost not a number at all. It overshadowed other numbers like the still-unborn Paul Bunyan. It was memorialized on the new American flag in the number of its stars and the number of its stripes. It was a number of which George Washington was the standard-bearer!—the head and only recently the strong right arm of the new Republic which had been born out of the blood and muscle of its integers. It was a number which was in the hearts and minds and mouths of all Americans.

"No. If George Washington, who was not merely the living symbol of all this but carried with him that extraordinary compulsion toward numbers which characterized his whole temperament besides, had wished to plant a number of oak trees to commemorate a birthday visit in the year 1791 . . . he would have, he could have, selected only one number out of all the mathematical trillions at his command—*the number thirteen*."

The sun was looking over the edge of Pennsylvania at Washington's Grove.

"George Washington planted thirteen trees here that day, and under one of them he buried Paul Revere's copper case. Twelve of the trees he arranged in an equilateral triangle, and we know that the historic treasure was not under any of the twelve. Therefore he must have buried the case under the thirteenth—a thirteenth oak sapling which grew to oakhood and, some time during the past century and a half, withered and died and vanished, vanished so utterly that it left no trace, not even its roots.

"Where would Washington have planted that thirteenth oak? Because beneath the spot where it once stood—there lies the copper case containing his sword and the first coin to be struck off in the new United States."

And Ellery glanced tenderly at the cherry sapling which Tobias Clarke had set into the earth in the middle of Washington's Grove six years before.

"Washington the surveyor, the geometer, the man whose mind cried out for integral symmetries? Obviously, in only one place: *In the center of the triangle*. Any other place would be unthinkable."

And Ellery hefted Tobias's ax and strode toward the six-year-old tree. He raised the ax.

But suddenly he lowered it, and turned, and said in a rather startled way: "See here! Isn't today . . . ?"

"Washington's Birthday," said Nikki.

Ellery grinned and began to chop down the cherry tree.

The Sa[illegible] ne the Drek[illegible] [illegible]

[illegible] a [illegible] plating [illegible] that [illegible] one of them he buried [illegible] copper [illegible] arranged all [illegible] and we know that [illegible] was not under any of the [illegible] under the chair [illegible] and [illegible] in the past [illegible] and [illegible] vanished [illegible] so utterly [illegible]

What would [illegible] have [illegible] the [illegible] tongue of [illegible] the [illegible] and the last coin [illegible] the new [illegible] States.

And [illegible] the [illegible] what [illegible] in the [illegible] tion.

At [illegible] the [illegible] for [illegible] Any [illegible] would [illegible] and [illegible] Tobias [illegible] as and [illegible] He raised the [illegible]

[illegible] and [illegible] Washington [illegible]

They [illegible] and [illegible] down [illegible]

The Case of the Late Pig

BY MARGERY ALLINGHAM

CHAPTER I

The Invitations to the Funeral Were Informal

THE MAIN THING to remember in autobiography, I have always thought, is not to let any damned modesty creep in to spoil the story. This adventure was mine, Albert Campion's, and I am fairly certain that I was pretty nearly brilliant in it in spite of the fact that I so nearly got myself and old Lugg killed that I hear a harp quintet whenever I consider it.

It begins with me eating in bed.

Lord Perowne's valet took lessons in elocution and since then has read *The Times* to his lordship while his lordship eats his unattractive nut-and-milk breakfast.

Lugg, who in spite of magnificent qualities has elements of the oaf about him, met his lordship's valet in the Mayfair mew pub where they cater for gentlemen in the service of gentlemen and was instantly inspired to imitation. Lugg has not taken lessons in elocution, at least not since he left Borstall in the reign of Edward the Seventh. When he came into my service he was a parole man with a stupendous record of misplaced bravery and ingenuity. Now he reads *The Times* to me when I eat, whether I like it or not.

Since his taste does not run towards the literary in journalism he reads to me the only columns in that paper which do appeal to him. He reads the Deaths.

"Peters . . ." he read, heaving his shirt-sleeved bulk between me and the light. "Know anyone called Peters, cock?"

I was reading a letter which had interested me particularly because it was both flowery and unsigned and did not hear him, so presently he laid down the paper with gentle exasperation.

"Answer me, can't you?" he said plaintively. "What's the good of me trying to give this place a bit of tone if you don't back me up? Mr Tuke says 'is lordship is most attentive during the readings. He chews everything 'e eats forty times before 'e swallers and keeps 'is mind on everything that's being read to 'im."

"So I should think," I said absently. I was taken by the letter. It was not the ordinary anonymous filth by any means.

"Peters—R. I. Peters, aged 37, on Thursday the ninth, at Tetheringham, after a short illness. Funeral, Tetheringham Church, 2:30 Saturday. No flowers. Friends will please accept this as the only intimation."

Lugg reads horribly and with effect.

The name attracted me.

"Peters?" I said, looking up from the letter with interest. "R. I. Peters . . . Pig Peters. Is it in there?"

"Oh, my *gawd!*" Lugg threw down the paper in disgust. "You're a philistine, that's what you are, a ruddy philis. After a perishing short illness, I keep tellin' you. Know 'im?"

"No," I said cautiously. "Not exactly. Not now."

Lugg's great white moon of a face took on an ignoble expression.

"I get you, Bert," he said smugly, tucking his chins into his collarless neck. "Not quite our class."

Although I realise that he is not to be altered, there are things I dare not pass.

"Not at all," I said with dignity. "And don't call me 'Bert'."

"All right." He was magnanimous. "Since you've asked me, cock, I won't. Mr Albert Campion to the world: Mr Albert to me. What about this bloke Peters we was discussin'?"

"We were boys together," I said. "Sweet, downy, blue-eyed little fellows at Botolph's Abbey. Pig Peters took three square inches of skin off my chest with a rusty penknife to show I was his branded slave. He made me weep till I was sick and I kicked him in the belly, whereupon he held me over an unlighted gas jet until I passed out."

Lugg was shocked.

"There was no doings like that at our college," he said virtuously.

"That's the evil of state control," I said gently, not anxious to appear unkind. "I haven't seen Peters since the day I went into the sicker with C.O. poisoning, but I promised him then I'd go to his funeral."

He was interested at once.

"I'll get out your black suit," he said obligingly. "I like a funeral—when it's someone you know."

I was not really listening to him. I had returned to the letter.

Why should he die? He was so young. There are thousands more fitting than he for the journey. "Peters, Peters," saith the angel. "Peters, Pietro, Piero, come," saith the angel. Why? Why should he follow him? He that was so strong, so unprepared, why should he die? The roots are red in the earth and the century creepeth on its way. Why should the mole move backwards?—it is not yet eleven.

It was typewritten on ordinary thin quarto, as are all these things, but it was not ill spelt and the punctuation was meticulous, which was an unusual feature in my experience. I showed it to Lugg.

He read it through laboriously and delivered himself of his judgment with engaging finality.

"Bit out of the Prayer Book," he said. "I remember learning it when I was a nipper."

"Don't be an ass," I said mildly, but he coloured and his little black eyes sank into his head.

"Call me a liar," he said truculently. "Go on, call me a liar, and then I'll do a bit of talking."

I know him in these moods and I realised from experience that it was impossible to shake him in a theory of this sort.

"All right," I said. "What does it mean?"

"Nothing," he said with equal conviction.

I tried another tack.

"What's the machine?"

He was helpful at once.

"A Royal portable, new or newish, no peculiarities to speak of. Even the E is as fresh as that bit of 'addock you've left. Paper's the ordinary Plantag.—they sell reams of it everywhere. Let's see the envelope. . . . London, W.C.1," he continued after a pause. "That's the old central stamp. Clear, isn't it? The address is from the telephone book. Chuck it in the fire."

I still held the letter. Taken in conjunction with the announcement in *The Times* it had, it seemed to me, definite points of interest. Lugg sniffed at me.

"Blokes like you who are always getting theirselves talked about are bound to get anonymous letters," he observed, allowing the critical note in his tone to become apparent. "While you remained strictly amateur you was fairly private, but now you keep runnin' round with the busies, sticking your nose into every bit of blood there is about, and you're gettin' talked of. We'll 'ave women sittin' on the stairs waitin' for you to sign their names on pillercases so they can embroider it if you go on the way you are going. Why can't you take a quiet couple o' rooms in a good neighbour'ood and play poker while you wait for your titled relative to die? That's what a gentleman would do."

"If you were female and could cook I'd marry you," I said vulgarly. "You nag like a stage wife."

That silenced him. He got up and waddled out of the room, the embodiment of dignified disgust.

I read the letter through again after I had eaten and it sounded just as lightheaded. Then I read *The Times* announcement.

R. I. Peters. . . . It was Pig all right. The age fitted in. I remembered him booting us to persuade us to call him "Rip." I thought of us as we were then, Guffy Randall and I and Lofty and two or three others. I was a neat little squirt with sleek white hair and goggles; Guffy was a tough for his age, which was ten and a quarter; and Lofty, who is now holding down his seat in the Peers with a passionate determination more creditable than necessary, was a cross between a small tapir and a more ordinary porker.

Pig Peters was a major evil in our lives at that time. He ranked with Injustice, the Devil and Latin Prose. When Pig Peters fed the junior study fire with my collection of skeleton leaves I earnestly wished him dead, and, remembering the incident that morning at breakfast, I was mildly surprised to find that I still did.

Apparently he was, too, according to *The Times*, and the discovery cheered me up. At twelve he was obese, red and disgusting, with sandy lashes, and at thirty-seven I had no doubt he had been the same.

Meanwhile, there was the sound of heavy breathing in the outer room and Lugg put his head round the door.

"Cock," he said in a tone of diffident friendliness which showed that all was forgiven, "I've had a squint at the map. See where Tetheringham is? Two miles west of Kepesake. Going down?"

I suppose it was that which decided me. At Highwaters, in the parish of Kepesake, there lives Colonel, the Hon. Leo Pursuivant, chief constable of the county and an extremely nice old boy. He has a daughter, Janet Pursuivant, whom I like still in spite of everything.

"All right," I said. "We'll drop in at Highwaters on our way back."

Lugg was in complete agreement. They had a nice piece of home-cured last time he was there, he said.

We went down in state. Lugg wore his flattest bowler, which makes him look like a thug disguised as a plain-clothes man, and I was remarkably neat myself.

Tetheringham was hardly *en fête*. If you consider three square miles of osier swamp surrounding a ploughed hill on which five cottages, a largish house and an ancient church crowd on each other's toes in order to keep out of a river's uncertain bed you have Tetheringham pretty accurately in your mind.

The churchyard is overgrown and pathetic and when we saw it in late winter it was a sodden mass of dead cow parsley. It was difficult not to feel sorry for Pig. He always had grand ideas, I remember, but there was nothing of pomp in his obsequies.

We arrived late—it is eighty miles from Town—and I felt a trifle loutish as I pushed open the mouldering lych gate and, followed by Lugg, stumbled over the ragged grass towards the little group by the grave.

The parson was old and I suspected that he had come on the bicycle I had seen outside the gate, for the skirts of his cassock were muddy.

The sexton was in corduroys and the bearers in dungarees.

The other members of the group I did not notice until afterwards. A funeral is an impressive business even among the marble angels and broken columns of civilisation. Here, out of the world in the rain-soaked silence of a forgotten hillside, it was both grim and sad.

As we stood there in the light shower the letter I had received that morning faded out of my mind. Peters had been an ordinary unlovable sort of twip, I supposed, and he was being buried in an ordinary unloved way. There was really nothing curious about it.

As the parson breathed the last words of the service, however, an odd thing happened. It startled me so much that I stepped back on Lugg and almost upset him.

Even at twelve and a half Pig had had several revolting personal habits and one of them was a particularly vicious way of clearing his throat. It was a sort of hoarse rasping noise in the larynx, followed by a subdued whoop and a puff. I cannot describe it any more clearly but it was a distinctive sort of row and one I never heard made by anyone else. I had completely forgotten it, but just as we were turning away from the yawning grave into which the coffin had been lowered I heard it distinctly after what must have been twenty years. It brought Pig back to my mind with a vividness which was unnerving and I gaped round at the rest of us with my scalp rising.

Apart from the bearers, the parson, the sexton, Lugg and myself, there were only four other people present and they all looked completely innocent.

There was a pleasant solid-looking person on my left and a girl in rather flashy black beyond him. She was more sulky than tearful and appeared to be alone. She caught my eye and smiled at me as I glanced at her and I looked on past her at the old man in the topper who stood in a conventional attitude of grief which was rather horrible because it was so unconvincing. I don't know when I took such a dislike to a fellow. He had little grey curly moustaches which glittered in the rain.

My attention was distracted from him almost at once by the discovery that the fourth unaccountable was Gilbert Whippet. He had been standing at my elbow for ten minutes and I had not seen him, which was typical of him.

Whippet was my junior at Botolph's Abbey and he followed me to the same school. I had not seen him for twelve or fourteen years, but, save that he had grown, of course, he was unchanged.

It is about as easy to describe Whippet as it is to describe water or a sound in the night. Vagueness is not so much his characteristic as his entity. I don't know what he looks like, except that presumably he has a face, since it would be an omission that I should have been certain to observe. He had on some sort of grey-brown coat which merged with the dead cow parsley and he looked at me with that vacancy which is yet recognition.

"Whippet!" I said. "What are you doing here?"

He did not answer and unconsciously I raised my hand to clip him. He never did answer until he was clipped and the force of habit was too much for me. Fortunately I restrained myself in time, recollecting that the years which had elapsed between our meetings had presumably given him ordinary rights of citizenship. All the same I felt unreasonably angry with him and I spoke sharply.

"Whippet, why did you come to Pig's funeral?" I said.

He blinked at me and I was aware of round pale grey eyes.

"I—er—I was invited, I think," he said in the husky diffident voice I remembered so well and which conveyed that he was not at all sure what he was talking about. "I—I—had one this—this morning, don't you know . . ."

He fumbled in his coat and produced a sheet of paper. Before I read it I knew what it was. Its fellow was in my pocket.

"Odd," said Whippet, "about the mole, you know. Informal invitation. I—er—I came."

His voice trailed away, as I knew it would, and he wandered off, not rudely but carelessly, as though there was nothing to keep him in place. He left the note in my hand by mistake, I was convinced.

I came out of the churchyard at the end of the straggling procession. As we emerged into the lane the stolid, pleasant-looking person I had noticed glanced at me with enquiry in his eyes and I went over to him. The question in my mind was not an easy one and I was feeling around for some fairly inoffensive way of putting it when he helped me out.

"A sad business," he said. "Quite young. Did you know him well?"

"I don't know," I said, looking like an idiot, while he stared at me, his eyes twinkling.

He was a big chap, just over forty, with a square capable face.

"I mean," I said, "I was at school with an R. I. Peters and when I saw *The Times* this morning I realised I was coming down this way and I thought I might look in, don't you know."

He remained smiling kindly at me as if he thought I was mental and I floundered on.

"When I got here I felt I couldn't have come to the right—I mean I felt it must be some other Peters," I said.

"He was a big heavy chap," he observed thoughtfully. "Deep-set eyes, too fat, light lashes, thirty-seven years old, went to a prep school at Ramsgate and then on to Totham."

I was shocked. "Yes," I said. "That's the man I knew."

He nodded gloomily. "A sad business," he repeated. "He came to me after an appendix operation. Shouldn't have had it: heart wouldn't stand it. Picked up a touch of pneumonia on the way down and"—he shrugged his shoulders—"couldn't save him, poor chap. None of his people here."

I was silent. There was very little to say.

"That's my place," he remarked suddenly, nodding towards the one big house. "I take a few convalescents. Never had a death there before. I'm in practice here."

I could sympathise with him and I did. It was on the tip of my tongue to ask him if Peters had let him in for a spot of cash. He had not hinted it but I guessed there was some such matter in his thoughts. However, I refrained; there seemed no point in it.

We stood there chatting aimlessly for some moments, as one does on these occasions, and then I went back to Town. I did not call in at Highwaters after all, much to Lugg's disgust. It was not that I did not want to see Leo or Janet, but I was inexplicably rattled by Pig's funeral and by the discovery that it actually was Pig's. It had been a melancholy little ceremony which had left a sort of "half-heard" echo in my ears.

The two letters were identical. I compared them when I got in. I supposed Whippet had seen *The Times* as I had. Still, it was queer he should have put two and two together. And there had been that extraordinary cough and the revolting old fellow in the topper, not to mention the sly-eyed girl.

The worst thing about it was that the incident had recalled Pig to my mind. I turned up some old football groups and had a good look at him. He had a distinctive face. One could see even then what he was going to turn into.

I tried to put him out of my head. After all, I had nothing to get excited about. He was dead. I shouldn't see him again.

All this happened in January. By June I had forgotten the fellow. I had just come in from a session with Stanislaus Oates at the Yard, where we had been congratulating each other over the evidence in the Kingston shooting business which had just flowered into a choice bloom for the judge's bouquet, when Janet rang up.

I had never known her hysterical before and it surprised me a little to hear her twittering away on the phone like a nest of sparrows.

"It's too filthy," she said. "Leo says you're to come at once. No, my dear, I can't say it over the phone, but Leo is afraid it's . . . Listen, Albert, it's M for mother, U for unicorn, R for rabbit, D for darling, E for—for egg, R for——"

"All right," I said, "I'll come."

Leo was standing on the steps of Highwaters when Lugg and I drove up. The great white pillars of the house, which was built by an architect who had seen the B.M. and never forgotten it, rose up behind him. He looked magnificent in his ancient shootin' suit and green tweed flower-pot hat—a fine specimen for anybody's album.

He came steadily down the steps and grasped my hand.

"My dear boy," he said, "not a word . . . not a word." He climbed in beside me and waved a hand towards the village. "Police station," he said. "First thing."

I've known Leo for some years and I know that the singleness of purpose which is the chief characteristic in a delightful personality is not to be diverted by anything less than a covey of Mad Mullahs. Leo had one thing in his mind and one thing only. He had been planning his campaign ever since he had heard that I was on my way, and, since I was part of that campaign, my only hope was to comply.

He would not open his mouth save to utter road directions until we stood together on the threshold of the shed behind the police station. First he dismissed the excited bobbies in charge and then paused and took me firmly by the lapel.

"Now, my boy," he said, "I want your opinion because I trust you. I haven't put a thought in your mind, I haven't told you a particle of the circumstances, I haven't influenced you in any way, have I?"

"No sir," I said truthfully.

He seemed satisfied, I thought, because he grunted.

"Good," he said. "Now, come in here."

He led me into a room, bare save for the trestle table in the centre, and drew back the sheet from the face of the thing that lay upon it.

"Now," he said triumphantly, "now, Campion, what d'you think of this?"

I said nothing at all. Lying on the table was the body of Pig Peters, Pig Peters unmistakable as Leo himself, and I knew without touching his limp, podgy hand that he could not have been dead more than twelve hours at the outside.

Yet in January . . . and this was June.

CHAPTER II

Decent Murder

NOT UNNATURALLY the whole thing was something of a shock to me and I suppose I stood staring at the corpse as though it were a beautiful view for some considerable time.

At last Leo grunted and cleared his throat.

"Dead, of course," he said, no doubt to recall my attention. "Poor feller. Damnable cad, though. Ought not to say it of a dead man, perhaps, but there you are. Truth must out."

Leo really talks like this. I have often thought that his conversation, taken down verbatim, might be worth looking at. Just then I was more concerned with the matter than the form, however, and I said, "You knew him, then?"

Leo grew red round the jawbone and his white moustache pricked up.

"I'd met the feller," he murmured, conveying that he thought it a shameful admission. "Had a most unpleasant interview with him only last night, I don't mind telling you. Extremely awkward in the circumstances. Still, can't be helped. There it is."

Since there was a considerable spot of mystery in the business already I saw no point in overburdening Leo's mind by adding my little contribution to it just then.

"What was he calling himself?" I enquired with considerable guile.

Leo had very bright blue eyes which, like most soldiers', are of an almost startling innocence of expression.

"Masqueradin', eh?" he said. "Upon my soul, very likely! Never thought of it. Untrustworthy customer."

"I don't know anything," I said hastily. "Who is he, anyway?"

"Harris," he said unexpectedly and with contempt. "Oswald Harris. More money than was good for him and the manners of an enemy noncommissioned officer. Can't put it too strongly. Terrible feller."

I looked at the dead man again. Of course it was Pig all right: I should have known him anywhere—and it struck me then as odd that the boy should really be so very much the father of the man. It's a serious thought when you look at some children.

Still, there was Pig and he was dead again, five months after his funeral, and Leo was growing impatient.

"See the wound?" he demanded.

He has a gift for the obvious. The top of the carroty head was stove in, sickeningly, like a broken soccer ball, and the fact that the skin was practically unbroken made it somehow even more distressing. It was such a terrific smash that it seemed incredible that any human arm could have delivered the blow. It looked to me as if he had been kicked through a felt hat by a cart horse and I said so to Leo.

He was gratified.

"Damn nearly right, my boy," he said with comforting enthusiasm. "Remarkable thing. Don't mind admitting don't follow this deducin' business myself, but substitute an urn for a cart horse and you're absolutely right. Remind me to tell Janet."

"An urn?"

"Geranium urn, stone," he explained airily. "Big so-called ornamental thing. Must have seen 'em, Campion. Sometimes have cherry pie in 'em. Madness to keep 'em on the parapet. Said so myself more than once."

I was gradually getting the thing straight. Apparently Pig's second demise had been occasioned by a blow from a stone flowerpot falling on him from a parapet. It seemed pretty final this time.

I looked at Leo. We were both being very decent and noncommittal, I thought.

"Any suggestion of foul play, sir?" I asked.

He hunched his shoulders and became very despondent.

"'Fraid so, my boy," he said at last. "No way out of it. Urn was one of several set all along the parapet. Been up to inspect 'em myself. All firm as the Rock of Gibraltar. Been there for years. Harris' urn couldn't have hopped off the ledge all by itself, don't you know. Must have been pushed by—er—human hands. Devilish situation in view of everything. Got to face it."

I covered Pig's body. I was sorry for him in a way, of course, but he seemed to have retained his early propensities for making trouble.

Leo sighed. "Thought you'd have to agree with me," he said.

I hesitated. Leo is not one of the great brains of the earth but I could hardly believe that he had dragged me down from London to confirm his suspicion that Pig had died from a bang on the head. I took it that there was more to come—and there was, of course; no end of it, as it turned out.

Leo stubbed a bony forefinger into my shoulder.

"Like to have a talk with you, my boy," he said. "One or two private matters to discuss. Have to come out sometime. We ought to go down to Halt Knights and have a look at things."

The light began to filter in.

"Was P—— Was Harris killed at Halt Knights?"

Leo nodded. "Poor Poppy! Decent little woman, you know, Campion. Never a suspicion of—er—anything of this sort before."

"I should hope not," I said, scandalised, and he frowned at me.

"Some of these country clubs . . ." he began darkly.

"Not murder," I said firmly and he relapsed into despondency.

"Perhaps you're right," he agreed. "Let's go down there. Drop in for a drink before dinner."

As we went out to the car I considered the business. To understand Halt Knights is to know Kepesake, and Kepesake is a sort of county paradise. It is a big village, just far enough from a town and a main road to remain exclusive without having to be silly about it. It has a Norman church, a village cricket green with elms, three magnificent pubs and a population of genuine countryfolk of proper independent views. It lies in a gentle valley on the shores of an estuary and is protected by a ring of modest little estates all owned by dear good fellers, so Leo says. The largest of these estates is Halt Knights.

At one period there was a nobleman at the Knights who owned the whole village, which had been left him by an ancestress who had had it, so the name would suggest, from a boy friend off to the Crusades. Changing times and incomes drove out the nobleman and his heirs; hence the smaller estates.

The house and some nine hundred acres of meadow and salting remained a millstone round somebody's neck until Poppy Bellew retired from the stage and, buying it up, transformed that part of it which had not collapsed into the finest hotel and country club in the kingdom.

Being a naturally expansive person of untiring energy, she did not let the nine hundred acres worry her but laid down an eighteen-hole golf course and reserved the rest for anything anyone might think of. It occurred to some intelligent person that there was a very fine point-to-point course there somewhere and at the time Pig got the urn on his head there had been four meetings there in each of five consecutive springs.

It was all very lazy and homely and comfortable. If anyone who looked as if he might spoil the atmosphere came along, somehow Poppy lost him. It was really very simple. She wanted to keep open house and the people round about were willing to pay their own expenses, or that was how it seemed to work out.

Leo's story was interesting. I could understand Pig getting himself killed at Halt Knights, but not how he managed to stay there long enough for it to happen.

Meanwhile, Leo had reached the car and was looking at Lugg with mistrust. Leo's ideas of discipline are military and Lugg's are not. I foresaw an impasse.

"Ah, Lugg," I said with forced heartiness, "I'm going to drive Sir Leo on to Halt Knights. You'd better go back to Highwaters. Take a bus or something."

Lugg stared at me and I saw rebellion in his eyes. His feet have been a constant source of conversation with him of late.

"A bus?" he echoed, adding "sir" as a belated afterthought as Leo's eyes fell upon him.

"Yes," I said foolishly. "One of those big green things. You must have seen them about."

He got out of the car heavily and with dignity and so far demeaned himself as to hold the door open for Leo, but me he regarded under fat white eyelids with a secret, contemplative expression.

"Extraordinary feller, your man," said Leo as we drove off. "Keep an eye on him, my dear boy. Save your life in the war?"

"Dear me, no!" I said in some astonishment. "Why?"

He blew his nose. "I don't know. Thought just crossed my mind. Now to this business, Campion. It's pretty serious and I'll tell you why." He paused and added so soberly that I started: "There are at least half-a-dozen good fellers, including myself, who were in more than half a mind to put that feller out of the way last night. One of us must have lost his head, don't you know. I'm being very frank with you, of course."

I pulled the car up by the side of the road. We were on the long straight stretch above The Dog and Pheasant.

"I'd like to hear about it," I said.

He came out with it quietly and damningly in his pleasant, worried voice. It was an enlightening tale in view of the circumstances.

Two of the estates near by had become vacant in the past year and each had been bought anonymously through a firm of London solicitors. No one thought much of it at the time but the blow had fallen about a week before our present conversation. Leo, going down to Halt Knights for a game of bridge and a drink, also had found the place in an uproar and Pig, of all people, installed. He was throwing his weight about and detailing his plans for the future of Kepesake, which included a hydro, a steeplechase course and a cinema-dance hall with special attractions to catch motorists from the none too far distant industrial town.

Taken on one side, Poppy had broken down and made a confession. Country ease and country hospitality had proven expensive and she, not wishing to depress her clients, who were also her nearest and dearest friends, had accepted the generous mortgage terms which a delightful gentleman from London had arranged, only to find that his charming personality had been but the mask to cloak the odious Pig, who had decided to foreclose at the precise moment when a few outstanding bills had been paid with the greater part of the loan.

Leo, who justified his name if ever man did, had padded forth gallantly to the rescue. He roared round the district, collected a few good souls of his own kidney, held a meeting, formed a syndicate, and approached the entrenched Pig armed with money and scrupulously fair words.

From that point, however, he had met defeat. Pig was adamant. Pig had all the money he required. Pig wanted Kepesake—and a fine old silver sty he was going to make of it.

Leo's solicitor, summoned from Norwich, had confirmed his client's worst fears. Poppy had trusted the charming gentleman too well. Pig had an option to purchase.

Realising that with money, Halt Knights and the two adjoining estates Pig could lay waste Kepesake, and their hearts with it, Leo and his friends had tried other methods. As Leo pointed out, men will fight for their homes. There is a primitive love inspired by tree and field which can fire the most correct heart to flaming passion.

Two or three of Halt Knights's oldest guests were asked by Pig to leave. Leo and most of the others stolidly sat their ground, however, and talk was high but quiet, while plots abounded.

"And then this morning, don't you know," Leo finished mildly, "one of the urns on the parapet crashed down on the feller as he sat sleepin' in a deck chair under the lounge window. Devilish awkward, Campion."

I let in the clutch and drove on without speaking. I thought of Kepesake and its gracious shadowy trees, its sweet meadows and clear waters, and thought what a howling shame it was. It belonged to these old boys and their children. It was their sanctuary, their little place of peace. If Pig wanted to make more money, why in heaven's name should he rot up Kepesake to do it? There are ten thousand other villages in England. Well, they'd saved it from Pig at any rate, or at least one of them had. So much looked painfully apparent.

Neither of us spoke until we turned in under the red Norman arch which is the main drive gate to the Knights. There Leo snorted.

"Another bounder!" he said explosively.

I looked at the little figure mincing down the drive towards us and all but let the car swerve on to the turf. I recognised him immediately, principally by the extraordinary sensation of dislike he aroused in me. He was a thoroughly unpleasant old fellow, affected and conceited, and the last time I had seen him he had been weeping ostentatiously into a handkerchief with an inch-wide black border at Pig's first funeral. Now he was trotting out of Halt Knights as if he knew the place and was very much at home there.

CHAPTER III

"That's Where He Died"

HE LOOKED AT ME with interest and I think he placed me, for I was aware of two beady bright eyes peering at me from beneath cairned eyebrows.

Leo, on the other hand, received a full salute from him, a wave of the panama delivered with one of those shrugs which attempt Old-World grace and achieve the slightly sissy.

Leo gobbled and tugged perfunctorily at his own green tweed.

"More people know Tom Fool than Tom Fool knows," he confided to me in an embarrassed rumble and hurried on so quickly that I took it he did not want the man discussed, which was curious.

"I want you to be careful with Poppy," he said. "Charmin' little woman. Had a lot to put up with the last day or two. Wouldn't like to see her browbeaten. Kid gloves, Campion. Kid gloves all the way."

I was naturally aggrieved. I have never been considered brutal, having if anything a mild and affable temperament.

"It's ten years since I beat a woman, sir," I said.

Leo cocked an eye at me. Facetiae are not his line.

"Hope you never have," he said severely. "Your mother—dear sweet lady—wouldn't have bred a son who could. I'm worried about Poppy, Campion. Poor charmin' little woman."

I felt my eyebrows rise. The man who could visualise Poppy as a poor little woman must also, I felt, be able to think of her being actually ill treated. I like Poppy. Charming she certainly is, but little—no. Leo was confusing the ideal with the conventional, and I might have told him so and mortally offended him had we not come through the trees at that moment to see the house awaiting us.

No English country house is worthy of the name if it is not breathtaking at half-past six on a June evening, but Halt Knights is in a street by itself. It is long and low, with fine windows. Built of crushed strawberry brick, the Georgian front does not look out of place against the Norman ruins which rise up behind it and melt into the high chestnuts massed at the back.

As in many East Anglian houses the front door is at the side, so that the lawn can come right up to the house in front.

As we pulled up I was glad to see that the door was open as usual, though the place seemed deserted save for the embarrassed bobby in bicycle clips who stood on guard by the lintel.

I could not understand his acute discomfort until I caught the gleam of a pewter tankard among the candytuft at his feet. Poppy has a great understanding of the creature man.

I touched Leo on the shoulder and made a suggestion and he blinked at me.

"Oh, all right, my boy. Make the examination first if you want to, by all means. This is where the feller was sittin'."

He led me round to the front of the house where the deck chairs, looking flimsy and oddly Japanese in their bright colours, straggled along under the windows.

"The urn," he said.

I bent down and pulled aside the couple of sacks which had been spread over the exhibit. As soon as I saw it I understood his depression. It was a large stone basin about two and a half feet high and two feet across and was decorated with amoretti and pineapples. It must have weighed the best part of three hundredweight with the earth it contained, and while I could understand it killing Pig I was amazed that it had not smashed him to pulp. I said so to Leo and he explained.

"Would have done—would have done, my boy, but only the edge of the rim struck his head where it jutted over the back of the chair. He had a hat on, you know. There's the chair—nothing much to see."

He kicked aside another sack and we looked down at a pathetic heap of splintered framework and torn canvas. Leo shrugged his shoulders helplessly.

I walked a little way down the lawn and looked up at the parapet. It is one of those long strips of plastered stone which finish off the flat fronts of Georgian houses and always remind me of the topping of marzipan icing on a very good fruitcake. The little windows of the second floor sit behind it in the sugar-loaf roof.

There were seven other urns set along the parapet at equal distances, and one significant gap. There was obviously nothing dangerous about them; they looked as if they had been there for ever.

We went towards the house.

"There's one thing I don't understand," I said. "Our murderer pal seems to have taken a tremendous risk. What an extremely dangerous thing to do."

Leo looked at me as though I had begun to gibber and I laboured on, trying to make myself clear.

"I mean," I said, "surely Harris wasn't sitting out here entirely alone? Someone might have come up to him to chat. The man who pushed the flowerpot over couldn't have made certain he was going to hit the right man unless he'd actually climbed out on the parapet to look first, which would have been lunatic."

Leo grew very red. "Harris was alone," he said. "He was sittin' out here when we turned up this mornin' and nobody felt like goin' to join him, don't you know. We left him where he was. He ignored us and no one felt like speakin' to him, so we all went inside. I was playin' a game of cards in the lounge through this window here when the infernal thing crashed down on him. You may think it childish," he added a little shamefacedly, "but there you are. The feller was an unmitigated tick."

I whistled. The clouds were blowing up.

"When you say 'all of you,' who do you mean?" I asked.

He looked wretched.

"About a dozen of us," he said. "All absolutely above suspicion. Let's go in."

As soon as we set foot on the stone flags of the entrance hall and sniffed the sweet cool fragrance of old wood and flowers which is the true smell of your good country house, Poppy appeared, fat, gracious and welcoming as always.

"Why, ducky," she said as she took my hands, "how very nice to see you. Leo, you're a lamb to send for him. Isn't it awful? Come and have a drink."

She piloted us down the broad stone corridor to the big white-panelled lounge with the deep, comfortable, chintz-covered chairs, chattering the whole time.

It is not easy to describe Poppy. She is over fifty, I suppose, with tight grey curls all over her head, a wide mouth and enormous blue eyes. That is the easy part. The rest is more difficult. She exudes friendliness, generosity, and a sort of naïve obstinacy. Her clothes are outrageous—vast flowery skirts and bodices embellished with sufficient frills to rig a frigate. However, they suit her personality if not her figure. You see her and you like her and that's all there is to it.

Leo was plainly batty about her.

"Such a horrid little man, Harris," she said as she gave me my whisky. "Has Leo told you all about him and me? How he tried to pinch the place. . . . He has? Oh well, that's all right. You see how it happened.

Still, it's very wrong of someone, very wrong indeed—although, my dear, I'm sure they meant to be kind."

Leo spluttered. "Isn't she a *dear?*" he said.

"I'm not being silly, am I, Albert?" She looked at me appealingly. "I did tell them it was dangerous last night. I said quite distinctly, 'This will lead to trouble,' and of course it did."

I intercepted a startled glance from Leo and sat up with interest. Poppy turned on him.

"Haven't you told him?" she said. "Oh, but you must. It's not fair."

Leo avoided my eyes. "I was comin' to that," he said. "I've only had Campion down here for half an hour."

"You were trying to shield them," said Poppy devastatingly, "and that's no good. When we've got the truth," she added naïvely, "then we can decide how much we're going to tell."

Leo looked scandalised and would have spoken but she forestalled him.

"It was like this," she said confidingly, giving my arm a friendly but impersonal pat. "Two or three of the more hearty old pets hatched up a plot last night. They were going to get Harris drunk and friendly first and then they were going to put the whole thing to him as man to man and in a burst of good fellowship he was going to sign a document they'd had prepared, relinquishing the option or whatever it is."

She paused and eyed me dubiously, as well she might, I thought. As my face did not change she came a little nearer.

"I didn't approve," she said earnestly. "I told them it was silly and in a way not quite honest. But they said Harris hadn't been honest with us and of course that was right, too, so they sat up in here with him last night. It might have been all right only instead of getting friendly he got truculent, as some people do, and while they were trying to get him beyond that stage he passed out altogether and they had to put him to bed. This morning he had a terrible hang-over and went to sleep it off on the lawn. He hadn't moved all the morning when that beastly thing fell on him."

"Awkward," murmured Leo. "Devilish awkward."

Poppy gave me the names of the conspirators. They were all eminently respectable people who ought to have known a great deal better. It sounded to me as if everybody's uncle had gone undergraduate again and I might have said so in a perfectly friendly way had not Poppy interrupted me.

"Leo's inspector—such a nice man; he's hoping to get promotion, he tells me—has been through the servants with a toothcomb and hasn't found anything, not even a brain, the poor ducks! I'm afraid there's going to be a dreadful scandal. It must be one of the visitors, you see, and I only have such dear people."

I said nothing, for at that moment a pudding-faced maid, who certainly did not look as though she had sufficient intelligence to drop an urn or anything else on the right unwanted guest, came in to say that if there was a Mr Campion in the house he was wanted on the telephone.

I took it for granted it was Janet and I went along to the hall with a certain pleasurable anticipation.

As soon as I took up the receiver, however, the exchange said brightly: "London call."

Considering I had left the city unexpectedly two hours before with the intention of going to Highwaters, and no one in the world but Lugg and Leo knew that I had come to Halt Knights, I thought there must be some mistake and I echoed her.

"Yes, that's right. London call," she repeated with gentle patience. "Hold on. You're through. . . ."

I held on for some considerable time.

"Hullo," I said at last. "Hullo. Campion here."

Still there was no reply, only a faint sigh, and the someone at the other end hung up. That was all.

It was an odd little incident, rather disturbing.

Before going back to the others I wandered upstairs to the top floor to have a look at the parapet. No one was about and most of the doors stood open, so that I had very little difficulty in finding the spot where Pig's urn had once stood.

It had been arranged directly in front of a box-room window and must, I thought, have obscured most of the light. When I came to look at the spot I saw that any hopeful theory I might have formed concerning a clumsy pigeon or a featherbrained cat was out of the question. The top of the parapet was covered with lichen save for the square space where the foot of the urn had stood. This was clear and brown save for the bodies of a few dead bugs of the kind one gets under stones, and in the centre of it there was a little slot, some three inches wide and two deep, designed to hold some sort of stone peg incorporated in the bottom of the urn all for safety's sake.

There was no question of the fall being accidental, therefore. Someone both strong and determined must have lifted the heavy thing up before pushing it out.

There was nothing unusual about the vacant space, as far as I could see, save that the lichen at the edge of the parapet was slightly damp. How important that was I did not dream.

I went down again to the lounge. I am a naturally unobtrusive person and I suppose I came in quietly, because neither Leo nor Poppy seemed to hear me, and I caught his words, which were loud and excited.

"My dear lady, believe me, I don't want to butt into your private affairs—nothing's farther from my mind—but it was a natural question. Hang it all, Poppy, the feller was a bounder, and there he was striding out of this place as though it belonged to him. However, don't tell me who he was if you'd rather not."

Poppy faced him. Her cheeks were pink and her eyes were bright with tears of annoyance.

"He came from the village to—to sell some tickets for a—a whist drive," she said, all in one breath, and I, looking at her, wondered if she could have been such a very great actress, after all, since she couldn't tell a lie better than that.

Then, of course, I realised who they were talking about.

CHAPTER IV

Among the Angels

I COUGHED DISCREETLY, and Leo turned round to glance at me guiltily. He looked miserable.

"Ah!" he said absently, but with a valiant attempt to make normal conversation. "Ah, Campion, not bad news, I hope?"

"No news at all," I said truthfully.

"Oh well, that's good. That's *good*, my boy," he bellowed suddenly, getting up and clapping me on the shoulder with unnecessary fervour. "No news is good news. We always say that, don't we? Well, Poppy, ought to go now, m'dear. People to dinner, you know. Good-bye. Come along, Campion. Glad you had good news."

The old boy was frankly blethering, and I was sorry for him. Poppy was still annoyed. Her cheeks were very pink and her eyes were tearful.

Leo and I went out.

I made him come onto the lawn again, where I had another look at the urn. The peg was intact. It protruded nearly two and a half inches from the flat surface of the stand.

Leo was very thoughtful when I pointed it out to him, but his mind could hardly have been on his work, for I had to explain the primitive arrangement to him twice before he saw any significance in it.

As we drove off under the trees he looked at me.

"Kittle cattle," he said sadly.

We drove back onto the main road in silence. I was glad of the spot of quiet because I took it that a little constructive thinking was overdue. I am not one of these intellectual sleuths, I am afraid. My mind does not work like an adding machine, taking the facts in neatly one by one and doing the work as it goes along. I am more like the bloke with the sack and spiked stick. I collect all the odds and ends I can see and turn out the bag at the lunch hour.

So far, I had netted one or two things. I had satisfied myself that Pig had been murdered; that is to say, whoever had killed him had done so intentionally, but not, I thought, with much premeditation. This seemed fairly obvious, since it was not reasonable to suppose that anyone could have insisted on him sitting just in that one spot, or made absolutely certain that he would stay there long enough to receive the urn when it came.

Considering the matter, I fancied some impulsive fellow had happened along to find the stage set, as it were; Pig sitting, porcine and undesirable, under the flowerpot, and, not being able to curb his murderous instinct, had trotted upstairs and done a thorough job of shoving all in the first fierce flush of inspiration.

Having arrived at this point, it struck me that the actual identification of the murderer must depend upon a process of elimination after an examination of alibis, and this, I thought, was definitely a job for the inspector. After all, he was the young hopeful out for promotion.

The real trouble, I foresaw, would be the question of proof. Since fingerprints on the rough cast would be too much to hope for, and an eyewitness would have come forward before now, it was in pinning the crime down that I imagined the real snag would arise.

Perhaps I ought to mention here that at that moment I was absolutely wrong. I was wrong not only about the position of the snag but about everything else as well. However, I had no ideas of it then. I leant back in the Lagonda, with Leo at my side, and drove through the yellow evening light thinking of Pig and his two funerals, past and present.

At that time, and I was hopelessly mistaken, of course, I was inclined to think that Pig's murderer was extraneous to the general scheme. The clever young gentleman from London innocently looked forward to a nice stimulating civil mystery with the criminal already under lock and key in the mortuary, and this in spite of the telephone call and Poppy's unpleasant visitor. Which proves to me now that the balmy country air had gone to my head.

I was sorry for Leo and Poppy and the overzealous old gentleman who had come so disastrously to the aid of Halt Knights. I sympathised with them over the scandal and the general rumpus. But at that moment I did not think that the murder itself was by any means the most exciting part of the situation.

Of course, had I known of the other odds and ends that the gods had in the bag for us, had I realised that the unpleasant Old Person with the Scythe was just sitting up in the garden resting on his laurels and getting his breath for the next bit of gleaning, I should have taken myself in hand, but I honestly thought the fireworks were over and that I had come in at the end of the party and not, as it turned out, at the beginning.

As we drove down the narrow village street past The Swan, I asked Leo a question as casually as I could.

"D'you know Tetheringham, sir?" I said. "There's a nursing home there, isn't there?"

"Eh?" He roused himself with a jerk from his unhappy meditations. "Tetheringham? Nursin' home? Oh yes, excellent place—excellent. Run by young Brian Kingston. A good feller. Very small, though, very small —the nursin' home, not Kingston. You'll like him. Big feller. Dear chap. Comin' to dinner tonight. Vicar's comin' too," he added as an afterthought. "Just the five of us. Informal, you know."

Naturally, I was interested.

"Has Kingston had the place long?"

Leo blinked at me. He seemed to wish I wouldn't talk.

"Oh, several years. Father used to practise there years ago. Left the son a large house and he, bein' an enterprisin' chap, made a goin' concern of it. Good doctor—wonderful doctor. Cured my catarrh."

"You know him well, then?" I asked, feeling sorry to intrude upon his thoughts but anxious to get on with the enquiry.

Leo sighed. "Fairly well," he said. "Well as one knows anyone, don't you know. Funny thing, I was playin' a hand with him and two other fellers this mornin' when that confounded urn fell on that bounder outside and made all this trouble. Came right down past the window where we were sittin'. Terrible thing."

"What were you playing? Bridge?"

Leo looked scandalised. "Before lunch? No, my dear boy. Poker. Wouldn't play bridge before lunch. Poker, that's what it was. Kingston had a queen pot and we were settlin' up, thinkin' about lunch, when there was a sort of shadow passed the window, and then a sort of thud that wasn't an ordinary thud. Damned unpleasant. I didn't like the look of him, did you? Looked a dangerous fellow, I thought, the sort of feller one'd set a dog on instinctively."

"Who?" I said, feeling I was losing the thread of the argument.

Leo grunted. "That feller we met in the drive at Poppy's place. Can't get him out of my mind."

"I think I've seen him before," I said.

"Oh?" Leo looked at me suspiciously. "Where? Where was that?"

"Er—at a funeral somewhere," I said, not wishing to be more explicit.

Leo blew his nose. "Just where you'd expect to see him," he said unreasonably, and we turned into the drive of Highwaters.

Janet came hurrying down the steps as we pulled up.

"Oh, darling, you're so late," she murmured to Leo and, turning to me, held out her hand. "Hello, Albert," she said, a little coldly, I thought.

I can't describe Janet as I saw her then. She was, and is, very lovely. I still like her.

"Hello," I said flatly and added idiotically because I felt I ought to say something else: "Give us to drink, ambrosia and sweet barm——"

She turned away from me and addressed Leo.

"You really must go and dress, pet. The vicar's here, all of a twitter, poor boy. The whole village is seething with excitement, he says, and Miss Dusey sent up to say that The Marquis is full of newspapermen. She wants to know if it's all right. Has anything turned up?"

"No, no, m'dear." Leo spoke absently and kissed her, unexpectedly, I felt sure.

He seemed to think the caress a little surprising himself, for he coughed as though to cover, or at least to excuse it, and hurried into the house, leaving her standing, dark haired and attractive, on the step beside me.

"He's worried, isn't he?" she said under her breath, and then went on, as though she had suddenly remembered who I was. "I'm afraid you must go and dress at once. You've only got ten minutes. Leave the car here and I'll send someone to take it round."

I have known Janet, on and off, for twenty-three years. When I first saw her she was bald and pinkly horrible. I was almost sick at the sight of her, and was sent out into the garden until I had recovered my manners. Her formality both hurt and astonished me, therefore.

"All right," I said, anxious to be accommodating at all costs. "I won't wash."

She looked at me critically. She has very fine eyes, like Leo's, only larger.

"I should," she said gently. "You show the dirt, don't you?—like a white fur."

I took her hand. "Friends, eh?" I said anxiously.

She laughed, but not very naturally.

"My dear, of course. Oh, by the way, your friend called at about half-past six but didn't stay. I said I expected you for dinner."

"Lugg," I said apprehensively, a great light dawning upon me. "What's he done?"

"Oh, not *Lugg*." She spoke with contempt. "I *like* Lugg. Your girl friend."

The situation was getting out of hand.

"It's all a lie," I said. "There is no other woman. Did she leave a name?"

"She did." There was grimness and, I thought, spite in Janet's tone. "Miss Effie Rowlandson."

"Never heard of her," I said honestly. "Was she a nice girl?"

"No," said Janet explosively and ran into the house.

I went into Highwaters alone. Old Pepper, pottering about in the hall doing the odd jobs that butlers do do, seemed pleased to see me, and I was glad of that. After a gracious though formal greeting, "A letter for you, sir," he said, in the same way as a man might say, "I am happy to present you with a medal." "It came this morning, and I was about to readdress it and send it on to you, when Sir Leo informed me that we were to expect you this evening."

He retired to his private cubbyhole at the back of the hall and returned with an envelope.

"You are in your usual room, sir, in the east wing," he said as he came up. "I will send George with your cases immediately. It wants but seven minutes before the gong."

I glanced at the envelope in my hand as he was sauntering off, and I suppose I hiccuped or something, for he glanced round at me with kindly concern.

"I beg your pardon, sir?"

"Nothing, Pepper," I said, confirming his worst fears, and, tearing open the envelope, I read the second anonymous letter as I went up to my room. It was as neatly typed and precisely punctuated as the first had been, quite a pleasure to read.

"O," saith the owl. "Oho," sobbeth the frog. "O-oh," mourneth the worm. "Where is Peters that was promised us?"

The angel weepeth behind golden bars. His wings cover his face. "Piero," weepeth the angel.

Why should these things be? Who was he to disturb the heavens?

Consider, o, consider, the lowly mole. His small hands are sore and his snout bleedeth.

CHAPTER V

Nice People

"IT'S THE nature-note motif I find confusing," I confided to Lugg as I dressed. "See any point in it at all?"

He threw the letter aside and smiled at me with unexpected sheepishness. Sentiment glistened all over his face.

"Pore little mole," he said.

I gaped at him, and he had the grace to look abashed. He recovered his truculence almost at once, however.

"That walk," he began darkly. "I'm glad you've come in. I've bin waitin' to talk to you. What do you think I am? A perishin' centipede? Green bus, my old sock!"

"You're getting old," I said offensively. "See if your mental faculties have failed as far as your physique has deteriorated. I have four minutes to get down to the dining room. Does that letter convey anything to you or not? It was sent here. It arrived this morning."

The dig touched him and his great white face was reproachful as he reread the note, his lips moving soundlessly.

"A owl, a frog, a worm and a angel are all upset because they can't find this 'ere Peters," he said at last. "That's clear, ain't it?"

"Dazzlingly," I agreed. "And it would suggest that the writer knew Peters was not dead, which is interesting, because he is. The fellow I've been to see in the mortuary is—or rather was—Peters himself. He died this morning."

Lugg eyed me. "'Avin' a game?" he enquired coldly.

I considered him with disgust as I struggled with my collar, and presently he continued without help, making an obvious effort to get his mind working.

"This mornin'? Reelly?" he said. "Died, did he? What of?"

"Flowerpot on the head, with intent."

"Done in? Reelly?" Lugg returned to the note. "Oh, well then, this is clear, ain't it? The bloke 'oo wrote this knew you was always anxious to snuff round a bit of blood, doin' the rozzers out of their rightful, and 'e kindly give you the tip to come along 'ere as fast as you could so's you wouldn't miss nothink."

"Yes, well, you're offensive, muddleheaded and vulgar," I said with dignity.

"Vulgar?" he echoed in sudden concern. "Not vulgar, cock. I may say what I mean, but I'm never vulgar."

He considered a moment.

"Rozzers," he announced with triumph. "You're right, rozzers is common. P'lice officers."

"You make me sick," I said truthfully. "The point you seem to have missed is that Peters died this morning, and that letter was posted to me at this address from central London some time before seven o'clock last night."

He took in the facts and surprised me by getting up.

"'Ere," he said, "see what this means? The bloke 'oo wrote you last night *knoo* Peters was goin' to die today."

I hesitated. It was the first time I had felt the genuine trickle up the spine. Meanwhile, he went on complaining.

"You've done it again," he mourned. "In spite of all I've done for you, here you are mixed up in the first bit of cheap mud that comes along. Lumme! You don't 'ave to whistle for it, even. It flies to you."

I looked at him. "Lugg," I said, "these words are in the nature of a prophecy. The puff paste has a sausage inside it, after all."

The gong forestalled him, but his comment followed me as I hurried to the door.

"Botulistic, most likely," he said.

I arrived in the dining room with half a second to spare, and Pepper regarded me with affection, which was more than Janet did, I was sorry to see.

Leo was talking to a slim black back in a clerical dinner jacket, and I sat down to find myself beside the pleasant-looking person with whom I had chatted at Pig's Tetheringham funeral.

He recognised me with a pleasing show of warmth and laughed at me with deep lazy grey eyes.

"Always in at the death?" he murmured.

We introduced ourselves, and I liked his manner. He was a big fellow, older than I was, with a certain shyness which was attractive. We chatted for some moments, and Janet joined us, and it was not until some minutes later that I became aware of someone hating me.

It is one of those odd but unmistakable sensations one experiences sometimes on busses or at private dinners, and I looked across the table to observe a young cleric whom I had never seen before regarding me with honest hostility. He was one of those tall, bony ascetics with high red cheeks and wrist bones, and the humourless round black eyes of the indignant-hearted.

I was so taken aback that I smiled at him foolishly, and Leo introduced us.

He turned out to be the Rev. Philip Smedley Bathwick, newly appointed to the parish of Kepesake. I could not understand his unconcealed hatred and was rather hurt by it until I saw him glance at Janet. Then I began to follow him. He positively goggled at her, and I might have felt sorry for him had it not been for something personal that there is no need to go into here.

He was doubly unfortunate, as it happened, because Leo monopolised him. As soon as we were safely embarked on the fish the old man bellowed, as he always does when he fancies the subject needs finesse: "That fellow we were talking about before dinner; where d'you say he's stayin'?"

"At Mrs Thatcher's, sir. Do you know the woman? She has a little cottage below The Swan."

Bathwick had a good voice, but there was a tremor in it which I put down to his suppressed anxiety to listen to the conversation at our end of the table.

Leo was not giving him any respite.

"Oh, I know old Mrs Thatcher," he said. "One of the Jepson family on Blucher's Hill. A good woman. What's she doin' with a feller like that in the house? Can't understand it, Bathwick."

"She lets rooms, sir." Bathwick's eyes wandered to Janet and away again, as if the sight hurt him. "This Mr Hayhoe has only been in the village a little under a week."

"Heigh-ho?" said Leo. "Idiotic name. Probably false."

As usual when he is irritated, he blared at the unfortunate young man, who gaped at him.

"Hayhoe is a fairly common name, sir," Bathwick ventured.

"Heigh-ho?" repeated Leo, looking at him as if he were demented. "I don't believe it. When you're as old as I am, Bathwick, you'll give up trying to be funny. This is a serious time, my dear feller, a serious time."

Bathwick grew crimson about the ears at the injustice, but he controlled himself and glowered silently. It was a ridiculous incident, but it constituted, I submit, the whole reason why Leo considers Bathwick a facetious ass to this day, which is a pity, of course, for a more serious-minded cove was never born.

At the time I was more interested in the information than the man, however, and I turned to Kingston.

"D'you remember a fantastic old man in a top hat weeping into an immense mourning handkerchief at that funeral at your place last winter?" I said. "That was Hayhoe."

He blinked at me. "Peters' funeral? No, I don't think I remember him. There was an odd sort of girl there, I know, and . . ."

He paused, and I saw a kind of excitement come into his eyes.

"I say!" he said.

We were all looking at him, and he became embarrassed and struggled to change the subject. As soon as the others were talking again, however, he turned to me.

"I've just thought of something," he said, his voice as eager as a boy's. "It may be useful. We'll have a chat after dinner, if you don't mind. You didn't know that fellow Peters well, did you?"

"Not intimately," I said guardedly.

"He wasn't a nice chap," he said and added, lowering his voice, "I believe I'm on to something. Can't tell you here."

He met my eyes, and my heart warmed to him. I like enthusiasm for the chase, or it's an inhuman business.

We did not have an opportunity to talk immediately we broke up, however, because the inspector in charge of the case came to see Leo while the port was still in circulation, and he excused himself.

Left with Bathwick, Kingston and I had our hands full. He was a red-hot innovator, we discovered. He spoke with passion of the insanitary condition of the thatched cottages and the necessity of bringing culture into the life of the average villager, betraying, I thought, a lack of acquaintance, with either the thatched cottage or, of course, the villager in question, who, as every countryman knows, does not exist.

Kingston and I were trying to convince him that the whole point of a village is that it is a sufficiently scattered community for a man to call his soul his own in it without seriously inconveniencing his neighbour, when Pepper arrived to ask me if I would join Sir Leo in the gun room.

I went into the fine old chamber on the first floor, where Leo does both his writing and his gun cleaning with impartial enthusiasm, to find him sitting at his desk. In front of him was an extremely attractive soul enjoying a glass of whisky. Leo introduced him.

"Inspector Pussey, Campion, my boy. Able feller. Been workin' like a nigger all day."

I liked Pussey on sight; anyone would.

He was lank and loose jointed and had one of those slightly comic faces which are both disarming and endearing, and it was evident that he regarded Leo with that amused affection and admiration which is the bedrock of the co-operation between man and master in rural England.

When I arrived they were both perturbed. I took it that the affair touched them both nearly. It was murder in the home meadow, so to speak. But there was more to it even than that, I found.

"Extraordinary thing, Campion," Leo said when Pepper had closed the door behind me. "Don't know what to make of it at all. Pussey here assures me of the facts, and he's a good man. Every reason to trust him every time."

I glanced at the inspector. He looked proudly puzzled, I thought, like a spaniel which has unexpectedly retrieved a dodo. I waited, and Leo waved to Pussey to proceed. He smiled at me disarmingly.

"It's a king wonder, sir," he said, and his accent was soft and broad. "Seems like we've made a mistake somewhere, but where that is I can't tell you, nor I can't now. We spent the whole day, my man and I, questioning of people, and this evening we got 'em all complete, as you'd say."

"And no one but Sir Leo has a decent alibi?" I said sympathetically. "I know. . . ."

"No sir." Pussey did not resent my interruption; rather he welcomed it. He had a natural flair for the dramatic. "No sir. Everyone has their alibi, and a good one, sir. The kitchen was eating of its dinner at the time of the—accident, and everyone was present, even the garden boy. Everyone else in the house was in the lounge or in the bar that leads out of it, and has two or three other gentlemen's word to prove it. There was no strangers in the place, if you see what I mean, sir. All the gentlemen who called on Miss Bellew this morning come for a purpose, as you might say. They all knew each other well. One of 'em couldn't have gone off and done it unless . . ."

He paused, getting very red.

"Unless what?" said Leo anxiously. "Go on, my man. Don't stand on ceremony. We're in lodge here. Unless what?"

Pussey swallowed.

"Unless *all the other gentlemen knew*, sir," he said and hung his head.

CHAPTER VI

Departed Pig

THERE WAS an awkward pause for a moment, not unnaturally. Pussey remained dumb stricken by his own temerity, I observed a customary diffidence, and Leo appeared to be struggling for comprehension.

"Eh!" he said at last. "Conspiracy, eh?"

Pussey was sweating. "Don't hardly seem that could be so, sir," he mumbled unhappily.

"I don't know . . ." Leo spoke judicially. "I don't know, Pussey. It's an idea. It's an idea. And yet, don't you know, it couldn't have been so in this case. They would all have had to be in it, don't you see, and *I was there.*"

It was a sublime moment. Leo spoke simply and with that magnificent innocence which is as devastating as it is blind. Pussey and I sighed with relief. The old boy had swept away the slender supports of fact and left us with a miracle, but it was worth it.

Leo continued to consider the case.

"No," he said at last. "No. Impossible. Quite impossible. We'll have to think of something else, Pussey. We'll go over the alibis together. Maybe there's a loophole somewhere; you never know."

They settled down to work, and I, not wishing to interfere in the inspector's province, drifted off to find Kingston. I discovered him in the drawing room with Janet and Bathwick, who stiffened and bristled as I came in. I wished he wouldn't. I am not oversensitive, I hope, but his violent dislike embarrassed me, and I offered him a cigarette on the gift principle. He refused it.

Kingston was as keen to chat as I was, and he suggested a cigar on the terrace. In any other drawing room, with the possible exception of Great-aunt Caroline's at Cambridge, such a remark might have sounded stilted or at least consciously period, but Highwaters is that sort of house. The late Lady Pursuivant liked her furniture gilt and her porcelain by the ton.

I saw Bathwick shoot him a glance of doglike gratitude which enhanced my sense of injustice, while Janet smouldered at me across the hearthrug.

We went out through the french windows onto as fine a marble terrace as any you'd find in Hollywood today, and Kingston took my arm.

"I say," he began, "that chap Peters . . ."

It took me back years to the little patch of grass behind the chapel at school and old Guffy taking me by the arm, with the same words uttered in exactly the same tone of mingled excitement and outrage.

"That chap Peters . . ."

"Yes?" I said encouragingly.

Kingston hesitated. "This is in the nature of a confession," he began unexpectedly, and I fancy I stared at him, for he coloured and laughed. "Oh, I didn't rob the blighter," he said. "But I took down his will for him. That's what I wanted to talk to you about. He came down to my place to recuperate after appendicitis, you know. He made the arrangements himself by letter, and on the way down he picked up a chill and developed roaring pneumonia and died in spite of everything. He came to me because I was fairly inexpensive, you know. Someone in the district recommended him, he said, and mentioned a chap I knew slightly. Well, when he was very ill he had a lucid period, and he sent for me and said he wanted to make a will. I wrote it down, and he signed it."

Kingston paused and fidgeted.

"I'm telling you this because I know about you," he went on at last. "I've heard about you from Janet, and I know Sir Leo called you down on this Harris business. Well, Campion, as a matter of fact, I altered the will a bit."

"Did you though?" I said foolishly.

He nodded. "Not in substance, of course," he said, "but in form. I had to. As he dictated it it ran something like this: 'To that unspeakable bounder and unjailed crook, my brother, born Henry Richard Peters—whatever he may be calling himself now—I leave all I possess at the time of my death, including everything that may accrue to my estate after I die. I do this not because I like him, am sorry for him, or sympathise in any way with any nefarious business in which he may be engaged, but simply because he is the son of my mother, and I know of no one else.' "

Kingston hesitated and regarded me solemnly in the moonlight.

"I didn't think it was decent," he said. "A thing like that can cause a lot of trouble. So I cleaned up the wording a bit. I simply made it clear that Mr Peters wanted everything to go to his brother, and left it at that. He signed it and died."

He smoked for a moment or so in silence, and I waited for him to continue.

"As soon as I saw Harris he reminded me of someone," he said, "and tonight at dinner, when you reminded me of that funeral, I realised who it was. Peters and Harris had a great deal in common. They were made of the same sort of material, if you see what I mean, and had the same colouring. Peters was larger and had more fat on him, but the more I think about it the stronger the likeness becomes. You see what I'm driving at, Campion? This man Harris may well be the legatee's brother."

He laughed apologetically.

"Now I've said it it doesn't sound so very exciting," he said.

I did not answer him at once. I knew perfectly well that the Peters in the mortuary was my Peters, and if there was a brother in the business I took it that it was he who had been Kingston's patient. It confirmed my earlier suspicions that Pig had been up to something characteristically fishy before retribution in the flowerpot had overtaken him.

"I sent the will along to his solicitors," Kingston continued. "I took all instructions about the funeral and so on from them, and they paid my account. I've got their name at home; I'll let you have it. Tomorrow morning do?"

I assured him it would, and he went on:

"I was down at the Knights this morning when it happened," he said, not without a certain pride. "We were playing poker. I'd just netted a queen pot when I heard the thud and we all rushed out. There was nothing to be done, of course. Have you seen the body?"

"Yes," I said. "I haven't examined it yet. Was that the first time you'd seen Harris?"

"Oh Lord, no! He's been there all the week. I've had to go along there every day to see Flossie Gage, one of the maids. She's had jaundice. I didn't talk to Harris much because—well, none of us did, you know. He was an offensive type. That incident with Bathwick showed you the type he was."

"Bathwick?"

"Oh, didn't you hear about that?" Kingston warmed to me. Like most country doctors he relished a spot of gossip. "It had its humorous side in a way. Bathwick is an earnest soul, as you may have noticed."

I agreed, and he chuckled and hurried on:

"Harris talked about a dance hall and a bathing beach he was going to build on that bit of land which runs down to the creek on the far side of the cricket pitch. Bathwick heard the gossip and was appalled by it. It didn't fit into his own scheme for Kepesake's development, which is more on welfare lines—communal kitchens and superintended crèches, and so on. He rushed down to see Harris in a panic, and I believe there was a grand scene. Harris had a sort of sense of humour and took a delight in teasing old Bathwick, who has none. They were in the lounge at the Knights, and Bill Duchesney and one or two other people were there, so Harris had an audience and let himself go. Bill told me Bathwick went off at last with his eyes bulging. Harris had promised him dancing houris, secret casinos and God knows what else, until the poor chap saw his dream yokel walking straight out of the church clinic on one side of the road into the jaws of hell on the other. Bill tried to soothe the vicar, I believe, but he said he was scared out of his wits and shocked to the marrow. You see the sort of fellow Harris was. He liked to show off. There was no need for him to tease old Bathwick, who'd be quite a good chap if he wasn't so solemn. However, that's not the point. The question is, who killed Harris? I'll bring down that solicitor's name, and any papers I can find, first thing in the morning, shall I?"

"I wish you would," I said trying not to sound too eager. "Thanks for telling me."

"Not at all. I wish I could be really helpful. It's so seldom anything happens down here." He laughed awkwardly. "That's a bit naïve, isn't it?" he murmured. "But you've no idea how dull the country is for a fairly intelligent man, Campion."

We were back to the drawing room, Janet and Bathwick were listening to the wireless, but she got up and switched it off as we appeared, and Bathwick sighed audibly at the sight of me.

Leo looked in after a bit, but he was plainly preoccupied, and he excused himself soon after. Not unnaturally the party broke up early. Kingston went home, taking the reluctant and smouldering cleric with him, and Janet and I wandered out on the terrace. It was warm and moonlit and rather exotic, what with night-scented stocks in the garden below and nightingales in the ilex.

"Albert . . ." said Janet.

"Yes?"

"You've some very peculiar friends, haven't you?"

"Oh, you meet all kinds of people at school," I said defensively, my mind still clinging to Peters. "It's like knowing a lot of eggs. You can't tell which one is going to grow into something definitely offensive."

She drew a long breath and her eyes glinted in the faint light.

"I didn't know you went to a co-ed," she said witheringly. "That accounts for you, I suppose."

"In a way," I agreed mildly. "I remember Miss Marshall. What a topping Head she was, to be sure. Such a real little sport on the hockey field. Such a demon for impositions. Such a regular little whirlwind with the birch."

"Shut up," said Janet unreasonably. "How d'you like Bathwick?"

"A dear fellow," I said dutifully. "Where does he live?"

"At the vicarage, just behind the Knights. Why?"

"Has he a nice garden?"

"Quite good. Why?"

"Does his garden adjoin the Knights garden?"

"The vicarage garden runs up to the chestnut copse at the back of Poppy's place. Why?"

"I like to know a man's background," I said. "He's rather keen on you, isn't he?"

She did not answer me, and I fancied she considered the question to be in bad taste. To my astonishment I felt her shiver at my side.

"Albert," she said in a very small voice, "do you know who did this beastly murder?"

"No, not yet."

"You think you'll find out?" She was almost whispering.

"Yes," I said. "I'll find out."

She put her hand in mine. "Leo's very fond of Poppy," she murmured.

I held her hand closely. "Leo has no more idea who killed Harris than a babe unborn," I said.

She shivered again. "That makes it worse, doesn't it? It'll be such a dreadful shock for him when he—he has to know."

"Poppy?" I said.

Janet clung to my arm. "They'd all shield her, wouldn't they?" she said unsteadily. "After all, she had most to lose. Go back to Town, Albert. Give it up. Don't find out."

"Forget it," I said. "Forget it for now."

We walked on in silence for a little. Janet wore a blue dress and I said I liked it. She also wore her hair in a knot low on her neck, and I said I liked that, too.

After a while she paid me a compliment. She said I was an eminently truthful person, and she was sorry to have doubted my word in a certain matter of the afternoon.

I forgave her readily, not to say eagerly. We turned back towards the french windows and had just decided not to go in, after all, when something as unforeseen as it was unfortunate occurred. Pepper came out, blowing gently. He begged our pardons, he said, but a Miss Effie Rowlandson had called to see Mr Campion and he had put her in the breakfast room.

CHAPTER VII

The Girl Friend

AS I FOLLOWED PEPPER through the house I ventured to question him.

"What's she like, Pepper?"

He turned and eyed me with a glance which conveyed clearly that he was an old man, an experienced man, and that dust did not affect his eyesight.

"The young woman informed me that she was a great friend of yours, sir, which was why she took the liberty of calling on you so late." He spoke sadly, intimating that the rebuke hurt him as much as it did me. He opened the breakfast-room door.

"Yoo-hoo!" said someone inside.

Pepper withdrew and Miss Effie Rowlandson rose to meet me.

"O-oh!" she said, glancing up at me under fluttering lashes, "you're not really, truly cross, are you?"

I am afraid I looked at her blankly. She was petite, blonde and girlish, with starry eyes and the teeth of tooth-paste advertisement. Her costume was entirely black save for a long white quill in her hat, and the general effect lay somewhere between Hamlet and Aladdin.

"O-oh, you don't remember me," she said. "O-oh, how awful of me to have come! I made sure you'd remember me. I am a silly little fool, aren't I?"

She conveyed that I was a bit of a brute, but that she did not blame me, and life was like that.

"Perhaps you've got hold of the wrong man?" I suggested helpfully.

"O-oh no . . ." Again her lashes fluttered at me. "I remember you—at the funeral, you know." She lowered her voice modestly on the last words.

Suddenly she came back to me with a rush. She was the girl at Peters's funeral. Why I should have forgotten her and remembered the old man I do not know, save that I recollect feeling that she was not the right person to stare at.

"Ah yes," I said slowly. "I do remember now."

She clapped her hands and squealed delightedly.

"I knew you would. Don't ask me why, but I just knew it. I'm like that sometimes. I just know things."

At this point the conversation came to an abrupt deadlock. I was not at my best, and she stood looking at me, a surprisingly shrewd expression in her light grey eyes.

"I knew you'd help me," she added at last.

I was more than ever convinced that I was not her man, and was debating how to put it when she made a surprising statement.

"He trampled on me," she said. "I don't know when I've been so mistaken in a man. Still, a girl does make mistakes, doesn't she, Mr Campion? I see I made a mistake in saying I was such an old friend of yours when we'd only met once—or really only just looked at each other. I know that now. I wouldn't do it again."

"Miss Rowlandson," I said, "why have you come? I—er—I have a right to know," I added stalwartly, trying to keep in the picture.

She peered at me. "O-oh, you're *hard*, aren't you?" she said. "All men are hard, aren't they? They're not all like him, though. O-oh, he was hard! Still," she added, with a wholly unconvincing attempt at gallant restraint, "I ought not to talk about him like that, did I, when he's dead—if he *is* dead. Is he?"

"Who?"

She giggled. "You're cautious, aren't you? Are all detectives cautious? I like a man to be cautious. Rowley Peters, of course. I used to call him

Rowley-Poly. That used to make him cross. You'd never guess how cross that used to make him. Poor Rowley-Poly! It's wrong to laugh when he's dead—if he *is* dead. Do you know?"

"My dear girl," I said. "We went to his funeral, didn't we?"

I suppose I spoke sharply, for her manner changed. She assumed a spurious dignity and sat down, arranging her short black skirts about her thin legs with great care.

"I've come to consult you, Mr Campion," she said. "I'm putting all my cards on the table. I want to know if you're satisfied about that funeral?"

"It wasn't much to do with me," I countered, temporarily taken aback.

"Oh, wasn't it? Well, why was you there? That's pinked you, hasn't it? I'm a straightforward girl, Mr Campion, and I want a straight answer. There was something funny about that funeral, and you know it."

"Look here," I said, "I'm perfectly willing to help you. Suppose you tell me why you think I can."

She looked at me steadily. "You've been to a good school, haven't you?" she said. "I always think it helps a man to have gone to a good school. Then you *know* he's a gentleman; I always say that. Well, I'll trust you. I don't often. And if you let me down, well, I've been silly again, that's all. I was engaged to marry Rowley Peters, Mr Campion, and then he went and died in a hole-and-corner nursing home and left all his money to his brother. If you don't think that's suspicious, I do."

I hesitated. "You think it's odd because he left his brother everything?" I began.

Effie Rowlandson interrupted me.

"I think it's funny he died at all, if you ask me," she said. "I'd threatened him with a lawyer, I had really. I had the letters and everything."

I said nothing, and she grew very pink.

"Think what you like about me, Mr Campion," she said, "but I've got feelings and I've worked very hard to get married. I think he's done the dirty on me. If he's hiding, I'll find him, if it's the last thing I do."

She sat looking at me like a suddenly militant sparrow.

"I came to you," she said, "because I heard you were a detective and I liked your face."

"Splendid! But why come here?" I demanded. "Why come to Kepesake, of all places?"

Effie Rowlandson drew a deep breath. "I'll tell you the truth, Mr Campion," she said.

Once again her lashes flickered, and I felt that our brief period of plain dealing was at an end.

"I've got a friend in this village, and he's seen my photographs of Rowley Peters. He's an old man, known me for years."

She paused and eyed me to see if I was with her or against her, and apparently she was reassured for she went on breathlessly:

"A few days ago he wrote me, this friend of mine did. 'There's a gentleman in the village very like a friend of yours,' he wrote. 'If I were you I'd come and have a look at him. It might be worth your while.' I came as soon as I could, and when I got here I found this man I'd come to see had got himself killed only this morning. I heard you were in the village, so I came along."

I began to follow her. "You want to identify him?" I said.

She nodded resolutely.

"Why come to me? Why not go to the authorities?"

Her reply was disarming. "Well, you see, I felt I knew you," she said.

I considered. The advantages of a witness at this juncture were inestimable.

"When can you be down at the police station?"

"I'd like to go now."

It was late for the country, and I said so, but she was adamant.

"I've made up my mind to it and I shan't sleep if I've got it hanging over me till tomorrow. Take me down now in your car. Go on, you know you can. I am being a nuisance, aren't I? But I'm like that. If I make up my mind to a thing, I fret till I've done it. I should be quite ill by the morning, I should really."

There was nothing else for it. I knew from experience that it is safest to catch a witness as soon as he appears on the scene.

I rang the bell and told the girl who answered it to send Lugg round with the car. Then, leaving Miss Rowlandson in the breakfast room, I went to find Janet.

It was not a very pleasant interview. Janet is a dear girl, but she can be most obtuse. When she went to bed, which she did with some dignity a few minutes after I had located her, I went back to the breakfast room.

Lugg seemed a little surprised when I appeared with Miss Rowlandson. I tucked her into the back of the car and climbed into the front seat beside him. He let in the clutch, and as we roared down the drive in fourth he leant towards me.

"Ever see a cat come out of a dawg kennel?" he murmured and added when I stared at him: "Gives you a bit of a turn. That's all."

We drove on in silence. I began to feel that my friend, Miss Effie Rowlandson, was going to be a responsibility.

It was a strange night with a great moon sailing in an infinite sky. Small odd-shaped banks of cumulus clouds swam over it from time to time, but for the most part it remained bland and bald as the knob on a brass bedstead.

Kepesake, which is a frankly picturesque village by day, was mysterious in the false light. The high trees were deep and shadowy and hid the small houses, while the square tower of the church looked squat and menacing against the transparent sky. It was a secret village through which we sped on what I for one felt was our rather ghastly errand.

When we pulled up outside the cottage which is also the police station there was only a single light in an upstairs room, and I leant over the back seat.

"Are you sure you wouldn't rather leave it until the morning?" I ventured.

She answered me through clenched teeth. "No, thank you, Mr Campion. I've made up my mind to go through with it. I've got to know."

I left them in the car and went down the path to rouse someone. Pussey himself came out almost at once and was wonderfully obliging, considering he had been on the point of going to bed. We conferred in whispers out of deference to the darkness.

"That's all right, sir," he said in reply to my apologies. "Us wants a bit o' help in this business and that's the truth now, so it is. If the lady can tell us anything about the deceased it's more than the landlord of his flat in London can. We'll go round the side, sir, if you don't mind."

I fetched the others, and together we formed a grim little procession on the gravel path leading round to the yard behind the cottage. Pussey unlocked the gates, and we crossed the tidy little square to the slate-roofed shed which looked like a small village schoolroom, and was not.

I took Effie Rowlandson's arm. She was shivering and her teeth were chattering, but she was not a figure of negligible courage.

Pussey was tact itself. "There's a light switch just inside the door," he said. "Now, miss, there ain't nothin' to shock you. Just a moment, sir; I'll go first."

He unlocked the door, and we stood huddled together on the stone step. Pussey turned over the light switch.

"Now," he said, and a moment later swallowed with a sound in which incredulity was mixed with dismay. The room remained as I had seen it that afternoon save for one startling innovation. The table in the middle of the floor was dismantled. The cotton sheet lay upon the ground, spread out as though a careless riser had flung it aside.

Pig Peters had gone.

CHAPTER VIII

The Wheels Go Round

THERE WAS a long uncomfortable pause. A moment before I had seen Pig's outline under the cotton clearly in my mind's eye. Now the image was dispelled so ruthlessly that I felt mentally stranded. The room was very cold and quiet. Lugg stepped ponderously forward.

"Lost the perishin' corpse now?" he demanded and he spoke so truculently that I knew he was rattled. "Lumme, Inspector, I 'ope your 'elmet's under lock and key."

Pussey stood looking down at the dismantled table, and his pleasant yokel face was pale.

"That's a wonderful funny thing," he began and looked round the ill-lit barren little room as though he expected to find an explanation for the mystery on its blank walls.

It was a moment of alarm, the night so silent, the place so empty and the bedraggled cotton pall on the ground.

Pussey would have spoken again had it not been for Effie Rowlandson's exhibition. Her nerve deserted her utterly and she drew away from me, her head strained back as she began to scream, her mouth twisted into an O of terror. It was nerve-racking, and I seized her by the shoulders and shook her so violently that her teeth rattled.

It silenced her, of course. Her final shriek was cut off in the middle, and she looked up at me angrily.

"Stop it!" I said. "Do you want to rouse the village?"

She put up her hands to push me away.

"I'm frightened," she said. "I don't know what I'm doing. What's happened to him? You told me he was here. I was going to look at him, and now he's gone."

She began to cry noisily. Pussey glanced at her and then at me.

"Perhaps that'd be best if the young lady went home," he suggested reasonably.

Miss Rowlandson clung to me. "Don't leave me," she said. "I'm not going down to The Feathers in the dark. I won't, I tell you, I won't! Not while he's about, *alive*."

"It's all right," I began soothingly. "Lugg'll drive you down. There's nothing to be alarmed about. There's been a mistake. The body's been moved. Perhaps the undertaker . . ."

Pussey raised his head as he heard the last word.

"No," he said. "That was in here an hour ago, because I looked."

Effie began to cry again. "I won't go with him," she said. "I won't go with anyone but you. I'm frightened. You got me into this. You must get me out of it. Take me home! Take me home!"

She made an astounding amount of noise, and Pussey looked at me beseechingly.

"Perhaps if you would drive the young lady down, sir," he suggested diffidently, "that would ease matters up here, in a manner of speaking. I better get on the telephone to Sir Leo right away."

I glanced at Lugg appealingly, but he avoided my eyes, and Miss Rowlandson laid her head on my shoulder in an ecstasy of tears.

The situation had all the unreality and acute discomfort of a nightmare. Outside the shed the yard was ghostly in the false light. It was hot, and there was not a breath of wind anywhere. Effie was trembling so violently that I thought she might collapse.

"I'll be back in a minute," I said to Pussey and hurried her down the gravel path to the waiting car.

The Feathers Inn is at the far end of the village. It stands by itself at the top of a hill and is reputed to have the best beer, if not the best accommodation, in the neighbourhood.

Effie Rowlandson scrambled into the front seat, and when I climbed in beside her she drew close to me, still weeping.

"I've had a shock," she snivelled. "I'd prepared myself and then it wasn't necessary. That was one thing. Then I realised Rowley got out by himself. You didn't know Rowley Peters as well as I did, Mr Campion. When I heard he'd been killed I didn't really believe it. He was clever, and he was cruel. He's about somewhere, hiding."

"He was dead this afternoon," I said brutally. "Very dead. And since miracles don't happen nowadays he's probably dead still. There's nothing to get so excited about. I'm sorry you should have had a rotten experience, but there's probably some very ordinary explanation for the disappearance of the body."

I was rather shocked to hear myself talking so querulously. There had been something very disturbing in the incident. The elusiveness of Pig dead was becoming illogical and alarming.

As we came out of the village onto the strip of heath which lay silent and deserted in the cold secretive light, she shuddered.

"I'm not an imaginative girl, Mr Campion," she said, "but you read of funny things happening, don't you? Suppose he was to rise up behind one of these banks of stones by the side of the road and come out towards us——"

"Shut up," I said, even more violently than I had intended. "You'll frighten yourself into a fit, my child. I assure you there's some perfectly reasonable explanation for all this. When you get into The Feathers make them give you a hot drink and go to bed. You'll find the mystery's been cleared up by the morning."

She drew away from me. "Oh, you're hard," she said with a return of her old manner. "I said you were hard. I like hard people, I do really."

Her lightning changes of mood disconcerted me, and I was glad when we pulled up outside the pub. The fine old lath-and-plaster front was in darkness, which was not astonishing, for it was nearly midnight.

"Which door is it?" I enquired.

"The one marked Club Room. I expect it'll be locked."

I left her in the car while I tapped on the door she indicated. For a time there was no response, and I was getting restive at the delay when

I heard a furtive movement on the inside. I tapped again, and this time the door was opened.

"I say, you're fearfully late," said the last voice I expected, and Gilbert Whippet, of all people, thrust a pale face out into the moonlight.

I gaped at him, and he had the grace to seem vaguely disturbed to see me.

"Oh . . . er . . . Campion," he said. "Hello! Terribly late, isn't it?"

He was backing into the dark pit of the doorway when I pulled myself together.

"Hey," I said, catching him by the sleeve. "Here, Whippet, where are you going?"

He did not resist me but made no attempt to come out into the light. Moreover, I felt that once I let him go he would fade quietly into the background.

"I was going to bed," he murmured, no doubt in reply to my question. "I heard you knock, so I opened the door."

"You stay and talk to me," I commanded. "What are you doing here, anyway?"

In spite of myself I heard the old censorious note creeping into my tone. Whippet is so very vague that he forces one into an unusual directness.

He did not answer me, and I repeated the question.

"Here?" he said, looking up at the pub. "Oh yes, I'm staying here. Only for a day or two."

He was infuriating, and I quite forgot the girl until I heard her step behind me.

"Mr Whippet," she began breathlessly, "he's gone! The body's gone! What shall we do?"

Whippet turned his pale eyes towards her, and I thought I detected a warning in the glance.

"Ah, Miss Rowlandson," he said. "You've been out? You're late, aren't you?"

I was glad to see she wasn't playing, either.

"The body's gone," she repeated. "Rowley Peters' body is gone."

The information seemed to sink in. For a moment he looked positively intelligent.

"Lost it?" he said. "Oh! . . . Awkward. Holds things up so."

His voice trailed away into silence, and he suddenly shook hands with me.

"Glad to have seen you, Campion. I'll look you up sometime. Er—good night."

He stepped back into the doorway, and Effie followed him. With great presence of mind I put my foot in the jamb.

"Look here, Whippet," I said, "if you can do anything to help us in this matter, or if you know anything, you'd better come out with it. What do you know about Peters, anyway?"

He blinked at me.

"Oh . . . nothing. I'm just staying here. I've heard the talk, of course. . . ."

I caught his sleeve again just as he was disappearing.

"You had one of those letters," I said. "Have you had any more?"

"About the mole? Yes. Yes, as a matter of fact, I have, Campion. I've got it somewhere. I showed it to Miss Rowlandson. I say, it's terribly awkward you losing the body. Have you looked in the river?"

It was such an unexpected question that it irritated me unreasonably.

"Why on earth in the river?" I said. "D'you know anything?"

In my excitement I must have held him a little more tightly than I had intended, for he suddenly shook himself free.

"I should look in the river," he said. "I mean, it's so obvious, isn't it?"

He stepped back and closed the door with himself and Miss Rowlandson inside. I still had my foot there, however, and he opened it again. He seemed embarrassed.

"It's fearfully late," he said. "I don't mean to be rude, Campion. I'll look you up tomorrow, if I may, but there's no point in your doing anything at all until you've found the body, is there?"

I hesitated. There was a great deal in what Whippet said. I was itching to get back, and yet there was evidently much he could explain. What on earth he was doing there with Effie Rowlandson, for one thing.

In that moment of hesitation I was lost. He moved forward, and as I stepped backward involuntarily the door was gently, almost politely, closed in my face.

I cursed him but decided he could wait. I hurried back to the car and turned her. As I raced down to the police station I tried to reconcile Whippet's reappearance with the whole mysterious business.

I covered the half mile in something under a minute, and pulled up outside Pussey's cottage at the same moment that another car arrived from the opposite direction. As I climbed out I recognised Leo's respectable Humber. Pepper Jr was driving, and Leo hailed me from the tonneau.

"Is that you, Campion? Most extraordinary business! Pussey told me over the phone."

I went up to the car and opened the door.

"Are you coming, sir?" I said.

"Yes, my boy, yes. Should have been here before, but I stopped to pick up Bathwick here. Seems to have had a little accident on the way home from our place tonight."

He put up his hand and turned on the light as he spoke, and I stared down into the pale, embarrassed face of the Rev. Philip Smedley Bathwick, who smiled at me with uncharacteristic friendliness. He was wringing wet. His dinner jacket clung to him, and his dog collar was a sodden rag.

"Been in the river, he tells me," said Leo.

CHAPTER IX

"And a Very Good Day to You, Sir"

"THE RIVER?" I echoed, Whippet's idiotic remark returning to me. "Really?"

Bathwick giggled. It was a purely nervous sound, but Leo scowled at him.

"Well, hardly," he said. "I was taking a short cut home across the saltings and I stumbled into one of the dikes. I'd come out without my torch. I made my way back to the road, and Sir Leo very kindly picked me up and gave me a lift."

It was a fantastic story in view of the moonlight, which was so bright that colours were almost distinguishable, and I thought Leo must notice it. He has a one-track mind, however. His one desire was to get back to the scene of the disappearance.

"Never mind, never mind. Soon get you home now," he said. "Pepper'll take you along. Make yourself a hot toddy. Wrap yourself in a blanket and you'll come to no harm."

"Er—thank you, thank you very much," said Bathwick. "I should like nothing better. I feel I must express . . ."

We heard no more, for Pepper Jr, who doubtless shared his employer's anxiety to get to the scene of the excitement in the shortest possible time, let in the clutch and Bathwick was whisked away.

I was sorry to lose him. His astonishing friendliness towards me was not the least fishy circumstance of his brief appearance.

"Where did you find him?" I asked Leo.

"On the lower road. Nearly ran him down. He's all right—just a duckin'." Leo was fighting with the catch of the police-station gate as he spoke and appeared profoundly disinterested.

"Yes, I know," I said. "But he left Highwaters at about a quarter to ten. I thought Kingston was going to run him home?"

"So he did, so he did," said Leo, sighing with relief as we got the wicket open. "Kingston put him down at the White Barn corner, and he said he'd strike his way home across the marshes. Can't be more than five hundred yards. But the silly feller stumbled into a dike, lost his nerve and made his way back to the road. Perfectly simple, Campion. No mystery there. Come on, my boy, come on. We're wastin' time."

"But it's now midnight," I objected. "It couldn't have taken him a couple of hours to scramble out of a dike."

"Might have done," said Leo irritably. "Backboneless feller. Anyway, we can't bother about him now. Got somethin' serious to think about. I don't like monkey business with a corpse. It's not a bit like my district. It's indecent. I tell you I feel it, Campion. Ah, here's Pussey. Anythin' to report, my man?"

Pussey and Lugg came up together. I could see their faces quite plainly, and I wondered how Bathwick could possibly have avoided seeing a rabbit hole, much less a dike.

Pussey, I saw at once, was well over his first superstitious alarm. At the moment he was less mystified than shocked.

"That's a proper nasty thing, sir," he said, "so that is, now."

He led us into the shed and, with Lugg remaining mercifully silent in the background, gave us a fairly concise account of his investigations.

"All these windows were bolted on the inside, sir, the same as you see them now, and the door was locked. At a quarter to eleven I went round the station just to see everything was all right for the night, and the body was here then. After that I went in to the front of the house, and I stayed there for some little time until I went up to my bedroom. I was just thinking about bed when Mr Campion here arrived with the young lady and Mr Lugg, and we come round here and made the discovery, sir."

He paused, took a deep breath, and Leo spluttered.

"Did the key leave your possession?"

"No sir."

Leo's natural reaction to the story of a miracle is to take it to read that someone is lying. I could hear him boiling quietly at my side.

"Pussey, I've always found you a very efficient officer," he began with dangerous calm, "but you're askin' me to believe in a fairy story. If the body didn't go through the windows it must have gone through the door, and if you had the only key . . ."

Pussey coughed. "Excuse me, sir," he began, "but Mr Lugg and me we made a kind of discovery, like. This building was put up by Mr Henry Royle, the builder in the Street, and Mr Lugg and me we noticed that several other buildings in this yard, sir, which were put up at the same time, all have the same locks, like."

Leo's rage subsided, and he became interested.

"Any of the other keys here missin'?"

"No sir; but as Mr Royle has done a lot of work hereabouts lately, it doesn't seem unlikely . . ."

He broke off on the question.

Leo swore, and it seemed to relieve him.

"Oh well, we shan't get any help there," he rumbled. "Wonder you trouble to lock the place at all, Pussey. Damned inefficient. Typical of the whole county," he added to me under his breath.

But Pussey had more to offer. With considerable pride he led us over the rough grass by the side of the shed to the tarred fence which marked the boundary line of police property. Three boards had been kicked down and there was a clear way into the narrow lane beyond.

"That's new," he said. "That's been done tonight."

A cursory search of the lane revealed nothing. The ground was hard and the surface was baked mud interspersed with tufts of grass. It was Pussey who put the general thought into words.

"Whoever moved him must 'a' done it between quarter to eleven and twenty-five minutes past. Seems very likely that was done from a car, or a cart. He was a heavy fellow. If you'll excuse me, sir, I think the best thing is for us to wait till the morning and then question all those as live near by. Seems like we can't do nothing while that's dark."

In the end we left it at that. Pepper Jr collected Leo and I sent Lugg back with the Lagonda. Pussey went to bed and I walked off down the grassy lane behind the shed. The moon was sinking and already there were faint streaks of light in the east. It was colder and I was in the mood to walk home.

The lane went on for some distance between high hedges. Pussey had given me clear directions how to get onto the road again and I sauntered on, my mind on the business.

Leo and Pussey, I saw, were outraged. The murder had shaken them up, but this apparently wanton disturbance of the dead shocked them both deeply.

As I thought of it, it seemed to me that this element was perhaps the most enlightening thing I had noticed so far, because although I knew I had no proof of it, it seemed to me that it constituted a complete let-out for Leo's particular band of friends who had gathered round Poppy in her trouble. Whereas any one of them might quite easily have staged the slightly ludicrous accident which had killed Pig, I could not see any of them dragging his body about afterwards in this extraordinarily pointless fashion.

I was considering those who were left, and Bathwick was figuring largely in my mind, when I turned out of the lane onto a grass field which rose up to form a considerable hill, circular against the sky line. I knew I had to skirt this field and pass through another before I came to the road, if I was to avoid an unnecessary couple of miles.

It was almost dark at the bottom of the hill, and as I plodded on, lost in my thoughts, there came to me suddenly over the brow of the hill a sound at once so human and so terrifying that I felt the hair on my scalp rising.

It was Pig's cough.

The night was very still, and I heard the rattle in the larynx, the whoop, and even the puff at the end of it.

For a moment I stood still, a prey to all the ridiculous fears of childhood. Then I set off up the hill at a double. The wind whistled in my ears and my heart was thumping.

Suddenly, as I reached the brow, I saw something silhouetted against the grey sky. This was so unexpected that I paused to gape at it. It was a tripod with something else which I at first took to be a small machine gun, and which turned out to be an old-fashioned telescope mounted upon it.

I approached this cautiously and had almost reached it when a figure rose up out of the earth beside it and stood waiting for me. He was against what light there was and I could only see his small silhouette. I stopped and, for want of something better, said what must have been the silliest thing in the world in the circumstances. I said "Good day."

"And a very good day to you, sir," answered one of the most unpleasant voices I have ever heard in all my life.

He came towards me and I recognised him with relief by his peculiar mincing walk.

"Perhaps I have the advantage of you, sir," he began. "You are Mr Campion?"

"Yes," I said. "And you're Mr Hayhoe."

He laughed, a little affected sound.

"It will serve," he murmured. "It will serve. I was looking forward to an interview with you today, sir. I was wondering how I could manage it with a certain amount of privacy. This is a most unexpected pleasure. I didn't expect to find a man of your age wandering about in the dawn. Most young men nowadays prefer to spend the best part of their day in their beds."

"You're up early yourself," I said, glancing at the telescope. "Waiting to see the sunrise?"

"Yes," he said and laughed again. "That and other things."

It was a mad conversation up there on the hill at two o'clock in the morning, and it went through my mind that he must be one of those fashionable nature lovers who rush round the country identifying birds. He soon disabused me of that idea, however.

"I take it you are making investigations concerning the death of that unfortunate fellow Harris?" he said. "Now, Mr Campion, I can be very useful to you. I wish to make you a proposition. For a reasonable sum, the amount to be settled between us, I will undertake to give you certain very interesting information, information which it would take you a very long time to collect alone and which should lead you to a very successful conclusion of the case. Your professional reputation will be enhanced, and I shall, of course, take none of the kudos. Now, suppose we come to terms."

I am afraid I laughed at him. This is the kind of offer which I have had so often. I thought of the cough I had heard.

"Harris was a relation of yours, I suppose?" I observed.

He stiffened a little and shrugged his shoulders.

"A nephew," he said, "and not a very dutiful one. He was quite a wealthy young man, you see, and I—well, as you can imagine, I am not the sort of man who normally spends his holidays in a wretched workman's hovel or his evenings trapesing about the barren countryside."

He was rather a terrible old man, but I was glad I had cleared up the mystery of the cough.

It was then that I remembered something. After all, so far, I myself was the only person to connect Rowley Peters with Oswald Harris, with the possible exception of Effie Rowlandson, who merely had her suspicions.

"Let me see," I murmured, "that was your nephew Rowland Peters, wasn't it?"

To my intense regret he brushed the inference aside.

"I have several nephews, Mr Campion, or, rather, I had," he said with spurious dignity. "I hate to press the point, but I regard this as a business interview. Terms first, if you please. Shall we say five hundred guineas for a complete and private explanation of the whole business? Or, of course, I might split up the lots, as it were."

While he was rambling on I was thinking, and at this point I had an inspiration.

"Mr Hayhoe," I said, "what about the mole?"

A little shrill sound escaped him, but he bit it off instantly.

"Oh!" he said, and there was cautiousness and respect in his voice, "you know about the mole, do you?"

CHAPTER X

The Parson's Dram

I DID NOT REPLY. In the circumstances of my extreme ignorance there was very little I could say. I remained silent, therefore, and, I hope, enigmatic. However, he was not to be drawn.

"I hadn't thought of the creature myself," he said unexpectedly, "but there may be something there. It's a valuable contribution. You seem to be unexpectedly intelligent, if I may say so without offence."

He sighed and sat down on the grass.

"Yes," he continued, clasping his knees. "Thinking it over, we ought to go far, you and I, once we can come to an understanding. Now, about this question of terms . . . I hate to insist upon the subject, but at the moment my financial affairs are in considerable disorder. How far would you be prepared to meet me?"

"Not to a pound," I said flatly, but with politeness. "If you know anything about the death of your nephew it's your obvious duty to go to the police with it."

Mr Hayhoe shrugged his shoulders. "Oh well," he said regretfully, "I gave you the opportunity. You can't deny that."

I turned away, expecting him to call me back, which he did.

"My dear young man," he protested when I had taken a few steps down the hill, "don't be precipitate. Let us talk this thing over reasonably. I have certain information which is of value to you. Why should we quarrel?"

"If you knew anything of importance," I said over my shoulder, "you'd hardly dare to talk about it."

"Ah, you don't understand." He seemed greatly relieved. "My own situation is perfectly safe. I have nothing to lose, everything to gain. My position is simple. I happen to possess an asset which I intend to realise. There are two likely purchasers: one is yourself, and the other is a certain person I need not name. Naturally, I shall dispose to the highest bidder."

I was growing weary of him. "Mr Hayhoe," I said, "I am tired. I want to go to bed. You are wasting my time. You are also making a fool of yourself. I'm sorry to be so explicit, but there it is."

He got up. "Look here, Campion," he said with a complete change of tone, his artificiality dropping from him and a wheedling note taking its place, "I could tell you something interesting if I wanted to. The police can pull me in and bullyrag me, but they can't hold me because they've nothing on me. I shan't talk to them and they can't make me. I can put you on to the right track for a consideration. What's it worth to you?"

"At this stage, very little," I said. "Half a crown, perhaps."

He laughed. "I think I can get more than that," he said softly. "Very much more. However, I'm not a rich man. Between ourselves, at the moment I'm very short indeed. Suppose we meet tomorrow morning, not quite as early as this? Say, seven o'clock. That gives me a clear twenty-four hours. If I can't get satisfaction in other quarters, well, I may bat my price a little. What do you say?"

He was an unpleasant piece of work, but I liked him better in this mood.

"We might have a chat about the mole," I conceded ungraciously.

He cocked an eye at me. "Very well," he agreed. "About the mole and

—other things. I'll meet you here, then, at seven o'clock tomorrow morning."

As I turned away an idea occurred to me.

"About your other purchaser," I said. "I shouldn't approach Sir Leo if I were you."

This time his laugh was spontaneous.

"You're not quite so clever as I thought you were," he said, and I went off down the hill with something to think about. Quite frankly, until that moment I had not seen him as a possible blackmailer.

At the time I thought I was justified in letting him cook for twenty-four hours, but at that time, as I have said, I did not know the type of person we were up against. Whenever I am apt to get overpleased with myself I remember that little chat on the hillside.

As I came wearily up the drive at Highwaters it was full dawn. The air was magnificent, the sky a translucent blue, and the birds were roaring at one another in undisturbed abandonment.

I suspected the french windows in the dining room had been left unlatched, and as I went round to them a rather unfortunate thing happened. Janet, who had no business to be awake at such an hour, came out on her balcony and caught me. I looked up to see her staring down at my slinking dinner-jacketed figure with mingled surprise and contempt.

"Good morning," I said innocently.

Two bright spots of colour appeared on her cheeks.

"I hope you saw Miss Rowlandson home safely," she said and went back to her room before I could explain.

I had a tepid bath and slept for a couple of hours, but I was waiting for Leo when he appeared round about eight o'clock. We went for a stroll round the garden before breakfast, and I put my request to him.

"Have the feller watched?" he said. "Good idea. I'll phone down to Pussey. Extraordinary name, Heigh-ho. Must be fictitious. Any reason above general suspicion?"

I told him about the conversation on the hilltop, and at first he wanted to have the man pulled in immediately.

"I don't think I would, sir," I objected. "I don't see how he can be involved himself, unless he's playing an incredibly dangerous game. Leave him loose, and he'll lead us to someone more interesting."

"As you like," he said. "As you like. Prefer the straightforward method myself."

As it happened, of course, he was perfectly right, but none of us knew that then.

Janet did not appear to breakfast, but I had no time to think about her, for Kingston arrived before the meal was over. He was bubbling with excitement and looked very young for his forty years as he came striding in, his coarse fair hair dishevelled and his rather lazy eyes unwontedly bright.

"I've found it," he announced before he was well in the room. "I've been up half the night turning over papers, but I tracked it down in the end. The firm I dealt with in Peters' affairs was Skinner, Sutain and Skinner, of Lincoln's Inn Fields. Any good?"

I took the name down, and he looked at me expectantly.

"I could take the day off and go up and see them for you, if you like," he said. "Or perhaps you'll go yourself?"

I didn't like to damp his enthusiasm, though it occurred to me that his life must be incredibly dull since he was so anxious to play the detective.

"Well, no," I said. "I think it'll have to wait for the time being. The body's disappeared, you see."

"Really? I say!" He seemed delighted and chattered on when I explained. "Things are moving, aren't they? I suppose you'll have to leave the solicitors for a day or two. Anything I can do? I've got to run down to Halt Knights to see my young patient, and there are one or two other people I ought to see, but after that I can be at your service entirely."

"I've got to go down to Poppy's," I said. "I'll come with you, if I may."

Leo had left us and was on the telephone in the gun room, talking to Pussey, when I disturbed him a minute or so later. He listened to my rather hurried story with unexpected intelligence.

"Wait a minute," he said when I had finished. "You think there may be some connection between this feller Peters you know and Harris, and you want me to get the London people to interview these solicitors with a view to their identifying the body. That right?"

"Yes," I said. "There may not be anything in it, but they might make general enquiries there about the two men, Peters and Harris. What I particularly want to know is where Harris got his money—if he was insured or anything. It's rather a shot in the dark, I know, but there's just a chance these people may be useful. I think they'll have to be handled delicately. I mean, I don't think it could be done by phone."

He nodded. "All right, my boy. Anything that helps us to get any nearer to this terrible thing, don't you know. . . . Pussey's going to put a man onto that feller Heigh-ho."

He paused abruptly and stood looking at me.

"Let's hope he doesn't lead us to anyone . . ."

He broke off helplessly.

"I'm going down to Halt Knights now," I murmured.

He coughed. "I'll follow you down. Don't alarm her, my boy; don't alarm her. Can't bring myself to believe that she's anything to do with it, poor little woman."

Kingston was waiting for me in the drive. He was exuberant. The turn affairs were taking seemed to stimulate him.

"I suppose it's all in the day's work for you?" he said a little enviously as I climbed in beside him. "But nothing ever happens down here, and

I should be inhuman if I wasn't interested. It's rather shocking how the human mind reacts to someone else's tragedy, isn't it? I didn't know Harris, of course, but what I did see of him didn't attract me. I should say the world's a better place without him. I saw him just before he died, you know, or at least an hour or so before, and I remember thinking at the time that he constituted a waste of space."

I was busy with my own problems, but I did not wish to be impolite. "When was this?" I said absently.

He was anxious to tell me.

"On the stairs at Halt Knights. I was going up to see my little patient with jaundice, and he came staggering down. I never saw a fellow with such a hang-over. He brushed past me, his eyes glazed and his tongue hanging out. Didn't say good morning or anything—you know the type."

"That patient of yours," I said. "She must have been upstairs all through the incident . . ."

He turned to me in surprise. "Flossie?" he said. "Yes, she was; but you're on the wrong tack there. She's away at the back of the house in a little top attic. Besides, you must have a look at her. The poor little beast is a bit better now, but a couple of days ago she couldn't stand, poor kid. However, she may have heard something. I'll ask her."

I told him not to bother, and he went on chattering happily, making all sorts of useless suggestions. When I listened to him at all, he had my sympathy. A life that needs a murder to make it interesting must, I thought, be very slow indeed.

When we arrived he went straight up to see his patient, and I sought out Poppy in the lounge. It was early, and we were alone. She seemed delighted to see me and, as usual, insisted on getting me a drink at once. I followed her into the bar while she mixed it, and hurried to put the question that was on my mind before Kingston should return.

"You say you remember yesterday morning very clearly?" I said. "Did you have a visitor who left here some little time before the accident? Someone who wasn't in the house at the time, but who wandered off within half an hour or so of the trouble?"

She paused in the act of scooping little blocks of ice out of the refrigerator tray.

"No, there was no one," she said, "unless you count the parson."

I took off my spectacles.

"Bathwick?"

"Yes. He always comes in round about twelve o'clock. He likes his highballs American fashion, like this thing I'm mixing for you. He never has more than one. Drops in about twelve o'clock, drinks it, and trots out again. I saw him to the door myself yesterday morning. He goes off through the kitchen garden to the stile leading into the vicarage meadow. Why?"

I stood looking down at the glass in my hand, twirling the ice round and round in the amber fluid, and it was then that I had the whole case under my nose.

Unfortunately, I only saw half of it.

CHAPTER XI

"Why Drown Him?"

I WAS STILL WORKING it out when Poppy laid her hand upon my arm. I turned to find her plump face flushed and anxious.

"Albert," she murmured confidently, "I can't talk now because Kingston's just coming down, but there's something I want to say to you. Ssh! There he is."

She turned back to the bar and began to bustle among the glasses. Kingston came in, cheerfully superior.

"She's all right now," he said, grinning at Poppy, "or will be in a day or two. Don't let her eat too much grease. Like to come up and see her, Campion?"

Poppy raised her eyebrows at him, and he explained. She began to laugh at us.

"The child hasn't the strength, and she hasn't the wits," she said. "And if she had she wouldn't do it. She's a good little girl, our Flossie. Flossie, indeed! I've never heard of anything so futile."

Kingston was very insistent, however, and his anxiety to keep in the picture might easily have been exasperating if there had been anything pressing to be done. As it was, I went upstairs with him through a maze of corridors and unexpected staircases until we found the little attic under the roof at the far end of the house from the box room.

As soon as I met Flossie I saw they were right. Her little yellow face was pathetic and disinterested. Kingston asked her questions—Had she heard anything? Had she been out of the room? Had anything unusual happened on the day before?—and she answered "No sir" to them all with the weary patience of the really ill.

We left her and went along to have another look at the box room. It was just as I had left it. Kingston was tremendously knowing and important. Evidently he fancied himself in his new role.

"There's a scratch there," he said, pointing to the one I had already noticed. "Does that tell you anything, Campion? It looks fairly new, doesn't it? How about getting some fingerprints?"

I looked at the rough cast sadly and led him away.

We got rid of him at last. He offered to drive me down to the police station, but I refused, explaining that Leo was coming to pick me up. I caught sight of Poppy as I spoke, and saw her turn colour.

We stood in the window together and watched Kingston's car disappear down the drive. She sighed.

"They're *bored,*" she said. "They're all bored, poor darlings. He's a nice boy, he doesn't want to be a ghoul; but it'll all give him something to talk about when he goes to see his patients. It must be terrible going to see people every day if you haven't got anything to tell them, don't you think?"

"Yes," I said dubiously. "I suppose it is. What have you got to tell *me,* by the way?"

She did not answer me immediately, but the colour came into her face, and she looked like some large guilty baby faced with confession.

"I had a few words with Leo yesterday," she began at last. "Not that I mind, of course, although it does do to keep in with one's clients and—er—friends. I can see that I've annoyed him. I told him a silly lie, and then I didn't like to explain. You can see that happening, can't you?"

She paused and eyed me.

"I can," I said cheerfully.

"The stupid thing is that it doesn't matter," she went on, playing with her rings. "People down here are terrible snobs, Albert."

I didn't quite follow her, and I said so.

"Oh well, it's Hayhoe," she said explosively. "An awful little bounder, Albert, but probably quite human, and he's got to live, like anybody else, hasn't he?"

"Wait a minute," I said. "I've got to get this straight. Is Hayhoe a friend of yours?"

"Oh no, not a *friend.*" She brushed the term away irritably. "But he came to me for help last week."

I was inspired.

"Did he borrow money?"

"Oh no!" She was shocked. "He was very hard up, poor man. He told me his story, and I may have lent him a pound or two. But you wouldn't say he'd borrowed *money.* You see, ducky, it was like this—he came to me about two days after that wretched man Harris settled here. I was just beginning to find out the sort of man Harris was when this poor old chap came along, asked to see me privately, and told me the whole thing. Harris was his nephew, you see, and there'd been a lot of jiggery-pokery going on, and somehow—I forget quite how—this little tick Harris had done the old man out of all his money. He wanted to see him on the quiet to get it back, and he wanted me to help him. I let him into Harris' room——"

"You what?" I said aghast.

"Well, I showed him where it was and let him go upstairs. That was some days ago. There was an awful row, and poor little Hayhoe came running out with a flea in his ear, since when he's never been near the place—until last night, when Leo happened to see him. I didn't want to explain the whole story—because there's no point in that man getting into a row when he wasn't even near the house yesterday morning—and so I was short with Leo, and he is cross. Put it all straight for me, Albert. Have another drink."

I refused the one and promised to do my best with the other.

"How do you know Hayhoe wasn't about yesterday morning?" I said.

She looked at me as though I was an imbecile.

"Well, I know what goes on in my own house, I hope," she said. "I know it's the fashion round here to think I'm a dear silly old fool, but I'm not completely demented. Besides, everybody's been questioned. That doesn't come into it."

"Why did Hayhoe come down here yesterday?"

"In the evening? Well"—she was hesitant again—"it's difficult to explain. He came to tell me that he knew how I felt being surrounded by snobby county people in a trouble like this, and he offered his help as a man of the world."

She was thoughtful for a moment or two.

"I really think he came to get a drink, if you ask me," she added with that touch of the practical which always redeems her.

"Did you lend him any more money?" I murmured diffidently.

"Only half a crown," she said. "Don't tell Leo. He thinks I'm such a fool."

My mind went back to Bathwick, and in the end she took me out and showed me the little path through the kitchen garden which led down to the vicarage stile. It was a quiet little path, almost entirely hidden by the foliage of the fruit trees. As we came back I turned to her.

"Look here," I said, "I know the police have badgered your staff about the events of yesterday morning, and I don't want to rattle them again, but do you think you could find out by unobtrusive, gossipy questioning if there was anybody pottering about the upper stories some little time before the accident? Bathwick could have come back, you see, quite easily."

"A parson!" said Poppy. "Well . . . You don't think . . . Oh, Albert, you can't!"

"Of course not," I said hastily. "I only wondered if he could have got upstairs. It'd be interesting, that's all."

"I'll find out," she said with decision.

I thanked her and added a warning note about the law of slander.

"Don't tell *me*," she said and added, brightening, "Is that the car?"

We hurried down to meet it, Poppy patting her tight grey curls as she went. But it was Lugg in the Lagonda and not Leo who pulled up outside the front door. He beckoned to me mysteriously, and as I hurried up I saw that his great moon of a face betrayed unusual excitement.

" 'Op in," he commanded. "The general wants you down at the station. Got something there for you."

"Have they found the body?"

He seemed disappointed. "Got your second-sight outfit workin' again, I see," he said. "Morning, ma'am." He leered at Poppy over my shoulder as he spoke, out of deference, I felt sure, to the memory of myriad past beers.

"I'm awfully sorry," I explained to her. "I've got to go. Leo's waiting for me down at the police station. Something's turned up. I'll send him along when the excitement's over."

She patted my arm. "Do," she said earnestly. "Do. He's a pet, Albert. One of the very best. Tell him I've been silly and I'm sorry, but—but he's not to mention it when he sees me."

I climbed in beside Lugg. "Where was it?" I demanded as we raced off.

"In the river. Calm as you please. Bloke in a fishin' boat picked it up. If we 'ad your magic sea shell 'ere p'raps that could tell us somethin'."

I was not listening to him. I was thinking of Whippet. Whippet and the anonymous letters, Whippet and Effie Rowlandson, and now Whippet and his extraordinary guess—if it was a guess. I couldn't imagine where he fitted into the picture. He upset all my calculations. I decided I must have a chat with him.

Lugg was sulking. "It seems to be a funny place we've come to," he said. "First they bang a chap on 'is 'ead and then they chuck 'im in the river . . . some persons aren't never satisfied, reelly."

I sat up. That was the point that had been bothering me all along. Why the river, where the corpse was almost certain to be found, sooner or later?

By the time we arrived at the little mortuary the obvious had sunk in. Leo was there and Pussey, and with them the two excited fishermen who had made the discovery. I took Leo on one side, but he would not listen to me immediately. He was bubbling.

"It's an outrage," he said. "It's a disgraceful thing. It shocks me, Campion. In my own village! There was no point in it. Wanton mischief."

"D'you think so?" I said, and I made a certain suggestion.

He stood looking at me and his blue eyes were incredulous. For a policeman, Leo has an amazing faith in the innate decency of his fellow men.

"We want an old man," I said. "Someone with the necessary skill, of course, but someone you can trust to hold his tongue. Anyone locally do?"

He considered. "There's old Professor Farringdon over at Rushberry," he said at last. "He did something of the sort for us some time ago. But you can see for yourself that the cause of death is obvious. Are we justified in having an autopsy?"

"In the case of violent death one's always justified in having an autopsy," I pointed out.

He nodded. "When you saw the body yesterday, did you notice anything then to put such an idea in your head?"

"No," I said truthfully. "No, I didn't. But this makes all the difference. Water has a peculiar property, hasn't it?"

He put his head on one side.

"How d'you mean?"

"Well, it washes things," I said, and I went off to find Whippet.

CHAPTER XII

The Disturbing Element

I HAD ALMOST REACHED the car when I remembered something which had slipped my mind in the excitement of the moment. I hurried back and sought out Pussey.

"Don't you worry, sir. We've put a man on him," he said reassuringly in reply to my question.

I still hesitated. "Hayhoe is slippery," I ventured, "and also it's most important that he's not alarmed."

Pussey was not offended, but he seemed to think that I was a little fussy.

"Young Birkin'll follow him and he won't know it no more than if he was being trailed by a ferret," he said. "You can set your mind at rest."

All this was very comforting, and I was going off again when Leo buttonholed me. He was still dubious about the necessity of an autopsy, and in the end I had to go back and take another look at Pig's pathetic body. There were one or two interesting signs when we looked for them, and in the end I left him convinced.

By this time it was comparatively late, and I arrived at The Feathers just before two o'clock. The landlady, a typical East Anglian, gaunt of body and reticent of speech, was not helpful. It took me some time to get it into her head that it was Whippet I wanted to see.

"Oh," she said at last, "a fair young gentleman, soft spoken like, almost a natural, as you might say. Well, he's not here."

"But he slept here last night," I persisted.

"Yes, yes, so he did, and that's the truth now," she agreed, "but he's not here now."

"Is he coming back?"

"I couldn't say."

It occurred to me that Whippet must have told her to keep quiet and this was extremely unlike him. My interest in him grew.

There was no sign of Miss Rowlandson, either. She, too, appeared to have gone out. But whether they went together or separately the landlady was not prepared to tell me.

In the end I had to go back to Highwaters unsatisfied. I was late for lunch, of course, and Pepper served me alone in the dining room, sorrow and disappointment apparent in every line of his sleek body.

What with one thing and another, I was falling headlong in his estimation.

When the meal was over he turned to me.

"Miss Janet is in the rose garden, sir," he said, conveying clearly that, murder or no murder, he thought a guest owed a certain deference to his hostess.

I took the rebuke meekly and went out to make amends. It was one of those vivid summer days which are hot without being uncomfortable. The garden was ablaze with flowers and the air serene and peaceful.

As I walked down the grass path between the lavender hedges I heard the sound of voices, and something familiar about one of them caught my attention. Two deck chairs were placed side by side on the rose lawn with their backs to me, and I heard Janet laugh.

At the sound of my approach her companion rose, and as I saw his head and shoulders appearing over the back of the chair I experienced an odd sensation which was half relief and half an unwarrantable exasperation. It was Whippet himself. Very cool and comfortable he looked, too, in his neat white flannels. His opening words were not endearing.

"Campion! Found you at last," he said. "Er—good. I've been searching for you, my dear fellow, searching all over the place. Here and there."

He moved a languid hand about a foot in either direction.

"I've been busy," I said gracelessly. "Hello, Janet."

She smiled up at me. "This is a nice friend of yours," she said with slightly unnecessary accent on the first word. "Do sit down."

"That's right, do," Whippet agreed. "There's a chair over there," he added, pointing to a pile on the other end of the lawn.

I fetched it, opened it, and sat down opposite them. Whippet watched me put it up with interest.

"Complicated things," he observed.

I waited for him to go on, but he seemed quite content to lie basking in the sun, with Janet, looking very lovely in white furbelows, at his side.

I began boldly. "It's been found, you know—in the river."

He nodded. "So I heard in the village. The whole place is terribly shaken by the tragedy, don't you think? Extraordinary restless spirit pervades the place—have you noticed it?"

He was infuriating, and again I experienced that desire to cuff him which I had felt so strongly on our first adult meeting.

"You've got rather a lot to explain yourself," I said, wishing that Janet would go away.

To my surprise he answered me intelligently.

"I know," he said. "I know. That's why I've been looking for you. There's Miss Rowlandson, for one thing. She's terribly upset. She's gone down to the vicarage now. I didn't know what to advise."

"The vicarage?" I echoed. "What on earth for?" Janet, I noticed, was sitting up with interest.

"Oh, help, you know," said Whippet vaguely. "When in doubt in a village one always goes to the parson, doesn't one? Good works and that sort of thing. Oh yes—and that reminds me, what about this? It came this morning. As soon as I saw it I thought 'Campion ought to have a look at this; this'll interest Campion.' Have you had one?"

He took a folded sheet of typing paper out of his wallet as he spoke, and handed it to me.

"The same postmark as the others," he said. "Funny, isn't it? I didn't know anyone knew I was staying at The Feathers, except you and—well, I mean you'd hardly have the time, would you, even if you . . ."

His voice trailed away into silence, and I read the third anonymous letter. This one was very short, typed on the same typewriter and with the same meticulous accuracy:

Although the skinner is at hand his ease is in the earth.
He waiteth patiently. Peace and hope are in his warm heart.
He foldeth his hands upon his belly.
Faith is his that can remove the mountain or his little hill.

And that was all.

"Do you make anything of it?" I enquired at last.

"No," said Whippet. "No."

I read it through again.

"Who's the 'he'?" I asked.

Whippet blinked at me. "One can't really say, can one? I took it to be the mole. 'His little hill,' you know."

Janet laughed. "I suppose you both know what you're talking about?" she said.

Whippet rose. "I fancy I ought to go, now that I've found Campion and cleared all this up. Thank you for allowing me to inflict myself upon you, Miss Pursuivant. You've been most kind."

I let him say good-bye and then insisted on escorting him to the gates myself.

"Look here, Whippet," I said as soon as we were out of earshot, "you'll have to explain. What are you doing in this business at all? Why are you here?"

He looked profoundly uncomfortable. "It's that girl, Effie, Campion," he said. "She's got a strong personality, you know. I met her at Pig's funeral, and she sort of collected me. When she wanted me to drive her down here yesterday I came."

It was an unlikely story from anybody but Whippet, but in his case I was rather inclined to accept it.

"Well, what about the letters?" I persisted.

He shrugged his shoulders. "One's supposed to tear up anonymous letters, isn't one?" he said. "Tear 'em up or keep 'em as mementos or frame 'em. Anything but take them seriously. And yet, you know, when they go on and on one seems to come to a point when one says to oneself, 'Who the hell is writing these things?' It's very disturbing, but I like the mole. I shall be at The Feathers, Campion. I give you my word I shall remain there. Look me up when you can spare the time, and we'll go into it. Good-bye."

I let him go. Talking to him, it seemed impossible that he should have the energy to involve himself very deeply in anything so disturbing as our case.

Walking back to the rose garden, I thought about the mole seriously for the first time. A great deal of what Whippet had said about anonymous letters was true. Hayhoe was an educated man, and so was Bathwick, but, even so, why should either of them send both to me and Whippet? It seemed inexplicable.

Janet came to meet me. She was not pleased.

"I don't want to interfere," she said, using the tone and the phrase to mean its exact opposite, "but I don't think you ought to allow her to annoy poor Bathwick."

"Who?" I said, momentarily off my guard.

Janet flared. "Oh, how you irritate me!" she said. "You know perfectly well who I mean . . . that wretched, stupid little girl, Effie Rowlandson. It's bad enough to bring her down here to our village, without letting her get her claws into people who couldn't possibly look after themselves. I hate to have to talk to you like this, Albert, but really you know it is rather disgusting of you."

I was not going to be dragged into a defence of Effie Rowlandson, but I was tired and I resented Bathwick being held up to me as an example of the innocent lamb.

"My dear girl," I said, "you heard about Bathwick getting wet last night. He told Leo an absurd story about falling into a dike on his way home. However, it took him nearly two hours to get out and onto the main road again, and I'm afraid he'll have to explain himself now that Harris' body has turned up—er—where it has."

I was not looking at her as I spoke, and her little cry brought me round to face her. Her cheeks were crimson and her eyes wide and alarmed.

"Oh!" she said. "Oh! Oh! How terrible!"

And then before I could stop her she had taken to her heels and fled back to the house. I followed her, of course, but she had shut herself in her bedroom, and once more I was given furiously to think.

I went into the library, which is a large old-fashioned room hardly ever used by the Pursuivants. It was cool and the air was aromatic with the smell of paper. I sat down in a big leather armchair to think things out, and I am afraid that my lack of sleep the night before was too much for me. I woke up to find Janet standing before me. She was pale but determined.

"I thought you'd gone out," she said breathlessly. "It's late, you know. Look here, Albert, I've got to tell you something. I can't let Bathwick get into trouble for something he didn't do, and I know he'd rather die than tell you himself. If you laugh I'll never speak to you again."

I got up and shook off the remnants of sleep. She looked very charming in her white dress, her eyes defiant.

"I've never felt less like laughing in my life," I said truthfully. "What's all this about Bathwick?"

She took a deep breath. "Mr Bathwick didn't fall in a dike," she said. "He fell in our lily pool."

"Really? How do you know?"

"I pushed him," said Janet in a small voice.

Pressed to continue, she explained:

"Last night, after you took Miss Rowlandson home, I didn't go to bed immediately. I went out on the balcony leading from my room. It was a very bright night, as you know, and I saw someone wandering about in the rose garden. I thought it was Daddy mooching about, worrying over the case, and I went out to talk to him. When I got there it was Bathwick. We walked round the garden together, and when we were quite near the lily pool he—er . . ."

She paused.

"Offered you his hand and heart in a slightly too forthright manner?" I suggested.

She nodded gratefully. "I pushed him away, and unfortunately he overbalanced and fell in the pool. As soon as I saw he was safe on land again I went back to the house. It seemed the nicest thing to do. I don't have to tell anybody else, do I?"

"No," I murmured. "No, I don't think so."

She smiled at me. "You're all right really, Albert," she said.

And then, of course, I was called to the telephone. It was Poppy on the end of the wire. She has never grown quite used to the instrument, and I had to hold the receiver some inches away from my ear before I could get her message.

"I've made those enquiries," she boomed. "I don't think the V. came back; anyway, no one saw him. But who do you think was seen roaming about the top story yesterday morning? My dear, I wouldn't have thought it of him. He seemed so *genuine*. . . . Who? Oh, didn't I tell you? Why, the uncle, *Hayhoe*, of course. Trotting round as though the place belonged to him. The girl who saw him naturally thought I'd given him permission. You never can tell with people, can you?"

CHAPTER XIII

Scarecrow in June

JANET WAS at my side when I hung up the receiver. "What is it?" she said anxiously. "That was Poppy's voice, wasn't it? Oh, Albert, I'm afraid! Something else terrible has happened."

"Good Lord, no!" I said, with an assurance I did not feel. "There's nothing to be frightened of. At least, I don't think so."

She stood looking up at me.

"You know it's all right about Bathwick now, don't you?"

"Of course," I assured her cheerfully. "I'd better go, though. There's something rather important to be fixed, something that's got to be done pretty quickly."

Lugg brought round the car and we went down to the police station together. Leo was still there in consultation with Pussey and I was sorry to see him so drawn and haggard. The affair was getting him down. There were deep lines in his face, and his bright eyes were darker than usual in their anxiety. I stated my case.

"Arrest Heigh-ho?" he said. "Really? I don't think we can arrest him, don't you know. We can bring him in and question him—wanted to in the beginnin'—but we can't hold him. There's not a tittle of solid evidence against the feller."

I didn't like to annoy him but I was desperately anxious.

"You must hold him, sir," I said. "That's the whole point. Pull him in for something else."

Leo looked aghast. "Trump up a charge?" he said. "Monstrous!"

There was not time to explain, and I had no proof, anyway.

"At least keep him here for twenty-four hours," I pleaded.

Leo frowned at me. "What's got on your mind, my boy?" he enquired. "Sound apprehensive. Anythin' in the wind?"

"I don't know," I said, trying not to appear as rattled as I felt. "Let's go and get him, anyway."

Leaving Leo to ponder over the question of arrest, Pussey and I went down in the Lagonda to Mrs Thatcher's cottage. We picked up young Birkin leaning against a fence on the opposite side of the road. He was a pleasant, shy youth in dilapidated khaki and he made his report in a stage whisper.

"He's been in all the day," he said. "That's 'is room where the light is. You can see 'im if you look."

He pointed to a blurred shadow on the faded chintz curtains and my heart sank. Birkin, I saw, was destined to confine his attentions to dog licences for some time to come. It was a coat and a bolster over the back of a chair, of course.

Pussey stood looking at it when we got into the stuffy little attic bedroom and his language was restrained and almost dignified.

The unfortunate Birkin rather enjoyed it, I fancy. In his private opinion it was a wonderful clever trick and something to tell the lads of the village.

Mrs Thatcher, a poor old woman who had been too busy all her life to have had time to develop an intelligence, was obstinately mystified. She had told Johnny Birkin that her lodger was in his room, and she honestly thought he was. He must have come downstairs in his stockinged feet, she reckoned. That was all we had to help us.

My scalp was rising. "We've got to find him," I said. "Don't you see it's desperately important?"

Pussey came out of his trance with alacrity.

"Well, he can't have gone far," he said. "This ain't a busy place. Someone will have seen him, bound to."

From Birkin's evidence the curtains had been drawn just after dusk and he had sat there peacefully watching the light ever since. It gave Hayhoe about an hour, and my spirits rose a little.

To do Pussey justice, he mobilised his small force with speed and efficiency. Leo and I had a meal at The Swan while they got busy. There were not many methods of exit from Kepesake and, since Mr Hayhoe did not possess a car, it seemed certain that we should get news of him within an hour or two.

I confess I was jumpy. I felt helpless. My own use in the search was practically nil. I was a comparative stranger, and as such did not inspire the confidence of the suspicious East Anglian.

We went down to The Feathers to interview Whippet and found him dining in the company of Effie Rowlandson and Bathwick. Leo was flabbergasted, and I was surprised myself—they were an odd trio.

When judiciously questioned, it became evident that they knew nothing about Hayhoe, but they looked so much like conspirators that I could have borne to stay and chat with them, had I not been so beset by the fear in my mind.

Round about eleven, Leo, Pussey and I had a conference. We sat round the stuffy little charge room at the station and Pussey put the case before us.

"He didn't leave by a bus and he didn't hire a car, and if he went on foot by any of the main roads he moves a deal faster than any ordinary animal." He paused and eyed us. "Seems like that's unnatural he ain't been seen at all," he said. "It isn't as though any strange car 'as been seen goin' through the village. We ain't on the road to anywhere here. It's been a quiet evening, everyone sittin' out on their doorsteps. Can't understand it, unless 'e's took to the fields."

I thought of the warm leafy darkness which surrounded us, of the deep meadows and grass-grown ditches, and I was afraid.

Leo was inclined to be relieved. "Seems to pin it on to him, this boltin'," he said. "Extraordinary thing! Took a dislike to the feller the moment I set eyes on him. Must have been skulkin' in the house all yesterday mornin'. Amazin'."

I didn't know whether to relieve his mind or enhance his fears and I kept silent. Pussey seemed to catch his superior officer's mood.

"Ah well, we'll get him sure enough," he said. "Now we know as who we're lookin' for we won't let 'im go. The whole village is on the lookout for 'im and none of us 'ere won't rest tonight. You go back to your bed, sir. You can leave 'im to us."

It seemed the only thing to do but I was loath to go.

"You've searched that hilltop?" I said.

"Every inch of it, sir. There's 'is telescope up there but nothin' else. Besides, 'e couldn't get there without bein' seen. 'E's got to come right through the village street with every man on the lookout for 'im. No, no, you won't find 'im on that hilltop—'lest 'e's a mowle."

I started and I suppose my face betrayed me, for he explained in deference to my city training.

"They mowles, they travel underground," he said, and I felt suddenly sick.

Before we left he brought up a matter which had gone clean out of my mind.

"That young lady," he began, "if she could identify . . ."

"In the morning," I said hastily. "There'll be a lot to do in the morning."

"Ah ha, you're right, sir," he agreed. "There'll be plenty if we catch un."

"There'll be more if you don't," I said and I went home with Leo.

I was climbing into bed for the first time for forty-eight hours when Pepper appeared with a telephone, which he plugged in by my bed.

"Doctor Kingston," he said and added, half in commiseration, half in reproach, "at *this* hour, sir."

Kingston was not only awake but aggressively bright and eager.

"Hope I didn't disturb you," he said. "I've been ringing up all the evening. I was down in the village on a case just after dinner and found the whole place seething. I hear you've got your man on the run. There's nothing I can do, I suppose?"

"I'm afraid not," I said, trying to keep polite.

"Oh, I see." He seemed genuinely disappointed. "I must apologise for being so inquisitive, but you know how it is. I feel I've got a sort of natural interest. You will let me know if anything happens or if I can possibly be of any use, won't you?"

"I will," I said, but he did not ring off.

"You sound tired. Don't overdo it. Oh, I say, there's some funny people staying at The Feathers. Strangers. The village doesn't know if it's just a case of ordinary immorality or if there's more to it. The fellow's name is Greyhound, or something. Like 'em looked into?"

I cursed him for his dull life.

"They're spies of mine," I said.

"What? I didn't quite catch you."

"Spies," I said. "Mine. I've got 'em everywhere. Good night."

I was awake at six. Lugg called me, protestingly.

"Conscientious, aren't you?" he said derisively. " 'Ayhoe's running away from a pack of narks who want to jug 'im for murder, but he's not going to pass up the little appointment 'e's made with you—Oh dear me no! I don't think."

"All the same, I think I'll go," I said. "You never know."

He stood before me, disconsolate, in an outrageous dressing gown.

"I'll come with you if you like," he offered magnanimously. "There's nothing I like better than a long country walk before the dew's off the grass—cools me feet."

I sent him back to bed, dressed and went out. It was one of those fine, clear mornings which promise great heat in the day to come. The sky was opal and the grass was soft and springy underfoot.

I went round by the field path and passed down the village street, where I caught a glimpse of the ingenuous Birkin. He gave me the news, or, rather, the smiling information that there was none.

"We'll be able to get 'im sure enough now the sun's up," he said. "We'll bring 'im back kicking."

I shivered although the morning was warm.

"I hope so," I said and went on.

The little sunken lane was deserted and it was a pleasant morning for walking, but I found my feet lagging and I entered the hill meadow with the deepest foreboding.

It was a longer climb to the top than I had thought and when I reached the summit I was momentarily relieved. It was clear and bare and I disturbed nothing but a brace of larks resting in the short grass. The old brass telescope was still mounted on its tripod. There was dew on the lenses and I wiped them with my handkerchief.

From where I stood I had a stupendous view of the surrounding country. I could see Halt Knights lying rose red and gracious on the grey saltings, the river mouth, dazzling in the morning sun, and, around it, the little pocket-handkerchief fields and meadows, the corn high and green, the pasture browned a little by the hot weather. It was a lovely country. Here and there little farms were dotted and among them the white ribbons of the roads twirled and turned.

I stood there for a long time looking at the scene. It was so peaceful, so quiet and so charming. There was nothing out of place, nothing frightening or remarkable.

And then I saw it. About half a mile away, in the midst of a field waist high in green corn, there was a dilapidated scarecrow, a grotesque, unnatural creature set up to terrify the not-quite-so-clever rooks.

But about this particular effigy there was a difference. Far from being frightened, the rooks were swarming upon it.

I looked through the telescope and straightened myself a moment or so later, sick and giddy, my worst fears realised. Mr Hayhoe had been found.

CHAPTER XIV

The Man They Knew

HE HAD A WOUND in his neck, a strong deep thrust over the collarbone which had severed the jugular, and when we found him he was not pretty to look at.

Pussey and Leo and I stood round the terrible thing hoisted on a piece of broken paling, and the green corn whispered around us.

After the usual preliminaries the police brought Hayhoe down on a tumbril to the little mortuary behind the station, and yet another trestle table was prepared there to receive him.

Leo looked pale and shaken, and Pussey, who had been turned up physically by the first sight of my discovery, presented a mottled ghost of his former cherubic self.

When we were alone together in the mortuary shed, standing between the two white-covered things which had come to upset so violently the time-honoured peace of Kepesake, Leo turned to me.

"This is what you were afraid of?" he said, accusingly.

I looked at him helplessly. "It did go through my mind that something like this might happen. He conveyed that he had definite information, you see."

He passed his hand over his sparse grey hair.

"But who? Who's done it, Campion?" he exploded. "Don't you see, my boy, a terrible thing is happening. It's the *strangers* who are getting killed off. The field's narrowing down to our own people. Good God! What's to be done now?"

"There's not much to go on," I pointed out. "The cornfield was bordered by the road, so the murderer would not have far to carry him even if he had to, although of course there's a chance he was killed on the spot. There was a great deal of blood about."

Leo avoided my eyes. "I know," he murmured. "I know. But what was the feller doing out in the middle of a cornfield with a murderer?"

"Having a very quiet private interview," I said. "I should like an opinion on this wound."

"You shall have it, my boy, you shall have it. The best in the world. Professor Farringdon will be along this morning to see the—ah—other body. This is frightful, Campion—I'm sorry I couldn't get someone at work on him yesterday, but Farringdon was unobtainable, and I didn't want to drag the Home Office into it if I could help it. This makes all the difference, though. 'Pon my soul, I don't know what I ought to do."

Any helpful suggestion I might have made was cut short by the return of Pussey, who had Kingston in tow. The doctor was excited and ashamed of himself for showing it. My opinion of him as a medical man went down a little as he made a cursory examination of Hayhoe. He was anxious to help and yet loath to commit himself by giving a definite opinion.

"I don't know what it was done with," he said at last. "Something narrow and sharp. A dagger, perhaps. One of those old-fashioned things—a trophy."

I glanced at Leo, and from the expression on his face I knew he was thinking of the fearsome array of native weapons on the walls of the billiard room at Halt Knights. All the same, I didn't see Poppy in the middle of the night in a cornfield with a dagger; that idea seemed to me farfetched and absurd.

Pussey seemed to find Kingston's guesses unsatisfactory, and he got rid of him in the end, but with considerable tact.

"It seems like we'd better leave that to the professor," he murmured to me. "Wonderful clever old man, the professor. I reckon he'll be over in half an hour or so. I don't know what he'll think on us—two on 'em instead of one," he added naïvely.

Leo turned away, his hands thrust deep into his pockets and his chin on his breast. We followed him into the station and Pussey made all the necessary arrangements for taking statements, making a search of the place where the body was found and the important enquiries into Mr Hayhoe's past history.

The routine work seemed to soothe Leo.

"I suppose we ought not to have moved him from the spot," he said, "until Farringdon arrived. But there seemed no point in leavin' the feller out in the sun hitched up on a spike like that. It was indecent. There's a brutal obviousness about these crimes, Campion. 'Pon my soul, I can't conceive the mind that arranged 'em—anyway, not among my own friends."

"Ah-h, there's still strangers about," said Pussey, with the intention of comforting him. "Likely there'll be *someone* who's had blood on's clothes. We'll find un. Don't you worry, sir."

Leo swung away from him and walked over to the window.

"Eh!" he said suddenly, "who's this?"

Looking over his shoulder I saw a sleek chauffeur-driven Daimler pull up outside the cottage gate. A tall thin grey-faced man descended and came hesitantly up to our door. A moment or so later we made the acquaintance of Mr Robert Wellington Skinner, junior partner of the ancient and respectable firm of solicitors whose name Kingston had given me.

He was a stiff, dignified personage, and he and Leo took to each other immediately, which was fortunate, or the subsequent interview would certainly have taken much longer and been doubly confusing. As it was, Mr Skinner came to the point in what was for him, I felt sure, record time.

"In view of everything, I thought I'd better come down myself," he murmured. "An affair of this sort in connection with one of our clients is, I can assure you, most unusual. I received your enquiries yesterday; I read the papers last night; I connected the two names immediately—Peters and Harris. In the circumstances I thought I had better come down myself."

Pussey and I exchanged glances. We were getting somewhere.

"The two men knew each other, then?" I asked.

He looked at me dubiously, as though he wondered if I could be trusted.

"They were brothers," he said. "Mr Harris changed his name for—ah—no doubt very good reasons of his own, and he is comparatively new to our books. Our principal client was his elder brother, Mr Rowland Isidore Peters, who died in this district last January."

After a certain amount of delay he went with Leo to view the body and came back a little green. He was also flustered.

"I wouldn't like to commit myself," he murmured. "I saw Mr Peters once twelve years ago, and I saw Mr Harris in London this spring. Those were the only two occasions on which I met either. The—ah—dead man I have just seen resembles both. Do you think I could have a glass of water?"

Pussey pressed him to be more exact and would have taken him back again, but he refused to go.

"Really, I see no point in it," he said. "I think you can take it that, in my opinion, the dead man is Mr Harris. After all, there's no reason to suppose that it shouldn't be. He called himself Harris down here, did he not?"

We let him cool down, and when he was more at ease I asked him cautiously about the dead man's estate.

"I really couldn't say, without reference to my books," he protested. "I know Mr Harris received a considerable sum of money under his brother's will. I can let you know the figures tonight. There was personal property and, of course, the insurance, as far as I remember. It all seemed perfectly in order to me at the time."

Pussey was relieved. "Anyway, we've cleared up his identity, that's one thing," he said. "No doubt one of us can get on with the P.M."

Leo and I escorted the solicitor back to his car. The unfortunate man was shaken by his experience, as well he might be, but he was an obliging soul and before he left he promised to let us know full details of the two estates.

"There's just one thing," I said as he got into the car. "Who was Mr Peters insured with? Do you know?"

He shook his head. "I'm afraid I couldn't tell you offhand. I think it was the Mutual Ordered Life. I'll look it up."

As soon as he had gone I made a suggestion to Leo and, having got his consent, sent Lugg and a constable down in the car to fetch Miss Effie Rowlandson. They were gone some little time, and when at last they reappeared they brought not only the girl herself but Bathwick, also, which was surprising. There was a considerable delay at the gate, and I went out. The vicar had got over his unexpected friendliness towards me of the night before, and I was aware that all his old antagonism had returned.

"I'm only doing what I'm told, sir," I heard the constable protesting as I came up. "Besides, the young lady suggested it 'erself only the night before last."

Bathwick ignored him and turned to me.

"This is an outrage," he said. "A young girl subjected to a disgusting sight just to satisfy a few inefficient policemen. . . . I must protest against it; I really must!"

Effie smiled at me wanly. "It's very nice of you, I'm sure," she said, "but I've made up my mind to it; I have, really. You wait here for me," she added, smiling at him.

However, he was not to be soothed. He protested so much and so vigorously that my interest in him revived, and I wondered what conceivable purpose he could have in making such a fuss.

In the end we left him in the car, and I took the girl into the little mortuary once more. I was never exactly attracted by Effie Rowlandson, but on that occasion I admired her pluck. She was not callous, and the shock must have been considerable, but she kept her head and played her part with dignity.

"Yes," she said huskily as I drew the sheet over the limp form once more. "Yes, it is Rowley. I wasn't in love with him, but I'm sorry he's dead. I . . ."

Her voice broke, and she began to cry. She controlled herself within a moment or so, however, and when I took her back to the bewildered Pussey she made her statement.

"I met him a little over a year ago," she said. "He had a flat in Knightsbridge, and he used to take me out a lot. We got engaged, or nearly engaged, and then . . . Oh, Mr Campion, you know the rest. I've told you."

Between us we got the story down on paper, and I took her back to the car. Bathwick had climbed out and was waiting for her at the gate. I suppose he saw that she had identified Harris from our faces, for he did not speak to me but, taking her arm, hurried her down the road towards The Feathers.

Lugg looked after him. "Funny bloke," he said. "Now, *where* 'ave you got to?"

"An impasse," I said truthfully and went back to Pussey.

We worked it out while we waited for Professor Farringdon. Pussey put his deductions in a reasonable if not too tidy nutshell.

"There's impersonation been going on," he said judicially. "Sounds like the old story—the good brother and the bad brother. We'll call 'em Peters and Harris for the sake of simplicity. Peters had the money, and on occasions Harris used to impersonate him; well, that's been done before. Harris carried on with this little bird under the name of Peters so that if she should look him up or make enquiries she'd find out he was a man of substance. As for the solicitor, he was in a proper muddle, poor gentleman. The two brothers doubtless looked powerful alike to begin with, and of course that poor bloke in there doesn't look like anything now. What would you say, sir?"

I hesitated. It is never safe to identify a man after twenty-five years, and Kingston had told me that his patient resembled Harris considerably. On the whole, I was inclined to back the inspector's theory, with one exception. When he talked of the "good brother" and the "bad brother" as Peters and Harris, I thought he should have reversed the names.

I told him so, and he eyed me. "Very likely," he said, "but that doesn't get us any nearer, does it? Who's done the murders? That's what I'd like to know."

We stood for a moment in silence looking at one another, and the professor's arrival took us by surprise. He came bustling in, a vigorous little Scotsman with short tufty grey hair and the shrewdest grey-blue eyes I have ever seen.

"Good morning, Inspector," he said. "You've got a remarkable amount of bodies, I hear."

His cheerfulness was disconcerting, and we escorted him to the shed in the yard in silence. As he pored over the man who had called himself Harris, however, his good humour changed, and he turned to me with a very grave face.

"I heard from Sir Leo what you were suggesting, and I take ma hat off to you," he said. "It's a diabolical thing—a diabolical thing."

"Then you think . . ." I began.

He waved me silent.

"I wouldn't dare to give an opeenion without a very careful autopsy," he said, "but I wouldn't be at all surprised if you were right; I wouldn't at all."

I walked over to the other side of the room while he was very busy. At last he straightened his back.

"Have it sent round to me," he said, "and I'll let you know for certain in a day or two. But I think I dare express an opinion—a very tentative one, you understand—that he met his death some little time before he had yon crack over the head."

I put a question and he nodded to me.

"Oh aye," he said, "it was poison. Chloral hydrate, I wouldn't wonder. That"—he indicated the terrible indentation of the skull—"that was in the nature of a blind. You've got a clever man up against you, Mr Campion. Now let's have a look at the other puir feller."

CHAPTER XV

Lugg Gives Notice

FOR TWO DAYS things hung fire; that is to say, for two days we were left in peace—Leo to struggle up from beneath the blow, and Pussey and I to collect what useful scraps of information we could.

The village was bright eyed and uncommunicative. People went to bed early behind locked doors, and sightseers who came to gape at the corner of the field where the wretched Hayhoe had been found were sent hastily on their way by outraged country folk.

Janet developed a strained expression, Poppy took to her bed, and even Whippet was more solicitous than I had supposed possible. He drifted up to see me at odd hours of the day and sat looking at me in enquiring silence until I packed him off to talk to Janet, who was kind enough to put up with him.

Kingston, of course, was very much in the foreground, and I even found him useful. He was an inveterate gossip, and the laws of libel and slander had no terrors for him.

The first piece of concrete information came from Mr Skinner, the solicitor. The Peters who had died in the Tetheringham nursing home, it transpired, had not been a poor man and had also had the perspicacity to insure himself for twenty thousand pounds with the Mutual Ordered Life Endowment. His intention, so Mr Skinner said, had been to borrow upon this policy in order to further some business scheme which he had on hand. As it happened, it had turned out very well indeed for Brother Harris.

Concerning Harris we found out very little. He had rented a flat in Knightsbridge under the name of Peters, but he had never been a wealthy man. Our difficulties were enhanced by the confusion in the actual identities of the two men: which was Harris and which was Peters?

In the end I went to Leo. He was sitting in his gun room, staring mournfully at his magnificent collection of sporting trophies, a mass of papers lying disregarded on his desk.

"We've got ten days, my dear feller," he said at last. "The two inquests have been adjourned to give us a breathing space, don't y'know, but that means we've got to get results. There's a lot of talk already. I don't mind telling you, my boy, the feeling round about is that I ought to have called in Scotland Yard at the first. It seemed simple at the beginning, but now, 'pon my soul, I don't know where things are leading. Every morning I wake up wonderin' what the day's going to bring forth. We've got a killer at large in the village. God knows where he's going to strike next."

He paused, and when I did not speak he looked at me sharply.

"I've known you since you were a child," he said, "and I know there's somethin' on your mind. If you know anythin' and you're waitin' for proof, don't hesitate to tell me your suspicions. I think I could bear anythin' rather than this uncertainty. Can you make any sense out of this puzzle?"

After working with Leo I knew that he was the most eminently trustworthy man in the world, but I hesitated to commit myself just then. It was too dangerous.

"Look here, Leo," I said, "I know how the first murder was done, and I think I know who did it, but at this stage proof is absolutely impossible, and without proof we can do nothing. Give me a day or two longer."

He was inclined to be annoyed at first, and I thought he was going to exercise his authority and force my confidence, but he quietened down at last, and I made my next request.

"Can you get a Home Office order for the exhumation of R. I. Peters, who was buried in the Tetheringham churchyard last January?"

He looked very grave. "I could try," he said at last. "But, my dear fellow, identification after all this time . . ." He grimaced and threw out his hands.

"I don't know," I persisted. "There are certain circumstances which make rather a lot of difference in that sort of thing."

He frowned at me. "Antimony in the body?" he suggested.

"Not necessarily," I said. "It's a question of the soil, mostly." In the end I got my own way, and afterwards I went out to find Kingston.

He was at home, I discovered by telephone, and Lugg and I went up. He received us in his uncomfortable consulting room with frank delight.

"Lord! you must be having an off day if you come up and see me," he said reproachfully. "Can I get you a drink?"

"No," I said. "Not now. This is hardly a social call. I want a bit of help."

His round pink face flushed with pleasure.

"Really?" he said. "That's very flattering. I had rather begun to feel that I was in the way down there, don't you know. As a matter of fact, I've been conducting a little private enquiry on my own. That's a most mysterious fellow staying down at The Feathers. Do you know anything about him?"

"Not much," I said truthfully. "I knew him a long while ago—we were at school together, as a matter of fact—but I haven't seen him much since."

"Ah!" He wagged his head mysteriously. "Mrs Thatcher says he used to come to see Hayhoe in the early part of the week. Did you know that?"

I hadn't, of course, and I thanked him.

"I'll look into it," I said. "Meanwhile, you wouldn't like to take me round your churchyard?"

He was only too anxious, and we left the great barrack of a house, which seemed servantless and neglected. He seemed conscious of its deficiencies and explained in a shamefaced fashion.

"I manage with a man from the village when I haven't any patients," he said. "He's a good fellow, a sort of general odd-job man, the son of the local builder, for whom he works when he's not being sexton or my charwoman. When I do get a patient, of course, I have to import a nurse and housekeeper."

We had wandered on ahead of Lugg, and he turned and grimaced at me.

"It's not much of a practice," he said, "otherwise, I suppose, I shouldn't find time for things to be so terribly dull."

As we passed the Lagonda, which was practically new, he looked at it a little wistfully, and I was sorry for him. There was something half childish in his unspoken envy. He had a genius for wasting time, and we spent some moments looking at it. He admired the engine, the gadgets and the polish on the bodywork, and quite won Lugg's heart.

In fact, we all got on very well together and, being in the mood for a confidant at the time, I took the risk and transferred the honour which I had been reserving for Whippet to himself. We talked about the soil of the churchyard. He was interesting and helpful.

"Yes," he said, "it's dry and it's hard, or there's some sort of preservative in it, I think, because I know old Witton, the gravedigger, dragged me out one morning to see a most extraordinary thing. He had opened a three-year-old grave to put in a relation of the dead woman, and somehow or other the coffin lid had become dislodged, and yet there was the body practically in a perfect state of preservation. How did you guess?"

"It's the cow parsley," I said. "You often find it growing in soil like that."

We went on talking about the soil for some time, and he suddenly saw the drift of my questioning.

"An exhumation?" he said. "Really? I say! That'll be rather . . ."

He stopped, suppressing the word "jolly," I felt sure.

". . . exciting," he added after a pause. "I've never been present at an exhumation. Nothing so startling ever happens down here."

"I can't promise," I protested. "Nothing's fixed, and for heaven's sake shut up about it. The one thing that's really dangerous at this stage is gossip."

"It's a question of identification, I suppose?" he said eagerly. "I say, Campion, you've got a very good chance. What a miracle he chose this particular place to die in! In ninety-nine cemeteries out of a hundred, you know——"

"Yes, but be quiet," I said. "Don't talk about it, for heaven's sake."

"I won't," he promised. "My dear old man, you can rely on me. Besides, I don't see a soul to talk to."

We got away from him eventually, having discovered what we wanted to know, and he stood watching us until we disappeared down the hill. Lugg sighed.

"Lonely life," he observed. "When you see a bloke like that it makes you feel you'd like to take him on a pub-crawl, don't it?"

"Does it?" I said.

He frowned. "You're getting so lah-di-dah and don't-speak-to-me-I'm-clever, you make me tired," he complained. "If I was in your position I wouldn't waste me time muckin' round with corpses. I'd ask a fellow like that up to Town for a week and show 'im the sights."

"My God," I said, "I believe you would."

He chose to be offended, and we drove home in silence.

The following day, which was the third since Hayhoe had been found, I woke up with a sensation that was half exhilaration and half apprehension. I had a premonition that things were going to move, although had I known in what direction I don't think I should have dared to go on.

It began with Professor Farringdon's report. He came over while I was at the station with Pussey, and made it verbally.

"Aye, it was chloral hydrate," he said, "as I told you. It was verra deeficult to decide just how much the man had taken before his death. So there is no way of knowing, you see, whether when yon stone crashed down on his head he was already dead, or if he was merely under the influence of the drug."

Pussey and I both knew the peculiar properties of chloral hydrate; it is a very favourite dope among con men, but we let him tell us all over again.

"It'd make him very sleepy, you understand. That's why it's so diabolically useful. If ye came upon a man suffering from a slight attack of this poison, ye'd simply think he was in a deep natural sleep."

Pussey looked at me. "All the time he was setting in that chair, I reckon he was just waiting for the thing to fall upon him, helpless, unable to move. Ah, that's a terrible thing, Mr Campion."

The professor went on to dilate upon the fate of Mr Hayhoe.

"Yon was an interesting wound," he said. "Remarkably lucky, or delivered by someone who was no fool. It caught him just over the collarbone, and went straight down into his neck. He must have died at once."

He went on to describe the knife that had been used, and even drew it for us, or at least he drew the blade. Pussey didn't know what to make of it at all, but it fitted in to my theory all right.

I left them together and went on to find Whippet. Neither he nor Effie

Rowlandson were at The Feathers when I arrived, but presently he came up alone in his little A.C.

"I've been house hunting," he said. "There's a little villa down the road that interests me. It's empty. I like empty houses. Do you? Whenever I'm in a district I go and look at empty houses."

I let him ramble on for some time, and when I thought he must have tired of the subject I put my question to him suddenly. If I hoped to surprise him I was disappointed.

"Hayhoe?" he said. "Oh yes. Oh yes, Campion, I had several conversations with him. Not a nice fellow; he tried to touch me."

"Very likely," I said. "But what did you talk to him about?"

Whippet raised his head, and I looked into his vague pale grey eyes.

"Natural history I think, mostly," he said. "Flora and fauna, you know."

At that moment another great wedge of the jigsaw slipped into place.

"Some are born blind," I said bitterly. "Some achieve blindness. And some have blindness thrust upon them. Moles come into the first category, don't they?"

He said nothing but remained quite still, looking out of the window.

I went back to Highwaters, and there the thing I had not foreseen, the thing for which I shall never forgive myself, awaited me.

Lugg had gone.

His suitcase, containing his few travelling things, had vanished, and on my dressing table, weighted down by an ash tray, was a crisp new pound note.

CHAPTER XVI

The Red Hair

AT FIRST I did not believe it. It was the one contingency which had never entered my mind, and for a moment I was completely thrown off my balance. I heard myself blethering around like a hysterical woman. Pepper did his best to help me.

"A telephone call came through to you, sir," he said. "I didn't take much notice of it, but I understood it was a London call. Mr Lugg took it, and some time afterwards he came down the back stairs with a suitcase in his hand. He went down to the village by the field path."

And that was all there was to it. That was all anybody could tell me. The exchange was not helpful. There had been a great many incoming calls. The girl at the post office had been run off her feet all day. No, she hadn't listened. Of course not! She never did.

I was beside myself. The question of time was so terribly important, and every now and again a variation of the ghastly vision which I had seen through the brass telescope rose up before my eyes.

The search began immediately.

Leo was sympathetic, and Janet did her best to be soothing. I had to explain to them all that the pound note meant nothing at all. Doubtless there are menservants who go off at a moment's notice, leaving a week's wages in lieu of warning, but Lugg is not of them. Besides, he had not been seen in the village nor at the bus stop. He had disappeared as mysteriously as Hayhoe had done; had wandered off into the fields and had vanished in precisely the same way.

I rang up Kingston. He listened to my excited story with disarming interest.

"I say, Campion!" His voice sounded young over the wire. "I've got an idea. I don't know if you remember it, but I said something to you yesterday. You didn't think much of it at the time—I saw that in your face—but I believe it's going to come in useful now. I'll be over right away."

He was. In less than twenty minutes he came panting up the drive in second gear, his face pink and his eyes burning with delighted enthusiasm. If it had been anybody but Lugg I could have forgiven him.

We held a consultation on the front lawn.

"It's that chap Whippet," he said. "I've been keeping an eye on him. I know how you feel—old school friends and that sort of thing—but you don't really know him at all, and things have been happening, haven't they? Someone must be behind them."

"Yes, well," I said impatiently, "go on."

He was a little overwhelmed to find me so receptive, I think, but he hurried on eagerly enough.

"There's a house," he said, "an empty villa which stands all by itself at the end of a partly made-up road. It was the beginning of a building scheme which got stopped when the parish council found out what was happening. Whippet's been down there once or twice. I don't say anything definite, but didn't it occur to you that that fellow Hayhoe must have been killed somewhere other than out in the open field? It's a lonely little place. Just the place for a spot of bother. Let's go down."

There was a great deal in what he said, and I did not want to waste time arguing. I moved over towards his car. He looked a little shamefaced.

"I'm afraid we'd better take yours," he said. "Mine's not very young, you know, and she developed a spot of her usual trouble coming along just now. The oil gets in somewhere and rots up the ignition. That is, unless you can wait while I clean a plug or two?"

I was not in the mood to wait, and I got out the Lagonda. He settled beside me with a little sigh of sheer pleasure at its comfort.

"Straight down the hill," he said, "and first on the left."

We turned out of the village and took the long lonely road which winds up through Tetheringham and on to Rushberry. Presently we turned again. There was a little beerhouse, The Dog and Pheasant, sitting coyly under a bank of elms about half a mile farther on, and as we neared it he touched my arm.

"You're rotting yourself up," he said. "You haven't been sleeping, and now this shock on top of it is getting you down. You'd better stop and have one."

I cursed at the delay, but he insisted and we went in.

It was an unattractive little place, old and incredibly dirty. The bar was a mass of cheap advertising trophies, and the only other customer at the time we entered was a toothless old person with a Newgate fringe.

Kingston insisted on beer. There was nothing like old beer for steadying one, he said, and while the half-witted landlady shambled off to fill our tankards, Kingston interrogated the old man concerning Lugg. He did it very well, all things considered, using the idiom of the county.

The old gentleman could not help us, however. He was short of sight and hard of hearing, so he said, and never took much count of strangers, anyway.

It was after the two greasy tankards had been pushed towards us that Kingston showed me the cottage we were going to investigate. It was just visible from the tiny window of the bar. I could see its hideously new red roof peering out amid a mass of foliage about half a mile away.

"Yes, well, let's get on," I said, for I had no great hopes of finding my unfortunate old friend there and time was getting short.

Kingston rose to the occasion.

"All right," he said. "We won't wait for another."

He drained his tankard and so did I. As I turned away from the bar I stumbled and inadvertently caught the old man's pewter mug with my elbow. Its contents were splattered all over the floor and there was another few minutes' delay while we apologised and bought him another drink.

When I got out to the car I stood for a moment looking down at the steering wheel.

"Look here, Kingston," I said, "d'you think it's really necessary to go to this place?"

"I do, old boy, I do." He was insistent. "It's odd, you know, a stranger hanging about an empty house."

I got in and began to drive. A quarter of a mile up the road the car swerved violently and I pulled up.

"I say," I said a little thickly, "would you drive this thing?"

He looked at me and I saw surprised interest on his round, unexpectedly youthful face.

"What's the matter, old man?" he said. "Feeling tired?"

"Yes," I said. "That stuff must have been frightfully strong. Drive on as quick as you can."

He climbed out, and I moved heavily over into the place he had vacated. A minute later we were roaring down the road again. I was slumped forward, my head on my chest, my eyes half closed.

"Can't understand it," I said, my words blurred. "Got to get ol' Lugg. I'm tired—terribly tired."

I was aware of him pulling up, and through my half-closed eyes I saw a dilapidated little villa, its white stucco streaked with many rains. At the side of the house there was a garage with a badly made little drive of a yard or so leading up to it.

I was aware of Kingston unlocking the doors of this garage and then I was down at the bottom of the car, my eyes closed and my breath coming at long regular intervals.

Kingston stepped behind the steering wheel again and we crawled into the narrow garage. I heard him stop and then I heard him laugh. It was like no sound I had ever heard from him before.

"Well, there you are, my clever Mr Campion," he said. "Sleep sound."

I think he must have pulled on some gloves, for I was aware of him wiping the steering wheel, and then he dragged me up and pressed my hands upon its smooth surface. He was talking all the time.

"Carbon monoxide is an easy death," he said. "That's why suicides choose it so often. It's so simple, isn't it? I just leave you in the car with the engine running, and close the garage doors as I go out, and the neurotic Mr Campion has done the inexplicable once again. Suicide of distinguished London criminologist."

He was some time completing his arrangements and then, when everything was set, he bent forward.

"I was too clever for you," he said, and there was a rather shocking note in his voice. "Too damned clever."

"By half," I added suddenly and leapt at him.

I hadn't spilt our poor old bearded friend's beer at The Dog and Pheasant for nothing. Showing a man something interesting out of a window while you put a spot of chloral hydrate in his tankard is poor chaff to catch old birds.

I caught him by the back of the neck and for a moment we grappled. What I hadn't realised, however, was the fellow's strength. Outwardly he appeared a rather flaccid type, but when we came to grips there was muscle there and weight to back it up. Besides, he was demented, he fought like a fiend. I had no longer any doubts about the identity of the hand which had sent that skilful thrust into Hayhoe's neck.

I struggled out of the car, but he was between me and the garage door. I saw his great shoulders hunched against the light. He leapt on me and we fell to the ground. I caught a glimpse of his eyes, and if ever I saw the "blood light" in a man's face it was then. I nearly escaped him once and had almost reached the doors when something like a vise seized me by the throat. I was lifted bodily and my head crashed down upon the concrete floor.

It was like going down very suddenly in a lift. It went on and on and at the end there was darkness.

I came up again painfully, in little jerks. I was aware that my arms were moving up and down with a slow rhythmic motion I could not control, and then I was gasping, fighting for breath.

"Look out—look out. You're doing nicely. Don't get excited. Steady yourself."

The voice came to me like a dream, and I saw through the fog a ridiculous small boy with ink smeared all over his face looking down at my bed in the sicker. Then the boy disappeared, but I still saw the same face, although the ink had been removed. It was Whippet. He was kneeling behind me giving me artificial respiration.

The whole business came back with a rush.

"Lugg!" I said. "My God, we've got to get Lugg!"

"I know." Whippet's voice sounded almost intelligent. "Fellow's positively dangerous, isn't he? I let Kingston get away before I got you out. I mean, I didn't want to have two of you on my hands."

I sat up. My head was throbbing and there was only one clear thought in my mind.

"Come on," I said. "We've got to get him before it's too late."

He nodded, and I was suddenly grateful for the understanding in his face.

"A fellow came by on a bicycle a moment or so ago," he said. "I put it to him and sent him off down to the village. He's going to send the whole crowd up to the nursing home. I thought that was the best way. I've got my car in the meadow round the back. Let's go to Tetheringham straight away, shall we?"

I don't remember the journey to Tetheringham. My head felt as though it was going to burst, my mouth was like an old rattrap, and I couldn't get rid of a terrible nightmare in which Lugg was hoisted on a scarecrow stake which was as high as the Nelson Column.

What I do remember is our arrival. We pulled up outside the front door of Kingston's barrack of a house, and when it wouldn't give we put our shoulders to it. I remember the tremendous sense of elation when it shattered open before our combined strength.

It was a movement on the first floor that sent us racing up the stairs, and, since five doors on the landing were open, we concentrated on the one that was not. It was unlocked, but someone held it on the other side. We could hear him snarling and panting as we fought with it.

And then, quite suddenly, it swung back. I was so beside myself that I should have charged in and taken what was coming to me, but it was Whippet who kept his head. He pulled me back and we waited.

Through the open door I could see a bed, and on it there was a large familiar form. The face was uncovered, and as far as I could see the colour was natural. But as I stared at it I saw the thing that sent the blood racing into my face and turned my body cold with the realisation of the thing I had not dreamed.

The faded grey-black fluff which surrounds Lugg's bald patch was as red as henna would make it. I saw the truth: the body of one fat man is much like the body of another once the features are obliterated, and what time can do can be done by other agencies. Kingston was going to have a body for his "jolly" exhumation, after all.

I dropped on my hands and knees. Ducking under the blow he aimed at me from his place of vantage behind the door, I caught him by the ankles. I was on his chest with my hands round his throat when I heard the second car pull up and Leo's voice on the stairs.

CHAPTER XVII

Late Final

IT TOOK THREE POLICEMEN to get Kingston into the car, and when he came up before the magistrates there was an unprecedented scene in the court. At the assizes his counsel pleaded insanity, a defence which failed, and I think justifiably; but that was later.

My own concern at the time was Lugg. Whippet and I worked upon him until Pussey got us a doctor from a neighbouring village, who saved him after an uncomfortably stiff fight. It was chloral hydrate again, of course. Kingston was not mad enough not to know what he was doing. He did not want any wound showing in his exhibition corpse. What his "finishing" process was to be, I can only guess, and I do not like to think of it even now.

Lugg told us his story as soon as we got him round. It was elementary. Kingston had simply phoned up Highwaters, made sure from Pepper that I was down in the village, and had then asked for Lugg. To him he gave a message purporting to come from me. According to this, I had work for him to do in town, but I wanted to see him first up at Tetheringham churchyard, where, Kingston hinted, I had discovered something. Lugg was to pack his bag and nip down the field path to the road to meet Kingston in the car. The pound note was to be left for Pepper in case I could not return. That was all. Lugg fell for the story, Kingston did meet him, and the reason they had not been seen was that the doctor's car was far too well known for anybody to notice it.

On arrival at Tetheringham, Lugg was left in the dining room, where he was given beer and told to wait. He drank the beer and the chloral which was in it and mercifully remembered no more.

Kingston must have got him upstairs alone and have just completed the hairdressing process when I phoned.

It was a pretty little trap, and Lugg's comments on it when he considered it are not reportable.

"You done it," he said reproachfully. "How was I to know you was leadin' the bloke up the garden with your 'come-and-'old-me-'and' every five minutes? You stuffed him full of the exhumation, thinkin' 'e'd go for you, I suppose? Never thought o' me. Isn't that you all over?"

I apologised. "Let's be thankful you're alive to tell the tale," I ventured.

He scowled at me. "I am. Got to shave me 'ead now. What are my London friends goin' to think about that? 'Oliday in the country . . . Oh yes, very likely!"

When we reached this point I thought it best to let him sleep, for there was still much to be done.

During the next twenty-four hours we worked incessantly, and at the end of it the case against Kingston was complete.

It was on the evening of the day on which the exhumation had taken place that Leo and I went down with Janet to Halt Knights. Leo was still simmering from the effects of that grimly farcical ceremony which had welded the final link in our chain of evidence.

"Bricks!" he said explosively. "Yellow bricks wrapped up in a blanket and nailed down in a coffin. . . . 'Pon my soul, Campion, the fellow was an impious blackguard as well as a murderer. Even now, I don't see how he did it alone."

"He wasn't alone," I pointed out mildly. "He had Peters to help him, to say nothing of that fellow who worked for him—the builder's son. In country places the builder is usually the undertaker, too, isn't he?"

"Royle!" Leo was excited. "Young Royle . . . that explains the key of the mortuary. Was the boy in it, do you think?"

"Hardly," I murmured. "I imagine Kingston simply managed him. He says his master offered to measure up the body while he did a repair job in the house. The nurse must have been an accomplice, of course, but we shall never get her. She and Kingston got the death certificate between them."

"You're terribly confusing," Janet cut in from the back of the car. "How many brothers were there?"

"None," I said, "as the clever young man from London suspected after he'd had it thrust well under his nose, poor chap. There was only the one inimitable Pig."

Janet will forgive me, I feel sure, if I say here that she is not a clever girl. On this occasion she was obtuse.

"Why go to all the trouble of pretending he died in January?"

"Because," I said sadly, "of the insurance, my poppet. Twenty thousand pounds. . . . He and Kingston were going to do a deal. Tie up with your medical man and let the Mutual Ordered Life settle your money troubles. Kingston met Pig in Town and they hatched the whole swindle up between them. Pig invented a wicked brother and laid the foundations by hoodwinking his own solicitors, who were a stuffy old firm at once reputable enough to impress the insurance company and sufficiently moribund to let Pig get away with his hole-and-corner death."

"Neat," said Janet judicially and added with that practicalness so essentially feminine, "Why didn't it work?"

"Because of the fundamental dishonesty of the man Pig. He wouldn't pay up. Once he had collected, he knew he had Kingston by the short hairs and, besides, by then the idea of developing this place had bitten him. I fancy he kept his doctor pal on a string, promising him and promising and then laughing at him. What he did not consider was the sort of fellow he had to deal with. Kingston is a conceited chap. He has a sort of blind courage coupled with no sense of proportion. Only a man with that type of mentality could have pulled off his share in the original swindle. The fact that he had been cheated by Pig wounded his pride unbearably, and then, of course, he found the man untrustworthy."

"Untrustworthy?" Leo grunted.

"Well, he began to get drunk, didn't he?" I said. "Think of Kingston's position. He saw himself cheated out of the share of the profits and at the same time at the complete mercy of a man who was in danger of getting too big for his boots, drinking too much and blowing the gaff. Admittedly, Pig could not give Kingston away without exposing his own guilt, but a man who gets very drunk may be careless. Then there was Hayhoe. The wicked uncle finds the wicked nephew in clover and wishes to browse also. He even installs a telescope on a neighbouring hillside in the hope of keeping an eye on developments at Highwaters. There is another danger for Kingston. I think the whole ingenious business came to him in a flash, and he acted on impulse moved by fury, gingered up by fear."

Leo made an expressive sound. "Terrible feller," he said. "Heigh-ho blackmailed him, I suppose, after guessin' the truth?"

"Uncle Hayhoe was bent on selling his discretion, certainly," I said, "but I don't think even he guessed Kingston had killed Pig. All he knew was that there was something infernally fishy about the first funeral. He made an appointment with Kingston to talk it over and they chose the empty villa to discuss terms. Kingston killed him there and later on carried him to the cornfield where we found him. He left the knife in the wound until he got him *in situ*, as it were; that's how he avoided a great deal of the blood."

Janet shuddered. "He deceived us all very well," she said. "I never dreamed . . ."

Leo coughed noisily. "Utterly deceived," he echoed. "Seemed a decent enough feller."

"He was amazing," I agreed. "My arrival at dinner that evening must have shaken him up a bit, in all conscience, since he'd seen me at the funeral, but he came out with the brother story immediately and made it sound convincing. The only mistake he made was in moving the body to the river when I said I was going to examine it. He acted on impulse there, you see; he saw his way and went straight for it every time."

Janet drew back. "You ought not to have walked into that last trap he set for you," she said.

"My dear girl," I said, anxious to defend myself, "we had to have proof of murder or attempted murder, for as far as proof was concerned he'd got clean away with his first two efforts. All the same, I don't think I'd have been so foolhardy if it hadn't been for Lugg."

"You'd have looked pretty green if it hadn't been for Gilbert," she said.

I looked at her sharply and saw that she was blushing.

"Whippet and I had a word or two on the phone after Kingston had agreed to pick me up at Highwaters," I admitted. "He spotted the empty villa and put me on to it. We guessed if there was to be an attempt on me Kingston would take me there. I shouldn't have been so brave without him. Mastermind is fond of life."

Janet dimpled. She is very pretty when her cheeks go pink.

"Then you know about Gilbert?" she said.

I stared at her. "How much do you know?"

"A little," she murmured.

"My hat!" I said.

Leo was on the point of demanding an explanation when we pulled up at the Knights. We found Poppy, Pussey and Whippet waiting for us in the lounge, and when we were all sitting round, with the ice cubes clinking in our tall glasses, Poppy suddenly turned on me.

"I'm sure you've made a mistake, Albert," she said. "I don't want to be unkind, dear, and I do think you're very clever. But how could Doctor Kingston have killed Harris, or Peters as you call him, when he was in this room playing poker with Leo when the vase fell upon him? You said yourself it couldn't have slipped off by accident."

The time had come for me to do my parlour trick, and I did my best to perform it in the ancient tradition.

"Poppy," I said, "do you remember Kingston coming to see your little maid on the morning of the murder? You took him up yourself, I suppose, and you both had a look at the kid? There was some ice in the water jug by her bed, wasn't there?"

She considered. "No," she said. "He came down, and I gave him a drink with ice in it. That was after I'd turned him into the bathroom to wash his hands. I came down here, and he followed me, and after he'd had his drink he took some tablets up to Flossie that he'd forgotten."

"Ah!" I said impressively. "Was he long following you down?"

She looked up with interest. "Why, yes, he was," she said. "Quite a while, now I think of it."

Having located my rabbit, as it were, I proceeded to produce it with a flourish.

"Kingston told us he met Harris, alias Pig, on the stairs, and that Pig had a hang-over," I began. "The first wasn't true, the second was. Pig was in his bedroom when Kingston slipped in to see him, having first got rid of you. Pig was dressed, but he wanted a corpse-reviver and he trusted Kingston, never dreaming that he'd goaded the man too far. After all, people don't go about expecting to be murdered. In his doctor's bag Kingston had some chloral, which is a reputable narcotic when used in moderation. He saw his opportunity. He administered a tidy dose and sent Pig to sit out on the lawn. He followed him downstairs and through the lounge windows saw him settle down. I think his original intention was to let him die and to trust the coroner to suspect a chronic case of dope. But this was risky, and the position of the chair, which was directly beneath the window, put the other idea into his head. If you notice, the windows on each floor in this house are directly above those on the last, and no one who knows the place can have missed the stone urns. They were originally intended to obscure the attic windows from the outside. It was while Kingston was drinking his highball that he had his brain wave. There were two or three solid rectangles of ice in his glass, and he pocketed two of them. Then he told you some story about forgotten tablets and went up to the top floor again, which was deserted at that time of the morning. There he discovered that, as he had suspected, Pig was sitting directly beneath the box-room urn. He knew he was unconscious already and would remain so. The rest was easy. He took the urn out of its socket and balanced it on its peg half over the ledge. Then he blocked it into position with the two pieces of ice and went quietly downstairs. The ledge is just below the level of the window sill, so the chance of anyone who passed the box-room door noticing that the urn was an inch or so out of place was remote. All he had to do, then, was to wait."

Poppy sat staring at me, her face pale.

"Until the ice melted and the urn fell?" she said. "How—how ghastly!"

Pussey wagged his head. "Powerful smart," he said. "Powerful smart. If I might ask you, sir, how did you come to think of that?"

"The moss on the ledge was damp when I arrived," I said. "The inference did not dawn on me at first, but when I had a highball here the other day I saw the ice and suddenly realised what it meant."

"Wonderful!" said Whippet without malice. "I was after the same fellow, of course, but the alibi put me out."

Leo stared at him as if he had only just become aware of his existence.

"Mr—er—Whippet," he said, "very pleased to have you here, of course, my boy. But where do you fit into this extraordinary story? What are you doin' here?"

There was a pause, and they all looked at me as though I was responsible for him. I looked at Whippet.

"His little hands are sore and his snout bleedeth," I said. "This is Gilbert Whippet, Jr, son of Q. Gilbert Whippet, of the Mutual Ordered Life Endowment Company, sometimes called the M.O.L.E. It didn't occur to me until that day at The Feathers, and then I could have kicked myself for missing it. You always were a lazy beast, Whippet."

He smiled faintly. "I—er—prefer writing to action, you know," he said hesitantly. "I am sorry, Campion, to have dragged you into this, but at the beginning we had nothing to go on at all except a sort of uneasy suspicion. I couldn't very well approach you direct because—well—er—there was nothing direct about it, so I—er—wrote."

His voice trailed away.

"Both Lugg and I appreciated your style," I said.

He nodded gravely. "It seemed the best way to ensure your interest," he said calmly. "Whenever I thought you might be flagging, I wrote again."

"Your people got hold of Effie, and you set her on to me, I suppose?" I said coldly.

"Er—yes," agreed Whippet without shame.

Poppy glanced round the room. "Where is she now?" she demanded.

Whippet beamed. It was the broadest smile I ever saw on his face.

"With—er—Bathwick," he murmured. "They've gone into the town, to the pictures. Very suitable, I thought. Happy endings and—er—all that."

I gaped at him. He had my respect.

When Lugg and I went back to London the next day, Poppy, who had come to Highwaters for lunch, stood with Leo and waved good-bye to us from the lawn. The sky was dappled blue and white, the birds sang, and the air smelt of hay.

Janet, with Whippet in tow, came running up to us just before we started. Her eyes were dancing, and she looked adorable.

"Congratulate us, Albert," she said. "We're engaged. Isn't it wonderful?"

I gave them my blessing with a good grace. Whippet blinked at me. "I'm indebted to you, Campion," he said.

We drove for some time in silence. I was thoughtful and Lugg, who was as bald as an egg, seemed depressed. As we reached the main road he nudged me.

"What a performance!" he said.

"Whose?" I enquired, not above appreciating a little honour where honour was due.

He leered. "That bloke Whippet. Come down to a place with Miss Effie Rowlandson, and go orf with Miss Janet Pursuivant. . . . That took a bit o' doing."

"Lugg," I said sadly, "would you like to walk home?"

[illegible]

[illegible] a [illegible] [illegible] [illegible] [illegible] [illegible] [illegible] a good [illegible]

"What a [illegible]," he [illegible].

[illegible] not about [illegible] a little [illegible] [illegible]

[illegible] "The [illegible] down to a [illegible] with a [illegible] [illegible] and [illegible] with [illegible] [illegible]. [illegible]

[illegible] "Would you like to walk home?"

No Motive

BY DAPHNE DU MAURIER

MARY FARREN WENT into the gun room one morning about half-past eleven and took her husband's revolver and loaded it, then shot herself. The butler heard the sound of the gun from the pantry. He knew Sir John was out and would not be back until lunch time, and no one had any business to be in the gun room at that hour of the day.

He went to investigate, and there he saw Lady Farren lying on the floor, in her own pool of blood. She was dead.

Aghast, he called the housekeeper, and after consultation they agreed he must first telephone the doctor, then the police, and lastly Sir John himself, who was at a board meeting.

The butler told the doctor and the police, who arrived within a few minutes of each other, what had happened; his message on the telephone had been the same to each.

"Her ladyship has had an accident. She is lying in the gun room with a gunshot wound in her head. I fear she is dead."

The message summoning Sir John home was worded differently. It just said, would Sir John please return home at once, as her ladyship had met with an accident.

The doctor, therefore, had to break the news to the husband when he came.

It was a painful, wretched business. He had known John Farren for years; both he and Mary Farren were patients of his; a happier married couple did not exist, and they were both looking forward to the baby that was to be born to them in the spring. No difficulties were expected; Mary Farren was normal, healthy, and delighted at the prospect of being a mother.

The suicide, therefore, did not make sense. Because it was suicide. There was no doubt about it. Mary Farren had scribbled three words on a writing pad, which she had put on the desk in the gun room. The words were, "Forgive me, darling."

The gun had been put away unloaded, as always. Mary Farren had quite definitely taken out the gun, loaded it, then shot herself.

The police corroborated with the doctor that the wound had been self-inflicted. Mercifully, she must have died at once.

Sir John Farren was a broken man. In that half hour, talking to the doctors and the police, he aged about twenty years. "But why did she do it?" he kept asking in agony. "We were so happy. We loved each other;

the baby was on its way. There was no motive, I tell you, absolutely no motive."

Neither the police nor the doctor had an answer for him.

The usual formalities were gone through, the official business of an inquest, with the expected verdict, "Suicide, with no evidence to show the state of mind of the deceased."

Sir John Farren talked to the doctor again and again, but neither of them could come to any conclusion.

"Yes, it is possible," said the doctor, "women can become temporarily deranged at such a time, but you would have noticed signs of it, and so would I. You tell me she was perfectly normal the night before, perfectly normal at breakfast. As far as you know, there was nothing on her mind at all?"

"Absolutely nothing," said Sir John. "We breakfasted together, as we always did; we made plans for the afternoon; after I returned from the board meeting I was going to take her for a drive. She was cheerful and completely happy."

Lady Farren's cheerfulness was also corroborated by the servants.

The housemaid, who had gone to the bedroom at half-past ten, found her ladyship examining shawls that had come by the parcel post. Lady Farren, delighted with the work, had shown the shawls to her and had said she would keep both pink and blue, for boy or girl.

At eleven a travelling salesman had called from a firm that made garden furniture. Her ladyship had seen the man, chosen two large garden seats from his catalogue. The butler knew this, because Lady Farren had shown him the catalogue after the man had gone, when he had come to enquire if there were any orders for the chauffeur, and her ladyship had said, "No, I shan't be going out until after lunch, when Sir John will be taking me for a drive."

The butler had gone from the room, leaving her ladyship drinking a glass of milk. He was the last person to see Lady Farren alive.

"It comes to this," said Sir John, "between that time, which was approximately twenty minutes past eleven, and eleven-thirty, when she shot herself, Mary went off her head. It doesn't make sense. There *must* have been something wrong. I've got to find out what it was. I shall never rest until I do."

The doctor did his best to dissuade him, but it was no use. He himself was convinced that Mary Farren had succumbed to a sudden brain storm, owing to her condition, and, not knowing what she was doing, had made an end of herself.

Let it stay there. Let it rest. And Time only would help John Farren to forget.

John Farren did not try to forget. He went to a private-detective agency and interviewed a man called Black, recommended by the firm as trustworthy and discreet. Sir John told him the story. Black was a canny Scot.

He didn't talk much, but he listened. It was his private opinion that the doctor's theory was right, and a sudden brain storm, owing to pregnancy, was the motive for the suicide. However, he was thorough at his job, and he went down to the country and interviewed the household. He asked many questions that the police had not asked, chatted with the doctor, checked up on the mail that had come for Lady Farren during the past few weeks, enquired about telephone calls and encounters with personal friends; and still there was no answer he could give to his client.

The one obvious solution that had come to his practised mind—that Lady Farren was expecting a child by a lover—did not work. Check and double check revealed no possibility of this. Husband and wife were devoted and had not been apart since their marriage three years previously. The servants all spoke of their great attachment for one another. There were no financial worries. Nor could the shrewd Black trace any infidelity on the part of Sir John. Servants, friends, neighbours, all spoke of his high integrity. Therefore, his wife had not shot herself through any fault of his that had come to light.

Temporarily Black was baffled. But not beaten. Once he took on a case, he liked to see it through to the end, and hardened though he was, he felt sorry to see Sir John's agony of mind.

"You know, sir," he said, "in cases of this sort we often have to go back in a person's life, rather further than the immediate past. I've been through every inch of your wife's desk, with your permission, and searched her papers and all correspondence, and I have found nothing to give the faintest clue to the trouble on her mind—if there was trouble.

"You have told me that you met Lady Farren—Miss Marsh, as she was then—while on a visit to Switzerland. She was living with an invalid aunt, Miss Vera Marsh, who had brought her up, her parents being dead."

"That is correct," said Sir John.

"They lived in Sierre and also in Lausanne, and you met both the Misses Marsh at the house of a mutual friend in Sierre. You struck up a friendship with the younger Miss Marsh, and by the end of your holiday you had fallen in love with her, and she with you, and you asked her to marry you."

"Yes."

"The elder Miss Marsh made no objection; in fact, she was delighted. It was arranged between you that you should make her an allowance to cover the expenses of a companion to take her niece's place, and within a couple of months or so you were married at Lausanne."

"Correct again."

"There was no question of the aunt coming to live with you in England?"

"No," said Sir John. "Mary wanted her to—she was much attached to her aunt—but the old lady refused. She had lived in Switzerland so long, she couldn't face the English climate or the English food. Incidentally, we have been out twice to see her since we married."

Black asked if Sir John had heard from his wife's aunt since the tragedy. Yes. He had written, of course, at once, and she had seen the news in the papers too. She was horrified. She could give no reason why Mary should have taken her life. A happy letter, written a week before, full of her happiness at the prospect of the future baby, had arrived in Sierre only a few days prior to the calamity. Miss Marsh had enclosed the letter for Sir John to read. And Sir John gave it to Black.

"I take it," said Black, "that the two ladies, when you met them first three years ago, were living very quietly?"

"They had this small villa, as I told you before," said Sir John, "and about twice a year they used to go down to Lausanne and take rooms in a pension. The old lady had some sort of trouble with her lungs, but not serious enough for a sanatorium or anything like that. Mary was a most devoted niece. It was one of the first things that drew me to her. Her gentleness and sweet temper to the old lady, who, like many elderly people, semi-invalid, was apt to be fractious at times."

"So your wife, the younger Miss Marsh, did not get about much? Not many friends her own age, and that sort of thing?"

"I suppose not. It did not seem to worry her. Hers was such a contented nature."

"And this had been her life since she was quite small?"

"Yes. Miss Marsh was Mary's only relative. She had adopted her when Mary's parents died. Mary was a child at the time."

"And how old was your wife when you married her?"

"Thirty-one."

"No history of a previous engagement or a love affair?"

"Absolutely none. I used to tease Mary about it. She said she had never seen anyone to give her the slightest flutter. And her aunt agreed. I remember Miss Marsh saying to me when we became engaged, 'It's rare to find anyone so unspoilt as Mary. She's got the prettiest face and is quite unaware of it, and the sweetest nature and doesn't realise that either. You're a very lucky man.' And I was."

Sir John sat staring at Black with such abject misery in his eyes that the tough Scot hardly liked to cross-question him further.

"So it really was a love match on both sides?" he said. "You are quite certain there was no pull in your title and position? I mean, the aunt might have told her niece that here was a chance she mustn't miss, another man like you might not come along. After all, ladies do think of these things."

Sir John shook his head.

"Miss Marsh might have had an eye to the main chance, I don't know," he said, "but certainly Mary had not.

"Right from the beginning it was I who sought out her, not the other way round. If Mary had been looking about for a husband, she would have shown signs of it when we first met. And you know what cats women can be. The friend at whose chalet I originally met the Marshes would have warned me that here was a girl, past thirty, in search of a husband. She said no such thing. She said, 'I want you to meet a perfect darling of a girl whom we all adore and feel rather sorry for because she leads such a lonely life.' "

"Yet she didn't appear lonely to you?"

"Not at all. She seemed perfectly content."

Black handed back Miss Marsh's letter to Sir John.

"You still want me to go on with this enquiry?" he said. "You don't think it would be simpler to decide, once and for all, that your doctor was right about Lady Farren, and she had some sort of a blackout which affected her mind and made her take her life?"

"No," said Sir John, "I tell you, somewhere there is a clue to this tragedy, and I shan't give up until I've found it. Or rather you find it for me. That's why I'm employing you."

Black rose from his chair.

"Very well," he said, "if that's the way you feel about it, I'll go right ahead with the case."

"What are you going to do?" asked Sir John.

"I shall fly to Switzerland tomorrow."

Black handed in his card at the Chalet Bon Repos at Sierre and was shown into a small salon that gave on to a balcony with a fine view across the Rhone Valley.

A woman, Miss Marsh's companion he supposed, led him through the salon on to the balcony. Black had time to notice that the room was furnished neatly, with good taste, but nothing out of the way, very much the room of an elderly English spinster living abroad who did not fling her money around.

There was a large picture of Lady Farren on the mantelpiece, taken recently, a duplicate of the one he had seen in Sir John's study. And another on a writing bureau of Lady Farren aged about twenty, he judged. A pretty, shy-looking girl, her hair worn rather longer than in the more recent portrait.

Black went on to the balcony and introduced himself to the elderly lady seated there in a wheeled chair as a friend of Sir John Farren's.

Miss Marsh had white hair, blue eyes, and a firm mouth. From the way she spoke to her companion, who immediately left them together, Black decided she was hard on those who served her. She seemed, however, genuinely pleased to see Black, and at once asked after Sir John with much concern and wanted to know if any light at all had been thrown on the tragedy.

"I'm sorry to say, none," answered Black. "In fact, I am here to ask you what you know about it. You knew Lady Farren better than any of us, even her husband. Sir John thinks you may have some ideas on the subject."

Miss Marsh looked surprised.

"But I wrote and told Sir John I was horrified and completely baffled," she said. "I enclosed Mary's last letter. Did he tell you?"

"Yes," said Black, "I saw the letter. And you have others?"

"I kept all her letters," said Miss Marsh. "She wrote me regularly, every week, after she married. If Sir John wants me to send him the letters I shall be pleased to do so. There is not one letter that isn't full of her affection for him, and her pride and delight in her new home. It was her one regret that I wouldn't stir myself to go and visit her. But you see, I am such an invalid."

"You look hearty enough," thought Black, "but perhaps you just didn't want to go."

"I gather you and your niece were much attached?" he said.

"I was deeply fond of Mary, and I like to think she was equally fond of me," was the swift reply. "Heaven knows I can be cantankerous at times, but Mary never seemed to mind. She was the sweetest-natured girl."

"You were sorry to lose her?"

"Of course I was sorry. I missed her terribly, and still do. But naturally her happiness came first."

"Sir John told me he made you an allowance to cover the cost of your present companion."

"Yes. It was generous of him. Will it continue, do you know?"

The inflection in her voice was sharp. Black decided that his original idea of Miss Marsh as someone who did not wholly disregard money was probably sound.

"Sir John didn't say. But I feel sure, if it was otherwise, you would have heard from him or from his lawyers," said Black.

Black looked at Miss Marsh's hands. They tapped the sides of the wheeled chair in a little nervous gesture.

"There was nothing in your niece's past that would account for her suicide?" he said.

She looked startled. "What on earth do you mean?"

"No previous engagement, or love affair gone wrong?"

"Good heavens, no."

Curious. She seemed relieved at the wording of his question.

"Sir John was Mary's only love. She led rather a solitary life with me, you know. Not many young people in the district. Even in Lausanne she never seemed to seek out people nearer her own age. It was not that she was particularly shy or reserved. Just self-contained."

"What about school friends?"

"I taught her lessons myself when she was small. She had a few terms in Lausanne when she was older, but as a day girl; we lived in a pension close by. I seem to remember one or two girls coming in for tea. But no especial friend."

"Have you any photographs of her at that age?"

"Yes. Several. I've got them all in an album somewhere. Would you care to see them?"

"I think I should. Sir John showed me several photographs, but I don't think he had any dating before their marriage."

Miss Marsh pointed to the bureau in the salon behind and told him to open the second drawer and bring back an album. He did so, and putting on spectacles, she opened the album, and he drew his seat beside her.

They went through the album at random. There were many snapshots, none of any particular interest. Lady Farren alone. Miss Marsh alone. Lady Farren and Miss Marsh in groups with other people. Snaps of the chalet. Snaps of Lausanne. Black turned the pages. No clue here.

"Is that the lot?" he said.

"I'm afraid it is," said Miss Marsh. "She was such a pretty girl, wasn't she? Those warm brown eyes. It is the most dreadful thing . . . Poor Sir John."

"You haven't any snaps of her when she was a child, I notice. These seem to start when she was around fifteen."

There was a pause, and then Miss Marsh replied, "No . . . no, I don't think I had a camera in those days."

Black had a well-trained ear. It was an easy matter for him to detect a falsehood. Miss Marsh was lying about something. About what?

"What a pity," he said. "I always think it's interesting to trace the child in the adult face. I'm a married man myself. My wife and I wouldn't be without the first albums of our youngster for the world."

"Yes, it was stupid of me, wasn't it?" said Miss Marsh.

She put the album down in front of her on the table.

"I expect you have the ordinary studio portraits?" said Black.

"No," said Miss Marsh, "or if I once had, I must have lost them. In the move, you know. We didn't come here until Mary was fifteen. We were in Lausanne before that."

"And you adopted Mary when she was five, I think Sir John said?"

"Yes. She would have been about five."

Again the momentary hesitation, the inflection in her voice.

"Have you any photographs of Lady Farren's parents?"

"No."

"Yet her father was your only brother, I understand?"

"My only brother, yes."

"What decided you to adopt Lady Farren as a child?"

"The mother was dead, and my brother did not know how to take care of her. She was a delicate child. We both of us felt it was the best solution."

"Of course your brother made you an allowance for the child's upkeep and education?"

"Naturally. I couldn't have managed otherwise." Then Miss Marsh made a mistake. But for this one mistake, Black might have let the whole thing go.

"You ask the most extraordinarily remote questions, Mr. Black," she said with a hard little laugh. "I don't see that the allowance paid to me by Mary's father can be of the slightest interest to you. What you want to know is why poor Mary killed herself, and so does her husband, and so do I."

"Anything even remotely connected with Lady Farren's past life is of interest to me," said Black. "You see, Sir John has employed me for that very purpose. Perhaps it is time that I explained to you I am not a personal friend of his. I am a private detective."

Miss Marsh turned grey. Her composure went. She became suddenly a very frightened old woman.

"What have you come to find out?" she said.

"Everything," said Black.

Now it was a favourite theory of the Scot's, which he often expounded to the director of the agency for whom he worked, that there are very few people in this world who haven't got something to hide. Time and time again he had seen men and women in the witness box, under cross-examination, and one and all were afraid; not of the questions put to them, which they must answer, and which might shed light on the particular case then under trial; but that in answering the questions, they would, by some mishap, by some slip of the tongue, reveal some personal secret pertaining to themselves which would discredit them.

Black was certain that Miss Marsh found herself in this position now. She might know nothing of Mary Farren's suicide or of its cause. But Miss Marsh herself was guilty of something that she had long sought to hide.

"If Sir John has found out about the allowance and thinks I have been defrauding Mary all these years, he might have had the decency to tell me himself, and not employ a detective," she said.

"Oh, ho, here we go," thought Black. "Give the old lady enough rope and she'll hang herself."

"Sir John did not mention the word fraud," he replied to Miss Marsh; "he merely thought the circumstances were rather strange."

Black was taking a chance, but he felt the result might be worth it.

"Of course they were strange," said Miss Marsh. "I tried to act for the best, and I believed I did. I can swear to you, Mr. Black, that I used very little money on myself, and that the most part of it went for Mary's upkeep, according to the agreement with the child's father. When Mary married, and as it happened married well, I did not think there was any harm in keeping the capital for myself. Sir John was rich, and Mary would not miss it."

"I take it," said Black, "that Lady Farren knew nothing of what was going on financially?"

"Nothing," said Miss Marsh. "She was never interested in money matters, and she believed herself entirely dependent on me. You don't think Sir John is going to prosecute me, Mr. Black? If he won a case against me, which he undoubtedly would, I should be destitute."

Black stroked his chin and pretended to consider.

"I don't think Sir John intends anything of the sort, Miss Marsh," he said. "But he would like to know the truth of what happened."

Miss Marsh sank back in her wheeled chair. No longer stiff and upright, she looked a tired old lady.

"Now that Mary is dead, it can't hurt her, the truth coming out," she said. "The fact is, Mr. Black, she wasn't my niece at all. I was paid a large sum of money to look after her. The money should have gone to her on her majority, but I kept it myself. Mary's father, with whom I signed the agreement, had died in the meantime. Living here in Switzerland, no one knew anything about the matter. It was so simple to keep it secret. I intended no harm."

"It was always the way," thought Black. "Temptation came to a man or a woman, and they gave way to it. They never 'intended' harm."

"I see," he said. "Well, Miss Marsh, I don't want to go into the details of what you did or how you spent the money intended for Lady Farren. What does interest me is this. If she wasn't your niece, who was she?"

"She was the only daughter of a Mr. Henry Warner. That is all I ever knew. He never told me his address, or where he lived. All I knew was the address of his bankers, and the branch in London; four cheques were paid to me from that address. After I took Mary in my care, Mr. Warner went to Canada and died there five years later.

"The bank informed me of this, and as I never heard from them again, I believed myself safe to do—what I did—with her money."

Black noted the name Henry Warner, and Miss Marsh gave him the address of the bank.

"Mr. Warner was not a personal friend of yours?" he asked.

"Oh no. I only met him twice. The first time was when I answered his advertisement to a box number for someone to take charge, indefinitely, of a delicate girl. I was very poor at the time and had just lost a post as governess to an English family returning to England.

"I did not want to take a position in a school, and this advertisement came as a godsend, especially as the sum to be paid for the child's upkeep, which the father intended to accumulate, was so generous. I knew I should be able to live as I had, frankly, never lived before. You can hardly blame me."

Something of her former confidence was returning. She looked sharply at Black.

"I am not blaming you," he said. "Tell me more about Henry Warner."

"There is little to tell," she said. "He asked very few questions about myself or my background. The only point he made clear was that he wanted Mary to remain with me for good; he had no intention of having her back with him again, or corresponding with her. He planned to go to Canada, he told me, and cut himself off from all former connections. I was entirely free to bring up his daughter as I thought fit. In other words, he washed his hands of her."

"A callous sort of customer?" suggested Black.

"Not exactly callous," replied Miss Marsh. "He looked anxious and careworn, as though the responsibility of looking after the child had been too much for him. His wife apparently was dead. Then I enquired in what way his daughter was delicate, because I knew little of nursing and did not particularly relish an ailing child.

"He explained to me that she was not physically delicate, but that she had witnessed a terrible train accident a few months previously, and the shock of this had caused her to lose her memory.

"She was perfectly normal otherwise, perfectly sane. But she remembered nothing previous to the shock. She did not even know he was her father. This was the reason, he told me, why he wanted her to begin a new life in another country."

Black jotted down some notes. The case at last was beginning to show possibilities.

"So you were willing to take the risk of having this child—suffering from mental shock—on your hands for life?" he asked.

He had not intended his question to be cynical, but Miss Marsh saw a sting in it. She flushed.

"I am used to teaching and used to children," she said; "also, independence was dear to me. I accepted Mr. Warner's offer, on condition I took to the child and the child took to me. At our second meeting he brought Mary with him. It was impossible not to feel an affection for her at once. That pretty little face, those large eyes, and the soft, gentle manner. She seemed quite normal, but young for her age. I chatted with her and asked her if she would like to come and stay with me, and she said she would; she put her hand in mine in the most confiding way. I told Mr. Warner 'Yes,' and the bargain was struck. He left Mary with me that evening, and we neither of us ever saw him again. It was easy enough to tell the child she was my niece, as she remembered nothing of her past; she accepted anything I cared to tell her about herself as gospel truth. It was all too easy."

"And from that day she did not once recover her memory, Miss Marsh?"

"Never. Life began for her when her father handed her over to me at that hotel in Lausanne, and it really began for me too. I could not have loved her better had she been in truth my niece."

Black glanced through his notes and put them in his pocket.

"So beyond the fact that you knew she was the daughter of a Mr. Henry Warner, you were completely ignorant as to her background?" he asked.

"Completely," said Miss Marsh.

"She was merely a little girl of five years old who had lost her memory?"

"Fifteen," corrected Miss Marsh.

"How do you mean, fifteen?" said Black.

Miss Marsh flushed again.

"I forgot," she said. "I misled you earlier in the afternoon. I always told Mary, and everybody else, that I had adopted my niece when she was five. It made it so much easier for me, and easier for Mary too, because she remembered nothing of her life previous to the time she came to live with me. She was, in point of fact, fifteen. You will realise now why I have no snapshots or photographs of Mary as a child."

"Indeed, yes," said Black. "And I must thank you, Miss Marsh, for being so helpful. I don't think Sir John is likely to raise any questions about the money, and for the present, at any rate, I shall keep the whole story of what you have told me as entirely confidential What I now have to find out is where Lady Farren—Mary Warner—was living for the first fifteen years of her life, and what that life was. It may have some bearing on the suicide."

Miss Marsh rang for her companion to show Black out. She had not quite recovered her equanimity.

"There is only one thing that has always puzzled me," she said. "I feel her father, Henry Warner, did not speak the truth. Mary showed no fear of trains at any time, and though I made several enquiries of many people, I could learn of no severe train accident that had happened in England, or anywhere else for that matter, during the months before Mary came to me."

Black returned to London, but he did not get in touch with Sir John Farren, because he thought it best to wait until he had more definite news to communicate.

It seemed to him unnecessary to reveal the truth about Miss Marsh and the adoption. It would only unsettle Sir John further, and it was hardly likely that this fact had suddenly come to light and driven his wife to suicide.

The more intriguing possibility was that Lady Farren had received a shock which, in the timing of a moment, had pierced the veil which had shrouded her memory for nineteen years.

It was Black's business to discover the nature of that shock. The first thing he did in London was to go to the branch of the bank where Henry

Warner had kept an account. He saw the manager and explained his mission.

It appeared that Henry Warner had indeed gone to Canada, had married again when he was out there, and had subsequently died. The widow had written, closing the account in England. The manager did not know whether Henry Warner had left a second family in Canada, nor did he know the address of the widow. Henry Warner's first wife had died many years previously. Yes, the manager knew about the daughter of the first marriage. She had been adopted by a Miss Marsh in Switzerland. Cheques had been paid to Miss Marsh, and they ceased when Henry Warner married a second time. The only positive information that the bank manager could give Black which might be helpful was Henry Warner's old address. And the piece of news, which Henry Warner had certainly not told Miss Marsh, that his profession was the Church, and that at the time Miss Marsh had adopted his daughter he was vicar of All Saints, in the parish of Long Common, Hampshire.

Black travelled down to Hampshire with a pleasurable feeling of anticipation. He always began to enjoy himself when the clues began to unravel. It reminded him of boyhood days of hide-and-seek. It was his interest in the unexpected that had called him to be a private detective in the first place, and he had never regretted his call.

He believed in keeping an open mind about his case, but it was difficult not to see the Reverend Henry Warner as the villain of this piece. The sudden handing over of a mentally sick daughter to a perfect stranger abroad, and then cutting himself loose from her and going to Canada seemed an extraordinarily heartless thing for a clergyman to do.

Black smelt scandal, and if the taint still lingered in Long Common after nineteen years, it would not be difficult to ferret out what the scandal had been.

Black put up at the local inn, describing himself as a writer on old churches in Hampshire, and with this same excuse he wrote a polite note to the present incumbent, asking if he might call.

His wish was granted, and the vicar, a young man, an enthusiast on architecture, showed him every corner of the church from nave to belfry, with a wealth of detail about fifteenth-century carving.

Black listened politely, disguising his own ignorance, and finally led the vicar round to talking of his predecessors.

Unfortunately the present vicar had been at Long Common for only six years, and he knew little about Warner, who had been succeeded by someone who had moved to Hull, but Warner had definitely held the living for twelve years, and his wife was buried in the churchyard.

Black saw the grave and noted the headstone. "Emily Mary, dearly beloved wife of Henry Warner who passed to rest safe in the arms of Jesus."

He also noted the date. The daughter Mary would have been ten years old at the time.

Yes, said the present vicar, he had heard that Warner had given up the living in a great hurry and gone to the Dominions, Canada, he believed. Some of the people in the village would remember him, especially the older ones. Possibly his own gardener would remember most. He had been gardener at the rectory for thirty years.

But as far as he, the vicar, knew, Warner had not been a historian or a collector; he had done no research work on the church.

If Mr. Black would care to come to the rectory, he, the present vicar, had many interesting books on Long Common history.

Mr. Black excused himself. He had got all he wanted out of the present incumbent. He felt that an evening at the bar of the inn where he was staying would prove more profitable, and it did.

He learnt no more about fifteenth-century carving, but a good deal about the Reverend Henry Warner.

The vicar had been respected in the parish, but never deeply liked because of his rigid views and his intolerance. He was not the sort of man to whom his parishioners went when they were in trouble; he was always more likely to condemn than to console. He never entered the bar of the inn, never mixed in friendly fashion with the humble.

He was known to have private means, and he was not dependent on his benefice. He liked to be invited to the few large houses in the neighbourhood, because he placed social values high; but he had not been particularly popular there either.

In short, the Reverend Henry Warner had been an intolerant, narrow-minded snob, which were three poor qualities for a vicar to hold. His wife, on the contrary, had been much loved by all, and it had been universally regretted when she died after an operation for cancer. She had been a most sweet-tempered lady, very thoughtful for others, most kind-hearted, and her little girl took after her.

Had the child been much affected by her mother's death?

No one remembered. It was thought not. She went away to school and was only home during the holidays. One or two recollected her riding about on her bicycle, a pretty, friendly little thing. The gardener and his wife had acted as married couple for the Reverend Henry Warner, the same gardener that was up at the rectory now. Old Harris. No, he did not come down to the pub of an evening. He was a teetotaller. He lived up in one of the cottages near the church. No, his wife was dead. He lived with a married daughter. He was a great rose fancier and won prizes for his roses every year at the local show.

Black finished his pint and departed. The evening was yet young. He dropped out of his disguise as a writer on old Hampshire churches and slipped into the role of a collector of Hampshire roses. He found old Harris smoking a pipe outside his cottage There were roses growing up his fence. Black stopped to admire them. The conversation was launched.

It took him the better part of an hour to lead Harris from roses to past vicars, from past vicars to Warner, from Warner to Mrs. Warner, from Mrs. Warner to Mary Warner, but the picture unfolded, and there was nothing very remarkable to see in it. The same tale was repeated that he had heard in the village.

The Reverend Warner was a hard man, not given to being friendly-like; very sparing, he was, with his praises. Took no interest in the garden. Stuck-up sort of chap. But down on you like a ton of bricks if anything was wrong. The lady was very different. Proper shame when she died. Miss Mary was a nice child too. His wife had been very fond of Miss Mary. Nothing stuck-up or proud about her.

"I suppose the Reverend Warner gave up the living because he was lonely after Mrs. Warner died?" said Black, offering Harris some of his own tobacco.

"No, it wasn't nothing to do with that. It was along of Miss Mary's health, and her having to live abroad after being so ill with the rheumatic fever. They went off to Canada, and we never heard from them no more."

"Rheumatic fever?" said Black. "That's a nasty thing to get."

"It wasn't anything to do with the beds here," said old Harris; "my wife kept the place aired and looked after everything, just as she used to when Mrs. Warner was living. It was at school Miss Mary caught it, and I remember saying to my wife that the vicar ought to sue the teachers up there for neglect. The child nearly died of it."

Black fingered the rose Harris had picked for him and placed it neatly in his buttonhole.

"Why didn't the vicar sue the school?" he asked.

"He never told us if he did or not," said the gardener; "all we was told was to pack up Miss Mary's things and send them off to the address in Cornwall he gave us, and then to get his own things packed, and dust covers put over the furniture, and before we knew what was happening a great van came to pack the furniture and take it to store, or to be sold—we heard afterwards it was sold, and then that the vicar had given up the living and they was going off to Canada. My wife was most upset about Miss Mary; she never had a word from her or from the vicar, and we had served them all those years."

Black agreed that it was a poor return for what they had done. "So the school was in Cornwall?" he observed. "I'm not surprised at anyone catching rheumatic fever in Cornwall. A very damp county."

"Oh no, sir," said old Harris. "Miss Mary went down to Cornwall for her convalescence. Place called Carnleath, I believe it was. She was at school at Hythe, in Kent."

"I have a daughter at school near Hythe," lied Black with ease. "I hope it's not the same place. What was the name of Miss Mary's school?"

"Couldn't tell you, sir," said old Harris, shaking his head, "it's too long ago. But I remember Miss Mary saying it was a lovely place, right on the sea, and she was very happy there, fond of the games and that."

"Ah," said Black, "can't be the same then. My daughter's school is inland. It's funny how people get hold of the wrong end of the stick. I heard Mr. Warner's name spoken down in the village this evening—queer, if you hear a name once in a day you hear it again—and someone was saying the reason they went to Canada was because the daughter had been badly injured in a train accident."

Old Harris laughed scornfully.

"Them fellows at the pub will say anything when they've a drop of beer inside them," he said. "Train accident indeed. Why, the whole village knew at the time it was rheumatic fever and that the vicar was almost out of his mind with the worry of it, being sent for so sudden up to the school and all. I've never seen a man so demented. To tell you the truth, neither the wife nor myself had ever thought him so fond of Miss Mary until that happened. He used to neglect her, we thought. She was so much her mother's girl. But his face was terrible when he came back from being sent for to the school, and he said to my wife that it was for God to punish the head teacher there for criminal negligence. Those were his words. Criminal negligence."

"Perhaps," said Black, "he had an uneasy conscience and blamed the school for neglect, when at heart he blamed himself."

"Could be," said old Harris, "could be. He'd always look for the fault in the other fellow."

Black considered the time had come to pass from the Warners to the roses once again. He lingered five more minutes, made a note of the blooms recommended for planting by an amateur like himself who wanted quick results, said good evening, and went back to the inn. He slept soundly and caught the first train back to London in the morning. He did not think he would secure any more information at Long Common. In the afternoon he took a train to Hythe. On this expedition he did not bother the local vicar, but addressed himself to the manageress of his hotel.

"I am looking around the coast for a suitable school for my daughter," he said, "and I understand that there are one or two in this part of the world that are very good indeed. I wonder if you happen to know the names of any you could recommend."

"Oh yes," said the manageress, "there are two very good schools in Hythe. There is Miss Braddock's, up at the top of the hill, and of course there is St. Bees, the big co-educational school right on the front. Here at the hotel we mostly get parents with children at St. Bees."

"Co-educational?" said Black. "Has it always been so?"

"Since it was first founded, thirty years ago," said the manageress. "Mr. and Mrs. Johnson are still the principals, though of course they are both elderly now. It's very well run and has an excellent tone. I know there is sometimes prejudice against a co-educational school, because people say it makes the girls masculine and the boys effeminate, but I've never seen a sign of that myself. The children always look very happy and just like other children, and they only take them up to fifteen anyway. Would you care for me to make an appointment for you to see either Mr. or Mrs. Johnson? I know them well."

Mr. Black wondered if she got a commission on pupils to whom she had recommended the school.

"Thank you very much," he said, "I would be pleased if you would." The appointment was made for eleven-thirty the next morning.

Black was surprised at St. Bees' being co-educational. He had not thought that the Reverend Henry Warner would have been open-minded on mixed tuition. St. Bees it must be, however, from the description given by old Harris, the gardener. St. Bees was certainly facing the sea, with a fine surround. The other school, Miss Braddock's, was tucked away behind the hill at the top of the town, with hardly any view at all, and no playing fields. Black had made sure of this by going to look at the outside before keeping his appointment at St. Bees.

A smell of shining linoleum, scrubbed floors, and varnish greeted him as he stood at the entrance, having mounted the school steps. A parlourmaid answered his bell and showed him into a large study on the right of the hall.

An elderly man with a bald head, horn spectacles, and an effusive smile rose to his feet and greeted him.

"Glad to meet you, Mr. Black," he said. "So you are looking for a school for your daughter? I hope you are going to leave St. Bees believing that you have found it."

Mr. Black summed him up in a word. "Salesman," he said to himself. Aloud he proceeded to spin a neat yarn about his daughter Phyllis, who was just reaching the awkward age.

"Awkward?" said Mr. Johnson. "Then St. Bees is the place for Phyllis. We have no awkward children here. All the odd spots get rubbed off. We pride ourselves on our happy, healthy boys and girls. Come and have a look at them."

He clapped Black upon the back and proceeded to lead him round the school. Black was not interested in schools, co-educational or otherwise; he was only interested in Mary Warner's rheumatic fever of nineteen years ago. But he was a patient man and allowed himself to be shown every classroom, every dormitory—the two wings were separated for the two sexes—the gymnasium, the swimming bath, the lecture hall, the playing fields, and finally the kitchen.

He then returned with a triumphant Mr. Johnson to the study.

"Well, Mr. Black?" said the principal, smiling behind his horn rims. "And are we to be allowed to have Phyllis?"

Black sat back and folded his hands, the picture of a fond father.

"Yours is a delightful school," he said, "but I must tell you that we have to be very careful of Phyllis' health. She is not a strong child and gets colds very easily. I am only wondering whether the air might not be too strong for her."

Mr. Johnson laughed and, opening a drawer in his desk, took out a book.

"My dear Mr. Black," he said, "St. Bees has one of the best health records of any school in England. A child develops a cold. He or she is isolated at once. That cold does not spread. In the winter months noses and throats are sprayed as a matter of routine. In the summer months the children do exercises for the lungs in front of open windows. We have not had an influenza epidemic for five years. One case of measles two years ago. One case of whooping cough three years ago. I have here a list of illnesses contracted by the boys and girls over the years, and it is a list I am proud to show to every parent."

He handed the book to Mr. Black, who took it with evidence of pleasure. It was just the evidence he wanted.

"This is remarkable," he said, turning the pages, "and of course modern methods of hygiene have helped you to have such a good health record. It can't have been the same some years ago."

"It has always been the same," said Mr. Johnson, getting up and reaching for another volume on his shelf. "Choose any year you fancy. You won't catch me out."

Without hesitation Black chose the year that Mary Warner had been removed from the school by her father.

Mr. Johnson ran his hand along the volumes and produced the year in question. Black turned the pages in search of rheumatic fever. There were cold cases, one broken leg, one German measles, one sprained ankle, one mastoid—but not the case he sought.

"Have you ever had a case of rheumatic fever?" he enquired. "My wife is particularly afraid of that for Phyllis."

"Never," said Mr. Johnson firmly. "We are far too careful. The boys and girls always have a rub-down after games, and the linen and clothing are most scrupulously aired."

Black shut up the book. He decided upon direct tactics.

"I like what I have seen of St. Bees," he said, "but I feel I must be frank with you. My wife was given a list of schools, with yours amongst it, and she at once struck it off the list because she remembered being very put off it by a friend many years ago. This friend had a friend—you know how it is—but the long and short of it was that the friend was obliged to remove his daughter from St. Bees and even talked of suing the school for negligence."

Mr. Johnson's smile had gone. His eyes looked small behind the horn-rimmed glasses.

"I should be very much obliged if you would give me the name of the friend," he said coldly.

"Certainly," said Black. "The friend afterwards left this country and went to Canada. He was a clergyman. And his name was the Reverend Henry Warner."

The horn-rimmed glasses did not disguise the odd, wary flicker in Mr. Johnson's eyes. He ran his tongue over his lips.

"The Reverend Henry Warner," he said, "now let me see." He leant back in his chair and seemed to be pondering. Black, trained to evasion, knew that the principal of St. Bees was thinking hard and playing for time.

"Criminal negligence was the word used, Mr. Johnson," he said, "and oddly enough I ran across a relative of Warner's only the other day, who happened to bring the matter up. I was told that Mary Warner nearly died."

Mr. Johnson took off his horn glasses and slowly polished them. His expression had quite changed. The over-genial schoolmaster had turned into the hardheaded businessman.

"You obviously know the story from the relative's point of view only," he said. "Any criminal negligence was on the part of the father, Henry Warner, and not on ours."

Black shrugged his shoulders.

"How can a parent be sure?" he murmured.

His words were calculated to draw the principal further.

"How can you be sure?" shouted Mr. Johnson, all pretence at geniality gone, and slapping his hand on his desk. "Because I would have you know that Mary Warner's case was one isolated incident that had never happened before and has never happened since.

"We were careful then. And we are careful now. I told the father that what had occurred must have occurred during the holidays, and most definitely and finally not at school. He would not believe me, and insisted that our boys here were to blame, through lack of supervision. I had every boy over a certain age up here before me, in this very room, and questioned them privately. My boys spoke the truth. They were not to blame. It was useless to try to get any sense out of the girl herself; she did not know what we were talking about or what we were asking her. I need hardly tell you, Mr. Black, that the whole thing was the most frightful shock to myself and my wife, and to the whole staff, and the story is one which, thank God, we have lived down and which we had hoped was forgotten."

His face showed fatigue and strain. The story may have been lived down, but it had definitely not been forgotten by the principal.

"What happened?" asked Black. "Did Warner tell you he was going to remove his daughter?"

"Did he tell us?" said Mr. Johnson. "No, indeed, we told him. How could we possibly keep Mary Warner here when we found she was five months pregnant?"

The jigsaw puzzle was fitting together rather nicely, thought Black. It was remarkable how the pieces came to hand if you set your mind to the job. Finding out the truth through other people's lies was always stimulating. First Miss Marsh; he had to break through her iron curtain. The Reverend Henry Warner, too, had certainly gone out of his way to build a fictitious barricade. A train accident to one, rheumatic fever to another. Poor devil, what a shock it must have been to him. No wonder he packed his daughter off to Cornwall to hide her secret, and shut up the house and left the neighbourhood.

Callous, though, to wash his hands of her when the business was through. The loss of memory must have been genuine enough. But Black wondered what had caused this. Had the world of childhood suddenly become nightmare to a schoolgirl of fourteen or fifteen, and nature taken charge and mercifully blotted out what had happened?

It looked this way to Black. But he was a thorough man; he was being paid well for his time of research, and he was not going to his client with a tale half told. It must be the whole story. He remembered Carnleath was the place where Mary Warner had gone for her convalescence after the supposed rheumatic fever. Black decided to go there.

The firm for which he worked supplied him with a car, and Black set out. It occurred to him that another word or two with old Harris, the gardener, might prove fruitful, and as it was on his way to the West Country, he stopped off at Long Common, bringing as excuse a small rose tree which he had purchased off a market gardener en route. He would tell the gardener this came from his own garden, as a small return for the advice given him the previous visit.

Black drew up outside the gardener's cottage at midday, at which hour he judged the old fellow would be home for his dinner.

Unfortunately Harris was not at home. He had gone to a flower show at Alton. The married daughter came to the door, a baby in her arms, and said she had no idea when he would be back. She seemed a pleasant, friendly sort of woman. Black lit a cigarette, handed over the rose tree, and admired the baby.

"I have a youngster like that at home," he said with his usual facility for playing fictitious roles.

"Really, sir?" said the woman. "I have two others, but Roy is the baby of the family."

They exchanged baby gossip while Black smoked his cigarette. "Tell your father I was in Hythe a day or two ago," he said, "seeing my girl, who is at school there. And curiously enough I met the headmaster of St. Bees, the school where Miss Mary Warner was educated—your father was telling me about it—and how angry the vicar was that his daughter caught rheumatic fever—and the headmaster remembered Miss Warner well. He insisted, after all these years, that it was not rheumatic fever, but some virus the child had picked up at home."

"Oh, really," said the woman. "Well, I suppose he had to say something for the sake of the school. Yes, that was the name. St. Bees. I remember Miss Mary talking about St. Bees often enough. We were much of an age, and when she was home she used to let me ride her bicycle. It seemed a great treat to me then."

"More friendly than the vicar then," said Black. "I gather your father had no great liking for him."

The woman laughed.

"No," she said, "I'm afraid nobody had much opinion of him, though I dare say he was a very good man. Miss Mary was a dear. Everyone liked Miss Mary."

"You must have been sorry," said Black, "that she went down to Cornwall and never came home to say good-bye."

"Oh, I was. I never could understand it. And I wrote to her down there, but never had no answer. It hurt me quite a bit, and Mother too. So unlike Miss Mary."

Black played with the tassle of the baby's shoe. The face was puckered to cry, and Black thought this might distract him. He did not want Harris' daughter to go back inside the cottage.

"It must have been lonely at the rectory all on her own," said Black. "I expect she was glad of your company during the holidays."

"I don't think Miss Mary was ever lonely," said the woman; "she was such a friendly soul, with a word for everyone, not stuck-up like the vicar. We used to have fine games together, pretending we were Indians and such. You know what kiddies are."

"No boy friends and cinemas then?"

"Oh no. Miss Mary wasn't that sort. The girls are terrible today, aren't they? Like young women. They chase the men."

"I bet you had admirers, both of you, for all that."

"No, really, sir, we didn't. Miss Mary was so used to boys at St. Bees, she never thought them out of the ordinary. Besides, the vicar would never have allowed anything like 'admirers.'"

"I suppose not. Was Miss Mary afraid of him?"

"I don't know about afraid. But she was careful not to displease him."

"Always had to be home before dark, I suppose."

"Oh yes. Miss Mary was never out after dark."

"I wish I could keep my daughter from coming back late," said Black. "In summer evenings it's sometimes nearly eleven o'clock before she is in. It's not right. Especially when you read the things that happen in the newspapers."

"Shocking, isn't it?" agreed the gardener's daughter.

"But this is a quiet neighbourhood. I don't suppose you get any bad characters around here, and didn't in those days either."

"No," said the woman, "though of course when the hoppers come it's a bit lively."

Black threw away his cigarette. It was burning his fingers.

"The hoppers?" he said.

"Yes, sir. It's a great district for growing hops. And in the summer the hoppers come down and camp in the neighbourhood, and they're quite a rough crowd, from some of the worst parts in London."

"How interesting. I had no idea they grew hops in Hampshire."

"Oh yes, sir. It's been an industry for a long time."

Black dangled a flower before the baby's eyes.

"I suppose you weren't allowed anywhere near them when you were young, or Miss Mary either," he said.

The woman smiled.

"We weren't supposed to, but we did," she said, "and we'd have got into a proper old row if we'd been found out. I remember one time—— What is it, Roy? Is it time for your nap? He's getting sleepy."

"You remember one time," said Black.

"Oh, the hoppers, yes. I remember one time we did go off to see them after supper—we'd got friendly with one of the families, you know—and they were having a celebration, what for I don't remember—someone's birthday, I suppose—and they gave me and Miss Mary beer to drink; we'd never tasted it before, and we got real tipsy.

"Miss Mary was worse than I was; she told me afterwards she didn't remember a thing that happened all evening—we were sitting round the tents, you know, where the people lived, and when we got home our heads were going round and round, we were quite scared. I've often thought since, whatever would the vicar have said if he'd known, and my old Dad too, for that matter. I would have got a thrashing, and Miss Mary a sermon."

"Deserved it too," said Black. "What age were you both then?"

"Oh, I was around thirteen, and Miss Mary had turned fourteen. It was the last summer holidays she ever had at the rectory. Poor Miss Mary. I often wonder what became of her. Married, no doubt, over in Canada. They say it's a lovely country."

"Yes, Canada's a fine place, by all accounts. Well, I mustn't stay here gossiping. Don't forget to give the rose tree to your father. And put that youngster to bed before he drops off in your arms."

"I will, sir, good day to you, and thank you."

"Thank you, on the contrary," thought Black. The visit had been worth while. Old Harris' daughter had been better value than old Harris. Hoppers and beer. Fair enough. Mr. Johnson of St. Bees would say conclusive. The time factor fitted too. The boys of St. Bees were absolved. What a damnable thing, though. Black let in the clutch and drove off through the village of Long Common towards the west. He felt it was important to discover at what point Mary Warner had lost her memory. That she remembered nothing of what must have happened at the hop-picking celebration was plain. A reeling head, a black-out, and two scared kids making for home at top speed before they were discovered.

Johnson of St. Bees, still warm in the defence of his school, had told Black that there was no doubt Mary Warner had been completely ignorant of her condition.

When the matron, aghast, had discovered the fact and taxed the child, Mary Warner was bewildered. She thought the matron had gone mad. "What do you mean?" she had said. "I'm not grown up, and I'm not married. Do you mean I'm like Mary in the Bible?"

She had not the remotest idea of the facts of life.

The school doctor had advised against questioning the child further. The father had been sent for. And Mary Warner was removed. That, so far as Mr. Johnson and the staff of St. Bees were concerned, was the end of the matter.

Black wondered what the vicar had said to his daughter. He suspected that the vicar had questioned the unfortunate child until he had given her brain fever. The shock must be enough to turn any child mental for life. Perhaps he would get the solution down at Carnleath. The only trouble was that Black did not know quite what he was looking for. The Reverend Warner must surely have changed their names.

Carnleath turned out to be a small fishing port on the south coast. It had probably enlarged itself during the past nineteen years, because there were three or four fair-sized hotels, a sprinkling of villas, and it was evident that the populace now devoted themselves to the business of catching tourists before catching fish.

Black's family, Phyllis and the boy, returned to the mythical land whence they sprang. Black was now a newly married man, and his wife, a girl of eighteen, was expecting her first baby. Black felt doubtful as he enquired for nursing homes. But he was not disappointed. There was a nursing home in Carnleath, and it did specialise in maternity cases only. Sea View, it was called. Right out on the cliff's edge, above the harbour.

He backed his car against a wall, got out, and went to the front door and rang the bell. He asked to see the matron. Yes, it was about booking a room for a future case.

He was shown into the matron's private sitting-room. She was small and plump and jolly, and he felt certain that he would be well advised to leave his mythical wife—Pearl, he decided to call her in a sudden flight of the imagination—in the matron's capable care.

"And when do you expect the happy event?"

No Cornish woman this, but a hearty, ringing Cockney. Black felt at home with her at once.

"In May," said Black. "My wife is with my in-laws at the moment, and so I've come on this little trip alone. She is determined to be beside the sea for the great occasion, and as we spent our honeymoon here, she feels a sentimental liking for the spot, and so do I." Black gave what he intended to be a sheepish, prospective father's smile. The matron was undaunted.

"Very nice too, Mr. Black," she said, "back to the scene of the crime, eh?" She laughed heartily. "Not all my patients are so fond of the backward glance. You'd be surprised."

Black handed the matron a cigarette. She took it and puffed at it with relish.

"I hope you aren't going to shatter my illusions," he said.

"Illusions?" said the matron. "We have few illusions here. They all go west in the labour ward. What was sauce for the gander turns out to be a pain under the pinny for the goose."

Black began to be sorry for the fictitious Pearl.

"Oh well," said Black, "my wife's a plucky girl. She's not frightened. I may say, she's considerably younger than myself. Only just turned eighteen. That's the one thing that worries me about this business. Is that too young to be having a baby, Matron?"

"They can't be too young," said the matron, puffing a cloud of smoke into the air; "the younger the better. Their bones aren't so set, and they're not muscle-bound. It's the old ones that give me my headaches. Come to me at thirty-five and think they're in for a picnic. We soon show 'em. Your wife play a lot of tennis?"

"Doesn't play at all."

"Good for her. Had a girl here last week, she was local champion over in Newquay, and she was so muscle-bound she was in labour for thirty-six hours. Sister and I were worn to a frazzle at the end of it."

"What about the girl?"

"Oh, she was all right once we stitched her up."

"You have had patients as young as eighteen before?" he asked.

"Younger than that," she said; "we cater for all ages here, fourteen to forty-five. And they haven't all had pleasant honeymoons. Would you like to see some of my babies? I've a little fellow born an hour ago, and Sister is just making him pretty for Mother."

Black steeled himself for the ordeal. If Matron was as forthright as this over one cigarette, how would she be after two double gins? He knew he must ask her to dinner. He went round the nursing home, saw one or two prospective mothers, saw several more whose illusions had apparently been shattered, and when he had inspected the babies, the labour ward, and the laundry, he made a silent vow to remain childless.

He booked a room with a view over the sea for Pearl, he gave the date in May—he even paid a deposit—and then he asked Matron to dine. "That's very nice of you," she said, "I'd enjoy it. The Smuggler's Rest is only a small place, nothing to look at from outside, but the bar's the best in Carnleath."

"Then the Smuggler's Rest it shall be," said Black, and they arranged to meet at seven.

By nine-thirty, after two double gins, lobster, and a bottle of Chablis, with brandy to follow, the difficulty was not to make Matron talk, but to get her to stop.

She launched into the finer sides of midwifery with a wealth of detail that nearly turned Black dizzy. He told her she should write her reminiscences. She said she would when she retired.

"No names, of course," he said, "and don't tell me all your patients have been married women, because I shan't believe you."

Matron tossed down her first brandy.

"I told you before we had all sorts at Sea View," she said, "but don't let that shock you. We're very discreet."

"I'm unshockable," said Black, "and so is Pearl."

Matron smiled.

"You know your onions," she said; "it's a pity all husbands don't. We'd have fewer tears at Sea View." She leant forward intimately. "You'd be staggered to know what some people pay," she said; "I don't mean the honest-to-God married people like yourself. But those who have slipped up. They come down here to get the business over, and they pretend to be above board, and everything nice and pretty, but they can't deceive me. I've been in the game too long. We've had titled patients at Sea View, pretending to be Mrs., and their husbands think they are having a holiday in the South of France. Not a bit of it. They're having what they didn't reckon to have—at Sea View."

Black ordered another brandy.

"What happens to the unwanted baby?" he asked.

"Oh, I have contacts," said Matron; "there're plenty of foster mothers in this part of the world who won't say no to twenty-five shillings a week until a child reaches school age. No questions asked. Sometimes I've seen the face of the real mother in the papers afterwards. I show it to Sister and we have a quiet laugh. 'She didn't wear that pretty smile in the labour ward,' I say to Sister. Yes, I'll write my memoirs one of these days. I dare say they'd be worth something, and they'd sell like hot cakes."

Matron took another of Black's cigarettes.

"I'm still worried about my wife's age," he said. "What's the youngest you've ever had?"

Matron paused for reflection, breathing smoke into the air.

"Sixteen, fifteen," she said. "Yes, we had a fifteen-year-old once, barely fifteen, if I remember rightly. That was a sad case. Long time ago now, though."

"Tell me about it," said Black.

Matron sipped her brandy.

"She came of well-to-do people too," she said; "the father would have paid anything I asked, but I'm not a grasper. I told him a sum I thought fair, and he was so pleased to dump his daughter on me, he gave me a bit extra. I had her here for five months, which is a thing I don't do as a rule, but he said it was either that or a remand home, and I felt so sorry for the poor kid I took her."

"How did it happen?" asked Black.

"Co-ed school, the father said. But I never believed that yarn. The amazing thing was that the little girl couldn't tell any of us what had happened. I generally get at the truth from my patients, but I never got it from her. She told us at Sea View that her father said it was the greatest disgrace could ever come upon any girl, and she couldn't make it out, she said, because her father was a clergyman, and he was forever preaching what had happened to the Virgin Mary as being the most wonderful thing in the world."

The waiter came with the bill, but Black waved him away.

"You mean to say the girl thought the whole business was supernatural?" he asked.

"That's exactly what she did think," said the matron, "and nothing would shake her. We told her the facts of life, and she wouldn't believe us. She said to Sister that something horrid like that might happen to other people, but it certainly hadn't happened to her. She said she had sometimes dreamt about angels, and probably one had come in the night, when she was asleep, and that her father would be the first to say he was sorry when the baby was born, because of course it would be a new messiah.

"Do you know, it was really pathetic to hear her talk, she was so sure of herself. She told us she loved children and wasn't a bit afraid, and she only hoped she was really good enough to be its mother; she knew this time he really would save the world."

"What a frightful story," said Black. He ordered coffee.

Matron became more human, more understanding. She forgot to smack her lips.

"We became ever so fond of the child, Sister and I," she said, "you couldn't help it. She had such a sweet nature. And we almost came to believe in her theory ourselves. She reminded us that Mary had only been a year or so younger than she was when Jesus was born, and that Joseph had tried to hide her away because he was shocked at her having a baby too. 'You see,' she told us, 'there'll be a great star in the sky the night my baby is born,' and sure enough, there was. It was only Venus, of course, but both Sister and I were glad for the child's sake it was there. It made it easier for her, took her mind off what was happening."

Matron drank her coffee and glanced at her watch.

"I ought to be going," she said; "we're doing a Caesarean at eight tomorrow morning, and I must have a good night's sleep."

"Finish your story first," said Black. "What was the end of it all?"

"She had her baby, and it was a boy, and I've never seen anything so sweet as that child sitting up in bed with her baby in her arms; it might have been a doll given her for a birthday present; she was so pleased she couldn't say a word. She just said, 'Oh, Matron, oh, Matron,' over and over again, and Lord knows I'm no softie, but I nearly cried, and so did Sister.

"But I can tell you one thing, whoever was responsible for that bit of work was a redhead. I remember saying to the child, 'Well, he's a proper little Carrots and no mistake,' and Carrots he became to all of us, and to the poor little girl as well. I don't ever want to go through again what happened when we parted them."

"Parted them?" asked Black.

"We had to do that. The father was taking her away, to begin a new life, and of course she couldn't do that with a baby, not a child her age. We kept her and Carrots for four weeks, and even then it was too long; she'd grown too attached to him. But it was all arranged, you see; the father was to fetch her, and the baby was to go to a home, and Sister and I talked it over, and we decided the only way to do it was to tell the poor child that Carrots had died in the night. So we told her that. But it was worse even than we thought. She turned dead white, and then she screamed. . . . I think I shall hear the sound of that scream to my dying day.

"It was terrible. High-pitched, queer. Then she fainted dead away, and we thought she would never come round and that she would die. We called in the doctor, which we don't do as a rule—we attend to our patients ourselves—and he said the whole thing was monstrous and that the shock of losing her baby might turn her mental. She came to, eventually. But do you know what had happened? She had lost her memory. She didn't recognise us, nor her father when he came, nor anyone. She remembered nothing of what had happened. Her memory had gone quite dead. She was well physically and mentally, but for that. The doctor said then it was the most merciful thing that could have happened. But if it ever came back, he said, it would be like waking up to hell for that poor little girl."

Black summoned the waiter and paid his bill.

"I'm sorry we've ended the evening on such a note of tragedy," he said, "but thank you very much for the story all the same. And I think you should include it in your memoirs when you come to write them. By the way, what happened to the baby?"

Matron reached for her gloves and her bag.

"They took him in at the St. Edmund's Home at Newquay," she said. "I had a friend on the Board of Governors and got it arranged, but it was quite a business. We called him Tom Smith—it seemed a safe, sound name—but I shall always think of him as Carrots. Poor lad, he will never know that in his mother's eyes he was destined to be the saviour of the world."

Black took Matron back to Sea View and promised to write as soon as he returned home, confirming the booking of the room. Then he ticked her and Carnleath off the list in his notebook, and beneath them wrote the words "St. Edmund's Home, Newquay." It seemed a pity to come all this way to the southwest and not drive a few miles further on what would be only a matter of routine. The matter of routine proved harder than he thought.

Homes for the offspring of unmarried mothers are not usually willing to discuss the whereabouts of the children handed to their care, and the superintendent of St. Edmund's Home was no exception to this rule.

"It doesn't do," he explained to Black; "the children know nothing but the home that brought them up. It would unsettle them if the parents ever tried to get in touch with them in after life. It might lead to all sorts of complications."

"I quite understand," said Black, "but in this case there could be no complications. The father was unknown, and the mother is dead."

"I have only your word for that," said the superintendent. "I'm sorry, but it's strictly against the rules to break silence. I can tell you one thing. The last we heard of the boy, he was going steady, in a good job as travelling salesman. I regret I cannot tell you any more than that."

"You've told me quite enough," said Black.

He went back to his car and looked at his notes.

It was not only in his mind that the superintendent's words had rung a bell, but in his notes as well.

The last person to see Lady Farren alive, except the butler, had been a travelling salesman touting orders for garden furniture.

Black drove north, to London.

The firm who made the garden furniture had its headquarters in Norwood, Middlesex. Black obtained the address by putting a call through to Sir John. The catalogue had been kept amongst all the other papers and letters belonging to Lady Farren.

"What is it? Are you on to anything?" Sir John asked over the telephone.

Black was cautious.

"Just a final checkup," he said; "I believe in being thorough. I will get in touch with you again as soon as possible."

He went to see the manager of the firm, and this time Black did not disguise his identity. He gave the manager his card and explained that he was employed by Sir John Farren to enquire into the last hours of the late Lady Farren, who—doubtless the manager had seen in the newspapers—had been found shot a week before. On the morning of her death she had given an order for garden seats to a travelling salesman for this firm. Would it be possible, Black asked, to see the man?

The manager was extremely sorry, but three salesmen were all away, and when they were travelling it was not possible to contact them. The distances they covered were large. Could Mr. Black give him the name of the particular salesman he wished to question? Yes, Tom Smith. The manager consulted his book. Tom Smith was quite a young fellow. This was his first round. He would not be due back at Norwood for another five days. If Mr. Black cared to see Smith at the earliest possible date, the manager suggested he should go to see him at his lodgings, on the evening of the fourth day, when he might have returned. He gave Black the address.

"Can you tell me," said Black, "if by any chance this young man has red hair?"

The manager smiled.

"Sherlock Holmes?" he said. "Yes, Tom Smith has a shock of red hair. You could warm your hands at it."

Black thanked him and left the office.

He wondered whether he should motor down to see Sir John right away. Was there any purpose in waiting four or five days to question young Smith? The pieces of the jigsaw fitted. The story was conclusive. Lady Farren must have recognised her son, and that was that. Yet . . . had she? The butler had taken in Lady Farren's glass of milk to the drawing-room after the salesman had left, and had found her perfectly normal. The pieces fitted, but there was still one little odd-shaped bit that was missing. Black decided to wait.

On the fourth evening he went down to Norwood about half-past seven, on the chance of finding that Tom Smith had returned. His luck held. The landlady, who opened the door to him, told him that Mr. Smith was having his supper, would he please come inside. She showed Black into a small sitting-room, where a young fellow, hardly more than a boy, was seated at the table, eating a plateful of kippers.

"Gentleman to see you, Mr. Smith," she said, and left the room.

Smith put down his knife and fork and wiped his mouth. He had a thin, rather pinched face, like a ferret, and his eyes were pale blue and close together. His red hair stuck up from his head like a brush. He was quite small in size.

"What's up?" he said. He was plainly on the defensive before Black had opened his lips to speak.

"My name is Black," said the detective pleasantly. "I'm from a private-enquiry agency, and I want to ask you a few questions if you don't mind."

Tom Smith rose to his feet. His eyes looked smaller than ever.

"What are you getting at?" he said. "I've not been doing anything."

Black lit a cigarette and sat down.

"I'm not suggesting you have," he said, "and I'm not here to look at your order book, if that's what's scaring you. But I happen to know that you visited a Lady Farren on your rounds just recently, and she gave you an order for two garden seats."

"What about it?"

"That's all. Tell me what happened at the interview."

Tom Smith continued to watch Black suspiciously. "All right," he said, "let's say I did go to this Lady Farren, let's say she did give me a couple of orders; I'll make it all right with the firm when I see them, if they've got wind of it. I can say I asked the cheque to be made out to me, through a mistake, and it won't happen again."

Black was reminded of Miss Marsh. Reminded, too, of the Reverend Henry Warner. Even of Mr. Johnson and his touchy self-defence. Why did people invariably lie when questioned about something else?

"I think," said Black, "it would be much simpler for you, and for your relations with your firm, if you told me the truth straightaway. If you do, I won't report on you, either to the firm or to the superintendent at St. Edmund's."

The young man shifted uneasily from one foot to the other. "You've come from them?" he said. "I might have known it. Always down on me, right from the start. Never had a chance, not me." A note of self-pity crept into his voice. He almost whined. The baby destined to save the world, thought Black, had obviously not made a conspicuous success of the job up to date.

"I'm not interested in your childhood," he said, "only in your very immediate past, and the interview you had with Lady Farren. You may not know it, but the lady is dead."

The boy nodded.

"Saw it in the evening paper," he said; "that's really what decided me to do it. She couldn't split on me."

"Do what?" asked Black.

"Spend the money," said Tom Smith, "and cross the order off my book, and say nothing to no one about it. Easy done."

Black smoked his cigarette, and he had a sudden vision of crowded tents, and lorries, and mattresses, dumped in a field where the hops grew beside tall poles, and bursts of laughter, and the smell of beer, and a shifty-eyed, redheaded fellow like this boy, hiding behind a lorry.

"Yes," said Black, "easy done, as you say. Tell me more."

Tom Smith became easier in manner. The detective wasn't going to say anything. Not if he told the truth. All right.

"Lady Farren was on the list of the big nobs in that district," he said, "plenty of money, I was told, and she'd be sure to give me an order. So I called there, and the butler showed me in, and I gave the lady my catalogue, and she chose two seats, and I asked for a cheque. She wrote it out, and I took it. No more to it than that."

"Wait a minute," said Black. "Was Lady Farren pleasant to you? Did she take any particular notice of you?"

The boy looked surprised.

"Notice of me?" he said. "No, why should she? I wasn't anyone. Just a chap trying to sell her garden seats."

"What did she say to you?" persisted Black.

"She just looked through the catalogue, and I stood by waiting, and she marked two items with a pencil, and then I said would she make out the cheque to bearer—I tried it on, see; she had that dumb sort of face that's easy to fool—and she didn't bat an eye, but went to the desk and wrote out the cheque.

"Twenty quid it was. Ten pound a seat. And I said good morning, and she rang for the butler, and he showed me out. I went off and cashed the cheque right away. I put the money in my wallet, and even then I wasn't sure about spending it or not, but when I saw in the paper the lady was dead, I said to myself, 'Here I go.' Well, you can't blame me. It's the first chance I ever had to make a bit of money no one knew anything about."

Black extinguished his cigarette.

"First chance, and you use it dishonestly," he said, "your choice, and your future. Ashamed of yourself?"

"No one's ashamed till he's caught out," said Tom Smith. And suddenly he smiled. The smile illuminated the pale ferret face, deepened the light blue eyes. The furtiveness went, and in its place shone a strange, engaging innocence.

"I see now that dodge didn't work," he said. "I'll try something else next time."

"Try saving the world," said Black.

"Eh?" said Tom Smith.

Black said good-bye and wished him good luck, and as he walked away down the street he was conscious that the boy had come out on to the doorstep and was watching him.

That afternoon Black went down to report to Sir John Farren, but before being shown into the library, he asked the butler to have a word with him alone. They went to the drawing-room.

"You brought the traveller into this room, and you left him with Lady Farren, then after five minutes or so Lady Farren rang, and you showed the salesman out. After that, you came in again with Lady Farren's glass of milk. Is that correct?"

"Quite correct, sir," said the butler.

"When you came with the glass of milk, what was her ladyship doing?"

"She was just standing, sir, much where you are now, and she was glancing through the catalogue."

"She looked just as usual?"

"Yes, sir."

"What happened then? I've asked you this before, but I must just check again before reporting to Sir John."

The butler considered.

"I gave her ladyship the milk. I asked if there were orders for the chauffeur, and she said no, Sir John would be driving her in the afternoon. She told me she had ordered two garden seats, and she showed me them marked in the catalogue. I said they would be useful. I saw her put the catalogue down on the desk, and she walked towards the window, to drink the glass of milk."

"She said nothing else? She didn't refer to the salesman at all who had brought the catalogue?"

"No, sir. Her ladyship didn't remark on him. But I remember I did, just as I was leaving the room, but I'm sure her ladyship didn't hear what I said, because she never answered me."

"What did you say?"

"I said, joking-like, her ladyship enjoyed a bit of humour, that if the traveller called again I'd know who he was because of his hair.

" 'Proper little Carrots he is, and no mistake,' I said. Then I closed the door and went to my pantry."

"Thank you," said Black, "that's all."

He stood looking out across the garden. Presently Sir John came into the room.

"I expected you in the library," he said. "Have you been here long?"

"Only a few minutes," said Black.

"Well. And what's the verdict?"

"The same as before, Sir John."

"You mean, we're back where we started from? You can't show me any reason why my wife should have killed herself?"

"None at all. I have come to the conclusion that the doctor's opinion was right. A sudden impulse, owing to her condition, made Lady Farren go to the gun room, take up your revolver, and shoot herself. She was happy, contented, and as you and everybody else knows, Sir John, she had led a blameless life.

"There was absolutely no motive for what she did."

"Thank God," said Sir John.

Black had never before considered himself a sentimentalist. Now he was no longer so sure.

"What happened then?" [illegible] on the stairs [illegible]
[illegible]
The [illegible]

[illegible]

[illegible]

[illegible]

"Where did [illegible]?"

[illegible]

[illegible]

[illegible]

[illegible]

[illegible]

[illegible]

Die like a Dog

BY REX STOUT

FROM "THREE WITNESSES" BY REX STOUT.

CHAPTER I

I DO SOMETIMES treat myself to a walk in the rain, though I prefer sunshine when there's not enough wind to give the dust a whirl. That rainy Wednesday, however, there was a special inducement: I wanted his raincoat to be good and wet when I delivered it. So with it on my back and my old brown felt on my head, I left the house and set out for Arbor Street, some two miles south in the Village.

Halfway there the rain stopped and my blood had pumped me warm, so I took the coat off, folded it wet side in, hung it on my arm, and proceeded. Arbor Street, narrow and only three blocks long, had on either side an assortment of old brick houses, mostly of four stories, which were neither spick nor span. Number 29 would be about the middle of the first block.

I reached it, but I didn't enter it. There was a party going on in the middle of the block. A police car was double-parked in front of the entrance to one of the houses, and a uniformed cop was on the sidewalk in an attitude of authority toward a small gathering of citizens confronting him. As I approached I heard him demanding, "Whose dog is this?"—referring, evidently, to an animal with a wet black coat standing behind him. I heard no one claim the dog, but I wouldn't have anyway, because my attention was diverted. Another police car rolled up and stopped behind the first one, and a man got out, pushed through the crowd to the sidewalk, nodded to the cop without halting, and went in the entrance, above which appeared the number 29.

The trouble was, I knew the man, which is an understatement. I do not begin to tremble at the sight of Sergeant Purley Stebbins of Manhattan Homicide West, which is also an understatement, but his presence and manner made it a cinch that there was a corpse in that house, and if I demanded entry on the ground that I wanted to swap raincoats with a guy who had walked off with mine, there was no question what would happen. My prompt appearance at the scene of a homicide would arouse all of Purley's worst instincts, backed up by reference to various precedents, and I might not get home in time for dinner, which was going to be featured by grilled squab with a brown sauce which Fritz calls *Vénitienne* and is one of his best.

Purley had disappeared within without spotting me. The cop was a complete stranger. As I slowed down to detour past him on the narrow sidewalk he gave me an eye and demanded, "That your dog?"

The dog was nuzzling my knee, and I stopped to give him a pat on his wet black head. Then, telling the cop he wasn't mine, I went on by. At the next corner I turned right, heading back uptown. I kept my eye peeled for a taxi the first couple of blocks, saw none, and decided to finish the walk. A wind had started in from the west, but everything was still damp from the rain.

Marching along, I was well on my way before I saw the dog. Stopping for a light on Ninth Avenue in the Twenties, I felt something at my knee, and there he was. My hand started for his head in reflex, but I pulled it back. I was in a fix. Apparently he had picked me for a pal, and if I just went on he would follow, and you can't chase a dog on Ninth Avenue by throwing rocks. I could have ditched him by taking a taxi the rest of the way, but that would have been pretty rude after the appreciation he had shown of my charm. He had a collar on with a tag, and could be identified, and the station house was only a few blocks away, so the simplest and cheapest way was to convoy him there. I moved to the curb to look for a taxi coming downtown, and as I did so a cyclone sailed around the corner and took my hat with it into the middle of the avenue.

I didn't dash out into the traffic, but you should have seen that dog. He sprang across the bow of a big truck, wiping its left front fender with his tail, braked landing to let a car by, sprang again, and was under another car—or I thought he was—and then I saw him on the opposite sidewalk. He snatched the hat from under the feet of a pedestrian, turned on a dime, and started back. This time his crossing wasn't so spectacular, but he didn't dally. He came to me and stood, lifting his head and wagging his tail. I took the hat. It had skimmed a puddle of water on its trip, but I thought he would be disappointed if I didn't put it on, so I did. Naturally that settled it. I flagged a cab, took the dog in with me, and gave the driver the address of Wolfe's house.

My idea was to take my hat hound upstairs to my room, give him some refreshment, and phone the ASPCA to send for him. But there was no sense in passing up such an opportunity for a little buzz at Wolfe, so after letting us in and leaving my hat and the raincoat on the rack in the hall, I proceeded to the door to the office and entered.

"Where the devil have you been?" Wolfe asked grumpily. "We were going over some lists at six o'clock, and it's a quarter to seven."

He was in his oversized chair behind his desk with a book, and his eyes hadn't left the page to spare me a glance. I answered him. "Taking that damn raincoat. Only I didn't deliver it, because—"

"What's that?" he snapped. He was glaring at my companion.

"A dog."

"I see it is. I'm in no temper for buffoonery. Get it out of here."

"Yes, sir, right away. I can keep him in my room most of the time, but of course he'll have to come downstairs and through the hall when I take him out. He's a hat hound. There is a sort of a problem. His name is

Nero, which, as you know, means 'black,' and of course I'll have to change it. Ebony would do, or Jet, or Inky, or—"

"Bah. Flummery!"

"No, sir. I get pretty darned lonesome around here, especially during the four hours a day you're up in the plant rooms. You have your orchids, and Fritz has his turtle, and Theodore has his parakeets up in the potting room, and why shouldn't I have a dog? I admit I'll have to change his name, though he is registered as Champion Nero Charcoal of Bantyscoot. I have suggested . . ."

I went on talking only because I had to. It was a fizzle. I had expected to induce a major outburst, even possibly something as frantic as Wolfe leaving his chair to evict the beast himself, and there he was gazing at Nero with an expression I had never seen him aim at any human, including me. I went on talking, forcing it.

He broke in. "It's not a hound. It's a Labrador retriever."

That didn't faze me. I'm never surprised at a display of knowledge by a bird who reads as many books as Wolfe does. "Yes, sir," I agreed. "I only said hound because it would be natural for a private detective to have a hound."

"Labradors," he said, "have a wider skull than any other dog, for brain room. A dog I had when I was a boy, in Montenegro, a small brown mongrel, had a rather narrow skull, but I did not regard it as a defect. I do not remember that I considered that dog to have a defect. Today I suppose I would be more critical. When you smuggled that creature in here did you take into account the disruption it would cause in this household?"

It had backfired on me. I had learned something new about the big fat genius: he would enjoy having a dog around, provided he could blame it on me and so be free to beef when he felt like it. As for me, when I retire to the country I'll have a dog, and maybe two, but not in town.

I snapped into reverse. "I guess I didn't," I confessed. "I do feel the need for a personal pet, but what the hell, I can try a canary or a chameleon. Okay, I'll get rid of him. After all, it's your house."

"I do not want to feel responsible," he said stiffly, "for your privation. I would almost rather put up with its presence than with your reproaches."

"Forget it." I waved a hand. "I'll try to. I promise not to rub it in."

"Another thing," he persisted. "I refuse to interfere with any commitment you have made."

"I have made no commitment."

"Then where did you get it?"

"Well, I'll tell you."

I went and sat at my desk and did so. Nero, the four-legged one, came and lay at my feet with his nose just not touching the toe of my shoe. I reported the whole event, with as much detail as if I had been reporting a vital operation in a major case, and, when I had finished, Wolfe was of course quite aware that my presentation of Nero as a permanent addition to the staff had been a plant. Ordinarily he would have made his opinion of my performance clear, but this time he skipped it, and it was easy to see why. The idea of having a dog that he could blame on me had got in and stuck.

When I came to the end and stopped there was a moment's silence, and then he said, "Jet would be an acceptable name for that dog."

"Yeah." I swiveled and reached for the phone. "I'll call the ASPCA to come for him."

"No." He was emphatic.

"Why not?"

"Because there is a better alternative. Call someone you know in the Police Department—anyone. Give him the number on the dog's tag, and ask him to find out who the owner is. Then you can inform the owner directly."

He was playing for time. It could happen that the owner was dead or in jail or didn't want the dog back, and if so Wolfe could take the position that I had committed myself by bringing the dog home in a taxi and that it would be dishonorable to renege. However, I didn't want to argue, so I phoned a precinct sergeant who I knew was disposed to do me small favors. He took Nero's number and said it might take a while at that time of day, and he would call me back. As I hung up, Fritz entered to announce dinner.

The squabs with that sauce were absolutely edible, as they always are, but other phenomena in the next couple of hours were not so pleasing. The table talk in the dining room was mostly one-sided and mostly about dogs. Wolfe kept it on a high level—no maudlin sentiment. He maintained that the basenji was the oldest breed on earth, having originated in Central Africa around 5000 B.C., whereas there was no trace of the Afghan hound earlier than around 4000 B.C. To me all it proved was that he had read a book I hadn't noticed him with.

Nero ate in the kitchen with Fritz and made a hit. Wolfe had told Fritz to call him Jet. When Fritz brought in the salad he announced that Jet had wonderful manners and was very smart.

"Nevertheless," Wolfe asked, "wouldn't you think him an insufferable nuisance as a cohabitant?"

On the contrary, Fritz declared, he would be most welcome.

After dinner, feeling that the newly formed Canine Canonizing League needed slowing down, I first took Nero out for a brief tour and, returning, escorted him up the two flights to my room and left him there. I had to admit he was well behaved. If I had wanted to take on a dog in town it could have been him. In my room I told him to lie down, and he did, and when I went to the door to leave, his eyes, which were the color of caramel, made it plain that he would love to come along, but he didn't get up.

Down in the office Wolfe and I got at the lists. They were special offerings from orchid growers and collectors from all over the world, and it was quite a job to check the thousands of items and pick the few that Wolfe might want to give a try. I sat at his desk, across from him, with trays of cards from our files, and we were in the middle of it, around ten-thirty, when the doorbell rang. I went to the hall and flipped a light switch and saw out on the stoop, through the one-way glass panel in the door, a familiar figure—Inspector Cramer of Homicide.

I went to the door, opened it six inches, and asked politely, "Now what?"

"I want to see Wolfe."

"It's pretty late. What about?"

"About a dog."

It is understood that no visitor, and especially no officer of the law, is to be conducted to the office until Wolfe has been consulted, but this seemed to rate an exception. Wolfe had been known to refuse an audience to people who topped inspectors, and, told that Cramer had come to see him about a dog, there was no telling how he might react in the situation as it had developed.

I considered the matter for about two seconds and then swung the door open and invited cordially, "Step right in."

CHAPTER II

"PROPERLY SPEAKING," Cramer declared as one who wanted above all to be perfectly fair and square, "it's Goodwin I want information from."

He was in the red leather chair at the end of Wolfe's desk, just about filling it. His big round face was no redder than usual, his gray eyes no colder, his voice no gruffer. Merely normal.

Wolfe came at me. "Then why did you bring him in here without even asking?"

Cramer interfered for me. "I asked for you. Of course you're in it. I want to know where the dog fits in. Where is it, Goodwin?"

That set the tone—again normal. He does sometimes call me Archie, after all the years, but it's exceptional. I inquired, "Dog?"

His lips tightened. "All right, I'll spell it. You phoned the precinct and gave them a tag number and wanted to know who owns the dog. When the sergeant learned that the owner was a man named Philip Kampf, who was murdered this afternoon in a house at twenty-nine Arbor

Street, he notified Homicide. The officer who had been on post in front of that house had told us that the dog had gone off with a man who had said it wasn't his dog. After we learned of your inquiry about the owner, the officer was shown a picture of you and said it was you who enticed the dog. He's outside in my car. Do you want to bring him in?"

"No, thanks. I didn't entice."

"The dog followed you."

I gestured modestly. "Girls follow me, dogs follow me, sometimes even your own dicks follow me. I can't help—"

"Skip the comedy. The dog belonged to a murder victim, and you removed it from the scene of the murder. Where is it?"

Wolfe butted in. "You persist," he objected, "in imputing an action to Mr. Goodwin without warrant. He did not 'remove' the dog. I advise you to shift your ground if you expect us to listen."

His tone was firm but not hostile. I cocked an eye at him. He was probably being indulgent because he had learned that Jet's owner was dead.

"I've got another ground," Cramer asserted. "A man who lives in that house, named Richard Meegan, and who was in it at the time Kampf was murdered, has stated that he came here to see you this morning and asked you to do a job for him. He says you refused the job. That's what he says." Cramer jutted his chin. "Now. A man at the scene of a murder admits he consulted you this morning. Goodwin shows up at the scene half an hour after the murder was committed, and he entices—okay, put it that the dog goes away with him, the dog that belonged to the victim and had gone to that house with him. How does that look?" He pulled his chin in. "You know damn well the last thing I want in a homicide is to find you or Goodwin anywhere within ten miles of it, because I know from experience what to expect. But when you're there, there you are, and I want to know how and why and what, and by God I intend to. Where's the dog?"

Wolfe sighed and shook his head. "In this instance," he said, almost genial, "you're wasting your time. As for Mr. Meegan, he phoned this morning to make an appointment and came at eleven. Our conversation was brief. He wanted a man shadowed, but divulged no name or any other specific detail because in his first breath he mentioned his wife—he was overwrought—and I gathered that his difficulty was marital. As you know, I don't touch that kind of work, and I stopped him. My vanity bristles even at an offer of that sort of job. My bluntness enraged him, and he dashed out. On his way he took his hat from the rack in the hall, and he took Mr. Goodwin's raincoat instead of his own. Archie. Proceed."

Cramer's eyes came to me, and I obeyed. "I didn't find out about the switch in coats until the middle of the afternoon. His was the same color as mine, but mine's newer. When he phoned for an appointment this morning he gave me his name and address, and I wanted to phone him to tell him to bring my coat back, but he wasn't listed, and Information said she didn't have him, so I decided to go get it. I walked, wearing Meegan's coat. There was a cop and a crowd and a PD car in front of twenty-nine Arbor Street, and, as I approached, another PD car came, and Purley Stebbins got out and went in, so I decided to skip it, not wanting to go through the torture. There was a dog present, and he nuzzled me, and I patted him. I will admit, if pressed, that I should not have patted him. The cop asked me if the dog was mine, and I said no and went on, and headed for home. I was—"

"Did you call the dog or signal it?"

"No. I was at Twenty-eighth and Ninth Avenue before I knew he was tailing me. I did not entice or remove. If I did, if there's some kind of a dodge about the dog, please tell me why I phoned the precinct to get the name of his owner."

"I don't know. With Wolfe and you I never know. Where is it?"

I blurted it out before Wolfe could stop me. "Upstairs in my room."

"Bring it down here."

"Right."

I was up and going, but Wolfe called me sharply. "Archie!"

I turned. "Yes, sir."

"There's no frantic urgency." He went to Cramer. "The animal seems intelligent, but I doubt if it's up to answering questions. I don't want it capering around my office."

"Neither do I."

"Then why bring it down?"

"I'm taking it downtown. We want to try something with it."

Wolfe pursed his lips. "I doubt if that's feasible. Sit down, Archie. Mr. Goodwin has assumed an obligation and will have to honor it. The creature has no master, and so, presumably, no home. It will have to be tolerated here until Mr. Goodwin gets satisfactory assurance of its future welfare. Archie?"

If we had been alone I would have made my position clear, but with Cramer there I was stuck. "Absolutely," I agreed.

"You see," he told Cramer. "I'm afraid we can't permit the dog's removal."

"Nuts. I'm taking it."

"Indeed? What writ have you? Replevin? Warrant for arrest as a material witness?"

Cramer opened his mouth and shut it again. He put his elbows on the chair arms, interlaced his fingers, and leaned forward. "Look. You and Meegan check, either because you're both telling it straight, or because you've framed it, I don't know which, and we'll see. But I'm taking the dog. Kampf, the man who was killed, lived on Perry Street, a few blocks away from Arbor Street. He arrived at twenty-nine Arbor Street, with the dog on a leash, about five-twenty this afternoon. The janitor of the house, named Olsen, lives in the basement, and he was sitting at his front window, and he saw Kampf arrive with the dog and turn in at the entrance. About ten minutes later he saw the dog come out, with no leash, and right after the dog a man came out. The man was Victor Talento, a lawyer, the tenant of the ground-floor apartment. Talento says he left his apartment to go to an appointment, saw the dog in the hall, thought it was a stray, and chased it out, and that's all he knows. Anyhow, Olsen says Talento walked off, and the dog stayed there on the sidewalk."

Cramer unlaced his fingers and sat back. "About twenty minutes later, around ten minutes to six, Olsen heard someone yelling his name and went to the rear and up one flight to the ground-floor hall. Two men were there, a live one and a dead one. The live one was Ross Chaffee, a painter, the tenant of the top-floor studio—that's the fourth floor. The dead one was the man that had arrived with the dog. He had been strangled with the dog's leash, and the body was at the bottom of the stairs leading up. Chaffee says he found it when he came down to go to an appointment, and that's all he knows. He stayed there while Olsen went downstairs to phone. A squad car arrived at five-fifty-eight. Sergeant Stebbins arrived at six-ten. Goodwin arrived at six-ten. Excellent timing."

Wolfe merely grunted. Cramer continued, "You can have it all. The dog's leash was in the pocket of Kampf's raincoat, which was on him. The laboratory says it was used to strangle him. The routine is still in process. I'll answer questions within reason. The four tenants of the house were all there when Kampf arrived: Victor Talento, the lawyer, on the ground floor; Richard Meegan, whose job you say you wouldn't take, second floor; Jerome Aland, a night-club performer, third floor; and Ross Chaffee, the painter with the studio. Aland says he was sound asleep until we banged on his door and took him down to look at the corpse. Meegan says he heard nothing and knows nothing."

Cramer sat forward again. "Okay, what happened? Kampf went there to see one of those four men, and had his dog with him. It's possible he took the leash off in the lower hall to leave the dog there, but I doubt it. At least it's just as possible that he took the dog along to the door of one of the apartments, and the dog was wet and the tenant wouldn't let it enter, so Kampf left it outside. Another possibility is that the dog was actually present when Kampf was killed, but we'll know more about that after we see and handle the dog. The particular thing we want—we're going to take the dog in that house and see which door it goes to. We're going to do that now. There's a man out in my car who knows dogs." Cramer stood up.

Wolfe shook his head. "You must be hard put. You say Mr. Kampf lived on Perry Street. With a family?"

"No. Bachelor. Some kind of a writer. He didn't have to make a living; he had means."

"Then the beast is orphaned. He's in your room, Archie?"

"Yes, sir." I got up and started for the door.

Wolfe halted me. "One moment. Go up and in, lock your door, and stay there till I notify you. Go!"

I went. It was either that or quit my job on the spot, and I resign only when we haven't got company. Also, assuming that there was a valid reason for refusing to surrender the dog to the cops, Wolfe was justified. Cramer, needing no warrant to enter the house because he was already in, wouldn't hesitate to mount to my room to do his own fetching, and stopping him physically would have raised some delicate points. Whereas breaking through a locked door would be another matter.

I didn't lock it, because it hadn't been locked for years and I didn't remember which drawer of my chest the key was in, and while I was searching Cramer might conceivably have made it up the carpeted stairs and come right in, so I left it open and stood on the sill to listen. If I heard him coming I would shut it and brace it with my foot. Nero, or Jet, depending on where you stand, came over to me, but I ordered him back, and he went without a murmur. From below came voices, not cordial, but not raised enough for me to get words. Before long there was the sound of Cramer's heavy steps leaving the office and tramping along the hall, and then the slam of the front door.

I called down, "All clear?"

"No!" It was a bellow. "Wait till I bolt it!" And after a moment: "All right!"

I shut my door and went to the stairs and descended. Wolfe was back in his chair behind his desk, sitting straight. As I entered he snapped at me, "A pretty mess! You sneak a dog in here to badger me, and what now?"

I crossed to my desk, sat, and spoke calmly. "We're way beyond that. You will never admit you bollixed it up yourself, so forget it. When you ask me what now, that's easy. I could say I'll take the dog down and deliver him at Homicide, but we're beyond that too. Not only have you learned that he is orphaned, as you put it, which sounds terrible, and therefore adopting him will probably be simple, but also you have taken a stand with Cramer, and of course you won't back up. If we sit tight with the door bolted I suppose I can take the dog out back for his outings, but what if the law shows up tomorrow with a writ?"

He leaned back and shut his eyes. I looked up at the wall clock: two minutes past eleven. I looked at my wristwatch: also two minutes past eleven. They both said six minutes past when Wolfe opened his eyes.

"From Mr. Cramer's information," he said, "I doubt if that case holds any formidable difficulties."

I had no comment.

"If it were speedily solved," he went on, "your commitment to the dog could be honored at leisure. I had thought until now that my disinclination to permit a policeman to storm in here and commandeer any person or object in this house that struck his fancy was shared by you."

"It is. Within reason."

"That's an ambiguous phrase, and I must be allowed my own interpretation short of absurdity. Clearly the simplest way to settle this matter is to find out who killed Mr. Kampf. It may not be much of a job; if it proves otherwise we can reconsider. An immediate exploration is the thing, and luckily we have a pretext for it. You can go there to get your raincoat, taking Mr. Meegan's with you, and proceed as the occasion offers. The best course would be to bring him here, but, as you know, I wholly rely on your discretion and enterprise in such a juncture."

"Thank you very much," I said bitterly. "You mean now."

"Yes."

"They may still have Meegan downtown."

"I doubt if they'll keep him overnight. In the morning they'll probably have him again."

"I'll have to take the dog out first."

"Fritz will take him out back in the court."

"I'll be damned." I arose. "No client, no fee, no nothing except a dog with a wide skull for brain room." I crossed to the door, turned, said distinctly, "I will be damned," went to the rack for my hat and Meegan's coat, and beat it.

CHAPTER III

THE RAIN HAD ENDED, and the wind was down. After dismissing the taxi at the end of Arbor Street, I walked to number 29, with the raincoat hung over my arm. There was light behind the curtains of the windows on the ground floor, but none anywhere above, and none in the basement. Entering the vestibule, I inspected the labels in the slots between the mailboxes and the buttons. From the bottom up they read: Talento, Meegan, Aland, and Chaffee. I pushed the button above Meegan, put my hand on the doorknob, and waited. No click. I twisted the knob, and it wouldn't turn. Another long push on the button, and a longer wait. I varied it by trying four short pushes. Nothing doing.

I left the vestibule and was confronted by two couples standing on the sidewalk staring at me, or at the entrance. They exchanged words, decided they didn't care for my returning stare, and passed on. I considered pushing the button of Victor Talento, the lawyer who lived on the ground floor, where light was showing, voted to wait a while for Meegan, with whom I had an in, moved down ten paces to a fire hydrant, and propped myself against it.

I hadn't been there long enough to shift position more than a couple of times when the light disappeared on the ground floor of number 29, and a little later the vestibule door opened and a man came out. He turned toward me, gave me a glance as he passed, and kept going. Thinking it unlikely that any occupant of that house was being extended the freedom of the city that night, I cast my eyes around, and sure enough, when the subject had gone some thirty paces a figure emerged from an areaway across the street and started strolling. I shook my head in disapproval. I would have waited until the guy was ten paces farther. Saul Panzer would have made it ten more than that, but Saul is the best tailer alive.

As I stood deploring that faulty performance, an idea hit me. They might keep Meegan downtown another two hours, or all night, or he might even be up in his bed asleep. This was at least a chance to take a stab at something. I shoved off, in the direction taken by the subject, who was now a block away. Stepping along, I gained on him. A little beyond the corner I was abreast of the city employee, who was keeping to the other side of the street; but I wasn't interested in him. It seemed to me that the subject was upping the stroke a little, so I did too, really marching, and as he reached the next intersection I was beside him. He had looked over his shoulder when he heard me coming up behind, but hadn't slowed. As I reached him I spoke.

"Victor Talento?"

"No comment," he said and kept going. So did I.

"Thanks for the compliment," I said, "but I'm not a reporter. My name's Archie Goodwin, and I work for Nero Wolfe. If you'll stop a second I'll show you my credentials."

"I'm not interested in your credentials."

"Okay. If you just came out for a breath of air you won't be interested in this either. Otherwise you may be. Please don't scream or look around, but you've got a Homicide dick on your tail. Don't look or he'll know I'm telling you. He's across the street, ninety feet back."

"Yes," he conceded, without changing pace, "that's interesting. Is this your good deed for the day?"

"No. I'm out dowsing for Mr. Wolfe. He's investigating a murder just for practice, and I'm looking for a seam. I thought if I gave you a break you might feel like reciprocating. If you're just out for a walk, forget it, and sorry I interrupted. If you're headed for something you'd like to keep private maybe you could use some expert advice. In this part of town at this time of night there are only two approved methods for shaking a tail, and I'd be glad to oblige."

He looked it over for half a block, with me keeping step, and then spoke. "You mentioned credentials."

"Right. We might as well stop under that light. The dick will keep his distance."

We stopped. I got out my wallet and let him have a look at my licenses, detective and driver's. He didn't skimp it, being a lawyer. I put my wallet back.

"Of course," he said, "I was aware that I might be followed."

"Sure."

"I intended to take precautions. But it may not be—I suppose it's not as simple as it seems. I have had no experience at this kind of maneuver. Who hired Wolfe to investigate?"

"I don't know. He says he needs practice."

"All right, if it's qualified." He stood sizing me up by the street light. He was an inch shorter than me, and some older, with his weight starting to collect around the middle. He was dark-skinned, with eyes to match, and his nose hooked to point down. I didn't prod him. My lucky stab had snagged him, and it was his problem. He was working on it.

"I have an appointment," he said.

I waited.

He went on. "A woman phoned me, and I arranged to meet her. My wire could have been tapped."

"I doubt it. They're not that fast."

"I suppose not. The woman had nothing to do with the murder, and neither had I, but of course anything I do and anyone I see is suspect. I have no right to expose her to possible embarrassment, and I can't be sure of shaking that man off."

I grinned at him. "And me too."

"You mean you would follow me?"

"Certainly, for practice. And I'd like to see how you handle it."

He wasn't returning my grin. "I see you've earned your reputation, Goodwin. You'd be wasting your time, because this woman has no connection with this business, but I should have known better than to make this appointment. I won't keep it. It's only three blocks from here. You might be willing to go and tell her I'm not coming, and I'll get in touch with her tomorrow. Yes?"

"Sure, if it's only three blocks. If you'll return the favor by calling on Nero Wolfe for a little talk. That's what I meant by reciprocating."

He considered it. "Not tonight."

"Tonight would be best."

"No. I'm all in."

"Tomorrow morning at eleven?"

"Yes, I can make it then."

"Okay." I gave him the address. "If you forget it, it's in the book. Now brief me."

He took a respectable roll of bills from his pocket and peeled off a twenty. "Since you're acting as my agent, you have a right to a fee."

I grinned again. "That's a neat idea, you being a lawyer, but I'm not acting as your agent. I'm doing you a favor on request and expecting one in return. Where's the appointment?"

He put the roll back. "Have it your way. The woman's name is Jewel Jones, and she's at the southeast corner of Christopher and Grove Streets, or will be." He looked at his wrist. "We were to meet there at midnight. She's medium height, slender, dark hair and eyes, very good-looking. Tell her why I'm not coming, and say she'll hear from me tomorrow."

"Right. You'd better take a walk in the other direction to keep the dick occupied, and don't look back."

He wanted to shake hands to show his appreciation, but that would have been just as bad as taking the twenty, since before another midnight Wolfe might be tagging him for murder, so I pretended not to notice. He headed east, and I headed west, moving right along without turning my head for a glimpse of the dick. I had to make sure that he didn't see a vision and switch subjects, but I let that wait until I got to Christopher Street. Reaching it, I turned the corner, went twenty feet to a stoop, slid behind it with only my head out, and counted a slow hundred. There were passers-by, a couple and a guy in a hurry, but no dick. I went on a block to Grove Street, passed the intersection, saw no loitering female, continued for a distance, and turned and backtracked. I was on the fifth lap, and it was eight minutes past twelve, when a taxi stopped at the corner, a woman got out, and the taxi rolled off.

I approached. The light could have been better, but she seemed to meet the specifications. I stopped and asked, "Jones?" She drew herself up. I said, "From Victor."

She tilted her head back to get my face. "Who are you?" She seemed a little out of breath.

"Victor sent me with a message, but naturally I have to be sure it reaches the right party. I've ante'd half of your name and half of his, so it's your turn."

"Who are you?"

I shook my head. "You go first, or no message from Victor."

"Where is he?"

"No. I'll count ten and go. One, two, three, four—"

"My name is Jewel Jones. His is Victor Talento."

"That's the girl. I'll tell you." I did so. Since it was desirable for her to grasp the situation fully, I started with my propping myself on the fire hydrant in front of 29 Arbor Street and went on from there, as it happened, including, of course, my name and status. By the time I finished she had developed a healthy frown.

"Damn it," she said with feeling. She moved and put a hand on my arm. "Come and put me in a taxi."

I stayed planted. "I'll be glad to, and it will be on me. We're going to Nero Wolfe's place."

"We?" She removed the hand. "You're crazy."

"One will get you ten I'm not. Look at it. You and Talento made an appointment at a street corner, so you had some good reason for not wanting to be seen together tonight. It must have been something fairly urgent. I admit the urgency didn't have to be connected with the murder of Philip Kampf, but it could be, and it certainly has to be discussed. I don't want to be arbitrary. I can take you to a Homicide sergeant named Stebbins, and you can discuss it with him; or I'll take you to Mr. Wolfe. I should think you'd prefer Mr. Wolfe, but suit yourself."

She had well-oiled gears. For a second, as I spoke, her eyes flashed like daggers, but then they went soft and appealing. She took my arm again, this time with both hands. "I'll discuss it with you," she said, in a voice she could have used to defrost her refrigerator. "I wouldn't mind that. We'll go somewhere."

I said come on, and we moved, with her maintaining contact with a hand hooked cozily on my arm. We hadn't gone far, toward Seventh Avenue, when a taxi came along and I flagged it and we got in. I told the driver, "Nine-eighteen West Thirty-fifth," and he started.

"What's that?" Miss Jones demanded.

I told her, Nero Wolfe's house. The poor girl didn't know what to do. If she called me a rat that wouldn't help her any. If she kicked and screamed I would merely give the hackie another address. Her best bet was to try to thaw me, and if she had had time for a real campaign, say four or five hours, she might conceivably have made some progress, because she had a knack for it. She didn't coax or argue; she just told me how she knew I was the kind of man she could tell anything to and I would believe her and understand her, and after she had done that she would be willing to go anywhere or do anything I advised, but she was sure I wouldn't want to take advantage . . .

There just wasn't time enough. The taxi rolled to the curb, and I had a bill ready for the driver. I got out, gave her a hand, and escorted her up the seven steps of the stoop, applauding her economy in not wasting breath on protests. My key wouldn't let us in, since the chain bolt would be on, so I pushed the button, and in a moment the stoop light shone on us, and in another the door opened. I motioned her in and followed. Fritz was there.

"Mr. Wolfe up?" I asked.

"In the office." He was giving Miss Jones a look, the look he gives any strange female who enters that house. There is always in his mind the possibility, however remote, that she will bewitch Wolfe into a mania for a mate. After asking him to conduct her to the front room, and putting my hat and the raincoat on the rack, I went on down the hall and entered the office.

Wolfe was at his desk, reading, and curled up in the middle of the room, on the best rug in the house, which was given to Wolfe years ago as a token of gratitude by an Armenian merchant who had got himself in a bad hole, was the dog. The dog greeted me by lifting his head and tapping the rug with his tail. Wolfe greeted me by raising his eyes from the book and grunting.

"I brought company," I told him. "Before I introduce her I should—"

"Her? The tenants of that house are all men! I might have known you'd dig up a woman!"

"I can chase her if you don't want her. This is how I got her." I proceeded, not dragging it out, but including all the essentials. I ended up, "I could have taken her to a spot I know of and grilled her myself, but it would have been risky. Just in a six-minute taxi ride she had me feeling —uh, brotherly. Do you want her or not?"

"Confound it." His eyes went to his book and stayed there long enough to finish a paragraph. He dog-eared it and put it down. "Very well, bring her."

I crossed to the connecting door to the front room, opened it, and requested, "Please come in, Miss Jones." She came, and as she passed through gave me a wistful smile that might have gone straight to my heart if there hadn't been a diversion. As she entered, the dog suddenly sprang to his feet, whirling, and made for her with sounds of unmistakable pleasure. He stopped in front of her, raising his head so she wouldn't have to reach far to pat it, and wagged his tail so fast it was only a blur.

"Indeed," Wolfe said. "How do you do, Miss Jones. I am Nero Wolfe. What's the dog's name?"

I claim she was good. The presence of the dog was a complete surprise to her. But without the slightest sign of fluster she put out a hand to give it a gentle pat, looked around, spotted the red leather chair, went to it, and sat.

"That's a funny question right off," she said, not complaining. "Asking me your dog's name."

"Pfui." Wolfe was disgusted. "I don't know what position you were going to take, but from what Mr. Goodwin tells me I would guess you were going to say that the purpose of your appointment with Mr. Talento was a personal matter that had nothing to do with Mr. Kampf or his death, and that you knew Mr. Kampf either slightly and casually or not at all. Now the dog has made that untenable. Obviously he knows you well, and he belonged to Mr. Kampf. So you knew Mr. Kampf well. If you try to deny that you'll have Mr. Goodwin and other trained men digging all around you, your past and your present, and that will be extremely disagreeable, no matter how innocent you may be of murder or any other wrongdoing. You won't like that. What's the dog's name?"

She looked at me, and I met it. In good light I would have qualified Talento's specification of "very good-looking." Not that she was unsightly, but she caught the eye more by what she looked than how she looked. It wasn't just something she turned on as needed; it was there even now, when she must have been pretty busy deciding how to handle it.

It took her only a few seconds to decide. "His name is Bootsy," she said. The dog, at her feet, lifted his head and wagged his tail.

"Good heavens," Wolfe muttered. "No other name?"

"Not that I know of."

"Your name is Jewel Jones?"

"Yes. I sing in a night club, the Flamingo, but I'm not working right now." She made a little gesture, very appealing, but it was Wolfe who had to resist it, not me. "Believe me, Mr. Wolfe, I don't know anything about that murder. If I knew anything that could help I'd be perfectly willing to tell you, because I'm sure you're the kind of man that understands and you wouldn't want to hurt me if you didn't have to."

That wasn't what she had fed me verbatim. Not verbatim.

"I try to understand," Wolfe said dryly. "You knew Mr. Kampf intimately?"

"Yes, I guess so." She smiled as one understander to another. "For a while I did. Not lately, not for the past two months."

"You met the dog at his apartment on Perry Street?"

"That's right. For nearly a year I was there quite often."

"You and Mr. Kampf quarreled?"

"Oh no, we didn't quarrel. I just didn't see him any more. I had other—I was very busy."

"When did you see him last?"

"Well—you mean intimately?"

"No. At all."

"About two weeks ago, at the club. He came to the club once or twice and spoke to me there."

"But no quarrel?"

"No, there was nothing to quarrel about."

"You have no idea who killed him, or why?"

"I certainly haven't."

Wolfe leaned back. "Do you know Mr. Talento intimately?"

"No, not if you mean—of course we're friends. I used to live there."

"With Mr. Talento?"

"Not *with* him." She was mildly shocked. "I never live with a man. I had the second-floor apartment."

"At twenty-nine Arbor Street?"

"Yes."

"For how long? When?"

"For nearly a year. I left there—let's see—about three months ago. I have a little apartment on East Forty-ninth Street."

"Then you know the others too? Mr. Meegan and Mr. Chaffee and Mr. Aland?"

"I know Ross Chaffee and Jerry Aland, but no Meegan. Who's he?"

"A tenant at twenty-nine Arbor Street. Second floor."

She nodded. "Well, sure, that's the floor I had." She smiled. "I hope they fixed that damn table for him. That was one reason I left. I hate furnished apartments, don't you?"

Wolfe made a face. "In principle, yes. I take it you now have your own furniture. Supplied by Mr. Kampf?"

She laughed—more of a chuckle—and her eyes danced. "I see you didn't know Phil Kampf."

"Not supplied by him, then?"

"A great big no."

"By Mr. Chaffee? Or Mr. Aland?"

"No and no." She went very earnest. "Look, Mr. Wolfe. A friend of mine was mighty nice about that furniture, and we'll just leave it. Archie told me what you're interested in is the murder, and I'm sure you wouldn't want to drag in a lot of stuff just to hurt me and a friend of mine, so we'll forget the furniture."

Wolfe didn't press it. He took a hop. "Your appointment on a street corner with Mr. Talento—what was that about?"

She nodded. "I've been wondering about that. I mean what I would say when you asked me, because I'd hate to have you think I'm a sap, and I guess it sounds like it. I phoned him when I heard on the radio about Phil and where he was killed, there on Arbor Street, and I knew Vic still lived there and I simply wanted to ask him about it."

"You had him on the phone."

"He didn't seem to want to talk about it on the phone."

"But why a street corner?"

This time it was more like a laugh. "Now, Mr. Wolfe, *you*'re not a sap. You asked about the furniture, didn't you? Well, a girl with furniture shouldn't be seen places with a man like Vic Talento."

"What is he like?"

She fluttered a hand. "Oh, he wants to get close."

Wolfe kept at her until after one o'clock, and I could report it all, but it wouldn't get you any further than it did him. He couldn't trip her or back her into a corner. She hadn't been to Arbor Street for two months. She hadn't seen Chaffee or Aland or Talento for weeks, and of course not Meegan, since she had never heard of him before. She couldn't even try to guess who had killed Kampf. The only thing remotely to be regarded as a return on Wolfe's investment of a full hour was her statement that as far as she knew there was no one who had both an attachment and a claim to Bootsy. If there were heirs she had no idea who they were. When she left the chair to go the dog got up too, and she patted him, and he went with us to the door. I took her to Tenth Avenue and put her in a taxi, and returned.

I got a glass of milk from the kitchen and took it to the office. Wolfe, who was drinking beer, didn't scowl at me. He seldom scowls when he is drinking beer.

"Where's Bootsy?" I inquired.

"No," he said emphatically.

"Okay." I surrendered. "Where's Jet?"

"Down in Fritz's room. He'll sleep there. You don't like him."

"That's not true, but you can have it. It means you can't blame him on me, and that suits me fine." I sipped milk. "Anyhow, that will no longer be an issue after Homicide comes in the morning with a document and takes him away."

"They won't come."

"I offer twenty to one. Before noon."

He nodded. "That was roughly my own estimate of the probability, so while you were out I phoned Mr. Cramer. I suggested an arrangement, and I suppose he inferred that if he declined the arrangement the dog might be beyond his jurisdiction before tomorrow, though I didn't say so. I may have given that impression."

"Yeah. You should be more careful."

"So the arrangement has been made. You are to be at twenty-nine Arbor Street, with the dog, at nine o'clock in the morning. You are to be present throughout the fatuous performance the police have in mind, and keep the dog in view. The dog is to leave the premises with you, before noon, and you are to bring him back here. The police are to make no further effort to constrain the dog for twenty-four hours. While in that house you may find an opportunity to flush something or someone more contributive than that volatile demirep. If you will come to my room before you go in the morning I may have a suggestion."

"I resent that," I said manfully. "When you call her that, smile."

CHAPTER IV

IT WAS A FINE bright morning. I didn't take Meegan's raincoat, because I didn't need any pretext and I doubted if the program would offer a likely occasion for the exchange.

The law was there in front, waiting for me. The one who knew dogs was a stocky middle-aged guy who wore rimless glasses. Before he touched the dog he asked me the name, and I told him Bootsy.

"A hell of a name," he observed. "Also that's a hell of a leash you've got."

"I agree. His was on the corpse, so I suppose it's in the lab." I handed him my end of the heavy cord. "If he bites you it's not on me."

"He won't bite me. Would you, Bootsy?" He squatted before the dog and started to get acquainted. Sergeant Purley Stebbins growled, a foot from my ear, "He should have bit you when you kidnaped him."

I turned. Purley was half an inch taller than me and two inches broader. "You've got it twisted," I told him. "It's women that bite me. I've often wondered what would bite you."

We continued exchanging pleasantries while the dog man, whose name was Loftus, made friends with Bootsy. It wasn't long before he announced that he was ready to proceed. He was frowning. "In a way," he said, "it would be better to keep him on leash after I go in, because Kampf probably did. Or did he? Maybe you ought to brief me a little more. How much do we know?"

"To swear to," Purley told him, "damn little. But putting it all together from what we've collected, this is how it looks, and I'll have to be shown different. When Kampf and the dog entered it was raining and the dog was wet. Kampf left the dog in the ground-floor hall. He removed the leash and had it in his hand when he went to the door of one of the apartments. The tenant of the apartment let him in, and they talked. The tenant socked him, probably from behind without warning, and used the leash to finish him. He stuffed the leash in the pocket of the raincoat. It took nerve and muscle both to carry the body out and down the stairs to the lower hall, but he damn well had to get it out of his place and away from his door, and any of those four could have done it in a pinch, and it sure was a pinch. Of course the dog was already outside, out on the sidewalk. While Kampf was in one of the apartments getting killed, Talento had come into the lower hall and seen the dog and chased it out."

"Then," Loftus objected, "Talento's clean."

"No. Nobody's clean. If it was Talento, after he killed Kampf he went out to the hall and put the dog out in the vestibule, went back in his apartment and carried the body out and dumped it at the foot of the stairs, and then left the house, chasing the dog on out to the sidewalk. You're the dog expert. Is there anything wrong with that?"

"Not necessarily. It depends on the dog and how close he was to Kampf. There wasn't any blood."

"Then that's how I'm buying it. If you want it filled in you can spend the rest of the day with the reports of the other experts and the statements of the tenants."

"Some other day. That'll do for now. You're going in first?"

"Yeah. Come on, Goodwin."

Purley started for the door, but I objected. "I'm staying with the dog."

"For God's sake. Then keep behind Loftus."

I changed my mind. It would be interesting to watch the experiment, and from behind Loftus the view wouldn't be good. So I went into the vestibule with Purley. The inner door was opened by a Homicide colleague, and we crossed the threshold and moved to the far side of the small lobby, which was fairly clean but not ornate. The colleague closed the door and stayed there. In a minute he pulled it open again, and

Loftus and the dog entered. Two steps in, Loftus stopped, and so did the dog. No one spoke. The leash hung limp. Bootsy looked around at Loftus. Loftus bent over and untied the cord from the collar, and held it up to show Bootsy he was free. Bootsy came over to me and stood, his head up, wagging his tail.

"Nuts," Purley said, disgusted.

"You know what I really expected," Loftus said. "I never thought he'd show us where Kampf took him when they entered yesterday, but I did think he'd go to the foot of the stairs, where the body was found, and I thought he might go on to where the body came from—Talento's door, or upstairs. Take him by the collar, Goodwin, and ease him over to the foot of the stairs."

I obliged. He came without urging, but gave no sign that the spot held any special interest for him. We all stood and watched him. He opened his mouth wide to yawn.

"Fine," Purley rumbled. "Just fine. You might as well go on with it."

Loftus came and fastened the leash to the collar, led Bootsy across the lobby to a door, and knocked. In a moment the door opened, and there was Victor Talento in a fancy rainbow dressing gown.

"Hello, Bootsy," he said, and reached down to pat.

"Goddamit!" Purley barked. "I told you not to speak!"

Talento straightened up. "So you did." He was apologetic. "I'm sorry, I forgot. Do you want to try it again?"

"No. That's all."

Talento backed in and closed the door.

"You must realize," Loftus told Purley, "that a Labrador can't be expected to go for a man's throat. They're not that kind of dog. The most you could expect would be an attitude, or possibly a growl."

"You can have 'em," Purley growled. "Is it worth going on?"

"By all means. You'd better go first."

Purley headed for me, and I gave him room and then followed him up the stairs. The upper hall was narrow and not very light, with a door at the rear end and another toward the front. We backed up against the wall opposite the front door to leave enough space for Loftus and Bootsy. They came, Bootsy tagging, and Loftus knocked. Ten seconds passed before footsteps sounded, and then the door was opened by the specimen who had dashed out of Wolfe's place the day before and taken my coat with him. He was in his shirt sleeves, and he hadn't combed his hair.

"This is Sergeant Loftus, Mr. Meegan," Purley said. "Take a look at the dog. Have you ever seen it before? Pat it."

Meegan snorted. "Pat it yourself. Go to hell."

"Have you ever seen it before?"

"No."

"Okay, thanks. Come on, Loftus."

As we started up the next flight the door slammed behind us, good and loud. Purley asked over his shoulder, "Well?"

"He didn't like him," Loftus replied from the rear, "but there are lots of people lots of dogs don't like."

The third-floor hall was a duplicate of the one below. Again Purley and I posted ourselves opposite the door, and Loftus came with Bootsy and knocked. Nothing happened. He knocked again, louder, and pretty soon the door opened to a two-inch crack, and a squeaky voice came through.

"You've got the dog."

"Right here," Loftus told him.

"Are you there, Sergeant?"

"Right here," Purley answered.

"I told you that dog don't like me. Once at a party at Phil Kampf's—I told you. I didn't mean to hurt it, but it thought I did. What are you trying to do, frame me?"

"Open the door. The dog's on a leash."

"I won't! I told you I wouldn't!"

Purley moved. His arm, out stiff, went over Loftus's shoulder, and his palm met the door and kept going. The door hesitated an instant and then swung open. Standing there, holding to its edge, was a skinny individual in red-and-green-striped pajamas. The dog let out a low growl and backed up a little.

"We're making the rounds, Mr. Aland," Purley said, "and we couldn't leave you out. Now you can go back to sleep. As for trying to frame you—"

He stopped because the door shut.

"You didn't tell me," Loftus complained, "that Aland had already fixed it for a reaction."

"No, I thought I'd wait and see. One to go." He headed for the stairs.

The top-floor hall had had someone's personal attention. It was no bigger than the others, but it had a nice clean tan-colored runner, and the walls were painted the same shade and sported a few small pictures. Purley went to the rear door instead of the front, and we made room for Loftus and Bootsy by flattening against the wall. When Loftus knocked footsteps responded at once, approaching the door, and it swung wide open. This was the painter, Ross Chaffee, and he was dressed for it, in an old brown smock. He was by far the handsomest of the tenants, tall, erect, with artistic wavy dark hair and features he must have enjoyed looking at.

I had ample time to enjoy them too as he stood smiling at us, completely at ease, obeying Purley's prior instructions not to speak. Bootsy was also at ease. When it became quite clear that no blood was going to be shed, Purley asked, "You know the dog, don't you, Mr. Chaffee?"

"Certainly. He's a beautiful animal."

"Pat him."

"With pleasure." He bent gracefully. "Bootsy, do you know your master's gone?" He scratched behind the black ears. "Gone forever, Bootsy, and that's too bad." He straightened. "Anything else? I'm working. I like the morning light."

"That's all, thanks." Purley turned to go, and I let Loftus and Bootsy by before following. On the way down the three flights no one had any remarks.

As we hit the level of the lower hall Victor Talento's door opened, and he emerged and spoke. "The District Attorney's office phoned. Are you through with me? They want me down there."

"We're through," Purley rumbled. "We can run you down."

Talento said that would be fine and he would be ready in a minute. Purley told Loftus to give me Bootsy, and he handed me the leash.

"I am willing," I said helpfully, "to give you a detailed analysis of the dog's conduct. It will take about a week."

"Go to hell," Purley growled, "and take the goddam dog along."

I departed. Outside the morning was still fine. The presence of two PD cars in front of the scene of a murder had attracted a small gathering, and Bootsy and I were objects of interest as we appeared and started off. We both ignored the stares. We moseyed along, in no hurry, stopping now and then to give Bootsy a chance to inspect something if he felt inclined. At the fourth or fifth stop, more than a block away, I saw the quartet leaving number 29. Stebbins and Talento took one car and Loftus and the colleague the other, and they rolled off.

I shortened up on Bootsy a little, walked him west until an empty taxi appeared, stopped it and got in, took a five-dollar bill from my wallet, and handed it to the hackie.

"Thanks," he said with feeling. "For what, down payment on the cab?"

"You'll earn it, brother," I assured him. "Is there somewhere within a block or so of Arbor and Court where you can park for anywhere from thirty minutes to three hours?"

"Not three hours for a finif."

"Of course not." I got another five and gave it to him. "I doubt if it will be that long."

"There's a parking lot not too far. On the street without a passenger I'll be solicited."

"You'll have a passenger—the dog. I prefer the street. He's a nice dog. When I return I'll be reasonable. Let's see what we can find."

He pulled the lever and we moved. There are darned few legal parking spaces in all Manhattan at that time of day, and we cruised around several corners before we found one, on Court Street two blocks from Arbor. He backed into it and I got out, leaving the windows down three inches. I told him I'd be back when he saw me, and headed south, turning right at the second corner.

There was no police car at 29 Arbor, and no gathering. That was satisfactory. Entering the vestibule, I pushed the button under Meegan and put my hand on the knob. No click. Pushing twice more and still getting no response, I tried Aland's button, and that worked. After a short wait the click came, and I shoved the door open, entered, mounted two flights, went to the door, and knocked with authority.

The squeaky voice came through. "Who is it?"

"Goodwin. I was just here with the others. I haven't got the dog. Open up."

The door swung slowly to a crack, and then wider. Jerome Aland was still in his gaudy pajamas. "For God's sake," he squeaked, "what do you want now? I need some sleep!"

I didn't apologize. "I was going to ask you some questions when I was here before," I told him, "but the dog complicated it. It won't take long." Since he wasn't polite enough to move aside, I had to brush him, skinny as he was, as I went in. "Which way?"

He slid past me, and I followed him across to chairs. They were the kind of chairs that made Jewel Jones hate furnished apartments, and the rest of the furniture didn't help any. He sat on the edge of one and demanded, "All right, what?"

It was a little tricky. Since he was assuming I was one of the Homicide personnel, it wouldn't do for me to know either too much or too little. It would be risky to mention Jewel Jones, because the cops might not have got around to her at all.

"I'm checking some points," I told him. "How long has Richard Meegan occupied the apartment below you?"

"Hell, I've told you that a dozen times."

"Not me. I said I'm checking. How long?"

"Nine days. He took it a week ago Tuesday."

"Who was the previous tenant? Just before him."

"There wasn't any. It was empty."

"Empty ever since you've been here?"

"No, I've told you, a girl had it, but she moved out about three months ago. Her name is Jewel Jones, and she's a fine artist, and she got me my job at the night club where I work now." His mouth worked. "I know what you're doing, you're trying to make it nasty, and you're trying to catch me getting my facts twisted. Bringing that dog here to growl at me—can I help it if I don't like dogs?"

He ran his fingers, both hands, through his hair. When the hair was messed good he gestured like a night-club performer. "Die like a dog," he said. "That's what Phil did, died like a dog. Poor Phil. I wouldn't want to see that again."

"You said," I ventured, "that you and he were good friends."

His head jerked up. "I did not. Did I say that?"

"More or less. Maybe not in those words. Why, weren't you?"

"We were not. I haven't got any good friends."

"You just said that the girl that used to live here got you a job. That sounds like a good friend. Or did she owe you something?"

"Not a damn thing. Why do you keep bringing her up?"

"I didn't bring her up, you did. I only asked who was the former tenant in the apartment below you. Why, would you rather keep her out of it?"

"I don't have to keep her out. She's not in it."

"Perhaps not. Did she know Philip Kampf?"

"I guess so. Sure she did."

"How well did she know him?"

He shook his head. "Now you're getting personal, and I'm the wrong person. If Phil was alive you could ask him, and he might tell you. Me, I don't know."

I smiled at him. "All that does, Mr. Aland, is make me curious. Somebody in this house murdered Kampf. So we ask you questions, and when we come to one you shy at, naturally we wonder why. If you don't like talking about Kampf and that girl, think what it could mean. For instance, it could mean that the girl was yours, and Kampf took her away from you, and that was why you killed him when he came here yesterday. Or it could—"

"She wasn't mine!"

"Uh-huh. Or it could mean that although she wasn't yours, you were under a deep obligation to her, and Kampf had given her a dirty deal, or he was threatening her with something, and she wanted him disposed of, and you obliged. Or of course it could be merely that Kampf had something on you."

He had his head tilted back so he could look down on me. "You're in the wrong racket," he asserted. "You ought to be writing TV scripts."

I stuck with him only a few more minutes, having got all I could hope for under the circumstances. Since I was letting him assume that I was a city employee, I couldn't very well try to pry him loose for a trip to Wolfe's place. Also I had two more calls to make, and there was no telling when I might be interrupted by a phone call or a courier to one of them from downtown. The only further item I gathered from Jerome Aland was that he wasn't trying to get from under by slipping in any insinuations about his co-tenants. He had no opinions or ideas about who had killed poor Phil. When I left he stood up, but he let me go and open the door for myself.

I went down a flight, to Meegan's door, and knocked and waited. Just as I was raising a fist to make it louder and better there were footsteps inside, and the door opened. Meegan was still in his shirt sleeves and still uncombed.

"Well?" he demanded.

"Back again," I said firmly but not offensively. "With a few questions. If you don't mind?"

"You know damn well I mind."

"Naturally. Mr. Talento has been called down to the District Attorney's office. This might possibly save you another trip there."

He sidestepped, and I went in. The room was the same size and shape as Aland's, above, and the furniture, though different, was no more desirable. The table against a wall was lopsided—probably the one that Jewel Jones hoped they had fixed for him. I took a chair at its end, and he took another and sat frowning at me.

"Haven't I seen you before?" he wanted to know.

"Sure, we were here with the dog."

"I mean before that. Wasn't it you in Nero Wolfe's office yesterday?"

"That's right."

"How come?"

I raised my brows. "Haven't you got the lines crossed, Mr. Meegan? I'm here to ask questions, not to answer them. I was in Wolfe's office on business. I often am. Now—"

"He's a fat, arrogant halfwit!"

"You may be right. He's certainly arrogant. Now, I'm here on business." I got out my notebook and pencil. "You moved into this place nine days ago. Please tell me exactly how you came to take this apartment."

He glared. "I've told it at least three times."

"I know. This is the way it's done. I'm not trying to catch you in some little discrepancy, but you could have omitted something important. Just assume I haven't heard it before. Go ahead."

"Oh, my God." His head dropped and his lips tightened. Normally he might not have been a bad-looking guy, with blond hair and gray eyes and a long bony face, but now, having spent the night, or most of it, with Homicide and the DA, he looked it, especially his eyes, which were red and puffy.

He lifted his head. "I'm a commercial photographer—in Pittsburgh. Two years ago I married a girl named Margaret Ryan. Seven months later she left me. I didn't know whether she went alone or with somebody. She just left. She left Pittsburgh too, or anyway I couldn't find her there, and her family never saw her or heard from her. About five months later, about a year ago, a man I know, a businessman I do work for, came back from a trip to New York and said he'd seen her in a theater here with a man. He went and spoke to her, but she claimed he was mistaken. He was sure it was her. I came to New York and spent a week looking around but didn't find her. I didn't go to the police because I didn't want to. You want a better reason, but that's mine."

"I'll skip that." I was writing in the notebook. "Go ahead."

"Two weeks ago I went to look at a show of pictures at the Institute in

Pittsburgh. There was a painting there, an oil, a big one. It was called 'Three Young Mares at Pasture,' and it was an interior, a room, with three women in it. One of them was on a couch, and two of them were on a rug on the floor. They were eating apples. The one on the couch was my wife. I was sure of it the minute I saw her, and after I stood and studied it I was even surer. There was absolutely no doubt of it."

"We're not challenging that," I assured him. "What did you do?"

"The artist's signature looked like Chapple, but of course the catalogue settled that. It was Ross Chaffee. I went to the Institute office and asked about him. They thought he lived in New York but weren't sure. I had some work on hand I had to finish, and it took a couple of days, and then I came to New York. I had no trouble finding Ross Chaffee; he was in the phone book. I went to see him at his studio—here in this house. First I told him I was interested in that figure in his painting, that I thought she would be just right to model for some photographs I wanted to do, but he said that his opinion of photography as a medium was such that he wouldn't care to supply models for it, and he was bowing me out, so I told him how it was. I told him the whole thing. Then he was different. He sympathized with me and said he would be glad to help me if he could, but he had painted that picture more than a year ago, and he used so many different models for his pictures that it was impossible to remember which was which."

Meegan stopped, and I looked up from the notebook. He said aggressively, "I'm repeating that that sounded phony to me."

"Go right ahead. You're telling it."

"I say it was phony. A photographer might use hundreds of models in a year, and he might forget, but not a painter. Not a picture like that. I got a little tactless with him, and then I apologized. He said he might be able to refresh his memory and asked me to phone him the next day. Instead of phoning I went back the next day to see him, but he said he simply couldn't remember and doubted if he ever could. I didn't get tactless again. Coming in the house, I had noticed a sign that there was a furnished apartment to let, and when I left Chaffee I found the janitor and rented it, and went to my hotel for my bags and moved in. I knew damn well my wife had modeled for that picture, and I knew I could find her. I wanted to be as close as I could to Chaffee and the people who came to see him."

I wanted something too. I wanted to say that he must have had a photograph of his wife along and that I would like to see it, but of course I didn't dare, since it was a cinch that he had already either given it to the cops, or refused to, or claimed he didn't have one. So I merely asked, "What progress did you make?"

"Not much. I tried to get friendly with Chaffee but didn't get very far. I met the other two tenants, Talento and Aland, but that didn't get me anywhere. Finally I decided I would have to get some expert help, and that was why I went to see Nero Wolfe. You were there, you know how that came out—that big blob."

I nodded. "He has dropsy of the ego. What did you want him to do?"

"I've told you."

"Tell it again."

"I was going to have him tap Chaffee's phone."

"That's illegal," I said severely.

"All right, I didn't do it."

I flipped a page of the notebook. "Go back a little. During that week, besides the tenants here, how many of Chaffee's friends and acquaintances did you meet?"

"Just two, as I've told you. A young woman, a model, in his studio one day, and I don't remember her name, and a man that was there another day, a man that Chaffee said buys his pictures. His name was Braunstein."

"You're leaving out Philip Kampf."

Meegan leaned forward and put a fist on the table. "Yes, and I'm going on leaving him out. I never saw him or heard of him."

"What would you say if I said you were seen with him?"

"I'd say you were a dirty liar!" The red eyes looked redder. "As if I wasn't already having enough trouble, now you set on me about a murder of a man I never heard of! You bring a dog here and tell me to pat it, for God's sake!"

I nodded. "That's your hard luck, Mr. Meegan. You're not the first man that's had a murder for company without inviting it." I closed the notebook and put it in my pocket. "You'd better find some way of handling your troubles without having people's phones tapped." I arose. "Stick around, please. You may be wanted downtown anyhow."

He went to open the door for me. I would have liked to get more details of his progress with Ross Chaffee, or lack of it, and his contacts with the other two tenants, but it seemed more important to have some words with Chaffee before I got interrupted. As I mounted the two flights to the top floor my wristwatch said twenty-eight minutes past ten.

CHAPTER V

"I KNOW THERE's no use complaining," Ross Chaffee said, "about these interruptions to my work. Under the circumstances." He was being very gracious about it.

The top floor was quite different from the others. I don't know what his living quarters in front were like, but the studio, in the rear, was big and high and anything but crummy. There were sculptures around, big and little, and canvases of all sizes were stacked and propped against racks. The walls were covered with drapes, solid gray, with nothing on them. Each of two easels—one much larger than the other—held a canvas that had been worked on. There were several plain chairs and two upholstered ones, and an oversized divan, nearly square. I had been steered to one of the upholstered numbers, and Chaffee, still in his smock, had moved a plain one to sit facing me.

"Only don't prolong it unnecessarily," he requested.

I said I wouldn't. "There are a couple of points," I told him, "that we wonder about a little. Of course it could be merely a coincidence that Richard Meegan came to town looking for his wife, and came to see you, and rented an apartment here just nine days before Kampf was murdered, but a coincidence like that will have to stand some going over. Frankly, Mr. Chaffee, there are those, and I happen to be one of them, who find it hard to believe that you couldn't remember who modeled for an important figure in a picture you painted. I know what you say, but it's still hard to believe."

"My dear sir." Chaffee was smiling. "Then you must think I'm lying."

"I didn't say so."

"But you do, of course." He shrugged. "To what end? What deep design am I cherishing?"

"I wouldn't know. You say you wanted to help Meegan find his wife."

"No, not that I wanted to. I was willing to. He was a horrible nuisance."

"He must have been a first-class pest."

"He was. He is."

"It should have been worth some effort to get rid of him. Did you make any?"

"I have explained what I did—in a statement, and signed it. I have nothing to add. I tried to refresh my memory. One of your colleagues suggested that I might have gone to Pittsburgh to look at the picture. I suppose he was being funny."

A flicker of annoyance in his fine dark eyes, which were as clear and bright as if he had had a good eight hours of innocent slumber, warned me that I was supposed to have read his statement, and if I aroused a suspicion that I hadn't he might get personal.

I gave him an earnest eye. "Look, Mr. Chaffee. This thing is bad for all concerned. It will get worse instead of better until we find out who killed Kampf. You men in this house must know things about one another, and maybe some things connected with Kampf, that you're not telling. I don't expect a man like you to pass out dirt just for the hell of it, but any dirt that's connected with this murder is going to come out, and if you know of any and are keeping it to yourself you're a bigger fool than you look."

"Quite a speech." He was smiling again.

"Thanks. You make one."

"I'm not as eloquent as you are." He shook his head. "No, I don't believe I can help you any. I can't say I'm a total stranger to dirt; that would be smug; but what you're after—no. You have my opinion of Kampf, whom I knew quite well; he was in some respects admirable but had his full share of faults. I would say approximately the same of Talento. I have known Aland only casually—certainly not intimately. I know no more of Meegan than you do. I haven't the slightest notion why any of them might have wanted to kill Philip Kampf. If you expect—"

A phone rang. Chaffee crossed to a table at the end of the divan and answered it. He told it yes a couple of times, and then a few words, and then, "But one of your men is here now. . . . I don't know his name, I didn't ask him. . . . He may be, I don't know. . . . Very well, one-fifty-five Leonard Street. . . . Yes, I can leave in a few minutes."

He hung up and turned to me. I spoke first, on my feet. "So they want you at the DA's office. Don't tell them I said so, but they'd rather keep a murder in the file till hell freezes over than have the squad crack it. If they want my name they know where to ask."

I marched to the door, opened it, and was gone.

There were still no PD cars out in front. After turning left on Court Street and continuing two blocks, I was relieved to find the cab still there, with its passenger perched on the seat looking out at the scenery. If the hackie had gone off with him to sell him, or if Stebbins had happened by and hijacked him, I wouldn't have dared to go home at all. He seemed pleased to see me, as he damned well should have been. During the drive to Thirty-fifth Street he sat with his rump braced against me for a buttress. The meter said only six dollars and something, but I didn't request any change. If Wolfe wanted to put me to work on a murder merely because he had got infatuated with a dog, let it cost him something.

I noticed that when we entered the office Jet went over to Wolfe, in place behind his desk, without any sign of bashfulness or uncertainty, proving that the evening before, during my absence, Wolfe had made approaches, probably had fed him something, and possibly had even patted him. Remarks occurred to me, but I saved them. I might be called on before long to spend some valuable time demonstrating that I had not been guilty of impersonating an officer, and that it wasn't my fault if murder suspects mistook me for one.

Wolfe put down his empty beer glass and inquired, "Well?"

I reported. The situation called for a full and detailed account, and I supplied it, with Wolfe leaning back with his eyes closed. When I came to the end he asked no questions. Instead, he opened his eyes, straightened up, and began, "Call the—"

I cut him off. "Wait a minute. After a hard morning's work I claim the satisfaction of suggesting it myself. I thought of it long ago. What's the name of the Institute in Pittsburgh where they have shows of pictures?"

"Indeed. It's a shot at random."

"I know it is, but it's only a buck. I just spent ten on a taxi. What's the name?"

"Pittsburgh Art Institute."

I swiveled for the phone on my desk, got the operator, and put in the call. I got through to the Institute in no time, but it took a quarter of an hour, with relays to three different people, to get what I was after.

I hung up and turned to Wolfe. "The show ended a week ago yesterday. Thank God I won't have to go to Pittsburgh. The picture was lent by Mr. Herman Braunstein of New York, who owns it. It was shipped back to him by express four days ago. He wouldn't give me Braunstein's address."

"The phone book."

I had it and was flipping the pages. "Here we are. Business on Broad Street, residence on Park Avenue. There's only one Herman."

"Get him."

"I don't think so. He may be a poop. It might take all day. Why don't I go to the residence without phoning? It's probably there, and if I can't get in you can fire me. I'm thinking of resigning anyhow."

He had his doubts, since it was my idea, but he bought it. After considering the problem a little, I went to the cabinet beneath the bookshelves, got out the Veblex camera, with accessories, slung the strap of the case over my shoulder, told Wolfe I wouldn't be back until I saw the picture, wherever it was, and beat it. Before going I dialed Talento's number to tell him not to bother to keep his appointment, but there was no answer. Either he was still engaged at the DA's office or he was on his way to Thirty-fifth Street, and if he came during my absence that was all right, since Jet was there to protect Wolfe.

A taxi took me to the end of a sidewalk canopy in front of one of the palace hives on Park Avenue in the Seventies, and I undertook to walk past the doorman without giving him a glance, but he stopped me. I said professionally, "Braunstein, taking pictures, I'm late," and kept going, and got away with it. After crossing the luxurious lobby to the elevator, which luckily was there with the door open, I entered, saying, "Braunstein, please," and the chauffeur shut the door and pulled the lever. We stopped at the twelfth floor, and I stepped out. There was a door to the right and another to the left, and I turned right without asking, on a fifty-fifty chance, listening for a possible correction from the elevator man, who was standing by with his door open.

It was one of the simplest chores I have ever performed. In answer to my ring the door was opened by a middle-aged female husky, in uniform with apron, and when I told her I had come to take a picture she let me in, asked me to wait, and disappeared. In a couple of minutes a tall dignified dame with white hair came through an arch and asked what I wanted. I apologized for disturbing her and said I would deeply appreciate it if she would let me take a picture of a painting which had recently been shown at the Pittsburgh Institute, on loan by Mr. Braunstein. It was called "Three Young Mares at Pasture." A Pittsburgh client of mine had admired it, and had intended to go back and photograph it for his collection, but the picture had gone before he got around to it.

She wanted some information, such as my name and address and the name of my Pittsburgh client, which I supplied gladly without a script, and then led me through the arch into a room not quite as big as Madison Square Garden. It would have been a pleasure, and also instructive, to do a little glomming at the rugs and furniture and other miscellaneous objects, especially the dozen or more pictures on the walls, but that would have to wait. She went across to a picture near the far end, said, "That's it," and lowered herself onto a chair.

It was a nice picture. I had half expected the mares to be without clothes, but they were fully dressed. Remarking that I didn't wonder that my client wanted a photograph of it, I got busy with my equipment, including flash bulbs. She sat and watched. I took four shots from slightly different angles, acting and looking professional, I hoped; got my stuff back in the case; thanked her warmly on behalf of my client; promised to send her some prints; and left. That was all there was to it.

Out on the sidewalk again, I walked west to Madison, turned downtown and found a drugstore, went in to the phone booth, and dialed a number.

Wolfe's voice came. "Yes? Whom do you want?"

I've told him a hundred times that's a hell of a way to answer the phone, but he's too damn pigheaded.

I spoke. "I want you. I've seen the picture, and I wouldn't have thought that stallion had it in him. It glows with color and life, and the blood seems to pulsate under the warm skin. The shadows are transparent, with a harmonious blending—"

"Shut up! Yes or no?"

"Yes. You have met Mrs. Meegan. Would you like to meet her again?"

"I would. Get her."

I didn't have to look in the phone book for her address, having already done so. I left the drugstore and flagged a taxi.

There was no doorman problem at the number on East Forty-ninth Street. It was an old brick house that had been painted a bright yellow and modernized, notably with a self-service elevator, though I didn't know that until I got in. Getting in was a little complicated. Pressing the button marked "Jewel Jones" in the vestibule was easy enough, and also unhooking the receiver and putting it to my ear, and placing my mouth close to the grille, but then it got more difficult.

A voice crackled. "Yes?"

"Miss Jones?"

"Yes. Who is it?"

"Archie Goodwin. I want to see you. Not a message from Victor Talento."

"What do you want?"

"Let me in and I'll tell you."

"No. What is it?"

"It's very personal. If you don't want to hear it from me I'll go and bring Richard Meegan, and maybe you'll tell him."

I heard the gasp. She should have known those house phones are sensitive. After a pause, "Why do you say that? I told you I don't know any Meegan."

"You're way behind. I just saw a picture called 'Three Young Mares at Pasture.' Let me in."

Another pause, and the line went dead. I put the receiver on the hook, and turned and placed my hand on the knob. There was a click, and I pushed the door and entered, crossed the little lobby to the elevator, pushed the button and, when the door opened, slid in, pushed the button marked 5, and was ascending. When the elevator stopped I opened the door and emerged into a tiny foyer. A door was standing open, and on the sill was Miss Jones in a blue negligee. She started to say something, but I rudely ignored it.

"Listen," I said, "there's no sense in prolonging this. Last night I gave you your pick between Mr. Wolfe and Sergeant Stebbins; now it's either Mr. Wolfe or Meegan. I should think you'd prefer Mr. Wolfe because he's the kind of man that understands; you said so yourself. I'll wait here while you change, but don't try phoning anybody, because you won't know where you are until you've talked with Mr. Wolfe, and also because their wires are probably tapped. Don't put on anything red. Mr. Wolfe dislikes red. He likes yellow."

She stepped to me and had a hand on my arm. "Archie. Where did you see the picture?"

"I'll tell you on the way down. Let's go."

She gave the arm a gentle tug. "You don't have to wait out here. Come in and sit down." Another tug, just as gentle. "Come on."

I patted her fingers, not wishing to be boorish. "Sorry," I told her, "but I'm afraid of young mares. One kicked me once."

She turned and disappeared into the apartment, leaving the door standing open.

CHAPTER VI

"DON'T CALL ME Mrs. Meegan!" Jewel Jones cried.

Wolfe was in as bad a humor as she was. True, she had been hopelessly cornered, with no weapons within reach, but he had been compelled to tell Fritz to postpone lunch until further notice.

"I was only," he said crustily, "stressing the fact that your identity is not a matter for discussion. Legally you are Mrs. Richard Meegan. That understood, I'll call you anything you say. Miss Jones?"

"Yes." She was on the red leather chair, but not in it. Just on its edge, she looked as if she were set to spring up and scoot any second.

"Very well." Wolfe regarded her. "You realize, madam, that everything you say will be received skeptically. You are a competent liar. Your offhand denial of acquaintance with Mr. Meegan last night was better than competent. Now. When did Mr. Chaffee tell you that your husband was in town looking for you?"

"I didn't say Mr. Chaffee told me."

"Someone did. Who and when?"

She was hanging on. "How do you know someone did?"

He wiggled a finger at her. "I beg you, Miss Jones, to realize the pickle you're in. It is not credible that Mr. Chaffee couldn't remember the name of the model for that figure in his picture. The police don't believe it, and they haven't the advantage of knowing, as I do, that it was you and that you lived in that house for a year, and that you still see Mr. Chaffee occasionally. When your husband came and asked Mr. Chaffee for the name, and Mr. Chaffee pleaded a faulty memory, and your husband rented an apartment there and made it plain that he intended to persevere, it is preposterous to suppose that Mr. Chaffee didn't tell you. I don't envy you your tussles with the police after they learn about you."

"They don't have to learn about me, do they?"

"Pfui. I'm surprised they haven't got to you already, though it's been only eighteen hours. They soon will, even if not through me. I know this is no frolic for you, here with me, but they will almost make it seem so."

She was thinking. Her brow was wrinkled and her eyes straight at Wolfe. "Do you know," she asked, "what I think would be the best thing? I don't know why I didn't think of it before. You're a detective, you're an expert at helping people in trouble, and I'm certainly in trouble. I'll pay you to help me. I could pay you a little now."

"Not now or ever, Miss Jones." Wolfe was blunt. "When did Mr. Chaffee tell you that your husband was here looking for you?"

"You won't even listen to me," she complained.

"Talk sense and I will. When?"

She edged back on the chair an inch. "You don't know my husband. He was jealous about me even before we married, and then he was worse. It got so bad I couldn't stand it, and that was why I left him. I knew if I stayed in Pittsburgh he would find me and kill me, so I came to New York. A friend of mine had come here—I mean, just a friend. I got a job at a modeling agency and made enough to live on, and I met a lot of people. Ross Chaffee was one of them, and he wanted to use me in a picture, and I let him. Of course he paid me, but that wasn't so important, because soon after that I met Phil Kampf, and he got me a tryout at a night club, and I made it. About then I had a scare, though. A man from Pittsburgh saw me at a theater and came and spoke to me, but I told him he was wrong, that I had never been in Pittsburgh."

"That was a year ago," Wolfe muttered.

"Yes. I was a little leery about the night club, in public like that, but months went by and nothing happened, and then all of a sudden this happened. Ross Chaffee phoned me that my husband had come and asked about the picture, and I asked him for God's sake not to tell him who it was, and he promised he wouldn't. You see, you don't know my husband. I knew he was trying to find me so he could kill me."

"You've said that twice. Has he ever killed anybody?"

"I didn't say anybody; I said me. I seem to have an effect on men." She gestured for understanding. "They just go for me. And Dick— Well, I know him, that's all. I left him a year and a half ago, and he's still looking for me, and that's what he's like. When Ross told me he was here I was scared stiff. I quit working at the club because he might happen to go there and see me, and I didn't hardly leave my apartment until last night."

Wolfe nodded. "To meet Mr. Talento. What for?"

"I told you."

"Yes, but then you were merely Miss Jones. Now you are also Mrs. Meegan. What for?"

"That doesn't change it any. I had heard on the radio about Phil being killed, and I wanted to know about it. I rang Ross Chaffee and I rang Jerry Aland, but neither of them answered, so I rang Vic Talento. He wouldn't tell me anything on the phone, but he said he would meet me."

"Did Mr. Aland and Mr. Talento know you had sat for that picture?"

"Sure they did."

"And that Mr. Meegan had seen it and recognized you, and was here looking for you?"

"Yes, they knew all about it. Ross had to tell them, because he thought Dick might ask them if they knew who had modeled for the picture, and he had to warn them not to tell. They said they wouldn't, and they didn't. They're all good friends of mine."

She stopped to do something. She opened her black leather bag on her lap, took out a purse, and fingered its contents, peering into it. She raised her eyes to Wolfe. "I can pay you forty dollars now, to start. I'm not just in trouble, I'm in danger of my life, really I am. I don't see how you can refuse— You're not listening!"

Apparently he wasn't. With his lips pursed, he was watching the tip of his forefinger make little circles on his desk blotter. Her reproach didn't stop him, but after a moment he moved his eyes to me and said abruptly, "Get Mr. Chaffee."

"No!" she cried. "I don't want him to know—"

"Nonsense," he snapped at her. "Everybody will have to know everything, and why drag it out? Get him, Archie. I'll speak to him."

I got at the phone and dialed. I doubted if he would be back from his session with the DA, but he was. His "hello" was enough to recognize his voice by. I pitched mine low so he wouldn't know it, not caring to start a debate as to whether I had or had not impersonated an officer, and merely told him that Nero Wolfe wished to speak to him.

Wolfe took it at his desk. "Mr. Chaffee? This is Nero Wolfe. . . . I've assumed an interest in the murder of Philip Kampf and have done some investigating. . . . Just one moment, please, don't ring off. . . . Sitting here in my office is Mrs. Richard Meegan, alias Miss Jewel Jones. . . . Please let me finish. . . . I shall of course have to detain her and communicate with the police, since they will want her as a material witness in a murder case, but before I do that I would like to discuss the matter with you and the others who live in that house. Will you undertake to bring them here as soon as possible? . . . No, I'll say nothing further on the phone, I want you here, all of you. If Mr. Meegan is balky, you might as well tell him his wife is here. I'll expect—"

She was across to him in a leap that any young mare might have envied, grabbing for the phone and shrieking at it, "Don't tell him, Ross! Don't bring him! Don't—"

My own leap and dash around the end of the desk was fairly good too. Getting her shoulders, I yanked her back, with enough enthusiasm so that I landed in the red leather chair with her on my lap, and since she was by no means through I wrapped my arms around her, pinning her arms to her sides, whereupon she started kicking my shins with her heels. She kept on kicking until Wolfe finished with Chaffee. When he hung up she suddenly relaxed and was limp, and I realized how warm she felt tight against me.

Wolfe scowled at us. "An affecting sight," he snorted.

CHAPTER VII

THERE WERE VARIOUS ASPECTS of the situation. One was lunch. For Wolfe it was unthinkable to have company in the house at mealtime, no matter what his or her status was, without feeding him or her, but he certainly wasn't going to sit at table with a female who had just pounced on him and clawed at him. That problem was simple. She and I were served in the dining room, and Wolfe ate in the kitchen with Fritz. We were served, but she didn't eat much. She kept listening and looking toward the hall, though I assured her that care would be taken to see that her husband didn't kill her on those premises.

A second aspect was the reaction of three of the tenants to their discovery of my identity. I handled that myself. When the doorbell rang and I admitted them, at a quarter past two, I told them I would be glad to discuss my split personality with any or all of them later, if they still wanted to, but they would have to file it until Wolfe was through. Victor Talento had another beef that he wouldn't file, that I had double-crossed him on the message he had asked me to take to Jewel Jones. He wanted to get nasty about it and demanded a private talk with Wolfe, but I told him to go climb a rope.

I also had to handle the third aspect, which had two angles. There was Miss Jones's theory that her husband would kill her on sight, which might or might not be well founded, and there was the fact that one of them had killed Kampf and might go to extremes if pushed. On that I took three precautions: I showed them the Carley .38 I had put in my pocket and told them it was loaded; I insisted on patting them from shoulders to ankles; and I kept Miss Jones in the dining room until I had them seated in the office, on a row of chairs facing Wolfe's desk, and until Wolfe had come in from the kitchen and been told their names. When he was in his chair behind his desk I went across the hall for her and brought her in.

Meegan jumped up and started for us. I stiff-armed him and made it good. She got behind me. Talento and Aland left their chairs, presumably to help protect the mare. Meegan was talking, and so were they. I detoured with her around back of them and got her to a chair at the end of my desk, and when I sat I was in an ideal spot to trip anyone headed for her. Talento and Aland had pulled Meegan down onto a chair between them, and he sat staring at her.

"With that hubbub over," Wolfe said, "I want to be sure I have the names right." His eyes went from left to right. "Talento, Meegan, Aland, Chaffee. Is that correct?"

I told him yes.

"Then I'll proceed." He glanced up at the wall clock. "Twenty hours ago Philip Kampf was killed in the house where you gentlemen live. The circumstances indicate that one of you killed him. But I won't rehash the multifarious details which you have already discussed at length with the police; you are familiar with them. I have not been hired to work on this case; the only client I have is a dog, and he came to my office by inadvertence. However, it is—"

The doorbell rang. I asked myself if I had put the chain bolt on, and decided I had. Through the open door to the hall I saw Fritz passing to answer it. Wolfe started to go on, but was annoyed by the sound of voices, Fritz's and another's, coming through, and stopped. The voices continued. Wolfe shut his eyes and compressed his lips. The audience sat and looked at him.

Then Fritz appeared in the doorway and announced, "Inspector Cramer, sir."

Wolfe's eyes opened. "What does he want?"

"I told him you are engaged. He says he knows you are, that the four men were followed to your house and he was notified. He says he expected you to be trying some trick with the dog, and he knows that's what you are doing, and he intends to come in and see what it is. Sergeant Stebbins is with him."

Wolfe grunted. "Archie, tell— No. You'd better stay where you are. Fritz, tell him he may see and hear what I'm doing, provided he gives me thirty minutes without interruptions or demands. If he agrees to that, bring them in."

"Wait!" Ross Chaffee was on his feet. "You said you would discuss it with us before you communicated with the police."

"I haven't communicated with them, they're here."

"You told them to come!"

"No. I would have preferred to deal with you men first and then call them, but here they are and they might as well join us. Bring them, Fritz, on that condition."

"Yes, sir."

Fritz went. Chaffee thought he had something more to say, decided he hadn't, and sat down. Talento said something to him, and he shook his head. Jerry Aland, much more presentable now that he was combed and dressed, kept his eyes fastened on Wolfe. For Meegan, apparently, there was no one in the room but him and his wife.

Cramer and Stebbins marched in, halted three paces from the door, and took a survey.

"Be seated," Wolfe invited them. "Luckily, Mr. Cramer, your usual chair is unoccupied."

"Where's the dog?" Cramer barked.

"In the kitchen. You had better suspend that prepossession. It's understood that you will be merely a spectator for thirty minutes?"

"That's what I said."

"Then sit down. But you should have one piece of information. You know the gentlemen, of course, but not the lady. Her current name is Miss Jewel Jones. Her legal name is Mrs. Richard Meegan."

"Meegan?" Cramer stared. "The one in the picture Chaffee painted? Meegan's wife?"

"That's right. Please be seated."

"Where did you get her?"

"That can wait. No interruptions and no demands. Confound it, sit down!"

Cramer went and lowered himself onto the red leather chair. Purley Stebbins got one of the yellow ones and planted it behind the row, between Chaffee and Aland.

Wolfe regarded the quartet. "I was about to say, gentlemen, that it was something the dog did that pointed to the murderer for me. But before—"

"What did it do?" Cramer barked.

"You know all about it," Wolfe told him coldly. "Mr. Goodwin related it to you exactly as it happened. If you interrupt again, by heaven, you can take them all down to your quarters, not including the dog, and stew it out yourself."

He went back to the four. "But before I come to that, another thing or two. I offer no comment on your guile with Mr. Meegan. You were all friends of Miss Jones's, having, I suppose, enjoyed various degrees of intimacy with her, and you refused to disclose her to a husband whom she had abandoned and professed to fear. I will even concede that there was a flavor of gallantry in your conduct. But when Mr. Kampf was murdered and the police swarmed in, it was idiotic to try to keep her out of it. They were sure to get to her. I got to her first only because of Mr. Goodwin's admirable enterprise and characteristic luck."

He shook his head at them. "It was also idiotic of you to assume that Mr. Goodwin was a police officer, and admit him and answer his questions, merely because he had been present during the abortive experiment with the dog. You should have asked to see his credentials. None of you had any idea who he was. Even Mr. Meegan, who had seen him in this office in the morning, was bamboozled. I mention this to anticipate any possible official complaint that Mr. Goodwin impersonated an officer. You know he didn't. He merely took advantage of your unwarranted assumption."

He shifted in his chair. "Another thing. Yesterday morning Mr. Meegan called here by appointment to ask me to do a job for him. With his first words I gathered that it was something about his wife, and I don't take that kind of work, and I was brusque with him. He was offended. He rushed out in a temper, getting his hat and raincoat from the rack in the hall, and he took Mr. Goodwin's coat instead of his own. Late in the afternoon Mr. Goodwin went to Arbor Street, with the coat that had been left in error, to exchange it. He saw that in front of number twenty-nine there were collected two police cars, a policeman on post, some people, and a dog. He decided to postpone his errand and went on by, after a brief halt during which he patted the dog. He walked home, and had gone nearly two miles when he discovered that the dog was following him. He brought the dog in a cab the rest of the way, to this house and this room."

He flattened a palm on his desk. "Now. Why did the dog follow Mr. Goodwin through the turmoil of the city? Mr. Cramer's notion that the dog was enticed is poppycock. Mr. Goodwin is willing to believe, as many men are, that he is irresistible to both dogs and women, and doubtless his vanity impeded his intellect or he would have reached the same conclusion that I did. The dog didn't follow him; it followed the coat. You ask, as I did, how to account for Mr. Kampf's dog following Mr. Meegan's coat. I couldn't. I can't. Then, since it was unquestionably Mr. Kampf's dog, it couldn't have been Mr. Meegan's coat. It is better than a conjecture, it is next thing to a certainty, that it was Mr. Kampf's coat."

His gaze leveled at the husband. "Mr. Meegan. Some two hours ago I learned from Mr. Goodwin that you maintain that you had never seen or heard of Mr. Kampf. That was fairly conclusive, but before sending for you I had to verify my conjecture that the model who had sat for Mr. Chaffee's picture was your wife. I would like to hear it straight from you. Did you ever meet with Philip Kampf alive?"

Meegan was meeting the gaze. "No."

"Don't you want to qualify that?"

"No."

"Then where did you get his raincoat?"

No answer. Meegan's jaw worked. He spoke. "I didn't have his raincoat, or if I did I didn't know it."

"That won't do. I warn you, you are in deadly peril. The raincoat that you brought into this house and left here is in the hall now, there on the rack. It can easily be established that it belonged to Mr. Kampf and was worn by him. Where did you get it?"

Meegan's jaw worked some more. "I never had it, if it belonged to Kampf. This is a dirty frame. You can't prove that's the coat I left here."

Wolfe's voice sharpened. "One more chance. Have you any explanation of how Kampf's coat came into your possession?"

"No, and I don't need any."

He may not have been pure boob. If he hadn't noticed that he wore the wrong coat home, and he probably didn't, in his state of mind, this had hit him from a clear sky and he had no time to study it.

"Then you're done for," Wolfe told him. "For your own coat must be somewhere, and I think I know where. In the police laboratory. Mr.

Kampf was wearing one when you killed him and pushed his body down the stairs—and that explains why, when they were making that experiment this morning, the dog showed no interest in the spot where the body had lain. It had been enveloped, not in his coat but in yours. That can be established too. If you won't explain how you got Mr. Kampf's coat, then explain how he got yours. Is that also a frame?"

Wolfe pointed a finger at him. "I note that flash in your eye, and I think I know what it means. But your brain is lagging. If, after killing him, you took your raincoat off of him and put on him the one that you thought was his, that won't help you any. For in that case the coat that was on the body is Mr. Goodwin's, and certainly that can be established, and how would you explain that? It looks hopeless, and—"

Meegan was springing up, but before he even got well started Purley's big hands were on his shoulders, pulling him back and down. And a new voice sounded.

"I told you he would kill me! I knew he would! He killed Phil!"

Jewel Jones was looking not at her husband, who was under control, but at Wolfe. He snapped at her, "How do you know he did?"

Judging by her eyes and the way she was shaking, she would be hysterical in another two minutes, and maybe she knew it, for she poured it out. "Because Phil told me—he told me he knew Dick was here looking for me, and he knew how afraid I was of him, and he said if I wouldn't come and be with him again he would tell Dick where I was. I didn't think he really would—I didn't think Phil could be as mean as that, and I wouldn't promise, but yesterday morning he phoned me and told me he had seen Dick and told him he thought he knew who had posed for that picture, and he was going to see him again in the afternoon and tell him about me if I didn't promise, and so I promised. I thought if I promised it would give me time to decide what to do. But Phil must have gone to see Dick again anyway—"

"Where had they met in the morning?"

"At Phil's apartment, he said. And he said—that's why I know Dick killed him—he said Dick had gone off with his raincoat, and he laughed about it and said he was willing for Dick to have his raincoat if he could have Dick's wife." She was shaking harder now. "And I'll bet that's what he told Dick! That was like Phil! I'll bet he told Dick I was coming back to him and he thought that was a good trade, a raincoat for a wife! That was like Phil! You don't—"

She giggled. It started with a giggle, and then the valves busted open and here it came. When something happens in that office to smash a woman's nerves, as it has more than once, it usually falls to me to deal with it, but that time three other guys, led by Ross Chaffee, came to her, and I was glad to leave it to them. As for Wolfe, he skedaddled. If there is one thing on earth he absolutely will not be in a room with it's a woman in eruption. He got up and marched out. As for Meegan, Purley and Cramer had him.

When they left with him, they didn't take the dog. To relieve the minds of any of you who have the notion, which I understand is widespread, that it makes a dog neurotic to change its name, I might add that he responds to Jet now as if his mother had started calling him that before he had his eyes open.

As for the raincoat, Wolfe had been right about the flash in Meegan's eye. Kampf had been wearing Meegan's raincoat when he was killed, and of course that wouldn't do, so after strangling him Meegan had taken it off and put on the one he thought was Kampf's. Only it was mine. As a part of the DA's case I went down to headquarters and identified it. At the trial it helped the jury to decide that Meegan deserved the big one. After that was over I suppose I could have claimed it, but the idea didn't appeal to me. My new one is a different color.

[illegible]

[illegible] but [illegible] for Macgregor [illegible]
and Cameron [illegible].

"When [illegible] with [illegible] didn't [illegible] there [illegible] [illegible] [illegible] I [illegible] and [illegible] [illegible] [illegible] [illegible] that [illegible] [illegible] [illegible] [illegible] [illegible]

[illegible] for [illegible] had been [illegible] death to Macgregor's [illegible] had [illegible] [illegible] was [illegible] and [illegible] that was [illegible] [illegible] Macgregor had [illegible] [illegible] [illegible] it was [illegible] went down [illegible] and [illegible] it. At the [illegible] [illegible] [illegible] I [illegible] [illegible] [illegible] after [illegible] I suppose I could [illegible] it, but [illegible] [illegible] [illegible]

The Dancing Detective

BY WILLIAM IRISH
(CORNELL WOOLRICH)

PATSY MARINO WAS CLOCKING us as usual when I barged in through the foyer. He had to look twice at his watch to make sure it was right when he saw who it was. Or pretended he had to, anyway. It was the first time in months I'd breezed in early enough to climb into my evening dress and powder up before we were due on the dance floor.

Marino said, "What's the matter, don't you feel well?"

I snapped, "D'ya have to pass a medical examination to get in here and earn a living?" and gave him a dirty look across the frayed alley-cat I wore on my shoulder.

"The reason I ask is you're on time. Are you sure you're feeling well?" he pleaded sarcastically.

"Keep it up and you won't be," I promised, but soft-pedalled it so he couldn't quite get it. He was my bread and butter after all.

The barn looked like a morgue. It always did before eight—or so I'd heard. They didn't have any of the "pash" lights on yet, those smoky red things around the walls that gave it atmosphere. There wasn't a cat in the box, just five empty gilt chairs and the coffin. They had all the full-length windows overlooking the main drag open to get some ventilation in, too. It didn't seem like the same place at all; you could actually breathe fresh air in it!

My high heels going back to the dressing-room clicked hollowly in the emptiness, and my reflection followed me upsidedown across the waxed floor, like a ghost. It gave me a spooky feeling, like tonight was going to be a bad night. And whenever I get a spooky feeling, it turns out to be a bad night all right.

I shoved the dressing-room door in and started: "Hey, Julie, why didn't you wait for me, ya getting too high-hat?" Then I quit again.

She wasn't here either. If she wasn't at either end, where the hell was she?

Only Mom Henderson was there, reading one of tomorrow morning's tabs. "Is it that late?" she wanted to know when she saw me.

"Aw, lay off," I said. "It's bad enough I gotta go to work on a empty stomach." I slung my cat-pelt on a hook. Then I sat down and took off my pumps and dumped some foot powder in them, and put them back on again.

"I knocked on Julie's door on my way over," I said, "and didn't get any answer. We always have a cup of Java together before we come to work. I don't know how I'm going to last the full fifteen rounds—"

An unworthy suspicion crossed my mind momentarily: Did Julie purposely dodge me to get out of sharing a cup of coffee with me like I always took with her other nights? They allowed her to make it in her rooming-house because it had a fire-escape; they wouldn't allow me to make it in mine. I put it aside as unfair. Julie wasn't that kind; you could have had the shirt off her back—only she didn't wear a shirt, just a brassière.

"Matter?" Mom sneered. "Didn't you have a nickel on you to buy your own?"

Sure I did. Habit's a funny thing, though. Got used to taking it with a side-kick and—I didn't bother going into it with the old slob.

"I got a feeling something's going to happen tonight," I said, hunching my shoulders.

"Sure," said Mom. "Maybe you'll get fired."

I thumbed my nose at her and turned the other way around on my chair. She went back to her paper. "There haven't been any good murders lately," she lamented. "Damn it, I like a good, juicy murder wanst in a while!"

"You're building yourself up to one right in here," I scowled into the mirror at her.

She didn't take offense; she wasn't supposed to, anyway. "Was you here when that thing happened to that Southern girl, Sally, I think, was her name?"

"No!" I snapped. "Think I'm as old as you? Think I been dancing here all my life?"

"She never showed up to work one night, and they found her—That was only, let's see now. . . ." She figured it out on her fingers. "Three years ago."

"Cut it out!" I snarled. "I feel low enough as it is!"

Mom was warming up now. "Well, for that matter, how about the Fredericks kid? That was only a little while before you come here, wasn't it?"

"I know," I cut her short. "I remember hearing all about it. Do me a favor and let it lie."

She parked one finger up alongside her mouth. "You know," she breathed confidentially, "I've always had a funny feeling one and the same guy done away with both of them."

"If he did, I know who I wish was third on his list!" I was glowering at her, when thank God the rest of the chain gang showed up and cut the death-watch short. The blonde came in, and then the Raymond tramp, and the Italian frail, and all the rest of them—all but Julie.

I said, "She was never as late as this before!" and they didn't even know who or what I was talking about. Or care. Great bunch.

A slush-pump started to tune up outside, so I knew the cats had come in too.

Mom Henderson got up, sighed. "Me for the white tiles and rippling waters," and waddled out to her beat.

I opened the door on a crack and peeped out, watching for Julie. The pash lights were on now and there were customers already buying tickets over the bird cage. All the other taxi-dancers were lining up—but not Julie.

Somebody behind me yelled, "Close that door! Think we're giving a free show in here?"

"You couldn't interest anyone in that second-hand hide of yours even with a set of dishes thrown in!" I squelched absent-mindedly, without even turning to find out who it was. But I closed it anyway.

Marino came along and banged on it and hollered, "Outside, you in there! What do I pay you for anyway?" and somebody yelled back: "I often wonder!"

The cats exploded into a razz-matazz just then with enough oompah to be heard six blocks away, so it would pull them in off the pave. Once they were in it was up to us. We all came out single file, to a fate worse than death, me last. They were putting the ropes up, and the mirrored tops started to go around in the ceiling and scatter flashes of light all over everything, like silver rain.

Marino said, "Where you goin', Ginger?" and when he used your front name like that it meant he wasn't kidding.

I said, "I'm going to phone Julie a minute, find out what happened to her."

"You get out there and goona-goo!" he said roughly. "She knows what time the session begins! How long's she been working here, anyway?"

"But she'll lose her job, you'll fire her," I wailed.

He hinged his watch. "She is fired already," he said flatly.

I knew how she needed that job, and when I want to do a thing I do it. A jive-artist was heading my way, one of those barnacles you can't shake off once they fasten on you. I knew he was a jive, because he'd bought enough tickets to last him all week; a really wise guy only buys them from stretch to stretch. The place might burn down for all he knows.

I grabbed his ticket and tore it quick, and Marino turned and walked away. So then I pleaded, "Gimme a break, will you? Lemme make a phone call first. It won't take a second."

The jive said, "I came in here to danst."

"It's only to a girl friend," I assured him. "And I'll smile pretty at you the whole time." (*Clink!* Volunteer 8-1111.) "And I'll make it up to you later, I promise I will." I grabbed him quick by the sleeve. "Don't go way, stand here!"

Julie's landlady answered. I said, "Did Julie Bennett come back yet?"

"I don't know," she said. "I ain't seen her since yesterday."

"Find out for me, will ya?" I begged. "She's late and she'll lose her job over here."

Marino spotted me, came back and thundered: "I thought I told you—"

I waved the half ticket in his puss. "I'm working," I said. "I'm on this gentleman's time," and I goona-gooed the jive with teeth and eyes, one hand on his arm.

He softened like ice cream in a furnace. He said, "It's all right, Mac," and felt big and chivalrous or something. About seven cents worth of his dime was gone by now.

Marino went away again, and the landlady came down from the second floor and said, "She don't answer her door, so I guess she's out."

I hung up and I said, "Something's happened to my girl friend. She ain't there and she ain't here. She wouldn'ta quit cold without telling me."

The goona-goo was beginning to wear off the jive by this time. He fidgeted, said, "Are you gonna danst or are you gonna stand there looking blue?"

I stuck my elbows out. "Wrap yourself around this!" I barked impatiently. Just as he reached, the cats quit and the stretch was on.

He gave me a dirty look. "Ten cents shot to hell!" and he walked off to find somebody else.

I never worry about a thing after it's happened, not when I'm on the winning end anyway. I'd put my call through, even if I hadn't found out anything. I got back under the ropes, and kept my fingers crossed to ward off garlic-eaters.

By the time the next stretch began, I knew Julie wasn't coming any more that night. Marino wouldn't have let her stay even if she had, and I couldn't have helped her get around him any more, by then, myself. I kept worrying, wondering what had happened to her, and that creepy feeling about tonight being a bad night came over me stronger than ever, and I couldn't shake it off no matter how I goona-gooed.

The cold orangeade they kept buying me during the stretches didn't brace me up any either. I wasn't allowed to turn it down, because Marino got a cut out of the concession profits.

The night was like most of the others, except I missed Julie. I'd been more friendly with her than the rest of the girls, because she was on the square. I had the usual run of freaks.

"With the feet, with the feet," I said wearily, "lay off the belt-buckle crowding."

"What am I supposed to do, build a retaining wall between us?"

"You're supposed to stay outside the three-mile limit," I flared, "and not try to go mountain climbing in the middle of the floor. Do I look like an Alp?" And I glanced around to see if I could catch Marino's eye.

The guy quit pawing. Most of them are yellow like that. But on the other hand, if a girl complains too often, the manager begins to figure her for a trouble-maker. "Wolf!" you know, so it don't pay.

It was about twelve when they showed up, and I'd been on the floor three and a half hours straight, with only one more to go. There are worse ways of earning a living. You name them. I knew it was about twelve because Duke, the front man, had just wound up *"The Lady Is a Tramp,"* and I knew the sequence of his numbers and could tell the time of night by them, like a sailor can by bells. Wacky, eh? Half-past—*"Limehouse Blues."*

I gandered at them when I saw them come in the foyer, because customers seldom come in that late. Not enough time left to make it worth the general admission fee. There were two of them; one was a fat, bloated little guy, the kind we call a "belly-wopper," the other was a pip. He wasn't tall, dark and handsome because he was medium-height, light-haired and clean-cut looking without being pretty about it, but if I'd had any dreams left he coulda moved right into them. Well, I didn't, so I headed for the dressing-room to count up my ticket stubs while the stretch was on; see how I was making out. Two cents out of every dime when you turn them in.

They were standing there sizing the barn up, and they'd called Marino over to them. Then the three of them turned around and looked at me just as I made the door, and Marino thumbed me. I headed over to find out what was up. Duke's next was a rhumba, and I said to myself: "If I draw the kewpie, I'm going to have kittens all over the floor."

Marino said, "Get your things, Ginger." I thought one of them was going to take me out; they're allowed to do that, you know, only they've got to make it up with the management for taking you out of circulation. It's not as bad as it sounds, you can still stay on the up and up, sit with them in some laundry and listen to their troubles. It's all up to you yourself.

I got the backyard sable and got back just in time to hear Marino say something about: "Will I have to go bail for her?"

Fat said, "Naw, naw, we just want her to build up the background a little for us."

Then I tumbled, got jittery, squawked: "What is this, a pinch? What've I done? Where you taking me?"

Marino soothed: "They just want you to go with them, Ginger. You be a good girl and do like they ast." Then he said something to them I couldn't figure. "Try to keep the place here out of it, will you, fellas? I been in the red for six months, as it is."

I cowered along between them like a lamb being led to the slaughter, looking from one to the other. "Where you taking me?" I wailed, going down the stairs.

Maiden's Prayer answered, in the cab. "To Julie Bennett's, Ginger." They'd gotten my name from Marino, I guess.

"What's she done?" I half sobbed.

"May as well tell her now, Nick," Fat suggested. "Otherwise she'll take it big when we get there."

Nick said, quietly as he could, "Your friend Julie met up with some tough luck, babe." He took his finger and he passed it slowly across his neck.

I took it big right there in the cab, Fat to the contrary. "Ah, no!" I whispered, holding my head. "She was on the floor with me only last night! Just this time last night we were in the dressing-room together having a smoke, having some laughs! No! She was my only friend." And I started to bawl like a two-year-old, straight down my make-up onto the cab floor.

Finally this Nick, after acting embarrassed as hell, took a young tent out of his pocket, said: "Have yourself a time on this, babe."

I was still working on it when I went up the rooming-house stairs sandwiched between them. I recoiled just outside the door. "Is she—is she still in there?"

"Naw, you won't have to look at her," Nick reassured me.

I didn't, because she wasn't in there any more, but it was worse than if she had been. Oh God, that sheet, with one tremendous streak down it as if a chicken had been—! I swivelled, played puss-in-the-corner with the first thing I came up against, which happened to be this Nick guy's chest. He sort of stood still like he liked the idea. Then he growled, "Turn that damn thing over out of sight, will you?"

The questioning, when I was calm enough to take it, wasn't a grill, don't get that idea. It was just, as they'd said, to fill out her background. "When was the last time you saw her alive? Did she go around much, y'know what we mean? She have any particular steady?"

"I left her outside the house door downstairs at one-thirty this morning, last night, or whatever you call it," I told them. "We walked home together from Joyland right after the session wound up. She didn't go around at all. She never dated the boys afterwards and neither did I."

The outside half of Nick's left eyebrow hitched up at this, like when a terrier cocks its ear at something. "Notice anyone follow the two of you?"

"In our racket they always do; it usually takes about five blocks to wear them out, though, and this is ten blocks from Joyland."

"You walk after you been on your pins all night?" Fat asked, aghast.

"We should take a cab, on our earnings! About last night, I can't swear no one followed us, because I didn't look around. That's a come-on, if you do that."

Nick said, "I must remember that," absent-mindedly.

I got up my courage, faltered: "Did it—did it happen right in here?"

"Here's how it went: She went out again after she left you the first time—"

"I knew her better than that!" I yipped. "Don't start that, Balloon

Lungs, or I'll let you have this across the snout!" I swung my cat-piece at him.

He grabbed up a little box, shook it in my face. "For this," he said. "Aspirin! Don't try to tell us different, when we've already checked with the all-night drugstore over on Sixth!" He took a couple of heaves, cooled off, sat down again. "She went out, but instead of locking the house-door behind her, she was too lazy or careless; shoved a wad of paper under it to hold it on a crack till she got back. In that five minutes or less, somebody who was watching from across the street slipped in and lay in wait for her in the upper hallway out here. He was too smart to go for her on the open street, where she might have had a chance to yell."

"How'd he know she was coming back?"

"The unfastened door woulda told him that; also the drug clerk tells us she showed up there fully dressed, but with her bare feet stuck in a pair of carpet-slippers to cool 'em. The killer musta spotted that too."

"Why didn't she yell out here in the house, with people sleeping all around her in the different rooms?" I wondered out loud.

"He grabbed her too quick for that, grabbed her by the throat just as she was opening her room-door, dragged her in, closed the door, finished strangling her on the other side of it. He remembered later to come out and pick up the aspirins which had dropped and rolled all over out there. All but one, which he overlooked and we found. She wouldn't 've stopped to take one outside her door. That's how we know about that part of it."

I kept seeing that sheet, which was hidden now, before me all over again. I couldn't help it, I didn't want to know, but still I had to know. "But if he strangled her, where did all that blood—" I gestured sickly, "come from?"

Fat didn't answer, I noticed. He shut up all at once, as if he didn't want to tell me the rest of it, and looked kind of sick himself. His eyes gave him away. I almost could have been a detective myself, the way I pieced the rest of it together just by following his eyes around the room. He didn't know I was reading them, or he wouldn't have let them stray like that.

First they rested on the little portable phonograph she had there on a table. By using bamboo needles she could play it late at night, soft, and no one would hear it. The lid was up and there was a record on the turntable, but the needle was worn down half-way, all shredded, as though it had been played over and over.

Then his eyes went to a flat piece of paper, on which were spread out eight or ten shiny new dimes; I figured they'd been put aside like that, on paper, for evidence. Some of them had little brown flecks on them, bright as they were. Then lastly his eyes went down to the rug; it was all pleated up in places, especially along the edges, as though something heavy, inert, had been dragged back and forth over it.

My hands flew up my head and I nearly went wacky with horror. I gasped it out because I hoped he'd say no, but he didn't, so it was yes. "You mean he danced with her *after* she was gone? Gave her dead body a dime each time, stabbed her over and over while he did?"

There was no knife, or whatever it had been, left around, so either they'd already sent it down for prints or *he'd* taken it out with him again.

The thought of what must have gone on here in this room, of the death dance that must have taken place. . . . All I knew was that I wanted to get out of here into the open, couldn't stand it any more. Yet before I lurched out, with Nick holding me by the elbow, I couldn't resist glancing at the label of the record on the portable. *"Poor Butterfly."*

Stumbling out the door I managed to say, "She didn't put that on there. She hated that piece, called it a drip. I remember once I was up here with her and started to play it, and she snatched it off, said she couldn't stand it, wanted to bust it then and there but I kept her from doing it. She was off love and men, and it's a sort of mushy piece, that was why. She didn't buy it, they were all thrown in with the machine when she picked it up secondhand."

"Then we know his favorite song, if that means anything. If she couldn't stand it, it would be at the bottom of the stack of records, not near the top. He went to the trouble of skimming through them to find something he liked."

"With her there in his arms, already!" That thought was about the finishing touch, on top of all the other horror. We were on the stairs going down, and the ground floor seemed to come rushing up to meet me. I could feel Nick's arm hook around me just in time, like an anchor, and then I did a clothespin act over it. And that was the first time I didn't mind being pawed.

When I could see straight again, he was holding me propped up on a stool in front of a lunch-counter a couple doors down, holding a cup of coffee to my lips.

"How's Ginger?" he said gently.

"Fine," I dribbled mournfully all over my lap. "How's Nick?"

And on that note the night of Julie Bennett's murder came to an end.

Joyland dance-hall was lonely next night. I came in late, and chewing cloves, and for once Marino didn't crack his whip over me. Maybe even he had a heart. "Ginger," was all he said as I went hurrying by, "don't talk about it while you're on the hoof, get me? If anyone asks you, you don't know nothing about it. It's gonna kill business."

Duke, the front man, stopped me on my way to the dressing-room. "I hear they took you over there last night," he started.

"Nobody took nobody nowhere, schmaltz," I snapped. He wore feathers on his neck, that's why I called him that; it's the word for long-haired musicians in our lingo.

I missed her worse in the dressing-room than I was going to later on out in the barn; there'd be a crowd out there around me, and noise and music, at least. In here it was like her ghost was powdering its nose alongside me at the mirror the whole time. The peg for hanging up her things still had her name penciled under it.

Mom Henderson was having herself a glorious time; you couldn't hear yourself think, she was jabbering away so. She had two tabloids with her tonight, instead of just one, and she knew every word in all of them by heart. She kept leaning over the gals' shoulders, puffing down their necks: "And there was a dime balanced on each of her eyelids when they found her, and another one across her lips, and he stuck one in each of her palms and folded her fingers over it, mind ye! D'ye ever hear of anything like it? Boy, he sure must've been down on you taxis—"

I yanked the door open, planted my foot where it would do the most good, and shot her out into the barn. She hadn't moved that fast from one place to another in twenty years. The other girls just looked at me, and then at one another, as much as to say: "Touchy, isn't she?"

"Get outside and break it down; what do I pay you for anyway?" Marino yelled at the door. A gob-stick tootled plaintively, out we trooped like prisoners in a lock-step, and another damn night had started in.

I came back in again during the tenth stretch (*"Dinah"* and *"Have You Any Castles, Baby?"*) to take off my kicks a minute and have a smoke. Julie's ghost came around me again. I could still hear her voice in my ears, from night-before-last! "Hold that match, Gin. I'm trying to duck a cement-mixer out there. Dances like a slap-happy pug. Three little steps to the right, as if he were priming for a standing broad-jump. I felt like screaming: For Pete's sake, if you're gonna jump, jump!"

And me: "What're you holding your hand for, been dancing upside-down?"

"It's the way he holds it. Bends it back on itself and folds it under. Like this, look. My wrist's nearly broken. And look what his ring did to me!" She had shown me a strawberry-size bruise.

Sitting there alone, now, in the half-light, I said to myself: "I bet *he* was the one! I bet *that's* who it was! Oh, if I'd only gotten a look at him, if I'd only had her point him out to me! If he enjoyed hurting her that much while she was still alive, he'd have enjoyed dancing with her after she was dead." My cigarette tasted rotten, I threw it down and got out of there in a hurry, back into the crowd.

A ticket was shoved at me and I ripped it without looking up. Gliding backward, all the way around on the other side of the barn, a voice finally said a little over my ear: "How's Ginger?"

I looked up and saw who it was, said, "What're you doing here?"

"Detailed here," Nick said.

I shivered to the music. "Do you expect him to show up *again*, after what he's done already?"

"He's a dance-hall killer," Nick said. "He killed Sally Arnold and the Fredericks girl, both from this same mill, and he killed a girl in Chicago in between. The prints on Julie Bennett's phonograph records match those in two of the other cases, and in the third case—where there were no prints—the girl was holding a dime clutched in her hand. He'll show up again sooner or later. There's one of us cops detailed to every one of these mills in the metropolitan area tonight, and we're going to keep it up until he does."

"How do you know what he looks like?" I asked.

He didn't answer for a whole bar. "We don't," he admitted finally. "That's the hell of it. Talk about being invisible in a crowd! We only know he isn't through yet, he'll keep doing it until we get him!"

I said, "He was here that night, he was right up here on this floor with her that night, before it happened; I'm sure of it!" And I sort of moved in closer. Me, who was always griping about being held too tight. I told him about the impression the guy's ring had left on her hand, and the peculiar way he'd held it, and the way he'd danced.

"You've got something there," he said, and he left me flat on the floor and went over to phone it in.

Nick picked me up again next dance.

He said, shuffling off, "That was him all right who danced with her. They found a freshly made impression still on her hand, a little offside from the first, which was almost entirely obliterated by then. Meaning the second one had been made after death, and therefore stayed uneffaced, just like a pinhole won't close up in the skin after death. They made an impression of it with moulage, my lieutenant just tells me. Then they filled that up with wax, photographed it through a magnifying lens, and now we know what kind of a ring he's wearing. A seal ring shaped like a shield, with two little jewel splinters, one in the upper right-hand corner, the other in the lower left."

"Any initials on it?" I gaped, awe-stricken.

"Nope, but something just as good. He can't get it off, unless he has a jeweler or locksmith file it off, and he'll be afraid to do that now. The fact that it would press so deeply into her hand proves that he can't get it off, the flesh of his finger has grown around it; otherwise it would have had a little give to it, the pressure would have shifted the head of it around a little."

He stepped all over my foot, summed up: "So we know how he dances, know what his favorite song is, '*Poor Butterfly*,' know what kind of a ring he's wearing. And we know he'll be back sooner or later."

That was all well and good, but I had my own health to look out for; the way my foot was throbbing! I hinted gently as I could, "You can't do very much watching out for him, can you, if you keep dancing around like this?"

"Maybe you think I can't. And if I just stand there with my back to the wall, it's a dead give-away. He'd smell me a mile away and duck out again. Keep it quiet what I'm doing here, don't pass it around. Your boss knows, of course, but it's to his interest to cooperate. A screwball like that can put an awful dent in his receipts."

"You're talking to the original sphinx," I assured him. "I don't pal with the rest of these twists anyway. Julie was the only one I was ever chummy with."

When the session closed and I came downstairs to the street, Nick was hanging around down there with the other lizards. He came over to me and took my arm and steered me off like he owned me.

"What's this?" I said.

He said, "This is just part of the act, make it look like the McCoy."

"Are you sure?" I said to myself, and I winked to myself without him seeing me.

All the other nights from then on were just a carbon copy of that one, and they started piling up by sevens. Seven, fourteen, twenty-one. Pretty soon it was a month since Julie Bennett had died. And not a clue as to who the killer was, where he was, what he looked like. Not a soul had noticed him that night at Joyland, too heavy a crowd. Just having his prints on file was no good by itself.

She was gone from the papers long ago, and she was gone from the dressing-room chatter, too, after a while, as forgotten as though she'd never lived. Only me, I remembered her, because she'd been my pal. And Nick Ballestier, he did because that was his job. I suppose Mom Henderson did too, because she had a morbid mind and loved to linger on gory murders. But outside of us three, nobody cared.

They did it the wrong way around, Nick's superiors at Homicide, I mean. I didn't try to tell him that, because he would have laughed at me. He would have said, "Sure! A dance-mill pony knows more about running the police department than the commissioner does himself! Why don't you go down there and show 'em how to do it?"

But what I mean is, the dance mills didn't need all that watching in the beginning, the first few weeks after it happened, like they gave them. Maniac or not, anyone would have known he wouldn't show up *that* soon after. They needn't have bothered detailing anyone at all to watch the first few weeks. He was lying low then. It was only after a month or so that they should have begun watching real closely for him. Instead they did it just the reverse. For a whole month Nick was there nightly. Then after that he just looked in occasionally, every second night or so, without staying through the whole session.

Then finally I tumbled that he'd been taken off the case entirely and was just coming for—er, the atmosphere. I put it up to him unexpectedly one night. "Are you still supposed to come around here like this?"

He got all red, admitted: "Naw, we were all taken off this duty long ago. I—er, guess I can't quit because I'm in the habit now or something."

"Oh, yeah?" I said to myself knowingly. I wouldn't have minded that so much, only his dancing didn't get any better, and the wear and tear on me was something awful. It was like trying to steer a steam-roller around the place.

"Nick," I finally pleaded one night, when he pinned me down flat with one of his size twelves and then tried to push me out from under with the rest of him, "be a detective all over the place, only please don't ask me to dance any more, I can't take it."

He looked innocently surprised. "Am I that bad?"

I tried to cover up with a smile at him. He'd been damn nice to me even if he couldn't dance.

When he didn't show up at all next night, I thought maybe I'd gone a little too far, offended him maybe. But the big hulk hadn't looked like the kind that was sensitive about his dancing, or anything else for that matter. I brought myself up short with a swift, imaginary kick in the pants at this point. "What the heck's the matter with *you?*" I said to myself. "You going soft? Didn't I tell you never to do that!" And I reached for the nearest ticket, and tore it, and I goona-gooed with a: "Grab yourself an armful, mister, it's your dime."

I got through that night somehow but I had that same spooky feeling the next night like I'd had *that* night—like tonight was going to be a bad night. Whenever I get that spooky feeling, it turns out to be a bad night all right. I tried to tell myself it was because Nick wasn't around. I'd got used to him, that was all, and now he'd quit coming, and the hell with it. But the feeling wouldn't go away. Like something was going to happen, before the night was over. Something bad.

Mom Henderson was sitting in there reading tomorrow morning's tab. "There hasn't been any good juicy murders lately," she mourned over the top of it. "Damn it, I like a good murder y'can get your teeth into wanst in a while!"

"Ah, dry up, you ghoul!" I snapped. I took off my shoes and dumped powder into them, put them on again. Marino came and knocked on the door. "Outside, freaks! What do I pay you for anyway?"

Someone jeered, "I often wonder!" and Duke, the front man, started to gliss over the coffin, and we all came out single file, me last, to a fate worse than death.

I didn't look up at the first buyer, just stared blindly at a triangle of shirt-front level with my eyes. It kept on like that for a while; always that same triangle of shirt-front. Mostly white, but sometimes blue, and once it was lavender, and I wondered if I ought to lead. The pattern of the tie across it kept changing too, but that was all.

"Butchers and barbers and rats from the harbors
Are the sweethearts my good luck has brought me."

"Why so downcast, Beautiful?"

"If you were standing where I am, looking where you are, you'd be downcast too."

That took care of him. And then the stretch.

Duke went into a waltz, and something jarred for a minute. My timetable. This should have been a gut bucket (low-down swing music) and it wasn't. He'd switched numbers on me, that's what it was. Maybe a request. For waltzes they killed the pash lights and turned on a blue circuit instead, made the place cool and dim with those flecks of silver from the mirror-top raining down.

I'd had this white shirt-triangle with the diamond pattern before; I remembered the knitted tie, with one tier unravelled on the end. I didn't want to see the face, too much trouble to look up. I hummed the piece mentally, to give my blank mind something to do. Then words seemed to drop into it, fit themselves to it, of their own accord, without my trying, so they must have belonged to it. *"Poor butterfly by the blossoms waiting."*

My hand ached, he was holding it so darned funny. I squirmed it, tried to ease it, and he held on all the tighter. He had it bent down and back on itself. . . .

"The moments pass into hours—"

Gee, if there's one thing I hate it's a guy with a ring that holds your mitt in a straight-jacket! And he didn't know the first thing about waltzing. Three funny little hops to the right, over and over and over. It was getting my nerves on edge. "If you're gonna jump, jump!" Julie's voice came back to me from long ago. She'd run into the same kind of a—

"I just must die, poor butterfly!"

Suddenly I was starting to get a little scared and a whole lot excited. I kept saying to myself: "Don't look up at him, you'll give yourself away." I kept my eyes on the knitted tie that had one tier unravelled. The lights went white and the stretch came on. We separated, he turned his back on me and I turned mine on him. We walked away from each other without a word. They don't thank you, they're paying for it.

I counted five and then I looked back over my shoulder, to try to see what he was like. He looked back at me at the same time, and we met each other's looks. I managed to slap on a smile, as though I'd only looked back because he'd made a hit with me, and that I hoped he'd come around again.

There was nothing wrong with his face, not just to look at anyway. It was no worse than any of the others around. He was about forty, maybe forty-five, hair still dark. Eyes speculative, nothing else, as they met mine. But he didn't answer my fake smile, maybe he could see through it. We both turned away again and went about our business.

I looked down at my hand, to see what made it hurt so. Careful not to raise it, careful not to bend my head, in case he was still watching. Just dropped my eyes to it. There was a red bruise the size of a small strawberry on it, from where his ring had pressed into it the whole time. I knew enough not to go near the box. I caught Duke's eye from where

I was and hitched my head at him, and we got together sort of casually over along the wall.

"What'd you play *'Poor Butterfly'* for that last time?" I asked.

"Request number," he said.

I said, "Don't point, and don't look around, but whose request was it?"

He didn't have to. "The guy that was with you the last two times. Why?" I didn't answer, so then he said, "I get it." He didn't at all. "All right, chiseler," he said, and handed me two dollars and a half, splitting a fiver the guy had slipped him to play it. Duke thought I was after a kick-back.

I took it. It was no good to tell him. What could he do? Nick Ballestier was the one to tell. I broke one of the singles at the orangeade concession —for nickels. Then I started to work my way over toward the phone, slow and aimless. I was within a yard of it when the cats started up again!

And suddenly *he* was right next to me, he must have been behind me the whole time.

"Were you going any place?" he asked.

I thought I saw his eyes flick to the phone, but I wasn't positive. One thing sure, there wasn't speculation in them any more, there was— decision.

"No place," I said meekly. "I'm at your disposal." I thought, "If I can only hold him here long enough, maybe Nick'll show up."

Then just as we got to the ropes, he said, "Let's skip this. Let's go out to a laundry and sit a while."

I said, smooth on the surface, panic-stricken underneath: "But I've already torn your ticket, don't you want to finish this one out at least?" And tried to goona-goo him for all I was worth, but it wouldn't take. He turned around and flagged Marino, to get his O.K.

His back was to me, and across his shoulder I kept shaking my head, more and more violently, to Marino—no, no, I don't want to go with him. Marino just ignored me. It meant more money in his pocket this way.

When I saw that the deal was going through, I turned like a streak, made the phone, got my buffalo in. It was no good trying to tell Marino, he wouldn't believe me, he'd think I was just making it up to get out of going out with the guy. Or if I raised the alarm on my own, he'd simply duck down the stairs before anyone could stop him and vanish again. Nick was the only one to tell, Nick was the only one who'd know how to nail him here.

I said, "Police headquarters, quick! Quick!" and turned and looked over across the barn. But Marino was already alone out there. I couldn't see where the guy had gone, they were milling around so looking over their prospects for the next one.

A voice came on and I said: "Is Nick Ballestier there? Hurry up, get him for me."

Meanwhile Duke had started to break it down again; real corny. It must have carried over the open wire. I happened to raise my eyes, and there was a shadow on the wall in front of me, coming across my shoulders from behind me. I didn't move, held steady, listening.

I said, "All right, Peggy, I just wanted to know when you're gonna pay me back that five bucks you owe me," and I killed it.

Would he get it when they told him? They'd say: "A girl's voice asked for you, Nick, from somewhere where there was music going on, and we couldn't make any sense out of what she said, and she hung up without waiting." A pretty slim thread to hold all your chances on.

I stood there afraid to turn. His voice said stonily, "Get your things, let's go. Suppose you don't bother any more tonight about your five dollars." There was a hidden meaning, a warning, in it.

There was no window in the dressing-room, no other way out but the way I'd come in, and he was right there outside the door. I poked around all I could, mourning: "Why don't Nick come?" and, boy, I was scared. A crowd all around me and no one to help me. He wouldn't stay; the only way to hang onto him for Nick was to go with him and pray for luck. I kept casing him through the crack of the door every minute or so. I didn't think he saw me, but he must have. Suddenly his heel scuffed at it brutally, and made me jump about an inch off the floor.

"Quit playing peek-a-boo, I'm waiting out here!" he called in sourly.

I grabbed up Mom Henderson's tab and scrawled across it in lipstick: "Nick: He's taking me with him, and I don't know where to. Look for my ticket stubs. Ginger."

Then I scooped up all the half tickets I'd accumulated all night long and shoved them loose into the pocket of my coat. Then I came sidling out to him. I thought I heard the phone on the wall starting to ring, but the music was so loud I couldn't be sure. We went downstairs and out on the street.

A block away I said, "There's a joint. We all go there a lot from our place," and pointed to Chan's. He said, "Shut up!" I dropped one of the dance checks on the sidewalk. Then I began making a regular trail of them.

The neon lights started to get fewer and fewer, and pretty soon we were in a network of dark lonely side streets. My pocket was nearly empty now of tickets. My luck was he didn't take a cab. He didn't want anyone to remember the two of us together, I guess.

I pleaded, "Don't make me walk any more, I'm awfully tired."

He said, "We're nearly there, it's right ahead." The sign on the next corner up fooled me; there was a chop-suey joint, there, only a second-class laundry, but I thought that was where we were going.

But in between us and it there was a long dismal block, with tumble-down houses and vacant lots on it. And I'd run out of dance checks. All my take gone, just to keep alive. He must have worked out the whole set-up carefully ahead of time, known I'd fall for that sign in the distance that we *weren't* going to.

Sure, I could have screamed out at any given step of the way, collected a crowd around us. But you don't understand. Much as I wanted to get away from him, there was one thing I wanted even more: To hold him for Nick. I didn't just want him to slip away into the night, and then do it all over again at some future date. And that's what would happen if I raised a row. They wouldn't believe me in a pinch, they'd think it was some kind of shakedown on my part. He'd talk himself out of it or scram before a cop came.

You have to live at night like I did to know the real callousness of passers-by on the street, how seldom they'll horn in, lift a finger to help you. Even a harness-cop wouldn't be much good, would only weigh my story against his, end up by sending us both about our business.

Maybe the thought came to me because I spotted a cop ahead just then, loitering toward us. I could hardly make him out in the gloom, but the slow steady walk told me. I didn't really think I was going to do it until we came abreast of him.

The three of us met in front of a boarded-up condemned house. Then, as though I saw my last chance slipping away—because Nick couldn't bridge the gap between me and the last of the dance checks any more, it was too wide—I stopped dead.

I began in a low tense voice: "Officer, this man here—"

Julie's murderer had involuntarily gone on a step without me. That put him to the rear of the cop. The whole thing was so sudden, it must have been one of those knives that shot out of their own hilts. The cop's eyes rolled, I could see them white in the darkness, and he coughed right in my face, warm, and he started to come down on top of me, slow and lazy. I sidestepped and he fell with a soft thud and rocked a couple of times with his own fall and then lay still.

But the knife was already out of him long ago, and its point was touching my side. And where the cop had been a second ago, *he* was now. We were alone together again.

He said in a cold, unexcited voice, "Go ahead, scream, and I'll give it to you right across him."

I didn't, I just pulled in all my breath.

He said, "Go ahead, down there," and steered me with his knife down a pair of steps into the dark area-way of the boarded-up house it had happened in front of. "Stand there, and if you make a sound—you know what I told you." Then he did something to the cop with his feet, and the cop came rolling down into the area-way after me.

I shrank back and my back was against the boarded-up basement door. It moved a little behind me. I thought, "This must be where he's taking me. If it is, then it's open." I couldn't get out past him, but maybe I could get *in* away from him.

I turned and clawed at the door, and the whole framed barrier swung out a little, enough to squeeze in through. He must have been hiding out in here, coming and going through here, all these weeks. No wonder they hadn't found him.

The real basement door behind it had been taken down out of the way. He'd seen what I was up to, and he was already wriggling through the gap after me. I was stumbling down a pitch-black hallway by then.

I found stairs going up by falling down on top of them full length. I sobbed, squirmed up the first few on hands and knees, straightened up as I went.

He stopped to light a match. I didn't have any, but his helped me too, showed me the outline of things. I was on the first-floor hall now, flitting down it. I didn't want to go up too high, he'd only seal me in some dead-end up there, but I couldn't stand still down here.

A broken-down chair grazed the side of my leg as I went by, and I turned, swung it up bodily, went back a step and pitched it down over the stair-well on top of him. I don't know if it hurt him at all but his match went out.

He said a funny thing then. "You always had a temper, Muriel."

I didn't stand there listening. I'd seen an opening in the wall farther ahead, before the match went out. Just a blackness. I dived through it and all the way across with swimming motions, until I hit a jutting mantel slab over some kind of fireplace. I crouched down and tucked myself in under it. It was one of those huge old-fashioned ones. I groped over my head and felt an opening there, lined with rough brickwork and furry with cobwebs, but it wasn't wide enough to climb up through. I squeezed into a corner of the fireplace and prayed he wouldn't spot me.

He'd lit another match, and it came into the room after me, but I could only see his legs from the fireplace opening, it cut him off at the waist. I wondered if he could see me; he didn't come near where I was.

The light got a little stronger, and he'd lit a candle stump. But still his legs didn't come over to me, didn't bend down, or show his face peering in at me. His legs just kept moving to and fro around the room. It was awfully hard, after all that running, to keep my breath down.

Finally he said out loud: "Chilly in here," and I could hear him rattling newspapers, getting them together. It didn't sink in for a minute what was going to happen next. I thought, "Has he forgotten me? Is he that crazy? Am I going to get away with it?" But there'd been a malicious snicker in his remark; he was crazy like a fox.

Suddenly his legs came over straight to me, without bending down to look he was stuffing the papers in beside me. I couldn't see out any more past them. I heard the scrape of a match against the floor boards. Then there was the momentary silence of combustion. I was sick, I wanted to die quick, but I didn't want to die that way. There was the hum of rising flame, and a brightness just before me, the papers all turned gold. I thought, "Oh, Nick! Nick! Here I go!"

I came plunging out, scattering sparks and burning newspapers.

He said, smiling, pleased with himself, casual, "Hello, Muriel. I thought you didn't have any more use for me? What are you doing in my house?" He still had the knife—with the cop's blood on it.

I said, "I'm not Muriel, I'm Ginger Allen from the Joyland. Oh, mister, please let me get out of here, please let me go!" I was so scared and so sick I went slowly to my knees. "Please!" I cried up at him.

He said, still in that casual way, "Oh, so you're not Muriel? You didn't marry me the night before I embarked for France, thinking I'd be killed, that you'd never see me again, that you'd get my soldier's pension?" And then getting a little more vicious, "But I fooled you, I was shell-shocked but I didn't die. I came back even if it was on a stretcher. And what did I find? You hadn't even waited to find out! You'd married another guy and you were both living on my pay. You tried to make it up to me, though, didn't you, Muriel? Sure; you visited me in the hospital, bringing me jelly. The man in the next cot died from eating it. Muriel, I've looked for you high and low ever since, and now I've found you."

He moved backwards, knife still in hand, and stood aside, and there was an old battered relic of a phonograph standing there on an empty packing-case. It had a great big horn to it, to give it volume. He must have picked it up off some ash-heap, repaired it himself. He released the catch and cranked it up a couple of times and laid the needle into the groove.

"We're going to dance, Muriel, like we did that night when I was in my khaki uniform and you were so pretty to look at. But it's going to have a different ending this time."

He came back toward me. I was still huddled there, shivering. "No!" I moaned. "Not me! You killed her, you killed her over and over again. Only last month, don't you remember?"

He said with pitiful simplicity, like the tortured thing he was: "Each time I think I have, she rises up again." He dragged me to my feet and caught me to him, and the arm with the knife went around me, and the knife pressed into my side.

The horrid thing over there was blaring into the emptiness, loud enought to be heard out on the street: "*Poor Butterfly*." It was horrible, it was ghastly.

And in the candle-lit pallor, with great shadows of us looming on the wall, like two crazed things we started to go round and round. I couldn't hold my head up on my neck; it hung way back over my shoulders like an overripe apple. My hair got loose and went streaming out as he pulled me and turned me and dragged me around. . . .

"*I just must die, poor butterfly!*"

Still holding me to him, he reached in his pocket and brought out a palmful of shiny dimes, and flung them in my face.

Then a shot went off outside in front of the house. It sounded like right in the area-way where the knifed cop was. Then five more in quick succession. The blare of the music must have brought the stabbed cop to. He must've got help.

He turned his head toward the boarded-up windows to listen. I tore myself out of his embrace, stumbled backwards, and the knife point seemed to leave a long circular scratch around my side, but he didn't jam it in in time, let it trail off me.

I got out into the hall before he could grab me again, and the rest of it was just kind of a flight-nightmare. I don't remember going down the stairs to the basement; I think I must have fallen down them without hurting myself—just like a drunk does.

Down there a headlight came at me from the tunnel-like passage. It must have been just a pocket-torch, but it got bigger and bigger, then went hurling on by. Behind it a long succession of serge-clothed figures brushed by me.

I kept trying to stop each one, saying: "Where's Nick? Are you Nick?"

Then a shot sounded upstairs. I heard a terrible death cry: "Muriel!" and that was all.

When I next heard anything it was Nick's voice. His arm was around me and he was kissing the cobwebs and tears off my face.

"How's Ginger?" he asked.

"Fine," I said, "and how's Nick?"

The Franchise Affair

BY JOSEPHINE TEY

CHAPTER I

IT WAS FOUR O'CLOCK of a spring evening; and Robert Blair was thinking of going home.

The office would not shut until five, of course. But when you are the only Blair, of Blair, Hayward, and Bennet, you go home when you think you will. And when your business is mostly wills, conveyancing, and investments your services are in small demand in the late afternoon. And when you live in Milford, where the last post goes out at 3.45, the day loses whatever momentum it ever had long before four o'clock.

It was not even likely that his telephone would ring. His golfing cronies would by now be somewhere between the fourteenth and the sixteenth hole. No one would ask him to dinner, because in Milford invitations to dinner are still written by hand and sent through the post. And Aunt Lin would not ring up and ask him to call for the fish on his way home, because this was her biweekly afternoon at the cinema, and she would at the moment be only twenty minutes gone with feature, so to speak.

So he sat there, in the lazy atmosphere of a spring evening in a little market town, staring at the last patch of sunlight on his desk (the mahogany desk with the brass inlay that his grandfather had scandalised the family by bringing home from Paris) and thought about going home. In the patch of sunlight was his tea-tray; and it was typical of Blair, Hayward, and Bennet that tea was no affair of a japanned tin tray and a kitchen cup. At 3.50 exactly on every working day Miss Tuff bore into his office a lacquer tray covered with a fair white cloth and bearing a cup of tea in blue-patterned china, and, on a plate to match, two biscuits; petit-beurre Mondays, Wednesdays and Fridays, digestive Tuesdays, Thursdays and Saturdays.

Looking at it now, idly, he thought how much it represented the continuity of Blair, Hayward, and Bennet. The china he could remember as long as he could remember anything. The tray had been used when he was very small by the cook at home to take the bread in from the baker, and had been rescued by his young mother and brought to the office to bear the blue-patterned cups. The cloth had come years later with the advent of Miss Tuff. Miss Tuff was a war-time product; the first woman who had ever sat at a desk in a respectable solicitor's in Milford. A whole revolution Miss Tuff was in her single gawky thin earnest person. But the firm had survived the revolution with hardly a jolt, and now, nearly a quarter of a century later, it was inconceivable that thin grey dignified

Miss Tuff had ever been a sensation. Indeed her only disturbance of the immemorial routine was the introduction of the tray-cloth. In Miss Tuff's home no meal was ever put straight on to a tray; if it comes to that, no cakes were ever put straight on to a plate; a tray-cloth or a doyley must intervene. So Miss Tuff had looked askance at the bare tray. She had, moreover, considered the lacquered pattern distracting, unappetising, and "queer." So one day she had brought a cloth from home; decent, plain, and white, as befitted something that was to be eaten off. And Robert's father, who had liked the lacquer tray, looked at the clean white cloth and was touched by young Miss Tuff's identification of herself with the firm's interests, and the cloth had stayed, and was now as much a part of the firm's life as the deed-boxes, and the brass plate, and Mr. Heseltine's annual cold.

It was when his eyes rested on the blue plate where the biscuits had been that Robert experienced that odd sensation in his chest again. The sensation had nothing to do with the two digestive biscuits; at least, not physically. It had to do with the inevitability of the biscuit routine; the placid certainty that it would be digestive on a Thursday and petit-beurre on a Monday. Until the last year or so, he had found no fault with certainty or placidity. He had never wanted any other life but this: this quiet friendly life in the place where he had grown up. He still did not want any other. But once or twice lately an odd, alien thought had crossed his mind; irrelevant and unbidden. As nearly as it could be put into words it was: "This is all you are ever going to have." And with the thought would come that moment's constriction in his chest. Almost a panic reaction; like the heart-squeezing that remembering a dentist appointment would cause in his ten-year-old breast.

This annoyed and puzzled Robert; who considered himself a happy and fortunate person, and adult at that. Why should this foreign thought thrust itself on him and cause that dismayed tightening under his ribs? What had his life lacked that a man might be supposed to miss?

A wife?

But he could have married if he had wanted to. At least he supposed he could; there were a great many unattached females in the district, and they showed no signs of disliking him.

A devoted mother?

But what greater devotion could a mother have given him than Aunt Lin provided; dear doting Aunt Lin.

Riches?

What had he ever wanted that he could not buy? And if that wasn't riches he didn't know what was.

An exciting life?

But he had never wanted excitement. No greater excitement, that is, than was provided by a day's hunting or being all-square at the sixteenth.

Then what?

Why the "This is all you are ever going to have" thought?

Perhaps, he thought, sitting staring at the blue plate where the biscuits had been, it was just that Childhood's attitude of something-wonderful-tomorrow persisted subconsciously in a man as long as it was capable of realisation, and it was only after forty, when it became unlikely of fulfilment, that it obtruded itself into conscious thought; a lost piece of childhood crying for attention.

Certainly he, Robert Blair, hoped very heartily that his life would go on being what it was until he died. He had known since his schooldays that he would go into the firm and one day succeed his father; and he had looked with good-natured pity on boys who had no niche in life ready-made for them; who had no Milford, full of friends and memories, waiting for them; no part in English continuity as was provided by Blair, Hayward, and Bennet.

There was no Hayward in the firm nowadays; there had not been one since 1843; but a young sprig of the Bennets was occupying the back room at this moment. Occupying was the operative word, since it was very unlikely that he was doing any work; his chief interest in life being to write poems of an originality so pristine that only Nevil himself could understand them. Robert deplored the poems but condoned the idleness, since he could not forget that when he had occupied that same room he had spent his time practising mashie shots into the leather arm-chair.

The sunlight slipped off the edge of the tray and Robert decided it was time to go. If he went now he could walk home down the High Street before the sunlight was off the east-side pavement; and walking down Milford High Street was still one of the things that gave him conscious pleasure. Not that Milford was a show-place. It could be duplicated a hundred times anywhere south of Trent. But in its unself-conscious fashion it typified the goodness of life in England for the last three hundred years. From the old dwelling-house flush with the pavement that housed Blair, Hayward, and Bennet and had been built in the last years of Charles the Second's reign, the High Street flowed south in a gentle slope—Georgian brick, Elizabethan timber-and-plaster, Victorian stone, Regency stucco—to the Edwardian villas behind their elm trees at the other end. Here and there, among the rose and white and brown, appeared a front of black glass, brazening it out like an overdressed parvenu at a party; but the good manners of the other buildings discounted them. Even the multiple businesses had dealt leniently with Milford. True, the scarlet and gold of an American bazaar flaunted its bright promise down at the south end, and daily offended Miss Truelove who ran the Elizabethan relic opposite as a tea-shop with the aid of her sister's baking and Ann Boleyn's reputation. But the Westminster Bank, with a humility rare since the days of usury, had adapted the Weavers Hall to their needs without so much as a hint of marble; and Soles, the wholesale chemists, had taken the old Wisdom residence and kept its tall surprised-looking front intact.

It was a fine, gay, busy little street, punctuated with pollarded lime trees growing out of the pavement; and Robert Blair loved it.

He had gathered his feet under him preparatory to getting up, when his telephone rang. In other places in the world, one understands, telephones are made to ring in outer offices, where a minion answers the thing and asks your business and says that if you will be good enough to wait just a moment she will "put you thrrrough" and you are then connected with the person you want to speak to. But not in Milford. Nothing like that would be tolerated in Milford. In Milford if you call John Smith on the telephone you expect John Smith to answer in person. So when the telephone rang on that spring evening in Blair, Hayward, and Bennet's it rang on Robert's brass-and-mahogany desk.

Always, afterwards, Robert was to wonder what would have happened if that telephone call had been one minute later. In one minute, sixty worthless seconds, he would have taken his coat from the peg in the hall, popped his head into the opposite room to tell Mr. Heseltine that he was departing for the day, stepped out into the pale sunlight and been away down the street. Mr. Heseltine would have answered his telephone when it rang and told the woman that he had gone. And she would have hung up and tried someone else. And all that followed would have had only academic interest for him.

But the telephone rang in time; and Robert put out his hand and picked up the receiver.

"Is that Mr. Blair?" a woman's voice asked; a contralto voice that would normally be a confident one, he felt, but now sounded breathless or hurried. "Oh, I am so glad to have caught you. I was afraid you would have gone for the day. Mr. Blair, you don't know me. My name is Sharpe, Marion Sharpe. I live with my mother at The Franchise. The house out on the Larborough road, you know."

"Yes, I know it," Blair said. He knew Marion Sharpe by sight, as he knew everyone in Milford and the district. A tall, lean, dark woman of forty or so; much given to bright silk kerchiefs which accentuated her gipsy swarthiness. She drove a battered old car, from which she shopped in the mornings while her white-haired old mother sat in the back, upright and delicate and incongruous and somehow silently protesting. In profile old Mrs. Sharpe looked like Whistler's mother; when she turned full-face and you got the impact of her bright, pale, cold, seagull's eye, she looked like a sibyl. An uncomfortable old person.

"You don't know me," the voice went on, "but I have seen you in Milford, and you look a kind person, and I need a lawyer. I mean, I need one now, this minute. The only lawyer we ever have business with is in London—a London firm, I mean—and they are not actually ours. We just inherited them with a legacy. But now I am in trouble and I need legal backing, and I remembered you and thought that you would——"

"If it is your car——" Robert began. "In trouble" in Milford meant one of two things; an affiliation order, or an offence against the traffic laws. Since the case involved Marion Sharpe, it would be the latter; but it made no difference because in neither case was Blair, Hayward, and Bennet likely to be interested. He would pass her on to Carley, the bright lad at the other end of the street, who revelled in court cases and was popularly credited with the capacity to bail the Devil out of hell. ("Bail him out!" someone said, one night at the Rose and Crown. "He'd do more than that. He'd get all our signatures to a guinea testimonial to the Old Sinner.")

"If it is your car——"

"Car?" she said, vaguely; as if in her present world it was difficult to remember what a car was. "Oh, I see. No. Oh, no, it isn't anything like that. It is something much more serious. It's Scotland Yard."

"Scotland Yard!"

To that douce country lawyer and gentleman, Robert Blair, Scotland Yard was as exotic as Xanadu, Hollywood, or parachuting. As a good citizen he was on comfortable terms with the local police, and there his connection with crime ended. The nearest he had ever come to Scotland Yard was to play golf with the local Inspector; a good chap who played a very steady game and occasionally, when it came to the nineteenth, expanded into mild indiscretions about his job.

"I haven't *murdered* anyone, if that is what you are thinking," the voice said hastily.

"The point is: are you *supposed* to have murdered anyone?" Whatever she was supposed to have done this was clearly a case for Carley. He must edge her off on to Carley.

"No; it isn't murder at all. I'm supposed to have kidnapped someone. Or abducted them, or something. I can't explain over the telephone. And anyhow I need someone now, at once, and——"

"But, you know, I don't think it is me you need at all," Robert said. "I know practically nothing about criminal law. My firm is not equipped to deal with a case of that sort. The man you need——"

"I don't want a criminal lawyer. I want a friend. Someone who will stand by me and see that I am not put-upon. I mean, tell me what I need not answer if I don't want to, and that sort of thing. You don't need a training in crime for that, do you?"

"No, but you would be much better served by a firm who were used to police cases. A firm that——"

"What you are trying to tell me is that this is not 'your cup of tea'; that's it, isn't it?"

"No, of course not," Robert said hastily. "I quite honestly feel that you would be wiser——"

"You know what I feel like?" she broke in. "I feel like someone drowning in a river because she can't drag herself up the bank, and instead of giving me a hand you point out that the other bank is much better to crawl out on."

There was a moment's silence.

"But on the contrary," Robert said, "I can provide you with an expert puller-out-of-rivers; a great improvement on my amateur self, I assure you. Benjamin Carley knows more about defending accused persons than anyone between here and——"

"What! That awful little man with the striped suits!" Her deep voice ran up and cracked, and there was another momentary silence. "I am sorry," she said presently in her normal voice. "That was silly. But you see, when I rang you up just now it wasn't because I thought you would be clever about things" ("*Wasn't* it, indeed," thought Robert) "but because I was in trouble and wanted the advice of someone of my own sort. And you looked my sort. Mr. Blair, do please come. I need you *now*. There are people from Scotland Yard here in the house. And if you feel that it isn't something you want to be mixed up in you could always pass it on to someone else afterwards; couldn't you? But there may be nothing after all to be mixed up in. If you would just come out here and 'watch my interests' or whatever you call it, for an hour, it may all pass over. I'm sure there is a mistake somewhere. Couldn't you please do that for me?"

On the whole Robert Blair thought that he could. He was too good-natured to refuse any reasonable appeal—and she had given him a loophole if things grew difficult. And he did not, after all, now he came to think of it, want to throw her to Ben Carley. In spite of her *bêtise* about striped suits he saw her point of view. If you had done something you wanted to get away with, Carley was no doubt God's gift to you; but if you were bewildered and in trouble and innocent, perhaps Carley's brash personality was not likely to be a very present help.

All the same, he wished as he laid down the receiver that the front he presented to the world was a more forbidding one—Calvin or Caliban, he did not care, so long as strange females were discouraged from flinging themselves on his protection when they were in trouble.

What possible kind of trouble could "kidnapping" be, he wondered as he walked round to the garage in Sin Lane for his car? *Was* there such an offence in English law? And whom could she possibly be interested in kidnapping? A child? Some child with "expectations"? In spite of the large house out on the Larborough road they gave the impression of having very little money. Or some child that they considered "ill-used" by its natural guardians? That was possible. The old woman had a fanatic's face, if ever he saw one; and Marion Sharpe herself looked as if the stake would be her natural prop if stakes were not out of fashion. Yes, it was probably some ill-judged piece of philanthropy. Detention "with intent to deprive parent, guardian, etc., of its possession." He wished he remembered more of his *Harris and Wilshere.* He could not remember off-hand whether that was a felony, with penal servitude in the offing, or a mere misdemeanour. "Abduction and Detention" had not sullied the Blair, Hayward, and Bennet files since December 1798, when the squire of Lessows, much flown with seasonable claret, had taken the young Miss Gretton across his saddle-bow from a ball at the Gretton home and ridden away with her through the floods; and there was no doubt at all, of course, as to the squire's motive on that occasion.

Ah, well; they would no doubt be open to reason now that they had been startled by the irruption of Scotland Yard into their plans. He was a little startled by Scotland Yard himself. Was the child so important that it was a matter for Headquarters?

Round in Sin Lane he ran into the usual war but extricated himself. (Etymologists, in case you are interested, say that the "Sin" is merely a corruption of "sand," but the inhabitants of Milford of course know better; before those council houses were built on the low meadows behind the town the lane led direct to the lovers' walk in High Wood.) Across the narrow lane, face to face in perpetual enmity, stood the local livery stable and the town's newest garage. The garage frightened the horses (so said the livery stable), and the livery stable blocked up the lane continually with delivery loads of straw and fodder and what not (so the garage said). Moreover the garage was run by Bill Brough, ex-R.E.M.E., and Stanley Peters, ex-Royal Corps of Signals; and old Matt Ellis, ex-King's Dragoon Guards, looked on them as representatives of a generation which had destroyed the cavalry and an offence to civilisation.

In winter, when he hunted, Robert heard the cavalry side of the story; for the rest of the year he listened to the Royal Corps of Signals while his car was being wiped, oiled, filled, or fetched. Today the Signals wanted to know the difference between libel and slander, and what exactly constituted defamation of character. Was it defamation of character to say that a man was "a tinkerer with tin cans who wouldn't know a nut from an acorn"?

"Don't know, Stan. Have to think over it," Robert said hastily, pressing the starter. He waited while three tired hacks brought back two fat children and a groom from their afternoon ride ("See what I mean?" said Stanley in the background) and then swung the car into the High Street.

Down at the south end of the High Street the shops faded gradually into dwelling houses with doorsteps on the pavement, then to houses set back a pace and with porticos to their doors, and then to villas with trees in their gardens, and then, quite suddenly, to fields and open country.

It was farming country; a land of endless hedged fields and few houses. A rich country, but lonely; one could travel mile after mile without meeting another human being. Quiet and confident and unchanged since the Wars of the Roses, hedged field succeeded hedged field, and skyline faded into skyline, without any break in the pattern. Only the telegraph posts betrayed the century.

Away beyond the horizon was Larborough. Larborough was bicycles, small arms, tin-tacks, Cowan's Cranberry Sauce, and a million human souls living cheek by jowl in dirty red brick; and periodically it broke bounds in an atavistic longing for grass and earth. But there was nothing in the Milford country to attract a race who demanded with their grass and earth both views and tea-houses; when Larborough went on holiday it went as one man west to the hills and the sea, and the great stretch of country north and east of it stayed lonely and quiet and unlittered as it had been in the days of the Sun in Splendour. It was "dull"; and by that damnation was saved.

Two miles out on the Larborough road stood the house known as The Franchise; set down by the roadside with the inconsequence of a telephone kiosk. In the last days of the Regency someone had bought the field known as The Franchise, built in the middle of it a flat white house, and then surrounded the whole with a high solid wall of brick with a large double gate, of wall height, in the middle of the road frontage. It had no relation with anything in the countryside. No farm buildings in the background; no side-gates, even, into the surrounding fields. Stables were built in accordance with the period at the back of the house, but they were inside the wall. The place was as irrelevant, as isolated, as a child's toy dropped by the wayside. It had been occupied as long as Robert could remember by an old man; presumably the same old man, but since The Franchise people had always shopped at Ham Green, the village on the Larborough side of them, they had never been seen in Milford. And then Marion Sharpe and her mother had begun to be part of the morning shopping scene in Milford, and it was understood that they had inherited The Franchise when the old man died.

How long had they been there, Robert wondered. Three years? Four years?

That they had not entered Milford socially was nothing to reckon by. Old Mrs. Warren, who had bought the first of the elm-shaded villas at the end of the High Street a small matter of twenty-five years ago in the hope that midland air would be better for her rheumatism than the sea, was still referred to as "that lady from Weymouth." (It was Swanage, incidentally.)

The Sharpes, moreover, might not have sought social contacts. They had an odd air of being self-sufficient. He had seen the daughter once or twice on the golf-course, playing (presumably as a guest) with Dr. Borthwick. She drove a long ball like a man, and used her thin brown wrists like a professional. And that was all Robert knew about her.

As he brought the car to a stop in front of the tall iron gates, he found that two other cars were already there. It needed only one glance at the nearer—so inconspicuous, so well-groomed, so discreet—to identify it. In what other country in this world, he wondered as he got out of his own car, does the police force take pains to be well-mannered and quiet?

His eye lighted on the further car and he saw that it was Hallam's; the local Inspector who played such a steady game on the golf-course.

There were three people in the police car: the driver, and, in the back, a middle-aged woman and what seemed to be either a child or a young girl. The driver regarded him with that mild, absent-minded, all-observing police eye, and then withdrew his gaze, but the faces in the back he could not see.

The tall iron gates were shut—Robert could not remember ever seeing them open—and Robert pushed open one heavy half with frank curiosity. The iron lace of the original gates had been lined, in some Victorian desire for privacy, by flat sheets of cast iron; and the wall was too high for anything inside to be visible; so that, except for a distant view of its roof and chimneys, he had never seen The Franchise.

His first feeling was disappointment. It was not the fallen-on-evil-times look of the house—although that was evident; it was the sheer ugliness of it. Either it had been built too late to share in the grace of a graceful period, or the builder had lacked an architect's eye. He had used the idiom of the time, but it had apparently not been native to him. Everything was just a little wrong: the windows the wrong size by half a foot, wrongly placed by not much more; the doorway the wrong width, and the flight of steps the wrong height. The total result was that instead of the bland contentment of its period the house had a hard stare. An antagonistic, questioning stare. As he walked across the courtyard to the unwelcoming door Robert knew what it reminded him of: a dog that has been suddenly wakened from sleep by the advent of a stranger, propped on his forelegs, uncertain for a moment whether to attack or merely bark. It had the same what-are-you-doing-here? expression.

Before he could ring the bell the door was opened; not by a maid but by Marion Sharpe.

"I saw you coming," she said, putting out her hand. "I didn't want you to ring because my mother lies down in the afternoons, and I am hoping that we can get this business over before she wakes up. Then she need never know anything about it. I am more grateful than I can say to you for coming."

Robert murmured something, and noticed that her eyes, which he had expected to be a bright gipsy brown, were actually a grey hazel. She drew him into the hall, and he noticed as he put his hat down on a chest that the rug on the floor was threadbare.

"The Law is in here," she said, pushing open a door and ushering him into a drawing-room. Robert would have liked to talk to her alone for a moment, to orientate himself; but it was too late now to suggest that. This was evidently the way she wanted it.

Sitting on the edge of a bead-work chair was Hallam, looking sheepish.

And by the window, entirely at his ease in a very nice piece of Hepplewhite, was Scotland Yard in the person of a youngish spare man in a well-tailored suit.

As they got up, Hallam and Robert nodded to each other.

"You know Inspector Hallam, then?" Marion Sharpe said. "And this is Detective-Inspector Grant, from Headquarters."

Robert noticed the "Headquarters," and wondered. Had she already at some time had dealings with the police, or was it that she just didn't like the slightly sensational sound of "the Yard"?

Grant shook hands, and said:

"I'm glad you've come, Mr. Blair. Not only for Miss Sharpe's sake but for my own."

"Yours?"

"I couldn't very well proceed until Miss Sharpe had some kind of support; friendly support if not legal, but if legal so much the better."

"I see. And what are you charging her with?"

"We are not charging her with anything——" Grant began, but Marion interrupted him.

"I am supposed to have kidnapped and beaten up someone."

"*Beaten up?*" Robert said, staggered.

"Yes," she said, with a kind of relish in enormity. "Beaten her black and blue."

"Her?"

"A girl. She is outside the gate in a car now."

"I think we had better begin at the beginning," Robert said, clutching after the normal.

"Perhaps I had better do the explaining," Grant said, mildly.

"Yes," said Miss Sharpe, "do. After all it is your story."

Robert wondered if Grant were aware of the mockery. He wondered a little, too, at the coolness that could afford mockery with Scotland Yard sitting in one of her best chairs. She had not sounded cool over the telephone; she had sounded driven, half-desperate. Perhaps it was the presence of an ally that had heartened her; or perhaps she had just got her second wind.

"Just before Easter," Grant began in succinct police-fashion, "a girl called Elisabeth Kane, who lived with her guardians near Aylesbury, went to spend a short holiday with a married aunt in Mainshill, the suburb of Larborough. She went by coach, because the London-Larborough coaches pass through Aylesbury, and also pass through Mainshill before reaching Larborough; so that she could get off the coach in Mainshill and be within a three-minute walk of her aunt's house, instead of having to go into Larborough and come all the way out again as she would have to if she travelled by train. At the end of a week her guardians—a Mr. and Mrs. Wynn—had a postcard from her saying that she was enjoying herself very much and was staying on. They took this to mean staying on for the duration of her school holiday, which would mean another three weeks. When she didn't turn up on the day before she was supposed to go back to school, they took it for granted that she was merely playing truant and wrote to her aunt to send her back. The aunt, instead of going to the nearest call-box or telegraph office, broke it to the Wynns in a letter, that her niece had left on her way back to Aylesbury a fortnight previously. The exchange of letters had taken the best part of another week, so that by the time the guardians went to the police about it the girl had been missing for four weeks. The police took all the usual measures but before they could really get going the girl turned up. She walked into her home near Aylesbury late one night wearing only a dress and shoes, and in a state of complete exhaustion."

"How old is the girl?" Robert asked.

"Fifteen. Nearly sixteen." He waited a moment to see if Robert had further questions, and then went on. (As one counsel to another, thought Robert appreciatively; a manner to match the car that stood so unobtrusively at the gate.) "She said she had been 'kidnapped' in a car, but that was all the information anyone got from her for two days. She lapsed into a semi-conscious condition. When she recovered, about forty-eight hours later, they began to get her story from her."

"They?"

"The Wynns. The police wanted it, of course, but she grew hysterical at any mention of police, so they had to acquire it second-hand. She said that while she was waiting for her return coach at the cross-roads in Mainshill, a car pulled up at the kerb with two women in it. The younger woman, who was driving, asked her if she was waiting for a bus and if they could give her a lift."

"Was the girl alone?"

"Yes."

"Why? Didn't anyone go to see her off?"

"Her uncle was working, and her aunt had gone to be god-mother at a christening." Again he paused to let Robert put further questions if he was so minded. "The girl said that she was waiting for the London coach, and they told her that it had already gone by. Since she had arrived at the cross-roads with very little time to spare, and her watch was not a particularly accurate one, she believed this. Indeed, she had begun to be afraid, even before the car stopped, that she had missed the coach. She was distressed about it because it was by then four o'clock, beginning to rain, and growing dark. They were very sympathetic, and suggested that they should give her a lift to a place whose name she did not catch, where she could get a different coach to London in half an hour's time. She accepted this gratefully and got in beside the elder woman in the back of the car."

A picture swam into Robert's mind of old Mrs. Sharpe, upright and intimidating, in her usual place in the back of the car. He glanced at

Marion Sharpe, but her face was calm. This was a story she had heard already.

"The rain blurred the windows, and she talked to the older woman about herself as they went along, so that she paid little attention to where they were going. When she at last took notice of her surroundings the evening outside the windows had become quite dark and it seemed to her that they had been travelling for a long time. She said something about its being extraordinarily kind of them to take her so far out of their way, and the younger woman, speaking for the first time, said that as it happened it was not out of their way, and that, on the contrary, she would have time to come in and have a cup of something hot with them before they took her on to her new cross-roads. She was doubtful about this, but the younger woman said it would be of no advantage to wait for twenty minutes in the rain when she could be warm and dry and fed in those same twenty minutes; and she agreed that this seemed sensible. Eventually the younger woman got out, opened what appeared to the girl to be drive gates, and the car was driven up to a house which it was too dark to see. She was taken into a large kitchen——"

"A kitchen?" Robert repeated.

"Yes, a kitchen. The older woman put some cold coffee on the stove to heat while the younger one cut sandwiches. 'Sandwiches without tops,' the girl called them."

"Smorgasbord."

"Yes. While they ate and drank, the younger woman told her that they had no maid at the moment and asked her if she would like to be a maid for them for a little. She said that she wouldn't. They tried persuasion, but she stuck to it that that was not at all the kind of job she would take. Their faces began to grow blurred as she talked, and when they suggested that she might at least come upstairs and see what a nice bedroom she would have if she stayed she was too fuddled in her mind to do anything but follow their suggestion. She remembers going up a first flight with a carpet, and a second flight with what she calls 'something hard' underfoot, and that was all she remembered until she woke in daylight on a truckle bed in a bare little attic. She was wearing only her slip, and there was no sign of the rest of her clothes. The door was locked, and the small round window would not open. In any case——"

"*Round* window!" said Robert, uncomfortably.

But it was Marion who answered him. "Yes," she said, meaningly. "A round window up in the roof."

Since his last thought as he came to her front door a few minutes ago had been how badly placed was the little round window in the roof, there seemed to Robert to be no adequate comment. Grant made his usual pause for courtesy's sake, and went on.

"Presently the younger woman arrived with a bowl of porridge. The girl refused it and demanded her clothes and her release. The woman said that she would eat it when she was hungry enough and went away, leaving the porridge behind. She was alone till evening, when the same woman brought her tea on a tray with fresh cakes and tried to talk her into giving the maid's job a trial. The girl again refused, and for days, according to her story, this alternate coaxing and bullying went on, sometimes by one of the women and sometimes by the other. Then she decided that if she could break the small round window she might be able to crawl out of it on to the roof, which was protected by a parapet, and call the attention of some passerby, or some visiting tradesman, to her plight. Unfortunately, her only implement was a chair, and she had managed only to crack the glass before the younger woman interrupted her, in a great passion. She snatched the chair from the girl and belaboured her with it until she was breathless. She went away, taking the chair with her, and the girl thought that was the end of it. But in a few moments the woman came back with what the girl thinks was a dog whip and beat her until she fainted. Next day the older woman appeared with an armful of bed-linen and said that if she would not work she would at least sew. No sewing, no food. She was too stiff to sew and so had no food. The following day she was threatened with another beating if she did not sew. So she mended some of the linen and was given stew for supper. This arrangement lasted for some time, but if her sewing was bad or insufficient, she was either beaten or deprived of food. Then one evening the older woman brought the usual bowl of stew and went away leaving the door unlocked. The girl waited, thinking it was a trap that would end in another beating; but in the end she ventured on to the landing. There was no sound, and she ran down a flight of uncarpeted stairs. Then down a second flight to the first landing. Now she could hear the two women talking in the kitchen. She crept down the last flight and dashed for the door. It was unlocked and she ran out just as she was into the night."

"In her slip?" Robert asked.

"I forgot to say that the slip had been exchanged for her dress. There was no heating in the attic, and in nothing but a slip she would probably have died."

"If she ever was in an attic," Robert said.

"If, as you say, she ever was in an attic," the Inspector agreed smoothly. And without his customary pause of courtesy went on: "She does not remember much after that. She walked a great distance in the dark, she says. It seemed a highroad but there was no traffic and she met no one. Then, on a main road, some time later, a lorry driver saw her in his headlight and stopped to give her a lift. She was so tired that she fell straight asleep. She woke as she was being set on her feet at the roadside. The lorry driver was laughing at her and saying that she was like a sawdust doll that had lost its stuffing. It seemed to be still night time. The lorry driver said this was where she said she wanted to be put off, and drove away. After a little she recognised the corner. It was less than two miles from her home. She heard a clock strike eleven. And shortly before midnight she arrived home."

CHAPTER II

THERE WAS a short silence.

"And this is the girl who is sitting in a car outside the gate of The Franchise at this moment?" said Robert.

"Yes."

"I take it that you have reasons for bringing her here."

"Yes. When the girl had recovered sufficiently she was induced to tell her story to the police. It was taken down in shorthand as she told it, and she read the typed version and signed it. In that statement there were two things that helped the police a lot. These are the relevant extracts:

'When we had been going for some time we passed a bus that had MILFORD in a lighted sign on it. No, I don't know where Milford is. No, I have never been there.'

"That is one. The other is:

'From the window of the attic I could see a high brick wall with a big iron gate in the middle of it. There was a road on the further side of the wall, because I could see the telegraph posts. No, I couldn't see the traffic on it because the wall was too high. Just the tops of lorry loads sometimes. You couldn't see through the gate because it had sheets of iron on the inside. Inside the gate the carriage-way went straight for a little and then divided in two into a circle up to the door. No, it wasn't a garden, just grass. Yes, lawn, I suppose. No, I don't remember any shrubs; just the grass and the paths.'"

Grant shut the little notebook he had been quoting from.

"As far as we know—and the search has been thorough—there is no other house between Larborough and Milford which fulfils the girl's description except The Franchise. The Franchise, moreover, fulfils it in every particular. When the girl saw the wall and the gate today she was sure that this was the place; but she has not so far seen inside the gate, of course. I had first to explain matters to Miss Sharpe, and find out if she was willing to be confronted with the girl. She very rightly suggested that some legal witness should be present."

"Do you wonder that I wanted help in a hurry?" Marion Sharpe said, turning to Robert. "Can you imagine a more nightmare piece of nonsense?"

"The girl's story is certainly the oddest mixture of the factual and the absurd. I know that domestic help is scarce," Robert said, "but would anyone hope to enlist a servant by forcibly detaining her, to say nothing of beating and starving her."

"No normal person, of course," Grant agreed, keeping his eye steadily fixed on Robert's so that it had no tendency to slide over to Marion Sharpe. "But believe me in my first twelve months in the force I had come across a dozen things much more incredible. There is no end to the extravagances of human conduct."

"I agree; but the extravagance is just as likely to be in the girl's conduct. After all, the extravagance begins with her. She is the one who has been missing for——" He paused in question.

"A month," Grant supplied.

"For a month; while there is no suggestion that the household at The Franchise has varied at all from its routine. Would it not be possible for Miss Sharpe to provide an alibi for the day in question?"

"No," Marion Sharpe said. "The day, according to the Inspector, is the 28th of March. That is a long time ago, and our days here vary very little, if at all. It would be quite impossible for us to remember what we were doing on March the 28th—and most unlikely that anyone would remember for us."

"Your maid?" Robert suggested. "Servants have ways of marking their domestic life that is often surprising."

"We have no maid," she said. "We find it difficult to keep one: The Franchise is so isolated."

The moment threatened to become awkward and Robert hastened to break it.

"This girl—— I don't know her name, by the way."

"Elisabeth Kane; known as Betty Kane."

"Oh, yes; you did tell me. I'm sorry. This girl—may we know something about her? I take it that the police have investigated her before accepting so much of her story. Why guardians and not parents, for instance?"

"She is a war orphan. She was evacuated to the Aylesbury district as a small child. She was an only child, and was billeted with the Wynns, who had a boy four years older. About twelve months later both parents were killed, in the same 'incident,' and the Wynns, who had always wanted a daughter and were very fond of the child, were glad to keep her. She looks on them as her parents, since she can hardly remember the real ones."

"I see. And her record?"

"Excellent. A very quiet girl, by every account. Good at her school work but not brilliant. Has never been in any kind of trouble, in school or out of it. 'Transparently truthful' was the phrase her form mistress used about her."

"When she eventually turned up at her home, after her absence, was there any evidence of the beatings she said she had been given?"

"Oh, yes. Very definitely. The Wynns' own doctor saw her early next morning, and his statement is that she had been very extensively knocked about. Indeed, some of the bruises were still visible much later when she made her statement to us."

"No history of epilepsy?"

"No; we considered that very early in the inquiry. I should like to say that the Wynns are very sensible people. They have been greatly distressed, but they have not tried to dramatise the affair, or allowed the girl to be an object of interest or pity. They have taken the affair admirably."

"And all that remains is for me to take my end of it with the same admirable detachment," Marion Sharpe said.

"You see my position, Miss Sharpe. The girl not only describes the house in which she says she was detained; she describes the two inhabitants—and describes them very accurately. 'A thin, elderly woman with soft white hair and no hat, dressed in black; and a much younger woman, thin and tall and dark like a gipsy, with no hat and a bright silk scarf round her neck.'"

"Oh, yes. I can think of no explanation, but I understand your position. And now I think we had better have the girl in, but before we do I should like to say——"

The door opened noiselessly, and old Mrs. Sharpe appeared on the threshold. The short pieces of white hair round her face stood up on end, as her pillow had left them, and she looked more than ever like a sibyl. She pushed the door to behind her and surveyed the gathering with a malicious interest.

"Hah!" she said, making a sound like the throaty squawk of a hen. "*Three* strange men!"

"Let me present them, Mother," Marion said, as the three got to their feet.

"This is Mr. Blair, of Blair, Hayward, and Bennet—the firm who have that lovely house at the top of the High Street."

As Robert bowed the old woman fixed him with her seagull's eye.

"Needs re-tiling," she said.

It did, but it was not the greeting he had expected.

It comforted him a little that her greeting to Grant was even more unorthodox. Far from being impressed or agitated by the presence of Scotland Yard in her drawing-room of a spring afternoon, she merely said in her dry voice: "You should not be sitting in that chair; you are much too heavy for it."

When her daughter introduced the local Inspector she cast one glance at him, moved her head an inch, and quite obviously dismissed him from further consideration. This, Hallam, to judge by his expression, found peculiarly shattering.

Grant looked inquiringly at Miss Sharpe.

"I'll tell her," she said. "Mother, the Inspector wants us to see a young girl who is waiting in a car outside the gate. She was missing from her home near Aylesbury for a month, and when she turned up again—in a distressed condition—she said that she had been detained by people who wanted to make a servant of her. They kept her locked up when she refused, and beat and starved her. She described the place and the people minutely, and it so happens that you and I fit the description admirably. So does our house. The suggestion is that she was detained up in our attic with the round window."

"Remarkably interesting," said the old lady, seating herself with deliberation on an Empire sofa. "What did we beat her with?"

"A dog whip, I understand."

"Have we got a dog whip?"

"We have one of those 'lead' things, I think. They make a whip if necessary. But the point is, the Inspector would like us to meet this girl, so that she can say if we are the people who detained her or not."

"Have you any objections, Mrs. Sharpe?" Grant asked.

"On the contrary, Inspector. I look forward to the meeting with impatience. It is not every afternoon, I assure you, that I go to my rest a dull old woman and rise a potential monster."

"Then if you will excuse me, I shall bring——"

Hallam made a motion, offering himself as messenger, but Grant shook his head. It was obvious that he wanted to be present when the girl first saw what was beyond the gate.

As the Inspector went out Marion Sharpe explained Blair's presence to her mother. "It was extraordinarily kind of him to come at such short notice and so quickly," she added, and Robert felt again the impact of that bright pale old eye. For his money, old Mrs. Sharpe was quite capable of beating seven different people between breakfast and lunch, any day of the week.

"You have my sympathy, Mr. Blair," she said, unsympathetically.

"Why, Mrs. Sharpe?"

"I take it that Broadmoor is a little out of your line."

"Broadmoor!"

"Criminal lunacy."

"I find it extraordinarily stimulating," Robert said, refusing to be bullied by her.

This drew a flash of appreciation from her; something that was like the shadow of a smile. Robert had the odd feeling that she suddenly liked him; but if so she was making no verbal confession of it. Her dry voice said tartly: "Yes, I expect the distractions of Milford are scarce and mild. My daughter pursues a piece of gutta-percha round the golf course——"

"It is not gutta-percha any more, Mother," her daughter put in.

"But at my age Milford does not provide even that distraction. I am reduced to pouring weedkiller on weeds—a legitimate form of sadism on a par with drowning fleas. Do you drown your fleas, Mr. Blair?"

"No, I squash them. But I have a sister who used to pursue them with a cake of soap."

"Soap?" said Mrs. Sharpe, with genuine interest.

"I understand that she hit them with the soft side and they stuck to it."

"How *very* interesting. A technique I have not met before. I must try that next time."

With his other ear he heard that Marion was being nice to the snubbed Inspector. "You play a very good game, Inspector," she was saying.

He was conscious of the feeling you get near the end of a dream, when waking is just round the corner, that none of the inconsequence really matters because presently you'll be back in the real world.

This was misleading because the real world came through the door with the return of Inspector Grant. Grant came in first, so that he was in a position to see the expressions on all the faces concerned, and held the door open for a police matron and a girl.

Marion Sharpe stood up slowly, as if the better to face anything that might be coming to her, but her mother remained seated on the sofa as one giving an audience, her Victorian back as flat as it had been as a young girl, her hands lying composedly in her lap. Even her wild hair could not detract from the impression that she was mistress of the situation.

The girl was wearing her school coat, and childish low-heeled clumpish black school shoes; and consequently looked younger than Blair had anticipated. She was not very tall, and certainly not pretty. But she had—what was the word?—appeal. Her eyes, a darkish blue, were set wide apart in a face of the type popularly referred to as heart-shaped. Her hair was mouse-coloured, but grew off her forehead in a good line. Below each cheek-bone a slight hollow, a miracle of delicate modelling, gave the face charm and pathos. Her lower lip was full, but the mouth was too small. So were her ears. Too small and too close to her head.

An ordinary sort of girl, after all. Not the sort you would notice in a crowd. Not at all the type to be the heroine of a sensation. Robert wondered what she would look like in other clothes.

The girl's glance rested first on the old woman, and then went on to Marion. The glance held neither surprise nor triumph, and not much interest.

"Yes, these are the women," she said.

"You have no doubt about it?" Grant asked her, and added: "It is a very grave accusation, you know."

"No, I have no doubt. How could I?"

"These two ladies are the women who detained you, took your clothes from you, forced you to mend linen, and whipped you?"

"Yes, these are the women."

"A remarkable liar," said old Mrs. Sharpe, in the tone in which one says: "A remarkable likeness."

"You say that we took you into the kitchen for coffee," Marion said.

"Yes, you did."

"Can you describe the kitchen?"

"I didn't pay much attention. It was a big one—with a stone floor, I think—and a row of bells."

"What kind of stove?"

"I didn't notice the stove, but the pan the old woman heated the coffee in was a pale blue enamel one with a dark blue edge and a lot of chips off round the bottom edge."

"I doubt if there is any kitchen in England that hasn't a pan exactly like that," Marion said. "We have three of them."

"Is the girl a virgin?" asked Mrs. Sharpe, in the mildly interested tone of a person inquiring: "Is it a Chanel?"

In the startled pause that this produced Robert was aware of Hallam's scandalised face, the hot blood running up into the girl's, and the fact that there was no protesting "Mother!" from the daughter as he unconsciously, but confidently, expected. He wondered whether her silence was tacit approval, or whether after a lifetime with Mrs. Sharpe she was shock-proof.

Grant said in cold reproof that the matter was irrelevant.

"You think so?" said the old lady. "If I had been missing for a month from my home it is the first thing that my mother would have wanted to know about me. However. Now that the girl has identified us, what do you propose to do? Arrest us?"

"Oh, no. Things are a long way from that at the moment. I want to take Miss Kane to the kitchen and the attic, so that her descriptions of them can be verified. If they are, I report on the case to my superior and he decides in conference what further steps to take."

"I see. A most admirable caution, Inspector." She rose slowly to her feet. "Ah, well, if you will excuse me I shall go back to my interrupted rest."

"But don't you want to be present when Miss Kane inspects—to hear the——" blurted Grant, surprised for once out of his composure.

"Oh, dear, no." She smoothed down her black gown with a slight frown. "They split invisible atoms," she remarked testily, "but no one so far has invented a material that does not crease. I have not the faintest doubt," she went on, "that Miss Kane will identify the attic. Indeed I should be surprised beyond belief if she failed to."

She began to move towards the door, and consequently towards the girl; and for the first time the girl's eyes lit with expression. A spasm of alarm crossed her face. The police matron came forward a step, protectively. Mrs. Sharpe continued her unhurried progress and came to rest a yard or so from the girl, so that they were face to face. For a full five seconds there was silence while she examined the girl's face with interest.

"For two people who are on beating terms, we are distressingly ill acquainted," she said at last. "I hope to know you much better before this affair is finished, Miss Kane." She turned to Robert and bowed. "Goodbye, Mr. Blair. I hope you will continue to find us stimulating." And, ignoring the rest of the gathering, she walked out of the door that Hallam held open for her.

There was a distinct feeling of anti-climax now that she was no longer there, and Robert paid her the tribute of a reluctant admiration. It was no small achievement to steal the interest from an outraged heroine.

"You have no objections to letting Miss Kane see the relevant parts of the house, Miss Sharpe?" Grant asked.

"Of course not. But before we go further I should like to say what I was going to say before you brought Miss Kane in. I am glad that Miss Kane is present to hear it now. It is this. I have never to my knowledge seen this girl before. I did not give her a lift anywhere, on any occasion. She was not brought into this house either by me or by my mother, nor was she kept here. I should like that to be clearly understood."

"Very well, Miss Sharpe. It is understood that your attitude is a complete denial of the girl's story."

"A complete denial from beginning to end. And now, will you come and see the kitchen?"

CHAPTER III

GRANT AND THE GIRL accompanied Robert and Marion Sharpe on the inspection of the house, while Hallam and the police matron waited in the drawing-room. As they reached the first-floor landing, after the girl had identified the kitchen, Robert said:

"Miss Kane said that the second flight of stairs was covered in 'something hard,' but the same carpet continues up from the first flight."

"Only to the curve," Marion said. "The bit that 'shows.' Round the corner it is drugget. A Victorian way of economising. Nowadays if you are poor you buy less expensive carpet and use it all the way up. But those were still the days when what the neighbours thought mattered. So the lush stuff went as far as eye could see and no further."

The girl had been right about the third flight, too. The treads of the short flight to the attic were bare.

The all-important attic was a low square little box of a room, with the ceiling slanting abruptly down on three sides in conformity with the slate roof outside. It was lit only by the round window looking out to the front. A short stretch of slates sloped from below the window to the low white parapet. The window was divided into four panes, one of which showed a badly starred crack. It had never been made to open.

The attic was completely bare of furnishing. Unnaturally bare, Robert thought, for so convenient and accessible a store-room.

"There used to be stuff here when we first came," Marion said, as if answering him. "But when we found that we should be without help half the time we got rid of it."

Grant turned to the girl with a questioning air.

"The bed was in that corner," she said, pointing to the corner away from the window. "And next it was the wooden commode. And in this corner behind the door there were three empty travelling-cases—two suit-cases and a trunk with a flat top. There was a chair but she took it away after I tried to break the window." She referred to Marion without emotion, as if she were not present. "There is where I tried to break the window."

It seemed to Robert that the crack looked much more than a few weeks old; but there was no denying that the crack was there.

Grant crossed to the far corner and bent to examine the bare floor, but it did not need close examination. Even from where he was standing by the door Robert could see the marks of castors on the floor where the bed had stood.

"There was a bed there," Marion said. "It was one of the things we got rid of."

"What did you do with it?"

"Let me think. Oh, we gave it to the cowman's wife over at Staples Farm. Her eldest boy got too big to share a room with the others any more and she put him up in their loft. We get our dairy stuff from Staples. You can't see it from here but it is only four fields away over the rise."

"Where do you keep your spare trunks, Miss Sharpe? Have you another box-room?"

For the first time Marion hesitated. "We do have a large square trunk with a flat top, but my mother uses it to store things in. When we inherited The Franchise there was a very valuable tallboy in the bedroom my mother has, and we sold it, and used the big trunk instead. With a chintz cover on it. My suitcases I keep in the cupboard on the first-floor landing."

"Miss Kane, do you remember what the cases looked like?"

"Oh, yes. One was a brown leather with those sort-of caps at the corners, and the other was one of those American-looking canvas-covered ones with stripes."

Well, that was definite enough.

Grant examined the room a little longer, studied the view from the window, and then turned to go.

"May we see the suitcases in the cupboard?" he asked Marion.

"Certainly," Marion said, but she seemed unhappy.

On the lower landing she opened the cupboard door and stood back to let the Inspector look. As Robert moved out of their way he caught the unguarded flash of triumph on the girl's face. It so altered her calm, rather childish, face that it shocked him. It was a savage emotion, primitive and cruel. And very startling on the face of a demure schoolgirl who was the pride of her guardians and preceptors.

The cupboard contained shelves bearing household linen, and on the floor four suitcases. Two were expanding ones, one of pressed fibre and one of rawhide; the other two were: a brown cowhide with protected corners, and a square canvas-covered hatbox with a broad band of multicoloured stripes down the middle.

"Are these the cases?" Grant asked.

"Yes," the girl said. "Those two."

"I am not going to disturb my mother again this afternoon," Marion said, with sudden anger. "I acknowledge that the trunk in her room is large and flat-topped. It has been there without interruption for the last three years."

"Very good, Miss Sharpe. And now the garage, if you please."

Down at the back of the house, where the stables had been converted long ago into garage, the little group stood and surveyed the battered old grey car. Grant read out the girl's untechnical description of it as recorded in her statement. It fitted, but it would fit equally well at least a thousand cars on the roads of Britain today, Blair thought. It was hardly evidence at all. " 'One of the wheels was painted a different shade from the others and didn't look as if it belonged. The different wheel was the one in front on my side as it was standing at the pavement,' " Grant finished.

In silence the four people looked at the darker grey of the near front wheel. There seemed nothing to say.

"Thank you very much, Miss Sharpe," Grant said at length, shutting his notebook and putting it away. "You have been very courteous and helpful and I am grateful to you. I shall be able to get you on the telephone any time in the next few days, I suppose, if I want to talk to you further?"

"Oh, yes, Inspector. We have no intention of going anywhere."

If Grant was aware of her too-ready comprehension he did not show it.

He handed over the girl to the matron and they left without a backward glance. Then he and Hallam took their leave, Hallam still with an air of apologising for trespass.

Marion had gone out into the hall with them, leaving Blair in the drawing-room, and when she came back she was carrying a tray with sherry and glasses.

"I don't ask you to stay for dinner," she said, putting down the tray and beginning to pour the wine, "partly because our 'dinner' is usually a very scratch supper and not at all what you are used to. (Did you know that your aunt's meals are famous in Milford? Even I had heard about them.) And partly because—well, because, as my mother said, Broadmoor is a little out of your line, I expect."

"About that," Robert said. "You do realise, don't you, that the girl has an enormous advantage over you. In the matter of evidence, I mean. She is free to describe almost any object she likes as being part of your household. If it happens to be there, that is strong evidence for her. If it happens not to be there, that is not evidence for you; the inference is merely that you have got rid of it. If the suitcases, for instance, had not been there, she could say that you had got rid of them because they had been in the attic and could be described."

"But she did describe them, without ever having seen them."

"She described two suitcases, you mean. If your four suitcases had been a matching set she would have only one chance in perhaps five of being right. But because you happened to have one of each of the common kinds her chances worked out at about even."

He picked up the glass of sherry that she had set down beside him, took a mouthful, and was astonished to find it admirable.

She smiled a little at him and said: "We economise, but not on wine," and he flushed slightly, wondering if his surprise had been as obvious as that.

"But there was the odd wheel of the car. How did she know about that? The whole set-up is extraordinary. How did she know about my mother and me, and what the house looked like? Our gates are never open. Even if she opened them—though what she could be doing on that lonely road I can't imagine—even if she opened them and looked inside she would not know about my mother and me."

"No chance of her having made friends with a maid? Or a gardener?"

"We have never had a gardener, because there is nothing but grass. And we have not had a maid for a year. Just a girl from the farm who comes in once a week and does the rough cleaning."

Robert said sympathetically that it was a big house to have on her hands unaided.

"Yes; but two things help. I am not a house-proud woman. And it is still so wonderful to have a home of our own that I am willing to put up with the disadvantages. Old Mr. Crowle was my father's cousin, but we didn't know him at all. My mother and I had always lived in a Kensington boarding-house." One corner of her mouth moved up in a wry smile. "You can imagine how popular Mother was with the residents." The smile faded. "My father died when I was very little. He was one of those optimists who are always going to be rich tomorrow. When he found one day that his speculations had not left even enough for a loaf of bread on the morrow, he committed suicide and left Mother to face things."

Robert felt that this to some extent explained Mrs. Sharpe.

"I was not trained for a profession, so my life has been spent in odd-jobs. Not domestic ones—I loathe domesticity—but helping in those lady-like businesses that abound in Kensington. Lampshades, or advising on holidays, or flowers, or bric-à-brac. When old Mr. Crowle died I was working in a tea-shop—one of those morning-coffee gossip shops. Yes, it is a little difficult."

"What is?"

"To imagine me among the tea-cups."

Robert, unused to having his mind read—Aunt Lin was incapable of following anyone's mental processes even when they were explained to her—was disconcerted. But she was not thinking of him.

"We had just begun to feel settled down, and at home, and safe, when this happened."

For the first time since she had asked his help Robert felt the stirring of partisanship. "And all because a slip of a girl needs an alibi," he said. "We must find out more about Betty Kane."

"I can tell you one thing about her. She is over-sexed."

"Is that just feminine intuition?"

"No. I am not very feminine and I have no intuition. But I have never known anyone—man or woman—with that colour of eye who wasn't. That opaque dark blue, like a very faded navy—it's infallible."

Robert smiled at her indulgently. She was very feminine after all.

"And don't feel superior because it happens not to be lawyers' logic," she added. "Have a look round at your own friends, and see."

Before he could stop himself he thought of Gerald Blunt, the Milford scandal. Assuredly Gerald had slate-blue eyes. So had Arthur Wallis, the potman at The White Hart, who was paying three different monetary levies weekly. So had—— Damn the woman, she had no right to make a silly generalisation like that and be right about it.

"It is fascinating to speculate on what she really did during that month," Marion said. "It affords me intense satisfaction that someone beat her black and blue. At least there is one person in this world who has arrived at a correct estimate of her. I hope I meet him someday, so that I may shake his hand."

"Him?"

"With those eyes it is bound to be a 'him'."

"Well," Robert said, preparing to go, "I doubt very much whether Grant has a case that he will want to present in court. It would be the girl's word against yours, with no other backing on either side. Against *you* would be her statement; so detailed, so circumstantial. Against *her* would be the inherent unlikeliness of the story. I don't think he could hope to get a verdict."

"But the thing is there, whether he brings it into court or not. And not only in the files of Scotland Yard. Sooner or later a thing like that begins to be whispered about. It would be no comfort to us not to have the thing cleared up."

"Oh, it will be cleared up, if I have anything to do with it. But I think we wait for a day or two to see what the Yard mean to do about it. They have far better facilities for arriving at the truth than we are ever likely to have."

"Coming from a lawyer, that is a touching tribute to the honesty of the police."

"Believe me, truth may be a virtue, but Scotland Yard discovered long ago that it is a business asset. It doesn't pay them to be satisfied with anything less."

"If he *did* bring it to court," she said, coming to the door with him, "and *did* get a verdict, what would that mean for us?"

"I'm not sure whether it would be two years' imprisonment or seven years penal servitude. I told you I was a broken reed where criminal procedure is concerned. But I shall look it up."

"Yes, do," she said. "There's quite a difference."

He decided that he liked her habit of mockery. Especially in the face of a criminal charge.

"Goodbye," she said. "It was kind of you to come. You have been a great comfort to me."

And Robert, remembering how nearly he had thrown her to Ben Carley, blushed to himself as he walked to the gate.

CHAPTER IV

"HAVE YOU HAD a busy day, dear?" Aunt Lin asked, opening her table napkin and arranging it across her plump lap.

This was a sentence that made sense but had no meaning. It was as much an overture to dinner as the spreading of her napkin, and the exploratory movement of her right foot as she located the footstool which compensated for her short legs. She expected no answer; or rather, being unaware that she had asked the question, she did not listen to his answer.

Robert looked up the table at her with a more conscious benevolence than usual. After his uncharted step-picking at The Franchise, the serenity of Aunt Lin's presence was very comforting, and he looked with a new awareness at the solid little figure with the short neck and the round pink face and the iron-grey hair that frizzed out from its large hairpins. Linda Bennet led a life of recipes, film stars, god-children, and church bazaars, and found it perfect. Well-being and contentment enveloped her like a cloak. She read the Women's Page of the daily paper (How To Make A Boutonnière From Old Kid Gloves) and nothing else as far as Robert was aware. Occasionally when she tidied away the paper that Robert had left lying about, she would pause to read the headlines and comment on them. ("MAN ENDS EIGHTY-TWO DAY FAST"—Silly creature! "OIL DISCOVERY IN BAHAMAS"—Did I tell you that paraffin is up a penny, dear?) But she gave the impression of never really believing that the world the papers reported did in fact exist. The world for Aunt Lin began with Robert Blair and ended within a ten-mile radius of him.

"What kept you so late tonight, dear?" she asked, having finished her soup.

From long experience Robert recognised this as being in a different category from: "Have you had a busy day, dear?"

"I had to go out to The Franchise—that house on the Larborough road. They wanted some legal advice."

"Those odd people? I didn't know you knew them."

"I didn't. They just wanted my advice."

"I hope they pay you for it, dear. They have no money at all, you know. The father was in some kind of importing business—monkey-nuts or something—and drank himself to death. Left them without a penny, poor things. Old Mrs. Sharpe ran a boarding-house in London to make ends meet, and the daughter was maid-of-all-work. They were just going to be turned into the street with their furniture, when the old man at The Franchise died. So providential!"

"Aunt Lin! Where do you get those stories?"

"But it's true, dear. Perfectly true. I forget who told me—someone who had stayed in the same street in London—but it was first-hand, anyhow. I am not one to pass on idle gossip, as you know. Is it a nice house? I always wondered what was inside that iron gate."

"No, rather ugly. But they have some nice pieces of furniture."

"Not as well kept as ours, I'll be bound," she said, looking complacently at the perfect sideboard and the beautiful chairs ranged against the wall. "The vicar said yesterday that if this house were not so obviously a home it would be a show place." Mention of the clergy seemed to remind her of something. "By the way, will you be extra patient with Christina for the next few days. I think she is going to be 'saved' again."

"Oh, poor Aunt Lin, what a bore for you. But I was afraid of it. There was a 'text' in the saucer of my early-morning tea today. 'Thou God seest me' on a pink scroll, with a tasteful design of Easter lilies in the background. Is she changing her church again, then?"

"Yes. She has discovered that the Methodists are 'whited sepulchres,' it seems, so she is going to those 'Bethel' people above Benson's bakery, and is due to be 'saved' any day now. She has been shouting hymns all the morning."

"But she always does."

"Not 'sword of the Lord' ones. As long as she sticks to 'pearly crowns' or 'streets of gold' I know it is all right. But once she begins on the 'sword of the Lord' I know that it will be my turn to do the baking presently."

"Well, darling, you bake just as well as Christina."

"Oh, no, she doesn't," said Christina, coming in with the meat course. A big soft creature with untidy straight hair and a vague eye. "Only one thing your Aunt Lin makes better than me, Mr. Robert, and that's hot cross buns, and that's only once a year. So there! And if I'm not appreciated in this house, I'll go where I will be."

"Christina, my love!" Robert said, "you know very well that no one could imagine this house without you, and if you left I should follow you to the world's end. For your butter tarts, if for nothing else. Can we have butter tarts tomorrow, by the way?"

"Butter tarts are no food for unrepentant sinners. Besides I don't think I have the butter. But we'll see. Meanwhile, Mr. Robert, you examine your soul and stop casting stones."

Aunt Lin sighed gently as the door closed behind her. "Twenty years," she said meditatively. "You won't remember her when she first came from the orphanage. Fifteen, and so skinny, poor little brat. She ate a whole loaf for her tea, and said she would pray for me all her life. I think she has, you know."

Something like a tear glistened in Miss Bennet's blue eye.

"I hope she postpones the salvation until she has made those butter tarts," said Robert, brutally materialistic. "Did you enjoy your picture?"

"Well, dear, I couldn't forget that he had five wives."

"Who has?"

"*Had*, dear. One at a time. Gene Darrow. I must say, those little programmes they give away are very informative but a little disillusioning. He was a student, you see. In the picture, I mean. Very young and romantic. But I kept remembering those five wives, and it spoiled the afternoon for me. So charming to look at too. They say he dangled his third wife out of a fifth-storey window by the wrists, but I don't really believe that. He doesn't look strong enough, for one thing. Looks as if he had chest trouble as a child. That peaky look, and thin wrists. Not strong enough to dangle anyone. Certainly not out of a fifth-storey . . ."

The gentle monologue went on, all through the pudding course; and Robert withdrew his attention and thought about The Franchise. He came to the surface as they rose from table and moved into the sitting-room for coffee.

"It is the most becoming garment, if maids would only realise it," she was saying.

"What is?"

"An apron. She was a maid in the palace, you know, and wore one of those silly little bits of muslin. So becoming. Did those people at The Franchise have a maid, by the way? No? Well, I am not surprised. They starved the last one, you know. Gave her——"

"Oh, Aunt *Lin!*"

"I assure you. For breakfast she got the crusts they cut off the toast. And when they had milk pudding . . ."

Robert did not hear what enormity was born of the milk pudding. In spite of his good dinner he was suddenly tired and depressed. If kind silly Aunt Lin saw no harm in repeating those absurd stories, what would the real gossips of Milford achieve with the stuff of a real scandal?

"And talking of maids—the brown sugar is finished, dear, so you will have to have lump for tonight—talking of maids, the Carleys' little maid has got herself into trouble."

"You mean someone else has got her into trouble."

"Yes. Arthur Wallis, the potman at The White Hart."

"What, Wallis *again!*"

"Yes, it really is getting past a joke, isn't it. I can't think why the man doesn't get married. It would be much cheaper."

But Robert was not listening. He was back in the drawing-room at The Franchise, being gently mocked for his legal intolerance of a generalisation. Back in the shabby room with the unpolished furniture, where things lay about on chairs and no one bothered to tidy them away.

And where, now he came to think of it, no one ran round after him with an ash-tray.

CHAPTER V

IT WAS MORE THAN a week later that Mr. Heseltine put his thin, small, grey head round Robert's door to say that Inspector Hallam was in the office and would like to see him for a moment.

The room on the opposite side of the hall where Mr. Heseltine lorded it over the clerks was always referred to as "the office," although both Robert's room and the little one behind it used by Nevil Bennet were, in spite of their carpets and their mahogany, plainly offices too. There was an official waiting-room behind "the office," a small room corresponding to young Bennet's, but it had never been popular with the Blair, Hayward, and Bennet clients. Callers stepped into the office to announce themselves and usually stayed there gossiping until such times as Robert was free to see them. The little "waiting-room" had long ago been appropriated by Miss Tuff for writing Robert's letters in, away from the distraction of visitors and from the office-boy's sniffings.

When Mr. Heseltine had gone away to fetch the Inspector, Robert noticed with surprise that he was apprehensive as he had not been apprehensive since in the days of his youth he approached a list of Examination Results pinned on a board. Was his life so placid that a stranger's dilemma should stir it to that extent? Or was it that the Sharpes had been so constantly in his thoughts for the last week that they had ceased to be strangers?

He braced himself for whatever Hallam was going to say; but what emerged from Hallam's careful phrases was that Scotland Yard had let them understand that no proceedings would be taken on the present evidence. Blair noticed the "present evidence" and gauged its meaning accurately. They were not dropping the case—did the Yard ever drop a case?—they were merely sitting quiet.

The thought of Scotland Yard sitting quiet was not a particularly reassuring one in the circumstances.

"I take it that they lacked corroborative evidence," he said.

"They couldn't trace the lorry driver who gave her the lift," Hallam said.

"That wouldn't surprise them."

"No," Hallam agreed, "no driver is going to risk the sack by confessing he gave anyone a lift. Especially a girl. Transport bosses are strict about that. And when it is a case of a girl in trouble of some kind, and when it's the police that are doing the asking, no man in his senses is going to own up to even having seen her." He took the cigarette that Robert offered him. "They needed that lorry driver," he said. "Or someone like him," he added.

"Yes," Robert said, reflectively. "What did you make of her, Hallam?"

"The girl? I don't know. Nice kid. Seemed quite genuine. Might have been one of my own."

This, Blair realised, was a very good sample of what they would be up against if it ever came to a case. To every man of good feeling the girl in the witness box would look like his own daughter. Not because she was a waif, but for the very good reason that she wasn't. The decent school coat, the mousy hair, the unmade-up young face with its appealing hollow below the cheek-bone, the wide-set candid eyes—it was a prosecuting counsel's dream of a victim.

"Just like any other girl of her age," Hallam said, still considering it. "Nothing against her."

"So you don't judge people by the colour of their eyes," Robert said idly, his mind still on the girl.

"Ho! Don't I!" said Hallam surprisingly. "Believe me, there's a particular shade of baby blue that condemns a man, as far as I'm concerned, before he has opened his mouth. Plausible liars every one of them." He paused to pull on his cigarette. "Given to murder, too, come to think of it—though I haven't met many killers."

"You alarm me," Robert said. "In the future I shall give baby-blue eyes a wide berth."

Hallam grinned. "As long as you keep your pocket book shut you needn't worry. All Baby-Blue's lies are for money. He only murders when he gets too entangled in his lies. The real murderer's mark is not the colour of the eyes but their setting."

"Setting?"

"Yes. They are set differently. The two eyes, I mean. They look as if they belonged to different faces."

"I thought you hadn't met many."

"No, but I've read all the case histories and studied the photographs. I've always been surprised that no book on murder mentions it, it happens so often. The inequality of setting, I mean."

"So it's entirely your own theory."

"The result of my own observation, yes. You ought to have a go at it sometime. Fascinating. I've got to the stage where I look for it now."

"In the street, you mean?"

"No, not quite as bad as that. But in each new murder case. I wait for the photograph, and when it comes I think: 'There! What did I tell you!' "

"And when the photograph comes and the eyes are of a mathematical identity?"

"Then it is nearly always what one might call an accidental murder. The kind of murder that might happen to anyone given the circumstances."

"And when you turn up a photograph of the revered vicar of Nether Dumbleton who is being given a presentation by his grateful parishioners to mark his fiftieth year of devoted service, and you note that the setting of his eyes is wildly unequal, what conclusion do you come to?"

"That his wife satisfies him, his children obey him, his stipend is sufficient for his needs, he has no politics, he gets on with the local big-wigs, and he is allowed to have the kind of services he wants. In fact, he has never had the slightest need to murder anyone."

"It seems to me that you are having your cake and eating it very nicely."

"Huh!" Hallam said disgustedly. "Just wasting good police observation on a legal mind. I'd have thought," he added, moving to go, "that a lawyer would be glad of some free tips about judging perfect strangers."

"All you are doing," Robert pointed out, "is corrupting an innocent mind. I shall never be able to inspect a new client from now on without my subconscious registering the colour of his eyes and the symmetry of their setting."

"Well, that's something. It's about time you knew some of the facts of life."

"Thank you for coming to tell me about the 'Franchise' affair," Robert said, returning to sobriety.

"The telephone in this town," Hallam said, "is about as private as the radio."

"Anyhow, thank you. I must let the Sharpes know at once."

As Hallam took his leave, Robert lifted the telephone receiver.

He could not, as Hallam said, talk freely over the telephone, but he would say that he was coming out to see them immediately and that the news was good. That would take the present weight off their minds. It would also—he glanced at his watch—be time for Mrs. Sharpe's daily rest, so perhaps he would have a hope of avoiding the old dragon. And also a hope of a tête-à-tête with Marion Sharpe, of course; though he left that thought unformulated at the back of his mind.

But there was no answer to his call.

With the bored and reluctant aid of the Exchange he rang the number for a solid five minutes, without result. The Sharpes were not at home.

While he was still engaged with the Exchange, Nevil Bennet strolled in clad in his usual outrageous tweed, a pinkish shirt, and a purple tie. Robert, eyeing him over the receiver, wondered for the hundredth time what was going to become of Blair, Hayward, and Bennet when it at last slipped from his good Blair grasp into the hands of this young sprig of the Bennets. That the boy had brains he knew, but brains wouldn't take him far in Milford. Milford expected a man to stop being undergraduate when he reached graduate age. But there was no sign of Nevil's acceptance of the world outside his coterie. He was still actively, if unconsciously, epaté-ing that world. As his clothes bore witness.

It was not that Robert had any desire to see the boy in customary suits of solemn black. His own suit was a grey tweed; and his country clientele would look doubtfully on "town" clothes. ("That awful little man with the striped suits," Marion Sharpe had said of a town-clad lawyer, in that unguarded moment on the telephone.) But there were tweeds and tweeds, and Nevil Bennet's were the second kind. Quite outrageously the second kind.

"Robert," Nevil said, as Robert gave it up and laid down the receiver, "I've finished the papers on the Calthorpe transfer, and I thought I would run into Larborough this afternoon, if you haven't anything you want me to do."

"Can't you talk to her on the telephone?" Robert asked; Nevil being engaged, in the casual modern fashion, to the Bishop of Larborough's third daughter.

"Oh, it isn't Rosemary. She is in London for a week."

"A protest meeting at the Albert Hall, I suppose," said Robert, who was feeling disgruntled because of his failure to speak to the Sharpes when he was primed with good news for them.

"No, at the Guildhall," Nevil said.

"What is it this time? Vivisection?"

"You are frightfully last-century now and then, Robert," Nevil said, with his air of solemn patience. "No one objects to vivisection nowadays except a few cranks. The protest is against this country's refusal to give shelter to the patriot Kotovich."

"The said patriot is very badly 'wanted' in his own country, I understand."

"By his enemies; yes."

"By the police; for two murders."

"Executions."

"You a disciple of John Knox, Nevil?"

"Good God, no. What has that to do with it?"

"*He* believed in self-appointed executioners. The idea has a little 'gone out' in this country, I understand. Anyhow, if it's a choice between Rosemary's opinion of Kotovich and the opinion of the Special Branch, I'll take the Special Branch."

"The Special Branch only do what the Foreign Office tells them. Everyone knows that. But if I stay and explain the ramifications of the Kotovich affair to you, I shall be late for the film."

"What film?"

"The French film I am going into Larborough to see."

"I suppose you know that most of those French trifles that the British intelligentsia bate their breath about are considered very so-so in their own country? However. Do you think you could pause long enough to drop a note into the letter-box of The Franchise as you go by?"

"I might. I always wanted to see what was inside that wall. Who lives there now?"

"An old woman and her daughter."

"Daughter?" repeated Nevil, automatically pricking his ears.

"Middle-aged daughter."

"Oh. All right, I'll just get my coat."

Robert wrote merely that he had tried to talk to them, that he had to go out on business for an hour or so, but that he would ring them up again when he was free, and that Scotland Yard had no case, as the case stood, and acknowledged the fact.

Nevil swept in with a dreadful raglan affair over his arm, snatched up the letter and disappeared with a "Tell Aunt Lin I may be late. She asked me over to dinner."

Robert donned his own sober grey hat and walked over to the Rose and Crown to meet his client—an old farmer, and the last man in England to suffer from chronic gout. The old man was not yet there, and Robert, usually so placid, so lazily good-natured, was conscious of impatience.

The pattern of his life had changed. Up to now it had been an even succession of equal attractions; he had gone from one thing to another without hurry and without emotion. Now there was a focus of interest, and the rest revolved round it.

He sat down on one of the chintz-covered chairs in the lounge and looked at the dog-eared journals lying on the adjacent coffee table. The only current number was *The Watchman,* the weekly review, and he picked it up reluctantly, thinking yet once more how the dry feel of the paper offended his finger tips and its serrated edges set his own teeth on edge. It was the usual collection of protests, poems, and pedantry; the place of honour among the protests being accorded to Nevil's future father-in-law, who spread himself for three-quarters of a column on England's shame in that she refused sanctuary to a fugitive patriot.

The Bishop of Larborough had long ago extended the Christian philosophy to include the belief that the underdog is always right. He was wildly popular with Balkan revolutionaries, British strike committees, and all the old lags in the local penal establishment. (The sole exception to this last being that chronic recidivist, Bandy Brayne, who held the good bishop in vast contempt, and reserved his affection for the Governor; to whom a tear in the eye was just a drop of H_2O, and who unpicked his most heartbreaking tales with a swift, unemotional accuracy.) There was *nothing,* said the old lags affectionately, that the old boy would not believe; you could lay it on with a trowel.

Normally Robert found the Bishop mildly amusing, but today he was merely irritated. He tried two poems, neither of which made sense to him, and flung the thing back on the table.

"England in the wrong again?" asked Ben Carley, pausing by his chair and jerking a head at *The Watchman.*

"Hullo, Carley."

"A Marble Arch for the well-to-do," the little lawyer said, flicking the paper scornfully with a nicotine-stained finger. "Have a drink?"

"Thanks, but I'm waiting for old Mr. Wynyard. He doesn't move a step more than he need, nowadays."

"No, poor old boy. The sins of the fathers. Awful to be suffering for port you never drank! I saw your car outside The Franchise the other day."

"Yes," said Robert, and wondered a little. It was unlike Ben Carley to be blunt. And if he had seen Robert's car he had also seen the police cars.

"If you know them you'll be able to tell me something I always wanted to know about them. Is the rumour true?"

"Rumour?"

"*Are* they witches?"

"Are they supposed to be?" said Robert lightly.

"There's a strong support for the belief in the countryside, I understand," Carley said, his bright black eyes resting for a moment on Robert's with intention, and then going on to wander over the lounge with their habitual quick interrogation.

Robert understood that the little man was offering him, tacitly, information that he thought ought to be useful to him.

"Ah well," Robert said, "since entertainment came into the country with the cinema, God bless it, an end has been put to witch-hunting."

"Don't you believe it. Give these midland morons a good excuse and they'll witch-hunt with the best. An inbred crowd of degenerates, if you ask me. Here's your old boy. Well, I'll be seeing you."

It was one of Robert's chief attractions that he was genuinely interested in people and in their troubles, and he listened to old Mr. Wynyard's rambling story with a kindness that won the old man's gratitude—and added, although he was unaware of it, a hundred to the sum that stood against his name in the old farmer's will—but as soon as their business was over he made straight for the hotel telephone.

There were far too many people about, and he decided to use the one in the garage over in Sin Lane. The office would be shut by now, and anyhow it was further away. And if he telephoned from the garage, so his thoughts went as he strode across the street, he would have his car at hand if she—if they asked him to come out and discuss the business further, as they very well might, as they almost certainly would—yes, of course they would want to discuss what they could do to discredit the girl's story, whether there was to be a case or not—he had been so relieved over Hallam's news that he had not yet come round in his mind to considering what——

"Evening, Mr. Blair," Bill Brough said, oozing his large person out of the narrow office door, his round calm face bland and welcoming. "Want your car?"

"No, I want to use your telephone first, if I may."

"Sure. Go ahead."

Stanley, who was under a car, poked his fawn's face out and asked: "Know anything?"

"Not a thing, Stan. Haven't had a bet for months."

"I'm two pounds down on a cow called Bright Promise. That's what comes of putting your faith in horseflesh. Next time you know something——"

"Next time I have a bet I'll tell you. But it will still be horseflesh."

"As long as it's not a cow——" Stanley said, disappearing under the car again; and Robert moved into the hot bright little office and picked up the receiver.

It was Marion who answered, and her voice sounded warm and glad. "You can't imagine what a relief your note was to us. Both my mother and I have been picking oakum for the last week. Do they still pick oakum, by the way?"

"I think not. It is something more constructive nowadays, I understand."

"Occupational therapy."

"More or less."

"I can't think of any compulsory sewing that would improve my character."

"They would probably find you something more congenial. It is against modern thought to compel a prisoner to do anything that he doesn't want to."

"That is the first time I have heard you sound tart."

"Was I tart?"

"Pure angostura."

Well, she had reached the subject of drink; perhaps now she would suggest his coming out for sherry before dinner.

"What a charming nephew you have, by the way."

"Nephew?"

"The one who brought the note."

"He is not my nephew," Robert said coldly. Why was it so ageing to be avuncular? "He is my first cousin once removed. But I am glad you liked him." This would not do; he would have to take the bull by the horns. "I should like to see you sometime to discuss what we can do to straighten things out. To make things safer——" He waited.

"Yes, of course. Perhaps we could look in at your office one morning when we are shopping? What kind of thing could we do, do you think?"

"Some kind of private inquiry, perhaps. I can't very well discuss it over the telephone."

"No, of course you can't. How would it do if we came in on Friday morning? That is our weekly shopping day. Or is Friday a busy day for you?"

"No, Friday would be quite convenient," Robert said, swallowing down his disappointment. "About noon?"

"Yes, that would do very well. Twelve o'clock the day after tomorrow, at your office. Goodbye, and thank you again for your support and help."

She rang off, firmly and cleanly, without all the usual preliminary twitterings that Robert had come to expect from women.

"Shall I run her out for you," Bill Brough asked as he came out into the dim daylight of the garage.

"What? Oh, the car. No, I shan't need it tonight, thanks."

He set off on his normal evening walk down the High Street, trying hard not to feel snubbed. He had not been anxious to go to The Franchise in the first instance, and had made his reluctance pretty plain; she was quite naturally avoiding a repetition of the circumstances. That he had identified himself with their interests was a mere business affair, to be resolved in an office, impersonally. They would not again involve him further than that.

Ah, well, he thought, flinging himself down in his favourite chair by the wood fire in the sitting-room and opening the evening paper (printed that morning in London), when they came to the office on Friday he could do something to put the affair on a more personal basis. To wipe out the memory of that first unhappy refusal.

The quiet of the old house soothed him. Christina had been closeted in her room for two days, in prayer and meditation, and Aunt Lin was in the kitchen preparing dinner. There was a gay letter from Lettice, his only sister, who had driven a truck for several years of a bloody war, fallen in love with a tall silent Canadian, and was now raising five blond brats in Saskatchewan. "Come out soon, Robin dear," she finished, "before the brats grow up and before the moss grows *right* round you. You know how *bad* Aunt Lin is for you!" He could hear her saying it. She and Aunt Lin had never seen eye to eye.

He was smiling, relaxed and reminiscent, when both his quiet and his peace were shattered by the irruption of Nevil.

"Why didn't you *tell* me she was like that!" Nevil demanded.

"Who?"

"The Sharpe woman! Why didn't you tell me?"

"I didn't expect you would meet her," Robert said. "All you had to do was drop the letter through the door."

"There was nothing in the door to drop it through, so I rang, and they had just come back from wherever they were. Anyhow, *she* answered it."

"I thought she slept in the afternoons."

"I don't believe she ever sleeps. She doesn't belong to the human family at all. She is all compact of fire and metal."

"I know she's a very rude old woman but you have to make allowances. She has had a very hard——"

"*Old?* Who are you talking about?"

"Old Mrs. Sharpe, of course."

"I didn't even see old Mrs. Sharpe. I'm talking about Marion."

"Marion Sharpe? And how did you know her name was Marion?"

"She told me. It does suit her, doesn't it? She couldn't be anything but Marion."

"You seem to have become remarkably intimate for a doorstep acquaintance."

"Oh, she gave me tea."

"Tea! I thought you were in a desperate hurry to see a French film."

"I'm never in a desperate hurry to do anything when a woman like Marion Sharpe invites me to tea. Have you noticed her eyes? But of course you have. You're her lawyer. That wonderful shading of grey into hazel. And the way her eyebrows lie above them, like the brush-mark of a painter genius. Winged eyebrows, they are. I made a poem about them on the way home. Do you want to hear it?"

"No," Robert said firmly. "Did you enjoy your film?"

"Oh, I didn't go."

"You didn't *go!*"

"I told you I had tea with Marion instead."

"You mean you have been at The Franchise *the whole afternoon!*"

"I suppose I have," Nevil said dreamily, "but, by God, it didn't seem more than seven minutes."

"And what happened to your thirst for French cinema?"

"But Marion *is* French film. Even you must see that!" Robert winced at the "even you." "Why bother with the shadow, when you can be with the reality? Reality. That is her great quality, isn't it? I've never met anyone as real as Marion is."

"Not even Rosemary?" Robert was in the state known to Aunt Lin as "put out."

"Oh, Rosemary is a darling, and I'm going to marry her, but that is quite a different thing."

"Is it?" said Robert, with deceptive meekness.

"Of course. People don't marry women like Marion Sharpe, any more than they marry winds and clouds. Any more than they marry Joan of Arc. It's positively blasphemous to consider marriage in relation to a woman like that. She spoke very nicely of you, by the way."

"That was kind of her."

The tone was so dry that even Nevil caught the flavour of it.

"Don't you like her?" he asked, pausing to look at his cousin in surprised disbelief.

Robert had ceased for the moment to be kind, lazy, tolerant Robert Blair; he was just a tired man who hadn't yet had his dinner and was suffering from the memory of a frustration and a snubbing.

"As far as I am concerned," he said, "Marion Sharpe is just a skinny woman of forty who lives with a rude old mother in an ugly old house, and needs legal advice on occasion like anyone else."

But even as the words came out he wanted to stop them, as if they were a betrayal of a friend.

"No, probably she *isn't* your cup of tea," Nevil said tolerantly. "You have always preferred them a little stupid, and blond, haven't you." This was said without malice, as one stating a dullish fact.

"I can't imagine why you should think that."

"All the women you nearly married were that type."

"I have never 'nearly married' anyone," Robert said stiffly.

"That's what you think. You'll never know how nearly Molly Manders landed you."

"Molly Manders?" Aunt Lin said, coming in flushed from her cooking and bearing the tray with the sherry. "Such a silly girl. Imagined that you used a baking-board for pancakes. And was always looking at herself in that little pocket mirror of hers."

"Aunt Lin saved you that time, didn't you, Aunt Lin?"

"I don't know what you are talking about, Nevil dear. Do stop prancing about the hearthrug, and put a log on the fire. Did you like your French film, dear?"

"I didn't go. I had tea at The Franchise instead." He shot a glance at Robert, having learned by now that there was more in Robert's reaction than met the eye.

"With those strange people? What did you talk about?"

"Mountains—Maupassant—hens——"

"*Hens*, dear?"

"Yes; the concentrated evil of a hen's face in a close-up."

Aunt Lin looked vague. She turned to Robert, as to terra firma.

"Had I better call, dear, if you are going to know them? Or ask the vicar's wife to call?"

"I don't think I would commit the vicar's wife to anything so irrevocable," Robert said, dryly.

She looked doubtful for a moment, but household cares obliterated the question in her mind. "Don't dawdle too long over your sherry or what I have in the oven will be spoiled. Thank goodness, Christina will be down again tomorrow. At least I hope so; I have never known her salvation take more than two days. And I don't really think that I *will* call on those Franchise people, dear, if it is all the same to you. Apart from being strangers and very odd, they quite frankly terrify me."

Yes; that was a sample of the reaction he might expect where the Sharpes were concerned. Ben Carley had gone out of his way today to let him know that, if there was police trouble at The Franchise, he wouldn't be able to count on an unprejudiced jury. He must take measures for the protection of the Sharpes. When he saw them on Friday he would suggest a private investigation by a paid agent. The police were overworked—had been overworked for a decade and more—and there was just a chance that one man working at his leisure on one trail might be more successful than the orthodox and official investigation had been.

CHAPTER VI

BUT BY FRIDAY MORNING it was too late to take measures for the safety of The Franchise.

Robert had reckoned with the diligence of the police; he had reckoned with the slow spread of whispers; but he had reckoned without the *Ack-Emma*.

The *Ack-Emma* was the latest representative of the tabloid newspaper to enter British journalism from the West. It was run on the principle that two thousand pounds for damages is a cheap price to pay for sales worth half a million. It had blacker headlines, more sensational pictures, and more indiscreet letterpress than any paper printed so far by British presses. Fleet Street had its own name for it—monosyllabic and unprintable—but no protection against it. The press had always been its own censor, deciding what was and what was not permissible by the principles of its own good sense and good taste. If a "rogue" publication decided not to conform to those principles then there was no power that could make it conform. In ten years the *Ack-Emma* had passed by half a million the daily net sales of the best selling newspaper in the country to date. In any suburban railway carriage seven out of ten people bound for work in the morning were reading an *Ack-Emma.*

And it was the *Ack-Emma* that blew the Franchise affair wide open.

Robert had been out early into the country on that Friday morning to see an old woman who was dying and wanted to alter her will. This was a performance she repeated on an average once every three months and her doctor made no secret of the fact that in his opinion she "would blow out a hundred candles one day without a second puff." But of course a lawyer cannot tell a client who summons him urgently at eight-thirty in the morning not to be silly. So Robert had taken some new will forms, fetched his car from the garage, and driven into the country. In spite of his usual tussle with the old tyrant among the pillows—who could never be brought to understand the elementary fact that you cannot give away *four* shares amounting to one third each—he enjoyed the spring countryside. And he hummed to himself on the way home, looking forward to seeing Marion Sharpe in less than an hour.

He had decided to forgive her for liking Nevil. After all, Nevil had never tried to palm her off on Carley. One must be fair.

He ran the car into the garage, under the noses of the morning lot going out from the livery stable, parked it, and then, remembering that it was past the first of the month, strolled over to the office to pay his bill to Brough, who ran the office side. But it was Stanley who was in the office; thumbing over dockets and invoices with the strong hands that so surprisingly finished off his thin forearms.

"When I was in the Signals," Stanley said, casting him an absent-minded glance, "I used to believe that the Quarter-bloke was a crook, but now I'm not so sure."

"Something missing?" said Robert. "I just looked in to pay my bill. Bill usually has it ready."

"I expect it's somewhere around," Stanley said, still thumbing. "Have a look."

Robert, used to the ways of the office, picked up the loose papers discarded by Stanley, so as to come on the normal tidy strata of Bill's arrangement below. As he lifted the untidy pile he uncovered a girl's face;

a newspaper picture of a girl's face. He did not recognise it at once but it reminded him of someone and he paused to look at it.

"Got it!" said Stanley in triumph, extracting a sheet of paper from a clip. He swept the remaining loose papers on the desk into a pile and so laid bare to Robert's gaze the whole front page of that morning's *Ack-Emma*.

Cold with shock, Robert stared at it.

Stanley, turning to take the papers he was holding from his grasp, noticed his absorption and approved it.

"Nice little number, that," he said. "Reminds me of a bint I had in Egypt. Same far-apart eyes. Nice kid she was. Told the most original lies."

He went back to his paper-arranging, and Robert went on staring.

THIS IS THE GIRL

said the paper in enormous black letters across the top of the page; and below it, occupying two-thirds of the page, was the girl's photograph. And then, in smaller but still obtrusive type, below:

IS THIS THE HOUSE?

and below it a photograph of The Franchise.

Across the bottom of the page was the legend:

THE GIRL SAYS YES: WHAT DO THE POLICE SAY?
See inside for the story.

He put out his hand and turned over the page.

Yes; it was all there, except for the Sharpes' name.

He dropped the page, and looked again at that shocking frontispiece. Yesterday The Franchise was a house protected by four high walls; so unobtrusive, so sufficient unto itself, that even Milford did not know what it looked like. Now it was there to be stared at on every bookstall; on every newsagent's counter from Penzance to Pentland. Its flat, forbidding front a foil for the innocence of the face above it.

The girl's photograph was a head-and-shoulders affair, and appeared to be a studio portrait. Her hair had an arranged-for-an-occasion look, and she was wearing what looked like a party frock. Without her school coat she looked—not less innocent, nor older; no. He sought for the word that would express it. She looked less—tabu, was it? The school coat had stopped one thinking of her as a woman, just as a nun's habit would. A whole treatise could probably be written, now he came to think of it, on the protective quality of school coats. Protective in both senses: armour and camouflage. Now that the coat was no longer there, she was feminine instead of merely female.

But it was still a pathetically young face, immature and appealing. The candid brow, the wide-set eyes, the bee-stung lip that gave her mouth the expression of a disappointed child—it made a formidable whole. It would not be only the Bishop of Larborough who would believe a story told by that face.

"May I borrow this paper?" he asked Stanley.

"Take it," Stanley said. "We had it for our elevenses. There's nothing in it."

Robert was surprised. "Didn't you find this interesting?" he asked, indicating the front page.

Stanley cast a glance at the pictured face. "Not except that she reminded me of that bint in Egypt, lies and all."

"So you didn't believe that story she told?"

"What do *you* think!" Stanley said, contemptuous.

"Where do you think the girl was, then, all that time?"

"If I remember what I *think* I remember about the Red Sea sadie, I'd say very definitely—oh, but definitely—on the tiles," Stanley said, and went out to attend to a customer.

Robert picked up the paper and went soberly away. At least one man-in-the-street had not believed the story; but that seemed to be due as much to an old memory as to present cynicism.

And although Stanley had quite obviously read the story without reading the names of the characters concerned, or even the place-names, only ten per cent of readers did that (according to the best Mass Observation); the other ninety per cent would have read every word, and would now be discussing the affair with varying degrees of relish.

At his own office he found that Hallam had been trying to reach him by telephone.

"Shut the door and come in, will you," he said to old Mr. Heseltine, who had caught him with the news on his arrival and was now standing in the door of his room. "And have a look at that."

He reached for the receiver with one hand, and laid the paper under Mr. Heseltine's nose with the other.

The old man touched it with his small-boned fastidious hand, as one seeing a strange exhibit for the first time. "This is the publication one hears so much about," he said. And gave his attention to it, as he would to any strange document.

"We are both in a spot, aren't we!" Hallam said, when they were connected. And raked his vocabulary for some epithets suitable to the *Ack-Emma*. "As if the police hadn't enough to do without having that rag on their tails!" he finished, being naturally absorbed in the police point of view.

"Have you heard from the Yard?"

"Grant was burning the wires at nine this morning. But there's nothing they can do. Just grin and bear it. The police are always fair game. Nothing you can do, either, if it comes to that."

"Not a thing," Robert said. "We have a fine free press."

Hallam said a few more things about the press. "Do your people know?" he asked.

"I shouldn't think so. I'm quite sure they would never normally see the *Ack-Emma,* and there hasn't been time for some kind soul to send it to them. But they are due here in about ten minutes, and I'll show it to them then."

"If it was ever possible for me to be sorry for that old battle-axe," Hallam said, "it would be at this minute."

"How did the *Ack-Emma* get the story? I thought the parents—the girl's guardians, I mean—were very strongly against that kind of publicity."

"Grant says the girl's brother went off the deep end about the police taking no action and went to the *Ack-Emma* off his own bat. They are strong on the champion act. 'The *Ack-Emma* will see right done!' I once knew one of their crusades run into a third day."

When he hung up Robert thought that if it was a bad break for both sides, it was at least an even break. The police would without doubt redouble their efforts to find corroborative evidence; on the other hand the publication of the girl's photograph meant for the Sharpes a faint hope that somebody, somewhere, would recognise it and say: "This girl could not have been in The Franchise on the date in question because she was at such-and-such a place."

"A shocking story, Mr. Robert," Mr. Heseltine said. "And if I may say so a quite shocking publication. Most offensive."

"That house," Robert said, "is The Franchise, where old Mrs. Sharpe and her daughter live; and where I went the other day, if you remember, to give them some legal advice."

"You mean that these people are our clients?"

"Yes."

"But, Mr. Robert, that is not at all in our line." Robert winced at the dismay in his voice. "That is quite outside our usual—indeed quite beyond our normal—we are not competent——"

"We are competent, I hope, to defend any client against a publication like the *Ack-Emma,*" Robert said, coldly.

Mr. Heseltine eyed the screaming rag on the table. He was obviously facing the difficult choice between a criminal clientele and a disgraceful journal.

"Did you believe the girl's story when you read it?" Robert asked.

"I don't see how she could have made it up," Mr. Heseltine said simply. "It is such a very circumstantial story, isn't it?"

"It is, indeed. But I saw the girl when she was brought to The Franchise to identify it last week—that was the day I went out so hurriedly just after tea—and I don't believe a word she says. Not a word," he added, glad to be able to say it loudly and distinctly to himself and to be sure at last that he believed it.

"But how could she have thought of The Franchise at all, or known all those things, if she wasn't there?"

"I don't know. I haven't the least idea."

"It is a most unlikely place to pick on, surely; a remote, invisible house like that, on a lonely road, in country that people don't visit very much."

"I know. I don't know how the job was worked, but that it *is* a job I am certain. It is a choice not between stories, but between human beings. I am quite certain that the two Sharpes are incapable of insane conduct like that. Whereas I don't believe the girl incapable of telling a story like that. That is what it amounts to." He paused a moment. "And you'll just have to trust my judgment about it, Timmy," he added, using his childhood's name for the old clerk.

Whether it was the "Timmy" or the argument, it was apparent that Mr. Heseltine had no further protest to make.

"You'll be able to see the criminals for yourself," Robert said, "because I hear their voices in the hall now. You might bring them in, will you."

Mr. Heseltine went dumbly out on his mission, and Robert turned the newspaper over so that the comparatively innocuous GIRL SMUGGLED ABOARD was all that would meet the visitors' eye.

Mrs. Sharpe, moved by some belated instinct for convention, had donned a hat in honour of the occasion. It was a flattish affair of black satin, and the general effect was that of a doctor of learning. That the effect had not been wasted was obvious by the relieved look on Mr. Heseltine's face. This was quite obviously not the kind of client he had expected; it was, on the other hand, the kind of client he was used to.

"Don't go away," Robert said to him, as he greeted the visitors; and to the others: "I want you to meet the oldest member of the firm, Mr. Heseltine."

It suited Mrs. Sharpe to be gracious; and exceedingly Victoria Regina was old Mrs. Sharpe when she was being gracious. Mr. Heseltine was more than relieved; he capitulated. Robert's first battle was over.

When they were alone Robert noticed that Marion had been waiting to say something.

"An odd thing happened this morning," she said. "We went to the Ann Boleyn place to have coffee—we quite often do—and there were two vacant tables, but when Miss Truelove saw us coming she very hastily tilted the chairs against the tables and said they were reserved. I might have believed her if she hadn't looked so embarrassed. You don't think that rumour has begun to get busy already, do you? That she did that because she has heard some gossip?"

"No," Robert said, sadly, "because she has read this morning's *Ack-Emma*." He turned the newspaper front side up. "I am sorry to have such bad news for you. You'll just have to shut your teeth and take it, as small boys say. I don't suppose you have ever seen this poisonous rag at close quarters. It's a pity that the acquaintance should begin on so personal a basis."

"Oh, no!" Marion said, in passionate protest as her eye fell on the picture of The Franchise.

And then there was unbroken silence while the two women absorbed the contents of the inner page.

"I take it," Mrs. Sharpe said at last, "that we have no redress against this sort of thing?"

"None," Robert said. "All the statements are perfectly true. And it is all statement and not comment. Even if it were comment—and I've no doubt the comment will come—there has been no charge so the case is not *sub judice*. They are free to comment if they please."

"The whole thing is one huge implied comment," Marion said. "That the police failed to do their duty. What do they think we did? Bribed them?"

"I think the suggestion is that the humble victim has less pull with the police than the wicked rich."

"Rich," repeated Marion, her voice curdling with bitterness.

"Anyone who has more than six chimneys is rich. Now. If you are not too shocked to think, consider. We *know* that the girl was never at The Franchise, that she could not——" But Marion interrupted him.

"Do *you* know it?" she asked.

"Yes," Robert said.

Her challenging eyes lost their challenge, and her glance dropped.

"Thank you," she said quietly.

"If the girl was never there, how could she have seen the house! . . . She did see it somehow. It is too unlikely for belief that she could be merely repeating a description that someone else gave her. . . . How could she see it? Naturally, I mean."

"You could see it, I suppose, from the top deck of a bus," Marion said. "But there are no double-decker buses on the Milford route. Or from on top of a load of hay. But it is the wrong time of year for hay."

"It may be the wrong time for hay," croaked Mrs. Sharpe, "but there is no season for lorry-loads. I have seen lorries loaded with goods as high as any hay wagon."

"Yes," Marion said. "Suppose the lift the girl got was not in a car, but on a lorry."

"There is only one thing against that. If a girl was given a lift on a lorry she would be in the cabin, even if it meant sitting on someone's knee. They wouldn't perch her up on top of the load. Especially as it was a rainy evening, you may remember. . . . No one ever came to The Franchise to ask the way, or to sell something, or to mend something—someone that the girl could have been with, even in the background?"

But no; they were both sure that no one had come, within the time the girl had been on holiday.

"Then we take it for granted that what she learned about The Franchise she learned from being high enough on one occasion to see over the wall. We shall probably never know when or how, and we probably could not prove it if we did know. So our whole efforts will have to be devoted, not to proving that she wasn't at The Franchise, but that she *was* somewhere else!"

"And what chance is there of that?" Mrs. Sharpe asked.

"A better chance than before this was published," Robert said, indicating the front page of the *Ack-Emma*. "Indeed it is the one bright spot in the bad business. *We* could not have published the girl's photograph in the hope of information about her whereabouts during that month. But now that *they* have published it—her own people, I mean—the same benefit should come to us. They have broadcast the story—and that is our bad luck; but they have also broadcast the photograph—and if we have any good luck at all someone, somewhere, will observe that the story and the photograph do not fit. That at the material time, as given in the story, the subject of the photograph could not possibly have been in the stated place, because they, personally, know her to have been elsewhere."

Marion's face lost a little of its bleak look, and even Mrs. Sharpe's thin back looked less rigid. What had seemed a disaster might be, after all, the means of their salvation.

"And what can we do in the way of private investigation?" Mrs. Sharpe asked. "You realise, I expect, that we have very little money; and I take it that a private inquiry is a spendthrift business."

"It does usually run away with more than one had bargained for, because it is difficult to budget for. But to begin with I am going, myself, to see the various people involved, and find out, if possible, on what lines any inquiry should be based. Find out what she was *likely* to do."

"Will they tell you that?"

"Oh, no. They are probably unaware themselves of her tendencies. But if they talk about her at all a picture must emerge. At least I hope so."

There was a few moments' silence.

"You are extraordinarily kind, Mr. Blair."

Victoria Regina had come back to Mrs. Sharpe's manner, but there was a hint of something else. Almost of surprise; as if kindness was not one of the things she had normally met with in life; nor expected. Her stiffly gracious acknowledgement was as eloquent as if she had said: "You know that we are poor, and that we may never be able to pay you adequately, and we are not at all the kind of people that you would choose to represent, but you are going out of your way to do us the best service in your power, and we are grateful."

"When do you go?" Marion asked.

"Directly after lunch."

"Today!"

"The sooner the better."

"Then we won't keep you," Mrs. Sharpe said, rising. She stood for a moment looking down at the paper where it lay spread on the table. "We enjoyed the privacy of The Franchise a great deal," she said.

When he had seen them out of the door and into their car, he called Nevil into his room and picked up the receiver to talk to Aunt Lin about packing a bag.

"I suppose you don't see the *Ack-Emma* ever?" he asked Nevil.

"I take it that the question is rhetoric," Nevil said.

"Have a look at this morning's. Hullo, Aunt Lin."

"Does someone want to sue them for something? It will be sound money for us, if so. They practically always settle out of court. They have a special fund for the——" Nevil's voice died away. He had seen the front page that was staring up at him from the table.

Robert stole a look at him over the telephone, and observed with satisfaction the naked shock on his cousin's bright young features. The youth of today, he understood, considered themselves shock-proof; it was good to know that, faced with an ordinary slab of real life, they reacted like any other human being.

"Be an angel, Aunt Lin, and pack a bag for me, will you? Just for overnight. . . ."

Nevil had torn the paper open and was now reading the story.

"Just London and back, I expect, but I'm not sure. Anyhow, just the little case; and just the minimum. Not all the things I *might* need, if you love me. Last time there was a bottle of digestive powder weighing nearly a pound, and when in heck did I ever need a digestive powder! . . . All right, then I *will* have ulcers. . . . Yes, I'll be in to lunch in about ten minutes."

"The blasted *swine!*" said the poet and intellectual, falling back in his need on the vernacular.

"Well, what do you make of it?"

"*Make* of it! Of what?"

"The girl's story."

"Does one have to *make* anything of it? An obvious piece of sensationalism by an unbalanced adolescent?"

"And if I told you that the said adolescent is a very calm, ordinary, well-spoken-of schoolgirl who is anything but sensational?"

"Have you seen her?"

"Yes. That was why I first went to The Franchise last week, to be there when Scotland Yard brought the girl to confront them." Put that in your pipe and smoke it, young Nevil. She may talk hens and Maupassant with you, but it is me she turns to in trouble.

"To be there on their behalf?"

"Certainly."

Nevil relaxed suddenly. "Oh, well; that's all right. For a moment I thought you were against her. Against them. But that's all right. We can join forces to put a spoke in the wheel of this——" he flicked the paper—"this moppet." Robert laughed at this typically Nevil choice of epithet. "What are you going to do about it, Robert?"

Robert told him. "And you will hold the fort while I am gone." He saw that Nevil's attention had gone back to the "moppet." He moved over to join him and together they considered the young face looking so calmly up at them.

"An attractive face, on the whole," Robert said. "What do you make of it?"

"What I should *like* to make of it," said the aesthete, with slow venom, "would be a *very nasty mess*."

CHAPTER VII

THE WYNNS' HOME outside Aylesbury was in a countrified suburb; the kind of district where rows of semi-detached houses creep along the edge of the still unspoiled fields; self-conscious and aware that they are intruders, or smug and not caring, according to the character their builders have given them. The Wynns lived in one of the apologetic rows; a red-brick string of ramshackle dwellings that set Robert's teeth on edge; so raw they were, so crude, so hang-dog. But as he drove slowly up the road, looking for the appropriate number, he was won over by the love that had gone to the decoration of these regrettable objects. No love had gone to their building; only a reckoning. But to each owner, as he took over, the bare little house had represented his "sufficient beauty," and having found it he served it. The gardens were small miracles of loveliness; each succeeding one a fresh revelation of some unsuspected poet's heart.

Nevil really ought to be here to see, Robert thought, slowing down yet once more as a new perfection caught his eye; there was more poetry here than in a whole twelve months of his beloved *Watchman*. All his clichés were here: form, rhythm, colour, total gesture, design, impact . . .

Or would Nevil see only a row of suburban gardens? Only Meadowside Lane, Aylesbury, with some Woolworth plants in the gardens?

Probably.

Number 39 was the one with the plain green grass bordered by a rockery. It was also distinguished by the fact that its curtains were invisible. No genteel net was stretched across the window-pane, no cream casement cloth hung at the sides. The windows were bare to the sun, the air, and the human gaze. This surprised Robert as much as it probably surprised the neighbours. It augured a nonconformity that he had not expected.

He rang the bell, wishing that he did not feel like a bagman. He was a suppliant; and that was a new role for Robert Blair.

Mrs. Wynn surprised him even more than her windows did. It was only when he had met her that he realised how complete a picture he had built in his mind of the woman who had adopted and mothered the child Betty Kane: the grey hair, the solid matronly comfortable figure, the plain broad sensible face; perhaps, even, an apron, or one of those flowered overalls that housewives wear. But Mrs. Wynn was not at all like that. She was slight and neat and young and modern and dark and pink-cheeked and still pretty, and had a pair of the most intelligent bright brown eyes Robert had ever seen.

When she saw a stranger she looked defensive, and made an involuntary closing movement with the door she was holding; but a second glance seemed to reassure her. Robert explained who he was, and she listened without interrupting him in a way he found quite admirable. Very few of his own clients listened without interrupting; male or female.

"You are under no obligation to talk to me," he finished, having explained his presence. "But I hope very much that you won't refuse. I have told Inspector Grant that I was going to see you this afternoon, on my clients' behalf."

"Oh, if the police know about it and don't mind——" She stepped back to let him come past her. "I expect you have to do your best for those people if you are their lawyer. And we have nothing to hide. But if it is really Betty you want to interview I'm afraid you can't. We have sent her into the country to friends for the day, to avoid all the fuss. Leslie meant well, but it was a stupid thing to do."

"Leslie?"

"My son. Sit down, won't you." She offered him one of the easy chairs in a pleasant, uncluttered sitting-room. "He was too angry about the police to think clearly—angry about their failure to do anything when it seemed so proved, I mean. He has always been devoted to Betty. Indeed until he got engaged they were inseparable."

Robert's ears pricked. This was the kind of thing he had come to hear. "Engaged?"

"Yes. He got engaged just after the New Year to a very nice girl. We are all delighted."

"Was Betty delighted?"

"She wasn't jealous, if that is what you mean," she said, looking at him with her intelligent eyes. "I expect she missed not coming first with him as she used to, but she was very nice about it. She *is* a nice girl, Mr. Blair. Believe me. I was a schoolmistress before I married—not a very good one, that is why I got married at the first opportunity—and I know a lot about girls. Betty has never given me a moment's anxiety."

"Yes. I know. Everyone reports excellently of her. Is your son's fiancée a schoolfellow of hers?"

"No, she is a stranger. Her people have come to live near here and he met her at a dance."

"Does Betty go to dances?"

"Not grown-up dances. She is too young yet."

"So she had not met the fiancée?"

"To be honest, none of us had. He rather sprang her on us. But we liked her so much we didn't mind."

"He must be very young to be settling down?"

"Oh, the whole thing is absurd, of course. He is twenty and she is eighteen. But they are very sweet together. And I was very young myself when I married and I have been very happy. The only thing I lacked was a daughter, and Betty filled that gap."

"What does she want to do when she leaves school?"

"She doesn't know. She has no special talent for anything as far as I can see. I have a notion that she will marry early."

"Because of her attractiveness?"

"No, because——" she paused and apparently changed what she had been going to say. "Girls who have no particular bent fall easily into matrimony."

He wondered if what she had been going to say had any remote connection with slate-blue eyes.

"When Betty failed to turn up in time to go back to school, you thought she was just playing truant? Although she was a well-behaved child."

"Yes; she was growing bored with school; and she had always said—which is quite true—that the first day back at school is a wasted one. So we thought she was just 'taking advantage' for once, as they say. 'Trying it on' as Leslie said, when he heard that she hadn't turned up."

"I see. Was she wearing school clothes on her holiday?"

For the first time Mrs. Wynn looked doubtfully at him; uncertain of his motive in asking.

"No. No, she was wearing her week-end clothes. . . . You know that when she came back she was wearing only a frock and shoes?"

Robert nodded.

"I find it difficult to imagine women so depraved that they would treat a helpless child like that."

"If you could meet the women, Mrs. Wynn, you would find it still more difficult to imagine."

"But all the worst criminals look innocent and harmless, don't they?"

Robert let that pass. He wanted to know about the bruises on the girl's body. Were they fresh bruises?

"Oh, quite fresh. Most of them had not begun to 'turn' even."

This surprised Robert a little.

"But there were older bruises as well, I take it."

"If there were they had faded so much as to be unnoticeable among all the bad new ones."

"What did the new ones look like? A whipping?"

"Oh, no. She had actually been knocked about. Even her poor little face. One jaw was swollen, and there was a big bruise on the other temple."

"The police say that she grew hysterical when it was suggested that she should tell them her story."

"That was when she was still ill. Once we had got the story out of her and she had had a long rest, it was easy enough to persuade her to repeat it to the police."

"I know you will answer this frankly, Mrs. Wynn: Has there never been any suspicion in your mind that Betty's story might not be true? Even a momentary suspicion?"

"Not even a momentary one. Why should there be? She has always been a truthful child. Even if she hadn't, how could she invent a long circumstantial story like that without being found out? The police asked her all the questions they wanted to; there was never any suggestion of accepting her statement as it stood."

"When she first told her story to you, did she tell it all in a piece?"

"Oh, no; it was spread over a day or two. The outline, first. And then filling in the details as she remembered them. Things like the window in the attic being round."

"Her days of coma had not blurred her memory."

"I don't think they would in any case. I mean, with Betty's kind of brain. She has a photographic memory."

Has she indeed! thought Robert; both ears erect and wide open.

"Even as a small child she could look at the page of a book—a child's book, of course—and repeat most of the contents from the picture in her mind. And when we played the Kim game—you know? the objects on the tray—we had to put Betty out of the game because she invariably won. Oh, no, she would remember what she saw."

Well, there was another game in which the cry was "Growing warm!" Robert remembered.

"You say she was always a truthful child—and everyone supports you in that—but did she never indulge in romanticising her own life, as children sometimes do?"

"Never," said Mrs. Wynn firmly. The idea seemed faintly to amuse her. "She couldn't," she added. "Unless it was the real thing it was no use to Betty. Even playing dolls' tea-parties, she would never imagine the things on the plates as most children are quite happy to do; there had to be a real thing there, even if it was only a little cube of bread. Usually it was something nicer, of course; it was a good way to wangle an extra and she was always a little greedy."

Robert admired the detachment with which she considered her longed-for and much-loved daughter. The remains of a schoolmistress's cynicism? So much more valuable, anyhow, for a child than a blind love. It was a pity that her intelligence and devotion had been so ill-rewarded.

"I don't want to keep on at a subject that must be unpleasant for you," Robert said. "But perhaps you could tell me something about the parents."

"Her parents?" Mrs. Wynn asked, surprised.

"Yes. Did you know them well? What were they like?"

"We didn't know them at all. We never even saw them."

"But you had Betty for—what was it?—nine months?—before her parents were killed, hadn't you?"

"Yes, but her mother wrote shortly after Betty came to us and said that to come to see her would only upset the child and make her unhappy and that the best thing for everyone would be to leave her to us until such times as she could go back to London. She said would I talk to Betty about her at least once every day."

Robert's heart contracted with pity for this unknown dead woman who had been willing to tear her own heart out for her only child. What treasure of love and care had been poured out in front of Betty Kane, child evacuee.

"Did she settle down easily when she came? Or did she cry for her mother?"

"She cried because she didn't like the food. I don't remember her ever crying for her mother. She fell in love with Leslie the first night—she was just a baby, you know—and I think her interest in him blotted out any grief she might have felt. And he, being four years older, was just the right age to feel protective. He still does—that is why we are in this mess today."

"How did this *Ack-Emma* affair happen? I know it was your son who went to the paper, but did you eventually come round to his——"

"Good heavens, no," Mrs. Wynn said indignantly. "It was all over before we could do anything about it. My husband and I were out when Leslie and the reporter came—they sent a man back with him when they heard his story, to get it first-hand from Betty—and when——"

"And Betty gave it quite willingly?"

"I don't know how willingly. I wasn't there. My husband and I knew nothing about it until this morning, when Leslie laid an *Ack-Emma* under our noses. A little defiantly, I may add. He is not feeling too good about it now that it is done. The *Ack-Emma*, I should like to assure you, Mr. Blair, is not normally my son's choice. If he had not been worked-up——"

"I know. I know exactly how it happened. And that tell-us-your-troubles-and-we'll-see-right-done is very insidious stuff." He rose. "You have been very kind indeed, Mrs. Wynn, and I am exceedingly grateful to you."

His tone was evidently more heartfelt than she had expected and she looked doubtfully at him. What have I said to help you? she seemed to be asking, half-dismayed.

He asked where Betty's parents had lived in London, and she told him. "There is nothing there now," she added. "Just the open space. It is to be part of some new building scheme, so they have done nothing to it so far."

On the doorstep he ran into Leslie.

Leslie was an extraordinarily good-looking young man who seemed to be entirely unaware of the fact—a trait that endeared him to Robert, who was in no mood to look kindly on him. Robert had pictured him as the bull-in-a-china-shop type; but on the contrary he was a rather delicate, kind-looking boy with shy earnest eyes and untidy soft hair. He glared at Robert with frank enmity when his mother presented him and had explained his business there; but, as his mother had said, there was a shade of defiance in the glare; Leslie was obviously not very happy with his own conscience this evening.

"No one is going to beat my sister and get away with it," he said fiercely when Robert had mildly deplored his action.

"I sympathise with your point of view," Robert said, "but I personally would rather be beaten nightly for a fortnight than have my photograph on the front page of the *Ack-Emma*. Especially if I was a young girl."

"If you had been beaten every night for a fortnight and no one did anything about it you might be very glad to have your photograph published in any rag if it got you justice," Leslie observed pertinently and brushed past them into the house.

Mrs. Wynn turned to Robert with a small apologetic smile, and Robert, taking advantage of her softened moment, said: "Mrs. Wynn, if it ever occurs to you that anything in that story of Betty's does not ring true, I hope you won't decide that sleeping dogs are best left."

"Don't pin your faith to that hope, Mr. Blair."

"You would let sleeping dogs lie, and the innocent suffer?"

"Oh no; I didn't mean that. I meant the hope of my doubting Betty's story. If I believed her at the beginning I am not likely to doubt her later."

"One never knows. Someday it may occur to you that this or that does not 'fit.' You have a naturally analytic mind; it may present you with a piece of subconscious when you least expect it. Something that has puzzled you deep down may refuse to be pushed down any more."

She had walked to the gate with him, and as he spoke the last sentence he turned to take farewell of her. To his surprise something moved behind her eyes at that light remark of his.

So she wasn't certain after all.

Somewhere, in the story, in the circumstances, there was some small thing that left a question in that sober analytical mind of hers.

What was it?

And then, with what he always remembered afterwards as the only perfect sample of telepathic communication in his experience, he paused as he was stepping into his car, and said: "Had she anything in her pockets when she came home?"

"She had only one pocket; the one in her dress."

"And was there anything in it?"

There was the faintest tightening of the muscles round her mouth. "Just a lipstick," she said, evenly.

"A lipstick! She is a little young for that, isn't she?"

"My dear Mr. Blair, they start experimenting with lipstick at the age of ten. As a wet-day amusement it has taken the place of dressing-up in Mother's things."

"Yes, probably; Woolworth is a great benefactor."

She smiled and said goodbye again and moved towards the house as he drove away.

What puzzled her about the lipstick? Robert wondered, as he turned from the uneven surface of Meadowside Lane on to the black smooth surface of the main Aylesbury-London road. Was it just the fact that the fiends at The Franchise should have left it with the girl? Was that what she found odd?

How amazing that the worry in her subconscious mind had communicated itself so instantly to him. He had not known that he was going to say that sentence about the girl's pockets until he heard himself saying it. It would never have occurred to him, left to himself, to wonder what was in the pocket of her frock. It would not occur to him that the frock might have a pocket at all.

So there was a lipstick.

And its presence was something that puzzled Mrs. Wynn.

Well; that was a straw that could be added to the little heap he had collected. To the fact that the girl had a photographic memory. To the fact that her nose had been put out of joint without warning only a month or two ago. To the fact that she was greedy. To the fact that she was bored with school. To the fact that she liked "reality."

To the fact—above all—that no one in that household, not even detached sensible Mrs. Wynn, knew what went on in Betty Kane's mind. It was quite unbelievable that a girl of fifteen who had been the centre of a young man's world could see herself supplanted overnight without reacting violently to the situation. But Betty had been "very nice about it."

Robert found this heartening. It was proof that that candid young face was no guide at all to the person who was Betty Kane.

CHAPTER VIII

ROBERT HAD DECIDED to kill a great many birds with one stone by spending the night in London.

To begin with, he wanted to have his hand held. And in the circumstances no one would hold his hand to better purpose than his old school friend Kevin Macdermott. What Kevin did not know about crime was probably not so anyhow. And as a well-known defending counsel his knowledge of human nature was extensive, varied, and peculiar.

At the moment the betting was evens whether Macdermott would die of high blood-pressure before he was sixty, or grace the Woolsack when he was seventy. Robert hoped the latter. He was very fond of Kevin.

They had first gravitated towards each other at school because they were both "going in for Law," but they had become and remained friends because they were complementary. To the Irishman, Robert's equanimity was amusing, provocative, and—when he was tired—restful. To Robert, Kevin's Celt flamboyance was exotic and fascinating. It was typical that Robert's ambition was to go back to the little country town and continue life as it was; while Kevin's was to alter everything that was alterable in the Law and to make as much noise as possible in the doing of it.

So far Kevin had not altered much—though he had done his best where some judges' rulings were concerned—but he had made considerable noise in his effortless, slightly malicious, fashion. Already the presence of Kevin Macdermott in a case added fifty per cent to its newspaper value—and a good deal more than that to its cost.

He had married—advantageously but happily—had a pleasant house near Weybridge and three hardy sons, lean and dark and lively like their father. For town purposes he kept a small flat in St. Paul's Churchyard, where, as he pointed out, he "could afford to look down on Queen Anne." And whenever Robert was in town—which was not oftener than Robert could help—they dined together, either at the flat or at the latest place where Kevin had found good claret. Outside the Law, Kevin's interests were show hacks, claret, and the livelier films of Warner Brothers.

Kevin was to be at some Bar dinner tonight, so his secretary had said when Robert had tried to reach him from Milford; but he would be delighted to have a legitimate excuse for dodging the speeches, so would Robert go along to St. Paul's Churchyard after dinner, and wait for him.

That was a good thing; if Kevin came from a dinner he would be relaxed and prepared to settle down for the evening; not restless and with three-quarters of his mind still back in the courtroom as he sometimes was.

Meanwhile, he would ring up Grant at Scotland Yard and see if he could spare him some minutes tomorrow morning. He must get it clear in his mind how he stood in relation with Scotland Yard: fellow sufferers, but on opposite sides of the fence.

At the Fortescue, the Edwardian old place in Jermyn Street, where he had stayed ever since he was first allowed to go to London on his own, they greeted him like a nephew and gave him "the room he had last time"; a dim comfortable box with a shoulder-high bed and a buttoned-plush settee; and brought him up a tray on which reposed an out-size brown kitchen teapot, a Georgian silver cream jug, about a pound of sugar lumps in a sixpenny glass dish, a Dresden cup with flowers and little castles, a red-and-gold Worcester plate made for "their Maj's" William IV and his Queen, and a much buckled kitchen knife with a stained brown handle.

Both the tea and the tray refreshed Robert. He went out into the evening streets feeling vaguely hopeful.

His search for the truth about Betty Kane brought him, only half consciously, to the vacant space where that block of flats had been; the spot where both her parents had died in one shattering burst of high explosive. It was a bare neat space, waiting its appointed part in some plan. Nothing was there to show that a building had ever stood on the spot. Round about, the unharmed houses stood with blank smug faces, like mentally deficient children too idiot to have understood the meaning of a disaster. It had passed them by and that was all they knew or cared about.

On the opposite side of the wide street, a row of small shops still stood as they had obviously stood for fifty years or more. Robert crossed to them and went into the tobacconist's to buy cigarettes; a tobacconist-and-newsagent knows everything.

"Were you here when that happened?" Robert asked, leaning his head towards the door.

"When what happened?" asked the rosy little man, so used to the blank space that he had long ago become unaware of it. "Oh, the incident? No, I was out on duty. Warden, I was."

Robert said that he had meant was he here in business at the time.

Oh, yes; yes, certainly he had the business then, and for long before it. Brought up in the neighbourhood, he was, and succeeded his father in the business.

"You would know the local people well, then. Do you remember the couple who were caretakers of the block of flats, by any chance?"

"The Kanes? Of course I do. Why wouldn't I remember them? They were in and out of this place all day. He for his paper in the morning, and then her for her cigarettes shortly after, and then back for his evening paper and her back for the third time probably for cigarettes again, and then he and I used to have a pint at the local when my boy had finished his lessons and would take over for me here. You knew them, sir?"

"No. But I met someone the other day who spoke of them. How was the whole place wrecked?"

The little pink man sucked his teeth with a derisive sound.

"Jerry-built. That's what it was. Just jerry-built. The bomb fell in the area there—that's how the Kanes were killed, they were down in their basement feeling fairly safe—and the whole thing just settled down like a house of cards. Shocking." He straightened the edge of a pile of evening papers. "It was just her bad luck that the only evening in weeks that she was at home with her husband, a bomb had to come." He seemed to find a sardonic pleasure in the thought.

"Where was she usually, then?" Robert asked. "Did she work somewhere in the evenings?"

"Work!" said the little man, with vast scorn. "Her!" And then, recollecting: "Oh, I'm sorry, I'm sure. I forgot for the minute that they might be friends of——"

Robert hastened to assure him that his interest in the Kanes was purely academic. Someone had remembered them as caretakers of the block of flats, that was all. If Mrs. Kane was not out working in the evenings what was she out doing?

"Having a good time, of course. Oh, yes, people managed to have a good time even then—if they wanted it enough and looked hard enough for it. Kane, he wanted her to go away to the country with that little girl of theirs, but would she? Not her! Three days of the country would kill her she said. She didn't even go to see the little thing when they evacuated her. The authorities, that is. With the rest of the children. It's my opinion she was tickled to death to have the child off her hands so that she could go dancing at nights."

"Whom did she go dancing with?"

"Officers," the little man said succinctly. "A lot more exciting than watching the grass grow. I don't say there was any actual harm in it, mind you," he said hastily. "She's dead, and I wouldn't like to pin anything on her that she isn't here to unpin, if you take my meaning. But she was a bad mother and a bad wife, that's flat and no one ever said anything to the contrary."

"Was she pretty?" Robert asked, thinking of the good emotion he had wasted on Betty's mother.

"In a sulky sort of way, yes. She sort of smouldered. You wondered what she would be like when she was lit up. Excited, I mean; not tight. I never saw her tight. She didn't get her excitement that way."

"And her husband?"

"Ah, he was all right, Bert Kane was. Deserved better luck than that woman. One of the best, Bert was. Terribly fond of the little girl. Spoiled her, of course. She had only to want something and he got it for her; but she was a nice kid, for all that. Demure. Butter wouldn't melt in her little mouth. Yes, Bert deserved better out of life than a good-time wife and a cupboard-love kid. One of the best, Bert was. . . ." He looked over the roadway at the empty space, reflectively. "It took them the best part of a week to find him," he said.

Robert paid for his cigarettes and went out into the street both saddened and relieved. Sad for Bert Kane, who had deserved better; but glad that Betty Kane's mother was not the woman he had pictured. All the way to London his mind had grieved for that dead woman; the woman who had broken her heart for her child's good. It had seemed to him unbearable that the child she had so greatly loved should be Betty Kane. But now he was free of that grief. Betty Kane's mother was exactly the mother he would have chosen for her if he were God. And she on her part looked very like being her mother's daughter.

"A cupboard-love kid." Well, well. And what was it Mrs. Wynn had said? "She cried because she didn't like the food, but I don't remember her crying for her mother."

Nor for that father who so devotedly spoiled her, apparently.

When he got back to the hotel he took his copy of the *Ack-Emma* from his despatch case, and over his solitary dinner at the Fortescue considered at his leisure the story on Page Two. From its poster-simplicity opening—

"On a night in April a girl came back to her home clad in nothing but a frock and shoes. She had left home, a bright happy schoolgirl with not a . . ."

to its final fanfare of sobs, it was of its kind a small masterpiece. It did perfectly what it set out to do. And that was to appeal to the greatest number of readers with one and the same story. To those who wanted sex-interest it offered the girl's lack of clothes, to the sentimentalist her youth and charm, to the partisan her helpless condition, to the sadist the details of her beatings, to the sufferer from class-hatred a description of the big white house behind its high walls, and to the warm-hearted British public in general the impression that the police had been, if not "nobbled," then at least lax, and that Right had not been Done.

Yes. It was clever.

Of course the story was a gift for them—which is why they had sent a man back immediately with young Leslie Wynn. But Robert felt that, when really on their mettle, the *Ack-Emma* could probably make a good story of a broken connecting-rod.

It must be a dreary business catering exclusively for the human failings. He turned the pages over, observing how consistently each story was used to appeal to the regrettable in the reader. Even GAVE AWAY A MILLION, he noticed, was the story of a disgraceful old man unloading on his income-tax and not of a boy who had climbed out of a slum by his own courage and enterprise.

With a slight nausea he put the thing back in his case, and took the case with him to St. Paul's Churchyard. There he found the "daily" woman waiting for him with her hat on. Mr. Macdermott's secretary had telephoned to say that a friend of his was coming and that he was to be given the run of the house and left alone in it without scruple; she had stayed merely to let him in; she would now leave him to it; there was whisky on the little table by the fire, and there was another bottle in the cupboard, but it might, if you asked her, be wise not to remind Mr. Macdermott about it or he would stay up too late and she had great trouble getting him up in the morning.

"It's not the whisky," Blair said, smiling at her, "it's the Irish in him. All the Irish hate getting up."

This gave her pause on the doorstep; evidently struck by this new idea.

"I wouldn't wonder," she said. "My old man's the same, and he's Irish. It's not whisky with him, just original sin. At least that's what I always thought. But perhaps it's just his misfortune in being a Murphy."

It was a pleasant little place; warm and friendly, and peaceful now that the roar of the city traffic was still. He poured himself a drink, went to the window to look down on Queen Anne, paused a moment to note once more how lightly the great bulk of the church floated on its base; so proportioned, so balanced, that it looked as if one could take it up on a palm and dandle it there; and then sat down and, for the first time since he had gone out that morning to see a maddening old woman who was changing her will again, relaxed.

He was half asleep when he heard Kevin's key in the lock, and his host was in the room before he could move.

Macdermott tweaked his neck in an evil pinch as he passed behind him to the decanters on the table. "It's beginning, old boy," he said, "it's beginning."

"What is?" Robert asked.

"The thickening of that handsome neck of yours."

Robert rubbed his neck lazily where it stung. "I do begin to notice draughts on the back of it, now you come to mention it," he said.

"Christ, Robert! does nothing distress you," Kevin said, his eyes pale and bright and mocking under their black brows, "even the imminent prospect of losing those good looks of yours?"

"I'm a little distressed at the moment, but it isn't my looks."

"Well, what with Blair, Hayward, and Bennet, it can't be bankruptcy; so I suppose it's a woman."

"Yes, but not the way you mean."

"Thinking of getting married? You ought to, Rob."

"You said that before."

"You want an heir for Blair, Hayward, and Bennet, don't you?" The calm certainty of Blair, Hayward, and Bennet had always pricked Kevin into small gibes, Robert remembered.

"There is no guarantee that it wouldn't be a girl. Anyhow, Nevil is taking care of that."

"The only thing that young woman of Nevil's will ever give birth to is a gramophone record. She was gracing a platform again the other day, I hear. If she had to earn the money for her train fares she mightn't be so willing to dash about the country being the Vocal Minority." He sat down with his drink. "I needn't ask if you are up on business. Sometime you really ought to come up and see this town. I suppose you dash off again tomorrow after a 10 a.m. interview with someone's solicitors."

"No," Robert said. "With Scotland Yard."

Keven paused with his glass half-way to his mouth. "Robert, you're slipping," he said. "What has the Yard to do with your Ivory Tower?"

"That's just it," Robert said equably, ignoring this additional flick at his Milford security. "It's there on the doorstep and I don't quite know how to deal with it. I want to listen to someone being intelligent about the situation. I don't know why I should unload it on you. You must be sick of problems. But you always did do my algebra for me."

"And you always reckoned the stocks and shares ones, if I remember rightly. I was always a fool about stocks. I still owe you something for saving me from a bad investment. Two bad investments," he added.

"Two?"

"Tamara, and Topeka Tin."

"I remember saving you from Topeka Tin, but I had nothing whatever to do with your breaking with Tamara."

"Oh, hadn't you, indeed! My good Robert, if you could have seen your face when I introduced you to her. Oh, no, not that way. Quite the contrary. The instantaneous *kindness* of your expression, that blasted English mask of courtesy and good breeding—it said everything. I saw myself going through life introducing Tamara to people and watching their faces being well-bred about it. It cured me of her in record time. I have never ceased to be grateful to you. So produce what is in the despatch case."

Nothing escaped Kevin, Robert thought, taking out his own copy of Betty Kane's statement to the police.

"This is a very short statement. I wish you would read it and tell me how it strikes you."

He wanted the impact on Kevin, without preliminaries to dull the edge of it.

Macdermott took it, read the first paragraph in one swift eye movement, and said: "This is the *Ack-Emma*'s protégée, I take it."

"I had no idea that you ever saw the *Ack-Emma*," Robert said, surprised.

"God love you, I feed on the *Ack-Emma*. No crime, no *causes célèbres*. No *causes célèbres*, no Kevin Macdermott. Or only a piece of him." He lapsed into utter silence. For four minutes his absorption was so complete that Robert felt alone in the room, as if his host had gone away. "Humph!" he said, coming out of it.

"Well?"

"I take it that your clients are the two women in the case, and not this girl?"

"Of course."

"Now you tell me your end," Kevin said, and listened.

Robert gave him the whole story. His reluctant visit, his growing partisanship as it became clear that it was a choice between Betty Kane and the two women, Scotland Yard's decision not to move on the available evidence, and Leslie Wynn's rash visit to the offices of the *Ack-Emma.*

"So tonight," Macdermott said, "the Yard is moving heaven and earth to find corroborative evidence that will back up the girl's story."

"I suppose so," said Robert, depressed. "But what I want to know is: Do you or do you not believe the girl's story?"

"I never believe anyone's story," Kevin pointed out with gentle malice. "What you want to know is: Do I find the girl's story believable? And of course I do."

"You do!"

"I do. Why not?"

"But it's an absurd story," Robert said, more hotly than he had intended.

"There is nothing absurd about it. Women who live lonely lives do insane things—especially if they are poor gentlewomen. Only the other day an elderly woman was found to have kept her sister chained up to a bed in a room no bigger than a good-sized cupboard. She had kept her like that for three years, and had fed her on the crusts and potato skins and the other scraps that she didn't want herself. She said, when it was discovered, that their money was going down too fast and this was her way of making ends meet. She had quite a good bank balance actually, but it was the fear induced by insecurity that had sent her crazy. That is a much more unbelievable—and from your point of view absurd—story than the girl's."

"Is it? It seems to me just an ordinary tale of insanity."

"Only because you know it happened. I mean, that someone had actually seen the thing. Suppose, on the contrary, that the rumour had merely gone round; that the crazy sister had heard it and released her victim before any investigation could be made; that the investigators found only two old ladies living an apparently normal life except for the invalidish nature of one of them. What then? Would you have believed the 'chained-up' tale? Or would you, more likely, have called it an 'absurd story'?"

Robert sank a little deeper into his depression.

"Here are two lonely and badly-dowered women saddled with a big house in the country; one of them too old to do much household work and the other loathing it. What is the most likely form for their mild insanity to take? The capture of a girl to be servant to them, of course."

Damn Kevin and his counsel's mind. He had thought that he had wanted Kevin's opinion, but what he had wanted was Kevin's backing for his own opinion.

"The girl they capture happens to be a blameless schoolgirl, conveniently far from her home. It is their bad luck that she is so blameless, because since she has never been caught out in a lie to date, everyone is going to take her word against theirs. If I were the police I would have risked it. It seems to me they are losing their nerve."

He shot an amused glance at Robert, sunk in his chair, glooming down his long legs at the fire. He sat for a moment or two enjoying his friend's discomfiture.

"Of course," he said, at length, "they may have remembered a parallel case, where everyone believed the girl's heart-rending story and were very thoroughly led up the garden."

"A parallel!" Robert said, folding his legs and sitting up. "When?"

"Seventeen-something. I forget the exact date."

"Oh," said Robert, dashed again.

"I don't know what is 'Oh' about it," Macdermott said mildly. "The nature of alibis has not changed much in two centuries."

"Alibis?"

"If the parallel case is any guide the girl's story is an alibi."

"Then you believe—I mean you find it believable—that the girl's story is all nonsense?"

"A complete invention from beginning to end."

"Kevin, you are maddening. You said you found it believable."

"So I do. I also find it believable that it is a tissue of lies. I am not briefed for either side. I can make a very good case out for either, at the shortest notice. On the whole I should prefer to be counsel for the young woman from Aylesbury. She would be wonderful in the witness box, and from what you tell me neither of the Sharpes would be much help, visually, to a counsel."

He got up to help himself to more whisky, holding out his other hand for Robert's glass. But Robert was in no mood for conviviality. He shook his head without lifting his gaze from the fire. He was tired and beginning to be out of temper with Kevin. He had been wrong to come. When a man had been a counsel in the criminal courts as long as Kevin had, his mind had only points of view, not convictions any more. He would wait until Kevin had half-finished the glass he was now sitting down with, and then make a movement to go. It would be good to put his head on a pillow and forget for a little that he was responsible for other people's problems. Or rather, for the solution of them.

"I wonder what she was doing all that month," Kevin said conversationally, taking a large gulp of practically neat whisky.

Robert's mouth opened to say: "Then you *do* believe the girl is a fake!"

but he stopped himself in time. He rebelled against dancing any more this evening to Kevin's piping.

"If you drink so much whisky on top of claret, what *you* will be doing for a month is a cure, my lad," he said. And to his surprise Kevin lay back and laughed like a schoolboy.

"Oh, Rob, I love you," he said delightedly. "You are the very essence of England. Everything we admire and envy in you. You sit there so mild, so polite, and let people bait you, until they conclude that you are an old tabby and they can do what they like with you, and then just when they are beginning to preen themselves they go that short step too far and wham! out comes that business-like paw with the glove off!" He picked Robert's glass out of his hand without a by-your-leave and rose to fill it and Robert let him. He was feeling better.

CHAPTER IX

THE LONDON-LARBOROUGH ROAD was a black straight ribbon in the sunshine, giving off diamond sparks as the crowded traffic caught the light and lost it again. Pretty soon both the air and the roads would be so full that no one could move in comfort and everyone would have to go back to the railways for quick travel. Progress, that was.

Kevin had pointed out last night that, what with present ease of communications, it was quite on the cards that Betty Kane had spent her month's vacation in Sydney, N.S.W. It was a daunting thought. She could be anywhere from Kamchatka to Peru, and all he, Blair, had to do was a little thing like proving she wasn't in a house on the Larborough-Milford road. If it were not a sunny morning, and if he were not sorry for Scotland Yard, and if he didn't have Kevin to hold his hand, and if he were not doing pretty well on his own so far, he might have felt depressed.

Feeling sorry for Scotland Yard was the last thing he had anticipated. But sorry he was. All Scotland Yard's energies were devoted to proving the Sharpes guilty and Betty Kane's story true; for the very good reason that they believed the Sharpes to be guilty. But what each one of them ached in his private soul to do was to push Betty Kane down the *Ack-Emma*'s throat; and they could only do that by proving her story nonsense. Yes, a really prize state of frustration existed in those large calm bodies at the Yard.

Grant had been charming in his quiet reasonable way—it had been rather like going to see a doctor, now he came to think of it—and had quite willingly agreed that Robert should be told about any letters that the *Ack-Emma* might provoke.

"Don't pin your hopes too firmly to that, will you," he had said, in friendly warning. "For one letter that the Yard gets that has any worth it gets five thousand that are nonsense. Letterwriting is the natural outlet of the 'odds.' The busybodies, the idle, the perverted, the cranks, the feel-it-my-duties——"

" 'Pro Bono Publico'——"

"Him and 'Civis'," Grant said with a smile. "Also the plain depraved. They all write letters. It's their *safe* outlet, you see. They can be as interfering, as long-winded, as obscene, as pompous, as one-idea'd, as they like on paper, and no one can kick them for it. So they write. My God, how they write!"

"But there is a chance——"

"Oh, yes. There is a chance. And all these letters will have to be weeded out, however silly they are. Anything of importance will be passed on to you, I promise. But I do remind you that the ordinary intelligent citizen writes only one time in five thousand. He doesn't like what he thinks of as 'poking his nose in'—which is why he sits silent in a railway carriage and scandalises the Americans, who still have a hick interest in other folk—and anyhow he's a busy man, full of his own affairs, and sitting down to a letter to the police about something that doesn't concern him is against all his instincts."

So Robert had come away pleased with the Yard, and sorry for them. At least he, Robert, had a straight row to hoe. He wouldn't be glancing aside every now and then and wishing it was the next row he was hoeing. And moreover he had Kevin's approval of the row he had chosen.

"I mean it," Kevin had said, "when I say that if I were the police I should almost have risked it. They have a good enough case. And a nice little conviction is always a hitch up the ladder of promotion for someone. Unfortunately—or fortunately for the citizen—the man who decides whether there is a case or not is the chap higher up, and he's not interested in any subordinate's speedy promotion. Amazing that wisdom should be the by-product of office procedure."

Robert, mellow with whisky, had let the cynicism flow past him.

"But let them just get one spot of corroboration, and they'll have a warrant at the door of The Franchise quicker than you can lift a telephone receiver."

"They won't get any corroboration," said the mellow Robert. "Why should they? How could they? What we want to do is to disprove the girl's story ourselves, so that it doesn't damn the Sharpes' lives for as long as they live. Once I have seen the aunt and uncle tomorrow we may have enough general knowledge about the girl to justify a start on our own investigation."

Now he was speeding down the black shining Larborough road on the way to seeing Betty's relations in Mainshill; the people she had stayed with on the memorable holiday. A Mr. and Mrs. Tilsit, they were. Tilsit,

93 Cherrill Street, Mainshill, Larborough—and the husband was travelling agent for a firm of brush-makers in Larborough and they had no children. That was all Robert knew about them.

He paused for a moment as he turned off the main road in Mainshill. This was the corner where Betty Kane waited for her bus. Or said she waited. Over there on the other side, it must have been. There was no side turning on that side; nothing but the long stretch of unbroken pavement as far as one could see in either direction. A busy enough road at this time of day; but empty enough, Robert supposed, in the doldrum hour of the late afternoon.

Cherrill Street was one long series of angular bay windows in dirty red brick, their forward surface almost scraping the low red-brick wall that hemmed them in from the pavement. The sour soil on either side of the window that did duty for a garden had none of the virtues of the new-turned earth of Meadowside Lane, Aylesbury; it grew only thin London Pride, weedy wall-flowers, and moth-eaten forget-me-not. The same housewife's pride obtained in Cherrill Street as in Aylesbury, of course, and the same crisp curtains hung at the windows; but if there were poets in Cherrill Street they found other outlets for their soul than gardens.

When he had rung unavailingly, and then knocked, at 93—indistinguishable from the others as far as he could see except by its painted numerals—a woman flung up the bedroom window next door, leaned out and said:

"You looking for Mrs. Tilsit?"

Robert said that he was.

"She's gone to get her groceries. The shop at the corner."

"Oh, thanks. If that's all, I'll wait."

"Shouldn't wait if you want to see her soon. Should go and fetch her."

"Oh. Is she going somewhere else?"

"No, just the grocer's; it's the only shop round here. But she takes half a morning deciding between two brands of wheat flakes. You take one packet up right firm and put it in her bag and she'll be quite pleased."

Robert thanked her and began to walk away to the end of the street, when she hailed him again.

"Shouldn't leave your car. Take it with you."

"But it's quite a little way, isn't it?"

"Maybe, but it's Saturday."

"Saturday?"

"School's out."

"Oh, I see. But there's nothing in it——" "to steal," he was going to say but amended it to "Nothing in it that's movable."

"Movable! Huh! That's good. We had window-boxes once. Mrs. Laverty over the way had a gate. Mrs. Biddows had two fine wooden clothes posts and eighteen yards of clothes rope. They all thought they weren't movable. You leave your car there for ten minutes you'll be lucky to find the chassis!"

So Robert got obediently into the car, and drove down to the grocer's. And as he drove he remembered something, and the memory puzzled him. This was where Betty Kane had been so happy. This rather dreary, rather grimy street; one of a warren of streets very like itself. So happy that she had written to say that she was staying on for the rest of her holidays.

What had she found here that was so desirable?

He was still wondering as he walked into the grocer's and prepared to spot Mrs. Tilsit among the morning customers. But there was no need for any guesswork. There was only one woman in the shop, and one glance at the grocer's patient face and the cardboard packet in the woman's either hand, made it plain that she was Mrs. Tilsit.

"Can I get you something, sir," the grocer said detaching himself for a moment from the woman's ponderings—it wasn't wheat flakes this morning, it was powdered soap—and moving towards Robert.

"No, thank you," Robert said. "I am just waiting for this lady."

"For me?" the woman said. "If it's the gas, then——"

Robert said hastily that he wasn't the gas.

"I *have* a vacuum cleaner, and it's going fine," she offered, and prepared to go back to her problem.

Robert said that he had his car outside and would wait until she had finished, and was beating a hasty retreat; but she said: "A car! Oh. Well, you can drive me back, can't you, and save me carrying all those things. How much, Mr. Carr, please?"

Mr. Carr, who had taken a packet of soap-flakes from her during her interest in Robert and wedged it into her shopping-bag, took her money, gave her change, wished her a thankful good-day, and cast a pitiful glance at Robert as he followed the woman out to his car.

Robert had known that it was too much to hope for another woman with Mrs. Wynn's detachment and intelligence, but his heart sank as he considered Mrs. Tilsit. Mrs. Tilsit was one of those women whose minds are always on something else. They chat brightly with you, they agree with you, they admire what you are wearing, and they offer advice, but their real attention is concentrated on what to do with the fish, or what Florrie told them about Minnie's eldest, or where they have left the laundry book, or even just what a bad filling that is in your right front tooth; anything, everything, except the subject in hand.

She seemed impressed with the appearance of Robert's car, and asked him in to have a cup of tea—there being apparently no hour of the day when a cup of tea was not a possible article of diet. Robert felt that he could not drink with her—even a cup of tea—without making plain his position of opposing counsel, so to speak. He did his best, but it was doubtful if she understood; her mind was so plainly already deciding whether to offer him the Rich Tea or the Mixed Fancy biscuits with his tea. Mention of her niece made none of the expected stir in her emotions.

"A most extraordinary thing, that was, wasn't it?" she said. "Taking her away and beating her. What good did they think that was going to do them? Sit down, Mr. Blayne, come in and sit down. I'll just——"

A bloodcurdling scream echoed through the house. An urgent, high-pitched, desperate screaming that went on and on, without even a pause for breath.

Mrs. Tilsit humped her parcels in a movement of exasperation. She leaned near enough to Robert to put her mouth within shouting distance of his ear. "My kettle," she yelled. "I'll be right back."

Robert sat down, and again considered the surroundings and wondered why Betty Kane had found them so good. Mrs. Wynn's front room had been a living-room; a sitting-room warm with human occupation and human traffic. But this was clearly a "best" room, kept for visitors who were not intimate enough to be admitted to the back regions; the real life of the house was in the poky room at the back. Either kitchen or kitchen-sitting-room. And yet Betty Kane had elected to stay. Had she found a friend? A girl-next-door? A boy-next-door?

Mrs. Tilsit came back in what seemed like two minutes, bearing a tray with tea. Robert wondered a little at this promptness of action until he saw the tray's contents. Mrs. Tilsit had not waited to make a decision; she had brought them both; Thin Wine and Sweet Shortbread. At least, he thought, watching her pour, that this woman explained one of the oddities in the affair: the fact that when the Wynns had written to have Betty sent home at once, her aunt had not flown to a telegraph office to break the news that Betty had left for home nearly a fortnight ago. The Betty who had gone a fortnight previously would be much less real in Mrs. Tilsit's mind than the jelly that was cooling on the back window-sill.

"I wasn't worried about her," Mrs. Tilsit said, as if in echo to his thoughts. "When they wrote from Aylesbury about her. I knew she would turn up. When Mr. Tilsit came home he was quite upset about it; he goes away for a week or ten days at a time you know; he's agent for Weekses; carried on like a mad thing, he did; but I just said you wait and she'll turn up all right, and she did. Well, nearly all right."

"She said she enjoyed her holiday here enormously."

"I suppose she did," she said vaguely, not looking gratified as Robert had expected. He glanced at her and realised that her mind was already on something else. The strength of his tea, if one was to judge by the direction of her eye.

"How did she pass her time? Did she make friends?"

"Oh, no, she was in Larborough most of the time."

"Larborough!"

"Oh, well, when I say most of the time, I do her an injustice. She helped with the house in the mornings, but in a house this size and me used to doing everything myself there isn't much to do. And she was here on holiday, wasn't she, poor thing, after all that school work. What good all that book work is to a young girl I don't know. Mrs. Harrap's daughter over the way could hardly write her name but she married the third son of a lord. Or perhaps it was the son of a third son," she said, looking doubtful. "I forget for the minute. She——"

"How did she spend her time in Larborough? Betty, I mean."

"Pictures, mostly."

"Pictures? Oh, the cinema. I see."

"You can do that from morning till night if you're given that way, in Larborough. The big ones open at half-past ten and they mostly change mid-week and there's about forty of them, so you can just go from one to another till it's time to go home."

"Is that what Betty did?"

"Oh, no. She's quite sensible, Betty is. She used to go in to the morning round because you get in cheaper before noon, and then she'd go bus-riding."

"Bus-riding. Where?"

"Oh, anywhere the fancy took her. Have another of these biscuits, Mr. Bain; they're fresh from the tin. She went to see the castle at Norton one day. Norton's the county town you know. Everyone imagines Larborough is because it's so big, but Norton's always been——"

"Did she not come home to lunch, then?"

"What? Oh, Betty. No, she'd have coffee lunch somewhere. We always have our real meal at night anyhow, you see, with Mr. Tilsit being out all day, so there was always a meal waiting when she came home. It's always been my pride to have a good nourishing sit-down meal ready for my——"

"What time would that be? Six?"

"No, Mr. Tilsit doesn't usually manage home before half-past seven."

"And I suppose Betty was home long before then?"

"Mostly she was. She was late once because she went to an afternoon show at the pictures, but Mr. Tilsit he created about it—though I'm sure he had no need to, what harm can you come to at the pictures?—and after that she was always home before him. When he was here, that is. She wasn't so careful when he was away."

So the girl had been her own mistress for a good fortnight. Free to come and go without question, and limited only by the amount of holiday money in her pocket. It was an innocent-sounding fortnight; and in the case of most girls of her age it undoubtedly would have been that. The cinema in the morning, or window gazing; a coffee lunch; a bus-ride into the country in the afternoon. A blissful holiday for an adolescent; the first taste of unsupervised freedom.

But Betty Kane was no normal adolescent. She was the girl who had told that long and circumstantial story to the police without a tremor.

The girl with four weeks of her life unaccounted for. The girl that someone had ended by beating unmercifully. How, then, had Betty Kane spent her unsupervised freedom?

"Did she go to Milford on the bus, do you know?"

"No, *they* asked me that, of course, but I couldn't say yes or not."

"They?"

"The police."

Yes, of course; he had forgotten for the moment that the police would have checked Betty Kane's every sentence to the limit of their power.

"You're not police, I think you said."

"No," Robert said yet once again, "I'm a lawyer. I represent the two women who are supposed to have detained Betty."

"Oh, yes. You told me. I suppose they have to have a lawyer like anyone else, poor things. To ask questions for them. I hope I'm telling you the things you want to know, Mr. Blayne."

He had another cup of tea in the hope that sooner or later she would tell him something he wanted to know. But it was mere repetition now.

"Did the police know that Betty was away on her own all day?" he asked.

She really thought about that. "That I can't remember," she said. "They asked me how she passed her time and I said that mostly she went to pictures or bus-riding, and they said did I go with her and I said—well, I'll have to admit I told a white lie about it and said that I did now and then. I didn't want them to think that Betty went to places alone. Though of course there was no harm in it."

What a mind!

"Did she have letters while she was here?" he asked as he was taking his leave.

"Just from home. Oh, yes, I would know. I always took the letters in. In any case they wouldn't have written to her, would they?"

"Who?"

"Those women who kidnapped her."

It was with a feeling of escape that Robert drove in to Larborough. He wondered if Mr. Tilsit had always been away "ten days at a time" from his home, or if he had got the travelling job as an alternative to flight or suicide.

In Larborough, Blair sought out the main garage of the Larborough And District Motor Services. He knocked at the door of the small office that guarded one side of the entrance, and went in. A man in a bus inspector's uniform was going through papers on the desk. He glanced up at Robert and without asking his business continued his own affairs.

Robert said that he wanted to see someone who would know about the Milford bus service.

"Time table on the wall outside," the man said without looking up.

"I don't want to know about times. I know them. I live in Milford. I want to know if you ever run a double-decker bus on that route."

There was silence for a long time; a silence expertly calculated to end at the point where Robert was about to open his mouth again.

"No," said the man.

"Never?" Robert asked.

This time there was no answer at all. The inspector made it plain that he was finished with him.

"Listen," Robert said, "this is important. I am a partner in a firm of solicitors in Milford, and I——"

The man turned on him. "I don't care if you are the Shah of Persia; there are *no double-decker buses on the Milford run!* And what do *you* want?" he added as a small mechanic appeared behind Robert in the doorway.

The mechanic hesitated, as if the business he had come on had been upset by a newer interest. But he pulled himself together and began to state his business. "It's about those spares for Norton. Shall I——"

As Robert was edging past him out of the office he felt a tug on his coat and realised that the little mechanic wanted him to linger until he could talk to him. Robert went out and bent over his own car, and presently the mechanic appeared at his elbow.

"You asking about double-decker buses? I couldn't contradict him straight out, you know; in the mood he's in now it'd be as much as my job's worth. You want to *use* a double-decker, or just to know if they ever run at all? Because you can't *get* a double-decker on that route, not to travel in, because the buses on that run are all——"

"I know, I know. They are single-decks. What I wanted to know was whether there *ever* are two-deck buses on the Milford route."

"Well, there are not supposed to be, you understand, but once or twice this year we've had to use a double-decker when one of the old single ones broke down unexpected. Sooner or later they'll be all double-deck, but there isn't enough traffic on the Milford run to justify a double, so all the old crocks of singles eventually land on that route and a few more like it. And so——"

"You're a great help. Would it be possible to find out exactly when a double-decker did run on that route?"

"Oh, certainly," the mechanic said, with a shade of bitterness. "In this firm it's recorded every time you spit. But the records are in there," he tilted back his head to indicate the office, "and as long as *he's* there there's nothing doing."

Robert asked at what hour there would be something doing.

"Well: he goes off at the same time as me: six. But I could wait a few minutes and look up the schedules when he's gone if it's very important to you."

Robert did not know how he was going to wait through the hours till six o'clock, but six o'clock it would have to be.

"Righto. I'll meet you in the Bell, that's the pub at the end of the street, about a quarter past six. That do?"

That would do perfectly, Robert said. Perfectly.

And he went away to see what he could bribe the lounge waiter at the Midland into giving him out of hours.

CHAPTER X

"I SUPPOSE YOU KNOW what you're doing, dear," Aunt Lin said, "but I can't help thinking it's very odd of you to defend people like that."

"I am not 'defending' them," Robert said patiently, "I am representing them. And there is no evidence whatever that they are 'people like that'."

"There is the girl's statement, Robert. She couldn't just have made all that up."

"Oh, couldn't she!"

"What advantage would it be to her to tell a lot of lies!" She was standing in his doorway passing her prayer-book from one hand to the other as she put on her white gloves. "What else could she have been doing if she wasn't at The Franchise?"

Robert bit back a "You'd be surprised!" It was always best with Aunt Lin to take the line of least resistance.

She smoothed her gloves into place. "If it's just that you're being noble, Robert dear, I must say you are just being wrongheaded. And do you have to go out to the *house!* Surely they could come to the office tomorrow. There's no hurry is there? It isn't as if someone was going to arrest them on the spot."

"It was my suggestion that I should go out to The Franchise. If someone accused *you* of stealing things off Woolworth's counter and you couldn't disprove it, I don't suppose you would enjoy walking down Milford High Street in broad daylight."

"I mightn't like it but I should most certainly do it, and give Mr. Hensell a piece of my mind."

"Who is Mr. Hensell?"

"The manager. Couldn't you come to church with me first and then go out to The Franchise; it's such a long time since you've been, dear."

"If you stand there much longer you'll be late for the first time in ten years. You go and pray that my judgment may be perfected."

"I shall most certainly pray for you, dear. I always do. I shall also put up a little one for myself. All this is going to be very difficult for me."

"For you?"

"Now that you're acting for those people I shan't be able to talk about it to anyone. It is quite maddening, dear, to sit silent and hear everyone telling for gospel truth things you know for a fact are wrong. It's like wanting to be sick and having to postpone it. Oh, dear, the bells have stopped, haven't they? I'll just have to slip into the Bracketts' pew. They won't mind. You won't stay to lunch at that place, will you, dear."

"I don't suppose that I shall be invited."

But his welcome at The Franchise was so warm that he felt that he might very well be invited after all. He would say no, of course; not because Aunt Lin's chicken was waiting but because Marion Sharpe would have to do the washing up afterwards. When there was no one there they probably ate off trays. Or in the kitchen, for all anyone knew.

"I am sorry we refused to answer the telephone last night," Marion said, apologising again. "But after the fourth or fifth time it really was too much. And we didn't expect you to have news so soon. After all you had only set out on Friday afternoon."

"Your telephone callers: were they male or female?"

"One male, and four female, as far as I remember. When you rang this morning I thought it was beginning again, but they seem to be late-sleepers. Or perhaps they don't really get evil-minded much before evening. We certainly provided the Saturday evening's entertainment for the country youths. They congregated in a group inside the gate and cat-called. Then Nevil found a bar of wood in the out-house——"

"Nevil?"

"Yes, your nephew. I mean, your cousin. He came to pay what he called a visit of condolence, which was very nice of him. And he found a bar that could be wedged in the gateway to keep the thing shut; we have no key for it, you see. But of course that didn't stop them for long. They hoisted each other up on the wall, and sat there in a row being offensive until it was time for them to go to their beds."

"Lack of education," old Mrs. Sharpe said thoughtfully, "is an extraordinary handicap when one is being offensive. They had no resource at all."

"Neither have parrots," Robert said. "But they can be provocative enough. We must see what police protection we can claim. Meanwhile I can tell you something pleasanter about that wall. I know how the girl saw over it."

He told them about his visit to Mrs. Tilsit and his discovery that the girl amused herself by bus-riding (or said she did) and his subsequent visit to the Larborough And District Motor Services garage.

"In the fortnight that the girl was at Mainshill there were two breakdowns of single-deck buses due to go out on the Milford run; and each time a double-decker had to be substituted. There are only three services each way daily, you know. And each time the breakdown happened to the bus due to go out on the mid-day service. So there were at least two occasions in that fortnight when she could have seen the house, the courtyard, you two, and the car, all together."

"But could anyone passing on top of a bus take in so much?"

"Have you ever travelled on the upper deck of a country bus? Even when the bus is going at a steady thirty-five, the pace seems funereal. What you can see is so much further away, and you can see it so much longer. Down below, the hedges brush the window and the pace seems good because things are closer. That is one thing. The other is that she has a photographic memory." And he told them what Mrs. Wynn had said.

"Do we tell the police this?" Mrs. Sharpe asked.

"No. It doesn't prove anything; just solves the problem of how she knew about you. When she needed an alibi she remembered you, and risked your not being able to prove that you were somewhere else. When you bring your car to the door, by the way, which side of the car is nearest the door?"

"Whether I bring it round from the garage or in from the road the off side is next the door, because it's easier to get out of."

"Yes; so that the near side, with the darker paint on the front wheel, would be facing the gate," Robert said conclusively. "That is the picture she saw. The grass and the divided path, the car at the door with the odd wheel, two women—both individual—the round attic window in the roof. She had only to look at the picture in her mind and describe it. The day she was using the picture for—the day she was supposed to have been kidnapped—was more than a month away and it was a thousand to one against your being able to say what you had done or where you had been on that day."

"And I take it," Mrs. Sharpe said, "that the odds are very much greater against our being able to say what she has done or where she has been in that month."

"The odds are against us, yes. As my friend Kevin Macdermott pointed out last night, there is nothing to hinder her having been in Sydney, N.S.W. But somehow I am far more hopeful today than I was on Friday morning. We know so much more about the girl now." He told them of his interviews in Aylesbury and Mainshill.

"But if the police inquiries didn't unearth what she was doing that month——"

"The police inquiries were devoted to checking her statement. They didn't start, as we do, with the premise that her statement is untrue from beginning to end. They checked it and it checked. They had no particular reason to doubt it. She had a blameless reputation, and when they inquired from her aunt how she had spent her holiday time they found that it had consisted of innocent visits to the cinema and country bus-rides."

"And what do *you* think it consisted of?" Mrs. Sharpe asked.

"I think she met someone in Larborough. That, anyhow, is the obvious explanation. It's from that supposition that I think any inquiry of ours should start."

"And what do we do about engaging an agent?" asked Mrs. Sharpe. "Do you know of one?"

"Well," Robert said, hesitating, "it had crossed my mind that you might let me pursue my own inquiries a little further before we engage a professional. I know that——"

"Mr. Blair," the old woman said, interrupting him, "you have been called into this unpleasant case without warning, and it cannot have been very willingly; and you have been very kind in doing your best for us. But we cannot expect you to turn yourself into a private inquiry agent on our behalf. We are not rich—indeed we have very little to live on—but as long as we have any money at all we shall pay for what services are proper. And it is not proper that you should turn yourself into a—what is it?—a Sexton Blake for our benefit."

"It may not be proper but it is very much to my taste. Believe me, Mrs. Sharpe, I hadn't planned it with any conscious thought of saving your pocket. Coming home in the car last night, very pleased with what I had done so far, I realised how much I should hate giving up the search to someone else. It had become a personal hunt. Please don't discourage me from——"

"If Mr. Blair is willing to carry on a little longer," Marion interrupted, "I think we should thank him heartily and accept. I know just how he feels. I wish I could go hunting myself."

"There will no doubt come a time when I shall have to turn it over to a proper inquiry agent whether I want to or not. If the trail leads far from Larborough, for instance. I have too many other commitments to follow it far. But as long as the search is on our doorsteps I do want to be the one to pursue it."

"How had you planned to pursue it?" Marion asked, interested.

"Well, I had thought of beginning with the coffee-lunch places. In Larborough, I mean. For one thing, there can't be so very many of them. And for another, we do know that, at any rate at the beginning, that was the kind of lunch she had."

"Why do you say 'at the beginning'?" Marion asked.

"Once she had met the hypothetical X, she may have lunched anywhere. But up till then she paid for her own lunches, and they were 'coffee' ones. A girl of that age prefers a bun lunch anyhow, even if she has money for a two-course meal. So I concentrate on the coffee-places. I flourish the *Ack-Emma* at the waitresses and find out as tactfully as a country lawyer knows how whether they have ever seen the girl in their place. Does that sound like sense to you?"

"Very good sense," Marion said.

Robert turned to Mrs. Sharpe. "But if you think you will be better served by a professional—and that is more than possible—then I shall bow out with——"

"I don't think we could be better served by anyone," Mrs. Sharpe said. "I have expressed my appreciation already of the trouble you have gone to on our behalf. If it would really please you to run down this—this——"

"Moppet," supplied Robert happily.

"Mopsy," Mrs. Sharpe amended, "then we can only agree and be grateful. But it seems to me likely to be a very long run."

"Why long?"

"There is a big gap, it seems to me, between meeting a hypothetical X in Larborough, and walking into a house near Aylesbury wearing nothing but a frock and shoes and well and truly beaten. Marion, there is still some of the Amontillado, I think."

In the silence that succeeded Marion's departure to fetch the sherry the quiet of the old house became apparent. There were no trees in the courtyard to make small noises in the wind and no birds to chatter. The silence was as absolute as the midnight silence of a small town. Was it peaceful, Robert wondered, after the crowded life of a boarding-house? Or was it lonely and a little frightening?

They had valued its privacy, old Mrs. Sharpe had said in his office on Friday morning. But was it a good life shut in behind the high walls in the perpetual silence?

"It seems to me," Mrs. Sharpe said, "that the girl took a great risk in choosing The Franchise, knowing nothing of the household or its circumstances."

"Of course she took a risk," Robert said. "She had to. But I don't think it was as big a gamble as you think."

"No?"

"No. What you are saying is that for all the girl knew there might be a large household of young people and three maidservants at The Franchise."

"Yes."

"But I think she knew quite well that there was no such thing."

"How could she?"

"Either she gossiped with the bus-conductor, or—and I think this is the more likely—she overheard comment from her fellow-passengers. You know the kind of thing: 'There are the Sharpes. Fancy living alone in a big house like that, just the two of them. And no maids willing to stay in a lonely place so far from shops and the pictures——' and so on. It is very much a 'local' bus, that Larborough-Milford one. And it is a lonely route, with no wayside cottages, and no village other than Ham Green. The Franchise is the only spot of human interest for miles. It would be more than human nature is capable of to pass the combined interest of the house, the owners, and their car without comments of some kind."

"I see. Yes, that makes sense."

"I wish, in a way, it *had* been through chatting with the conductor that she learned about you. That way, he would be more likely to remember her. The girl says she was never in Milford and doesn't know where it is. If a conductor remembered her, we could at least shake her story to that extent."

"If I know anything of the young person she would open those child-like eyes of hers and say: 'Oh, was that Milford? I just got on a bus and went to the terminus and back.'"

"Yes. It wouldn't take us very far. But if I fail to pick up the girl's trail in Larborough, I'll try her picture on the local conductors. I do wish she was a more memorable creature."

The silence fell round them again while they contemplated the unmemorable nature of Betty Kane.

They were sitting in the drawing-room, facing the window, looking out on the green square of the courtyard and faded pink of the brick wall. And as they looked the gate was pushed open and a small group of seven or eight people appeared and stood at gaze. Entirely at their ease they were; pointing out to each other the salient points of interest—the favourite being apparently the round window in the roof. If last night The Franchise had provided the country youth with its Saturday evening entertainment, it was now, so it would seem, providing Sunday morning interest for Larborough. Certainly a couple of cars were waiting for them outside the gate, since the women of the party wore silly little shoes and indoor frocks.

Robert glanced across at Mrs. Sharpe, but except for a tightening of her always grim mouth she had not moved.

"Our public," she said at last, witheringly.

"Shall I go and move them on?" Robert said. "It's my fault for not putting back the wooden bar you left off for me."

"Let them be," she said. "They will go presently. This is what royalty puts up with daily; we can support it for a few moments."

But the visitors showed no sign of going. Indeed, one group moved round the house to inspect the out-buildings; and the rest were still there when Marion came back with the sherry. Robert apologised again for not having put up the bar. He was feeling small and inadequate. It went against the grain to stay there quietly and watch strangers prowling round as if they owned the place or were contemplating buying it. But if he went out and asked them to move on and they refused to, what power had he to make them go? And how would he look in the Sharpes' eyes if he had to beat a retreat to the house and leave these people in possession?

The group of explorers came back from their tour round the house and reported with laughter and gesticulation what they had seen. He heard Marion say something under her breath and wondered if she were cursing. She looked like a woman who would have a very fine line in curses.

She had put down the sherry tray and had apparently forgotten about it; it was no moment for hospitality. He longed to do something decisive and spectacular to please her, just as he had longed to rescue his lady-love from burning buildings when he was fifteen. But alas, there was no surmounting the fact that he was forty-odd and had learned that it is wiser to wait for the fire-escape.

And while he hesitated, angry with himself and with those crude human creatures outside, the fire-escape arrived in the person of a tall young man in a regrettable tweed suit.

"Nevil," breathed Marion, watching the picture.

Nevil surveyed the group with his most insufferable air of superiority, and it seemed that they wilted slightly, but they were evidently determined to stand their ground. Indeed, the male with the sports jacket and the pin-striped trousers was clearly preparing to make an issue of it.

Nevil looked at them silently for a further few seconds and then fished in his inner pocket for something. At the first movement of his hand a strange difference came over the group. The outer members of it detached themselves and faded unobtrusively through the gate; the nearer ones lost their air of bravado, and became placatory. Finally the sports-jacket made small rejecting movements of surrender and joined the retreat through the gate.

Nevil banged the gate to behind them, levered the wooden bar into place, and strolled up the path to the door wiping his hands fastidiously on a really shocking handkerchief. And Marion ran out to the door to meet him.

"Nevil!" Robert heard her say. "How did you do it?"

"Do what?" Nevil asked.

"Get rid of those creatures."

"Oh, I just asked their names and addresses," Nevil said. "You've no idea how discreet people become if you take out a notebook and ask for their name and address. It's the modern equivalent to: 'Fly, all is discovered.' They don't wait to ask your credentials in case you may actually have some. Hello, Robert. Good morning, Mrs. Sharpe. I'm actually on my way to Larborough, but I saw the gate open and these two frightful cars outside so I stopped to investigate. I didn't know Robert was here."

This quite innocent implication that of course Robert was capable of dealing equally well with the situation was the unkindest cut of all. Robert could have brained him.

"Well, now that you are here and have so expertly rid us of the nuisance you must stay and drink a glass of sherry," Mrs. Sharpe said.

"Could I come in and drink it on my way home in the evening?" Nevil said. "You see, I'm on my way to lunch with my prospective father-in-law and it being Sunday there is a ritual. One must be there for the warming-up exercises."

"But of course come in on your way home," Marion said. "We shall be delighted. How shall we know it is you? For the gate, I mean." She was pouring sherry and handing it to Robert.

"Do you know Morse?"

"Yes, but don't tell me you do."

"Why not?"

"You look a most unlikely Morse addict."

"Oh, when I was fourteen I was going to sea, and I acquired in the heat of my ambition a lot of incidental idiocies. Morse was one of them. I shall hoot the initials of your beautiful name on the horn, when I come. Two longs and three shorts. I must fly. The thought of talking to you tonight will support me through luncheon at the Palace."

"Won't Rosemary be any support?" Robert asked, overcome by his baser self.

"I shouldn't think so. On Sundays Rosemary is a daughter in her father's house. It is a role that does not become her. *Au revoir*, Mrs. Sharpe. Don't let Robert drink all the sherry."

"And when," Robert heard Marion ask as she went with him to the door, "did you decide not to go to sea?"

"When I was fifteen. I took up ballooning instead."

"Theoretical, I suppose."

"Well, I gassed about gases."

Why did they sound so friendly, so at ease, Robert wondered. As if they had known each other a long time. Why did she like that lightweight Nevil?

"And when you were sixteen?"

If she knew how many things Nevil had taken up and dropped in his time she might not be so pleased to be the latest of them.

"Is the sherry too dry for you, Mr. Blair?" Mrs. Sharpe asked.

"No, oh no, thank you, it is excellent." Was it possible that he had been looking sour? Perish the thought.

He stole a cautious glance at the old lady and thought that she was looking faintly amused. And old Mrs. Sharpe being amused was no comfortable sight.

"I think I had better go before Miss Sharpe bars the gate behind Nevil," he said. "Otherwise she will have to come to the gate again with me."

"But won't you stay and have lunch with us? There is no ritual about it at The Franchise."

But Robert made his excuses. He didn't like the Robert Blair he was becoming. Petty and childish and inadequate. He would go back and have ordinary Sunday lunch with Aunt Lin and be again Robert Blair of Blair, Hayward, and Bennet, equable and tolerant and at peace with his world.

Nevil had gone by the time he reached the gate, in a flurry of sound that shattered the Sabbath quiet, and Marion was about to close the gate.

"I can't think that the Bishop approves of his future son-in-law's means of transport," she said looking after the roaring object as it streaked down the road.

"Exhausting," Robert said, still caustic.

She smiled at him. "I think that is the first witty pun I have ever heard anyone make," she said. "I hoped you would stay for lunch, but in a way I'm rather relieved that you aren't."

"Are you indeed?"

"I made a 'shape' but it didn't stand up. I'm a very bad cook. I do faithfully what it says in the book but it hardly ever works out. Indeed I'm surprised to death when it does. So you will be better off with your Aunt Lin's apple tart."

And Robert suddenly and illogically wished that he was staying, to share the "shape" that had not stood up and to be gently mocked by her along with her cooking.

"I'll let you know tomorrow night how I get on in Larborough," he said matter-of-factly. Since he was not on hens-and-Maupassant terms with her he would keep the conversation to practicalities. "And I'll ring up Inspector Hallam and see if one of their men can give a look round The Franchise once or twice a day; just to show the uniform, so to speak, and to discourage idlers."

"You are very kind, Mr. Blair," she said. "I can't imagine what it would be without you to lean on."

Well, if he couldn't be young and a poet, he could be a crutch. A dull thing, a thing resorted to only in emergencies, but useful; useful.

CHAPTER XI

BY HALF-PAST TEN ON Monday morning he was sitting in front of a steaming cup of coffee in the Karena. He began with the Karena because when one thinks of coffee at all one thinks of a Karena, with the smell of the roasting coffee downstairs in the shop and the liquid version waiting upstairs among the little tables. And if he was going to have a surfeit of coffee he might as well have some good stuff while he could still taste it.

He was holding the *Ack-Emma* in his hand with the girl's photograph open to the gaze of the waitresses as they passed, hoping vaguely that his interest in it might cause one of them to say: "That girl used to come in here every morning." To his surprise the paper was gently removed from his grasp, and he looked up to see his waitress regarding him with a kind smile. "That is last Friday's," she said. "Here." And she proffered that morning's *Ack-Emma.*

He thanked her and said that while he would be glad to see this morning's paper he would like to keep the Friday one. Did this girl, this girl on the front page of Friday's, ever come in there for coffee?

"Oh, no, we'd have remembered her if she did. We were all discussing that case on Friday. Imagine beating her half to death like that."

"Then you think they did."

She looked puzzled. "The paper says they did."

"No, the paper reports what the girl said."

She obviously did not follow that. This was the democracy we deified.

"They wouldn't print a story like that if it wasn't true. It would be as much as their life's worth. You a detective?"

"Part time," Robert said.

"How much do you get an hour for that?"

"Not nearly enough."

"No, I suppose not. Haven't got a Union, I suppose. You don't get your rights in this world unless you have a Union."

"Too true," said Robert. "Let me have my bill, will you?"

"Your check, yes."

At the Palace, the biggest and newest of the cinemas, the restaurant occupied the floor behind the balcony and had carpets so deep that one tripped on them, and lighting so subdued that all the cloths looked dirty. A bored houri with gilt hair, an uneven hem to her skirt, and a wad of chewing gum in her right jaw, took his order without ever glancing at him, and fifteen minutes later put down a cup of washy liquid in front of him without letting her eyes stray even approximately in his direction. Since in the fifteen minutes Robert had discovered that the never-look-at-the-customers technique was universal—presumably they were all going to be film stars the year after next and could not be expected to take any interest in a provincial clientele—he paid for the untasted liquid and left.

At the Castle, the other big cinema, the restaurant did not open until afternoon.

At the Violet—royal purple everywhere and yellow curtains—no one had seen her. Robert, casting subtleties aside, asked them bluntly.

Upstairs at Griffon and Waldron's, the big store, it was rush hour and the waitress said: "Don't *bother* me!" The manageress, looking at him with absent-minded suspicion, said: "We never give information about our customers."

At the Old Oak—small and dark and friendly—the elderly waitresses discussed the case interestedly with him. "Poor love," they said. "What an experience for her. Such a nice face, too. Just a baby. Poor love."

At the Alençon—cream paint and old-rose couches against the walls—they made it plain that they had never heard of the *Ack-Emma* and could not possibly have a client whose photograph appeared in such a publication.

At the Heave Ho—marine frescos and waitresses in bell-bottomed trousers—the attendants gave it as their unanimous opinion that any girl who took a lift should expect to have to walk home.

At the Primrose—old polished tables with raffia mats and thin unprofessional waitresses in flowered smocks—they discussed the social implications of lack of domestic service and the vagaries of the adolescent mind.

At the Tea-Pot there was no table to be had, and no waitress willing to attend to him; but a second glance at the fly-blown place made him sure that, with the others to choose from, Betty Kane would not have come here.

At half-past twelve he staggered into the lounge of the Midland, and called for strong waters. As far as he knew he had covered all the likely eating-places in the centre of Larborough and in not one of them had anyone remembered seeing the girl. What was worse, everyone agreed that if she had been there they would have remembered her. They had pointed out, when Robert was sceptical of that, that a large proportion of their customers on any one day were regulars, so that the casuals stood out from the rest and were noted and remembered automatically.

As Albert, the tubby little lounge waiter, set his drink in front of him, Robert asked, more out of habit than volition: "I suppose you've never seen this girl in your place, Albert?"

Albert looked at the front page of the *Ack-Emma* and shook his head. "No, sir. Not that I recollect. Looks a little young, sir, if I may say so, for the lounge of the Midland."

"She mightn't look so young with a hat on," Robert said, considering it.

"A hat." Albert paused. "Now, wait a minute. A *hat*." Albert laid his little tray down and picked up the paper to consider it. "Yes, of course; that's the girl in the green hat!"

"You mean she came in here for coffee?"

"No, for tea."

"Tea!"

"Yes, of course, that's the girl. Fancy me not seeing that, and we had that paper in the pantry last Friday and chewed the rag over it for hours! Of course it's some time ago now, isn't it. About six weeks or so, it must be. She always came early; just about three, when we start serving teas."

So that is what she did. Fool that he was not to have seen that. She went into the morning round at the cinema in time to pay the cheaper price—just before noon, that was—and came out about three, and had tea, not coffee. But why the Midland, where the tea was the usual dowdy and expensive hotel exhibit, when she could wallow in cakes elsewhere?

"I noticed her because she always came alone. The first time she came I thought she was waiting for relations. That's the kind of kid she looked. You know: nice plain clothes and no airs."

"Can you remember what she wore?"

"Oh, yes. She always wore the same things. A green hat and a frock to match it under a pale grey coat. But she never met anyone. And then one day she picked up the man at the next table. You could have knocked me over with a feather."

"You mean: he picked her up."

"Don't you believe it! He hadn't even thought of her when he sat down there. I tell you, sir, she didn't look that sort. You'd expect an aunt or a mother to appear at any moment and say: 'So sorry to have kept you waiting, darling.' She just wouldn't occur to any man as a possible. Oh, no; it was the kid's doing. And as neat a piece of business, let me tell you, sir, as if she had spent a lifetime at it. Goodness, and to think that I didn't spot her again without her hat!" He gazed in wonder at the pictured face.

"What was the man like? Did you know him?"

"No, he wasn't one of our regulars. Dark. Youngish. Business gent, I should say. I remember being a little surprised at her taste, so I don't think he could have been up to much, now I come to think of it."

"You wouldn't know him again, then."

"I might, sir, I might. But not to swear to. You—er—planning any swearing to, sir?"

Robert had known Albert for nearly twenty years and had always found him of an excellent discretion. "It's like this, Albert," he said. "These people are my clients." He tapped the photograph of The Franchise, and Albert gave vent to a low whistle.

"A tough spot for you, Mr. Blair."

"Yes, as you say: a tough spot. But mostly for them. It is quite unbelievably tough for them. The girl comes out of the blue one day accompanied by the police, to whom she has told this fantastic story. Until then neither of the two women has ever set eyes on her. The police are very discreet, and decide that they haven't enough evidence to make it a good case. Then the *Ack-Emma* hears about it and makes capital out of it, and the story is all over Britain. The Franchise is wide open, of course. The police can't spare men to afford constant protection, so you can imagine the lives these women are leading. My young cousin, who looked in before dinner last night, says that from lunch-time on crowds of cars arrived from Larborough, and people stood on the roofs or hoisted themselves up on the wall to stare or take photographs. Nevil got in because he arrived at the same time as the policeman on the evening beat, but as soon as they left the cars were swarming again. The telephone went continually until they asked the Exchange not to put through any more calls."

"Have the police dropped it for good, then?"

"No, but they can't do anything to help *us*. What they are looking for is corroboration of the girl's story."

"Well, that's not very likely, is it? For them to get, I mean."

"No. But you see the spot we are in. Unless we can find out where the girl was during the weeks she says she was at The Franchise, the Sharpes will be in the position of being permanently convicted of a thing they haven't even been accused of!"

"Well, if it's the girl in the green hat—and I'm sure it is, sir—I'd say she was what is known as 'out on the tiles,' sir. A very cool customer she was for a girl that age. Butter wouldn't melt in her mouth."

"Butter wouldn't melt in her little mouth," the tobacconist had said of the child Betty.

And "on the tiles" was Stanley's verdict on the pictured face that was so like "the bint he had had in Egypt."

And the worldly little waiter had used both phrases in his estimate of her. The demure girl in the "good" clothes, who had come every day by herself to sit in the hotel lounge.

"Perhaps it was just a childish desire to be 'grand'," the nice side of him prompted; but his common sense refused it. She could have been grand at the Alençon, and eaten well, and seen smart clothes at the same time.

He went in to have lunch, and then spent a large part of the afternoon trying to reach Mrs. Wynn on the telephone. Mrs. Tilsit had no telephone and he had no intention of involving himself in a Tilsit conversation again if he could help it. When he failed he remembered that Scotland Yard would most certainly, in that painstaking way of theirs, have a description of the clothes the girl was wearing when she went missing. And in less than seven minutes, he had it. A green felt hat, a green wool frock to match, a pale grey cloth coat with large grey buttons, fawn-grey rayon stockings and black court shoes with medium heels.

Well, at last he had it, that setting-off place; that starting-point for inquiry. Jubilation filled him. He sat down in the lounge on his way out and wrote a note to tell Kevin Macdermott that the young woman from Aylesbury was not such an attractive brief as she had been on Friday night; and to let him know, of course—between the lines—that Blair, Hayward, and Bennet could get a move on when it was necessary.

"Did she ever come back?" he asked Albert, who was hovering. "I mean, after she had 'got her man'."

"I don't remember ever seeing either of them again, sir."

Well, the hypothetical X had ceased to be hypothetical. He had become plain X. He, Robert, could go back tonight to The Franchise in triumph. He had put forward a theory, and the theory had proved fact, and it was he who had proved it a fact. It was depressing, of course, that the letters received so far by Scotland Yard had all been merely anonymous revilings of the Yard for their "softness" to the "rich," and not claims to have seen Betty Kane. It was depressing that practically everyone he had interviewed that morning believed the girl's story without question; were, indeed, surprised and at a loss if asked to consider any other point of view. "The paper said so." But these were small things compared to the satisfaction of having arrived at that starting-point; of having unearthed X. He didn't believe that fate could be so cruel as to show that Betty Kane parted with her new acquaintance on the steps of the Midland and never saw him again. There *had* to be an extension of that incident in the lounge. The history of the following weeks demanded it.

But how did one follow up a young dark business gent who had tea in the lounge of the Midland about six weeks previously? Young dark business gents were the Midland's clientele; and as far as Blair could see all as like as two peas anyhow. He was very much afraid that this was where he bowed out and handed over to a professional bloodhound. He had no photograph this time to help him; no knowledge of X's character or habits as he had had in the case of the girl. It would be a long process of small inquiries; a job for an expert. All he could do at the moment, so far as he could see, was to get a list of residents at the Midland for the period in question.

For that he went to the Manager; a Frenchman who showed great delight and understanding in this *sub rosa* proceeding, was exquisitely sympathetic about the outraged ladies at The Franchise, and comfortingly cynical about smooth-faced young girls in good clothes who looked as if butter wouldn't melt in their mouths. He sent an underling to copy the entries from the great ledger, and entertained Robert to a *sirop* from his own cupboard. Robert had never subscribed to the French taste for small sweet mouthfuls of unidentifiable liquids drunk at odd times, but he swallowed the thing gratefully and pocketed the list the underling brought as one pockets a passport. Its actual value was probably nil, but it gave him a nice feeling to have it.

And if he had to turn over the business to a professional, the professional would have somewhere to start his burrowing. X had probably never stayed at the Midland in his life; he had probably just walked in for tea one day. On the other hand, his name might be among that list in his pocket; that horribly long list.

As he drove home he decided that he would not stop at The Franchise. It was unfair to bring Marion to the gate just to give her news that could be told over the telephone. He would tell the Exchange who he was, and the fact that the call was official, and they would answer it. Perhaps by tomorrow the first flood of interest in the house would have subsided, and it would be safe to unbar the gate again. Though he doubted it. Today's *Ack-Emma* had not been calculated to have an appeasing effect on the mob mind. True, there were no further front-page headlines; the Franchise affair had removed itself to the correspondence page. But the letters the *Ack-Emma* had chosen to print there—and two-thirds of them were about the Franchise affair—were not likely to prove oil on troubled waters. They were so much paraffin on a fire that was going quite nicely anyhow.

Threading his way out of the Larborough traffic, the silly phrases came back to him; and he marvelled all over again at the venom that these unknown women had roused in the writers' minds. Rage and hatred spilled over on to the paper; malice ran unchecked through the largely-illiterate sentences. It was an amazing exhibition. And one of the oddities of it was that the dearest wish of so many of those indignant protesters against violence was to flog the said women within an inch of their lives. Those who did not want to flog the women wanted to reform the police. One writer suggested that a fund should be opened for the poor young victim of police inefficiency and bias. Another suggested that every man of goodwill should write to his Member of Parliament about it, and make their lives a misery until something was done about this miscarriage of justice. Still another asked if anyone had noticed Betty Kane's marked resemblance to Saint Bernadette.

There was every sign, if today's correspondence page of the *Ack-Emma* was any criterion, of the birth of a Betty Kane cult. He hoped that its corollary would not be a Franchise vendetta.

As he neared the unhappy house, he grew anxious; wondering if Monday, too, had provided its quota of sightseers. It was a lovely evening, the low sun slanting great golden swathes of light over the spring fields; an evening to tempt even Larborough out to the midland dullness of Milford; it would be a miracle if, after the correspondence in the *Ack-Emma*, The Franchise was not the mecca of an evening pilgrimage. But when he came within sight of it he found the long stretch of road deserted; and as he came nearer he saw why. At the gate of The Franchise, solid and immobile and immaculate in the evening light, was the dark-blue-and-silver figure of a policeman.

Delighted that Hallam had been so generous with his scanty force, Robert slowed down to exchange greetings; but the greeting died on his lips. Along the full length of the tall brick wall, in letters nearly six feet high was splashed a slogan. "FASCISTS!" screamed the large white capitals. And again on the further side of the gate: "FASCISTS!"

"Move along, please," the Force said, approaching the staring Robert with slow, polite menace. "No stopping here."

Robert got slowly out of the car.

"Oh, Mr. Blair. Didn't recognise you, sir. Sorry."

"Is it whitewash?"

"No, sir; best quality paint."

"Great Heavens!"

"Some people never grow out of it."

"Out of what?"

"Writing things on walls. There's one thing: they might have written something worse."

"They wrote the worst insult they knew," said Robert wryly. "I suppose you haven't got the culprits?"

"No, sir. I just came along on my evening beat to clear away the usual gapers—oh, yes, there were dozens of them—and found it like that when I arrived. Two men in a car, if all reports are true."

"Do the Sharpes know about it?"

"Yes, I had to get in to telephone. We have a code now, us and the Franchise people. I tie my handkerchief on the end of my truncheon and wave it over the top of the gate when I want to speak to them. Do you want to go in, sir?"

"No. No, on the whole I think not. I'll get the Post Office to let me through on the telephone. No need to bring them to the gate. If this is going to continue they must get keys for the gate so that I can have a duplicate."

"Looks as though it's going to continue all right, sir. Did you see today's *Ack-Emma!*"

"I did."

"Strewth!" said the Force, losing his equanimity at the thought of the *Ack-Emma*, "you would think to listen to them we were nothing but a collection of itching palms! It's a holy wonder we're not, come to that. It would suit them better to agitate for more pay for us instead of slandering us right and left."

"You're in very good company, if it's any consolation to you," Robert said. "There can't be anything established, respectable, or praiseworthy that they haven't slandered at some time or other. I'll send someone either tonight or first thing in the morning to do something about this—obscenity. Are you staying here?"

"The sergeant said when I telephoned that I was to stay till dark."

"No one overnight?"

"No, sir. No spare men for that. Anyhow, they'll be all right once the light's gone. People go home. Especially the Larborough lot. They don't like the country once it gets dark."

Robert, who remembered how silent the lonely house could be, felt doubtful. Two women, alone in that big quiet house after dark, with hatred and violence just outside the wall—it was not a comfortable thought. The gate was barred, but if people could hoist themselves on to the wall for the purpose of sitting there and shouting insults, they could just as easily drop down the other side in the dark.

"Don't worry, sir," the Force said, watching his face. "Nothing's going to happen to them. This is England, after all."

"So is the *Ack-Emma* England," Robert reminded him. But he got back into the car again. After all, it *was* England; and the English countryside at that; famed for minding its own business. It was no country hand that had splashed that "FACISTS!" on the wall. It was doubtful if the country had ever heard the term. The country, when it wanted insults, used older, Saxon words.

The Force was no doubt right; once the dark came everyone would go home.

CHAPTER XII

AS ROBERT TURNED his car into the garage in Sin Lane and came to a halt, Stanley, who was shrugging off his overalls outside the office door, glanced at his face and said: "Down the drain again?"

"It isn't a bet," Robert said, "it's human nature."

"You start to be sorry about human nature and you won't have time for anything else. You been trying to reform someone?"

"No, I've been trying to get someone to take some paint off a wall."

"Oh, work!" Stanley's tone indicated that even to expect someone to do a job of work these days was being optimistic to the point of folly.

"I've been trying to get someone to wipe a slogan off the walls of The Franchise, but everyone is extraordinarily busy all of a sudden."

Stanley stopped his wriggling. "A slogan," he said. "What kind of slogan?" And Bill, hearing the exchange, oozed himself through the narrow office door to listen.

Robert told them. "In best quality white paint, so the policeman on the beat assures me."

Bill whistled. Stanley said nothing; he was standing with his overalls shrugged down to his waist and concertinaed about his legs.

"Who've you tried?" Bill asked.

Robert told them. "None of them can do anything tonight, and tomorrow morning, it seems, all their men are going out early on important jobs."

"It's not to be believed," Bill said. "Don't tell me they're afraid of reprisals!"

"No, to do them justice I don't think it's that. I think, although they would never say so to me, that they think those women at The Franchise deserve it." There was silence for a moment.

"When I was in the Signals," Stanley said, beginning in a leisurely fashion to pull up his overalls and get into the top half again, "I was given a free tour of Italy. Nearly a year it took. And I escaped the malaria, and the Ities, and the Partisans, and the Yank transport, and most of the other little nuisances. But I got a phobia. I took a great dislike to slogans on walls."

"What'll we get it off with?" Bill asked.

"What's the good of owning the best equipped and most modern garage in Milford if we haven't something to take off a spot of paint?" Stanley said, zipping up his front.

"Will you really try to do something about it?" Robert asked, surprised and pleased.

Bill smiled his slow expansive smile. "The Signals, the R.E.M.E. and a couple of brooms. What more do you want?" he said.

"Bless you," Robert said. "Bless you both. I have only one ambition tonight; to get that slogan off the wall before breakfast tomorrow. I'll come along and help."

"Not in that Savile Row suit, you won't," Stanley said. "And we haven't a spare suit of——"

"I'll get something old on and come out after you."

"Look," Stanley said patiently, "we don't need any help for a little job like that. If we did we'd take Harry." Harry was the garage boy. "You haven't eaten yet and we have, and I've heard it said that Miss Bennet doesn't like her good meals spoiled. I suppose you don't mind if the wall looks smeary? We're just good-intentioned garage hands, not decorators."

The shops were shut as he walked down the High Street to his home at Number 10, and he looked at the place as a stranger walking through on a Sunday might. He had been so far from Milford during his day in Larborough that he felt that he had been away for years. The comfortable quiet of Number 10—so different from the dead silence of The Franchise—welcomed and soothed him. A faint smell of roasting apples escaped from the kitchen. The firelight flickered on the wall of the sitting-room, seen through its half-open door. Warmth and security and comfort rose up in a gentle tide and lapped over him.

Guilty at being the owner of this waiting peace, he picked up the telephone to talk to Marion.

"Oh, *you!* How nice," she said, when at last he had persuaded the Post Office that his intentions were honourable; and the warmth in her voice catching him unawares—his mind being still on white paint—caught him under the heart and left him breathless for a moment. "I'm so glad. I was wondering how we were going to talk to you; but I might have known that you would manage it. I suppose you just say you're Robert Blair and the Post Office gives you the freedom of the place."

How like her, he thought. The genuine gratitude of "I might have known that you would manage"; and then the faint amusement in the sentence that followed.

"I suppose you've seen our wall decoration?"

Robert said yes, but that no one ever would again, because by the time the sun rose it would have gone.

"Tomorrow!"

"The two men who own my garage have decided to obliterate it tonight."

"But—could seven maids with seven mops——?"

"I don't know; but if Stanley and Bill have set their minds on it, obliterated it will be. They were brought up in a school that doesn't tolerate frustrations."

"What school is that?"

"The British Army. And I have more good news for you: I have established the fact that X exists. She had tea with him one day. Picked him up at the Midland, in the lounge."

"Picked him up? But she is just a child, and so—— Oh, well, she told that story, of course. After that anything is possible. How did you find out that?"

He told her.

"You've had a bad day at The Franchise, haven't you," he said, when he had finished the saga of the coffee shops.

"Yes, I feel dirty all over. What was worse than the audience and the wall was the post. The postman gave it to the police to take in. It is not often that the police can be accused of disseminating obscene literature."

"Yes, I imagine it must have been pretty bad. That was only to be expected."

"Well, we have so few letters that we have decided that in future we shall burn everything without opening them, unless we recognise the writing. So don't use typescript if you write to us."

"But do you know my handwriting?"

"Oh, yes, you wrote us a note, you remember. The one Nevil brought that afternoon. Nice handwriting."

"Have you seen Nevil today?"

"No, but one of the letters was from him. At least, it wasn't a letter."

"A document of some kind?"

"No, a poem."

"Oh. Did you understand it?"

"No, but it made quite a nice sound."

"So do bicycle bells."

He thought she laughed a little. "It is nice to have poems made to one's eyebrows," she said. "But still nicer to have one's wall made clean. I do thank you for that—you and what's-their-names—Bill and Stanley. If you want to be very kind perhaps you would bring or send us some food tomorrow?"

"Food!" he said, horrified that he had not thought of that before; that was what happened when you lived a life where Aunt Lin put everything down in front of you, all but put the stuff in your mouth; you lost your capacity for imagination. "Yes, of course. I forgot that you would not be able to shop."

"It isn't only that. The grocer's van that calls on Monday didn't come today. Or perhaps," she added hastily, "it came and just couldn't call our attention. Anyhow, we should be so grateful for some things. Have you got a pencil there?"

She gave him a list of things, and then asked: "We didn't see today's *Ack-Emma*. Was there anything about us?"

"Some letters on the correspondence page, that is all."

"All anti, I suppose."

"I'm afraid so. I shall bring a copy out tomorrow morning when I bring the groceries, and you can see it for yourselves."

"I'm afraid we are taking up a great deal of your time."

"This has become a personal matter with me," he said.

"Personal?" She sounded doubtful.

"The one ambition of my life is to discredit Betty Kane."

"Oh; oh, I see." Her voice sounded half relieved, half—could it be?—disappointed. "Well, we shall look forward to seeing you tomorrow."

But she was to see him long before that.

He went to bed early, but lay long awake; rehearsing a telephone conversation that he planned to have with Kevin Macdermott; considering different approaches to the problem of X; wondering if Marion was asleep, in that silent old house, or lying awake listening for sounds.

His bedroom was over the street, and about midnight he heard a car drive up and stop, and presently through the open window he heard Bill's cautious call; not much more than a throaty whisper. "Mr. Blair! Hey, Mr. Blair!"

He was at the window almost before the second utterance of his name.

"Thank goodness," whispered Bill. "I was afraid the light might be Miss Bennet's."

"No, she sleeps at the back. What is it?"

"There's trouble at The Franchise. I've got to go for the police because the wire is cut. But I thought you'd want to be called, so I——"

"What kind of trouble?"

"Hooligans. I'll come in for you on my way back. In about four minutes."

"Is Stanley with them?" Robert asked, as Bill's great bulk merged with the car again.

"Yes, Stan's having his head bound up. Back in a minute." And the car fled away up the dark silent High Street.

Before Robert had got his clothes on he heard a soft "ssshush" go past his window, and realised that the police were already on their way. No screaming sirens in the night, no roaring exhausts; with no more sound than a summer wind makes among the leaves the Law was going about its business. As he opened the front door, cautiously so as not to wake Aunt Lin (nothing but the last trump was likely to wake Christina) Bill brought his car to a standstill at the pavement.

"Now tell me," Robert said, as they moved away.

"Well, we finished that little job by the light of the headlamps—not very professional, it isn't, but a lot better than it was when we got there—and then we switched off the heads, and began to put away our things.

Sort of leisurely like; there was no hurry and it was a nice night. We'd just lit a cigarette and were thinking of pushing off when there was a crash of glass from the house. No one had got in our side while we were there, so we knew it must be round the sides or the back. Stan reached into the car and took out his torch—mine was lying on the seat because we'd been using it—and said: 'You go round that way and I'll go the other and we'll nip them between us.'"

"Can you get round?"

"Well, it was no end of a business. It's hedge up to the wall end. I wouldn't like to have done it in ordinary clothes, but in overalls you just push hard and hope for the best. It's all right for Stan; he's slim. But short of lying on the hedge till it falls down there's no way through for me. Anyhow we got through, one on each side, and through the one at the back corners, and met in the middle of the back without seeing a soul. Then we heard more crashing of glass, and realised that they were making a night of it. Stan said: 'Hoist me up, and I'll give you a hand after me.' Well, a hand would be no good to me, but it happens that the field level at the back comes fairly high up the wall—in fact I think it was probably cut away to build the wall—so that we got over fairly easily. Stan said had I anything to hit with besides my torch and I said yes, I had a spanner. Stan said: 'Forget your bloody spanner and use your ham fist; it's bigger.'"

"What was he going to use?"

"The old rugby tackle, so he said. Stan used to be quite a good stand-off half. Anyhow we went on in the dark towards the sound of the crashing glass. It seemed as if they were just having a breaking tour round the house. We caught up with them near the front corner again, and switched on our torches. I think there were seven of them. Far more than we had expected, anyhow. We switched off at once, before they could see that we were only two, and grabbed the nearest. Stan said: 'You take that one, sergeant,' and I thought at the time he was giving me my rank out of old habit, but I realise now he was bluffing them we were police. Anyhow some of them beat it, because though there was a mix-up there couldn't have been anything like seven of them in it. Then, quite suddenly it seemed, there was quiet—we'd been making a lot of noise—and I realised that we were letting them get away, and Stan said from somewhere on the ground: 'Grab one, Bill, before they get over the wall!' And I went after them with my torch on. The last of them was just being helped over, and I grabbed his legs and hung on. But he kicked like a mule, and what with the torch in my hand he slipped from my hands like a trout and was over before I could grab him again. That finished me, because from inside that wall at the back is even higher than it is at the front of the house. So I went back to Stan. He was still sitting on the ground. Someone had hit him a wallop over the head with what he said was a bottle and he was looking very cheap. And then Miss Sharpe came out to the top of the front steps, and said was someone hurt? She could see us in the torchlight. So we got Stan in—the old lady was there and the house was lit by this time—and I went to the phone, but Miss Sharpe said: 'That's no use. It's dead. We tried to call the police when they first arrived.' So I said I'd go and fetch them. And I said I'd better fetch you too. But Miss Sharpe said no, you'd had a very hard day and I wasn't to disturb you. But I thought you ought to be in on it."

"Quite right, Bill, I ought."

The gate was wide open as they drew up, the police car at the door, most of the front rooms lit, and the curtains waving gently in the night wind at the wrecked windows. In the drawing-room—which the Sharpes evidently used as a living-room—Stanley was having a cut above his eyebrow attended to by Marion, a sergeant of police was taking notes, and his henchman was laying out exhibits. The exhibits seemed to consist of half bricks, bottles, and pieces of paper with writing on them.

"Oh, Bill, I told you not to," Marion said as she looked up and saw Robert.

Robert noted how efficiently she was dealing with Stanley's injury; the woman who found cooking beyond her. He greeted the sergeant and bent to look at the exhibits. There was a large array of missiles but only four messages; which read, respectively: "Get out!" "Get out or we'll make you!" "Foreign bitches!" and "This is only a sample!"

"Well, we've collected them all, I think," the sergeant said. "Now we'll go and search the garden for footprints or whatever clues there may be." He glanced professionally at the soles that Bill and Stanley held up at his request, and went out with his aide to the garden, as Mrs. Sharpe came in with a steaming jug and cups.

"Ah, Mr. Blair," she said. "You still find us stimulating?"

She was fully dressed—in contrast to Marion who was looking quite human and un-Joan-of-Arc in an old dressing-gown—and apparently unmoved by these proceedings, and he wondered what kind of occasion would find Mrs. Sharpe at a disadvantage.

Bill appeared with sticks from the kitchen and lighted the dead fire, Mrs. Sharpe poured the hot liquid—it was coffee and Robert refused it, having seen enough coffee lately to lose interest in it—and the colour began to come back to Stan's face. By the time the policemen came back from the garden the room had acquired a family-party air, in spite of the waving curtains and the non-existent windows. Neither Stanley nor Bill, Robert noticed, appeared to find the Sharpes odd or difficult; on the contrary they seemed relaxed and at home. Perhaps it was that the Sharpes took them for granted; accepting this invasion of strangers as if it were an every-day occurrence. Anyhow, Bill came and went on his ploys as if he had lived in the house for years; and Stanley put out his cup for a second helping without waiting to be asked. Involuntarily, Robert thought that Aunt Lin in their place would have been kind and fussy and they would have sat on the edge of the chairs and remembered their dirty overalls.

Perhaps it was the same taking-for-granted that had attracted Nevil.

"Do you plan to stay on here, ma'am?" the sergeant asked as they came in again.

"Certainly," Mrs. Sharpe said, pouring coffee for them.

"No," Robert said. "You mustn't, you really must not. I'll find you a quiet hotel in Larborough, where——"

"I never heard anything more absurd. Of course we are going to stay here. What do a few broken windows matter?"

"It may not stop at broken windows," the sergeant said. "And you're a great responsibility to us as long as you are here; a responsibility we haven't really got the force to deal with."

"I'm truly sorry we are a nuisance to you, sergeant. We wouldn't have bricks flung at our windows if we could help it, believe me. But this is our home, and here we are staying. Quite apart from any question of ethics, how much of our home would be left to come back to if it was left empty? I take it if you are too short of men to guard human beings, you certainly have no men to guard empty property?"

The sergeant looked slightly abashed, as people so often did when Mrs. Sharpe dealt with them. "Well, there is that, ma'am," he acknowledged, with reluctance.

"And that, I think, disposes of any question of our leaving The Franchise. Sugar, sergeant?"

Robert returned to the subject when the police had taken their departure, and Bill had fetched a brush and shovel from the kitchen and was sweeping up the broken glass in room after room. Again he urged the wisdom of a hotel in Larborough, but neither his emotion nor his common sense was behind the words. He would not have gone if he had been in the Sharpes' place, and he could not expect them to; and in addition he acknowledged the wisdom of Mrs. Sharpe's view about the fate of the house left empty.

"What you want is a lodger," said Stanley, who had been refused permission to sweep up glass because he was classed as walking-wounded. "A lodger with a pistol. What d'you say I come and sleep here of nights? No meals, just sleeping night watchman. They all sleep anyhow, night watchmen do."

It was evident by their expressions that both the Sharpes appreciated the fact that this was an open declaration of allegiance in what amounted to a local war; but they did not embarrass him with thanks.

"Haven't you got a wife?" Marion asked.

"Not of my own," Stanley said demurely.

"Your wife—if you had one—might support your sleeping here," Mrs. Sharpe pointed out, "but I doubt if your business would, Mr.—er—Mr. Peters."

"My business?"

"I imagine that if your customers found that you had become night watchman at The Franchise they would take their custom elsewhere."

"Not them," Stanley said comfortably. "There's nowhere else to take it. Lynch is drunk five nights out of seven, and Biggins wouldn't know how to put on a bicycle chain. Anyhow, I don't let my customers tell me what I do in my spare time."

And when Bill returned, he backed Stanley up. Bill was a much married man and it was not contemplated that he would ever sleep anywhere except at home. But that Stanley should sleep at The Franchise seemed to both of them a natural solution of the problem.

Robert was mightily relieved.

"Well," Marion said, "if you are going to be our guest at nights you might as well begin now. I am sure that head feels like a very painful turnip. I'll go and make up a bed. Do you prefer a south view?"

"Yes," said Stanley gravely. "Well away from kitchen and wireless noises."

"I'll do what I can."

It was arranged that Bill should slip a note into the door of Stanley's lodgings to say that he would be in for lunch as usual. "She won't worry about me," Stanley said, referring to his landlady. "I've been out for nights before now." He caught Marion's eye, and added: "Ferrying cars for customers; you can do it in half the time at night."

They tacked down the curtains in all the ground-floor rooms to provide some protection for their contents if it rained before morning, and Robert promised to get glaziers out at the earliest possible moment, deciding privately to go to a Larborough firm, and not risk another series of polite rebuffs in Milford.

"And I shall also do something about a key for the gate, so that I can have a duplicate," he said as Marion came out with them to bar the gate, "and save you from being gate-keeper as well as everything else."

She put out her hand, to Bill first. "I shall never forget what you three have done for us. When I remember tonight it won't be these clods that I shall remember," she tilted her head to the windowless house, "but you three."

"Those clods were local, I suppose you know," Bill said as they drove home through the quiet spring night.

"Yes," Robert agreed. "I realised that. They had no car, for one thing. And 'Foreign bitches!' smells of the conservative country, just as 'Fascists!' smells of the progressive town."

Bill said some things about progress.

"I was wrong to let myself be persuaded yesterday evening. The man on the beat was so sure that 'everyone would go home when it grew dark' that I let myself believe it. But I should have remembered a warning I got about witch-hunts."

Bill was not listening. "It's a funny thing how unsafe you feel in a house without windows," he said. "Take a house with the back blown clean off, and not a door that will shut; you can live quite happily in a front room provided it still has windows. But without windows even a whole undamaged house feels unsafe."

Which was not an observation that provided Robert with any comfort.

CHAPTER XIII

"I WONDER if you would mind calling for the fish, dear," Aunt Lin said on the telephone on Tuesday afternoon. "Nevil is coming to dinner, and so we are going to have an extra course of what we were going to have for breakfast. I really don't see why we should have anything extra just for Nevil, but Christina says that it will keep him from making what she calls 'inroads' on the tart that is going to do again on her night-out tomorrow. So if you wouldn't mind, dear."

He was not looking forward greatly to an extra hour or two of Nevil's society, but he was feeling so pleased with himself that he was in a better humour to support it than usual. He had arranged with a Larborough firm for the replacement of the Franchise windows; he had miraculously unearthed a key that fitted the Franchise gate—and there would be two duplicates in existence by tomorrow; and he had personally taken out the groceries—together with an offering of the best flowers that Milford could supply. His welcome at The Franchise had been such that he had almost ceased to regret the lack of light exchanges on Nevil lines. There were, after all, other things than getting to Christian-name terms in the first half-hour.

In the lunch hour he had rung up Kevin Macdermott, and arranged with his secretary that when Kevin was free in the evening he would call him at 10 High Street. Things were getting out of hand, and he wanted Kevin's advice.

He had refused three invitations to golf, his excuse to his astounded cronies being that he had "no time to chase a piece of gutta-percha round a golf-course."

He had gone to see an important client who had been trying to interview him since the previous Friday and who had been provoked into asking him on the telephone if "he still worked for Blair, Hayward, and Bennet."

He had got through his arrears of work with a mutely reproachful Mr. Heseltine; who, although he had allied himself on the Sharpe side, still obviously felt that the Franchise affair was not one for a firm like theirs to be mixed up in.

And he had been given tea by Miss Tuff out of the blue-patterned china on the lacquer tray covered by the fair white cloth and accompanied by two digestive biscuits on a plate.

It was lying on his desk now, the tea-tray; just as it had been a fortnight ago when the telephone had rung and he had lifted the receiver to hear Marion Sharpe's voice for the first time. Two short weeks ago. He had sat looking at it in its patch of sunlight, feeling uneasy about his comfortable life and conscious of time slipping past him. But today, the digestive biscuits held no reproach for him because he had stepped outside the routine they typified. He was on calling terms with Scotland Yard; he was agent for a pair of scandalous women; he had become an amateur sleuth; and he had been witness of mob violence. His whole world looked different. Even the people he met looked different. The dark skinny woman he used to see sometimes shopping in the High Street, for instance, had turned into Marion.

Well, one result of stepping out of a routined life was, of course, that you couldn't put on your hat and stroll home at four o'clock of an afternoon. He pushed the tea-tray out of his way, and went to work, and it was half-past six before he looked at the clock again, and seven before he opened the door of Number 10.

The sitting-room door was ajar as usual—like many doors in old houses it swung a little if left off the latch—and he could hear Nevil's voice in the room beyond.

"On the contrary, I think you are being extremely silly," Nevil was saying.

Robert recognised the tone at once. It was the cold rage with which a four-year-old Nevil had told a guest: "I am extremely sorry that I asked you to my party." Nevil must be very angry indeed about something.

With his coat half off Robert paused to listen.

"You are interfering in something you know nothing whatever about; you can hardly claim that is an intelligent proceeding."

There was no other voice, so he must be talking to someone on the telephone; probably keeping Kevin from getting through, the young idiot.

"I am not infatuated with anyone. I never *have* been infatuated with anyone. It is you who are infatuated—with ideas. You are being extremely silly, as I said before. . . . You are taking the part of an unbalanced adolescent in a case you know nothing about; I should have thought that was sufficient evidence of infatuation . . . You can tell your father from me that there is nothing Christian about it, just unwarranted interference. I'm not sure it isn't incitement to violence. . . . Yes, last night. . . . No, all their windows broken, and things painted on their walls. . . . If he is so interested in justice he might do something about that. But your lot are never interested in justice, are they? Only in injustice. . . . What do I mean by your lot? Just what I say. You and all your crowd who are for ever adopting good-for-nothings and championing them against the world. You wouldn't put out a finger to keep a hard-working little man from going down the drain, but let an old lag lack the price of a meal and your sobs can be heard in Antarctica. You make me sick. . . . Yes, I said you make me sick. . . . Cat-sick. Sick to my stomach. I retch!"

And the bang of the receiver on its rest indicated that the poet had said his say.

Robert hung up his coat in the cupboard and went in. Nevil with a face like thunder was pouring himself out a stiff whisky.

"I'll have one too," Robert said. "I couldn't help overhearing," he added. "That wasn't Rosemary, by any chance?"

"Who else? Is there anyone else in Britain capable of an ineffable silliness like that?"

"Like what?"

"Oh, didn't you hear that bit? She has taken up the cause of the persecuted Betty Kane." Nevil gulped some whisky, and glared at Robert as if Robert were responsible.

"Well, I don't suppose her stepping on the *Ack-Emma* band-wagon will have much effect one way or another."

"The *Ack-Emma!* It isn't the *Ack-Emma.* It's the *Watchman.* That mental deficient she calls father has written a letter about it for Friday's issue. Yes, you may well look squeamish. As if we weren't coping with enough without that highfalutin nugget of perverted sentimentality putting in its sixpenceworth!"

Remembering that the *Watchman* was the only paper ever to have published any of Nevil's poems, Robert thought this showed slight ingratitude. But he approved the description.

"Perhaps they won't print it," he said, less in hope than looking for comfort.

"You know very well they will print anything he chooses to send them. Whose money saved them just when they were going down for the third time? The Bishop's, of course."

"His wife's, you mean." The Bishop had married one of the two granddaughters of Cowan's Cranberry Sauce.

"All right, his wife's. And the Bishop has the *Watchman* for a lay pulpit. And there isn't anything too silly for him to say in it, or too unlikely for them to print. Do you remember that girl who went round shooting taxi-drivers in cold blood for a profit of about seven-and-eleven a time? That girl was just his meat. He sobbed himself practically into a coma about her. He wrote a long heart-breaking letter about her in the *Watchman,* pointing out how under-privileged she had been, and how she had won a scholarship to a secondary school and hadn't been able to 'take it up' because her people were too poor to provide her with books or proper clothes, and so she had gone to blind-alley jobs and then to bad company —and so, it was inferred, to shooting taxi-drivers, though he didn't actually mention that little matter. Well, all the *Watchman* readers *lahved* that, of course; it was just their cup of tea; all criminals according to the *Watchman* readers are frustrated angels. And then the Chairman of the Board of Governors of the school—the school she was supposed to have won a scholarship to—wrote to point out that so far from winning anything was she that her name was 159th out of two hundred competitors; and that someone as interested in education as the Bishop was should have known that no one was prevented from accepting a scholarship through lack of money, since in needy cases books and money grants were forthcoming automatically. Well, you would have thought that that would shake him, wouldn't you? But not a bit. They printed the Chairman's letter on a back page, in small print; and in the very next issue the old boy was sobbing over some other case that he knew nothing about. And on Friday, so help me, he'll be sobbing over Betty Kane."

"I wonder—if I went over to see him tomorrow——"

"It goes to press tomorrow."

"Yes, so it does. Perhaps if I telephoned——"

"If you think that anyone or anything will make His Lordship keep back a finished composition from the public gaze, you're being naïve."

The telephone rang.

"If that's Rosemary, I'm in China," Nevil said.

But it was Kevin Macdermott.

"Well, sleuth," said Kevin. "My congratulations. But next time don't waste an afternoon trying to ring up civilians in Aylesbury, when you can get the same information from Scotland Yard by return."

Robert said that he was still sufficiently civilian not to think in terms of Scotland Yard at all; but that he was learning; rapidly.

He sketched the happenings of last night for Kevin's benefit, and said: "I can't afford to be leisurely about it any more. Something must be done as quickly as possible to clear them of this thing."

"You want me to give you the name of a private agent, is that it?"

"Yes, I suppose it has come to that. But I did wonder——"

"Wonder what?" Kevin asked, as he hesitated.

"Well, I did think of going to Grant at the Yard and saying quite frankly that I had found out how she could have known about the Sharpes and about the house; and that she had met a man in Larborough and that I had a witness of the meeting."

"So that they could do what?"

"So that they could investigate the girl's movements during that month instead of us."

"And you think they would?"

"Of course. Why not?"

"Because it wouldn't be worth their while. All they would do when they found out that she was not trustworthy would be to drop the case thankfully into oblivion. She has not sworn to anything so they could not prosecute her for perjury."

"They could proceed against her for having misled them."

"Yes, but it wouldn't be worth their while. It won't be easy to unearth her movements for that month, we may be sure. And on top of all that unnecessary investigation they would have the job of preparing and presenting a case. It's highly unlikely that an overworked department, with serious cases flooding in at their doors, are going to all that bother when they could quietly drop the thing on the spot."

"But it's supposed to be a department of Justice. It leaves the Sharpes——"

"No, a department of the Law. Justice begins in court. As you very well know. Besides, Rob, you haven't brought them any proof of anything. You don't know that she ever went to Milford. And the fact that she picked up a man at the Midland, and had tea with him, doesn't do anything to disprove her story that she was picked up by the Sharpes. In fact the only leg you have to stand on is Alec Ramsden, 5 Spring Gardens, Fulham, South West."

"Who is he?"

"Your private sleuth. And a very good one, take it from me. He has a flock of tame operators at call, so if he is busy himself he can supply you with a fairly good substitute. Tell him I gave you his name and he won't palm off a dud on you. Not that he would, anyhow. He's the salt of the earth. Pensioned from the Force because of a wound 'received in the course of duty.' He'll do you proud. I must go. If there's anything else I can do just give me a ring sometime. I wish I had time to come down and see The Franchise and your witches for myself. They grow on me. Goodbye."

Robert laid down the receiver, picked it up again, asked for Information, and obtained the telephone number of Alec Ramsden. There was no answer and he sent a telegram saying that he, Robert Blair, needed some work done urgently and that Kevin Macdermott had said that Ramsden was the man to do it.

"Robert," said Aunt Lin coming in pink and indignant, "did you know that you left the fish on the hall table and it has soaked through to the mahogany and Christina was waiting for it."

"Is the gravamen of the charge the mahogany or keeping Christina waiting?"

"Really, Robert, I hardly know what's come over you. Since you got involved in this Franchise affair you've changed entirely. A fortnight ago you would never have dreamed of putting a parcel of fish down on polished mahogany and forgetting all about it. And if you had you would be sorry about it and apologise."

"I do apologise, Aunt Lin; I am truly contrite. But it is not often I am saddled with a responsibility as serious as the present one and you must forgive me if I am a little jaded."

"I don't think you are jaded at all. On the contrary, I have never seen you so pleased with yourself. I think you are positively *relishing* this sordid affair. Only this morning Miss Truelove at the Anne Boleyn was condoling with me on your being mixed up in it."

"Was she indeed? Well, I condole with Miss Truelove's sister."

"Condole about what?"

"On having a sister like Miss Truelove. You *are* having a bad time, aren't you, Aunt Lin."

"Don't be sarcastic, dear. It is not pleasant for anyone in this town to see the notoriety that has overtaken it. It has always been a quiet and dignified little place."

"I don't like Milford as much as I did a fortnight ago," Robert said reflectively, "so I'll save my tears."

"No less than four separate charabancs arrived from Larborough at one time or another today, having come for nothing but to inspect The Franchise *en route*."

"And who catered for them?" Robert asked, knowing that coach traffic was not welcome in Milford.

"No one. They were simply furious."

"That will larn them to go poking their noses. There is nothing Larborough minds about as much as its stomach."

"The vicar's wife insists on being Christian about it, but I think that that is the wrong point of view."

"Christian?"

"Yes; 'reserving our judgment,' you know. That is merely feebleness, not Christianity. Of course I don't discuss the case, Robert dear; even with her. I am the soul of discretion. But of course she knows how I feel, and I know how she feels, so discussion is hardly necessary."

What was clearly a snort came from Nevil where he was sunk in an easy chair.

"Did you say something, Nevil dear?"

The nursery tone clearly intimidated Nevil. "No, Aunt Lin," he said meekly.

But he was not going to escape so easily; the snort had only too clearly been a snort. "I don't grudge you the drink, dear, but is that your *third* whisky? There is a Traminer for dinner, and you won't taste it at all after that strong stuff. You mustn't get into bad habits if you are going to marry a Bishop's daughter."

"I am not going to marry Rosemary."

Miss Bennet stared, aghast. "Not!"

"I would as soon marry a Public Assistance Board."

"But, Nevil!"

"I would as soon marry a radio set." Robert remembered Kevin's remark about Rosemary giving birth to nothing but a gramophone record. "I would as soon marry a crocodile." Since Rosemary was very pretty Robert supposed that "crocodile" had something to do with tears. "I would as soon marry a soap-box." Marble Arch, Robert supposed. "I would as soon marry the *Ack-Emma.*" That seemed to be final.

"But Nevil, dear, *why!*"

"She is a very silly creature. Almost as silly as the *Watchman.*"

Robert heroically refrained from mentioning the fact that for the last six years the *Watchman* had been Nevil's bible.

"Oh, come, dear; you've had a tiff; all engaged couples do. It's a good thing to get the give-and-take business on a firm basis before marriage; those couples who never quarrel during their engagement lead surprisingly rowdy lives after marriage; so don't take a small disagreement too seriously. You can ring her up before you go home tonight——"

"It is a quite fundamental disagreement," Nevil said coldly. "And there is no prospect whatever of my ringing her up."

"But Nevil, dear, what——"

The three thin cracked notes of the gong floated through her protest and gave her pause. The drama of broken engagements gave place on the instant to more immediate concerns.

"That is the gong. I think you had better take your drink in with you, dear. Christina likes to serve the soup as soon as she has added the egg, and she is not in a very good mood tonight because of getting the fish so late. Though why that should make any difference to her I can't think. It is only grilled, and that doesn't take any time. It's not as if she had had to wipe the fish juice off the mahogany, because I did that myself."

CHAPTER XIV

IT FURTHER UPSET Aunt Lin that Robert should have breakfast next morning at 7.45 so that he could go early to the office. It was another sign of the degeneration that the Franchise affair was responsible for. To have early breakfast so that he might catch a train, or set out for a distant meet, or attend a client's funeral, was one thing. But to have early breakfast just so that he could arrive at work at an office-boy hour was a very odd proceeding, and unbefitting a Blair.

Robert smiled, walking up the sunny High Street still shuttered and quiet. He had always liked the early morning hours, and it was at this hour that Milford looked its best; its pinks and sepias and creams as delicate in the sunlight as a tinted drawing. Spring was merging into summer, and already the warmth of the pavement radiated into the cool air; the pollarded limes were full out. That would mean shorter nights for the lonely women at The Franchise, he remembered thankfully. But perhaps—with any luck—by the time the summer was actually here their vindication would be complete and their home no longer a beleaguered fortress.

Propped against the still closed door of the office was a long thin grey man who seemed to be all bones and to have no stomach at all.

"Good-morning," Robert said. "Did you want to see me?"

"No," said the grey man. "You wanted to see me."

"*I* did?"

"At least so your telegram said. I take it you're Mr. Blair?"

"But you can't be here already!" Robert said.

"It's not far," the man said laconically.

"Come in," said Robert trying to live up to Mr. Ramsden's standard of economy in comment.

In the office he asked as he unlocked his desk: "Have you had breakfast?"

"Yes, I had bacon and eggs at the White Hart."

"I am wonderfully relieved that you could come yourself."

"I had just finished a case. And Kevin Macdermott has done a lot for me."

Yes; Kevin, for all his surface malice and his overcrowded life, found the will and the time to help those who deserved help. In which he differed markedly from the Bishop of Larborough, who preferred the undeserving.

"Perhaps the best way would be for you to read this statement," he said, handing Ramsden the copy of Betty Kane's statement to the police, "and then we can go on with the story from there."

Ramsden took the typescript, sat down in the visitors' chair—folded up would be a more accurate description of his action—and withdrew himself from Robert's presence very much as Kevin had done in the room in St. Paul's Churchyard. Robert, taking out his own work, envied them their power of concentration.

"Yes, Mr. Blair?" he said presently; and Robert gave him the rest of the story: the girl's identification of the house and its inmates, Robert's own entrance into the affair, the police decision that they would not proceed on the available evidence, Leslie Wynn's resentment and its result in the *Ack-Emma* publicity, his own interviews with the girl's relations and what they revealed, his discovery that she went bus-riding and that a double-decker did run on the Milford bus-route during the relevant weeks, and his unearthing of X.

"To find out more about X is your job, Mr. Ramsden. The lounge waiter, Albert, knows what he looked like, and this is a list of residents for the period in question. It would be too great luck that he should be staying at the Midland, but one never knows. After that you're on your own. Tell Albert I sent you, by the way. I've known him a long time."

"Very good. I'll get over to Larborough now. I'll have a photograph of the girl by tomorrow, but perhaps you could lend me your *Ack-Emma* one for today."

"Certainly. How are you going to get a proper photograph of her?"

"Oh. Ways."

Robert deduced that Scotland Yard had been given one when the girl was reported missing, and that his old colleagues at Headquarters would not be too reluctant to give him a copy; so he left it at that.

"There's just a chance that the conductor of one of those double-decker buses may remember her," he said as Ramsden was going. "They are Larborough And District Motor Services buses. The garage is in Victoria Street."

At half-past nine the staff arrived—one of the first being Nevil; a change in routine which surprised Robert: Nevil was usually the last to arrive and the last to settle down. He would wander in, divest himself of his wrappings in his own small room at the back, wander into "the office" to say good morning, wander into the "waiting-room" at the back to say hello to Miss Tuff, and finally wander into Robert's room and stand there thumbing open the bound roll of one of the esoteric periodicals that came for him by post and commenting on the permanently deplorable state of affairs in England. Robert had grown quite used to running through his morning post to a Nevil obbligato. But today Nevil came in at the appointed time, went into his own room, shut the door firmly after him, and, if the pulling in and out of drawers was any evidence, settled down to work at once.

Miss Tuff came in with her notebook and her dazzling white peter-pan collar, and Robert's normal day had begun. Miss Tuff had worn peter-pan collars over her dark frock for twenty years, and would have looked undressed, almost indecent, without them now. A fresh one went on every morning; the previous day's having been laundered the night before and laid ready for putting on tomorrow. The only break in the routine was on Sundays. Robert had once met Miss Tuff on a Sunday and entirely failed to recognize her because she was wearing a jabot.

Until half-past ten Robert worked, and then realised that he had had breakfast at an abnormally early hour and was now in need of more sustenance than an office cup of tea. He would go out and have coffee and a sandwich at the Rose and Crown. You got the best coffee in Milford at the Anne Boleyn, but it was always full of shopping females ("*How* nice to see you, my dear! We *did* miss you so at Ronnie's party! And *have* you heard . . .") and that was an atmosphere he would not face for all the coffee in Brazil. He would go across to the Rose and Crown, and afterwards he would shop a little on behalf of the Franchise people, and after lunch he would go out and break to them gently the bad news about the *Watchman*. He could not do it on the telephone because they had no telephone now. The Larborough firm had come out with ladders and putty and recalcitrant sheets of glass and had replaced the windows without fuss or mess. But they, of course, were Private Enterprise. The Post Office, being a Government department, had taken the matter of the telephone into avizandum and would move in their own elephantine good time. So Robert planned to spend part of his afternoon telling the Sharpes the news he could not tell them by telephone.

It was still early for mid-morning snacks and the chintz and old oak of the Rose and Crown lounge was deserted except for Ben Carley, who was sitting by the gate-legged table at the window reading the *Ack-Emma*. Carley had never been Robert's cup of tea—any more than, he suspected, he was Carley's—but they had the bond of their profession (one of the strongest in human nature) and in a small place like Milford that made them very nearly bosom friends. So Robert sat down as a matter of course at Carley's table; remembering as he did so that he still owed Carley gratitude for that unheeded warning of his about the feeling in the countryside.

Carley lowered the *Ack-Emma* and regarded him with the too-lively dark eyes that were so alien in this English Midland serenity. "It seems to be dying down," he said. "Only one letter today; just to keep something in the kitty."

"The *Ack-Emma*, yes. But the *Watchman* is beginning a campaign of its own on Friday."

"The *Watchman!* What's *it* doing climbing into the *Ack-Emma*'s bed?"

"It wouldn't be the first time," Robert said.

"No, I suppose not," Carley said, considering it. "Two sides of the same penny, when you come to think of it. Oh, well. That needn't worry you. The total circulation of the *Watchman* is about twenty thousand. If that."

"Perhaps. But practically every one of those twenty thousand has a second cousin in the permanent Civil Service in this country."

"So what? Has anyone ever known the permanent Civil Service to move a finger in any cause whatever outside their normal routine?"

"No, but they pass the buck. And sooner or later the buck drops into—into a—a——"

"A fertile spot," Carley offered, mixing the metaphor deliberately.

"Yes. Sooner or later some busybody or sentimentalist or egotist, with not enough to do, thinks that something should be done about this and begins to pull strings. And a string pulled in the Civil Service has the same effect as a string pulled in a peep-show. A whole series of figures is yanked into action, willy-nilly. Gerald obliges Tony, and Reggie obliges Gerald, and so on, to incalculable ends."

Carley was silent a moment. "It's a pity," he said. "Just when the *Ack-Emma* was losing way. Another two days and they would have dropped it for good. In fact they're two days over their normal schedule, as it is.

I have never known them carry a subject longer than three issues. The response must have been terrific to warrant that amount of space."

"Yes," Robert agreed, gloomily.

"Of course, it was a gift for them. The beating of kidnapped girls is growing very rare. As a change of fare it was beyond price. When you have only three or four dishes, like the *Ack-Emma*, it's difficult to keep the customers' palates properly tickled. A tit-bit like the Franchise affair must have put up their circulation by thousands in the Larborough district alone."

"Their circulation will slack off. It's just a tide. But what I have to deal with is what's left on the beach."

"A particularly smelly beach, let me say," Carley observed. "Do you know that fat blonde with the mauve powder and the uplift brassière who runs that Sports Wear shop next the Anne Boleyn? She's one of the things on your beach."

"How?"

"She lived at the same boarding-house in London as the Sharpes, it seems; and she has a lovely story as to how Marion Sharpe once beat a dog half to death in a rage. Her clients loved that story. So did the Anne Boleyn customers. She goes there for her morning coffee." He glanced wryly at the angry flush on Robert's face. "I needn't tell you that she has a dog of her own. It has never been corrected in its spoiled life, but it is rapidly dying of fatty degeneration through the indiscriminate feeding of morsels whenever the fat blonde is feeling gooey."

There were moments, Robert thought, when he could very nearly hug Ben Carley, striped suits and all.

"Ah, well, it will blow over," said Carley, with the pliant philosophy of a race long used to lying low and letting the storm blow past.

Robert looked surprised. Forty generations of protesting ancestors were surprised in his sole person. "I don't see that blowing over is any advantage," he said. "It won't help my clients at all."

"What can you do?"

"Fight, of course."

"Fight what? You wouldn't get a slander verdict, if that's what you're thinking of."

"No. I hadn't thought of slander. I propose to find out what the girl was really doing during those weeks."

Carley looked amused. "Just like that," he said, commenting on this simple statement of a tall order.

"It won't be easy and it will probably cost them all they have, but there is no alternative."

"They could go away from here. Sell the house and settle down somewhere else. A year from now no one outside the Milford district will remember anything about this affair."

"They would never do that; and I shouldn't advise them to, even if they would. You can't have a tin can tied to your tail and go through life pretending it isn't there. Besides, it is quite unthinkable that that girl should be allowed to get away with her tale. It's a matter of principle."

"You can pay too high a price for your damned principles. But I wish you luck, anyhow. Are you considering a private inquiry agent? Because if you are I know a very good——"

Robert said that he had got an agent and that he was already at work.

Carley's expressive face conveyed his amused congratulation at this swift action on the part of the conservative Blair, Hayward, and Bennet.

"The Yard had better look to its laurels," he said. His eyes went to the street beyond the leaded panes of the window, and the amusement in them faded to a fixed attention. He stared for a moment or two and then said softly: "Well! of all the nerve!"

It was an admiring phrase, not an indignant one; and Robert turned to see what was occasioning his admiration.

On the opposite side of the street was the Sharpes' battered old car; its odd front wheel well in evidence. And in the back, enthroned in her usual place and with her usual air of faint protest at this means of transport, was Mrs. Sharpe. The car was pulled up outside the grocer's, and Marion was presumably inside shopping. It could have been there only a few moments or Ben Carley would have noticed it before, but already two errand boys had paused to stare, leaning on their bicycles with voluptuous satisfaction in this free spectacle. And even while Robert took in the scene people came to the doors of neighbouring shops as the news flew from mouth to mouth.

"What incredible folly!" Robert said angrily.

"Folly nothing," said Carley, his eyes on the picture. "I wish they were clients of mine."

He fumbled in his pocket for change to pay for his coffee, and Robert fled from the room. He reached the near side of the car just as Marion came out on to the pavement at the other side. "Mrs. Sharpe," he said sternly, "this is an extraordinarily silly thing to do. You are only exacerbating——"

"Oh, good morning, Mr. Blair," she said, in polite social tones. "Have you had your morning coffee, or would you like to accompany us to the Anne Boleyn?"

"Miss Sharpe!" he said appealing to Marion, who was putting her packages down on the seat. "You must know that this is a silly thing to do."

"I honestly don't know whether it is or not," she said, "but it seems to be something that we must do. Perhaps we have grown childish with living too much to ourselves, but we found that neither of us could forget that snub at the Anne Boleyn. That condemnation without trial."

"We suffer from spiritual indigestion, Mr. Blair. And the only cure is a hair of the dog that bit us. To wit, a cup of Miss Truelove's excellent coffee."

"But it is so unnecessary! So——"

"We feel that at half-past ten in the morning there must be a large number of free tables at the Anne Boleyn," Mrs. Sharpe said tartly.

"Don't worry, Mr. Blair," Marion said. "It is a gesture only. Once we have drunk our token cup of coffee at the Anne Boleyn we shall never darken its doors again." She burlesqued the phrase in characteristic fashion.

"But it will merely provide Milford with a free——"

Mrs. Sharpe caught him up before he could utter the word. "Milford must get used to us as a spectacle," she said dryly, "since we have decided that living entirely within four walls is not something that we can contemplate."

"But——"

"They will soon grow used to seeing monsters and take us for granted again. If you see a giraffe once a year it remains a spectacle; if you see it daily it becomes part of the scenery. We propose to become part of the Milford scenery."

"Very well, you plan to become part of the scenery. But do one thing for me just now." Already the curtains of first-floor windows were being drawn aside and faces appearing. "Give up the Anne Boleyn plan—give it up for today at least—and have your coffee with me at the Rose and Crown."

"Mr. Blair, coffee with you at the Rose and Crown would be delightful, but it would do nothing to relieve my spiritual indigestion, which, in the popular phrase, 'is killing me'."

"Miss Sharpe, I appeal to you. You have said that you realise that you are probably being childish, and—well, as a personal obligation to me as your agent, I ask you not to go on with the Anne Boleyn plan."

"*That* is blackmail," Mrs. Sharpe remarked.

"It is unanswerable, anyhow," Marion said, smiling faintly at him. "We seem to be going to have coffee at the Rose and Crown." She sighed. "Just when I was all strung up for a gesture!"

"Well, of all the nerve!" came a voice from overhead. It was Carley's phrase over again but held none of Carley's admiration; it was loaded with indignation.

"You can't leave the car here," Robert said. "Quite apart from the traffic laws it is practically Exhibit A."

"Oh, we didn't intend to," Marion said. "We were taking it round to the garage so that Stanley can do something technical to its inside with some instrument he has there. He is exceedingly scornful about our car, Stanley is."

"I dare say. Well, I shall go round with you; and you had better step on it before we are run in for attracting a crowd."

"Poor Mr. Blair," Marion said, pressing the starter. "It must be horrid for you not to be part of the landscape any more, after all those years of comfortable merging."

She said it without malice—indeed there was genuine sympathy in her voice—but the sentence stuck in his mind and made a small tender place there as they drove round into Sin Lane, avoided five hacks and a pony that were trailing temperamentally out of the livery stable, and came to rest in the dimness of the garage.

Bill came out to meet them, wiping his hands on an oily rag. "Morning, Mrs. Sharpe. Glad to see you out. Morning, Miss Sharpe. That was a neat job you did on Stan's forehead. The edges closed as neat as if they had been stitched. You ought to have been a nurse."

"Not me. I have no patience with people's fads. But I might have been a surgeon. You can't be very faddy on the operating table."

Stanley appeared from the back, ignoring the two women who now ranked as intimates, and took over the car. "What time do you want this wreck?" he asked.

"An hour do?" Marion asked.

"A year wouldn't do, but I'll do all that can be done in an hour." His eye went on to Robert. "Anything for the Guineas?"

"I've had a good tip for Bali Boogie."

"Nonsense," old Mrs. Sharpe said. "None of that Hippocras blood were any good when it came to a struggle. Just turned it up."

The three men stared at her, astonished.

"You are interested in racing?" Robert said, unbelieving.

"No, in horseflesh. My brother bred thoroughbreds." Seeing their faces she gave her dry cackle of laughter, so like a hen's squawk. "Did you think I went to rest every afternoon with my Bible, Mr. Blair? Or perhaps with a book on black magic. No, indeed; I take the racing page of the daily paper. And Stanley would be well advised to save his money on Bali Boogie; if anything in horseflesh ever deserved so obscene a name that animal does."

"And what instead?" Stanley asked, with his usual economy.

"They say that horse sense is the instinct that keeps horses from betting on men. But if you must do something as silly as betting, then you had better put your money on Kominsky."

"Kominsky!" Stanley said. "But it's at sixties!"

"You can of course lose your money at a shorter price if you like," she said dryly. "Shall we go, Mr. Blair?"

"All right," Stan said. "Kominsky it is; and you're on to a tenth of my stake."

They walked back to the Rose and Crown; and as they emerged from the comparative privacy of Sin Lane into the open street Robert had the exposed feeling that being out in a bad air-raid used to give him. All the attention and all the venom in the uneasy night seemed to be concentrated on his shrinking person. So now in the bright early-summer sunlight he crossed the street feeling naked and unprotected. He was ashamed to see how relaxed and seemingly indifferent Marion swung along at his side, and hoped that his self-consciousness was not apparent. He talked as naturally as he could, but he remembered how easily her mind had always read the contents of his, and felt that he was not making a very good job of it.

A solitary waiter was picking up the shilling that Ben Carley had left on the table, but otherwise the lounge was deserted. As they seated themselves round the bowl of wallflowers on the black oak table Marion said: "You heard that our windows are in again?"

"Yes; P. C. Newsam looked in on his way home last night to tell me. That was smart work."

"Did you bribe them?" Mrs. Sharpe asked.

"No. I just mentioned that it was the work of hooligans. If your missing windows had been the result of blast you would no doubt still be living with the elements. Blast ranks as misfortune, and therefore a thing to be put up with. But hooliganism is one of those things that Something Must Be Done About. Hence your new windows. I wish that it was all as easy as replacing windows."

He was unaware that there had been any change in his voice, but Marion searched his face and said: "Some new development?"

"I'm afraid there is. I was coming out this afternoon to tell you about it. It appears that just when the *Ack-Emma* is dropping the subject—there is only one letter today and that a mild one—just when the *Ack-Emma* has grown tired of Betty Kane's cause the *Watchman* is going to take it up."

"Excelsior!" said Marion. "The *Watchman* snatching the torch from the failing hands of the *Ack-Emma* is a charming picture."

"Climbing into the *Ack-Emma*'s bed," Ben Carley had called it; but the sentiment was the same.

"Have you spies in the *Watchman* office, Mr. Blair?" Mrs. Sharpe asked.

"No; it was Nevil who got wind of it. They are going to print a letter from his future father-in-law, the Bishop of Larborough."

"Hah!" said Mrs. Sharpe. "Toby Byrne."

"You know him?" asked Robert, thinking that the quality of her tone would peel the varnish off wood if spilt on it.

"He went to school with my nephew. The son of the horse-leech brother. Toby Byrne, indeed. He doesn't change."

"I gather that you didn't like him."

"I never knew him. He went home for the holidays once with my nephew but was never asked back."

"Oh?"

"He discovered for the first time that stable lads got up at the crack of dawn, and he was horrified. It was slavery, he said; and he went round the lads urging them to stand up for their rights. If they combined, he said, not a horse would go out of the stable before nine o'clock in the morning. The lads used to mimic him for years afterwards; but he was not asked back."

"Yes; he doesn't change," agreed Robert. "He has been using the same technique ever since, on everything from Kaffirs to crêches. The less he knows about a thing the more strongly he feels about it. Nevil was of the opinion that nothing could be done about the proposed letter, since the Bishop had already written it, and what the Bishop has written is not to be contemplated as waste-paper. But I couldn't just sit and do nothing about it; so I rang him up after dinner and pointed out as tactfully as I could that he was embracing a very doubtful cause, and at the same time doing harm to two possibly innocent people. But I might have saved my breath. He pointed out that the *Watchman* existed for the free expression of opinion, and inferred that I was trying to prevent such freedom. I ended up by asking him if he approved of lynching, because he was doing his best to bring one about. That was after I saw it was hopeless and had stopped being tactful." He took the cup of coffee that Mrs. Sharpe had poured out for him. "He's a sad come-down after his predecessor in the See; who was the terror of every evil-doer in five counties, and a scholar to boot."

"How did Toby Byrne achieve gaiters?" Mrs. Sharpe wondered.

"I assume that Cowan's Cranberry Sauce had no inconsiderable part in his translation."

"Ah, yes. His wife. I forgot. Sugar, Mr. Blair?"

"By the way, here are the two duplicate keys to the Franchise gate. I take it that I may keep one. The other you had better give to the police, I think, so that they can look round as they please. I also have to inform you that you now have a private agent in your employ." And he told them about Alec Ramsden, who appeared on doorsteps at half-past eight in the morning.

"No word of anyone recognising the *Ack-Emma* photograph and writing to Scotland Yard?" Marion asked. "I had pinned my faith to that."

"Not so far. But there is still hope."

"It is five days since the *Ack-Emma* printed it. If anyone was ever going to recognise it they would have by now."

"You don't make allowances for the discards. That is nearly always the way it happens. Someone spreads open their parcel of chips and says: 'Dear me, where did I see that face?' Or someone is using a bundle of newspapers to line drawers in a hotel. Or something like that. Don't lose hope, Miss Sharpe. Between the good Lord and Alec Ramsden, we'll triumph in the end."

She looked at him soberly. "You really believe that, don't you," she said as one noting a phenomenon.

"I do," he said.

"You believe in the ultimate triumph of Good."

"Yes."

"Why?"

"I don't know. I suppose because the other thing is unthinkable. Nothing more positive or more commendable than that."

"I should have a greater faith in a God who hadn't given Toby Byrne a bishopric," Mrs. Sharpe said. "When does Toby's letter appear, by the way?"

"On Friday morning."

"I can hardly wait," said Mrs. Sharpe.

CHAPTER XV

ROBERT WAS LESS SURE about the ultimate triumph of good by Friday afternoon.

It was not the Bishop's letter which shook his faith. Indeed the events of Friday did much to take the wind out of the Bishop's sails; and if Robert had been told on Wednesday morning that he would bitterly regret anything that served to deflate the Bishop he would not have believed it.

His Lordship's letter had run very true to form. The *Watchman*, he said, had always set its face against violence and was not now, of course, proposing to condone it, but there were occasions when violence was but a symptom of a deep social unrest, resentment, and insecurity. As in the recent Nullahbad case, for instance. (The "unrest, resentment, and insecurity" in the Nullahbad case lay entirely in the bosoms of two thieves who could not find the opal bracelet they had come to steal and by way of reprisal killed the seven sleeping occupants of the bungalow in their beds.) There were undoubtedly times when the proletariat felt themselves helpless to redress a patent wrong, and it was not to be marvelled at that some of the more passionate spirits were moved to personal protest. (Robert thought that Bill and Stanley would hardly recognise the louts of Monday night under the guise of "passionate spirits"; and he held that "personal protest" was a slight understatement for the entire wrecking of the ground floor windows of The Franchise.) The people to be blamed for the unrest (the *Watchman* had a passion for euphemism: unrest, under-privileged, backward, unfortunate; where the rest of the world talked about violence, the poor, mentally deficient, and prostitutes; and one of the things that the *Ack-Emma* and the *Watchman* had in common, now he thought about it, was the belief that all prostitutes were hearts-of-gold who had taken the wrong turning)—the people to be blamed for the unrest were not those perhaps misguided persons who had demonstrated their resentment so unmistakably, but the powers whose weakness, ineptitude and lack of zeal had led to the injustice of a dropped case. It was part of the English heritage that justice should not only be done but that it should be shown to be done; and the place for that was in open court.

"What good does he think it would do anyone for the police to waste time preparing a case that they were foreordained to lose?" Robert asked Nevil, who was reading the letter over his shoulder.

"It would have done *us* a power of good," Nevil said. "He doesn't seem to have thought of that. If the Magistrate dismissed the case the suggestion that his poor bruised darling was telling fibs could hardly be avoided, could it! Have you come to the bruises?"

"No."

The bruises came near the end. The "poor bruised body" of this young and blameless girl, his lordship said, was a crying indictment of a law that had failed to protect her and now failed to vindicate her. The whole conduct of this case was one that demanded the most searching scrutiny.

"That must be making the Yard very happy this morning," Robert said.

"This afternoon," amended Nevil.

"Why this afternoon?"

"No one at the Yard would read a bogus publication like the *Watchman*. They won't see it until someone sends it to them this afternoon."

But they had seen it, as it turned out. Grant had read it in the train. He had picked it off the bookstall with three others; not because it was his choice but because it was a choice between that and coloured publications with bathing-belle covers.

Robert deserted the office and took the copy of the *Watchman* out to The Franchise together with that morning's *Ack-Emma*, which had quite definitely no further interest in the Franchise affair. Since the final, subdued letter on Wednesday it had ceased to mention the matter. It was a lovely day; the grass in the Franchise courtyard absurdly green, the dirty-white front of the house glorified by the sun into a semblance of grace, the reflected light from the rosy brick wall flooding the shabby drawing-room and giving it a smiling warmth. They had sat there, the three of them, in great contentment. The *Ack-Emma* had finished its undressing of them in public; the Bishop's letter was not after all as bad as it might have been; Alec Ramsden was busy on their behalf in Larborough and would without doubt unearth facts sooner or later that would be their salvation; the summer was here with its bright short nights; Stanley was proving himself "a great dear"; they had paid a second short visit to Milford yesterday in pursuance of their design to become part of the scenery, and nothing untoward had happened to them beyond stares, black looks, and a few audible remarks. Altogether, the feeling of the meeting was that it all might be worse.

"How much ice will this cut?" Mrs. Sharpe asked Robert, stabbing her skinny index finger at the correspondence page of the *Watchman.*

"Not much, I think. Even among the *Watchman* clique the Bishop is looked at slightly sideways nowadays, I understand. His championship of Mahoney didn't do him any good."

"Who was Mahoney?" Marion asked.

"Have you forgotten Mahoney? He was the Irish 'patriot' who put a bomb in a woman's bicycle basket in a busy English street and blew four people to pieces, including the woman, who was later identified by her wedding ring. The Bishop held that Mahoney was merely misguided, not a murderer; that he was fighting on behalf of a repressed minority—the Irish, believe it or not—and that we should not make him into a martyr. That was a little too much for even *Watchman* stomachs, and since then the Bishop's prestige is not what it was, I hear."

"Isn't it shocking how one forgets when it doesn't concern oneself," Marion said. "Did they hang Mahoney?"

"They did, I am glad to say—much to his own pained surprise. So many of his predecessors had benefited from the plea that we should not make martyrs, that murder had ceased to be reckoned in their minds as one of the dangerous trades. It was rapidly becoming as safe as banking."

"Talking of banking," Mrs. Sharpe said, "I think it would be best if our financial position were made clear to you, and for that you should get in touch with old Mr. Crowle's solicitors in London, who manage our affairs. I shall write to them explaining that you are to be given full details, so that you may know how much we have to come and go on, and can make corresponding arrangements for the spending of it in defence of our good name. It is not exactly the way we had planned to spend it."

"Let us be thankful we have it to spend," Marion said. "What does a penniless person do in a case like this?"

Robert quite frankly did not know.

He took the address of the Crowle solicitors and went home to lunch with Aunt Lin, feeling happier than he had at any time since he had first caught sight of the *Ack-Emma*'s front page on Bill's desk last Friday. He felt as one feels in a bad thunderstorm when the noise ceases to be directly overhead; it will still continue, and probably still be very unpleasant, but one can see a future through it, whereas but a moment ago there was nothing but the dreadful "now."

Even Aunt Lin seemed to have forgotten The Franchise for a spell and was at her woolly and endearing best—full of the birthday presents she was buying for Lettice's twins in Saskatchewan. She had provided his favourite lunch—cold ham, boiled potatoes, and brown-betty with thick cream—and moment by moment he was finding it more difficult to realise that this was the Friday morning he had dreaded because it would see the beginning of a *Watchman* campaign against them. It seemed to him that the Bishop of Larborough was very much what Lettice's husband used to call " a busted flush." He couldn't imagine now why he had wasted a thought on him.

It was in this mood that he went back to the office. And it was in this mood that he picked up the receiver to answer Hallam's call.

"Mr. Blair?" Hallam said. "I'm at the Rose and Crown. I'm afraid I've got bad news for you. Inspector Grant's here."

"At the Rose and Crown?"

"Yes. And he's got a warrant."

Robert's brain stopped functioning. "A search warrant?" he asked stupidly.

"No; a warrant to arrest."

"No!"

"I'm afraid so."

"But he *can't* have!"

"I expect it's a bit of a shock for you. I admit I hadn't anticipated it myself."

"You mean he has managed to get a witness—a corroborative witness?"

"He has two of them. The case is sewn up and tied with ribbon."

"I can't believe it."

"Will you come over, or shall we go to you? I expect you'll want to come out with us."

"Out where? Oh, yes. Yes, of course I shall. I'll come over to the Rose and Crown now. Where are you? In the lounge?"

"No, in Grant's bedroom. Number Five. The one with the casement window on the street—over the bar."

"All right. I'm coming straight over. I say!"

"Yes?"

"A warrant for both?"

"Yes. For two."

"All right. Thank you. I'll be with you in a moment."

He sat for a moment getting back his breath, and trying to orientate himself. Nevil was out on business, but Nevil was not much of a moral support at any time. He got up, took his hat, and went to the door of "the office."

"Mr. Heseltine, please," he said, in the polite formula always used in the presence of the younger staff; and the old man followed him into the hall and out to the sunlit doorway.

"Timmy," Robert said. "We're in trouble. Inspector Grant is here from Headquarters with a warrant to arrest the Franchise people." Even as he said the words he could not believe that the thing was really happening.

Neither could old Mr. Heseltine; that was obvious. He stared, wordless; his pale old eyes aghast.

"It's a bit of a shock, isn't it, Timmy?" He shouldn't have hoped for support from the frail old clerk.

But shocked as he was, and frail, and old, Mr. Heseltine was nevertheless a law clerk, and the support was forthcoming. After a lifetime among formulae his mind reacted automatically to the letter of the situation.

"A warrant," he said. "Why a *warrant?*"

"Because they can't arrest anyone without one," Robert said a trifle impatiently. Was old Timmy getting past his work?

"I don't mean that. I mean, it's a misdemeanour they're accused of, not a felony. They could surely make it a summons, Mr. Robert? They don't need to *arrest* them, surely? Not for a misdemeanour."

Robert had not thought of that. "A summons to appear," he said. "Yes, why not? Of course there's nothing to hinder them arresting them if they want to."

"But why should they want to? People like the Sharpes wouldn't run away. Nor do any further harm while they are waiting to appear. Who issued the warrant, did they say?"

"No, they didn't say. Many thanks, Timmy; you've been as good as a stiff drink. I must go over to the Rose and Crown now—Inspector Grant is there with Hallam—and face the music. There's no way of warning The Franchise because they have no telephone. I'll just have to go out there with Grant and Hallam hanging round my neck. And only this morning we were beginning to see daylight, so we thought. You might tell Nevil when he comes in, will you? And stop him doing anything foolish or impulsive."

"You know very well, Mr. Robert, I've never been able to stop Mr. Nevil doing anything he wanted to do. Though it has seemed to me that he has been surprisingly sober this last week. In the metaphorical sense, I mean."

"Long may it last," Robert said, stepping out into the sunlit street.

It was the dead period of the afternoon at the Rose and Crown and he passed through the hall and up the wide shallow stairs without meeting anyone, and knocked at the door of Number Five. Grant, calm and polite as always, let him in. Hallam, vaguely unhappy-looking, was leaning against the dressing-table in the window.

"I understand that you hadn't expected this, Mr. Blair," Grant said.

"No, I hadn't. To be frank, it is a great shock to me."

"Sit down," Grant said. "I don't want to hurry you."

"You have new evidence, Inspector Hallam says."

"Yes; what we think is conclusive evidence."

"May I know what it is?"

"Certainly. We have a man who saw Betty Kane being picked up by the car at the bus-stop——"

"By *a* car," Robert said.

"Yes, if you like, by *a* car—but its description fits that of the Sharpes'."

"So do ten thousand others in Britain. And?"

"The girl from the farm, who went once a week to help clean The Franchise, will swear that she heard screams coming from the attic."

"*Went* once a week? Doesn't she go any longer?"

"Not since the Kane affair became common gossip."

"I see."

"Not very valuable pieces of evidence in themselves, but very valuable as proof of the girl's story. For instance she really did miss that Larborough-London coach. Our witness says that it passed him about half a mile down the road. When he came in sight of the bus-stop a few moments later the girl was there waiting. It is a long straight road, the main London road through Mainshill——"

"I know. I know it."

"Yes; well, when he was still some way from the girl he saw the car stop by her, saw her get in, and saw her driven away."

"But not who drove the car?"

"No. It was too far away for that."

"And this girl from the farm—did she volunteer the information about the screaming?"

"Not to us. She spoke about it to her friends, and we acted on information, and found her quite willing to repeat the story on oath."

"Did she speak about it to her friends before the gossip about Betty Kane's abduction got round?"

"Yes."

That was unexpected, and Robert was rocked back on his heels. If that was really true—that the girl had mentioned screaming before there was any question of the Sharpes being in trouble—then the evidence would be damning. Robert got up and walked restlessly to the window and back. He thought enviously of Ben Carley. Ben wouldn't be hating this as he hated it, feeling inadequate and at a loss. Ben would be in his element; his mind delighting in the problem and in the hope of outwitting established authority. Robert was dimly aware that his own deep-seated respect for established authority was a handicap to him rather than an asset; he needed some of Ben's native belief that authority is there to be circumvented.

"Well, thank you for being so frank," he said at last. "Now, I'm not minimising the crime you are accusing these people of, but it *is* misdemeanour not felony, so why a warrant? Surely a summons would meet the case perfectly?"

"A summons would be in order certainly," Grant said smoothly. "But in cases where the crime is aggravated—and my superiors take a grave view of the present one—a warrant is issued."

Robert could not help wondering how much the gadfly attentions of the *Ack-Emma* had influenced the calm judgments at the Yard. He caught Grant's eye and knew that Grant had read his thought.

"The girl was missing for a whole month—all but a day or two," Grant said, "and had been very badly knocked about, very deliberately. It is not a case to be taken lightly."

"But what do you gain from arrest?" Robert asked, remembering Mr. Heseltine's point. "There is no question of these people not being there to answer the charge. Nor any question of a similar crime being committed by them in the interval. When did you want them to appear, by the way?"

"I planned to bring them up at the police court on Monday."

"Then I suggest that you serve them with a summons to appear."

"My superiors have decided on a warrant," Grant said, without emotion.

"But you could use your judgment. Your superiors can have no knowledge of local conditions, for instance. If The Franchise is left without occupants it will be a wreck in a week. Have your superiors thought of that? And if you arrest these women, you can only keep them in custody until Monday, when I shall ask for bail. It seems a pity to risk hooliganism at The Franchise just for the gesture of arrest. And I know Inspector Hallam has no men to spare for its protection."

This right-and-left gave them both pause. It was amazing how ingrained the respect for property was in the English soul; the first change in Grant's face had occurred at the mention of the possible wrecking of the house. Robert cast an unexpectedly kind thought to the louts who had provided the precedent, and so weighted his argument with example. As for Hallam, quite apart from his limited force he was not likely to look kindly on the prospect of fresh hooliganism in his district and fresh culprits to track down.

Into the long pause Hallam said tentatively: "There is something in what Mr. Blair says. Feeling in the countryside is very strong, and I doubt if they would leave the house untouched if it was empty. Especially if news of the arrest got about."

It took nearly half an hour to convince Grant, however. For some reason there was a personal element in the affair for Grant, and Robert could not imagine what it could be, or why it should be there.

"Well," the Inspector said at length, "you don't need me to serve a summons." It was as if a surgeon was contemptuous at being asked to open a boil, Robert thought, amused and vastly relieved. "I'll leave that to Hallam and get back to town. But I'll be in court on Monday. I understand that the Assizes are imminent, so if we avoid a remand the case can go straight on to the Assizes. Can you be ready with your defence by Monday, do you think?"

"Inspector, with all the defence my clients have we could be ready by tea-time," Robert said bitterly.

To his surprise, Grant turned to him with a broader smile than was usual with him; and it was a very kind smile. "Mr. Blair," he said, "you have done me out of an arrest this afternoon, but I don't hold it against you. On the contrary, I think your clients are luckier than they deserve in their solicitor. It will be my prayer that they are less lucky in their counsel! Otherwise I may find myself talked into voting them a testimonial."

So it was not with "Grant and Hallam hanging round his neck" that Robert went out to The Franchise; not with a warrant at all. He went out in Hallam's familiar car with a summons sticking out of the pocket of it; and he was sick with relief when he thought of the escape they had had, and sick with apprehension when he thought of the fix they were in.

"Inspector Grant seemed to have a very personal interest in executing that warrant," he said to Hallam as they went along. "Is it that the *Ack-Emma* has been biting him, do you think?"

"Oh, no," Hallam said. "Grant's as nearly indifferent to that sort of thing as a human being can be."

"Then why?"

"Well, it's my belief—strictly between ourselves—that he can't forgive them for fooling him. The Sharpes, I mean. He's famous at the Yard for his good judgment of people, you see; and, again between ourselves, he didn't much care for the Kane girl *or* her story; and he liked them even less when he had seen the Franchise people, in spite of all the evidence. Now he thinks the wool was pulled over his eyes, and he's not taking it lightly. It would have given him a lot of pleasure, I imagine, to produce that warrant in their drawing-room."

As they pulled up by the Franchise gate and Robert took out his key, Hallam said: "If you open both sides I'll drive the car inside, even for the short time. No need to advertise the fact that we're here." And Robert, pushing open the solid iron leaves, thought that when visiting actresses said "Your policemen are wonderful" they didn't know the half of it. He got back into the car and Hallam drove up the short straight drive and round the circular path to the door. As Robert got out of the car Marion came round the corner of the house, wearing gardening gloves and a very old skirt. Where her hair was blown up from her forehead by the wind it changed from the heavy dark stuff that it was to a soft smoke. The first summer sun had darkened her skin and she looked more than ever like a gipsy. Coming on Robert unexpectedly she had not time to guard her expression, and the lighting of her whole face as she saw him made his heart turn over.

"How nice!" she said. "Mother is still resting but she will be down soon and we can have some tea. I——" Her glance went on to Hallam and her voice died away uncertainly. "Good afternoon, Inspector."

"Good afternoon, Miss Sharpe. I'm sorry to break into your mother's rest, but perhaps you would ask her to come down. It's important."

She paused a moment, and then led the way indoors. "Yes, certainly. Has there been some—some new development? Come in and sit down." She led them into the drawing-room that he knew so well by now—the lovely mirror, the dreadful fireplace, the bead-work chair, the good "pieces," the old pink carpet faded to a dirty grey—and stood there, searching their faces, savouring the new threat in the atmosphere.

"What is it?" she asked Robert.

But Hallam said: "I think it would be easier if you fetched Mrs. Sharpe and I told you both at the same time."

"Yes. Yes, of course," she agreed, and turned to go. But there was no need to go. Mrs. Sharpe came into the room, very much as she had on that previous occasion when Hallam and Robert had been there together: her short strands of white hair standing on end where they had been pushed up by her pillow, her seagull's eyes bright and inquiring.

"Only two kinds of people," she said, "arrive in noiseless cars. Millionaires and the police. Since we have no acquaintances among the former—and an ever-widening acquaintance with the latter—I deduced that some of *our* acquaintances had arrived."

"I'm afraid I'm even less welcome than usual, Mrs. Sharpe. I've come to serve a summons on you and Miss Sharpe."

"A summons?" Marion said, puzzled.

"A summons to appear at the police court on Monday morning to answer a charge of abduction and assault." It was obvious that Hallam was not happy.

"I don't believe it," Marion said slowly. "I don't believe it. You mean you are charging us with this thing?"

"Yes, Miss Sharpe."

"But how? Why now?" She turned to Robert.

"The police think they have the corroborative evidence they needed," Robert said.

"What evidence?" Mrs. Sharpe asked, reacting for the first time.

"I think the best plan would be for Inspector Hallam to serve you both with the summonses, and we can discuss the situation at greater length when he has gone."

"You mean, we have to accept them?" Marion said. "To appear in the public court—my mother too—to answer a—to be accused of a thing like that?"

"I'm afraid there is no alternative."

She seemed half intimidated by his shortness, half resentful at his lack of championship. And Hallam, as he handed the document to her, seemed to be aware of this last and to resent it in his turn.

"And I think I ought to tell you, in case he doesn't, that but for Mr. Blair here it wouldn't be a mere summons, it would be a warrant; and you would be sleeping tonight in a cell instead of in your own beds. Don't bother, Miss Sharpe: I'll let myself out."

And Robert, watching him go and remembering how Mrs. Sharpe had snubbed him on his first appearance in that room, thought that the score was now game all.

"Is that true?" Mrs. Sharpe asked.

"Perfectly true," Robert said; and told them about Grant's arrival to arrest them. "But it isn't me you have to thank for your escape: it is old Mr. Heseltine in the office." And he described how the old clerk's mind reacted automatically to stimulus of a legal sort.

"And what is this new evidence they think they have?"

"They have it all right," Robert said dryly. "There is no thinking about it." He told them about the girl being picked up on the London road through Mainshill. "That merely corroborates what we have always suspected: that when she left Cherrill Street, ostensibly on her way home, she was keeping an appointment. But the other piece of evidence is much more serious. You told me once that you had a woman—a girl—from the farm, who came in one day a week and cleaned for you."

"Rose Glyn, yes."

"I understand that since the gossip got round she doesn't come any more."

"Since the gossip——? You mean, the Betty Kane story? Oh, she was sacked before that ever came to light."

"*Sacked?*" Robert said sharply.

"Yes. Why do you look so surprised? In our experience of domestic workers sacking is not an unexpected occurrence."

"No, but in this case it might explain a lot. What did you sack her for?"

"Stealing," said old Mrs. Sharpe.

"She had always lifted a shilling or two from a purse if it was left around," supplemented Marion, "but because we needed help so badly we turned a blind eye and kept purses out of her way. Also any small liftable articles, like stockings. And then she took the watch I'd had for twenty years. I had taken it off to wash some things—the soapsuds rise up one's arms, you know—and when I went back to look for it it had gone. I asked her about it, but of course she 'hadn't seen it.' That was too much. That watch was part of me, as much a part of me as my hair or my fingernails. There was no recovering it, because we had no evidence at all that she had taken it. But after she had gone we talked it over and next morning we walked over to the farm, and just mentioned that we would not be needing her any more. That was a Tuesday—she always came on Mondays—and that afternoon after my mother had gone up to rest Inspector Grant arrived, with Betty Kane in the car."

"I see. Was anyone else there when you told the girl at the farm that she was sacked?"

"I don't remember. I don't think so. She doesn't belong to the farm—to Staples, I mean; they are delightful people. She is one of the labourer's daughters. And as far as I remember we met her outside their cottage and just mentioned the thing in passing."

"How did she take it?"

"She got very pink and flounced a bit."

"She grew beetroot red and bridled like a turkeycock," Mrs. Sharpe said. "Why do you ask?"

"Because she will say on oath that when she was working here she heard screams coming from your attic."

"Will she indeed," said Mrs. Sharpe, contemplatively.

"What is much worse, there is evidence that she mentioned the screams before there was any rumour of the Betty Kane trouble."

This produced a complete silence. Once more Robert was aware how noiseless the house was, how dead. Even the French clock on the mantelpiece was silent. The curtain at the window moved inwards on a gust of air and fell back to its place as soundlessly as if it were moving in a film.

"That," said Marion at last, "is what is known as a facer."

"Yes. Definitely."

"A facer for you, too."

"For us, yes."

"I don't mean professionally."

"No? How then?"

"You are faced with the possibility that we have been lying."

"Really, Marion!" he said impatiently, using her name for the first time and not noticing that he had used it. "What I am faced with, if anything, is the choice between your word and the word of Rose Glyn's friends."

But she did not appear to be listening. "I wish," she said passionately, "oh, how I wish that we had one small, just one small piece of evidence on our side! She gets away—that girl gets away with everything, everything. We keep on saying 'It is not true,' but we have no way of *showing* that it is not true. It is all negative. All inconclusive. All feeble denial. Things combine to back up her lies, but nothing happens to help prove that we are telling the truth. Nothing!"

"Sit down, Marion," her mother said. "A tantrum won't improve the situation."

"I could kill that girl; I could kill her. My God, I could torture her twice a day for a year and then begin again on New Year's day. When I think what she has done to us I——"

"Don't think," Robert interrupted. "Think instead of the day when she is discredited in open court. If I know anything of human nature that will hurt Miss Kane a great deal worse than the beating someone gave her."

"You still believe that that is possible?" Marion said incredulous.

"Yes. I don't quite know how we shall bring it about. But that we shall bring it about I do believe."

"With not one tiny piece of evidence for us, not one; and evidence just—just *blossoming* for her?"

"Yes. Even then."

"Is that just native optimism, Mr. Blair," Mrs. Sharpe asked, "or your innate belief in the triumph of Good, or what?"

"I don't know. I think Truth has a validity of its own."

"Dreyfus didn't find it very valid; nor Slater; nor some others of whom there is record," she said dryly.

"They did in the end."

"Well, frankly, I don't look forward to a life in prison waiting for Truth to demonstrate its validity."

"I don't believe that it will come to that. Prison, I mean. You will have to appear on Monday, and since we have no adequate defence you will no doubt be sent for trial. But we shall ask for bail, and that means that you can go on staying here until the Assizes at Norton. And before that I hope that Alec Ramsden will have picked up the girl's trail. Remember we don't even have to know what she was doing for the rest of the month. All we have to show is that she did something else on the day she says you picked her up. Take away that first bit and her whole story collapses. And it is my ambition to take it away in public."

"To undress her in public the way the *Ack-Emma* has undressed us? Do you think she would mind?" Marion said. "Mind as we minded?"

"To have been the heroine of a newspaper sensation, to say nothing of the adored centre of a loving and sympathetic family, and then to be uncovered to the public gaze as a liar, a cheat and a wanton? I think she would mind. And there is one thing she would mind particularly. One result of her escapade was that she got back Leslie Wynn's attention; the attention she had lost when he became engaged. As long as she is a wronged heroine she is assured of that attention; once we show her up she has lost it for good."

"I never thought to see the milk of human kindness so curdled in your gentle veins, Mr. Blair," Mrs. Sharpe remarked.

"If she had broken out as a result of the boy's engagement—as she very well might—I should have nothing but pity for her. She is at an unstable age, and his engagement must have been a shock. But I don't think that had very much to do with it. I think she is her mother's daughter; and was merely setting out a little early on the road her mother took. As selfish, as self-indulgent, as greedy, as plausible as the blood she came of. Now I must go. I said that I would be at home after five o'clock if

Ramsden wanted to ring up to report. And I want to ring Kevin Macdermott and get his help about counsel and things."

"I'm afraid that we—that I, rather—have been rather ungracious about this," Marion said. "You have done, and are doing, so much for us. But it was such a shock. So entirely unexpected and out of the blue. You must forgive me if——"

"There is nothing to forgive. I think you have both taken it very well. Have you got someone in the place of the dishonest and about-to-commit-perjury Rose? You can't have this huge place entirely on your hands."

"Well, no one in the locality would come, of course. But Stanley—what would we do without Stanley?—Stanley knows a woman in Larborough who might be induced to come out by bus once a week. You know, when the thought of that girl becomes too much for me, I think of Stanley."

"Yes," Robert said, smiling. "The salt of the earth."

"He is even teaching me how to cook. I know how to turn eggs in the frying-pan without breaking them now. 'D'you have to go at them as if you were conducting the Philharmonic?' he asked me. And when I asked him how he got so neat-handed he said it was with 'cooking in a bivvy two feet square'."

"How are you going to get back to Milford?" Mrs. Sharpe asked.

"The afternoon bus from Larborough will pick me up. No word of your telephone being repaired, I suppose?"

Both women took the question as comment, not interrogation. Mrs. Sharpe took leave of him in the drawing-room, but Marion walked to the gate with him. As they crossed the circle of grass enclosed by the branching driveway, he remarked: "It's a good thing you haven't a large family or there would be a worn track across the grass to the door."

"There is that as it is," she said, looking at the darker line in the rough grass. "It is more than human nature could bear to walk round that unnecessary curve."

Small talk, he was thinking; small talk. Idle words to cover up a stark situation. He had sounded very brave and fine about the validity of Truth, but how much was mere sound? What were the odds on Ramsden's turning up evidence in time for the court on Monday? In time for the Assizes? Long odds against, wasn't it? And he had better grow used to the thought.

At half-past five Ramsden rang up to give him the promised report; and it was one of unqualified failure. It was the girl he was looking for, of course; having failed to identify the man as a resident at the Midland, and having therefore no information at all about him. But nowhere had he found even a trace of her. His own men had been given duplicates of the photograph and with them had made inquiries at the airports, the railway termini, travel agencies, and the more likely hotels. No one claimed to have seen her. He himself had combed Larborough, and was slightly cheered to find that the photograph he had been given was at least easily recognisable, since it had been readily identified at the places where Betty Kane had actually been. At the two main picture houses, for instance—where, according to the box-office girls' information, she had always been alone—and at the ladies' cloakroom of the bus-station. He had tried the garages, but had drawn blank.

"Yes," Robert said. "He picked her up at the bus-stop on the London road through Mainshill, where she would normally have gone to catch her coach home." And he told Ramsden of the new developments. "So things really are urgent now. They are being brought up on Monday. If only we could prove what she did that first evening. That would bring her whole story crashing down."

"What kind of car was it?" Ramsden asked.

Robert described it, and Ramsden sighed audibly over the telephone.

"Yes," Robert agreed. "A rough ten thousand of them between London and Carlisle. Well, I'll leave you to it. I want to ring up Kevin Macdermott and tell him our woes."

Kevin was not in chambers, nor yet at the flat in St. Paul's Churchyard, and Robert eventually ran him to earth at his home near Weybridge. He sounded relaxed and amiable, and was instantly attentive when he heard the news that the police had got their evidence. He listened without remark while Robert poured out the story to him.

"So you see, Kevin," Robert finished, "we're in a frightful jam."

"A schoolboy description," Kevin said, "but exquisitely accurate. My advice to you is to 'give' them the police court, and concentrate on the Assizes."

"Kevin, couldn't you come down for the week-end, and let me talk about it to you? It's six years, Aunt Lin was saying yesterday, since you spent a night with us, so you're overdue anyhow. Couldn't you?"

"I promised Sean I'd take him over to Newbury on Sunday to choose a pony."

"But couldn't you postpone it? I'm sure Sean wouldn't mind if he knew it was in a good cause."

"Sean," said his doting parent, "has never taken the slightest interest in any cause that was not to his own immediate advantage. Being a chip off the old block. If I came would you introduce me to your witches?"

"But of course."

"And would Christina make me some butter tarts?"

"Assuredly."

"And could I have the room with the text in wools?"

"Kevin, you'll come?"

"Well, it's a damned dull country, Milford, except in the winter"—this was a reference to hunting, Kevin's only eye for country being from the back of a horse—"and I was looking forward to a Sunday riding on the downs. But a combination of witches, butter tarts, and a bedroom with a text in wools is no small draw."

As he was about to hang up, Kevin paused and said: "Oh, I say, Rob?"

"Yes?" Robert said, and waited.

"Have you considered the possibility that the police have the right of it?"

"You mean, that the girl's absurd tale may be true?"

"Yes. Are you keeping that in mind—as a possibility, I mean?"

"If I were I shouldn't——" Robert began angrily, and then laughed. "Come down and see them," he said.

"I come, I come," Kevin assured him, and hung up.

Robert called the garage, and when Bill answered asked if Stanley was still there.

"It's a wonder you can't hear him from where you are," Bill said.

"What's wrong?"

"We've just been rescuing that bay pony of Matt Ellis's from our inspection pit. Did you want Stan?"

"Not to speak to. Would you be very kind and ask him to pick up a note for Mrs. Sharpe on his way past tonight?"

"Yes, certainly. I say, Mr. Blair, is it true that there is fresh trouble coming about the Franchise affair—or shouldn't I ask that?"

Milford! thought Robert. How did they do it? A sort of information-pollen blown on the wind?

"Yes, I'm afraid there is," he said. "I expect they'll tell Stanley about it when he goes out tonight. Don't let him forget about the note, will you?"

"No, that's all right."

He wrote to The Franchise to say that Kevin Macdermott was coming down for Saturday night, and could he bring him out to see them on Sunday afternoon before he left to go back to town?

CHAPTER XVI

"DOES KEVIN MACDERMOTT *have* to look like a tout when he comes to the country?" Nevil asked, the following evening as he and Robert waited for the guest to finish his ablutions and come down to dinner.

What Kevin in country clothes actually looked like, Robert considered, was a rather disreputable trainer of jumpers for the smaller meetings; but he refrained from saying that to Nevil. Remembering the clothes that Nevil had startled the countryside with for the last few years, he felt that Nevil was in no position to criticise anyone's taste. Nevil had turned up to dinner in a chaste dark grey suit of the most irreproachable orthodoxy, and seemed to think that his new conformity made him free to forget the experimentalism of his immediate past.

"I suppose Christina is in the usual lather of sentiment?"

"A lather of white of egg, as far as I have been able to judge."

Christina regarded Kevin as "Satan in person," and adored him. His Satanic qualities came not from his looks—though Kevin did indeed look a little like Satan—but from the fact that he "defended the wicked for the sake of worldly gain." And she adored him because he was good-looking, and a possibly reclaimable sinner, and because he praised her baking.

"I hope it's a soufflé, then, and not that meringue stuff. Do you think that Macdermott could be lured into coming down to defend them at Norton Assizes?"

"I think he is much too busy for that, even if he were interested. But I'm hoping that one of his dogs-bodies will come."

"Primed by Macdermott."

"That's the idea."

"I really don't see why Marion should have to slave to provide Macdermott with lunch. Does he realise that she has to prepare and clear away and wash up every single thing, to say nothing of carting them to and fro a day's journey to that antediluvian kitchen?"

"It was Marion's own idea that he should come to lunch with them. I take it that she considers the extra trouble worth while."

"Oh, you were always crazy about Kevin; and you simply don't know how to begin to appreciate a woman like Marion. It's—it's *obscene* that she should be wasting her vitality on household drudgery, a woman like that. She should be hacking her way through jungles, or scaling precipices, or ruling a barbarous race, or measuring the planets. Ten thousand nit-wit blondes dripping with mink have nothing to do but sit back and have the polish on their predatory nails changed, and Marion carts coal. Coal! *Marion!* And I suppose by the time this case is finished they won't have a penny to pay a maid even if they could get one."

"Let us hope that by the time this case is finished they are not doing hard labour by order."

"Robert, it *couldn't* come to that! It's unthinkable."

"Yes, it's unthinkable. I suppose it is always unbelievable that anyone one knows should go to prison."

"It's bad enough that they should go into the dock. Marion. Who never did a cruel, or underhand, or shabby thing in her life. And just because a—— Do you know. I had a lovely time the other night. I found a book on torture, and I stayed awake till two o'clock choosing which one I would use on the Kane."

"You should get together with Marion. That is her ambition too."

"And what would yours be?" There was a faint hint of scorn in the tone, as though it was understood that the mild Robert would have no strong feelings on the subject. "Or haven't you considered it?"

"I don't need to consider it," Robert said slowly. "I'm going to undress her in public."

"*What!*"

"Not that way. I'm going to strip her of every rag of pretence, in open court, so that everyone will see her for what she is."

Nevil looked curiously at him for a moment. "Amen," he said quietly. "I didn't know you felt like that about it, Robert." He was going to add something, but the door opened and Macdermott came in, and the evening had begun.

Eating solidly through Aunt Lin's superb dinner, Robert hoped that it was not going to be a mistake to take Kevin to Sunday lunch at The Franchise. He was desperately anxious that the Sharpes should make a success with Kevin; and there was no denying that Kevin was temperamental and the Sharpes not everyone's cup of tea. Was lunch at The Franchise likely to be an asset to their cause? A lunch cooked by Marion? For Kevin who was a gourmet? When he had first read the invitation—handed in by Stanley this morning—he was glad that they had made the gesture, but misgiving was slowly growing in him. And as one perfection succeeded the other in unhurried procession across Aunt Lin's shining mahogany, with Christina's large face hovering in eager benevolence beyond the candle-light, the misgiving swelled until it took entire possession of him. "Shapes that did not stand up" might fill his breast with a warm, protective affection; but they could hardly be expected to have the same effect on Kevin.

At least Kevin seemed glad to be here, he thought, listening to Macdermott making open love to Aunt Lin, with a word thrown to Christina every now and then to keep her happy and faithful. Dear Heaven, the Irish! Nevil was on his best behaviour, full of earnest attention, with a discreet "sir" thrown in now and again; often enough to make Kevin feel superior but not often enough to make him feel old. The subtler English form of flattery, in fact. Aunt Lin was like a girl, pink-cheeked and radiant; absorbing flattery like a sponge, subjecting it to some chemical process, and pouring it out again as charm. Listening to her talk Robert was amused to find that the Sharpes had suffered a sea-change in her mind. By the mere fact of being in danger of imprisonment, they had been promoted from "these people" to "poor things." This had nothing to do with Kevin's presence; it was a combination of native kindness and woolly thinking.

It was odd, Robert thought, looking round the table, that this family party—so gay, so warm, so secure—should be occasioned by the dire need of two helpless women in that dark silent house set down among the endless fields.

He went to bed with the warm aura of the party still round him, but in his heart a chill anxiety and an ache. Were they asleep out there at The Franchise? How much sleep had they had lately?

He lay long awake, and wakened early; listening to the Sunday morning silence. Hoping that it would be a good day—The Franchise looked its worst in rain, when its dirty-white became almost grey—and that whatever Marion made for lunch would "stand up." Just before eight o'clock a car came in from the country and stopped below the window, and someone whistled a soft bugle call. A company call, it was. B Company. Stanley, presumably. He got up and put his head out of the window.

Stanley, hatless as usual—he had never seen Stanley in any kind of head covering—was sitting in the car regarding him with tolerant benevolence.

"You Sunday snoozers," said Stanley.

"Did you get me up just to sneer at me?"

"No. I have a message from Miss Sharpe. She says when you come out you're to take Betty Kane's statement with you, and you're on no account to forget it because it's of the first importance. I'll say it's important! She's going round looking as if she had unearthed a million."

"Looking happy!" Robert said, unbelieving.

"Like a bride. Indeed I haven't seen a woman look like that since my cousin Beulah married her Pole. A face like a scone, Beulah has; and believe me that day she looked like Venus, Cleopatra, and Helen of Troy rolled into one."

"Do you know what it is that Miss Sharpe is so happy about?"

"No. I did cast out a few feelers, but she's saving it up, it seems. Anyhow, don't forget the copy of the statement, or the responses won't come right, or something. The pass-word's in the statement."

Stanley proceeded on his way up the street towards Sin Lane, and Robert took his towel and went to the bathroom greatly puzzled. While he waited for breakfast he took out the statement from among the papers in his despatch case, and read it through again with a new attention. What had Marion remembered or discovered that was making her so happy? Betty Kane had slipped somewhere, that was obvious. Marion was radiant, and Marion wanted him to bring the Kane statement when he came. That could only mean that somewhere in the statement was proof that Betty Kane was lying.

He reached the end of the statement without finding any likely sentence and began to hunt through it again. What could it be? That she had said it was raining, and that it—perhaps—had not been raining? But that would not have been vital, or even important to the credibility of her story. The Milford bus, then? The one she said she had passed, when being driven in the Sharpes' car. Were the times wrong? But they had checked the times long ago, and they fitted nearly enough. The "lighted sign" on the bus? Was the time too early for a sign to be lighted? But that would have been merely a slip of memory, not a discrediting factor in her statement.

He hoped passionately that Marion in her anxiety to obtain that "one small piece of evidence" on their side was not exaggerating some trifling discrepancy into proof of dishonesty. The descent from hope would be worse than no hope at all.

This real worry almost obliterated the social worry of the lunch from his mind, and he ceased to care greatly whether Kevin enjoyed his meal at The Franchise or not. When Aunt Lin said to him, covertly, as she set off for church: "What do you think they'll give you for lunch, dear? I'm quite sure they live on those toasted flake things out of packets, poor things," he said shortly: "They know good wine when they taste it; that should please Kevin."

"What has happened to young Bennet?" Kevin asked as they drove out to The Franchise.

"He wasn't asked to lunch," Robert said.

"I didn't mean that. What has happened to the strident suits and the superiority and the *Watchman* aggressiveness?"

"Oh, he has fallen out with the *Watchman* over this case."

"Ah!"

"For the first time he is in a position to have actual personal knowledge of a case the *Watchman* is pontificating about, and it has been a bit of a shock to him, I think."

"Is the reformation going to last?"

"Well, do you know, I shouldn't be a bit surprised if it did. Apart from the fact that he has got to an age when they normally give up childish things, and was due for a change, I think he has been doing some revision and wondering if any of the other *Watchman* white-headed boys were any more worthy of championing than Betty Kane. Kotovich, for instance."

"Hah! The patriot!" Kevin said expressively.

"Yes. Only last week he was holding forth on our duty to Kotovich; our duty to protect and cherish him—and eventually provide him with a British passport, I suppose. I doubt if today he would be quite so simple. He has grown up wonderfully in the last few days. I didn't know he even possessed a suit like the one he was wearing last night. It must be one he got to go to his school prize-giving in, for he certainly has worn nothing so sober since."

"I hope for your sake it lasts. He has brains, the boy; and once he got rid of his circus tricks would be an asset to the firm."

"Aunt Lin is distressed because he has split with Rosemary over the Franchise affair, and she is afraid he won't marry a Bishop's daughter after all."

"Hooray! More power to him. I begin to like the boy. You put a few wedges into that split, Rob—casual-like—and see that he marries some nice stupid English girl who will give him five children and give the rest of the neighbourhood tennis parties between showers on Saturday afternoons. It's a much nicer kind of stupidity than standing up on platforms and holding forth on subjects you don't know the first thing about. Is this the place?"

"Yes, this is The Franchise."

"A perfect 'mystery house'."

"It wasn't a mystery house when it was built. The gates, as you can see, were scroll work—rather nice work, too—so that the whole place was visible from the road. It was the simple operation of backing the gate with the iron sheeting that converted the house from something quite ordinary to something rather secret."

"A perfect house for Betty Kane's purpose anyhow. What a piece of luck for her that she remembered it."

Robert was to feel guilty afterwards that he had not had greater faith in Marion; both over the matter of Betty Kane's statement and over the lunch. He should have remembered how cool-minded she was, how analytic; and he should have remembered the Sharpe gift for taking people as they found them and its soothing effect on the persons concerned. The Sharpes had made no effort to live up to Aunt Lin's standard of hospitality; no effort to provide a formal dining-room lunch. They had set a table for four in the window of the drawing-room where the sun fell on it. It was a cherry-wood table, very pleasant in grain but sadly needing polishing. The wine glasses, on the other hand, were polished to a diamond brilliance. (How like Marion, he thought, to concentrate on the thing that mattered and to ignore mere appearance.)

"The dining-room is an incredibly gloomy place," Mrs. Sharpe said. "Come and see it, Mr. Macdermott."

That too was typical. No sitting round with their sherry making small talk. Come and see our horrible dining-room. And the visitor was part of the household before he knew it.

"Tell me," Robert said to Marion as they were left alone, "what is this about the——"

"No, I am not going to talk about it until after lunch. It is to be your liqueur. It is a piece of the most astonishing luck that I should have thought of it last night, when Mr. Macdermott was coming to lunch today. It makes everything quite different. It won't stop the case, I suppose, but it does make everything different for us. It is the 'small thing' that I was praying for to be evidence for *us*. Have you told Mr. Macdermott?"

"About your message. No, I haven't said anything. I thought it better —not to."

"Robert!" she said looking at him with a quizzical amusement. "You didn't trust me. You were afraid I was havering."

"I was afraid you might be building more on a small foundation than —than it would hold. I——"

"Don't be afraid," she said, reassuringly. "It will hold. Would you like to come to the kitchen and carry the tray of soup for me?"

They had even managed the service without fuss or flurry. Robert carried the tray with four flat bowls of soup, and Marion came after him with a large dish under a Sheffield plate cover, and that seemed to be all. When they had drunk their soup, Marion put the large dish in front of her mother, and a bottle of wine in front of Kevin. The dish was a pot-au-feu chicken with all its vegetables round it; and the wine was a Montrachet.

"A Montrachet!" Kevin said. "You wonderful woman."

"Robert told us you were a claret lover," Marion said, "but what is left in old Mr. Crowle's cellar is long past its best. So it was a choice between that and a very heavy red burgundy that is wonderful on winter evenings but not so good with one of the Staples' fowls on a summer day."

Kevin said something about how seldom it was that women were interested in anything that did not bubble, or alternatively explode.

"To be frank," Mrs. Sharpe said, "if these parcels had been saleable we should probably have sold them, but we were exceedingly glad that they were too scrappy and varied for that. I was brought up to appreciate wine. My husband had a fairly good cellar, though his palate was not as good as mine. But my brother at Lessways had a better one, and a fine palate to match."

"Lessways?" Kevin said, and looked at her as if searching for a resemblance. "You're not Charlie Meredith's sister, are you?"

"I am. Did you know Charles? But you couldn't. You are too young."

"The first pony I ever had of my own was bred by Charlie Meredith," Kevin said. "I had him for seven years and he never put a foot wrong."

And after that, of course, both of them ceased to take any further interest in the others, and not over-much in the food.

Robert caught Marion's amused and congratulatory glance at him, and said: "You did yourself grave injustice when you said you couldn't cook."

"If you were a woman you would observe that I have not cooked anything. The soup I emptied out of a can, heated it, and added some sherry and flavouring; the fowl I put into a pot just as it came from Staples, poured some boiling water over it, added everything I could think of and left it on the stove with a prayer; the cream cheese also came from the farm."

"And the wonderful rolls to go with the cream cheese?"

"Stanley's landlady made those."

They laughed a little together, quietly.

Tomorrow she was going into the dock. Tomorrow she was going to be a public spectacle for the delight of Milford. But today her life was still her own, and she could share amusement with him; could be content with the hour. Or so it seemed if her shining eyes were any evidence.

They took the cheese plates from under the noses of the other two, who did not even pause in their conversation to remark the action, carried the trays of dirty dishes away to the kitchen and made the coffee there. It was a great gloomy place with a floor of stone slabs, and an old-fashioned sink that depressed him at sight.

"We put the range on only on Mondays when the scrubbing is done," Marion said, seeing his interest in the place. "Otherwise we cook on the little oil stove."

He thought of the hot water that ran so instantly into the shining bath when he turned the tap this morning, and was ashamed. He could hardly visualise, after his long years of soft living, an existence where one's bathing was done in water that was heated over an oil burner.

"Your friend is a charmer, isn't he," she said, pouring the hot coffee into its jug. "A little Mephistophelian—one would be terribly afraid of him as opposing counsel—but a charmer."

"It's the Irish," Robert said, gloomily. "It comes as natural to them as breathing. Us poor Saxons plod along our brutish way and wonder how they do it."

She had turned to give him the tray to carry, and so was facing him with their hands almost touching. "The Saxons have the two qualities that I value most in this world. Two qualities that explain why they have inherited the earth. Kindness and dependability—or tolerance and responsibility, if you prefer the terms. Two qualities the Celt never had; which is why the Irish have inherited nothing but squabbles. Oh damn, I forgot the cream. Wait a moment. It's keeping cold in the wash-house." She came back with the cream and said, mock rustic: "I have heard tell as how there's things called refrigerators in some folks' houses now, but we don't need none."

And as he carried the coffee to the sunlight of the drawing-room he visualised the bone-chilling cold of those kitchen quarters in winter with no roaring range as there had been in the palmy days of the house when a cook had lorded it over half a dozen servants and you ordered coal by the wagon load. He longed to take Marion away from the place. Where he would take her he did not quite know—his own home was filled with the aura of Aunt Lin. It would have to be a place where there was nothing to polish and nothing to carry and practically everything was done by pressing a button. He could not see Marion spending her old age in service to some pieces of mahogany.

As they drank their coffee he brought the conversation gently round to the possibility of their selling The Franchise at some time or other and buying a cottage somewhere.

"No one would buy the place," Marion said. "It is a white elephant. Not big enough for a school, too remote for flats, and too big for a family these days. It might make a good madhouse," she added, thoughtfully, her eyes on the high pink wall beyond the window; and Robert saw Kevin's glance flash over her and run away again. "It is quiet, at least. No trees to creak, or ivy to tap at the window-panes, or birds to go yap-yap-yap until you want to scream. It is a very peaceful place for tired nerves. Perhaps someone would consider it for that."

So she liked the silence; the stillness that had seemed to him so dead. It was perhaps what she had longed for in her London life of noise and elbowing and demands; her life of fret and cramped quarters. The big quiet ugly house had been a haven.

And now it was a haven no longer.

Some day—Oh-please-God-let-it-happen—some day he would strip Betty Kane for ever of credit and love.

"And now," Marion said, "you are invited to inspect the 'fatal attic'."

"Yes," Kevin said, "I should be greatly interested to see the things that the girl professed to identify. All her statements seemed to me the result of logical guesses. Like the harder carpet on the second flight of stairs. Or the wooden commode—something that you would almost certainly find in a country house. Or the flat-topped trunk."

"Yes, it was rather terrifying at the time, the way she kept hitting on things we had—and I hadn't had time to gather my wits—it was only afterwards I saw how little she really had identified in her statement. And she did make one complete bloomer, only no one thought of it until last night. Have you got the statement, Robert?"

"Yes." He took it out of his pocket.

They had climbed, she and Robert and Macdermott, the last bare flight of stairs and she led them into the attic. "I came up here last night on my usual Saturday tour round the house with a mop. That is our solution to the housekeeping problem, in case you are interested. A good large mop well soaked in absorbent polish-stuff run over every floor once a week. It takes five minutes per room and keeps the dust at bay."

Kevin was poking round the room, and inspecting the view from the window. "So this is the view she described," he said.

"Yes," Marion said, "that is the view she described. And if I remember the words of her statement, as I remembered them last night, correctly, then she said something that she can't—Robert, would you read the bit where she describes the view from the window?"

Robert looked up the relevant passage, and began to read. Kevin was bending slightly forward staring out of the little round window, and Marion was standing behind him, smiling faintly like a sibyl.

"'From the window of the attic,'" read Robert, "'I could see a high brick wall with a big iron gate in the middle of it. There was a road on the further side of the wall, because I could see the telegraph posts. No, I couldn't see the traffic on it because the wall was too high. Just the tops of lorry loads sometimes. You couldn't see through the gate because it had sheets of iron on the inside. Inside the gate the carriage-way went straight for a little and then divided in two into a circle up to the door. No, it wasn't a garden, just——' "

"What!" yelled Kevin, straightening himself abruptly.

"What what?" Robert asked, startled.

"Read that last bit again, that bit about the carriage-way."

" 'Inside the gate the carriage-way went straight for a little and then divided into two into a circle up to the——' "

Kevin's shout of laughter stopped him. It was an abrupt monosyllable of amused triumph.

"You see?" Marion said into the sudden silence.

"Yes," Kevin said softly, his pale bright eyes gloating on the view. "That was something she didn't reckon with."

Robert moved over as Marion gave way to let him have her place, and so saw what they were talking about. The edge of the roof with its small parapet cut off the view of the courtyard before the carriage-way branched at all. No one imprisoned in that room would know about the two half circles up to the doorway.

"You see," Marion said, "the Inspector read that description when we were all in the drawing-room. And all of us knew that the description was accurate. I mean, an accurate picture of what the courtyard is like; so we unconsciously treated it as something that was finished with. Even the Inspector. I remember his looking at the view from the window but it was quite an automatic gesture. It didn't occur to any of us that it would not have been as described. Indeed, except for one tiny detail it was as described."

"Except for one tiny detail," Kevin said. "She arrived in darkness and fled in darkness, and she says she was locked in the room all the time, so she could have known nothing of that branching drive. What does she say, again, about her arrival, Rob?"

Robert looked it up and read:

" 'The car stopped at last and the younger woman, the one with the black hair, got out and pushed open big double gates on to a drive. Then she got back in and drove the car up to a house. No, it was too dark to see what kind of a house, except that it had steps up to the door. No, I don't remember how many steps; four or five, I think. Yes, definitely a small flight of them.' And then she goes on about being taken to the kitchen for coffee."

"So," Kevin said. "And her account of her flight? What time of night was that?"

"Sometime after supper if I remember rightly," Robert said, shuffling through the pages. "After dark, anyhow. Here it is." And he read:

" 'When I got to the first landing, the one above the hall, I could hear them talking in the kitchen. There was no light in the hall. I went on down the last flight, expecting every moment that one of them would come out and catch me, and then made a dash for the door. It wasn't locked and I ran straight out and down the steps to the gate and out to the road. I ran along the road—yes, it was hard like a highroad—until I couldn't run any longer and I lay in the grass till I was feeling able to go on.' "

" 'It was hard, like a highroad,' " Kevin quoted. "The inference being that it was too dark to see the surface she was running on."

There was a short silence.

"My mother thinks that this is enough to discredit her," Marion said. She looked from Robert to Kevin, and back again, without much hope. "But you don't, do you." It was hardly a question.

"No," Kevin said. "No. Not alone. She might wriggle out of it with a clever counsel's help. Might say that she had deduced the circle from the swing of the car when she arrived. What she would normally have deduced, of course, would be the ordinary carriage sweep. No one would spontaneously think of anything as awkward as that circular drive. It makes a pretty pattern, that's all—which is probably why she remembered it. I think this tit-bit should be kept as make-weight for the Assizes."

"Yes, I thought you would say that," Marion said. "I'm not really disappointed. I was glad about it, not because I thought that it would free us of the charge, but because it frees us of the doubt that must have—must have——" She stammered unexpectedly, avoiding Robert's eyes.

"Must have muddied our crystal minds," finished Kevin, briskly; and cast a glance of pleased malice at Robert. "How did you think of this last night when you came to sweep?"

"I don't know. I stood looking out of the window, and at the view she described, and wishing that we might have just one small tiny microscopic piece of evidence on *our* side. And then, without thinking, I heard Inspector Grant's voice reading that bit in the drawing-room. Most of the story he told us in his own words, you know. But the bits that brought him to The Franchise he read in the girl's words. I heard his voice—it's a nice voice—saying the bit about the circular carriage-way, and from where I was at that moment there was no circular carriage-way. Perhaps it was an answer to unspoken prayer."

"So you still think that we had best 'give' them tomorrow and bank everything on the Assizes?" Robert said.

"Yes. It makes no difference actually to Miss Sharpe and her mother. An appearance in one place is very like an appearance in another—except that the Assizes at Norton will probably be less unpleasant than a police court in one's home town. And the shorter their appearance tomorrow the better from their point of view. You have no evidence to put before the court tomorrow, so it should be a very short and formal affair. A parade of *their* evidence, an announcement that you reserve your defence, an application for bail, and *voilà!*"

This suited Robert well enough. He did not want to prolong tomorrow's ordeal for them; he had more confidence in any case in a judgment framed outside Milford; and most of all he did not want, now that it had come to a case, a half-decision, a dismissal. That would not be sufficient for his purpose where Betty Kane was concerned. He wanted the whole story of that month told in open court, in Betty Kane's presence. And by the time the Assizes opened at Norton, he would, please God, have the story ready to tell.

"Whom can we get to defend them?" he asked Kevin as they drove home to tea.

Kevin reached into a pocket, and Robert took it for granted that what he was looking for was a list of addresses. But what he produced was obviously an engagement book.

"What is the date of the Assizes at Norton, do you know?" he asked.

Robert told him, and held his breath.

"It's just possible that I might be able to come down myself. Let me see, let me see."

Robert let him see in complete silence. One word, he felt, might ruin the magic.

"Yes," Kevin said. "I don't see why I shouldn't—short of the unforeseen. I like your witches. It would give me great pleasure to defend them against that very nasty piece of work. How odd that she should be old Charlie Meredith's sister. One of the best, the old boy was. About the only approximately honest horse-coper known in history. I have never ceased to be grateful to him for that pony. A boy's first horse is very important. It colours his whole after-life; not only his attitude to horseflesh; everything else as well. There is something in the trust and friendship that exists between a boy and a good horse that——"

Robert listened, relaxed and amused. He had realised, with a gentle irony untinged with any bitterness, that Kevin had given up any thought of the Sharpes' guilt long before the evidence of that view from the window was presented to him. It was not possible that old Charlie Meredith's sister could have abducted anyone.

CHAPTER XVII

"IT'S A PERPETUAL wonder to me," Ben Carley said, eyeing the well-populated benches in the little court, "how so many of the lieges have so little to do on a Monday morning. Though I must say it's some time since the gathering has had so much tone. Have you noticed the Sports Wear? Back row but one, in a yellow hat that doesn't go with her mauve powder *or* her hair. If she's left that little Godfrey girl in charge, she's going to be short of change tonight. I got that girl off when she was fifteen. She'd been swiping cash since she could walk and she's still swiping it. No female to be left alone with a till, believe me. And that Anne Boleyn woman. First time I've ever seen her in court. Though how she's avoided it so long I don't know. Her sister's for ever paying out cheques to cover her R.D. ones. No one's ever discovered what she does with the money. Someone blackmailing her, perhaps. I wonder who. I wouldn't put it past Arthur Wallis, at the White Hart. Three different orders to pay every week, and another on the way, just won't come out of a potman's pay."

Robert let Carley burble on without listening to him. He was only too conscious that the audience in court was not the usual Monday morning collection of loafers putting off time until they opened. The news had gone round, by the mysterious Milford channels, and they had come to see the Sharpes charged. The normal drabness of the court was gay with women's clothes; and its normal drowsy silence sibilant with their chatter.

One face he saw which should have been hostile but was oddly friendly: that of Mrs. Wynn, whom he had last seen standing in her lovely little patch of garden in Meadowside Lane, Aylesbury. He could not think of Mrs. Wynn as an enemy. He liked her, admired her, and was sorry for her in advance. He would have liked to go over and say how d'you do to her, but the game had been laid out on the squares now and they were chequers of different colour.

Grant had not appeared so far, but Hallam was there, talking to the sergeant who had come to The Franchise the night the hooligans wrecked the windows.

"How's your sleuth doing?" Carley asked, during a pause in his running commentary.

"The sleuth's all right, but the problem is colossal," Robert said. "The proverbial needle just gives itself up by comparison."

"One girl against the world," mocked Ben. "I'm looking forward to seeing this floosie in the flesh. I suppose after all the fan mail she's had, and the offers of marriage, and the resemblance to Saint Bernadette, she'll think a country police court too small an arena for her. Did she have any stage offers?"

"I wouldn't know."

"I suppose Mama would repress them anyhow. That's her there with the brown suit, and she looks a very sensible woman to me. I can't think how she ever came to have a daughter like—— Oh, but she was adopted, wasn't she? An Awful Warning. It's a constant wonder to me how little folk know about the people they live with. There was a woman over at Ham Green had a daughter that was never out of her sight as far as she knew, but daughter walked out in a pet one day and didn't come back and frantic mother goes howling to the police and police discover that the girl who has apparently never been away from mother for a night is a married woman with a child and has merely collected child and gone to live with husband. See police records if not believing Ben Carley. Ah, well, if you grow dissatisfied with your sleuth let me know and I'll give you the address of a very good one. Here we go."

He rose in deference to the Bench, while continuing a monologue on the Bench's complexion, possible temper, and probable occupation yesterday.

Three routine cases were disposed of; old offenders apparently so used to the procedure that they anticipated the drill, and Robert half expected someone to say "Wait for it, can't you!"

Then he saw Grant come in quietly and sit in an observer's position at the back of the Press bench, and he knew that the time had come.

They came in together when their names were called, and took their places in the horrid little pew as if they were merely taking their places in church. It *was* rather like that, he thought: the quiet, and observant eyes, and the suggestion of waiting for a performance to begin. But he suddenly realised what he would be feeling if it were Aunt Lin in Mrs. Sharpe's place, and was fully aware for the first time of what Marion must be suffering on her mother's behalf. Even if the Assizes saw them cleared of the charge, what would compensate them for what they had endured? What punishment fit Betty Kane's crime?

For Robert, being old-fashioned, believed in retribution. He might not go all the way with Moses—an eye was not always compensation for an eye—but he certainly agreed with Gilbert: the punishment should fit the crime. He certainly did not believe that a few quiet talks with the chaplain and a promise to reform made a criminal into a respect-worthy citizen. "Your true criminal," he remembered Kevin saying one night, after a long discussion on penal reform, "has two unvarying characteristics, and it is these two characteristics which make him a criminal. Monstrous vanity and colossal selfishness. And they are both as integral, as ineradicable, as the texture of the skin. You might as well talk of 'reforming' the colour of one's eyes."

"But," someone had objected, "there have been monsters of vanity and selfishness who were not criminal."

"Only because they have victimised their wives instead of their bank," Kevin had pointed out. "Tomes have been written trying to define the criminal, but it is a very simple definition after all. The criminal is a person who makes the satisfaction of his own immediate personal wants the mainspring of his actions. You can't cure him of his egotism, but you can make the indulgence of it not worth his while. Or almost not worth his while."

Kevin's idea of prison reform, Robert remembered, was deportation to a penal colony. An island community where everyone worked hard.

This was not a reform for the benefit of the prisoners. It would be a nicer life for the warders, Kevin said; and would leave more room in this crowded island for good citizens' houses and gardens; and since most criminals hated hard work more than they hated anything in this world, it would be a better deterrent than the present plan which, in Kevin's estimation, was no more punitive than a third-rate public school.

Looking at the two figures in the dock Robert thought that in the "bad old days" only the guilty were put in the pillory. Nowadays, it was the untried who bore the pillory and the guilty went immediately into a safe obscurity. Something had gone wrong somewhere.

Old Mrs. Sharpe was wearing the flat black satin hat in which she had appeared at his office on the morning of the *Ack-Emma* irruption into their affairs, and looked academic, respectable, but odd. Marion too was wearing a hat—less, he supposed, out of deference to the court than as some protection against the public gaze. It was a country felt, with a short brim; and its orthodoxy lessened to some extent her normal air of being a law unto herself. With her black hair hidden and her brilliant eyes shadowed she looked no swarthier than a normal out-of-doors woman might. And though Robert missed the black hair and the brilliance he thought that it was all to the good that she should look as "ordinary" as possible. It might lessen the pecking-to-death instinct in her hostile fellows.

And then he saw Betty Kane.

It was the stir on the Press bench that told him she was in court. Normally the Press bench was occupied by two bored apprentices in the art of reporting: one for the *Milford Advertiser* (once weekly, on Fridays) and one combining the *Norton Courier* (twice weekly, Tuesdays and Fridays) with the *Larborough Times* and anyone else who would take the stuff. But today the Press bench was filled, and the faces there were neither young nor bored. They were the faces of men invited to a meal and quite ready for it.

And Betty Kane was two-thirds of what they had come for.

Robert had not seen her since she stood in the drawing-room at The Franchise in her dark blue school coat, and he was surprised all over again by her youth and her candid innocence. In the weeks since he had first seen her she had grown into a monster in his mind; he thought of her only as the perverted creature who had lied two human beings into the dock. Now, seeing the actual physical Betty Kane again, he was nonplussed. He *knew* that this girl and his monster were one, but he found it difficult to realise. And if he, who felt that he now knew Betty Kane so well, reacted like that to her presence, what effect would her childlike grace have on good men and true when the time came?

She was wearing "week-end" clothes, not her school things. A cloudy blue outfit that made one think of forget-me-nots and wood-smoke and bluebells and summer distances, and was further calculated to bedevil the judgment of sober men. Her young and simple and very-well-brought-up hat stood back from her face and showed the charming brow and the wide-set eyes. Robert absolved Mrs. Wynn, without even having to consider the matter, from any conscious dressing of the girl for the occasion, but was bitterly aware that if she had lain awake at nights devising the outfit it could not have served its purpose better.

When her name was called and she walked to the witness stand, he stole a glance at the faces of those who could see her clearly. With the sole exception of Ben Carley—who was looking at her with the interest one accords a museum exhibit—there was only one expression on the faces of the men: a sort of affectionate compassion. The women, he observed, had not surrendered so easily. The more motherly ones obviously yearned to her youth and her vulnerability, but the younger ones were merely avid; without emotion other than curiosity.

"I—don't—believe—it!" Ben said, *sotto voce*, while she was taking the oath. "You mean that child was on the loose for a month? I don't believe she's ever kissed anything but the book!"

"I'll bring witnesses to prove it," muttered Robert, angry that even the worldly and cynical Carley was succumbing.

"You could bring ten irreproachable witnesses and still not get a jury to believe it; and it's the jury who count, my friend."

Yes, what jury would believe any bad of her!

Watching her as she was led through her story, he reminded himself of Albert's account of her: the "nicely brought-up girl" whom no one would have thought of as a woman at all, and the cool expertness with which she attached the man she had chosen.

She had a very pleasant voice; young and light and clear; without accent or affectation. And she told her tale like a model witness; volunteering no extras, explicit in what she did say. The pressmen could hardly keep their eyes on their shorthand. The Bench was obviously doting. (God send there was something tougher at the Assizes!) The members of the police force were gently perspiring in sympathy. The body of the court breathless and motionless.

No actress had ever had a better reception.

She was quite calm, as far as anyone could see; and apparently unaware of the effect she was having. She made no effort to make a point, or to use a piece of information dramatically. And Robert found himself wondering whether the understatement was deliberate and whether she realised quite clearly how effective it was.

"And did you in fact mend the linen?"

"I was too stiff from the beating, that night. But I mended some later."

Just as if she were saying: "I was too busy playing bridge." It gave an extraordinary air of truth to what she said.

Nor was there any sign of triumph in the account of her vindication. She had said this and that about the place of her imprisonment, and this and that had proved to be so. But she showed no overt pleasure in the fact. When she was asked if she recognised the women in the dock, and if they were in fact the women who had detained and beaten her, she looked at them gravely for a moment of silence and then said that she did and they were.

"Do you want to examine, Mr. Blair?"

"No, sir. I have no questions."

This caused a slight stir of surprise and disappointment in the body of the court, who had looked forward to drama; but it was accepted by the initiates without remark; it was taken for granted that the case would go forward to another court.

Hallam had already given his statement, and the girl was now followed by the corroborative witnesses.

The man who had seen her picked up by the car proved to be a Post Office sorter called Piper. He worked on a postal van which the L.M.S. ran between Larborough and London, and he was dropped off at Mainshill station on the return journey because it was near his home. He was walking up the long straight London road through Mainshill, when he noticed that a young girl was waiting at the stop for the London coaches. He was still a long distance from her but he noticed her because the London coach had overtaken him about half a minute previously, before he had come within sight of the bus-stop; and when he saw her waiting there he realised that she must just have missed it. While he was walking towards her but still some distance away, a car overtook him at a good pace. He did not even glance at it because his interest was concentrated on the girl and on whether when he came up with her he should stop and tell her that the London bus had passed. Then he saw the car slow down alongside the girl. She bent forward to talk to whoever was in it, and then got in herself and was driven away.

By this time he was near enough to describe the car but not to read the number. He had not thought of reading the number anyhow. He was merely glad that the girl had got a lift so quickly.

He would not take an oath that the girl in question was the girl he had seen give evidence, but he was certain in his own mind. She had worn a palish coat and hat—grey he thought—and black slippers.

Slippers?

Well, those shoes with no straps across the instep.

Court shoes.

Well, court shoes, but he called them slippers. (And had every intention, his tone made it clear, of going on calling them slippers.)

"Do you want to examine, Mr. Blair?"

"No, thank you, sir."

Then came Rose Glyn.

Robert's first impression was of the vulgar perfection of her teeth. They reminded him of a false set made by a not very clever dentist. There surely never had been, never could be, any natural teeth as flashily perfect as those Rose Glyn had produced as substitutes for her milk teeth.

The Bench did not like her teeth either, it seemed, and Rose soon stopped smiling. But her tale was lethal enough. She had been in the habit of going to The Franchise every Monday to clean the house. On a Monday in April she had been there as usual, and was preparing to leave in the evening when she heard screaming coming from upstairs somewhere. She thought something had happened to Mrs. or Miss Sharpe and ran to the foot of the stairs to see. The screaming seemed to be far away, as if it came from the attic. She was going to go upstairs, but Mrs. Sharpe came out of the drawing-room and asked her what she was doing. She said someone was screaming upstairs. Mrs. Sharpe said nonsense, that she was imagining things, and wasn't it time that she was going home. The screaming had stopped then, and while Mrs. Sharpe was talking Miss Sharpe came downstairs. Miss Sharpe went with Mrs. Sharpe into the drawing-room, and Mrs. Sharpe said something about "ought to be more careful." She was frightened, she did not quite know why, and went away to the kitchen and took her money from where it was always left for her on the kitchen mantelpiece, and ran from the house. The date was April the 15th. She remembered the date because she had decided that next time she went back, on the following Monday, she would give the Sharpes her week's notice; and she had in fact done that, and had not worked for the Sharpes since Monday April the 29th.

Robert was faintly cheered by the bad impression she was patently making on everyone. Her open delight in the dramatic, her Christmas Supplement glossiness, her obvious malice, and her horrible clothes, were unhappily contrasted with the restraint and good sense and good taste of her predecessor in the witness box. From the expressions on the faces of her audience she was summed up as a slut and no one would trust her with sixpence.

But that did nothing to discount the evidence she had just given on oath.

Robert, letting her go, wondered if there was any way of pinning that watch on her, so to speak. Being a country girl, unversed in the ways of pawnshops, it was unlikely that she had stolen that watch to sell it; she had taken it to keep for herself. That being so, was there perhaps some way of convicting her of theft and so discrediting her evidence to that extent?

She was succeeded by her friend Gladys Rees. Gladys was as small and pale and skinny as her friend was opulent. She was scared and ill at ease, and took the oath hesitatingly. Her accent was so broad that even the Court found difficulty in following her, and the prosecution had several times to translate her wilder flights of English into something nearer common speech. But the gist of her evidence was clear. On the evening of Monday the 15th April she had gone walking with her friend,

Rose Glyn. No, not anywhere special, just walking after supper. Up to High Wood and back. And Rose Glyn had told her that she was scared of The Franchise because she had heard someone screaming in an upstairs room, although there was supposed not to be anyone there. She, Gladys, knew that it was Monday the 15th that Rose had told her that, because Rose had said that when she went next week she was going to give notice. And she had given notice and had not worked for the Sharpes since Monday the 29th.

"I wonder what dear Rose has got on her," Carley said, as she left the witness box.

"What makes you think she has anything?"

"People don't come and perjure themselves for friendship; not even country morons like Gladys Rees. The poor silly little rat was frightened stiff. She would never have come voluntarily. No, that oleograph has a lever of some sort. Worth looking into if you're stuck, perhaps."

"Do you happen to know the number of your watch?" he asked Marion as he was driving them back to The Franchise. "The one Rose Glyn stole."

"I didn't even know that watches had numbers," Marion said.

"Good ones do."

"Oh, mine was a good one, but I don't know anything about its number. It was very distinctive, though. It had a pale blue enamel face with gold figures."

"Roman figures?"

"Yes. Why do you ask? Even if I got it back I could never bear to wear it after that girl."

"It wasn't so much getting it back I thought of, as convicting her of having taken it."

"That would be nice."

"Ben Carley calls her 'the oleograph,' by the way."

"How lovely. That is just what she is like. Is that the little man you wanted to push us off on to, that first day?"

"That's the one."

"I am so glad that I refused to be pushed."

"I hope you will still be as glad when this case is over," Robert said, suddenly sober.

"We have not yet thanked you for standing surety for our bail," Mrs. Sharpe said from the back of the car.

"If we began to thank him for all we owe him," Marion said, "there would be no end to it."

Except, he thought, that he had enlisted Kevin Macdermott on their side—and that was an accident of friendship—what had he been able to do for them? They would go for trial at Norton little more than a fortnight hence, and they had no defence whatever.

CHAPTER XVIII

THE NEWSPAPERS HAD a field-day on Tuesday.

Now that the Franchise affair was a court case, it could no longer provide a crusade for either the *Ack-Emma* or the *Watchman*—though the *Ack-Emma* did not fail to remind its gratified readers that on such and such a date *they* had said so and so, a plain statement which was on the surface innocent and unexceptionable but was simply loaded with the forbidden comment; and Robert had no doubt that on Friday the *Watchman* would be taking similar credit to itself, with similar discretion. But the rest of the Press, who had not so far taken any interest in a case that the police had no intention of touching, woke with a glad shout to report a case that was news. Even the soberer dailies held accounts of the court appearance of the Sharpes, with headings like: EXTRAORDINARY CASE, and: UNUSUAL CHARGE. The less inhibited had full descriptions of the principal actors in the case, including Mrs. Sharpe's hat and Betty Kane's blue outfit, pictures of The Franchise, the High Street in Milford, a school friend of Betty Kane, and anything else that was even approximately relevant.

And Robert's heart sank. Both the *Ack-Emma* and the *Watchman*, in their different ways, had used the Franchise affair as a stunt. Something to be used for its momentary worth and dropped tomorrow. But now it was a national interest, reported by every kind of paper from Cornwall to Caithness; and showed signs of becoming a *cause célèbre*.

For the first time he had a feeling of desperation. Events were hounding him, and he had no refuge. The thing was beginning to pile up into a tremendous climax at Norton and he had nothing to contribute to that climax; nothing at all. He felt as a man might feel if he saw a stacked heap of loaded crates begin to lean over towards him and had neither retreat nor a prop to stay the avalanche.

Ramsden grew more and more monosyllabic on the telephone, and less and less encouraging. Ramsden was sore. "Baffled" was a word used in boys' detective stories; it had not until now had even the remotest connection with Alec Ramsden. So Ramsden was sore, monosyllabic, and dour.

The one bright spot in the days that followed the court at Milford was provided by Stanley, who tapped on his door on Thursday morning, poked his head in, and seeing that Robert was alone came in, pushing the door to with one hand and fishing in the pocket of his dungarees with the other.

"Morning," he said. "I think you ought to take charge of these. Those women at The Franchise have no sense at all. They keep pound notes in tea-pots and books and what not. If you're looking for a telephone number you're as likely as not to find a ten-shilling note marking the butcher's address." He fished out a roll of money and solemnly counted twelve ten-pound notes on to the desk under Robert's nose.

"A hundred and twenty," he said. "Nice, ain't it?"

"But what *is* it?" Robert asked, bewildered.

"Kominsky."

"Kominsky?"

"Don't tell me you didn't have anything on! After the old lady giving us the tip herself. Mean to say you *forgot* about it!"

"Stan, I haven't even remembered lately that there was such a thing as the Guineas. So you backed it?"

"At sixties. And that's the tenth I told her she was on to, for the tip."

"But—a tenth? You must have been plunging, Stan."

"Twenty pounds. Twice as much as my normal ceiling. Bill did a bit of good too. Going to give his missus a fur coat."

"So Kominsky won."

"Won by a length and a half on a tight rein; and was that a turn up for the book!"

"Well," Robert said, stacking the notes and banding them, "if the worst comes to the worst and they end up bankrupt, the old lady can always do a fair trade as a tipster."

Stanley eyed his face for a moment in silence, apparently not happy about something in his tone. "Things are pretty bad, 'm?" he said.

"Fierce," said Robert, using one of Stanley's own descriptions.

"Bill's missus went to the court," Stan said, after a pause. "She said she wouldn't believe that girl even if she told her there were twelve pennies in a shilling."

"Oh?" Robert said, surprised. "Why?"

"Much too good to be true, she said she was. She said no girl of fifteen was ever as good as that."

"She's sixteen now."

"All right, sixteen. She said she was fifteen once and so were all her girl friends, and that wide-eyed-wonder didn't fool her for a moment."

"I'm very much afraid it will fool a jury."

"Not if you had an all-woman jury. I suppose there's no way of wangling that?"

"Not short of Herod measures. Don't you want to give this money to Mrs. Sharpe yourself, by the way?"

"Not me. You'll be going out there sometime today, and you can give it to her if you like. But see you get it back and put it in the bank or they'll be picking it out of flower vases years hence and wondering when they put that there."

Robert smiled as he put the money away in his pocket to the sound of Stanley's departing feet. Endlessly unexpected, people were. He would have taken it for granted that Stan would have revelled in counting those notes out in front of the old lady. But instead he had turned shy. That tale of money in tea-pots was just a tale.

Robert took the money out to The Franchise in the afternoon, and for the first time saw tears in Marion's eyes. He told the tale as Stanley had told it—tea-pots and all—and finished: "So he made me his deputy"; and it was then that Marion's eyes had filled.

"Why did he mind about giving it to us?" she said, fingering the notes. "He's not usually so—so——"

"I think it may be that he considers that you need it now, and that that makes it a delicate affair instead of a matter-of-fact one. When you gave him the tip you were just the well-off Sharpes who lived at The Franchise, and he would have turned over the proceeds to you with éclat. But now you are two women out on bail of £200 each in your personal recognizances and of a similar sum by one surety on behalf of you each; to say nothing of having the expenses of a counsel to come; and are therefore, I think, in Stan's mind not people that one can hand over money to easily."

"Well," said Mrs. Sharpe, "not all my tips have had a margin of a length-and-a-half on the right side. But I don't deny that I am very glad to see the percentage. It was very kind of the boy."

"Should we keep as much as ten per cent?" Marion asked doubtfully.

"That was the arrangement," Mrs. Sharpe said equably. "If it hadn't been for me he would be short by the amount of a bet on Bali Boogie at this moment. What *is* a Bali Boogie, by the way?"

"I am glad you came," Marion said, ignoring her mother's quest for education, "because something unexpected has happened. My watch has come back."

"You mean you've found it?"

"No, oh, no. She sent it back through the post. Look!"

She produced a small, very dirty, white cardboard box, which contained her watch with the blue enamel face and the wrapping that had been round the watch. The wrapping was a square of pinkish tissue paper with a circular stamp reading SUN VALLEY, TRANSVAAL, and had evidently started life embracing an orange. On a torn piece of paper was printed: I DON'T WANT NONE OF IT. The capital I was dotted like a small letter, after the fashion of illiterates.

"Why do you think she turned squeamish about it?" Marion wondered.

"I don't for a moment think she did," Robert said. "I couldn't imagine that girl ever relinquishing anything that her hand had closed over."

"But she did. She sent it back."

"No. Someone sent it back. Someone who was frightened. Someone with a rudimentary conscience, too. If Rose Glyn had wanted to be rid of it she would have thrown it into a pond, without a second thought.

But X wants to be rid of it and to make restitution at the same time. X has both a bad conscience and a frightened soul. Now who would have a bad conscience about you just now? Gladys Rees?"

"Yes, of course you are right about Rose. I should have thought of that. She never would have sent it back. She would have put her heel on it sooner. You think perhaps she gave it to Gladys Rees?"

"That might explain a lot. It might explain how Rose got her to court to back up that 'screaming' story. I mean, if she had been the receiver of stolen goods. When you come to think of it, Rose could have very little chance of wearing a watch that the Staples people must quite often have seen on your wrist. It is much more likely that she was 'large' with it in favour of her friend. 'A little thing I picked up.' Where does the Rees girl belong to?"

"I don't know where she belongs to; somewhere the other side of the county, I think. But she has come to work for that isolated farm beyond Staples."

"Long ago?"

"I don't know. I don't think so."

"So she could wear a new watch without question. Yes, I think it was Gladys who sent back your watch. If ever there was an unwilling witness it was Gladys on Monday. And if Gladys is shakeable to the point of sending back your property, a faint hope begins to dawn."

"But she has committed perjury," Mrs. Sharpe said. "Even a moron like Gladys Rees must have some glimmering of awareness that that is not well seen in a British court."

"She could plead that she was blackmailed into it. If someone suggested that course to her."

Mrs. Sharpe eyed him. "Isn't there anything in English law about tampering with a witness?" she asked.

"Plenty. But I don't propose to do any tampering."

"What do you propose to do?"

"I must think it over. It is a delicate situation."

"Mr. Blair, the intricacies of the Law have always been beyond me, and are always likely to be, but you won't get yourself put away for contempt of court, or something like that, will you? I can't imagine what the present situation would be like without your support."

Robert said that he had no intention of getting himself put away for anything. That he was a blameless solicitor of unblemished reputation and high moral principles and that she need have no fear either for herself or for him.

"If we could knock the prop of Gladys Rees from under Rose's story it would undermine their whole case," he said. "It's their most valuable piece of evidence: that Rose had mentioned the screaming before there was any suggestion of a charge against you. I suppose you couldn't see Grant's face when Rose was giving evidence? A fastidious mind must be a great handicap in the C.I.D. It must be sad to have your whole case depend on someone you would hate to touch with a barge-pole. Now I must be getting back. May I take the little cardboard box and the scrap of paper with the printing?"

"It was clever of you to have seen that Rose would not have sent it back," Marion said, putting the scrap of paper into the box and giving it to him. "You should have been a detective."

"Either that or a fortune-teller. Everything deduced from the egg-stain on the waistcoat. *Au revoir.*"

Robert drove back to Milford with his mind full of this new possibility. It was no solution to their predicament, but it might be a lifeline.

In the office he found Mr. Ramsden waiting for him; long, grey, lean, and dour.

"I came to see you, Mr. Blair, because it wasn't a thing that could be said over the telephone very well."

"Well?"

"Mr. Blair, we're wasting your money. Do you happen to know what the white population of the world is?"

"No, I don't."

"Neither do I. But what you're asking me to do is to pick this girl out of the white population of the world. Five thousand men working for a year mightn't do it. One man might do it tomorrow. It's a matter of pure chance."

"But it always has been that."

"No. In the first days the chances were fair. We covered the obvious places. The ports, the airports, the travel places, the best known 'honeymoon' places. And I didn't waste your time or money in any travelling. I have contacts in all the big towns and in a lot of the smaller ones, and I just send them a request saying: 'Find out if such and such a person stayed at one of your hotels,' and the answer is back in a few hours. Answers from all over Britain. Well, that done, we are left with a small proposition called the rest of the world. And I don't like wasting your money, Mr. Blair. Because that is what it will amount to."

"Do I understand that you are giving up?"

"I don't put it like that, exactly."

"You think I should give you notice because you have failed."

Mr. Ramsden stiffened noticeably at the word "failed."

"It's throwing good money away on a long chance. It isn't a business proposition, Mr. Blair. It isn't even a good gamble."

"Well, I have something for your consideration that is definite enough to please you, I think." He fished the little cardboard box out of his pocket. "One of the witnesses on Monday was a girl called Gladys Rees. Her role was to supply evidence that her friend Rose Glyn had talked to her about screams at The Franchise long before the police were interested in the place. Well, she supplied the evidence all right, but not *con amore,* as you might say. She was nervous, unwilling, and was obviously hating it—in contrast to her friend Rose who was having the time of her life. One of my local colleagues suggested that Rose had got her there by pressure, but that didn't seem very likely at the time. This morning, however, the watch that Rose stole from Miss Sharpe came back by post in this box, with the printed message enclosed. Now Rose would never have bothered to return the watch; she has no conscience at all. Nor would she have written the note; having no desire to repudiate anything. The conclusion is inescapable, that it was Gladys who received the watch—Rose could not have worn it without detection anyhow—and that that was how Rose got her to back up her lies."

He paused to let Ramsden comment. Mr. Ramsden nodded; but it was an interested nod.

"Now we can't approach Gladys with any kind of argument without being accused of intimidating witnesses. I mean, getting her to go back on her story before the Assizes is not possible. All we can do is to concentrate on breaking her down at the Assizes. Kevin Macdermott could probably do it by force of personality and persistent questions, but I doubt it; and anyhow the Court might stop him before he had achieved anything. They are apt to look sideways on him when he begins to ride a witness."

"They are?"

"What I want to do is to be able to put this printed scrap into court as evidence. To be able to say that it is Gladys Rees's writing. With the evidence that it was she who had the stolen watch, we make the suggestion that Rose used pressure on her to testify to what is not true, Macdermott assures her that if she was blackmailed into giving false evidence she will probably not be punished for it, and she breaks down and confesses."

"So you want another specimen of Gladys Rees's printing."

"Yes. And coming along just now I was thinking about it. I have the impression that her present job is her first one, so it can't be very long since she left school. Perhaps her school could furnish one. Or anyhow, provide a starting-off place. It would be enormously to our advantage if we could come by a specimen without *provocateur* methods. Do you think you could do something about it?"

"I'll get you a specimen, yes," Ramsden said; as who should say: Give me any reasonable commission and it will be executed. "Did the Rees girl go to school here?"

"No, I understand she comes from the other side of the county."

"All right, I'll find out. Where is she working now?"

"At an isolated place called Bratt's Farm; over the fields from Staples, the place behind The Franchise."

"And about the search for the Kane girl——"

"Isn't there anything you could still do in Larborough itself? I can't teach you anything about your business, I know that, but she *was* in Larborough."

"Yes, and where she was we traced her. In public places. But X may *live* in Larborough, for all we know. She may just have gone to ground there. After all, a month—or practically a month—is an odd time for that sort of disappearance, Mr. Blair. That sort of thing usually ranges from a week-end to ten days but not longer. She may just have gone home with him."

"Do you think that is what happened?"

"No," Ramsden said slowly. "If you want my honest opinion, Mr. Blair, it is that we have missed her at one of the exits."

"Exits?"

"That she went out of the country, but looking so different that that butter-wouldn't-melt photograph didn't convey her at all."

"Why different?"

"Well, I don't suppose she was provided with a phoney passport, so she would presumably travel as his wife."

"Yes, of course. I took that for granted."

"And she couldn't do that looking as she does. But with her hair swept up and some make-up on, she would look quite different. You have no idea the difference sweeping-up hair-dressing makes to a woman. The first time I saw my wife with one I didn't recognise her. It made her so different, if you want to know, that I felt quite shy with her; and we'd been married twenty years."

"So that's what you think happened. I expect you're right," Robert said sadly.

"That's why I don't want to waste any more of your money, Mr. Blair. Looking for the girl in the photograph is not much use, because the girl we're looking for didn't look a bit like that. When she *did* look like that, people recognised her at first glance. At the cinemas and what not. We traced her easily enough during her time on her own in Larborough. But from then on it's a complete blank. Her photograph doesn't convey her to anyone who saw her after she left Larborough."

Robert sat doodling on Miss Tuff's nice fresh blotting-paper. A herring-bone pattern; very neat and decorative. "You see what this means, don't you? We are sunk."

"But you have this," Ramsden protested, indicating the printed scrap of paper that had come with the watch.

"That merely destroys the police case. It doesn't disprove Betty Kane's story. If the Sharpes are ever to be rid of this thing the girl's story has to be shown to be nonsense. Our only chance of doing that is to find out where she was during those weeks."

"Yes. I see."

"I suppose you have checked on private owners?"

"Planes? Oh, yes. The same thing goes there. We have no photograph of the man, so he might be any one of the hundreds of private owners who went abroad with female companions in the specified time."

"Yes. Pretty well sunk. Not much wonder Ben Carley was amused."

"You're tired, Mr. Blair. You've been having a worrying time."

"Yes. It isn't very often a country solicitor has something like this dumped on his shoulders," Robert said wryly.

Ramsden regarded him with what amounted on the Ramsden visage to a smile. "For a country solicitor," he said, "it seems to me you're not doing badly, Mr. Blair. Not badly at all."

"Thanks," Robert said, really smiling. Coming from Alec Ramsden that was practically an O.M.

"I shouldn't let it get you down. You've got an insurance against the very worst happening—or will, when I get that printed evidence."

Robert flung down the pen he had been doodling with. "I'm not interested in insurance," he said with sudden heat. "I'm interested in justice. I have only one ambition in life at this moment. And that is to have Betty Kane's story disproved in open court. To have the full account of what she did during those weeks made public in her presence and duly backed up by irreproachable witnesses. What are our chances of that, do you think? And what—tell me—what have we left untried that could possibly help us?"

"I don't know," Mr. Ramsden said, seriously. "Prayer, perhaps."

CHAPTER XIX

THIS, ODDLY ENOUGH, was also Aunt Lin's reaction.

Aunt Lin had become gradually reconciled to Robert's connection with the Franchise affair as it moved from the provincial-unsavoury to the national-celebrated. It was, after all, no disgrace to be connected with a case that was reported in *The Times*. Aunt Lin did not, of course, read *The Times*, but her friends did. The vicar, and old Colonel Whittaker, and the girl at Boots and old Mrs. Warren from Weymouth (Swanage); and it was vaguely gratifying to think that Robert should be solicitor for the defence in a famous trial, even if the defence was against a charge of beating a helpless girl. And of course it had never even remotely shadowed her mind that Robert would not win the case. She had taken that quite placidly for granted. In the first place Robert himself was so clever; and in the second Blair, Hayward, and Bennet could not conceivably be connected with a failure. She had even regretted in her own mind, in passing, that his triumph would take place over at Norton and not in Milford where everyone might be there to see.

So that the first hint of doubt came as a surprise to her. Not a shock, since she still could not visualise the prospect of failure. But definitely as a new thought.

"But, Robert," she said, sweeping her foot round under the table in an effort to locate her footstool, "you don't suppose for a moment that you are going to *lose* the case, do you?"

"On the contrary," Robert said, "I don't suppose for a moment that we shall win it."

"Robert!"

"In trial by jury it is customary to have a case to put to the jury. So far we have no case. And I don't think that the jury is going to like that at all."

"You sound quite pettish, dear. I think you are allowing the thing to get on your nerves. Why don't you take tomorrow afternoon off and arrange a golf four? You have hardly golfed at all lately and it can't be good for your liver. Not golfing, I mean."

"I can't believe," Robert said wonderingly, "that I was ever interested in the fate of 'a piece of gutta-percha' on a golf-course. That must have been in some other life."

"That is what I say, dear. You are losing your sense of proportion. Allowing this affair to worry you quite unnecessarily. After all, you have Kevin."

"That I take leave to doubt."

"What do you mean, dear?"

"I can't imagine Kevin taking time off and travelling down to Norton to defend a case that he is fore-ordained to lose. He has his quixotic moments, but they don't entirely obliterate his common sense."

"But Kevin promised to come."

"When he made that promise there was still time for a defence to materialise. Now we can almost count the days to the Assizes and still we have no evidence—and no prospect of any."

Miss Bennet eyed him over her soup spoon. "I don't think, you know, dear," she said, "that you have enough faith."

Robert refrained from saying that he had none at all. Not, anyhow, where divine intervention in the Franchise affair was concerned.

"Have faith, my dear," she said happily, "and it will all come right. You'll see." The charged silence that succeeded this evidently worried her a little, for she added: "If I had known you were doubtful or unhappy about the case, dear, I should have said extra prayers about it long ago. I am afraid I took it for granted that you and Kevin would manage it between you." "It" being British justice. "But now that I know you are worrying about it I shall most certainly put up some special petitions."

The matter-of-fact application-for-relief tone with which this was uttered restored Robert's good humour.

"Thank you, darling," he said in his normal good-natured voice.

She laid the spoon down on her empty plate and sat back; and a small teasing smile appeared on her round pink face. "I know that tone," she said. "It means that you're humouring me. But there's no need to, you know. It's I who am right about this, and you are wrong. It says quite distinctly that faith will move mountains. The difficulty always is that it takes a quite colossal faith to move a mountain; and it is practically impossible to assemble so large a faith, so mountains are practically never moved. But in lesser cases—like the present one—it is possible to have enough faith for the occasion. So instead of being deliberately hopeless, dear, do *try* to have some confidence in the event. Meanwhile I shall go along to St. Matthew's this evening and spend a little time praying that you will be given a piece of evidence tomorrow morning. That will make you feel happier."

When Alec Ramsden walked into his room next morning with the piece of evidence, Robert's first thought was that nothing could prevent Aunt Lin taking credit for it. Nor was there any hope of his not mentioning it, since the first thing she would ask him at luncheon, in bright confident tones, would be: "Well, dear, did you get the evidence I prayed for?"

Ramsden was both pleased with himself and amused; so much could be translated, at any rate, from the Ramsden idiom into common knowledge.

"I had better confess frankly, Mr. Blair, that when you sent me to that school I had no great hopes. I went because it seemed to be as good a starting-place as any, and I might find out from the staff some good way of getting acquainted with Rees. Or rather, letting one of my boys get acquainted. I had even worked out how we could get printed letters from her without any fuss, once one of my boys got off with her. But you're a wonder, Mr. Blair. You had the right idea after all."

"You mean you've got what we wanted!"

"I saw her form mistress, and was quite frank about what we wanted and why. Well, as frank as need be. I said Gladys was suspected of perjury—a penal servitude affair—but that we thought she'd been blackmailed into giving her evidence, and to prove it was blackmail we needed a sample of any printed letters she ever wrote. Well, when you sent me there I took it for granted that she would not have printed a single letter since she left the kindergarten. But the form mistress—a Miss Baggaly—said to give her a minute to think. 'Of course,' she said, 'she was very good at drawing, and if I have nothing perhaps the visiting art-mistress might have something. We like to keep good work when our pupils produce it.' As a comfort for all the duds they have to put up with, I suppose, poor things. Well, I didn't have to see the art-mistress, because Miss Baggaly hunted through some things, and produced this."

He laid a sheet of paper down on the desk in front of Robert. It appeared to be a free-hand map of Canada, showing the principal divisions, towns and rivers. It was inaccurate but very neat. Across the bottom was printed DOMINION OF CANADA. And in the right-hand corner was the signature: Gladys Rees.

"It seems that every summer, at breaking-up time, they have an exhibition of work, and they normally keep the exhibits until the next exhibition the following year. I suppose it would seem too callous just to toss them out the day after. Or perhaps they keep them to show to visiting big-wigs and inspectors. Anyhow, there were drawers full of the stuff. This," he indicated the map, "was a product of a competition—'Draw a map of any country from memory in twenty minutes'—and the three prize winners had their answers exhibited. This was a 'third equal'."

"I can hardly believe it," Robert said, feasting his eyes on Gladys Rees's handiwork.

"Miss Baggaly was right about her being good with her hands. Funny, when she stayed so illiterate. You can see where they corrected her dotted Capital I's."

You could indeed. Robert was gloating over the place.

"She has no mind, the girl, but a good eye," he said, considering Gladys's idea of Canada. "She remembered the shape of things but not the names. And the spelling is entirely her own. I suppose the 'third equal' was for the neat work."

"Neat work for us anyhow," Ramsden said, laying down the scrap of paper that had come with the watch. "Let us be thankful she didn't choose Alaska."

"Yes," Robert said. "A miracle." (Aunt Lin's miracle, his mind said.) "Who is the best man at this sort of thing?"

Ramsden told him.

"I'll take it up to town with me now, tonight, and have the report before morning, and I'll take it round to Mr. Macdermott at breakfast time, if that's all right with you."

"Right?" said Robert. "It's perfect."

"I think it might be a good idea to fingerprint them too—and the little cardboard box. There *are* judges who don't like handwriting experts, but the two together would convince even a judge."

"Well," Robert said, handing them over, "at least my clients are not going to be sentenced to hard labour."

"There's nothing like looking on the bright side," Ramsden commented dryly; and Robert laughed.

"You think I'm ungrateful for such a dispensation. I'm not. It's a terrific load off my mind. But the real load is still there. Proving that Rose Glyn is a thief, liar, and blackmailer—with perjury thrown in as a sideline—leaves Betty Kane's story still untouched. And it is Betty Kane's story that we set out to disprove."

"There's still time," Ramsden said; but half-heartedly.

"About all there is time for is a miracle."

"Well? Why not? They happen. Why shouldn't they happen to us? What time shall I telephone you tomorrow?"

But it was Kevin who telephoned on the morrow; full of congratulations and jubilation. "You're a marvel, Rob. I'll make mincemeat of them."

Yes, it would be a lovely little exercise in cat-and-mouse play for Kevin; and the Sharpes would walk out of the court "free." Free to go back to their haunted house and their haunted existence; two half-mad witches who had once threatened and beaten a girl.

"You don't sound very gay, Rob. Is it getting you down?"

Robert said what he was thinking; that the Sharpes saved from prison would still be in a prison of Betty Kane's making.

"Perhaps not, perhaps not," Kevin said. "I'll do my best with the Kane over that howler about the divided path. Indeed, if Miles Allison weren't prosecuting I could probably break her with it; but Miles will probably be quick enough to retrieve the situation. Cheer up, Rob. At the very least her credit will be seriously shaken."

But shaking Betty Kane's credit was not enough. He knew just how little effect that would have on the general public. He had had a large experience lately of the woman-in-the-street, and had been appalled by the general inability to analyse the simplest statement. Even if the newspapers were to report that small bit about the view from the window—and they would probably be much too busy reporting the more sensational matter of Rose Glyn's perjury—even if they reported it, it would have no effect on the average reader. "They tried to put her in the wrong but they were very quickly put in their place." That is all it would convey to them.

Kevin might successfully shake Betty Kane's credit with the Court, the reporters, the officials, and any critical minds who happened to be present; but on the present evidence he could do nothing to alter the strong feeling of partisanship that Betty Kane's case had aroused throughout the country. The Sharpes would stay condemned.

And Betty Kane would "get away with it."

That to Robert was a thought that was even worse than the prospect of the Sharpes' haunted life. Betty Kane would go on being the centre of an adoring family; secure, loved, hero-worshipped. The once easy-going Robert grew homicidal at the thought.

He had had to confess to Aunt Lin that a piece of evidence had turned up at the time specified in her prayers, but had pusillanimously refrained from telling her that the said evidence was good enough to destroy the police case. She would call that winning the case; and "winning," to Robert, meant something very different.

To Nevil too, it seemed. And for the first time since young Bennet came to occupy the back room that used to be his, Robert thought of him as an ally; a communal spirit. To Nevil, too, it was unthinkable that

Betty Kane should "get away with it." And Robert was surprised all over again at the murderous rage that fills the pacifist-minded when their indignation is roused. Nevil had a special way of saying "Betty Kane": as if the syllables were some poison he had put in his mouth by mistake and he was spitting it out. "Poisonous," too, was his favourite epithet for her. "That poisonous creature." Robert found him very comforting.

But there was little comfort in the situation. The Sharpes had accepted the news of their probable escape from a prison sentence with the same dignity that had characterised their acceptance of everything, from Betty Kane's first accusation to the serving of a summons and an appearance in the dock. But they, too, realised that the thing would be escape but not vindication. The police case would break down, and they would get their verdict. But they would get it because in English law there was no middle course. In a Scots court the verdict would be Not Proven. And that, in fact, would be what the result of the Assizes verdict next week would amount to. Merely that the police had not had good enough evidence to prove their case. Not that the case was necessarily a bad one.

It was when the Assizes were only four days away that he confessed to Aunt Lin that the evidence did suffice to defeat the charge. The growing worry on that round pink face was too much for him. He had meant merely to give her that sop and leave the matter there; but instead he found himself pouring it all out to her as he had poured out his troubles as a small boy; in the days when Aunt Lin was an omniscient and omnipotent angel and not just kind, silly Aunt Lin. She listened to this unexpected torrent of words—so different from the normal phrases of their meal-time intercourse—in surprised silence, her jewel-blue eyes attentive and concerned.

"Don't you see, Aunt Lin, it isn't victory; it's defeat," he finished. "It's a travesty of justice. It isn't a verdict we're fighting for; it's justice. And we have no hope of getting it. Not a ghost of a hope!"

"But why didn't you tell me all this, dear? Did you think I would not understand, or agree, or something?"

"Well, you didn't feel as I did about——"

"Just because I didn't much like the look of those people at The Franchise—and I must confess, dear, even now, that they aren't the kind of people I naturally take to—just because I didn't much like them doesn't mean that I am indifferent to seeing justice done, surely?"

"No, of course not; but you said quite frankly that you found Betty Kane's story believable, and so——"

"That," said Aunt Lin calmly, "was before the police court."

"The court? But you weren't at the court."

"No, dear, but Colonel Whittaker was, and he didn't like the girl at all."

"Didn't he, indeed."

"No. He was quite eloquent about it. He said he had once had a—a what-do-you-call-it—a lance-corporal in his regiment, or battalion or something, who was exactly like Betty Kane. He said he was an injured innocent who set the whole battalion by the ears and was more trouble than a dozen hard-cases. Such a nice expression: hard-cases, isn't it. He finished up in the greenhouse, Colonel Whittaker said."

"The glasshouse."

"Well, something like that. And as for the Glyn girl from Staples, he said that one glance at her and you automatically began to reckon the number of lies there would be per sentence. He didn't like the Glyn girl either. So you see, dear, you needn't have thought that I would be unsympathetic about your worry. I am just as interested in abstract justice as you are, I assure you. And I shall redouble my prayers for your success. I was going over to the Gleasons' garden party this afternoon, but I shall go along to St. Matthew's instead and spend a quiet hour there. I think it is going to rain in any case. It always does rain at the Gleasons' garden party, poor things."

"Well, Aunt Lin, I don't deny we need your prayers. Nothing short of a miracle can save us now."

"Well, I shall pray for the miracle."

"A last-minute reprieve with the rope round the hero's neck? That happens only in detective stories and the last few minutes of horse-operas."

"Not at all. It happens every day, somewhere in the world. If there was some way of finding out and adding up the times it happens you would no doubt be surprised. Providence does take a hand, you know, when other methods fail. You haven't enough faith, my dear, as I pointed out before."

"I don't believe that an angel of the Lord is going to appear in my office with an account of what Betty Kane was doing for that month, if that is what you mean," Robert said.

"The trouble with you, dear, is that you think of an angel of the Lord as a creature with wings, whereas he is probably a scruffy little man in a bowler hat. Anyhow, I shall pray very hard this afternoon, and tonight too, of course; and by tomorrow perhaps help will be sent."

CHAPTER XX

THE ANGEL of the Lord was not a scruffy little man, as it turned out; and his hat was a regrettably continental affair of felt with a tightly rolled brim turned up all round. He arrived at Blair, Hayward, and Bennet's about half-past eleven the following morning.

"Mr. Robert," old Mr. Heseltine said, putting his head in at Robert's door, "there's a Mr. Lange in the office to see you. He——"

Robert, who was busy, and not expecting angels of the Lord, and quite used to strangers turning up in the office and wanting to see him, said: "What does he want? I'm busy."

"He didn't say. He just said he would like to see you if you were not too busy."

"Well, I'm scandalously busy. Find out tactfully what he wants, will you? If it is nothing important Nevil can deal with it."

"Yes, I'll find out; but his English is very thick, and he doesn't seem very willing to——"

"English? You mean, he has a lisp?"

"No, I mean his pronunciation of English isn't very good. He——"

"The man's a foreigner, you mean?"

"Yes. He comes from Copenhagen."

"Copenhagen! Why didn't you tell me that before!"

"You didn't give me a chance, Mr. Robert."

"Show him in, Timmy, show him in. Oh, merciful Heaven, do fairy-tales come true?"

Mr. Lange was rather like one of the Norman pillars of Notre Dame. Just as round, just as high, just as solid and just as dependable-looking. Far away at the top of this great round solid erect pillar his face shone with friendly rectitude.

"Mr. Blair?" he said. "My name is Lange. I apologise for bothering you"—he failed to manage the TH—"but it was important. Important to you, I mean. At least, yes I think."

"Sit down, Mr. Lange."

"Thank you, thank you. It is warm, is it not? This is perhaps the day you have your summer?" He smiled on Robert. "That is an idiom of the English, that joke about one-day summer. I am greatly interested in the English idiom. It is because of my interest in English idiom that I come to see you."

Robert's heart sank to his heels with the plummet swoop of an express lift. Fairy-tales, indeed. No; fairy-tales stay fairy-tales.

"Yes?" he said encouragingly.

"I keep a hotel in Copenhagen, Mr. Blair. The hotel of the Red Shoes it is called. Not, of course, because anyone wears red shoes there but because of a tale of Andersen, which you perhaps may——"

"Yes, yes," Robert said. "It has become one of our tales too."

"Ah, so! Yes. A great man, Andersen. So simple a man and now so international. It is a thing to marvel at. But I waste your time, Mr. Blair, I waste your time. What was I saying?"

"About English idiom."

"Ah, yes. To study English is my hubby."

"Hobby," Robert said, involuntarily.

"Hobby. Thank you. For my bread and butter I keep a hotel—and because my father and his father kept one before me—but for a hub . . . a hobby? yes; thank you—for a hobby I study the idiomatic English. So every day the newspapers that they leave about are brought to me."

"They?"

"The English visitors."

"Ah, yes."

"In the evening, when they have retired, the page collects the English papers and leaves them in my office. I am busy, often, and I do not have time to look at them, and so they go into the pile and when I have leisure I pick one up and study it. Do I make myself clear, Mr. Blair?"

"Perfectly, perfectly, Mr. Lange." A faint hope was rising again. Newspapers?

"So it goes on. A few moments of leisure, a little reading in an English paper, a new idiom—perhaps two—all very without excitement. How do you say that?"

"Placid."

"So. Placid. And then one day I take this paper from the pile, just as I might take any of the others, and I forget all about idiom." He took from his capacious pocket a once-folded copy of the *Ack-Emma,* and spread it in front of Robert on the desk. It was the issue of Friday, May the 10th, with the photograph of Betty Kane occupying two-thirds of the page. "I look at this photograph. Then I look inside and read the story. Then I say to myself that this is most extraordinary. Most extraordinary it is. The paper say this is the photograph of Betty Kann. Kann?"

"Kane."

"Ah. So. Betty Kane. But it is also the photograph of Mrs. Chadwick, who stay at my hotel with her husband."

"What!"

Mr. Lange looked pleased. "You are interested? I so hoped you might be. I did so hope."

"Go on. Tell me."

"A fortnight they stayed with me. And it was most extraordinary, Mr. Blair, because while that poor girl was being beaten and starved in an English attic, Mrs. Chadwick was eating like a young wolf at my hotel—the cream that girl could eat, Mr. Blair, even I, a Dane, was surprised—and enjoying herself very much."

"Yes?"

"Well, I said to myself: It is after all a photograph. And although it is just the way she looked when she let down her hair to come to the ball——"

"Let it down!"

"Yes. She wore her hair brushed up, you see. But we had a ball with costume—Costume?"

"Yes. Fancy dress."

"Ah. So. Fancy dress. And for her fancy dress she lets her hair hang down. Just like that there." He tapped the photograph. "So I say to myself: It is a photograph, after all. How often has one seen a photograph that does not in the least resemble the real person. And what has this girl in the paper to do, possibly, with little Mrs. Chadwick who is here with her husband during that time! So I am reasonable to myself. But I do not throw away the paper. No. I keep it. And now and then I look at it. And each time I look at it I think: But that *is* Mrs. Chadwick. So I am still puzzled, and going to sleep I think about it when I should be thinking about tomorrow's marketing. I seek explanation from myself. Twins, perhaps? But no; the Betty girl is an only child. Cousins. Coincidence. Doubles. I think of them all. At night they satisfy me, and I turn over and go to sleep. But in the morning I look at the photograph, and all comes to pieces again. I think: But certainly beyond a doubt that is Mrs. Chadwick. You see my dilemma?"

"Perfectly."

"So when I am coming to England on business, I put the newspaper with the Arabic name——"

"Arabic? Oh, yes, I see. I didn't mean to interrupt."

"I put it into my bag, and after dinner one night I take it out and show it to my friend where I am staying. I am staying with a compatriot of mine in Bayswater, London. And my friend is instantly very excited and say: But it is now a police affair, and these women say that never have they seen the girl before. They have been arrested for what they are supposed to have done to this girl and they are about to be tried for it. And he calls to his wife: 'Rita! Rita! Where is the paper of a week last Tuesday?' It is the kind of household, my friend's, where there is always a paper of a week last Tuesday. And his wife come with it and he shows me the account of the trial—no, the—the——"

"Court appearance."

"Yes. The appearance in court of the two women. And I read how the trial is to be at some place in the country in a little more than a fortnight. Well, by now, that would be in a very few days. So my friend say: How sure are you, Einar, that that girl and your Mrs. Chadwick are one? And I say: Very sure indeed I am. So he say: Here in the paper is the name of the solicitor for the women. There is no address but this Milford is a very small place and he will be easy to find. We shall have coffee early tomorrow—that is breakfast—and you will go down to this Milford and tell what you think to this Mr. Blair. So here I am, Mr. Blair. And you are interested in what I say?"

Robert sat back, took out his handkerchief, and mopped his forehead. "Do you believe in miracles, Mr. Lange?"

"But of course. I am a Christian. Indeed, although I am not yet very old I have myself seen two."

"Well, you have just taken part in a third."

"So?" Mr. Lange beamed. "That makes me very content."

"You have saved our bacon."

"Bacon?"

"An English idiom. You have not only saved our bacon. You have practically saved our lives."

"You think, then, as I think, that they are one person, that girl and my guest at the Red Shoes?"

"I haven't a doubt of it. Tell me, have you the dates of her stay with you."

"Oh, yes, indeed. Here they are. She and her husband arrived by air on Friday the 29th of March, and they left—again by air, I think, though of that I am not so certain—on the 15th of April, a Monday."

"Thank you. And her 'husband,' what did he look like?"

"Young. Dark. Good-looking. A little—now, what is the word? Too-bright. Gaudy? No."

"Flashy?"

"Ah. There is it. Flashy. A little flashy, I think. I observe that he was not greatly approved of by the other Englishmen who came and went."

"Was he just on holiday?"

"No, oh, no. He was in Copenhagen on business."

"What kind of business?"

"That I do not know, I regret."

"Can't you even make a guess? What would he be most likely to be interested in in Copenhagen?"

"That depends, Mr. Blair, on whether he was interested in buying or selling."

"What was his address in England?"

"London."

"Beautifully explicit. Will you forgive me a moment while I telephone? Do you smoke?" He opened the cigarette box and pushed it towards Mr. Lange.

"Milford 195. You will do me the honour of having lunch with me, Mr. Lange, won't you? Aunt Lin? I have to go to London directly after lunch. . . . Yes, for the night. Will you be an angel and pack a small bag for me? . . . Thank you, darling. And would it be all right if I brought someone back to take pot-luck for lunch today? . . . Oh, good. . . . Yes, I'll ask him." He covered the mouthpiece, and said: "My aunt, who is actually my cousin, wants to know if you eat pastry?"

"Mr. Blair!" Mr. Lange said, with a wide smile and a wide gesture for his girth. "And you ask a Dane?"

"He loves it," Robert said into the telephone. "And I say, Aunt Lin. Were you doing anything important this afternoon? . . . Because what I think you ought to do is to go to St. Matthew's and give thanks . . . Your angel of the Lord has arrived."

Even Mr. Lange could hear Aunt Lin's delighted: "*Robert!* No, not really!"

"In the flesh. . . . No, not a bit scruffy . . . Very tall and beautiful and altogether perfect for the part. . . . You'll give him a good lunch, won't you? . . . Yes, that's who is coming to lunch. An angel of the Lord."

He put down the telephone and looked up at the amused Mr. Lange.

"And now, Mr. Lange, let us go over to the Rose and Crown and have some bad beer."

CHAPTER XXI

WHEN ROBERT WENT out to The Franchise, three days later, to drive the Sharpes over to Norton for the Assizes on the morrow, he found an almost bridal atmosphere about the place. Two absurd tubs of yellow wallflowers stood at the top of the steps; and the dark hall gleamed with flowers like a church decorated for a wedding.

"Nevil!" Marion said, with an explanatory wave of her hand to the massed glory. "He said the house should be *en fête*."

"I wish that I had thought of it," Robert said.

"After the last few days, it surprises me that you can think at all. If it were not for you, it is not rejoicing we should be today!"

"If it weren't for a man called Bell, you mean."

"Bell?"

"Alexander Bell. He invented the telephone. If it weren't for that invention we should still be groping in the dark. It will be months before I can look at a telephone without blenching."

"Did you take turn about?"

"Oh, no. We each had our own. Kevin and his clerk at his chambers, me at his little place in St. Paul's Churchyard, Alec Ramsden and three of his men at his office and wherever they could find a telephone that they could use uninterruptedly."

"That was six of you."

"Seven of us with six telephones. And we needed them!"

"Poor Robert!"

"At first it was fun. We were filled with the exhilaration of the hunt, of knowing that we were on the right track. Success was practically in our laps. But by the time we had made sure that none of the Chadwicks in the London telephone book had any connection with a Chadwick who had flown to Copenhagen on the 29th of March, and that all the Air line knew about him was that two seats had been booked from Larborough on the 27th, we had lost any feeling of fun we had started with.

The Larborough information cheered us, of course. But after that it was pure slog. We found out what we sold to Denmark and what she bought from us, and we divided them up between us."

"The merchandise?"

"No, the buyers and sellers. The Danish tourist office was a god-send. They just poured information at us. Kevin, his clerk, and I took the exports, and Ramsden and his men took the imports. From then on it was a tedious business of being put through to managers and asking: 'Have you a man called Bernard Chadwick working for you?' The number of firms who *haven't* got a Bernard Chadwick working for them is unbelievable. But I know a lot more about our exports to Denmark than I did before."

"I have no doubt of it!"

"I was so sick of the telephone that when it rang at my end I nearly didn't pick it up. I had almost forgotten that telephones were two-way. A telephone was just a sort of quiz instrument that I could plug into offices all over the country. I stared at it for quite a while before I realised that it was after all a mutual affair and that someone was trying to call me for a change."

"And it was Ramsden."

"Yes, it was Alec Ramsden. He said: 'We've got him. He buys porcelain and stuff for Brayne, Havard and Co.'"

"I am glad it was Ramsden who unearthed him. It will comfort him for his failure to run down the girl."

"Yes, he's feeling better about it now. After that it was a rush to interview the people we needed and to obtain subpoenas and what not. But the whole lovely result will be waiting for us in the court at Norton tomorrow. Kevin can hardly wait. His mouth waters at the prospect."

"If it was ever in my power to be sorry for that girl," Mrs. Sharpe said, coming in with an over-night bag and dumping it on a mahogany wall-table in a way that would have turned Aunt Lin faint, "it would be in a witness-box facing a hostile Kevin Macdermott." Robert noticed that the bag, which had originally been a very elegant and expensive one—a relic of her prosperous early married life, perhaps—was now deplorably shabby. He decided that when he married Marion his present to the bride's mother would be a dressing-case; small, light, elegant and expensive.

"It will never be in my power," Marion said, "to have even a passing sensation of sorrow for that girl. I would swat her off the earth's face as I would swat a moth in a cupboard—except that I am always sorry about the moth."

"What had the girl intended to do?" Mrs. Sharpe asked. "Had she intended to go back to her people at all?"

"I don't think so," Robert said. "I think she was still filled with rage and resentment at ceasing to be the centre of interest at 39 Meadowside

Lane. It is as Kevin said long ago: crime begins in egotism; inordinate vanity. A normal girl, even an emotional adolescent, might be heart-broken that her adopted brother no longer considered her the most important thing in his life; but she would work it out in sobs, or sulks, or being difficult, or deciding that she was going to renounce the world and go into a convent, or half a dozen other methods that the adolescent uses in the process of adjustment. But with an egotism like Betty Kane's there is no adjustment. She expects the world to adjust itself to her. The criminal always does, by the way. There was never a criminal who didn't consider himself ill-done-by."

"A charming creature," Mrs. Sharpe said.

"Yes. Even the Bishop of Larborough would find some difficulty in thinking up a case for her. His usual 'environment' hobby-horse is no good this time. Betty Kane had everything that he recommends for the cure of the criminal: love, freedom to develop her talents, education, security. It's quite a poser for his lordship when you come to consider it, because he doesn't believe in heredity. He thinks that criminals are made, and therefore can be unmade. 'Bad blood' is just an old superstition, in the Bishop's estimation."

"Toby Byrne," Mrs. Sharpe said with a snort. "You should have heard Charles's stable lads on him."

"I've heard Nevil," Robert said. "I doubt if anyone could improve on Nevil's version of the subject."

"Is the engagement definitely broken, then?" Marion asked.

"Definitely. Aunt Lin has hopes of the eldest Whittaker girl. She is a niece of Lady Mountleven, and a grand-daughter of Karr's Krisps."

Marion laughed with him. "Is she nice, the Whittaker girl?" she asked.

"Yes. Fair, pretty, well-brought-up, musical but doesn't sing."

"I should like Nevil to get a nice wife. All he needs is some permanent interest of his own. A focus for his energies and his emotions."

"At the moment the focus for both is The Franchise."

"I know. He has been a dear to us. Well, I suppose it is time that we were going. If anyone had told me last week that I should be leaving The Franchise to go to a triumph at Norton I wouldn't have believed it. Poor Stanley can sleep in his own bed from now on, instead of guarding a couple of hags in a lonely house."

"Isn't he sleeping here tonight?" Robert asked.

"No. Why should he?"

"I don't know. I don't like the idea of the house being left entirely empty."

"The policeman will be round as usual on his beat. Anyhow, no one has even tried to do anything since the night they smashed our windows. It is only for tonight. Tomorrow we shall be home again."

"I know. But I don't much like it. Couldn't Stanley stay one more night? Until the case is over."

"If they want to wreck our windows again," Mrs. Sharpe said, "I don't suppose Stanley's being here will deter them."

"No, I suppose not. I'll remind Hallam, anyhow, that the house is empty tonight," Robert said, and left it there.

Marion locked the door behind them, and they walked to the gate, where Robert's car was waiting. At the gate Marion paused to look back at the house. "It's an ugly old place," she said, "but it has one virtue. It looks the same all the year round. At midsummer the grass gets a little burnt and tired-looking, but otherwise it doesn't change. Most houses have a 'best' time; rhododendrons, or herbaceous borders, or virginia creeper, or almond blossom, or something. But The Franchise is always the same. It has no frills. What are you laughing at, Mother?"

"I was thinking how *bedizened* the poor thing looks with those tubs of wallflower."

They stood there for a moment, laughing at the forbidding, dirty-white house with its incongruous decoration of frivolity; and laughing, shut the gate on it.

But Robert did not forget; and before having dinner with Kevin at The Feathers in Norton he called the police station at Milford and reminded them that the Sharpes' house would be empty for that one night.

"All right, Mr. Blair," the sergeant said, "I'll tell the man on the beat to open the gate and look round. Yes, we still have a key. That'll be all right."

Robert did not quite see what that would achieve; but then he did not see what protection could be afforded in any case. Mrs. Sharpe had said, if anyone was minded to break windows then the windows would inevitably be broken. He decided that he was being fussy, and joined Kevin and his law friends with relief.

The Law talks well, and it was late before Robert went to bed in one of the dark panelled rooms that made The Feathers famous. The Feathers—one of the "musts" of American visitors to Britain—was not only famous but up to date. Pipes had been led through the linen-fold oak, wires through the beamed ceilings, and a telephone line through the oak planks of the floor. The Feathers had been providing comfort for the travelling public since 1480, and saw no reason why it should stop.

Robert fell asleep as soon as his head touched the pillow and the telephone at his ear had been ringing for some moments before he became aware of it.

"Well?" he said, still half-asleep. And became instantly wide awake.

It was Stanley. Could he come back to Milford? The Franchise was on fire.

"Badly?"

"It's got a good hold, but they think they can save it."

"I'll be over as soon as I can make it."

He made the twenty miles in a door-to-door time that the Robert Blair of a month ago would have considered reprehensible in the achievement of another, and quite inconceivable as an achievement of his own. As he tore past his own home at the lower end of Milford High Street and out into the country beyond, he saw the glow against the horizon, like the rising of a full moon. But the moon hung in the sky, a young silver moon in the pale summer night. And the glow of the burning Franchise wavered in sickening gusts that tightened Robert's heart with remembered horror.

At least there was no one in the building. He wondered if anyone had been there in time to rescue what was valuable from the house. Would there be anyone there who could distinguish what was valuable from what was worthless?

The gates were wide open and the courtyard—bright in the flames—was crowded with the men and machines of the Fire Service. The first thing he saw, incongruous on the grass, was the bead-work chair from the drawing-room; and a wave of hysteria rose in him. Someone had saved that, anyhow.

An almost unrecognisable Stanley grabbed his sleeve and said: "There you are. I thought you ought to know, somehow." Sweat trickled down his blackened face, leaving clear rivulets behind them, so that his young face looked seamed and old. "There isn't enough water. We've got quite a lot of the stuff out. All the drawing-room stuff that they used every day. I thought that's what they'd want, if it had to be a choice. And we flung out some of the upstairs stuff but all the heavy stuff has gone up."

Mattresses and bed-linen were piled on the grass out of the way of the firemen's boots. The furniture stood about the grass as it had been set down, looking surprised and lost.

"Let's take the furniture further away," Stanley said. "It's not safe where it is. Either some lighted bits will fall on it or one of those bastards will use it to stand on." The bastards were the Fire Service, doing their sweating and efficient best.

So Robert found himself prosaically carting furniture through a fantastic scene; miserably identifying pieces that he had known in their proper sphere. The chair that Mrs. Sharpe had considered Inspector Grant too heavy for; the cherry-wood table they had given Kevin luncheon at; the wall-table that Mrs. Sharpe had dumped her bag down on only a few hours ago. The roar and crackle of the flames, the shoutings of the firemen, the odd mixture of moonlight, head-lights, and wavering flame, the mad juxtaposition and irrelevance of the bits of furniture, reminded him of how it felt to be coming round from an anaesthetic.

And then two things happened together. The first floor fell in with a crash. And as the new spout of flame lit the faces round him he saw two youths alongside whose countenances were alive with gloating. At the same moment he became aware that Stanley had seen them too. He saw Stanley's fist catch the further one under the chin with a crack that could be heard even over the noise of the flames, and the gloating face disappeared into the darkness of the trampled grass.

Robert had not hit anyone since he gave up boxing when he left school, and he had no intention of hitting anyone now. His left arm seemed to do all that was necessary of its own accord. And the second leering face went down into obscurity.

"Neat," remarked Stanley, sucking his broken knuckles. And then, "Look!" he said.

The roof crumpled like a child's face when it is beginning to cry; like a melting negative. The little round window, so famous and so ill-reputed, leaned forward a little and sank slowly inwards. A tongue of flame leapt up and fell again. Then the whole roof collapsed into the seething mass below, falling two floors to join the red wreck of the rest of the interior. The men moved back from the furnace heat. The fire roared in unrestricted triumph into the summer night.

When at last it died away Robert noticed with a vague surprise that the dawn had come. A calm, grey dawn, full of promise. Quiet had come too; the roar and the shoutings had faded to the soft hiss of water on the smoking skeleton. Only the four walls stood, blurred and grimy, in the middle of the trampled grass. The four walls and the flight of steps with their warped iron railing. On either side of the doorway stood what remained of Nevil's gay little tubs, the soaked and blackened flowers hanging in unrecognisable shreds over their edges. Between them the square opening yawned into a black emptiness.

"Well," said Stanley, standing beside him, "that seems to be that."

"How did it begin?" asked Bill, who had arrived too late to see anything but the wreck that was left.

"No one knows. It was well alight when P. C. Newsam arrived on his beat," Robert said. "What became of those two chaps, by the way?"

"The two we corrected?" Stanley said. "They went home."

"It's a pity that expression is no evidence."

"Yes," Stanley said. "They won't get anyone for this any more than they got anyone for the window-breaking. And I still owe someone for a crack on the head."

"You nearly broke that creature's neck tonight. That ought to be some kind of compensation to you."

"How are you going to tell them?" Stanley said. This obviously referred to the Sharpes.

"God knows," Robert said. "Am I to tell them first and let it spoil their triumph in court for them; or am I to let them have their triumph and face the awful come-down afterwards?"

"Let them have their triumph," Stanley said. "Nothing that happens afterwards can take that away from them. Don't mess it up."

"Perhaps you are right, Stan. I wish I knew. I had better book rooms at the Rose and Crown for them."

"They wouldn't like that," Stan said.

"Perhaps not," Robert said, a shade impatiently. "But they have no choice. Whatever they decide to do they will want to stay here a night or two to arrange about things, I expect. And the Rose and Crown is the best available."

"Well," Stanley said, "I've been thinking. And I'm sure my landlady would be glad to have them. She's always been on their side, and she has a spare room, and they could have that sitting-room in front that she never uses, and it's very quiet down there, that last row of Council houses facing on the Meadows. I'm sure they'd rather have that than a hotel where they would be stared at."

"They would indeed, Stan. I should never have thought of it. You think your landlady would be willing?"

"I don't think; I'm sure. They're her greatest interest in life at the moment. It would be like royalty coming to stay."

"Well, find out definitely, would you, and telephone me a message to Norton. To The Feathers at Norton."

CHAPTER XXII

IT SEEMED TO ROBERT that at least half Milford had managed to pack itself into the Court at Norton. Certainly a great many citizens of Norton were milling round the outer doors, vocal and frustrated; furious that when a case of national interest was being decided at "their" Assizes they should be done out of their right to witness it by an influx of foreigners from Milford. Wily and deceitful foreigners, too, who had suborned the Norton youth to keep places in the queue for them; a piece of forethought which had not occurred to Norton adults.

It was very warm, and the packed court stirred uneasily throughout the preliminaries and through most of Miles Allison's account of the crime. Allison was the antithesis of Kevin Macdermott; his fair, delicate face that of a type rather than a person. His light dry voice was unemotional, his method matter-of-fact. And since the story he was telling was one which they had all read about and discussed until it was threadbare, they withheld their attention from him and amused themselves by identifying friends in court.

Robert sat turning over and over in his pocket the little oblong of pasteboard that Christina had pressed into his hand on his departure yesterday, and rehearsing phrases for afterwards. The pasteboard was a bright Reckitt's blue and bore in gold letters the words: NOT A SPARROW SHALL FALL, and a picture in the right upper corner of a robin with an out-size red breast. How, wondered Robert, turning the little text over and over in his fingers, did you tell someone that they had no home any more?

The sudden movement of a hundred bodies and the subsequent silence brought him back to the court-room, and he realised that Betty Kane was taking the oath preparatory to giving evidence. "Never kissed anything but the book," Ben Carley had said of her appearance on a similar occasion. And that is what she looked like today. The blue outfit still made one think of youth and innocence; speedwell, and camp-fire smoke, and harebells in the grass. The tilted-back brim of her hat still showed the childish forehead with its charming hair line. And Robert, who knew now all about her life in the weeks she was missing, found himself being surprised all over again at sight of her. Plausibility was one of the first endowments of the criminal; but up to now such plausibility as he had had to deal with was of the old-soldier-ten-bob-note kind. Easily recognised for what it was. The work of amateurs at the job. It occurred to him that for the first time he was seeing the real thing at work.

Once again she gave her evidence in model fashion; her clear young voice audible to everyone in court. Once again she had her audience breathless and motionless. The only difference this time was that the Bench was not doting. The Bench, indeed, if one was to judge by the expression on the face of Mr. Justice Saye, was very far from doting. And Robert wondered how much the judge's critical gaze was due to natural distaste for the subject, and how much to the conclusion that Kevin Macdermott would not be sitting there ready to defend the two women in the dock unless they had a thundering good defence.

The girl's own account of her sufferings did what her counsel's had not done: roused the audience to an emotional reaction. More than once they had given vent to a united sigh, a murmur of indignation; never overt enough to rank as a demonstration, and so bring down the Court's rebuke, but audible enough to show which way their sympathies lay. So that it was in a charged atmosphere that Kevin rose to cross-examine.

"Miss Kane," began Kevin in his gentlest drawl, "you say that it was dark when you arrived at The Franchise. Was it *really* so dark?"

This question, with its coaxing tone, made her think that he did not want it to be dark, and she reacted as he intended.

"Yes. Quite dark," she said.

"Too dark to see the outside of the house?"

"Yes, much too dark."

He appeared to give that up and try a new tack.

"Then the night you escaped. Perhaps that was not quite dark?"

"Oh, yes. That was even darker, if possible."

"So that you could not possibly have seen the outside of the house on some occasion?"

"Never."

"Never. Well, having settled that point, let us consider what you say you could see from the window of your prison in the attic. You said in your statement to the police, when you were describing this unknown place where you were imprisoned, that the carriage-way from the gate to the door 'went straight for a little and then divided in two into a circle up to the door'."

"Yes."

"How did you know it did that?"

"How did I know it? I could see it."

"From where?"

"From the window in the attic. It looked out on the courtyard in front of the house."

"But from the window in the attic it is possible to see only the straight part of the carriage-way. The edge of the roof cuts off the rest. How did you know that the carriage-way divided in two and made a circle up to the door?"

"I saw it!"

"How?"

"From that window."

"You want us to understand that you see on a different principle from ordinary beings? On the principle of the Irishman's gun that shoots round corners. Or is it all done by mirrors?"

"It is the way I described!"

"Certainly it is the way you described; but what you described was the view of the courtyard as seen by, let us say, someone looking over the wall at it; not by someone looking at it from the window in the attic. Which you assure us was your only view of it."

"I take it," said the Court, "that you have a witness to the extent of the view from the window."

"Two, my lord."

"One with normal vision will be sufficient," said the Court dryly.

"So you cannot explain how, speaking to the police that day in Aylesbury, you described a peculiarity that you could not possibly have known about, if your story was true. Have you ever been abroad, Miss Kane?"

"Abroad?" she said, surprised by the change of subject. "No."

"Never?"

"No, never."

"You have not, for instance, been to Denmark lately? To Copenhagen, for instance."

"No." There was no change in her expression but Robert thought that there was the faintest uncertainty in her voice.

"Do you know a man called Bernard Chadwick?"

She was suddenly wary. Robert was reminded of the subtle change in an animal that has been relaxed and becomes attentive. There is no alteration in pose; no actual physical change. On the contrary, there is only an added stillness; an awareness.

"No." The tone was colourless; uninterested.

"He is not a friend of yours."

"No."

"You did not, for instance, stay with him at a hotel in Copenhagen?"

"No."

"Have you stayed with anyone in Copenhagen?"

"No, I have never been abroad at all."

"So that if I were to suggest that you spent those missing weeks in a hotel in Copenhagen and not in an attic at The Franchise, I should be mistaken."

"Quite mistaken."

"Thank you."

Miles Allison, as Kevin had anticipated, rose to retrieve the situation.

"Miss Kane," he said, "you arrived at The Franchise by car."

"Yes."

"And that car, you say in your statement, was driven up to the door of the house. Now, if it was dark, as you say, there must have been side-lights on the car, if not head-lights; which would illuminate not only the carriage-way but most of the courtyard."

"Yes," she broke in, before he could put it to her, "yes, of course I must have seen the circle then. I knew I had seen it. I knew it." She glanced at Kevin for a moment, and Robert was reminded of her face when she saw that she had guessed correctly about the suitcases in the cupboard, that first day at The Franchise. If she knew what Kevin had waiting for her, Robert thought, she would have no spare thought for a passing triumph.

She was succeeded in the witness-box by Carley's "oleograph"; who had bought both a new frock and a new hat for her appearance at Norton—a tomato-red frock and a puce hat with a cobalt ribbon and a pink rose—and looked more luscious and more revolting than ever. Again Robert was interested to note how her relish of her part discounted, even with this more emotional audience, the effect of what she said. They didn't like her, and in spite of their *parti pris* attitude their English distrust of malice cooled their minds towards her. When Kevin, cross-examining, suggested that she had in fact been dismissed and had not "given in her notice" at all, there was a So-that's-it! expression on every second face in court. Apart from an attempt to shake her credit, there was not much that Kevin could do with her, and he let her go. He was waiting for her poor stooge.

The stooge, when she arrived, looked even less happy than she had looked in the police court at Milford. The much more impressive array of robes and wigs clearly shook her. Police uniforms were bad enough, but in retrospect they seemed positively home-like compared with this solemn atmosphere, this ritual. If she was out of her depth in Milford, she was obviously drowning here. Robert saw Kevin's considering eye on her, analysing and understanding; deciding on his approach. She had been scared stiff by Miles Allison, in spite of his patient quietness; evidently regarding anything in a wig and gown as hostile and a potential dispenser of penalties. So Kevin became her wooer and protector.

It was positively indecent, the caress that Kevin could get into his voice, Robert thought, listening to his first sentences to her. The soft unhurried syllables reassured her. She listened for a moment and then began to relax. Robert saw the small skinny hands that had been clutched so tightly together on the rail of the box slacken and spread slowly to a prone position. He was asking about her school. The fright had faded from her eyes and she was answering quite calmly. Here, she quite obviously felt, was a friend.

"Now, Gladys, I am going to suggest to you that you did not want to come here today and give evidence against these two people at The Franchise."

"No, I didn't. Indeed I didn't!"

"But you came," he said; not accusing, just making the statement.

"Yes," she said; shamefaced.

"Why? Because you thought it was your duty?"

"No, oh no."

"Was it because someone forced you to come?"

Robert saw the judge's instant reaction to this, but so out of the tail of his eye did Kevin. "Someone who held something over your head?" finished Kevin smoothly, and his lordship paused. "Someone who said: 'You say what I tell you to say or I'll tell about you'?"

She looked half-hopeful, half-bewildered. "I don't know," she said, falling back on the escape of the illiterate.

"Because if anyone made you tell lies by threatening what they would do to you if you didn't, they can be punished for it."

This was clearly a new idea to her.

"This court, all these people you see here, have come here today to find out the truth about something. And his lordship up there would deal very sternly with anyone who had used threats to make you come here and say something that was not true. What is more, there is a very heavy punishment for persons who take an oath to speak truth and tell what is not true; but if it so happened that they had been frightened into telling lies by someone threatening them, then the person who would be punished most would be the person who made the threats. Do you understand that?"

"Yes," she said in a whisper.

"Now I am going to suggest to you what really happened, and you will tell me whether I am right." He waited for her agreement, but she said nothing, so he went on. "Someone—a friend of yours, perhaps—took something from The Franchise—let us say, a watch. She did not want the watch herself, perhaps, and so she handed it on to you. It may be that you did not want to take it, but your friend is perhaps a domineering person and you did not like to refuse her gift. So you took it. Now I suggest that presently that friend proposed to you that you should back up a story she was going to tell in court and you, being averse to telling lies, said no. And that she then said to you: 'If you don't back me up I shall say that you took that watch from The Franchise one day when you came to see me'—or some other threat of that sort."

He paused a moment but she merely looked bewildered.

"Now, I suggest that because of those threats you did actually go to a police court and did actually back up your friend's untrue story, but that when you got home you were sorry and ashamed. So sorry and ashamed that the thought of keeping that watch any longer was unbearable to you. And that you then wrapped up the watch, and sent it back to The Franchise by post with a note saying: 'I don't want none of it.'" He paused. "I suggest to you, Gladys, that that is what really happened."

But she had had time to take fright. "No," she said. "No, I never had that watch."

He ignored the admission, and said smoothly: "I am quite wrong about that?"

"Yes. It wasn't me sent back the watch."

He picked up a paper and said, still mildly: "When you were at that school we were talking about, you were very good at drawing. So good that you had things put up for show at the school exhibition."

"Yes."

"I have here a map of Canada—a very neat map—which was one of your exhibits and which indeed won you a prize. You have signed it here in the right-hand corner, and I have no doubt that you were proud to sign such a neat piece of work. I expect you will remember it."

It was taken across the court to her, while Kevin added:

"Ladies and Gentlemen of the Jury, it is a map of Canada which Gladys Rees made in her last year at school. When his lordship has inspected it he will no doubt pass it on to you." And then, to Gladys: "You made that map yourself?"

"Yes."

"And wrote your name in the corner."

"Yes."

"And printed DOMINION OF CANADA across the bottom?"

"Yes."

"You printed those letters across the bottom that read: DOMINION OF CANADA. Good. Now, I have here the scrap of paper on which someone wrote the words: I DON'T WANT NONE OF IT. This scrap of paper, with its printed letters, was enclosed with the watch that was sent back to The Franchise. The watch that had gone missing while Rose Glyn was working there. And I suggest that the printing of I DON'T WANT NONE is the same as the printing of DOMINION OF CANADA. That it was written by the same hand. And that that hand was yours."

"No," she said, taking the scrap of paper as it was handed to her and putting it hastily down on the ledge as though it might sting her. "I never. I never sent back no watch."

"You didn't print those letters that read: I DON'T WANT NONE OF IT?"

"No."

"But you did print those letters that read DOMINION OF CANADA?"

"Yes."

"Well, later in this case I shall bring evidence that these two printings are by the same hand. In the meantime the jury can inspect them at their leisure and arrive at their own conclusions. Thank you."

"My learned friend has suggested to you," said Miles Allison, "that pressure was brought on you to come here. Is there any truth in that suggestion?"

"No."

"You did not come here because you were frightened of what might happen to you if you didn't?"

She took some time to think over this, evidently disentangling it in her mind. "No," she ventured at last.

"What you said in the witness-box at the police court, and what you have said today, is the truth?"

"Yes."

"Not something that someone suggested you might say?"

"No."

But the impression that was left with the jury was just that: that she was an unwilling witness repeating a story that was someone else's invention.

That ended the evidence for the prosecution and Kevin went straight on with the matter of Gladys Rees; on the housewife principle of "getting his feet clear" before he began the real work of the day.

A handwriting expert gave evidence that the two samples of printing which had been put into court were by the same hand. Not only had he no doubt about it, but he had rarely been given an easier task. Not only were letters duplicated in the two samples but combinations of letters were similarly duplicated, combinations such as DO and AN and ON. As it was evident that the jury had already made up their minds for themselves on this point—no one who saw the two samples could doubt that they were by the same hand—Allison's suggestion that experts could be wrong was automatic and half-hearted. Kevin demolished it by producing his fingerprint witness, who deponed that the same fingerprints were to be found on each. And Allison's suggestion that the fingerprints might not be those of Gladys Rees was a last-stand effort. He had no wish that the Court might put it to the test.

Now that he had established the fact that Gladys Rees had, when she made her first declaration, been in possession of a watch stolen from The Franchise and had returned it immediately after that declaration, with a conscience-stricken note, Kevin was free to deal with Betty Kane's story. Rose Glyn and her story had been sufficiently discredited for the police to be already laying their heads together. He could safely leave Rose to the police.

When Bernard William Chadwick was called, there was a craning forward and a murmur of interrogation. This was a name that the newspaper readers did not recognise. What could he be doing in the case? What was he here to say?

He was here to say that he was a buyer of porcelain, fine china, and fancy goods of various kinds for a wholesale firm in London. That he was married and lived with his wife in a house in Ealing.

"You travel for your firm," Kevin said.

"Yes."

"In March of this year did you pay a visit to Larborough?"

"Yes."

"While you were in Larborough did you meet Betty Kane?"

"Yes."

"How did you meet her?"

"She picked me up."

There was an instant and concerted protest from the body of the court. Whatever discrediting Rose Glyn and her ally had suffered, Betty Kane was still sacrosanct. Betty Kane, who looked so much like Bernadette, was not to be spoken of lightly.

The judge rebuked them for the demonstration, involuntary though it had been. He also rebuked witness. He was not quite clear, he inferred, what "picking up" involved and would be grateful if the witness would confine himself to standard English in his replies.

"Will you tell the Court just how you did meet her," Kevin said.

"I had dropped into the Midland lounge for tea one day, and she—er—began to talk to me. She was having tea there."

"Alone?"

"Quite alone."

"You did not speak to her first?"

"I didn't even notice her."

"How did she call attention to her presence, then?"

"She smiled, and I smiled back and went on with my papers. I was busy. Then she spoke to me. Asked what the papers were, and so on."

"So the acquaintance progressed."

"Yes. She said she was going to the flicks—to the pictures—and wouldn't I come too? Well, I was finished for the day and she was a cute kid so I said yes, if she liked. The result was that she met me next day and went out to the country in my car with me."

"On your business trips, you mean."

"Yes; she came for the ride, and we would have a meal somewhere in the country and tea before she went home to her aunt's place."

"Did she talk about her people to you?"

"Yes, she said how unhappy she was at home, where no one took any notice of her. She had a long string of complaints about her home, but I didn't take much notice of them. She looked a pretty sleek little outfit to me."

"A what?" asked the judge.

"A well-cared for young girl, my lord."

"Yes?" Kevin said. "And how long did this idyll in Larborough persist?"

"It turned out that we were leaving Larborough on the same day. She was going back to her people because her holiday was over—she had already extended it so that she could run about with me—and I was due to fly to Copenhagen on business. She then said she had no intention of going home and asked me to take her with me. I said nothing doing. I didn't think she was so much of an innocent child as she seemed in the lounge at the Midland—I knew her better by that time—but I still thought she was inexperienced. She was only sixteen, after all."

"She told you she was sixteen."

"She had her sixteenth birthday in Larborough," Chadwick said with a wry twist of the mouth under the small dark moustache. "It cost me a gold lipstick."

Robert looked across at Mrs. Wynn and saw her cover her face with her hands. Leslie Wynn, sitting beside her, looked unbelieving and blank.

"You had no idea that actually she was still fifteen."

"No. Not until the other day."

"So when she made the suggestion that she should go with you you considered her an inexperienced child of sixteen."

"Yes."

"Why did you change your mind about her?"

"She—convinced me that she wasn't."

"Wasn't what?"

"Inexperienced."

"So after that you had no qualms about taking her with you on the trip abroad?"

"I had qualms in plenty, but by then I had learned—what fun she could be, and I couldn't have left her behind if I had wanted to."

"So you took her abroad with you."

"Yes."

"As your wife?"

"Yes, as my wife."

"You had no qualms about any anxiety her people might suffer?"

"No. She said she still had a fortnight's holiday to come, and that her people would take it for granted that she was still with her aunt in Larborough. She had told her aunt that she was going home, but had told her people that she was staying on. And as they never wrote to each other it was unlikely that her not being in Larborough would become known to her people."

"Do you remember the date on which you left Larborough?"

"Yes; I picked her up at a coach stop in Mainshill on the afternoon of March the 28th. That was where she would normally have got her bus home."

Kevin left a pause after this piece of information, so that its full significance should have a chance. Robert, listening to the momentary quiet, thought that if the court-room were empty the silence could not be more absolute.

"So you took her with you to Copenhagen. Where did you stay?"

"At the Red Shoes Hotel."

"For how long?"

"A fortnight."

There was a faint murmur of comment or surprise at that.

"And then?"

"We came back to England together on the 15th of April. She had told me that she was due home on the 16th. But on the way over she told me that she had actually been due back on the 11th and would now have been missing for four days."

"She misled you deliberately?"

"Yes."

"Did she say why she had misled you?"

"Yes. So that it would be impossible for her to go back. She said she was going to write to her people and say that she had a job and was quite happy and that they were not to look for her or worry about her."

"She had no compunction about the suffering that would cause parents who had been devoted to her?"

"No. She said her home bored her so much she could scream."

Against his will, Robert's eyes went to Mrs. Wynn, and came away again at once. It was crucifixion.

"What was your reaction to the new situation?"

"I was angry to begin with. It put me in a spot."

"Were you worried about the girl?"

"No, not particularly."

"Why?"

"By that time I had learned that she was very well able to take care of herself."

"What exactly do you mean by that?"

"I mean: whoever was going to suffer in any situation she created, it wouldn't be Betty Kane."

The mention of her name suddenly reminded the audience that the girl they had just been hearing about was "the" Betty Kane. "Their" Betty Kane. The one like Bernadette. And there was a small uneasy movement; a taking of breath.

"So?"

"After a lot of rag-chewing——"

"Of what?" said his lordship.

"A lot of discussion, my lord."

"Go on," said his lordship, "but do confine yourself to English, standard or basic."

"After a lot of talk I decided the best thing to do would be to take her down to my bungalow on the river near Bourne End. We used it for week-ends in the summer and for summer holidays, but only rarely for the rest of the year."

"When you say 'we,' you mean your wife and you."

"Yes. She agreed to that quite readily, and I drove her down."

"Did you stay there with her that night?"

"Yes."

"And on the following nights?"

"The following night I spent at home."

"In Ealing."

"Yes."

"And afterwards?"

"For a week after that I spent most nights at the bungalow."

"Was your wife not surprised that you did not sleep at home?"

"Not unbearably."

"And how did the situation at Bourne End disintegrate?"

"I went down one night and found that she had gone."

"What did you think had happened to her?"

"Well, she had been growing very bored for the last day or two—she found housekeeping fun for about three days but not more, and there wasn't much to do down there—so when I found she had gone I took it that she was tired of me and had found someone or something more exciting."

"You learned later where she had gone, and why?"

"Yes."

"You heard the girl Betty Kane give evidence today?"

"I did."

"Evidence that she had been forcibly detained in a house near Milford."

"Yes."

"That is the girl who went with you to Copenhagen, stayed there for a fortnight with you, and subsequently lived with you in a bungalow near Bourne End?"

"Yes, that is the girl."

"You have no doubt about it?"

"No."

"Thank you."

There was a great sigh from the crowd as Kevin sat down and Bernard Chadwick waited for Miles Allison. Robert wondered if Betty Kane's face was capable of showing any emotion other than fear and triumph. Twice he had seen it pulse with triumph and once—when old Mrs. Sharpe crossed the drawing-room towards her that first day—he had seen it show fear. But for all the emotion it showed just now she might have been listening to a reading of Fat Stock prices. Its effect of inward calm, he decided, must be the result of physical construction. The result of wide-set eyes, and placid brow, and inexpensive small mouth always set in the same childish pout. It was that physical construction that had hidden, all those years, the real Betty Kane even from her intimates. A perfect camouflage, it had been. A façade behind which she could be what she liked. There it was now, the mask, as child-like and calm as when he had first seen it above her school coat in the drawing-room at The Franchise; although behind it its owner must be seething with unnameable emotions.

"Mr. Chadwick," Miles Allison said, "this is a very *belated* story, isn't it?"

"Belated?"

"Yes. This case has been a matter for press-report and public comment for the past three weeks, or thereabouts. You must have known that two women were being wrongfully accused—if your story was true. If, as you say, Betty Kane was with you during those weeks, and not, as she says, in the house of these two women, why did you not go straight to the police and tell them so?"

"Because I didn't know anything about it."

"About what?"

"About the prosecution of these women. Or about the story that Betty Kane had told."

"How was that?"

"Because I have been abroad again for my firm. I knew nothing about this case until a couple of days ago."

"I see. You have heard the girl give evidence; and you have heard the doctor's evidence as to the condition in which she arrived home. Does anything in your story explain that?"

"No."

"It was not you who beat the girl?"

"No."

"You say you went down one night and found her gone."

"Yes."

"She had packed up and gone?"

"Yes; so it seemed at the time."

"That is to say, all her belongings and the luggage that contained them had disappeared with her."

"Yes."

"And yet she arrived home without belongings of any sort, and wearing only a dress and shoes."

"I didn't know that till much later."

"You want us to understand that when you went down to the bungalow you found it tidy and deserted, with no sign of any hasty departure."

"Yes. That's how I found it."

When Mary Frances Chadwick was summoned to give evidence there was what amounted to a sensation in court, even before she appeared. It was obvious that this was "the wife"; and this was fare that not even the most optimistic queuer outside the court had anticipated.

Frances Chadwick was a tallish good-looking woman; a natural blonde with the clothes and figure of a girl who has "modelled" clothes; but growing a little plump now, and, if one was to judge from the good-natured face, not much caring.

She said that she was indeed married to the previous witness, and lived with him in Ealing. They had no children. She still worked in the clothes trade now and then. Not because she needed to, but for pocket-money and because she liked it. Yes, she remembered her husband's going to Larborough and his subsequent trip to Copenhagen. He arrived back from Copenhagen a day later than he had promised, and spent that night with her. During the following week she began to suspect that her husband had developed an interest elsewhere. The suspicion was confirmed when a friend told her that her husband had a guest at their bungalow on the river.

"Did you speak to your husband about it?" Kevin asked.

"No. That wouldn't have been any solution. He attracts them like flies."

"What did you do, then? Or plan to do?"

"What I always do with flies."

"What is that?"

"I swat them."

"So you proceeded to the bungalow with the intention of swatting whatever fly was there."

"That's it."

"And what did you find at the bungalow?"

"I went late in the evening hoping I would catch Barney there too——"

"Barney is your husband?"

"And how. I mean, yes," she added hastily, catching the judge's eye.

"Well?"

"The door was unlocked so I walked straight in and into the sitting-room. A woman's voice called from the bedroom: 'Is that you, Barney? I've been so lonely for you.' I went in and found her lying on the bed in the kind of negligée you used to see in vamp films about ten years ago. She looked a mess, and I was a bit surprised at Barney. She was eating chocolates out of an enormous box that was lying on the bed alongside her. Terribly nineteen-thirty, the whole set-up."

"Please confine your story to the essentials, Mrs. Chadwick."

"Yes. Sorry. Well, we had the usual exchange——"

"The usual?"

"Yes. The what-are-you-doing-here stuff. The wronged-wife and the light-of-love, you know. But for some reason or other she got in my hair. I don't know why. I had never cared very much on other occasions. I mean, we just had a good row without any real hard feelings on either side. But there was something about this little tramp that turned my stomach. So——"

"Please, Mrs. Chadwick!"

"All right. Sorry. But you did say tell it in my own words. Well, there came a point where I couldn't stand this floo—— I mean, I got to a stage when she riled me past bearing. I pulled her off the bed and gave her a smack on the side of the head. She looked so surprised it was funny. It would seem no one had ever hit her in her life. She said: 'You hit me!' just like that; and I said: 'A lot of people are going to hit you from now on, my poppet,' and gave her another one. Well, from then on it was just a fight. I own quite frankly that the odds were all on my side. I was bigger for one thing and in a flaming temper. I tore that silly negligée off her, and it was ding-dong till she tripped over one of her mules that was lying on the floor and went sprawling. I waited for her to get up, but she didn't, and I thought she had passed out. I went into the bathroom to get a cold wet cloth and mopped her face. And then I went into the kitchen to make some coffee. I had cooled off by then and thought she would be glad of something when she had cooled off too. I brewed the coffee and left it to stand. But when I got back to the bedroom I found that the faint had been all an act. The little—the girl had lit out. She had had time to dress, so I took it for granted that she had dressed in a hurry and gone."

"And did you go too?"

"I waited for an hour, thinking Barney might come. My husband. All the girl's things were lying about, so I slung them all into her suitcase and put it in the cupboard under the stairs to the attic. And I opened all the windows. She must have put her scent on with a ladle. And then when Barney didn't come I went away. I must just have missed him, because he did go down that night. But a couple of days later I told him what I had done."

"And what was his reaction?"

"He said it was a pity her mother hadn't done the same thing ten years ago."

"He was not worried as to what had become of her?"

"No. I was, a bit, until he told me her home was only over at Aylesbury. She could quite easily cadge a lift that distance."

"So he took it for granted that she had gone home?"

"Yes. I said, hadn't he better make sure. After all, she was a kid."

"And what did he say in answer to that?"

"He said: 'Frankie, my girl, that "kid" knows more about self-preservation than a chameleon.'"

"So you dismissed the affair from your mind."

"Yes."

"But it must have come to your mind again when you read accounts of the Franchise affair?"

"No, it didn't."

"Why was that?"

"For one thing, I never knew the girl's name. Barney called her Liz. And I just didn't connect a fifteen-year-old schoolgirl who was kidnapped and beaten somewhere in the Midlands with Barney's bit. I mean, with the girl who was eating chocolates on my bed."

"If you had realised that the girls were identical, you would have told the police what you knew about her?"

"Certainly."

"You would not have hesitated owing to the fact that it was you who had administered the beating?"

"No. I would administer another tomorrow if I got the chance."

"I will save my learned friend a question and ask you: Do you intend to divorce your husband?"

"No. Certainly not."

"This evidence of yours and his is not a neat piece of public collusion?"

"No. I wouldn't need collusion. But I have no intention of divorcing Barney. He's fun, and he's a good provider. What more do you want in a husband?"

"I wouldn't know," Robert heard Kevin murmur. Then in his normal voice he asked her to state that the girl she had been talking about was the girl who had given evidence; the girl who was now sitting in court. And so thanked her and sat down.

But Miles Allison made no attempt to cross-examine. And Kevin moved to call his next witness. But the foreman of the jury was before him.

The jury, the foreman said, would like his lordship to know that they had all the evidence they required.

"What was this witness that you were about to call, Mr. Macdermott?" the judge asked.

"He is the owner of the hotel in Copenhagen, my lord. To speak to their having stayed there over the relevant period."

The judge turned inquiringly to the foreman.

The foreman consulted the jury.

"No, my lord; we don't think it is necessary, subject to your lordship's correction, to hear the witness."

"If you are satisfied that you have heard enough to arrive at a true verdict—and I cannot myself see that any further evidence would greatly clarify the subject—then so be it. Would you like to hear counsel for the defence?"

"No, my lord, thank you. We have reached our verdict already."

"In that case, any summing-up by me would be markedly redundant. Do you want to retire?"

"No, my lord. We are unanimous."

CHAPTER XXIII

"WE HAD BETTER WAIT until the crowd thins out," Robert said. "Then they'll let us out the back way."

He was wondering why Marion looked so grave; so unrejoicing. Almost as if she were suffering from shock. Had the strain been as bad as all that?

As if aware of his puzzlement, she said: "That woman. That poor woman. I can't think of anything else."

"Who?" Robert said, stupidly.

"The girl's mother. Can you imagine anything more frightful? To have lost the roof over one's head is bad—— Oh, yes, Robert my dear, you don't have to tell us——" She held out a late edition of the *Larborough Times* with a Stop Press paragraph reading: THE FRANCHISE, HOUSE MADE FAMOUS BY MILFORD ABDUCTION CASE, BURNT TO THE GROUND LAST NIGHT. "Yesterday that would have seemed to me an enormous tragedy. But compared with that woman's calvary it seems an incident. What *can* be more shattering than to find that the person you have lived with and loved all those years not only doesn't exist but has never existed? That the person you have so much loved not only doesn't love you but doesn't care two hoots about you and never did? What is there *left* for someone like that? She can never again take a step on to green grass without wondering if it is bog."

"Yes," Kevin said, "I couldn't bear to look at her. It was indecent, what she was suffering."

"She has a charming son," Mrs. Sharpe said. "I hope he will be a comfort to her."

"But don't you *see*," Marion said. "She *hasn't* got her son. She has nothing now. She thought she had Betty. She loved her and was as sure of her as she loved and was sure of her son. Now the very foundations of her life have given way. How is she to judge, any longer, if appearances can be so deceptive? No, she has nothing. Just a desolation. I am bleeding inside for her."

Kevin slipped an arm into hers and said: "You have had sufficient trouble of your own lately without saddling yourself with another's. Come; they'll let us go now, I think. Did it please you to see the police converging in that polite casual way of theirs on the perjurers?"

"No, I could think of nothing but that woman's crucifixion."

So she too had thought of it as that.

Kevin ignored her. "And the indecent scramble for a telephone that the Press indulged in the moment his lordship's red tail was through the door? You will be vindicated at great length in every newspaper in Britain, I promise you. It will be the most public vindication since Dreyfus. Wait here for me, while I get out of these. I shan't be a moment."

"I suppose we had best go to a hotel for a night or two?" Mrs. Sharpe said. "Have we any belongings at all?"

"Yes, quite a few, I'm glad to say," Robert told her; and described what had been saved. "But there is an alternative to the hotel." And he told them of Stanley's suggestion.

So it was to the little house on the outer rim of the "new" town that Marion and her mother came back; and it was in the front room at Miss Sim's that they sat down to celebrate; a sober little group: Marion, her mother, Robert, and Stanley. Kevin had had to go back to town. There was a large bunch of garden flowers on the table which had come with one of Aunt Lin's best notes. Aunt Lin's warm and gracious little notes had as little actual meaning as her "Have you had a busy day, dear?" but they had the same cushioning effect on life. Stanley had come in with a copy of the *Larborough Evening News* which carried on its front page the first report of the trial. The report was printed under a heading which read: ANANIAS ALSO RAN.

"Will you golf with me tomorrow afternoon?" Robert asked Marion. "You have been cooped up too long. We can start early, before the two-rounders have finished their lunch and have the course to ourselves."

"Yes, I should like that," she said. "I suppose tomorrow life will begin again and be just the usual mixture of good and bad. But tonight it is just a place where dreadful things can happen to one."

When he called for her on the morrow, however, all seemed well with life. "You can't imagine what bliss it is," she said. "Living in this house, I mean. You just turn a tap and hot water comes out."

"It is also very educational," Mrs. Sharpe said.

"Educational?"

"You can hear every word that is said next door."

"Oh, come, Mother! Not every word!"

"Every third word," amended Mrs. Sharpe.

So they drove out to the golf-course in high spirits, and Robert decided that he would ask her to marry him when they were having tea in the club-house afterwards. Or would there be too many people interrupting there, with their kind words on the result of the trial? Perhaps on the way home again?

He had decided that the best plan was to leave Aunt Lin in possession of the old house—the place was so much hers that it was unthinkable that she should not live there until she died—and to find a small place for Marion and himself somewhere else in Milford. It would not be easy, these days, but if the worst came to the worst they could make a tiny flat on the top floor of Blair, Hayward, and Bennet's. It would mean removing the records of two hundred years or so; but the records were rapidly arriving at museum quality and should be moved in any case.

Yes, he would ask her on the way home again.

This resolution lasted until he found that the thought of what was to come was spoiling his game. So on the ninth green he suddenly stopped waggling his putter at the ball, and said: "I want you to marry me, Marion."

"Do you, Robert?" She picked her own putter out of her bag, and dropped the bag at the edge of the green.

"You will, won't you?"

"No, Robert dear, I won't."

"But Marion! Why? Why not, I mean."

"Oh—as the children say, 'because'."

"Because why?"

"Half a dozen reasons, any one of them good by themselves. For one, if a man is not married by the time he is forty, then marriage is not one of the things he wants out of life. Just something that has overtaken him; like flu and rheumatism and income-tax demands. I don't want to be just something that has overtaken you."

"But that is——"

"Then, I don't think that I should be in the least an asset to Blair, Hayward, and Bennet. Even——"

"I'm not asking you to marry Blair, Hayward, and Bennet."

"Even the proof that I didn't beat Betty Kane won't free me of being 'the woman in the Kane case'; an uncomfortable sort of wife for the senior partner. It wouldn't do you any good, Robert, believe me."

"Marion, for heaven's sake! Stop——"

"Then, you have Aunt Lin and I have my mother. We couldn't just park them like pieces of chewing-gum. I not only love my mother, I *like* her. I admire her and enjoy living with her. You, on the other hand, are used to being spoiled by Aunt Lin—— Oh, yes, you are!—and would miss far more than you know all the creature comforts and the cosseting that I wouldn't know how to give you—and wouldn't give you if I knew how," she added, flashing a smile at him.

"Marion, it is *because* you don't cosset me that I want to marry you. Because you have an adult mind and a——"

"An adult mind is very nice to go to dinner with once a week, but after a lifetime with Aunt Lin you would find it a very poor exchange for good pastry in an uncritical atmosphere."

"There is one thing you haven't even mentioned," Robert said.

"What is that?"

"Do you care for me at all?"

"Yes. I care for you a great deal. More than I have ever cared for anyone, I think. That is, partly, why I won't marry you. The other reason has to do with myself."

"With you?"

"You see, I am *not* a marrying woman. I don't want to have to put up with someone else's crotchets, someone else's demands, someone else's colds in the head. Mother and I suit each other perfectly because we make no demands on each other. If one of us has a cold in the head she retires to her room without fuss and doses her disgusting self until she is fit for human society again. But no husband would do that. He would expect sympathy—even though he brought on the cold himself by pulling off clothes when he grew warm instead of waiting sensibly to get cool—sympathy and attention and feeding. No, Robert. There are a hundred thousand women just panting to look after some man's cold; why pick on me?"

"Because you are that one woman in a hundred thousand, and I love you."

She looked slightly penitent. "I sound flippant, don't I? But what I say is good sound sense."

"But, Marion, it is a lonely life——"

"A 'full' life in my experience is usually full only of other people's demands."

"—and you will not have your mother for ever."

"Knowing Mother as I do, I have no doubt that she will outlive me with perfect ease. You had better hole out: I see old Colonel Whittaker's four on the horizon."

Automatically he pushed his ball into the hole. "But what will you do?" he asked.

"If I don't marry you?"

He ground his teeth. She was right: perhaps her mocking habit of mind would not be a comfort to live with.

"What had you and your mother thought of doing now that you have lost The Franchise?"

She delayed over her answer, as if it were difficult to say. Fussing with her bag, and keeping her back to him.

"We are going to Canada," she said.

"Going away!"

She still had her back to him. "Yes."

He was aghast. "But Marion, you can't. And why to Canada?"

"I have a cousin who is a professor at McGill. A son of Mother's only sister. He wrote some time ago to ask Mother if we would go out to keep house for him, but by that time we had inherited The Franchise and were very happy in England. So we said no. But the offer is still open. And we—we both will be glad to go now."

"I see."

"Don't look so downcast. You don't know what an escape you are having, my dear."

They finished the round in a business-like silence.

But driving back to Sin Lane after having dropped Marion at Miss Sim's, Robert smiled wryly to think that to all the new experiences that knowing the Sharpes had brought to him was now added that of being a rejected suitor. The final, and perhaps the most surprising, one.

Three days later, having sold to a local dealer what had been saved of their furniture, and to Stanley the car he so much despised, they left Milford by train. By the odd toy train that ran from Milford to the junction at Norton. And Robert came to the junction with them to see them on to the fast train.

"I always had a passion for travelling light," Marion said, referring to their scanty luggage, "but I never imagined it would be indulged to the extent of travelling with an over-night case to Canada."

But Robert could not think of small-talk. He was filled with a misery and desolation that he had not known since his small soul was filled with woe at going back to school. The blossom foamed along the line side, the fields were burnished with buttercups, but the world for Robert was grey ash and drizzle.

He watched the London train bear them away, and went home wondering how he could support Milford without the hope of seeing Marion's thin brown face at least once a day.

But on the whole he supported it very well. He took to golfing of an afternoon again; and although a ball would always in the future be for him a "piece of gutta-percha," his form had not seriously deteriorated. He rejoiced Mr. Heseltine's heart by taking an interest in work. He suggested to Nevil that between them they might sort and catalogue the records in the attic and perhaps make a book of them. By the time Marion's goodbye letter from London came, three weeks later, the soft folds of life in Milford were already closing round him.

My very dear Robert (wrote Marion),

This is a hasty *au revoir* note, just to let you know that we are both thinking of you. We leave on the morning plane to Montreal the day after tomorrow. Now that the moment is almost here we have discovered that what we both remember are the good and lovely things, and that the rest fades to comparative insignificance. This may be only nostalgia in advance. I don't know. I only know that it will always be happiness to remember you. And Stanley, and Bill—and England.

Our united love to you, and our gratitude

Marion Sharpe.

He laid the letter down on his brass and mahogany desk. Laid it down in the afternoon patch of sunlight.

Tomorrow at this time Marion would no longer be in England.

It was a desolating thought, but there was nothing to do but be sensible about it. What, indeed, was there to do about it?

And then three things happened at once.

Mr. Heseltine came in to say that Mrs. Lomax wanted to alter her will again, and would he go out to the farm immediately.

Aunt Lin rang up and asked him to call for the fish on his way home.

And Miss Tuff brought in his tea.

He looked for a long moment at the two digestive biscuits on the plate. Then, with a gentle finality, he pushed the tray out of his way and reached for the telephone.

CHAPTER XXIV

The summer rain beat on the air-field with a dreary persistence. Every now and then the wind would lift it and sweep the terminus buildings with it in one long brush-stroke. The covered way to the Montreal plane was open on either side and the passengers bent their heads against the weather as they filed slowly into it. Robert, moving up at the tail of the queue, could see Mrs. Sharpe's flat black satin hat, and the short strands of white hair being blown about.

By the time he boarded the plane they were seated, and Mrs. Sharpe was already burrowing in her bag. As he walked up the aisle between the seats Marion looked up and saw him. Her face lighted with welcome and surprise.

"Robert!" she said. "Have you come to see us off?"

"No," Robert said. "I'm travelling by this plane."

"Travelling!" she said, staring. "*You* are?"

"It's a public conveyance, you know."

"I know, but—you're going to Canada?"

"I am."

"What for?"

"To see my sister in Saskatchewan," Robert said demurely. "A much better pretext than a cousin at McGill."

She began to laugh; softly and consumedly.

"Oh, Robert, my dear," she said, "you can't imagine how revolting you are when you look smug!"